Present
Together We Are Strong

Carey Anderson

DEDICATION

I would like to dedicate this book to #TheTeenager. Babygirl, it was your original idea that created the idea for the TWAS in the first place. You may not be a reader like I am, but your love and constant support has been the fuel to my fire. I love you with all my heart, and thank you for always believing in me.

Cover design: Art Nuance

Join me on Facebook – www.facebook.com/careythewriteranderson

Twitter - @CareyTheWriter

Blog - http://careyanderson.blogspot.com

Website – http://www.careythewriteranderson.com

<u>**Editorial – Treasures of Joy Editorial**</u>

ACKNOWLEDGMENTS

I would like to thank my Rough Rider team as a whole. All of you are truly amazing and extremely supportive. Thank you for giving me your free time to dance in my imagination. Also, my virtual rough riders, those of you who continue to support me. You read my stories, you write lovely reviews that I cherish and read over and over again, and then you recommend my work to others. Your loyalty and support are utterly amazing and I truly appreciate you.

Mrs. Dyes! You opened a world to me, that I don't know, that I would've ever known existed. My thirst for all things creative began with your class. My teacher was and forever will be amazing.

Prolog

Then Andrew and Andre walked in the door. Andre was so happy to see me; he ran to me and threw his arms around my neck. My heart was pounding as Andrew eyed me as he stood by the door. Amber took Andre to the backyard, he didn't really want to go, but his father flashed him a look. Andrew stood by the door trying to read me, so I eyed him back. We were having a stare down.

"So, how come you didn't know I was coming?" I asked.

He cocked his head to the side. Then he sat down in the recliner across from me. "You normally do things a certain way. My man is used to having Yussef as a back up. He slipped up. He's been dealt with."

"What does that mean?" Andrew blank stared at me. "Was that really the first time you saw her at Berkeley?"

"Yes."

"How did you end up Hooking up for lunch?"

"She called my office. I figured lunch would be harmless."

"In what way?"

He blew air, "in what way what Tracy?"

Through clinched lips I said, "in what way was lunch supposed to be harmless Andrew?"

Andrew was reading my face. He wasn't gonna bully me out of my feelings. "It was the easiest option." He said like he wasn't interested in talking to me.

"So it was the easiest way to hurt me." I huffed.

Then he leaned forward, "so your staying out all night wasn't to hurt me?"

"Of course it was." I blurted out.

He wasn't expecting me to admit that. I could tell I caught him off guard. He squirmed in his seat. Then he sat back, and released a little chuckle. "So what about fighting her?"

"She knew exactly what she was doing. She was just as guilty."

His smile got bigger, "you hit me."

I had to think about it. Everything was happening so fast. "Yes I did. I apologize for doing that."

"Where did you go?"

"I don't know where I was exactly."

His smile went away. "Who were you with?" I swallowed hard, but I didn't say anything. "Tracy! So help me God I'm not playing with you! Who were you with?" I stared at him. He got up very angry. He picked up the recliner effortlessly, and then he put it down. He started getting really big, and tears started pouring out of my eyes. He stood over me with his hands flexing and unflexing.

"ANSWER ME WOMAN!" He looked really scary and huge. I kept staring at his eyes. If he was gonna hit me I wasn't gonna close my eyes. "YOU'RE CHEATING ON ME!"

"NO I'M NOT!" I said standing up on the couch to match his growl. "I'M NOT THE CHEATER YOU ARE!"

"I DIDN'T CHEAT ON YOU! I WASN'T GOING TO CHEAT ON YOU! I JUST HAD LUNCH!!" He yelled.

"I SAW YOU! I WAS THERE!"

"What?" He backed down.

"I left the office even earlier then I said, cause I wanted to surprise you and take you out to lunch. Imagine my surprise when I see you holding the door open for her. You opened your car door for her. I followed you, I saw everything! You're so used to following me, you forget it can go both ways." He sat down. "I saw the cocktails, saw the touching, I saw everything!"

"Just like I saw Yussef driving your car." His expression was full of pain. I looked at him. "I wasn't sure if that was him. When no one had you, I knew it was him. Did you call him?" I shook my head no. He got angry.

"Andrew, Yussef has nothing but respect for you. He looks up to you. He admires you."

His expression changed multiple times. "He wants to be me you mean."

"No!"

"Yes!"

"No! Andrew stop trying to assign some kind of evil plot to him."

"Stop defending him!" He barked.

"Ok!"

"Are you in love with him?"

I looked at him, "how could you ask me that?"

"Answer the question!"

"No! Are you in love with Jennay?" He blew air. I mimicked him and blew air too.

"No!"

It was silent for a few minutes. "Do you think we should be together?"

My question wounded him; as soon as I saw the affect I wanted to take it back. "You want to break up?"

"That's not what I meant."

"Then please tell me, what do you mean?" He sat back in the chair waiting for me to speak.

"I mean we've had one drama after another. I liked us when this drama didn't exist. I liked us when it was simpler to be together." I said.

"The deeper in you get the more that has to be settled. You told me you were with me until death do us part. You told me as long as I didn't cheat or hit you, we'd work it out. Now you want out!" He was getting big again. "You wanna go run after Yussef? I'll kill him! That's not a threat! He's a dead man!"

"Andrew! Please! That's not what I meant." I started crying again.

"Oh so now you're gonna cry because he's a dead man!" Andrew said hitting his fist into his hand. The sound of the hit echoed.

"Andrew!" I tried to talk through my tears. "That's not what I meant!"

Tears started running down his face. "THEN TELL ME WHAT YOU MEAN! CAUSE IT SOUNDS TO ME LIKE YOU'RE CHOOSING SOMEONE ELSE OVER ME!" He was screaming in my face.

I tried to talk over the tears, but I could barely talk. I touched his face. He was furious! "Andrew!" I could barely get his name out my mouth. I kept shaking my head no. "I love you!" I tried to calm down so that I could speak. "I don't want to break up! I figured you didn't want me anymore. You stopped talking to me." He looked confused. "You have been shutting me out. Every time I ask you questions you tell me not now. Then the other morning didn't help. I figured you wanted out but didn't know how to tell me."

"I'm gonna ask you one more time. Did you cheat on me? Tell me the truth!"

"No, I've never slept with anyone other than you since we've been together."

Then he stood me up, I didn't want to, but I dare not deny him in this state. I thought I was about to be hit so many times. "STOP! Stop running from me! It hurts me when you do that. Make me feel like you're not a flight risk."

"What do you mean?" I asked.

"You want me to open up to you, but every time something happens you run away from me. Stuff like this doesn't make you the most trust worthy in my book."

"Ok" I said.

Then he hugged me. More like squeezed the life out of me. I hugged him back, we both stood there crying our eyes out. Then he checked my hand, "NEVER take this off!"

"Ok," I said feeling relieved that he said that. I had him sit down and then I took my favorite seat, on his lap. I laid my head on his chest. His heart was beating so fast. I know it's stupid but it did feel good to know he was jealous about me. I wasn't the only person looking stupid.

"You smell like my mom." He said taking me in.

I thought about what Amber said about me smelling like a man earlier. I was happy I didn't go straight home. That could've been a death warrant for Yussef. "I used her stuff". Then I inhaled and exhaled, "so you still want to be with me?"

His heart started speeding up. "Yes."

"Why?"

"Because I love you! I don't want to be without you. No, I can't be without you!" Then he squeezed my thigh. "You still want to be with me?"

"Yes."

"Why?"

"Because no one has ever made me feel loved like you do. Outside of today you've never scared me, although I get it. You're a scary guy, you've never been that to me."

"I scared you?"

I blew air. "Yea right! You know you were being scary! Picking up chairs, and screaming in my face."

"I was going crazy yesterday and all last night. I couldn't find you; I knew you were mad at me. Then to know you were here and not coming home. I know I promised mom's, but you were stalling and probably would've stayed gone another night if I didn't come over."

"I was scared."

"You never have to be afraid of me." He said kissing my forehead.

I got butterflies in my stomach. "On that note, can you do something for me?"

"ANYTHING!" He said as he squeezed my thigh again.

"Leave Yussef alone."

In one quick move I was on the couch and he was on his feet. "You gotta be kidding me! He's dead!"

"Andrew! Please! What did he do?"

"HE KNOWS EXACTLY WHAT HE'S DONE!" He started pacing. "YOU DON'T MESS WITH YOUR BOSS'S GIRL!"

"Andrew! I'm still here, and it's not like that. He knows I love you, he encourages it. He has your back."

"Yea my way back!" He said visibly unraveled. "I can't Tracy! He knows better!"

"Please Andrew!"

"I was going to leave him alone as long as he stayed out of my way, but he crossed the line yesterday!"

"What did he do?"

Still pacing, "I'm over here trying to calm down. And you're stirring things up again! I don't want to talk about this. You can't change my mind!"

"Please Andrew! He's my friend! You know how many of those I have these days. Please!"

He gave me an evil look. "I bet he's your friend alright!" He started to walk away. Then he turned towards me. "If I ever find out you slept with him!" He said pointing his finger at me. "I'm not responsible for what happens next!"

I flew off the couch. "So if you cheat basically you want me to deal with it. Get over it and keep loving you, but if I cheat on you you're threatening me?" He didn't say anything, his face was stone. "That doesn't work for me!"

"It is what it is!"

"Then I don't want this! I have no intentions of sleeping with anyone other than you, but you will not threaten me. You will not impose double standards on me. I will not live like this!" Then I walked past him to go upstairs to get my purse.

As I was going up the stairs he grabbed my shoulder, it spun me. My back hit the wall, he grabbed me and put me in another bear hug. It happened so fast that I screamed. "Ok! Ok! Ok!" He said holding me. "I'll kill both of us, ok?"

I laughed, "you'll kill both of us?"

"Yea you first then me, but only after I'm sure you're dead. Then I'll kill myself." He said laughing.

"How about no one dies, including my friend?"

He squeezed tighter. "I can't promise you he won't die. I can't. Tell him he needs to stay away."
"Andrew!"
He squeezed tighter, "Ssshhhh! I don't want to talk about him anymore."
"But.."
He squeezed tighter, "no more".
"Can't! Breathe!" I said turning red.
"Oh my bad!" He loosened his grip. We stood there hugging so long that we were swaying. Then my stomach grumbled. "Are you hungry?"
"I haven't eaten since breakfast."
"Lets go eat." He invited his mother to come with us.
She hugged both of us so tight. Then she said, "if I didn't get to wear my dress, heads were gonna roll!" Then she smacked the back of Andrew's head. He rolled his eyes.

Amber

I took a deep breath, and exhaled. I laid on my bed. "Then that would make you a liar, and me a fool for all the times I believed you when you offered more. If this is all you have, then it's all you have, but it's not good enough. Maybe for someone else but not me."
"How do I become a liar?"
"Every time you dangled something more in front of my face, that means you were lying to me just to get what you wanted. And if this is truly all you have to offer I can't go back to that condo either."
"Why?" I could hear irritation in his voice.
"I was under the impression that that condo was on the road to something real. Now it feels like it was all a ruse."
"What's not real about me and you? It doesn't get more real than us!" He was angry.
"You're too smart not to get it Malcolm. And it's beneath me to have to explain all this to you. If this living is fine for you, who am I to make you change it. I just find it funny that everyone else ALWAYS wanted to give me more. But you, you're the only one who wouldn't." I was about to explode into tears. I didn't want to give up my nonchalant tone. So I had to end the conversation. "It hurts but at least you've stay consistent. You'll give me what I want to a point. I gotta go, I have a flight in the morning."
"So you're telling me this was all for nothing?"
"It was if your only aspiration was to be a boyfriend." Then I thought about it. "And no it wasn't for nothing. You finally have a good relationship with all three of your sons." Tears started pouring out of my eyes. "I gotta go!" I hung up my phone. I laid there crying my eyes out. I cried so hard that I cried myself to sleep. I almost didn't hear my alarm. I was moving slow, but I was moving. I pulled my hair back into a low ponytail and I braided the ends. I put on my comfortable travel clothes then I went to the airport. The ticket counter guy tried to cheer me up as I checked my bags. I couldn't pull out of my funk. I called Sophia when I got to my gate. First, I apologized for calling her so early. Then, I unloaded everything from the night before. She said she couldn't believe it, and I told her I couldn't either. I couldn't stop saying how disappointed I was. She asked me if there was any way he could've been messing with me to throw me off his scent. I told her he was mad last night, and he doesn't fake getting mad. Then I told her that a proposal from him at this point would feel fake and forced so I was through with the whole idea. I told her the next person to propose to me outside of Tag I was accepting. At least that way I could say I was married at least once in my life. She told me I didn't mean that, and I promised her I did. They were announcing boarding for my flight. I had a brief layover in Phoenix and then I was on my way to Atlanta. Fortunately we had rehearsals at North Star, so filming on location should wrap up hopefully in three days. I told Sophia I loved her and that I'd call her as soon as I made it to Atlanta. As soon as I sat in my First Class seat I put on my seat belt, put my pillow behind my head, pulled out my blanket and went back to sleep. I woke up as we were pulling up to the Phoenix Gate. I went to a restaurant and ordered bacon and eggs. I heard female screams and women running. I looked up to see Shameless an East Coast Rapper

surrounded by women requesting autographs. When he looked up he saw me and smiled. I waved then I made my way to my gate. I ate my breakfast as Shameless made his way towards me. His bodyguard stopped people from approaching us. "Hey shorty! How you doing? Long time no see!" He said coming in for a hug.

"How you doing? It's been a long time. Do you remember my name?"

"Of course I do Amber." He said sitting down. "Why wouldn't I?"

"It's not like we talked much when I worked on your stuff. Where you heading to?"

"I'm going to ATL to do this little cameo in my boy's video. How about you?"

"Choreography for T Ruiz's video."

"Studio or location?"

"My portion is studio."

"Ooh! Ooh! Which one? You gotta stop by." He said getting excited.

"News Worthy studios."

"Yea! Yea! You gotta swing by." Then he took a pen and paper out and wrote down his number. I didn't know where the excitement was coming from; Shame and I never had any kind of a real connection. If anything I figured Ramell was involved in here somewhere. I put the number in my wallet. We chatted until we boarded the plane he was on one side of first class and I was on the other. As we were boarding he was texting somebody and he was all smiles. I tried not to think about Malcolm and relax. I watched the inflight movie best I could without my mind drifting to all the times Malcolm mentioned marriage. Every time he mentioned or even implied that we would get married it had a baby attached to the idea. I never understood that especially when we already one and then three. That last time, when he referred to me as his wife. I don't know if there was a baby attached to that idea or not. Up until then we thought I couldn't have anymore. And I'm sorry now that I'm a Nana; I don't want to have any more babies. He better not come at me with no lame request for a baby or some junk like that. Malcolm wouldn't play the game like he wasn't interested in marriage to try to surprise me with a proposal; he's never been that cheesy. That's what makes this hurt. I've waited all my life for him to put it on paper, and still this is where we sit almost three decades later. Shame asked me what hotel I was staying at, it turns out we were staying at the same one, so I shared a car service with him. I was gonna catch a cab, but he had a car so it worked out. He asked if I wanted to catch a bite to eat, but I declined. I wanted to unwind and get some rest. The time difference was gonna kick my butt if I didn't. I called Sophia and I told her about Shameless. She asked me if I thought he was trying to hook up. I told her that I thought he was friends with Ramell, and probably trying to arrange for us to meet up somewhere. She asked me if I felt up to seeing him. I told her that seeing Ramell wasn't a problem, we were never a couple and he knew that. She told me to be careful and to call her if I needed her.

The studio called and said they were sending a car at 6am to pick me up. I cursed in my mind at the thought of being ready for work at 3am on my internal clock. I grabbed a quick bite to eat and then I went to bed. It wasn't hard to sleep cause I was depressed anyways.

When I got to the studio Corey greeted me with a big sleepy hug. Once I got the dancers warmed up, I wasn't so sleepy anymore. Day One was good. Day Two was even better. Day Three was best! At the close of day three I asked Corey what lot Shame was on since he told me he talked to him earlier. We hopped in a golf cart and he took me over to lot 63. The bass was pumping and the set was designed to look like a club. Everyone had on suits and hats like they were at an OG event. The director came over to Corey and asked him for his opinion. They started speaking director jargon. Shame came over and he was very excited to see me. He said I was supposed to call him before I came. I told him I wanted to pop my head in real quick and that I wasn't gonna stay. He told everyone in the booth to wave at me. I didn't focus on anyone specifically, I waved and said hello. He begged me to go out with them tonight. I kept trying to think of a reason to get out of it, but he was persistent. I asked Corey if he would come with me. He frowned at me, I told him I was gonna tell Shame he was the reason I couldn't go. Corey said he knew who my man was and he didn't want any problems. I told him as long as we stuck together there wouldn't be any. Corey said he had to get up in the morning, I told him that would be my excuse to leave. I told Shame I would come, but I had to leave when Corey left. Shame frowned, but he agreed. I had a nice massage and facial back at the hotel. Since it was really warm out there and I didn't know where we were going I put on pants, sandals, and a halter-top. No makeup just gloss and big hoop earrings. Corey gave me a quick up and down, he was on guard but so was I. Shame came to the lobby and greeted us, his bodyguard stayed to the side. He said the rest of the group was gonna meet us at the restaurant. In the limo Corey asked me if I heard from Malcolm today. I smirked and said no. Shame looked at Corey then he asked me who Malcolm was. I told him he was my boyfriend. He didn't seem bothered or anything by that, and I shot Corey a "See!" look because I kept trying to explain to him that Shameless wasn't trying to push up on me. When we got to the restaurant we went to the private room in the back, which was huge and full of people. I could see Corey relax when Shame greeted a girl with his tongue, and we saw the director from their video. She was like a sponge soaking up anything Corey would share with her. I followed Shame and his girl to a booth in the corner. His bodyguard sat on the end his girl scooted next to him, then Shame, and I sat on the end. Someone came in and Shame waved them over. I looked across the room and Corey's eyes were big. I didn't wanna turn around; I knew it was Ramell I'd just say hi. Enjoy the evening and leave when Corey was ready. Then I heard, "hello Amber" I got Goosebumps as soon as I heard the voice. Shame smiled at me real big while his girl looked like she wished she was me, and I wished I was anybody else other than me. "Hi" is all I could muster to say in that moment.

"Amber scoot over so my man can sit." Shame said scooting in to give me space.

I scooted over. "So how have you been?"

"Ok" I said sipping my water.

He gave me that award-winning smile. "Since when are you shy?" He asked.

"Since I started feeling setup. Since when you start hanging out with rappers?"

"You know what, we should give them some privacy." Shame said scooting towards his girl who didn't want to leave. "We'll be back."

"They've come to a few games. Lewis and I have become good friends. What does Malcolm think about you being here?"

"He won't like it once he finds out you're here." I knew I should've gotten up, but that would've been doing the right thing, not that it was what I wanted to do.

"He has a problem with me?" He asked innocently.

I blank stared at him. "Come on Dwayne, what would Michelle think?" Corey looked like he was on the edge of his seat.

"Michelle and I are throwing in the towel again, for good this time." He said with his eyes locked on me.

"Why? After four kids you can't make it work even for them?"

He swallowed, "five we had twins."

"Whoa!" I said feeling horrible for them. "Why?"

He told me how once they moved they both tried really hard to put their best foot forward. Then they had the boys it was ok for a while. Eventually it turned back into everything it was when they split the first time. And like last time she had him served. He said he doesn't want to put his kids through this especially when she pushed the issue about having them and now this. He showed me pictures of his beautiful clan. His boys looked just like him. I guess Michelle felt like she hit the jackpot getting twins in her last go around. Then I shared how my last conversation with him destroyed my life, and almost ended his. He didn't look phased by the thought. "Honestly, I feel like I've just been existing anyways." He said staring at me.

I looked at Corey whose eyes were still glued to me. I scooted the long way out of the booth.

"Dwayne I can't do this."

He gave me sad eyes, "do what?"

"I haven't recovered from our last conversation. Somehow some way Malcolm's gonna find out about this. I don't want to have to explain." I looked at Corey, "you ready?" He nodded at me. I mouthed I was gonna run to the bathroom and then I'd be ready. Corey nodded again.

In the bathroom there were some groupies having their loud conversation not paying attention to who was in the bathroom.

"Girl! Dwayne Reed! Did you see him?" Tramp one said.

"Yea, but he came looking for somebody otherwise he wouldn't be here." Tramp two said.

"How you know?" Tramp one said.

"He run with Shame sometimes. He spends most of the time whining about his ending marriage. The only time he hooks up with a female is if she reminds him of this chick he dated back in the day." Tramp two said.

"Did she look like me?" Tramp one said.

They laughed. "Heck if I know! I'm assuming she's light skinned though. Cause they always caramel colored." Tramp two said.

"So why he here tonight?" Tramp one asked.

"Well you saw where he was. That girl is the cookie cutter type. They all be like that. He'll probably leave here with her; don't spin your wheels on him. There are so many other choices here tonight." Tramp two said.

"Who's the girl with Shame tonight?" Tramp one asked.

"Ask me if I care! We all know who's name he's gonna calling tonight! And who's going on a shopping spree in the morning!"

I heard clapping and laughter, they continued their conversation as they left the bathroom. I washed my hands telling myself not to cry or get emotionally caught up. I couldn't even think about how good it felt to see Dwayne after all these years. And to see him look at me with that same love in his eyes was amazing. No! No! I couldn't think about him, cause no matter how good he was I still wanted Malcolm. No, I'm going back to my hotel and staying there until its time to go to the airport. I took a deep breath and I walked out the bathroom. Dwayne was standing there, he looked desperate. He grabbed me by the hand and pulled me down the hallway through the kitchen and to this area just off the kitchen. When I started to ask him what was going on, he kissed me. Oh my bleeding heart it was a good kiss too. My arms wrapped around his neck like they used to and I leaned in to the kiss. All the wonderful memories of how much this man loved me and how he wanted to marry me. If I even gave him the look like I wanted to marry him, I bet he'd be all over it. But for now it didn't matter, my heart still belonged to Malcolm. I pushed away from him and both our eyes filled with tears. I walked back through the kitchen, down the hallway by the bathroom and back into the private room. Dwayne silently walked behind me; I walked in the room and held the door open for him. Then I found Corey's eyes, he excused himself and walked out with me. The host called a cab for us. I knew I looked sad when Corey put his arm around me and told me to cheer up. Dwayne came over still glassy eyed but no tears dropping. He put a paper in my hand and told me if anything ever changed to contact him. Then he walked out and got in a rental car. Corey asked me if I was ok, and I inhaled deeply and exhaled. I couldn't wait to get to my room and cry my eyes out again. I shook my leg the whole car ride like that was the only thing holding in my tears. In the lobby I hugged Corey and thanked him for going with me. Corey asked me if I wanted to get something to eat at the restaurant, but I told him I wanted to go lay down. When really I just wanted to wallow in my even bigger depression now. I barely made it in the door before I started balling. I went in the bathroom and blew my nose. As I washed my hands I looked in the mirror, that fast my eyes and nose were red. When I walked out the bathroom I reached for my suitcase that's when the big white box on the dresser caught my attention, it wasn't there before I left. I immediately stopped crying and my alarm went up. I had the feeling someone was in my room. Dwayne did leave before us, what if he somehow got in my room? But if he came in here it was all bad cause he already knows it can't happen, so was he here to hurt me? I moved forward enough to look in the mirror to see the reflection of whoever was in the room. I saw blackness with piercing eyes. Even though I knew that was Malcolm my first reaction was to scream. "What are you doing here?" I said walking around the corner.

His face was very serious. "Why are you crying?"

"What do you mean? You know why."

"Do I?" He said reading my face. I rolled my eyes at him. "Why are you crying? Act like I don't know, explain it to me." He sat back in his chair.

"No!"

"No?"

"Right. No! I'm tired of explaining stuff to you. I'm tired of going round and round with you. You should know me by now. You know why I'm crying."

He stood up and walked into my face. He inhaled deeply. "You smell like a few different colognes so you hugged a few guys tonight. Let me see if I can tell you how your evening went." He straightened up and walked over to the box on the dresser. "Lewis is out here, a long with quite a few others that he runs tight with. He invited you out to dinner with them. I saw that you took Corey with you. Very wise choice. Judging by how early you came home, the pretty boy showed up right away. He told you how he's getting a divorce, and wishes there was some way you could get back together. Seeing that your back so soon you left like my good girl would, but why are you upset about it?" He looked at me in my eyes. "Could it be because you were torn about what you wanted to do and you did the right thing by default?" Then he bent down in my face. "Doing right by me upsets you that much?" He peck kissed my lips. "So I've spent the last few days thinking about our last conversation. I'm gonna tell you, spending my night perplexed is not the way I saw that evening ending. I saw us laughing, joking around, me finally getting some. You know the way it should've went but instead you're mad at me, and I can't sleep. It bothers me that you still love him. You know how I'd like to handle it; I'm trying this new thing where I try and act like an adult and not a savage, but don't test me!" He looked me in my eyes. "So here's your chance. Choose where you wanna be, who do you want to be with me or him?"

I frowned, "what?"

"You can go be with the pretty boy. I promise to only pistol-whip him. He'll live and you guys can live happily ever after. Or you can choose me?" He stood up straight and crossed his arms.

I looked at him and smiled, "why do you let him bother you?"

He exhaled, tackled me on the bed kissing me all over. "You are gonna be the death of me I can feel it!"

"What's in the box?" I asked through a smile

"Go see" he said moving so I could see inside.

I opened the box it was a dozen long stem roses. I smiled, "just like the ones you used to give me after my performances." I smiled even bigger. "Thank you they're beautiful!"

"Why were you crying?"

"You don't want to marry me. How do you think that makes me feel? Then to make matters worse seeing someone who desperately wants to, but they aren't you is depressing. I could runaway and marry him."

"And die the very next day!" There was no joke to his tone.

I rolled my eyes, "I wouldn't be satisfied cause he still wouldn't be you. I'm frustrated for now. But like I told you the other day, I'm not gonna play this game indefinitely with you."

"I'm not asking you to. Now you know you're slipping right!" I looked confused. "It took you too long to see that box on the dresser. If I was here to hurt you, you'd be hurt. I gotta put somebody back on you, you were wide open."

"I'm not one of your soldiers."

"I can see that."

I kicked my sandals off, took my hair down. He stood in front of me and put his hands in my hair. "No one will ever love you like I do, no matter what they offer you. There isn't anything I wouldn't do for you." Then he kissed me.

Anything but marry me, I said to myself. I was happy he was there, and I was happy he didn't propose cause it wouldn't seem genuine. I want him to want to marry me. Not like he feels forced into it. I wish Momma was here, she'd tell me what to do.

Yussef

Andrew sat back; I could tell he was struggling with feeling remorseful for what he just did, but then I could see it turn off. Andrew was in pain and in destructive mode. "Let's go meet these chicken heads." He said to me looking around the club.

I looked up, and that's when I saw her. She was beautiful! Long curly hair, soft skin, and beautiful smile. Andrew was looking in the opposite direction. I saw her about the same time as she saw me. She smiled and I felt lightning hit my stomach. "Whoa!" is all I could muster. I had to go meet this girl.

"You ready?" Andrew said looking in the other direction.

"I'm gonna go this way, maybe we can meet up in the middle in a little bit." I said with urgency in my voice.

"Cool!" I'll take both of them then." Andrew went to the right and I went to the left.

As I went to the left, my hands felt clammy and I couldn't believe how nervous I felt about approaching this girl. I guess I could understand how Comfort was nervous that night when he met Amber. If the emotion I saw in him matches anything that I'm feeling right now! I completely understand it. She whispered to her friend as I approached and they both seemed to get bashful, she likes me right? I cleared my throat, be cool! Just be calm and natural. "How you doing tonight?" She smiled real big, "I'm good and you?" She said blushing.

"I'm good now. What's your name pretty lady?"

"Sylvia, and this is my friend Monica."

"Nice to meet you, hello Monica." I tried to take all nervousness out of my voice.

"Hello," she said then she giggled again for her friend.

"You wanna dance?" I asked not knowing what else to say to her that would matter to me at that moment. I just wanted to be in her space. I wanted to see her move, I wanted to smell her. I wanted her! This is a first!

"Depends," she said putting her little hand on her hip. My stomach flipped at the thought of rejection.

"On?" I swallowed.

"You didn't even tell me your name." She smiled again.

I tried to hide my exhale of almost relief. "I'm Yussef." I said reaching out to shake her hand.

"Yussef, that's Hebrew for Joseph right?"

That did it! My heart was beating out of my chest! No one has ever known anything about my name before. "That's right, so how about that dance?" Be COOL! I kept telling myself. She handed her purse to Monica and we were off to the dance floor. Now, I wasn't a master dancer like Andrew or Jeff, but I did ok. We had a good time, and we were both smiling on the dance floor. We stayed out there almost all night dancing up a storm. Randi looked at us and smiled real big as she seemed to shut down the place with Jeff. Sylvia and Monica went to the bathroom as the club closed. We decided to go get something to eat.

Andrew came over, "I got a hook up." He said pointing at the two girls he was talking about earlier. "You cool or you wanna come with?"

"I met somebody, I'm good." I said with a big smile.

"Alright then. Stay strapped up, and I'll catch up with you later." He said giving me a pound, and then he left.

Randi and Jeff came over, "we wanna go get something to eat. You down?" Jeff asked.

"Yeah, we were just saying the same thing." I said.

"We? Did you meet somebody?" Randi asked somewhat surprised.

"Why is that surprising? You think you the only one who can hook up?"

She blushed at Jeff, "no, I was just asking."

Then Sylvia and Monica seemed like they were walking in slow motion towards us. "Whoa!" Jeff said turning his eyes away.

"Are you ready?" Sylvia asked.

"Yes, these are my friends Randi and Jeff. And this is Sylvia and her friend Monica." Everyone said hello and shook hands. "Anywhere we all wanna go to eat?"

"Benny's is 24 hours right?" Monica said.

"Yes, but there's a National's Hamburger right here in Jack London that's open 24 as well. How does that sound to everybody?" Jeff said.

"Good to us." Monica said.

Randi shook her head yes as well. "National's it is, did you guys drive here?" I was praying they said no, I wanted as much time with her as possible.

"Her brother dropped us off, we're supposed to call him when we're ready." Sylvia said.

My heart jumped for joy. "I can take you guys home if you like." I was trying to be cool, but everything in me felt like I was bursting.

"That would be nice." Then she gave me that smile.

Doesn't this girl know how gorgeous she is! Her smile kills me every time she unleashes it on me. She keeps looking at me like she likes me too. This almost feels too good to be true. I told myself to stop being so pessimistic and just go with it. I opened the car doors for Sylvia and Monica, while Randi and Jeff got in the back on the other side. We decided to take one car to keep it simple. At National's the conversation flowed wonderfully. Sylvia and Monica went to Laney college in Oakland, and they lived in San Leandro. Every time she said my name that slight accent captured my attention. Everything about her is sexy to me, and I know better than to dig her this fast, but something about her keeps pulling me in. Jeff kept looking at me, but he was digging Randi in the same way. And Monica who was equally beautiful was just happy to be out with us. We sat in National's for hours talking. I asked her how she was familiar with the origin of my name. She said as a child she was friends with a Jewish family, they had an Uncle Yussef. We sat in National's so long we watched the sky turn from dark to light. None of us wanted the night to end. Jeff offered his house to hang out for a while longer. So we took him back to his car, then Randi rode with him as we followed him to his house. Monica told him his house was too big for one person. He said his brother stayed between there and LA, while he was in school getting his Master's Degree. Then he shared that he inherited the house from his parents. He grew up in this house. Randi was all smiles as he gave us the tour and pointed Monica to the guest bed where she could sleep. We called ourselves attempting to watch a movie, and one by one we all passed out. I was the last one though. Sylvia laid her head on my shoulder and I sat there staring at her for a long time. She was so beautiful to me; her snore didn't even bother me. This was the start of something great I could feel it in my stomach.

Sasha

We drove to Berkeley up University Ave. to Shattuck Ave., a couple blocks up we parked. There was a long line outside of "No Words" a poetry club. Carina, Tanisha's girlfriend was going to speak. I hadn't met her yet, but Tanisha is the happiest I've ever seen her since they got together. I honestly thought she'd go back to men. But I guess she's waiting for Andrew in order for that to happen. This place was very dimly lit, with flickering candles on each table. It smelled like fresh baked apple pie in there. There was a full bar and a barista, and tons of fresh pastries and Italian desserts. So I ordered a cappuccino, tiramisu, and Hennessy. Tanisha got us a table pretty close to the front. Carina looked very excited to finally meet me. We hugged like old best friends. Carina told me she was so happy to finally meet me in person. She said she was a little nervous, but excited to perform. We listened to numerous artistic expressions of love and hate. A hour and a half in Carina went up. She was good; she read her poem with passion and enthusiasm. Tanisha sat there so proud of Carina, even though everyone snapped I clapped and stood up. Everyone laughed at my excitement. A few more regulars went up and the MC said, "Last but certainly not least!" Then he turned to the side. "Brotha I didn't even see you walk in!" He smiled, "everybody give up snaps for The Invisible Poet!" My mouth dropped when I saw Yussef walk up to take the stage. I looked at Tanisha and she had no idea as well. I shifted in my seat, after only seconds of being in his presence I couldn't stop my body from responding. I sat forward in my chair waiting for his voice. Yussef winked at me and I melted. I felt like such a groupie. Tanisha touched my arm telling me to calm down. I shook my head letting her know I was cool.

"Darkness surrounds me, am I sleep or am I dead?" He licked his lips, *"inside I feel numb, searching for confirmation and acceptance, and I must be dead."* He takes one step backwards and then one forward. *"I reached out to her, gave her my everything, when she doesn't feel me, it must mean that I'm dead. Like brothers of a Royal family we have been, my life I risk to protect you, but still you betray me. I know, I know! You weren't in your right mind; your soul was suspended from the pain of your ancestor's tumultuous life. However, why do I pay the price? Applying the good book I put on the Christian cloth of love, brothers we remain. When presented with the chance of a lifetime, a moment to be free and feel alive. I walk away from this lady of the court; my loyalty is to the King. Her touch fades again, my soul screams to live again. The most trusted of the Knights, most highly favored one, I was awarded the primary responsibility to guard your future queen. Now I understand Sir Lancelot, but the question is. How does my story end?"*

Forget the snapping everybody was on their feet in thunderous applause! I clapped but I felt sad, who is she? Was he talking about me? The audience demanded an "ENCORE!"
As if he was asking for my input he looked at me. I put on a brave smile and clapped harder, when truthfully I was afraid of what I was gonna hear. When everyone was convinced he would give us one more taste, they sat down and anxiously waited for him to speak.

"She walks in the room unsure of herself, **Intriguing***! Fake it until you make it,* **Inspiring***! Her uncertainty is what attracts me,* **Desire***!"* He smiled, *"Surrounded by the overly confident your uncertainty,* **Refreshing***! When I talk she listens, only one before her was able to figure me out,* **Yearning***!"* He gave me eye contact, *"I live in her everyday smell, and peppermint is her biting base,* **Stimulating***! Watching him disrespect you,* **Infuriating***!"* He sounded mad. *"Thinking only of your heart I build him up,* **Deception***! Longing to live in your lap,* **Betrayal***! Hiding what I feel,* **Fraudulent***! Speaking what is on my heart to you,* **Freedom***! Disappointing my brother,* **Growth***! No longer choosing to be Invisible because I know your eyes see. Your sight has resurrected me; given me the love for my life that I need to set matters straight. No longer content with being Invisible, I demand to be seen. Your love has done this for me. Without the ability to say it, I read your mind. Thank you for not being blind, thank you for seeing me. Your Sight has been the cocoon that gave me wings. I know you love me, although we could never be!"*

Then he walked off the stage and hugged Tanisha.
Everyone was applauding again, "The Invisible Poet you guys!"
He hugged Carina, and then he hugged me. "What are you guys doing here? This is my honeycomb hideout." He smiled at me.
As people walked by they patted him on the shoulders or back to tell him how much they enjoyed his poems. "I came to support Carina. I wasn't expecting all that. My brain is still going trying to figure out all that it means."
Yussef patted my hand. "What you drinking?"
"Hennessy"
He smiled, "thug!" Then he walked towards the bar. He came and then the bartender came with four shots. "1, 2, 3, 4!" We took our shots. Then we sat back in our chairs relaxing.
"Yussef you're playing with fire! Please don't do this!" Tanisha said looking really sad.
"So...." I drummed my fingers on the table. "Yussef, we need to talk once and for all. Clear the air! Everything!"
Yussef sat all the way back in his chair taking me in. Then he shook his head no, "nope! Can't do it!"

"What?" AGAIN! He's always rejecting me! I can't do like I used to and push up on someone else to try to make myself feel desirable.

"You're clouding up this place with pheromones! I know as soon as one of those things hit my nose I'm a goner!" We laughed

That made me feel a little better. "Goner?"

"You're always seducing me just being you. You almost got me killed last time, I didn't want to leave. But it was the right thing to do."

I started shaking my leg, "can we move over one table for some privacy then. I'll try my best not to attack you."

He smiled then he agreed. Carina smiled at us, while Tanisha looked disgusted. He asked me about El, and I told him honestly. El and I got together before Andrew and Tracy, and here we are stagnant not able to move forward. I told him how much his being a gentleman has affected me. He said he was glad that I stopped putting physical attributes in the way of everything else. He said there was so much more to me than just being pretty. He said he was happy that I found someone who redirects my attention. I asked him why he didn't want me; I braced myself for his answer. He waited for me to lift my eyes to his. Then he asked me who said that he didn't want me? I told him that he never called, and whenever I saw him he was distant. He touched my hands, "Sasha! I wanted you, but that would've been a disaster. Besides you're only truly single for a matter of days." We laughed. Then he asked again if I loved El. When I said yes, he laughed and shook his head. He said one day he'll get to be first, that hurt. I told him his poetry was really nice. He looked me in my eyes and said it's amazing that I was here tonight to hear both of them. So at some point he was talking about me right? I asked what was going on in his world, and he said a lot of nonsense. I asked him if he was single, and he said it depends. It depends on whether I meant physically, mentally, or emotionally. Cause he had a different answer in each space. I told him he was being vague on purpose and he smiled at me. He told me to be good to El.

Chantel

When I got to The Place Where Jazz is Played, Gus was more excited than normal to see me. He was really animated and he told me I looked beautiful as usual. Everybody kept smiling at me like they knew something I didn't. The band Narration and I rehearsed and then I went back to my dressing room like I always do. The hostess Candice came in my room with big eyes. "GUESS WHO'S HERE! YOU WILL NEVER GUESS!" She didn't give me a chance to answer. "SHAMELESS!"

"The rapper?" I asked.

"YES GIRL!!! AND HE'S SITTING AT THE FRONT TABLE!!"

I got butterflies, after a few months when I didn't hear anything from Darryl I assumed he forgot about me. "That's nice, don't make me nervous. My nerves girl, my nerves!"

She did a happy dance, "I know I'm just so excited!"

Then there was a knock at the door. Candice opened it. It was Gus and he was wearing that huge smile. "Candy tell you who's in the house?"

"Yes, I just didn't expect a rapper." I said turning to my mirror.

Gus frowned, "that's not who..."

I looked in the mirror as he walked in my door. It felt like I lost all of my air. I couldn't take my eyes off him; it had been too long since I'd seen him. "Chantel," he said flashing his dimples. I could've melted right out of my chair.

"Derrick," I said as calmly as I could.

We stared at each other for a minute neither one of us speaking then Derrick looked at Candice and Gus who forgot they were standing in the middle of the room ear hustling. "Oh! Yeah! Come on Candice!" Gus clumsily ordered.

When they left the room I watched Derrick but I didn't say anything. My heart was beating too fast. He actually looked nervous. "I didn't realize you were here." I deflated a little bit. He wasn't coming for me. "I... I'm caught off guard by all this." He didn't seem like his normal calm self.

"Have a seat." I said pointing to the couch.

"Ok," he said agreeing with me. "You look beautiful!"

I couldn't help it I smiled. "Thank you, you look good."

He pointed behind him with his thumb, "I'm here with somebody. But she's not really somebody. She's just who I'm with."

"Ok" I said getting a kick out of seeing him unglued.

"The point! I have a point! Did I tell you, you look beautiful?"

I smiled bigger, "you can tell me again. I don't mind."

He chuckled, sat back on the couch and exhaled. "I wanted to know if you wanna sing your song?" I didn't respond right away. "I brought the music if you forgot the words."

"I know the words. I'm trying to gauge my nerves right in this moment."

He flashed his dimples again. "Is that a yes?"

"Sure, you think Narration will be able to keep up?"

"Yes" then he stood up. "I guess saying we need to talk is an understatement huh?"

"You would know." I said trying to be cool.

"I missed you." Then he exhaled, "we're gonna talk." He stood up. "I'm gonna play a song, then I'll invite you out."

"Ok," then I smiled at him.

He smiled then he walked out the room. I exhaled the most dramatic exhale. I checked my face and dress in the mirror. Who cares who was in the audience Derrick was here.

I walked backstage as Narration was finishing their opening song. Brady went out and introduced D-Rick and everyone went wild. Derrick glanced at me one last time before he provided the saxophone vocals to the song. It was almost as if he was singing. "Over time, I've been building my castle of love...." Gus put his arm around me and swayed with me. When the song was over the house gave him a standing ovation. But how could they not? He was magnificent! When he invited me out the house got loud again and that made me feel really good. I gave each member a hug; I was stalling to calm my nerves. When I got to Derrick he held me as tightly as I held him. The first time we touched in years and his body was warm. We let go at the same time. I took my mark on the stage and the music began. I sang the song Derrick wrote for me with all my heart. Everyone erupted into applause the stage rumbled from the sound of everyone's applause. We held onto each other as we bowed for the audience. Derrick and I walked off the stage together. I could tell he wanted to hug me again but he didn't. Derrick grabbed my hand and led me to the table. It wasn't hard to tell which one was there with Derrick they were all paired off. I smiled at Yussef as Derrick introduced everyone at the table. The girl with Shameless was Yussef's sister, Latia. They looked just a like, no question of whether they were related. Then he introduced me to Valerie. If looks could kill I would've been dead, I understood the feeling. "Should I leave?" I asked wanting to be respectful of his date.

"No, you stay." He said pulling up two extra chairs.

"I need to get with you. That song has to get out to main stream." Lewis said

Derrick had no noticeable reaction. "You think so?"

"I know so. Can I get your info from Latia?"

Derrick handed him a card. "Really Derrick? You're gonna have her sit at our table?" Valerie said like she couldn't take it any more.

Everybody looked at her with a sucks to be you look. "Derrick I'll leave." I said as I attempted to stand.

"Chantel sit! Valerie if you have a problem with my friend sitting here, then you leave. If you choose to stay, I don't want to hear another peep from you about it. Chantel is just as welcome here as you are, if not more." He said in a low rumble.

Valerie looked stuck and like she didn't know what to do. She looked at Latia like she was asking for advice. Latia didn't give her a reaction either. Then Valerie stood up. She gathered her purse and sweater, and then she left. Derrick didn't appear to be phased by her walkout at all. He pushed Valerie's chair away and pulled my chair next to him.

Then the table relaxed, and everyone started talking and enjoying the rest of Narration's set. When it was time I went back on the stage to perform. I sang a couple of my dad's songs, my songs, and then I closed with the song that Derrick dedicated to me. It was perfect that he was there and that I planned my music this way without knowing he'd be here. The house went crazy! Derrick looked like he wanted to kiss me; he stayed in his seat almost smiling at me holding those dimples prisoner. Derrick hung around after closing waiting for me. "Valerie's not gonna be waiting for you?" I asked as we walked to my car.

"We weren't deep. She'd be a fool." He said staring at me.

I glanced at him and then I glanced away. "What are the odds that you'd show up here tonight?" I said

"I know! How have you been?" He asked still staring.

I shrugged, "ok I guess. How about you?"

He exhaled and looked at the ground. "Chantel I don't do emotional well. Showing feelings has never been my strength. I shut down when things get emotional." He exhaled again.

"You smiled more tonight than I've seen you smile in one setting before. You're making progress."

"That's because you're here. Are you seeing anybody? Anybody I need to kill?" He almost smiled.

"Is that a joke or are you serious?"

"It's only a joke if there's no one."

"Let me think of how to answer that." He stared at me. "There was this guy who was checking for me. Then he said he got into a fight with three guys, and his jaw got broken. Haven't talked to him since. I think he's still recovering, but he wasn't my man, just a friend."

"Sounds like he popped off at the mouth to the wrong person."

"I think he did."

"That's too bad." Derrick faked sympathy.

"So I hear you're an uncle?"

Derrick actually smiled releasing the dimples. "Yeah, he's nothing like his mother thank goodness! And you're an auntie too."

I smiled, "you talked to Cyrus?"

"No," he said staring.

"So what's the deal Derrick?"

"I want you back, but I have a feeling you're gonna be difficult." He sucked his teeth.

"Tell me the truth...."

He cut me off, "I already know what one of your questions is gonna be. I was younger and dumber. My intention was not to hurt you."

"So you were cheating on me?" I stared at his eyes. His eyes hit the ground. "You kept saying it was gonna be me. Deflecting!"

"I know, you're right." He said

"Is that why you kept me away from your mother?"

"Her reaction was just as painful as yours. I wasn't ready."

"How do I know you're ready now?"

"I guess you'd have to trust me."

"You do know we have no foundation for trust."

"I know, which means I have to start from scratch. Can't you see it's killing me not to kiss you right now?"

"Derrick I haven't been with anyone else!" I felt my anger.

"I know!"

"You know?"

He looked in my eyes. "I know!"

"You hurt me and acted like I was overreacting."

"I know!"

"Why are you always testing me?"

xv

"It's hard to trust someone outside of your family." He said

"I know, but I trusted you!"

He exhaled, "I know. Look, I don't expect this to all be ironed out tonight; but I won't stop until I have you back."

"Whatever Derrick!" I said walking to my car.

I unlocked the door, and then he pushed the door shut. He stood in my face. "Don't disregard me like that. I know I was wrong, but that doesn't stop me from getting angry about being disregarded."

I could feel the warmth from his breath and body. I wanted to kiss him, but I wasn't gonna do it. "Fine."

"You know it only makes you human if you let me kiss you right now."

"A weak human!"

"I won't tell if you won't."

That was the longest and most delicious kiss of my life.

Kendra

"KB! When's your prom?"

"You want to take me?"

"I'm asking aren't I? I thought you knew it was me and you this year."

"I wasn't sure if you were going with Nellie or not."

He blew air, "when are you going dress shopping?"

"I honestly haven't thought about it."

I could hear the smile in his voice, "you want me to come?"

"If you want to."

"If I want to? KB! I get to watch you model different dresses for me. Of course I want to. The dress you wore last year was cool. But this year you need something that highlights your main assets."

"You've put a lot of thought into this I see."

"I've definitely got some ideas. But here's the thing you gotta trust me."

"What does that mean?"

"Ok so here's my plan." He cleared his throat, "for kicks and giggles we have you try on some styles and see what you like best. THEN!!!! My momma has this dress designer friend who can make your dress for you. That way your dress is original and you don't have to worry about anyone having your dress. Sound good?"

"Sounds expensive!"

"Don't worry about the cost. I got you!"

"You got me? What does that mean?"

"Means I'm paying for everything. I want your night out with me to be unlike any night you've ever known."

"Everything with you has been unlike anything I've ever known."

"KB! Don't go there with me right now! I'm trying to be strong." He cleared his throat, "sound like a plan?"

"Sounds like a plan."

After work on a Saturday Kalani, Ryder, Darryl, and I went all over the Bay Area looking at and trying on dresses. I asked Kalani to try on dresses for me as well as another reference point. But we really used that time to whisper about how silly Darryl and Ryder were. The dresses I liked I took pictures in. I told Darryl what I liked about each dress and then he asked me what color I wanted the dress to be. When I said black, he smiled. He asked me if I wanted to add silver to make it perfect. I told him that was fine. He told us he had reservations for us so we went to Point Richmond to the Mac Hotel. He had a banquet room reserved for our party of four. There was a piano in the room. He told me to come sit at the piano with him.

He held his hands just above the keys, "just so you guys know. I'm an artist, but Ryder has the pipes. So we're going to play a little melody for you. We hope you like it." Then he took a deep breath.

He looked at Ryder and he nodded, Darryl started banging on the piano making a bunch of horrible noise. Then Ryder started singing calmly, but equally horribly. Kalani and I laughed so hard we couldn't keep it together. I don't know why this fool wasn't concerned about someone hearing us. Our waitress came in the room and she looked like she was sent to tell him to stop. "Mr. Wallace?"

"I'm sorry I don't take request yet." He said smiling at her as he continued banging.

"Ok but, Mr. Wallace…"

"I know! I know! Music has been known to soothe the average beast!"

"Yes, but Mr. Wallace…"

"You want me to sing directly to you. You got it," Ryder said. He pointed at Darryl, "Hit it!"

Ryder dramatically walked towards the waitress singing his horrible song while Darryl pounded on the keyboard with an evil grin. "Don't hurt her now!" He said to Ryder. Ryder took the waitress in his arms and spun her around. Then he slow danced with her while singing his song. It was so horrible, she couldn't help but laugh. "MR. WALLACE PLEASE!" She yelled in between laughs.

Darryl stopped pounding, "you can call me Darryl!" Then he went back to pounding.

"Darryl! Please! You're gonna get me fired!" She pleaded while laughing.

"Ok!! Ok! Point Richmond is not ready for our musical genius." He said to Ryder, "but waitress. You gotta admit, you have never heard musical styling's like ours before."

"I agree! I have never heard anything like that before." She said still laughing.

Lanie

"Mmmmooooommmmmmaaaaaa!" Lanie yelled from her bathroom.

"What I tell you about screaming like that?"

She put her big brown eyes on me, "sorry momma. I'm just frustrated!" Her hair was all over her head. It looked like she tried to do something and ended up in a war with her hair. "I need help!" She pointed to her head.

I tried to hold back my laughter, "what are you trying to do?"

"I don't know, something cute."

"Lately you care so much about how you look when we go to service. This wouldn't happen to have anything to do with that new family? Would it?"

The Jamison family moved to Berkeley from Palo Alto. They have a son about Lanie's age and one a little younger. Now that I think about it Lanie has been my number one partner to service. Erica, Zoey, and EJ come as well, but they don't come as religiously as Lanie has been coming these days. Now that I think about it, her little shopping sprees have been somewhat centered around what she's going to wear to service. Lanie put her eyes to the floor, "maybe."

I smiled, "he is a little cutie pie isn't he?"

"I think I might be too much woman for him."

I couldn't help it, I cracked up! "Too much woman?"

"Yes, sometimes he doesn't say anything to me."

"He does seem shy."

"Yea, he's not like daddy. Daddy just doesn't talk much. Not because he's shy, he's just sitting there thinking of mean things to say half the time. Dorian is just shy. That makes me want to grab him. I don't know why."

"Grab him?"

"At the congregation picnic, he was following us around. We were walking up this hill and he started falling so I grabbed him and pulled him up. His eyes got big and after that I kept grabbing him when he was about to step wrong. I couldn't have my man falling off the hill."

I cracked up, "your man?"

She blushed, "yes momma. Why is this funny?" Her eyes were serious as she looked at me. "It seems like all the boys like Erica and girls like her. I'm not that sweet and I'm not that innocent." I crossed my arms, "explain that."

Lanie's eyes danced around the room, "I mean. I don't know how to be gentle like that. Erica's got that never been kissed look down real good, I don't. She's been kissed and I haven't."

I closed the door, "you can't be saying that. What if your father hears, he'll have a heart attack."

"Come on! Erica's almost in college, he can't think she's never been kissed. Just like you can't think EJ and Eric are still virgins."

Irritation ran through my veins, "funny how you're telling me everyone's business except your own! I don't want to know that my sons are taking advantage of little girls. I don't want to know that you want some boy putting the most diseased part of his body in yours!" Lanie turned green, "stop trying to grow up so fast. You are not a woman little girl. Erica and the twins are a lot older than you. There's certain things they will experience that you need A LOT of time before you experience. Right now you should focus on enjoying being a little girl. You will be an adult soon enough and once you're an adult you can't go backwards." Then I started taming her hair.

She watched my eyes in the mirror, "are you mad at me?"

"No, but I don't want to know that my sons are squishing about in little girl's guts, or that my daughter is letting a little boy get close enough to her to put any part of his body in hers. It all leads to trouble, and its not the way I'm trying to raise any of you. Are you sexually active?"

She gasped, "what? Momma no! I haven't even been kissed."

Ethan opened the door, "GOOD! And you better never!"

Lanie and I jumped, "where did you come from?"

Ethan focused on Lanie, "who did Erica kiss?"

Lanie stiffened, "nobody! I was just saying that to have something to say."

Ethan gave her that fatherly death stare, "when is it ever ok to lie to me?"

Lanie flinched, "I'm sorry."

"Who?"

Lanie put her eyes on the floor. "Daddy I love you so much! You're an amazing father."

"Who?"

"You are the best father, there's no one better than you. I tell the girls at school all the time about how good of a daddy I've got."

"ELAINE!"

Lanie gasped, "DADDY! We've discussed this!"

"Answer me!" Lanie kept her eyes to the floor. Ethan took the comb from me. He put it in her hair and started pulling it through.

"DADDY!" She screamed in agony. "Ok! Daddy! Ok! I'll talk. I'll talk!" She said grabbing for the comb.

"What's going on?" Erica said walking into the bathroom. Zoey was peeking in from the hallway.

"RUN! Save yourself! Daddy's gonna torture you too!" Lanie said with tears pouring out of her eyes.

Erica started to run and Ethan called her back. Still holding Lanie's hair in one hand and the comb in the other, Ethan asked Erica who's the boy she's been kissing on. When Erica stood there looking stuck, Ethan put the comb back in Lanie's hair. As he pulled the comb through again Lanie screamed again. Erica started crying and she begged her father to stop. Zoey looked terrified by the whole scene. Now this would seem horrible if Lanie's hair was tangled. This girl just takes tender headed to a whole other level. The comb passed through her hair nicely each time, but Lanie don't like getting her hair done period. Lanie started screaming that this was child abuse. To save her sister Erica sang like a canary. Ethan told Erica to invite the boy over. When she hesitated he warned her that if she didn't, he'd make her go to school right here in the Bay and she wouldn't be allowed to date until she was fifty years old. Lanie stood there crying her eyes out as if she was reliving the whole experience.

Episode 1

Kendra

Jason was looking over the contracts with me. I couldn't help but smile at his discerning frown as his eyes glided over everything. He had a yellow highlighter in his hand. Every so many sentences he would stop and highlight. Once he was finished, like any good father would, he went over everything with me. He asked me if I had any questions. I told him I wanted a second pair of eyes to go over everything to make sure I didn't miss anything or misunderstand. Jason smiled and said business was going to pick up, and I needed to get ready. I took a deep breath and prepared myself for greatness.

I'm taking subcontracts from Mitigated Staffing Solutions. Mitigated is one of the biggest temporary staffing companies in the country. This company spans from Coast to Coast. My tiny house cleaning and janitorial service was going to provide them with more employment opportunities. Also, I would be able to use their services for staff as well, whether I needed temporary or permanent help it would be covered.

My ex-boyfriend Darryl really came through for me on this one. He's been saying that he could help me expand my business but I really thought he was trying to use my business as an excuse to talk to me. I know Anton my fiancé didn't like the idea of Darryl helping me. But it's really not his call to make. He's so focused on his own business that he can't remember to do simple things I ask of him that would help me.

I thought the engagement period was supposed to be a happy blissful time, at least before you set the date and all the planning craziness begins. Anton and I have been fine, but that's just it. We're only fine. We're not fantastic; we're not all over each other. I would be lying if I said that was his entire fault. I know Anton loves me. I know he's completely open when it comes to me. I just... I just.... I don't know how I feel. I guess the best I can say is I feel stuck. My mind says that marrying Anton is the right thing to do; having children with him is a stable investment in a father who would be hands-on, loving, and patient. However, my heart screams obscenities at me and remains stuck in yesteryear when it was full of fantasies of Darryl. Last night I dreamed about us making love and it felt so real like it just happened. Darryl hadn't cheated on me and my heart and body were free to be with him. Instead I woke up to the disappointment of the fact that it was all a dream. I tried to shake it off, remind myself of where everything stands today. Darryl can't be alone as far as I can tell. Part of me wonders if he even really loved me like he says he does or does he want me because he knows I don't sleep around. I feel like he needs to take the time to determine where he wants to be in his life. I want someone stable and content being with me ONLY! If he's got to have so many women how could he ever be what I need?

Chantel

"Thank you for staying tuned. We are talking to the lovely and tantalizing Chantel Shaw everybody!" The audience applauded. "Now Chantel I couldn't help but notice this ice dripping from your finger. Is somebody engaged?" My interviewer asked.

I blushed, "yes I am." The audience went crazy.

"We have more questions from the audience." Then she gave the person manning the microphone permission to allow the person to speak.

The girl was very excited. "Hi Chantel! I love you so much!" She screamed! "You have no idea how much your music has helped me through some stormy times in my life. I follow everything you do. I even went to see that movie *Heartless* three times because it was perfectly scored with your music." She started jumping around and fanning herself. "I noticed that your body seems different." She smiled real big and started jumping around again. "Are you pregnant? And if you are how does Shameless feel about it?"

I smiled because I knew this would happen but I thought I'd have more time before I'd have to announce my pregnancy. "Do I look different?"

"Oh come on, we won't tell anyone." My interviewer said.

I put my hand on my stomach, "I'm four months. And my big brother is very happy for me."

"Oh my goodness! Do you know what you're having?"

"Not yet, I won't know for another month and a half."

"What are you hoping for a boy or a girl?"

"It doesn't matter to me as long as the baby is healthy."

"So does this ring mean you're getting married soon?"

I exhaled, "I am."

"To whom?" She asked getting all in my business.

"To my fiancé and the father of my child. He's not in the business so it's pointless to say his name."

"Will you have cameras at your wedding?"

"I doubt it. If anything I'll release pictures later. But right now I'm promoting my latest release." I steered the topic back to my music.

When the interview was over Bruce was standing directly next to me. Derrick is nervous about overly enthusiastic fans possibly knocking me over. He didn't want me to sign autographs at all. This was the compromise. Bruce escorted me back to the airport as I prepared for the flight home.

Tracy

"Tracy's here," I said announcing my presence on the conference call. I drummed my fingers on the desk while my mind wandered all over the place. In this office is the last place I want to be. I'd rather be in the bed with Andrew doing what only comes natural. Instead I'm back to normal life, conference calls and trying not to drive myself crazy. It's been two months why aren't I pregnant yet? But then again I could be pregnant right now and I just don't know yet. I touched my stomach and smiled at the idea. No longer the fear that could ruin my life. Now I sit anxiously anticipating when it will happen. Meanwhile I keep asking myself about the bakery. Andrew's uncle offered to finance my shop if I decide to open one. Like Amber said, the thought of making a living by doing something I love is scary. What if only a small group of people like my creations? Every time I think about it I break out in a sweat. My mom said I should do it. She said my job is too stressful at times. She even volunteered my dad to help me with whatever I needed. I think she just wants to get him out of the house. Joy says I should do it too, but I'm scared. I've been independent all my adult life. And although Andrew is very generous, I'm scared. What if he changes up on me one day? Although, he decided against a pre-nup, stating that I was stuck with him for the rest of my life. I feel like that's the fairytale answer. And since nothing outside of our fairytale wedding ever happens for me like it should; I feel like I should continue to work as a safety net.

"Tracy?" Neil tapped on my cubicle wall. I looked at him. "They're waiting for your response."

I made an embarrassed face. "What did they ask me?"

"They wanna know the status on your implementation piece."

I took my line off mute and I responded. I did my best to stay plugged in the remainder of the call. After the call wrapped up Neil asked where I wanted to order lunch from and he'd reserve a conference room to go over the latest from our project call. I said I wanted a salad from Trisha's in the center. He told me he knew which one I wanted, then he went to talk to Danielle the receptionist. I drummed my fingers again. I'm sure he meant nothing by telling me he knew what I liked, but I'm nervous about everything I say and do. I'm careful not to say too much or get too comfortable. I don't want any repeats of my previous assistant. Even though that was a special circumstance, still.

Neil said we were in Sundance conference room. I left the door open even though he closed it, and then we dove into our project. Danielle brought our lunch once it was delivered. Neil shared that he and his sister were going to have lunch with his father this weekend. He wasn't excited about it; he said he was going to comfort his sister. He said he could care less whether his father lived or died. He said all of his life his father was a faceless man and then all of a sudden he appears. Like Santa Claus with bags of money trying to right all the wrongs. He said it feels forced and he doesn't trust him. I listened empathetically, I couldn't say I understood. My dad was always there for me. When Neil calmed down and changed back to his normal spray tan complexion from red, I returned the focus of our conversation back on our project. When I finally got back to my desk it was only two. I sighed; four o'clock couldn't get here fast enough.

Sasha

"I was looking through this magazine trying to get an idea for my hair."

Ava tisked at me, "Sasha, you shouldn't pick your hair until you pick your dress. What if you pick a style that doesn't compliment the look?"

"You picked your hair," I reminded her.

"I also knew the style of dress I was getting. You're all over the place. Let's focus on the engagement party first anyways. When are you getting your dress for that?"

"Saturday, I'm going to a shop in San Francisco. My momma knows the owner of the bridal store. Apparently Tracy found her shop by chance while she was dress shopping. This lady used to babysit me when I was little. Drew seems to remember her. She just seems familiar to me, but I can't say I remember her." I frowned.

"Why does that make you mad?"

"It doesn't, I'm still struggling with being mad at Drew. Everybody and I do mean everybody was in the wedding except me."

"Tanisha wasn't."

I blew air, "she wasn't gonna put on a dress. But still she was a part of the planning. I'm over here in isolation just because I live a car ride away. He's been kissing my butt asking for forgiveness. But it hurts, cause naturally I want my twin in my wedding. Especially since we know Tanisha won't do it."

"How do you know? I think you should ask her. You might be surprised."

"Yea but as what?"

"Duh! Your maid of honor of course! That's your sister. Besides she's going to be a part of your planning either way. Seems only right."

"If she says no...."

She cut me off, "I know! I got your back." Then she got excited. "Call her now! I wanna know if I'm doing her hair or not."

I don't know why my heart was beating a mile a minute. Tanisha answered the phone. "Officer Seaver!"

"You're on duty? You can call me back."

"Girl! I thought I was answering my work phone. What's up I can talk for a minute."

"I wanna ask you something, please don't be offended by it. It would mean the world to me...." Tanisha didn't say anything. I inhaled then exhaled. "Will you be my maid of honor?"

It was silent for a long time. Then Tanisha started laughing. "You mean put on a dress?"

"Yes, dress, make-up, and hair the whole bit," I said nervously.

She laughed then she got quiet. "Please don't make me walk with Drew!" She pleaded.

I felt like I was going to float away! "You'll do it???"

"You can't say I don't love you!"

"Oh my goodness Tanisha! I love you so much! I was scared to ask you! But Ava told me to ask you and then you said yes! I can't believe this! I'm even happier than I thought I'd be!"

"Let's do this. Don't tell anyone. Let them see me walking down the aisle." She laughed.

"Un huh, you don't want Amber to ask you to be in hers." I laughed.

"Right!" She laughed, "This is my last time in a dress!"

"Deal! Mum's the word!"

Yussef

"Do you like them?" I asked the girls, "Angela picked them out."

"We love them! Thank you daddy!" Yezzy ran over to kiss my cheek.

"Yes, thank you!" Syd said following suit.

"Good, put them in your room. Then we're going over our cousin Bernadette's house."

"Yay!" They cheered. "But why can't we bring them?" Yezzy asked.

"Because these dolls are really special. You have to be gentle with them and I can see them getting messed up over there."

"Ok daddy!" Syd said running to her room with her doll with Yezzy following suit.

"How do I look?" Angela said coming out of the bathroom.

"Beautiful as usual!" I said admiring her form.

"Should I change? Am I too casual?"

"Come here," I said waving her over. I made her sit in my lap. "Cargo pants are the way to go. This is not a life-altering event. You're going to meet more of my family. In all honesty I'm still meeting a lot of them too. The girls know more people personally than I do and that's because they're in school together. There's no pressure here. The only anticipated tension is from Drew, but he's a ball of emotion. I cannot waste any more energy on him." I rubbed her back.

She exhaled. "You sure you gonna be ok seeing her?"

I kissed her, "I'm in love with you. That was just a crush. They're married and happy. I have you and my girls and I'm happy."

"That wasn't a yes Yussef," she said dryly.

"I'm gonna be fine." I was trying to convince her that I was telling the truth. I didn't honestly know how I would feel seeing Tracy casually again. I haven't found the words to explain Sasha yet. So I thank God she's not gonna be there too. Although last time I saw her I think we landed on a mutual understanding. She's in love with her man, I have Angela... How many directions can a man's heart go in? System overload! I kissed Angela again, hoping my kiss assured her that I was ok. Even if I wasn't too sure myself. When I opened the garage, the girls got excited cause we were riding in Grand poppa's car and they loved it as much as I do. Angela looked completely nervous even though she smiled to try to mask it. It was a beautiful day out so I took the top down, passed the girls their scarves and shades that Angela bought them for such occasions. I looked in the mirror and paused for a minute. All I saw was my father; it was like I disappeared the moment I took off my locs. Nobody seems to recognize me except Malcolm. My momma claims that she grew my hair long because she wanted me to be my own person. I honestly think she really wanted a little girl. Once she saw my hair she couldn't bare to cut it. That's my theory anyways; its not like it matters now.

I've been laying low these last few months. Once I got DNA confirmation on both of my girls, I've been focused on them and Angela. I've been working from home and only talking to the baby momma's over the phone. Sylvia's still in shock so she's on good behavior. I haven't looked into Melissa's eyes to tell you what's going on with her. That girl is crazy, so I'm in no hurry to look into anything with her.

Darryl pulled up at the same time as I did. He whistled, "I can't believe it man! You went from no kids to two kids in no time flat! Automatic fatherhood! How you lovely ladies doing?" He said to my girls.

"Good!" The girls said in unison.

"And you?" He said to Angela.

"Oh me? I'm good. I mean I'm ok. How are you?" She said nervously.

Darryl walked over and put his arm around her shoulders. "I'm good! You seem nervous, and you know what? That's good! That means you care, but there's no reason to be nervous. It's just a bunch of loud and crazy Latour's in there. We're good people you'll see, no matter what anyone else may have told you."

"I'm from Richmond I don't know about Oakland people."

"Richmond?" He smiled, "you know any Mason's?"

"Tons!"

"Darryl Mason, nice to meet you!" He smiled.

Angela forgot she was nervous. "Dana Mason is my girl!"

"She's crazy! You run with crazy folks so see it's all good." Angela smiled at me really big. I thanked Darryl then we followed him inside. "Paulette this is Angela, break her in easily like you did Chantel. Don't unleash all the craziness right away," he said.

"Well then you better check yourself as well. How are you?" She said giving Angela a hug. Then she looked at me and inhaled, "hey cousin!" Then she hugged me.

"Hey cousin," I liked the sound of that. "I guess at some point, we'll have to sit down and have you guys map out the family tree for me."

"Definitely!"

"Hey! Hey!" Latia said as she came in the door with Lewis in tow.

"Hello," Angela said at the recognition of a familiar face.

"Auntie!" Yezzy said running to Latia.

Syd was still adjusting to this new life just like the rest of us. "Um, Sydney? Come give me some love sweetheart." Latia commanded. Syd smiled widely and ran to her auntie.

"How are auntie's babies?"

"Good!"

"Hold on! Hold on!" Darryl said getting everybody's attention. "What I gotta do? Who I gotta be? To get hugs like that?" The girls smiled. "When you see me, I want you to come running! Jump on me! Scream Darryl, you ain't gotta call me uncle, cause we cousins, but I wanna feel the love, got it?"

"Ok," Syd giggled.

"So now let's rehearse." He cleared his throat and bent down with his arms stretched. "Hi girls!" He said real corny.

"DARRYL!" The girls yelled and ran to him giving him hugs like he asked for.

Darryl fake cried, "that was beautiful ladies! Just beautiful!"

"What you in here crying about?" Andrew said walking in the door.

"You had to be there." Darryl said straightening up. Then he told Andre to come over. "Andre, these are your big cousins. Introduce yourselves."

"Hi I'm Andre, but you can call me Dre."

"Yesmina, but you can call me Yezzy. And this is my sister Sydney, but you can call her Syd."

"There are more cousins out back, how about we all go." Paulette said probably because of the obvious tension in the room.

"Andrew," He said extending his hand to Lewis. "This is my wife, Tracy."

Angela grabbed my hand. "Nice to meet you, I'm Lewis."

"Hey Latia," Andrew said giving her a hug. His expression was weird. Latia said an awkward hello. "Yussef." He stood tall in front of me.

"Andrew, this is my girlfriend Angela. Angela this is Andrew and his wife

Tracy." I heard myself say but it still sounded weird.

"It's nice to finally meet you." Tracy said to Angela and Latia, "I've heard so much about both of you."

Angela and Latia smiled, then Paulette reminded us to follow her to the backyard. Angela and I walked first and I held on to her hand. I wanted the ridiculousness to go away. In the backyard there were a ton of people. Older and younger, everyone was introducing their selves to Latia and I. And falling all over their selves cause Lewis was here. Lewis is a very well-known rapper who goes by the name Shameless. When Derrick and Chantel arrived some of the attention was off of Lewis but not by a whole lot. Chantel grew up around my family so they were used to seeing her even though she was a big star now. Having Chantel did buffer a lot of the awkwardness. She got the women interacting and relaxing. Derrick brought me a drink; he asked how things were going. I told him being here feels like a dream come true. He said this is the way it should've always been. Andrew was talking to our cousin Fuzzy, and he kept looking in our direction. Derrick called him over, Andrew frowned and came over. Derrick told him to stop acting like a girl, to say what he needed to say and then let's be done with everything. Then Derrick walked away. I asked Andrew if there was anything else that needed to be said. "I'm still mad at you!" Andrew said like a big ole kid.

"So! I'm mad at you!"

"So!"

"So!" I exhaled. "We family or what?"

Andrew rolled his eyes, "we mad family!"

I laughed, "we're what?"

"We family man," he said in a defeated tone.

"Did Malcolm tell you about my Sydney?"

"I knew about the one, I thought the other was Angela's?"

"They're mine. I got the DNA test to prove it." Andrew's eyes got big as he waited for the story. So I told him the story about how I found out about Sydney by chance. He was standing, then he was leaning, then he was holding himself up and looking at me like I had to be making this story up. I wished I was, but so much had happened recently in my life that I didn't get to share with one of my closest friends. Andrew said no wonder I cut my locs off, he almost didn't recognize me at first. He said he thought he was seeing my father when he walked in the door. Malcolm and Amber showed up. Malcolm saw us talking and he stayed away. Amber came over and gave us HUGE hugs then she made her way around the picnic. Andrew and I sat over to the side reestablishing our relationship.

Lanie

I saw Yussef's car and I got excited. I've been missing his knucklehead self. He's been missing in action for too long! I looked at my sisters with a grin. Each of us stood up straight and sucked in our stomachs. It's no secret that I've had a crush on Yussef since I was a child. Even though I love Dorian my longtime boyfriend. I *wants me some* Yussef like you wouldn't believe! It makes me mad every time he pats me on the head like I'm a kid to him. LET THE RECORD REFLECT, I could marry him and have all of his babies. Zoey had the nerve to develop her own crush on him. He doesn't respond to her either, he gives her the same respectful dismissal that he gives me, but he doesn't dismiss her like she's a kid.

I'm going to walk in, take a handful of Yussef's locs, and inhale them. His hair always smells good and it's always neat, clean, and soft. When we stepped out in the yard, I scanned the yard for a second and then a third time. Maybe he's inside. I was about to go back inside when I noticed the guy talking to Drew. I grabbed the railing to catch myself.

I slowly sat on the stair. Yussef cut his hair off! Lord! Why? I wiped my mouth cause I caught myself drooling. "Lanie! Cut it out!" Darryl called out from across the yard smiling at me. He gets on my nerves!

Donzae came over to me with a big smile. She sat next to me on the step and she scooted real close to me. She whispered in my ear. "He's our cousin girl!" I flared my nostrils at her. "Turns out he's Troy's son, do you remember him?"

"Of course I do."

"Look at Yussef girl! You can see it."

I weakly pointed my eyes at Yussef. I wanted to cry but nothing would come out. "NO!" I screamed. Everybody looked at me, "Carry on! Nothing to see here." D laughed at me as if he knew why I screamed. "So what! Just because he's your cousin, that doesn't make him mine."

"Oh, so now you're picking and choosing who you claim. What happened to us being blood relatives?"

I growled at Donzae, "you're getting on my nerves! I don't care anyways! I got a man! Yussef is eye candy nothing more. I can look at him like I look at D or Ryder." I cast my eyes across the yard again. I started crying. Donzae put her arms around me and rocked me telling me it was going to be ok.

"What's wrong with her?" Bump asked.

"She's just adjusting to the new family dynamics! Dang you nosy!" Bump looked at me and started cracking up as he walked away. "Oh no girl! D's coming!"

I got up to run away. "Don't run, cause I will chase you." He said with a big smile. I ran anyways, "*Lanie! Lanie! Don't run from me girl! I just wanna ask you something!*" He said all dramatically like, if he wanted to he couldn't catch me.

"Stop talking while you run! Show.... Off!" I said trying to run and scream.

"I just wanna ask you something Lanie, slow down." I stopped to catch my breath. D was laughing, "I take it you know about the latest development in our family tree." He smiled real big.

"I hate you so much sometimes."

"Yep! He's kin, so I guess this means you have to leave your silly little crush at the door."

"He's not *my* cousin!"

"Come on! Lanie! Lanie!"

I looked across the yard, "why did he cut his hair? All those beautiful locs? I find myself looking for him amongst all the loc'ed guys I see now." I sighed, "I'm gonna miss his hair the most."

D pointed his finger to the sky, "fear not! His little girls inherited his pretty hair gene."

"**HIS WHAT**?" I screamed.

D cracked up, "you ok? You need a valium?"

I scanned the yard; I spotted a little girl with long hair in a ponytail. "Not fair!"

"That's one, the other one is over there."

I marched over to Drew and Yussef, "How could you do this to me?"

"Do what?" Yussef was clueless.

"Hi Lanie," Drew smiled.

"Hi, Hi! Two babies, what about our kids? You're still going to have babies with me when we get married, right?"

Yussef put his finger up, "sssssshhhh! My girlfriend might think you're serious."

I stumbled back a step, "your WHAT?"

D was cracking up, "Why aren't I recording this? I need to remember this moment whenever I need a good laugh."

"SHUT UP!" I looked at the women with Chantel. "That PLAIN girl? Cargo shorts?

Who wears cargo shorts to a picnic?"

"Lanie, please be nice to her. She's very nervous about meeting all of you."

"She should be!" I pouted.

"You play too much, you need to stop before I think you're serious." Then Yussef gave me a family hug like usual and completely dismissed me while D and Drew smiled at me cause they knew.

I joined Donzae with the other ladies. It was now my mission to pick this chick apart. Nothing on my list of things important compared to me. What does she have that I don't?

Amber

"But Nana bought my house for me!' I said feeling defeated. Malcolm sat there watching me get emotional about the idea. He suggested having a house built up in the hills close to Derrick's house. I liked the idea of having something together; I didn't want to give up my house either. I love my house! But Malcolm was right too much had happened in both of our houses. Since we have the means for a fresh start why not? I didn't care what he did with his house, but I wasn't living in a house where all of his previous mistresses ran free. He could say the same about my house although; I will say in my defense that my house hasn't seen nearly as many overnight guests as his. Malcolm asked me if I wanted a fresh start or not. I exhaled cause this battle wasn't worth fighting. "Fine Malcolm!" I exhaled in defeat. Malcolm smiled at me and then he called my Uncle Dale. He told him as soon as we finished breakfast we'd be on our way up the hill. Malcolm was looking at his phone checking emails for work while I sulked. It looked like his brain was going a mile a minute as he swung from business matter to business matter. Some of them made him mad, and others had no effect on him. I sat there wondering how he kept everything straight; he had so many balls in the air at once.

He stopped and looked at me, he asked me if Tracy had made a decision about the bakery yet? I exhaled and I told him she's scared. Malcolm looked at me like it was so simple, he told me to go over the business plan with her. He said she's educated, she should understand what I was showing her. I said she should but there was more to it than just saying here's the plan now go out and make it work. Malcolm said there really wasn't, that was it, and that was all. I told him he's all about business and in his mind it was a win-win situation. But for her it was emotional as well as business. Malcolm exhaled; he said Andrew and Tracy are an emotional couple. He said he was glad they found a way to make it work cause they would drive him crazy. I reminded him that I could relate to Tracy. He said he could relate more to Chantel. He said she was still way more emotional than he could understand, but she was more his temperament than Tracy if he had to choose. I told him that was only because he has all those years of working with Chantel to know her better. With Tracy, well he was still getting to know her.

After breakfast, we drove up the Oakland hills and up to the security gate for Derrick and Chantel's community. "Good morning Mr. Latour! Have a good day." The guard at the gate said as he opened the gate. Derrick's house was over to the left tucked away in the corner and not extremely noticeable. Chantel's brother Cyrus' house was ahead of us. Malcolm went to Uncle Dale's trailer on the right. Sharon and I hugged big hugs, and then she asked to see my ring again. She whistled loudly and told me she was happy for me, I smiled. Uncle Dale had Sharon bring up the lot he had in mind for our house. He showed us the planned structure of the house and explained a lot of the upgrades and modifications that we could make to the house. Malcolm asked me what I thought, I exhaled, and then I told him I liked it. But why did we need so many bedrooms? He said we were about to start having a busload of grandchildren. He said it only seemed right that we would have space for them. I exhaled because I didn't feel old enough to have a busload of grandchildren. I didn't think of myself as twenty-five, but I didn't see myself moving to a retirement community in Florida either. As if he was reading my mind Malcolm said the kids were getting older not us. I asked how long it would take to have this house built. He said he'd need to get some of the modifications approved by the city, which could take a little bit. Malcolm asked him about the unapproved modifications. Uncle Dale smiled and said like Derrick's house he'd incorporate them during the building process. We walked to the location of our future home together. Uncle Dale explained because of the location within this project we would have an AMAZING view of the Bay, similar to the one seen from Derrick's house. Then Uncle Dale mentioned that Malachi was going to purchase a house in this development. I asked about Jade, and he said she and Sonny hadn't decided yet. Timothy and Grace wanted to stay in Daddy's house, but Timothy may change his mind yet again. He keeps going back and forth struggling with himself. Uncle Dale said Timothy's lot is ready for him whenever he decides to get it together.

Malachi

I had a dream I was talking to my parents. This was nothing unusual. I dream about them all the time. I miss my crazy momma so much! And my dad was my best friend. Sometimes I can't believe they're gone cause I see them so clearly. Denise put her arms around me, which made me open my eyes, but I didn't move. She rubbed my back, as she was aware that I was having a dream. I love my wife, she patiently waited for me to get it together and officially give her my last name. But sometimes I feel like this life is all wrong! In my dreams when I'm talking to my momma she asks me why my wife doesn't look like her. I tell her that Denise is a good woman and I love her. My momma reminds me that I love chocolate, women who look like her. She says she just knew that Timothy would bring home someone who reminded him of her. I tell her that Grace does remind him of her she just happens to be Asian. My momma doesn't argue but she's still disappointed. My momma reminds me that I'm a black man, as if I could forget. I normally wake up sweating and upset, I can't tell Denise about these dumb dreams. It seems so petty to have dreams like this.

Most times I make love to Denise, my coping mechanism. Lately I feel... I feel like I'm suffocating! Wife and kids, that's the dream right? My wife is gorgeous and loves me to death. Two of the best kids ever! Shouldn't I feel like I've got it all locked up? Like I'm sitting on top of the world? I don't, not even a little bit. I'm a good man, but that inner struggle is always hard for me. Sometimes Malcolm and I talk about some of the things we've done when we were younger. When I get to Momma, Malcolm always gets quiet. He lets me get it out, and then he tells me I need to see Joanne. Joanne is the therapist who sees a lot of my family members, and if she can help Malcolm get out of his own way she has to be good. I just haven't gotten around to seeing her yet. I wanna come to terms on my own with why the bosom of another woman makes me feel so alive? Cora is a fellow engineer at my plant. I didn't pay her any mind at first we always were about our business. I think it was one business trip too many. I don't even remember what I was mad about now. At the time it was justified anger. One drink too many, one dance too many, and I was tasting the full lips of a woman I had been penalizing myself for desiring. We didn't go further than the kiss that night, but the foundation for my turmoil was laid. Cora reminded me of momma in a lot of ways I guess, she was smart and strong. Her skin was a deep ebony black. Her eyes pierce you when she's angry, and they salute you when she's happy. She knew I was married and she was engaged at the time. She's gotten married and divorced since then. I'm so disappointed in myself; Denise doesn't say anything but how could she not know? Maybe she doesn't know or maybe she doesn't care. I'd hate to find out which one it is. Either way I'd feel like I was drowning. Cora and I have broken the whole thing off so many times. She understands that I will never leave my wife, and she doesn't want me to. Neither of us ever thought we'd be caught up like this. It's not something we planned or were looking for. So far we've been discreet, I've told no one about my indiscretion. And she says she's told no one. With the way my sisters always shared things I'm sure she's told at least someone. I used to share everything with Denise. There wasn't anything I couldn't tell her. When her mother got sick it took the life out of her for a minute. I understood it though, she was focused on her mother and I took care of the kids. We were still communicating and even though she shut down, I understood that was her way of dealing with the whole thing. Then she shut down completely. She couldn't be a wife or a mother. I was selfish and ridiculous for trying to talk to her about it. Denise went to therapy to help with the loss of her mother. She and I have never spoken about what happened or how seeing her like that has affected me. We found a new routine and carried on with business as usual. Then Cora happened, I love my wife. I love our family together, but I also care about this woman who's been able to fill a need.

Episode 2

Tracy

"Malcolm isn't too particular, so I was thinking I wanted a Caramel Rum cake for our cake table. What do you think?" Amber said with a smile.
"That's simple enough." I wrote it down.
Amber was surprised, "simple enough? If you say so."
"What type of design do you want? You want a round cake, box shaped, sheet cake?"
"Oh I don't know honey whatever you think is best. But I want PURPLE the most important color, GREEN, and GOLD. Those colors represent me, Jade, and my momma."
"Aw! That is so sweet!" I said. I told Becca I was having lunch with my mother in-law today. So she knew I wasn't coming back exactly at an hour. Suddenly we got three weddings coming up. Amber and Malcolm's, Chantel and Derrick's, and Sasha and El's. So someone came up with the idea to have a big engagement party for all three couples since a lot of the same people would be at all three. Amber asked me to make the cake for their cake table at their engagement party. I don't know who's making the other cakes, but of course I'm all over anything Amber asks me to do. I love these moments when it's just she and I, like it used to be. I guess all the drama kind of kept us isolated. Now that Malcolm and Andrew have a better relationship we see more of his family. I don't mind being with them. They're quite funny and entertaining, but I also enjoy the moments where I get to be one on one with each one. I find myself falling in love with each person individually. Fortunately Andrew hasn't brought up Yussef or his girlfriend yet, but I can see it coming. I about wanted to DIE when I saw Yussef with his locs all gone. My first reaction was like WHAT DID YOU DO? I loved his locs, they complimented him so well. Then it was like oh WOW look at you. Without the locs you see him, and as much as I don't think about it Yussef is FINE! Never as FINE as my baby though. Never to be mistaken I LOVE my husband! At the end of the day, I know how good I got it, and I would never give him up. I'm just saying WHOA! I know his girlfriend knows about everything as well... Yussef is such a stand-up guy. I still admire that about him, when others become slaves to the wrong thing he always does the right thing no matter how painful it is. Angela was watching me the whole picnic though. Chantel did a good job of getting us to interact. I don't know if Chantel knows about everything, but I was thankful that she was there. She had us playing games and teaming up, I'd say our interaction went well. Sometimes you can't tell with females. I just knew to steer clear of Andrew and

Yussef. Andrew said they had a good conversation but he didn't go into detail, and I know better than to ask. Andrew was going to need time to adjust to the idea of Yussef being around. "Amber, how is all of this going to take place? Who's getting married first?"

Amber explained that Derrick and Chantel were going to get married first. Then Sasha was going next, she said she's working on patience cause she's waited on Malcolm for a long time and now she has to get in line. Then she got really excited as she threw out ideas for her special day. If I thought I was excited about my day, then I'd say we tied for first place. Amber was up in arms about who would give her away though. She said she always thought her daddy would be there. Now that he's gone she doesn't know, should it be one of her uncles or one of her brothers. Or should it be one of her boys. She said she needed to decide. Then she exhaled. She said she wanted her sister Jade to be her matron of honor and Sophia to be her maid of honor. She said she didn't know about Rosalind. She said Rosalind was her oldest friend, but when they lost Troy, Yussef's father, it felt like she lost her best friend too. I thought about Joy and the time we spent apart. Fortunately for me, Joy and I picked up where we left off and that was all due to the fact that she's that good of a person, but everyone isn't so fortunate. I told her she still had time to figure out if she wanted to have her in her wedding. She nodded, and then she got excited and looked at her ring. She kept saying she was engaged and how excited she was. I smiled remembering the feeling.

Last thing I wanted to do was go back to the office. I wished I could've spent the rest of the day with Amber talking about her wedding and basking in her joy of her upcoming nuptials. When I got back to the office there was a fire that needed extinguishing within one of my projects. As if his spidy-senses were going off Andrew called me to check in. He asked if I was leaving on time today. I exhaled and I told him I doubted it. He told me to call him when I left. He said his day was going pretty good, so he'd make dinner. I thanked him and blew him kisses over the phone.

When I walked in the puppies met me at the door. All of the lights were off and there was a line of flickering lights leading to the bedroom. You know those battery-operated lights that look like tea lights. I assume he didn't use candles in case the puppies knocked them over. I smiled really big as I felt my heart bubble over. I set the alarm on the doors and windows and then I made my way up the stairs. Andrew had soft music playing and the lights led to my bathroom where my baby was waiting in the bathtub with a bottle of wine and two glasses. I smiled as I was getting in my favorite retreat when I got home anyways. Andrew smiled as he poured my glass. I stripped and sat in front of him in my tub. He said Andre was with Amber and Malcolm; they were going out to dinner. I exhaled and leaned into him letting all the stress of the day melt into the water. He asked me about my day and I rambled off the ridiculousness of our work levels right now. Andrew listened and asked me questions but he basically let me vent saying the same things over again sometimes cause I needed to get it out. He moved my hair and softly kissed my neck, which made me stop talking, I liked the way that felt. Then I started adding up the scene he wanted to talk to me about something otherwise why would he make sure I was so relaxed? I started tensing; Andrew chuckled and kissed my neck again. Then he said this wasn't a setup, I said un huh and I waited for a possible boom to come from him. Since I was now suspicious he knew he should just go ahead and say what was needed to be said. He told me that he had lunch with Malcolm and they talked about the bakery idea. He said Malcolm was offering to put a business plan together for me if I wanted to go in that direction. I exhaled and tried not to tense up. "Andrew the thought of going into business for myself is terrifying. What if it fails?"

"Why did you marry me?" He asked calmly.

"Because I love you."

"I married you because I love you and I believe in you. Do you believe me when I say we can't fail?"

"For the most part."

"Only for the most part?"

"We're not perfect, although I believe we will do our best to stick together. No one is promised tomorrow."

Andrew blew irritated air. "Well I believe we're perfectly matched. And you're stuck with me the rest of your life, that's it and that's all. I feel like if you're confident enough to take this journey it's time for you to take another leap of faith. You are good at what you do. Your cakes and pies are delicious and although you may feel like my family likes them because they're family. I'm gonna tell you from firsthand experience that they are the most critical. You have a gift and you should be stressed doing what you love and not working for someone else."

I sat there quiet for a minute, "I can't see the Bay Area liking me enough to make a living doing it. My cakes may be good, but I don't think they're good enough."

"Ok so maybe you don't turn a profit from opening a shop. What if all you do is provide me with a viable loss that I can write off each year in taxes, what's the harm in that? You're doing what you were born to do and it's still helping out the family. I'd rather you come home stressed about filling an order than you ever come home stressed about someone else's business."

"But you don't work for yourself. You come home stressed about someone else's business. You're not asking me to do something that you even do."

"What is it Tracy? Why are you holding on to this job? Anyone else would be happy to let go of a job they don't even like to do something they love."

"You're asking me to be dependent on you. I've only ever depended on my parents to take care of me. I've been working since I could work. You're asking me to give up everything I know. Everything I've work very hard to establish and to rely on you. You have no idea how scary that is to me." I said tensing up.

"I do know how scary that is, but I think we can manage the scary. It's not like you need that job to pay your bills. I pay them. Your paychecks are only collecting interest. Your checking account should be swollen at this point. What could I do to assure you that it's ok to leave that job?"

"I don't know Andrew, I have a 401K, my medical benefits, my independence."

"You can rollover your IRA's and I'll make contributions to them. We can set up our own account if you like. I know you're scared, but I believe you can be great at this. And you'd get to set your own hours. You could ask Joy to help you."

"She has a job already!"

"Yes but once Tracy's Tasty Treats takes off I know she's the first person you'd loop in."

"And Nicole!"

"And your whole family. The only thing stopping you right now from greatness is yourself." Then he exhaled, "besides I don't know if I want you stressed like that when you're pregnant." All my disappointment came gushing forward, and my body tensed as I started to cry. He exhaled as he pulled me in closer. "Tracy, its gonna happen when it's supposed to. I bet you're obsessing over it and it's just not time yet. We're still on our honeymoon anyways." I turned and laid my head on his shoulder while I cried. "Don't cry, I like it this way. We have more time just the three of us."

"It's all your fault!" I said in between sobs.

"Why is it my fault?" He rubbed my back.

"The Beast probably went in there and banged everything up. So now my uterus is all squished up in the corner and I can't get pregnant!" I cried a little more.

Andrew snickered and then he belly laughed, I looked at him with an irritated face. How dare he laugh at what hurts me. "It's not funny Andrew!"

"I'm sorry, you should've heard it. If you weren't so sensitive you would be laughing

13

too."

"I wanna go to the doctor. What if that miscarriage messed me up and I can't get pregnant without help?"

"Tracy, let's let it ride for now. If anything your body is still in shock from all the damage we did on our honeymoon. It will happen when it's time."

Chantel

I thought it was called morning sickness cause you only get sick in the morning. I'm hating the feeling of being sick. Derrick made this lovely dinner for me and I just flushed most of it. I sat on the floor tired and sweating from that violent display. Derrick used a cool towel as he wiped my face, then he picked me up and carried me to our bed. He took my clothes off and told me to get in the bed and he'd bring me broth. Broth didn't sound good after what I gave to the porcelain goddess. Beef Bourguignon with new potatoes, even my nose loved it! My taste buds sang! The baby hated it and sent it back to the kitchen. His cousin Sophia made it at her restaurant and Derrick duplicated it. If I wouldn't have been hungry I would've punished this baby by not eating another thing. However, I tore up that broth like it was a second helping of Derrick's stew. As I laid there listening to Derrick go to town on the piano downstairs in the music room my cellphone rang. It was Lewis, when I answered the phone I could hear tons of noise in the background and Lewis was overly excited. "Chantel!"

"Yes Lewis, what's going on?" I tried to hear everything.

"She said YES! She finally said yes!" I had no doubt that he was talking about Latia; I just didn't know what he meant. "My love said yes! She'll have me! We're getting married!"

I popped up! "Seriously? It's about time! Congratulations! I'm so happy for you."

"We're literally going to be family now!"

"I know right! Congratulations! Let me know how planning goes."

"You ok you don't sound too hot?" He said switching gears.

"Derrick made the best dinner and the baby made me throw it up." Lewis started laughing. "Glad that amuses you."

"Where's my man?"

"He's downstairs creating a masterpiece. I'll tell him your news when he comes up. Congratulations again."

"Alright! I'll see you guys at your engagement party in a couple of weeks."

As soon as we hung up my daddy was calling me. I stared at the phone debating whether to answer it or not, "hi Daddy."

"You don't sound good."

"I'm pregnant, this is what pregnant Chantel sounds like when her baby makes her throw up a perfectly delicious dinner."

"So that explains why you weren't at Gus'. We killed it!"

"You always do!"

"Will you be flying out soon?"

"No, I'll be around at least until the engagement party."

"Babygirl, I don't understand why you guys don't have your own party. Why are you sharing your moment with two other couples?"

"This is why you called isn't it?" He didn't respond. "If you asked me if I cared about any of this I would tell you no. Derrick wants to get married. I don't have to be married. He wants to share these moments with his family. That's fine with me. I honestly don't care, you should be happy that I'm getting married at all."

"Why do you say it like that?" He sounded like I offended him.

"Because I could've went without marriage it doesn't change anything about Derrick and

I."

"I'm glad you're doing it. Are you going to film at your wedding?"

I rolled my eyes, "no daddy. I want my wedding day to be private."

"As soon as paparazzi finds out that all these celebrities are coming to The Bay, they're gonna get suspicious."

"I'm not inviting a bunch of people to my wedding."

"Oh come on, what's the point of making all those connections if you're not going to invite them?"

Derrick walked in the room and I rolled my eyes again. I agreed to allow my father to perform at my reception. I know he's hoping to make some business connections through his performance. I asked him to remember to be happy for me, and that the day was about Derrick and I not about his music. Thankfully he backed down because I wasn't in the mood to go round and round with him. Derrick started kissing my stomach and I no longer had any interest in talking to my father. I got off the phone quickly. I told Derrick about Lewis and Latia, he didn't have a noticeable reaction. Derrick could be over protective at times. He continued to kiss my stomach and talk to the baby. He told the baby how excited he was that they were coming and he couldn't wait to hold them. I smiled at him and watched all the sincerity in his face as he talked to his child.

In the morning I ate a saltine like Sherrell told me to. Then I made my way down to the kitchen. Derrick said he needed to go into the office today and he was on his way out. As he walked out the door I called my sister in-law Sherrell and asked if she made breakfast yet. She said she just walked in the kitchen. I told her we should go to Sophia's for breakfast. She got excited and said she'd walk over as soon as she had little Rosa dressed. I got showered and dressed. I pulled my SUV with the booster seat for little Rosa already installed out the garage. Sherrell and Rosa were walking over. Rosa got really excited when she saw me. As if I didn't see her almost every day. Sherrell asked if Amber was going to come with us. I called Amber and she was already there, she said great minds think alike. So we headed over to Walnut Creek.

"Cyrus left early this morning?"

"Yea, he's not too happy with me right now," She sighed.

"Why?"

"Cause I told him that we should wait until you've delivered before we have our next one. This is your moment to shine. He says you don't care about stuff like that."

"Cause I don't."

"But I feel like you should have this time. You and Derrick have waited so long."

"Sherrell it's fine. Besides our babies will be closer in age this way. The best way to entertain a baby is with another baby. You need to hurry up," I smiled.

"Are you sure?"

"I'm positive!" Then I exhaled, "now that, that's out of the way I have a pickle of my own." I gripped the steering wheel. "I want Cyrus to give me away." Sherrell gasped and covered her mouth. "I know! I know! Help me figure out how to get my way in this."

"Your dad is gonna be heartbroken!"

"I know, but it would mean more to me if Cyrus did it. Help me!"

"Un un, I'm not touching that! That has drama written all over it." We were quiet for a little bit then she said. "You've got to barter something he really wants in exchange and hope that he picks that instead."

I exhaled, "like what? I'm not naming my baby Daniel or Danielle."

"You've got a few weeks to figure it out."

When we got to the restaurant Sophia was kissing Travis goodbye. She came over to the car to greet my belly. I told her about last night and she had a gentle conversation with the baby. She told the baby to let me enjoy my breakfast. Amber and Andre came out to us. We hugged hello and then we went inside the restaurant. There were a few customers inside but not overly crowded. So we sat in a booth on the main floor. Andre and Rosa were cracking up while we were talking. Amber told us that Tracy was going to make her cake for the engagement party. I asked her if Tracy could decorate cakes. I knew her cakes were good, but I didn't want to take a chance on my cake looking homemade. Amber smiled and told me I would just have to see. Sophia said Tracy needed to hurry up and open her bakery so that she could order desserts from her. Sherrell asked if Tracy was that good and they said, "YES!" in unison. Sophia told the chef to bring out a special omelet for me; Sherrell said it sounded good so she ordered the same and a waffle for Rosa. After breakfast we took the kids to a nearby park to burn off energy. While we discussed the party and how much fun it was going to be. My phone rang and I smiled when I saw it was Alexa. She wanted to know why she had to hear about my engagement through celebrity gossip. She said she wouldn't have believed it if she didn't know how sprung I was off of my man. She said Meredith called her to verify if the story was true. Since we were friends I felt obligated to invite her to the wedding. I told her I'd send her an invitation.

Sasha

If this man puts his hands on his hips one more time! I guess my presence is a little intimidating for him, but be a man about it. I'm asking this fool questions about his books and although I can tell he's telling the truth he's too nervous. "Claude, I'm not here cause you've done anything wrong. You're actually doing a wonderful job. Random pop ups is what I do." Claude relaxed a lot. Since I was out here in New York taking care of business, El came and we visited with his family. However, at this particular moment I was checking up on the Shylight lounge out here. I asked Tracy's twin sisters to meet me here but I wasn't expecting them for another thirty minutes. I hit it off with Tara, but I didn't want to be mean and only invite her. I told Claude that I was meeting friends there in a few minutes, but everything looked good. Claude relaxed a lot; I wanted him to relax to the point that he stopped putting his hands on his hips. Anything to stop that! When the girls arrived it wasn't hard to tell who was who. Tia had her hair pulled back in a neat ponytail, dark blue jeans with a white button up tucked in, coffee colored leather jacket, glasses, and heels. Tara on the other hand, she had her hair down with big barrel curls, mid-thigh length dress, boots that came to her knees, fishnet stockings, waist length jacket. I gave them hugs and kisses. We had a table over to the side and we had dinner and people watched. Eventually we graced the dance floor with our presence. Tia stayed at the table.

On the dance floor Tara and I talked about the engagement party coming up. I told her she had to come. She asked me if there were going to be any men there. My mind instantly wondered if Yussef was going to be there. I shook off the thought. I smiled when I saw El and his friend Brody as they were approaching. I asked Brody what happened to his girlfriend. He made a wounded face as he said he was once again single. When I asked him what happened he said they went in different directions. I introduced him to Tara; she had a goofy grin and said he needed to meet her sister. We went back to the table and Tara introduced Brody to Tia. Tara raised her eyebrow at me; I didn't think Tia was interested until I saw her take a second glance when she thought no one was looking. Brody was all right, definitely didn't have enough game for me. Maybe that's what Tia was looking for. Tara said Tia used to be a lot of fun, lately she's been laying low. El invited me to dance, Brody invited Tia to dance, and then a guy invited Tara to dance. We had a nice time. When we dropped the girls off Brody started asking questions about Tia. I wished I had answers for him, but I was happy to hear his enthusiasm about her.

In the morning we had breakfast with Mr. & Mrs. Parsons, they brought their daughter

Brielis' son with them. They were excited about coming to the engagement party, and they wanted to know about the wedding plans. We didn't have a date yet, but I assured them that my family would be covering everything including their airfare to the West Coast. Mrs. Parsons rubbed her hands together; she said Zoila heard about the engagement. Then she asked me if it was ok with me that she told us what happened. I told her it was ok, cause I honestly wanted to know. She said Zoila came over early in the morning in tears. She apologized over and over for how disrespectful she was the last time she saw her. Then she said Zoila fell on her knees crying her eyes out cause she couldn't believe that El had given his heart to someone else. After all they had been through she thought he was coming back to her. I looked at El to read his face about how all of this was hitting him. He adjusted in his seat but he kept his face even. Mrs. Parsons said she felt sorry for her, but it was time that she accepted that her baby had moved on. She said she told her that she had years to accept it, obviously she hadn't. Mr. Parsons asked El if he was going to invite his sister to our engagement party and wedding. I looked at El to see what he said. El was quiet for a minute, and then he told his father that he would discuss it with me and that he'd get back to him. I liked that he didn't make decisions for us and then told me to deal with it. Sometimes he came to me with a decision and he was making sure it was ok with me, and if there was a concern on my end he'd take it into consideration. My baby is a man's man! I love that about him!

Kendra

"KB!" I heard Darryl's voice and I closed my eyes hoping it was my imagination. I turned around and sure enough it was him, I smiled. "Please call me Kendra." Darryl pursed his lips at me like I was ridiculous for trying. "KB, how's business?" Ahjanae, Kalani, and I were picking out the last finishing touches for our office space. It was a small but nice office in the Rockridge shopping center. I was going to be next door to Carina's Events as soon as it opens, an event and wedding planner. All of the shops and businesses in this center were nicely decorated and put together. We were going over the design of the office and the furniture we wanted to get with Ryder's Uncle Darren. "Hey Darryl, how's it going?" Darren said.
"I can't complain." Darryl said staring at me. "KB, I need to talk to you."
"So talk," I returned my attention to the catalog.
Darryl took my hand and led me out of the office. "KB! Are you avoiding me?" I swallowed and said an unconvincing no. Darryl smiled, "you are avoiding me! I knew it! You're still in love with me. Break off the engagement and come to daddy." He put his arms out.
"Look Darryl, I don't want you getting the wrong idea. We were at a wedding, you dang near sang to me. It was an open bar for crying out loud. I shouldn't have kissed you."
"Un huh! Yes you should've. I would've been devastated if you didn't kiss me. My heart would've stopped beating! My system would've shut down and I would've died! My brother got married, my other brother got engaged, MY PARENTS GOT ENGAGED! You would've wanted me to be the only person without love that night? That's what you want for me?"
I stretched my eyes at him. "Your parents got engaged?"
His smile got bigger, "can you dig it? Yes! Malcolm even seems excited about it, go figure." This smile was different. He was proud of his parents.
"So what does that mean for your theory on marriage?" I don't know why my heart sped up.
"KB! I need a woman that loves me. I don't need a wife!" I rolled my eyes as I flat lined. "The sooner you accept the fact that you're that woman, the sooner we can start making some pretty big booty babies." He smiled.

"As flattering as that may have sounded in your head, I want to be a wife. I'm going to be a wife, I have a fiancé and I'm going to have plenty of babies with him."

Darryl chuckled, "don't irritate me." Then he exhaled, "so the plan is to have a big engagement party for my parents, brother, and cousin. I need you to go with me."

"Darryl!"

"Now say it breathlessly like you used to," he teased.

"I can't go out with you, I'm engaged to Anton. You may not respect my relationship, but I do!"

Darryl exhaled and crossed his arms like he was letting me get it out of my system. "Go ahead, tell me about it! Tell me how he's better than me! Loves you more than I do! Knows you better, all that."

"He loves me enough to be faithful to me."

Darryl stepped into my face and he looked me in my eyes. "I was faithful to you when we were together. We broke up because of you not me." I deflated, and then he faked cried. "You broke my heart KB! And yet, I still want you. I don't let the past affect what I feel for you today."

"The reason we aren't together today is because of your constant need for too many females. If you weren't such a hoe, we wouldn't have broken up in the first place. What is the point of going back and forth about what happened yesterday when we were kids?" He smiled and said we still are kids. I exhaled. "I'm not going!"

"KB! Don't make me do this, don't make me blackmail you cause I will stoop that low."

"You've got nothing." I dared him.

"Maybe I do, maybe I don't. Your baby daddy is asking, no begging you. You always gotta play hard to get. Can you please for once just say yes?"

"Stop referring to yourself as my baby daddy that hurts."

"Stop acting like you don't love me. Stop acting like you don't want me. KB!" He paused for dramatic effect, "stop acting."

I rolled my eyes at him, "Darryl! I'm in the middle of setting up my office. Can we please talk about this another time?"

He took out his phone, "of course. When would you like to get together?"

"What are you doing?"

He looked at me completely serious. "I'm going over my schedule. You know I travel a lot for work. Let's bump schedules."

I laughed, "well I was thinking Thursday for lunch."

He held his serious face. "Yea, yea sure. Lunch, you wanna go to Addis again?" He smiled at me.

I held back the urge to curse him right there. "NO!"

He chuckled, "oh come on! You know that food was good!"

"It was delicious! No doubt about that."

"So then what's the problem?"

"The dessert almost cost me my life!"

Darryl smiled and looked off into the distance, "sweet! Sweet! Sweet Death! How many times did you orgasm that day?" He smiled at me.

"Not enough to be stupid enough to ever do that again."

He was quiet for a long time smiling at me and staring at my eyes. When his phone rang, his face turned serious as he looked at it. "Ok, I'm gonna see you Thursday for lunch. I'll pick you up from here." Then he walked away answering his phone slowly. He stood at the stairs watching me while he spoke seriously on the phone. When I realized he was waiting for me to go inside before he walked away, I smiled.

Wednesday night I screamed at the butterflies in my stomach. Anton asked me why I barely touched my dinner; I told him my stomach was acting weird. Anton asked me for an opinion on his sketch for a landscaping job. I told him I liked it, and then he asked for suggestions, so I gave him some. That night when we went to bed, I threw the covers over my shoulder fast and put my back to him. Anton asked what was wrong cause I was quiet all evening. I told him I was tired and needed to rest. That night I think it was a flashback or maybe it was just a dream, but I was at home and in my bed with Darryl. My body was responding to him like it always does and I was in bliss. I realized I was dreaming when I started choking. Anton was sitting with the light on watching me. When I stopped coughing and caught my breath I asked him what was wrong with him. He said I was dreaming out loud and he was waiting for me to wake up. Panic hit me as I wondered if I said Darryl's name. When he smiled at me I knew I didn't. "Your body may be tired, but it sounds like your mind is missing me." I smiled and turned back on my side. He scooted in close to me, kissing my shoulder. "You got a little nap, you sure you can't go for a quickie?"

I yawned, "I'm already sleep Anton." Then I pretended to be sleep until I was sleep. In the morning he tried to wake me, but I held on to my fake sleep until he had been gone for thirty minutes. Then I sat up, his place was nice. However, every time I'm here I fight the urge to clean something. We spend most of our time together here, just because Darryl could pop up at any given moment at my place and although I haven't slept with Darryl since before Anton and I were even a thought on my end. I don't want him to question me. Darryl tends to be a sensitive subject between us and rightfully so. I showered, dressed, and then slowly made my way out the door. The whole time I was prepping myself on how to respond to Darryl, I didn't want to lead him on or have him thinking that I felt anything for him. I was locking the top lock to Anton's door when a girl approached me. "Excuse me, does Anton Tafoya live here?"

The first thing I saw were her blue eyes. "Yes," I turned to face her.

"Is he home, I need to speak with him."

"And you are?"

"Megan," she said like I should know who she is.

"Megan?" I rolled my hands, to tell her to give me more.

She exhaled as she smiled and tucked her long black hair on the right side of her face behind her ear. "I'm his ex-girlfriend Megan."

I guess she figured that I should know who she was by that very vague introduction. I chewed back my irritation. "Anton's not home right now."

"Do you know where I can find him?"

"He's at work," I dug in my purse and pulled out a pen and paper. "Write down your number and I'll have him call you tonight."

She smiled, "thank you. Are you his roommate?" She asked while writing down her number.

"Fiancé," Then I watched her hand stop writing.

"Fiancé?" Her eyes traveled from my feet to my face. She looked completely surprised. "Is that surprising?"

She turned pink as she tried to choose her words. "Good for him, congratulations." She faked enthusiasm.

"Un huh! You're weird." I took the paper from her. "He'll call you later."

"Thanks," she looked like she wanted to run. "So when's the happy day?"

"It's not set yet, are you here to win him back or something?"

My bluntness surprised her, "um…. well. Not quite, but we do have unfinished business."

"Great! Bring it on! We need a test anyways, it might as well be you." Then I walked away from her. I sat in my car and I watched her get into her obvious rental car and drive away.

I sat in my car at the shopping center trying to process what I was feeling. This girl appears out of thin air. Is that the possible baby momma? She didn't look like anybody's momma, but she could've been. Anton said he hadn't dated anyone black since he was in junior high school and that drove his momma crazy. It didn't matter what the girl's background was, I wanted to know what she wanted and what she wanted with my man. Darryl appeared out of nowhere and told me to get in the passenger seat. He drove all the way out to Fairfield and then to this little unnoticeable place. It was a barbecue spot. He said the tri-tip here was delicious and I wouldn't be sorry, so I agreed. Then he stared at me. "What?"

"You are bothered by something, I'm just happy it's not me." He watched me.

"Have you ever dated a white girl?"

"Me? Date?" He gave me a get real look.

I exhaled, "whatever you call what you do then."

"I am an equal opportunity lover.... I love the many." He leaned back in his chair, "you think Anton wants to marry you only because you're black?"

"WHAT?" I hadn't thought of that. "NO!"

"Have you ever dated a guy who wasn't black?"

"No, it's not that I would be against it, it's just never happened."

"Does it matter? People are the same no matter the color of their skin."

"True," I shook my head. "Mr. Mason why are we here?"

He frowned, "I'm gonna change my name to Wallace or Latour." Then he exhaled, "we're here so you can stop acting like you don't know my name. Who I am, what I'm capable of, and agree to go with me to the engagement party." I opened my mouth like I was going to object. "KB, if you try to reject me I'm going to sit in that chair next to you. All my raw sexiness will draw you in and you will forget the square. Not that I would hate that, but I'm bringing you in gradually."

I exhaled, "I suppose I need to wear a dress to this thing?"

Darryl shook his head yes very happily. "YES!" Then he licked his lips, "the sexier the better."

When I got to Anton's he was working on his invoicing for the week. I kissed his cheek and asked how his day went and he said it was fine nothing to write home about. I grabbed a glass of juice and then I sat on the couch watching his face. He was concentrating on what he was doing and barely paying me attention. "What you doing?" I asked even though I already knew.

"Invoicing, adding up my men's hours. The jobs they did for me, the norm." He said in a monotone.

"Are you hungry?"

"Un huh," he said focusing.

"What would you like to eat?"

"Un huh," he said still looking down.

"You had a visitor today."

"Un huh..."

"Don't you want to know who?"

"Un huh..."

"Megan."

He frowned, "what did you say?" He narrowed his eyes; I had his full attention now.

"A girl named Megan came here looking for you. She acted like I should've known who she is. Who is she?" He was speechless for a minute, "oh and she was surprised that you're engaged as well."

"What did she look like?"

"A little taller than me, white, dark brown almost black hair, blue eyes, very pretty."

Anton's mouth fell open, "she came here? What did she want?" I blank stared at him. "Whoa!"

"Who is she?"

"She's the one, the one that moved away. Did she have a kid?"

"I didn't see one, doesn't mean she doesn't have one. Let's call her." I reached for his house phone.

"No!" He reached out for me to pause. "I can't handle this right now! Can we stay at your place?"

"Why?" I asked suspiciously.

"How does she know where I live? She's never been here! This is more involved than I can handle being right now. Can we call tomorrow?"

"You seriously don't want to know what she wants?"

"Not tonight I don't."

"Fine, you can go stay at your mom's if it's all that. I'm staying here and I'm waiting for her to show up again." Anton got up irritated and stormed into his bedroom. "Just so you know! It doesn't sit well with me that you would run from a female no matter what the situation is!"

Yussef

I took a deep breath then I got out of the car. Angela and the girls were waiting for me. The girls were excited to be at the place where a kid could be a kid. When we walked in the door Melissa and her husband Jackson and their son little Jackson were waiting. "Mommy!" Yezzy ran over to hug her mother and stepfather. The greeter stamped us with the same number on our hands as the kids. Sylvia came in right behind us and Syd ran to her mother, "Mommy!" Melissa was visibly irritated at the sight of Sylvia. I bought three big buckets of tokens and gave each of the kids a bucket and I told them to go crazy. The kids squealed in excitement and then they took off. We went to the opposite side of the restaurant where it was less crowded. Melissa's body language was angry and annoyed. Angela was watching everyone taking everything in. Sylvia, I could tell she didn't know what to expect, we sat at a table with chairs. Melissa sat directly across from me with her husband next to her. Sylvia sat at the head of the table, and Angela sat next to me. "We want to thank everyone for coming out tonight, we figure the sooner we get this paperwork out of the way the better." I gestured between Angela and I.

"Who are you supposed to be?" Melissa said trying to pull back her irritation.

"I'm Angela, we've spoken over the phone."

"Oh right, the girlfriend." Melissa rolled her eyes. "Yussef why is she even here? She's not your wife, I don't want to talk to her to discuss our daughter."

"Too bad this isn't a meeting about what Melissa wants. Yussef I think especially with her, all communication should go through me." Angela said matching Melissa's attitude.

"Hold on! Hold on!" Jackson said, "Melissa it may not be a bad idea for you to go through Angela. You're too upset about this whole thing."

Melissa glared at Jackson but she didn't say anything and he gave her a look like she needed to stand down. Sylvia cleared her throat, "so. You were saying Yussef?"

I put a folder in front of each of them. "I had a lawyer draw up these custody agreements for child support and visitation. Take them to your lawyers and then give them to me signed in a week."

Sylvia laughed, "like I can afford a lawyer. What are you going to do take Sydney from me?" She opened her folder. She started laughing again when she got to the child support payments. "This is a joke? You can afford to do this?" Her eyes were big.

Jackson was looking in their folder, "we don't need your money Yussef!" Melissa barked.

"Hold on Melissa. If nothing else we could put this money into her college fund." Jackson was annoyed with her.

"Jackson if you don't stop contradicting me!" Melissa barked.

"Woman if you don't stop acting like this." He barked back.

"Jackson maybe you and I should talk and then you could let her know how it's going to go." I said.

"NO! This is my daughter! I make decisions for my daughter!"

"Your daughter?" Jackson was beyond irritated. "Who's been supporting you and your daughter? You need to calm down."

Sylvia touched my hand; she had tears in her eyes. "Thank you Yussef!"

I moved my hand as Angela and Melissa looked at her hand like they were trying to shoot lasers. "Ok, so maybe we can't do this on our own. Maybe we need the court room." I looked between my ex's.

"Well yea, if you think I'm going to accept the same package you're giving her." Melissa said.

"Why would you think you deserve something better than I would get?" Sylvia said getting irritated.

"Because we know how you did him. Yussef was only a payday to you. At least my daughter was conceived in love." Melissa said.

"Yea, while you were engaged to him!" Sylvia spit.

Angela shot me an irritated look. "Ok! Look! None of that matters today! Melissa you are a happily married woman with a family with or without Yesmina. Sylvia you need my help and support as it should be. I just want to warn you that my lawyers are pretty good, and you will not come out as pretty if we have to go to court."

"You have a pen? I don't have the money to go to court and this contract is beautiful. Melissa you can go to court if you want, but I'm signing."

Angela handed Sylvia a pen. Melissa looked like she was going to explode. "There's no way I'm going to allow him to do more for your daughter than mine. I'll sign too." Melissa said grabbing the pen that Sylvia laid on the table.

"Don't you think we should discuss it first?" Jackson said.

"Yesmina is my daughter!"

"Our daughter!" Jackson glared at Melissa like he wanted to choke the life out of her. The kids came over all thoroughly excited, they were asking if we were going to eat pizza. I didn't want to be in this hostile environment any longer than I had to be. The kids were having so much fun, I sucked it up. I ordered two large pizzas and pitchers of sodas that the kids picked out. As the adults all sat there awkwardly watching the time pass. Melissa refused to be cordial, but I knew that was her jealousy talking. If it was only the two of us, she'd agree to anything she thought would make me happy. I guess some other guy would feel like a King sitting up here with these women ready to come to blows about him. But for me it was just a reminder of how things went for me. Angela is the only one that things have worked out the way they're supposed to. She was single, and so was I. She accepted me for who I am, all my instant drama and loves me anyways. As soon as the girls finished eating Angela and I stood up and said goodbye. I put my arm around her as we turned to walk out, I heard Melissa stop breathing. When we got in the car, Angela told me to switch phones with her. She said she could tell that especially Melissa but Sylvia was going to be calling me in the next twenty-four hours. She said Sylvia's eyes doubled when she saw how much I was going to pay her in child support. She said Sylvia's gonna be coming after the money and Melissa was still in love with me. She said she felt bad for her husband. I thanked her for coming with me. She was quiet for a minute. "Sylvia is really pretty!" She said sadly.

"Why does that matter? I told you what happened. She broke my heart, I can't look at her the same."

"Melissa's pretty too, and you have so much history!"

"Right! And you know how she kept my daughter from me. She knows she committed an unforgivable sin. If it wasn't for my girls I'd NEVER speak to either of them again."

She exhaled, "They're prettier than I thought. I should've known they would be beautiful. Look at their daughters." She said in a defeated tone.

"Angela! Please don't fall apart on me. I don't know what you saw in there, but they've got nothing on you. You're beautiful! I love you!"

As if she didn't hear me, "I think I need to lose weight."

"WHY? I DON'T LIKE SKINNY WOMEN!"

"Yea, but you didn't see what I just saw!"

"And you don't see what I see! Please baby; don't make me feel like those idiots have any effect on us. I'm with you."

That night I made love to Angela like my life depended on it. As soon as her leg stopped trembling I went in again. I couldn't handle her feeling like anything less than the Queen she is. Besides if she felt like this about Sylvia I dreaded the day she met Sasha.

Lanie

"Amen!" I said wholeheartedly to Dorian's prayer of thanks and blessings for our group. I stood there watching Dorian speak to Brother Stapp about service tonight.

"Elaine it's so good to see you. I missed you Sunday."

Fire burned in my stomach as my momma touched my arm to try to calm me. "Um Dotty, you know no one calls her that. Please don't do that."

"I was just saying that I didn't see her Sunday."

"I didn't see you either!" I snapped.

"I was here!"

"Are you sure, cause I didn't see you Dotty. Are you sure?"

Dotty narrowed her eyes at me, "that's Sister Chapman to you."

"Oh come on Dotty, don't start none won't be none." I smiled.

Dotty angrily turned her back to me as she gathered her stuff. Dorian chuckled as he walked over. "Good evening Sister Wallace." He gave my momma a hug and kiss. "How are you tonight?"

My momma looked at the back of Dotty. "Once this moment passes I'll go back to great. How about you?"

"I'm good now that I see this young lady." He reached out to shake my hand.

I looked at his hands, "handshake?"

He dropped his smile, "stop playing Lanie."

He could hug me in our place of worship. I don't see what the big deal is. Dorian and my momma glared at me with the same look. I turned my back on them then I picked up my things. I wanted a hug and since Dorian feels like playing Brother Righteous right now, it was feeling like a waste of a Tuesday night to be here. Don't get me wrong, I enjoy coming to service with my momma. I get to see my sister in-law, my nieces and nephew, sometimes EJ comes. I have friends here that I always seem to forget about until I'm here. Dotty put me in a bad mood and now I'm just irritated about everything. I walked away from Dorian and my momma and I gave Shelby a hug. She asked me why I was frowning and I told her people get on my nerves. She asked me which people Dorian people or Sister Chapman people. I told her to take her pick. Shelby is sweet like my momma and my sister Erica where I'm different. Thank goodness for my sister Zoey or else I might not feel like I fit in around these parts. I looked back at Dorian who was watching me as I walked out.

I said hi to my daddy as I passed his office. He asked if my momma was still talking when I left. He was trying to gauge how much time he had before she came home and they disappeared into their room for the night.

I took a shower then I went into my walk in closet. I converted the back of a few of my

23

shelves into my little personal liquor cabinet. My momma had a problem with drinking years ago so my daddy said as long as she didn't know we had liquor in our rooms it was ok. If she by some chance discovered it then we had to get rid of it. I poured a shot of cognac then my phone started ringing. I downed it then I dove for my phone. "Hello?"

"Come meet me." Dorian commanded.

"No thanks, I don't need to see Brother Righteous anymore tonight."

"Lanie, I don't have time for this! Get your tail up and come meet me!"

I tried to pretend like I didn't like him telling me what to do. "Or else what?"

"Or else you won't see me until I get back."

"Where you going?"

"You're wasting time, get your butt over here and bring my sugar."

"Fine!" I tried to sound annoyed.

I opened the door as my momma was coming in. "Where you going?"

"HUH?" I hurried past her.

"You heard me."

I fast walked to my car, "I'll be right back momma. Love you! Goodnight!" I got in my car and hurried away.

I parked in the parking lot of the apartment building around the corner from Dorian. There was a gate between his parking lot and the one I parked in. I went up the back stairs and opened the back door. Dorian was busting suds when I walked in. He smiled at me. I stood there with my arms folded. "Good evening Lanie, good to see you."

"I could sock you in your face! Of all people you will not play me Dorian!"

"What did I supposedly do now?"

"I heard about your little date."

"Date?" He looked like he was trying to figure out what I was talking about. "Oh! That wasn't no date. It was a group of us at Yoshi's. We listened to jazz. I came home."

I gritted my teeth, "you sat next to April and you bought her food."

"Who's telling you all this?"

"Don't worry about my source!"

"I knew as soon as I saw Oneika she was gonna run back and tell you half-truths."

"Call it whatever you want! I'm tired of playing this game with you! I'm going to get me a real man!"

"I am a real man!" He put his soapy hands up, " I come in peace. Don't start swinging." He approached me. "I'm sorry that false information got back to you like that. I was not on a date with April. I did not invite her; I didn't know she was coming. Yes, she sat next to me but I didn't have anything to do with that. She forgot her wallet so I paid for her food that's it." He put his arms around me. "Now be a good girl and give me a kiss."

I kissed him; I kissed him with everything in me. When I pulled at his pants he backed up. "Come on Dorian! No one will know!"

"We're not married." He returned to the sink.

"That's not my fault! Marry me already!"

I could tell he was irritated. "We will not get married just to have sex." He looked at me with kindness in his eyes. "You've got to get stronger spiritually. Not for me, but for you. I want to worship side by side with you."

I growled in frustration. "Who determines how spiritually strong I am? I don't need you judging me." I started whining. "Dorian! Don't you want me?" I pressed my breast against his back as I put my arms around him.

He took a deep breath, "yes."

"I'm tired of my virginity aren't you? I want to make love to you in the worst way. I want to know what orgasms feel like. I'm tired of imagining I want to know. I've got to be the oldest virgin alive. Outside of Erica, but that's her problem." She's engaged to Josh, he's alright. A softie like her. My man has controlled fire just like I like. No one understands how or why we are together. At first glance of course you see me, and old square britches. THEN!!!! He lets his hair down and it's like "WATCH OUT!" Passion, Power, Perception! He's kind of shy at first, but I think I've broken him of his shyness. He used to get so embarrassed behind the things I'd say; now he rolls with me. He even sounds like me sometimes.

"You're focusing on the physical part. There's more to being married than just sex."

"Baby we got everything else together. You know you wanna give it to me."

"Lanie stop playing on my weakness for you. I promise to be a strong spiritual head for the both of us. It is not easy to be strong. I want you more than you could understand. I love you Elaine. I will never love anyone like I love you."

It never makes my skin crawl when he calls me by my birth name. Outside of my parents he's the only one to get away with it. "Dorian I love you!" I turned him around. I put my leg up, "baby I want you! I need you!"

Dorian put his head back. "I love you! Please stop! If I gave in I would be so mad at myself!"

"So why did you invite me over here? We could've talked over the phone. When I see you I want it, you know it, but you forever playing *Brother Righteous*! I'm not going to wait for you forever! You got so many rules. You want to control everything. I'm gonna get me a real man! We are grown! Why I gotta sneak over here like we're kids?"

"You know it would look bad if someone saw your car outside my place and we were here alone."

"Like I care what it looks like! I'm willing to marry you, but you got too many rules. I'm too much woman for you! I told you that when we were kids but you must get your kicks off of controlling me. I'm done! I can't do this anymore!" I started walking away from him.

"Lanie!" I kept walking and fussing. "Come back!" I was almost to the door. He slammed the door shut right after I opened it. He spun me around and threw me up against my door. "You are so spoiled! I love you and I want you for more than what's between your legs. You know we are supposed to have a chaperone whenever we're together. If we're going to keep having this argument every time I see you! All I ask you to do is be consistent in your attendance to service. That's it! Every Sunday and Tuesday night be at our place of worship for a couple of hours. I'm not asking you to be a missionary or any other demands that I could request of my spouse. You can't do that simple thing and you want to act like I'm the one! I'm tired of my virginity too! I want you! But! I want you for something more than sex! I want to share my life with you! All those females come in droves when you're not there. I want you and you can't do this simple thing? What happens when we get married you gonna be hit or miss like your brothers? I don't want to be Shelby or your momma. Sitting by myself looking at all the other families. I want to worship with my wife. If you can't comply with my simple request maybe you should go. Go out there and find someone who will be done with you as soon as they have what they want. Maybe then you'll understand what you lost in me." Then he walked away. He walked out of the kitchen and into the living room.

I know he's right but this virginity crap was for the birds. Z makes sex sound pretty amazing and I want that. Although, every time her heart gets broken whenever mister wonderful turns out to be mister milk-bone we gotta go shoot him, clear any links from her to him, you know. Times like those I appreciate Dorian even though Yussef seems more my speed. He'd do me and then go to service when I did. Oh but right! He thinks of me as a little girl! I walked in the living room and Dorian was staring at me with a tent in his pants. "Can I help you with that?"

"Don't touch me!"

I sat on the edge of the couch. "You want to break up with me? Maybe we should."

He locked his jaw, "if that's all you got from what I just said, then maybe we should."

"That's not all I got, but I can't promise to be better." He exhaled, "you don't understand! I like shooting people! I'm too violent! Why can't we be like my parents? I promise to come more than my father does."

He exhaled, "you're killing me! I don't want to go alone. Would our kids stay home with you or go with me? I can make them go, but eventually they'll choose to stay with you. Staying with you is easier. Of all the things we'll fight about during our marriage, service shouldn't be one of them."

"You really want to break up with me over this one little thing?"

He looked at me; the tent was still there. "I don't want to break up with you. Like you said, I'm tired of my virginity too."

"Dorian just marry me!"

"I can't!" I got irritated. He should know I'm about to do something. I grabbed my skirt and I got on top of him and I kissed him. He tried to fight the kiss at first, but he can't resist me. I kissed him and when I started sucking on his neck he was so focused on trying to make me stop kissing his neck that he failed to realize that I was undoing his pants. He lost his air when my hand stroked him. Zoey showed me how to give a hand job so many times I can do it without looking, but I wanted to see him. Dorian tried to ask me to stop but my rhythm had him speechless. Seeing him respond to me was a complete turn on. With one quick move I was mounting him. Dorian bucked his eyes at me as he turned completely red. He turned to shake his head no, I kissed his cheek and I shook my head yes. As I started to descend on him he sucked all his air in then he grabbed me by the waist and moved me off of him. He took a minute to catch his breath. "Lanie you... Have to... Go!"

"Dorian!"

"You don't respect me! You have to go!"

"Fine!"

Episode 3

Amber

I sat there waiting for him to get off the phone. I finally decided it was time as his fiancé to pop by his office from time to time. Fortunately he was working at the Oakland kiosk today. His face lit up when Ms. Laverne led me into his office. He put one finger up and then he spoke to the person over the phone. I could hear her excited tone. I walked around his office looking at his pictures and books. I smiled at the picture from Andrew's wedding with all of us. The pictures here were different than the ones he has in his home office. When he hung up he came around the desk and kissed me. He asked me what he owed the honor of my visit to. I told him to sit, and when he did I took my seat in his lap. I told him I loved him and this was for his own good. He frowned as he waited for my point. I hit the intercom button, I asked Ms. Laverne to ask Yussef to come in. Malcolm smirked at me and asked what I was up to. Yussef knocked on the door, I told him to come in. "Whoa! Uncle Blackie in love is a wonderful sight!" He said chuckling.

"Stop calling me that!" Malcolm said with a smile.

"Yussef and I were talking. You've never taken a real vacation. Whenever you took quote unquote vacations before it was to handle other business. I don't want our honeymoon to be your first vacation. I would like to *break you in* a little early."

Malcolm started laughing, "break me in? I can't just up and leave, I have an empire to run."

"That's where Yussef, Sasha, Darryl, and Derrick come into play. I think the four of them could manage to cover things for a week. I could probably even get Andy to take a week off and pitch in if you think you'd need him."

"Uncle Blackie you have been going since you got out. You've never taken a vacation;

you need to take some time with your woman. Isn't there somewhere you'd like to go and just relax?" Malcolm stared at him but didn't respond. "Calling you that is our thing, don't act brand-new just because you're woman is in here." Yussef smiled at him.
Malcolm grabbed my thigh, "I honestly didn't think about our honeymoon. I guess you wanna go somewhere good huh?"
"Not just good, somewhere fantastic at least. All you ever do is work, you need to take a moment to step back and smell the roses."
Malcolm's body was tense, and he didn't look happy about the idea. Not that I expected him to. We've never done anything like a vacation together. He's always been working and working. He told us he would consider the idea, but he couldn't say yes or no at the moment. I kissed him and told him not to take too long. Then I asked Yussef if he was hungry, he said he could eat. I invited Ms. Laverne and then the four of us went out to lunch. As we were sitting at our table in a restaurant a guy kept looking in our direction. He looked familiar, but I couldn't place why. He walked over to our table. "I am so sorry to bother you, but aren't you Malcolm?"
"Yes, and you're Kent." Malcolm's expression didn't change.
The guy smiled and his eyes glazed over. "Yes! You remember me! I never got a chance to thank you."
I smiled, "for what?"
"Oh my God Amber! I didn't see you there. You look exactly the same too!" He smiled, Yussef pulled out the chair next to him and we waited for him to speak. Kent told us he went to Oakland High with us. I guess that's why he looked familiar. He said while we were in school Kent said he was kind of lost and didn't know what he was going to do with himself. He said back then there weren't a lot of opportunities for young black men. He said he saw the way Malcolm and people like him were living so he thought if he hustled like Malcolm he would come up. He said he didn't even know Malcolm knew who he was. He said Malcolm came to him and told him he was in over his head and he would most likely end up dead if he continued on his course. He told us that Malcolm told him he was smart and deserved better than the life he was heading to. He said basically Malcolm made him give it all up and focus on school. Then he looked at Malcolm he told him he saved his life. He said he didn't go to school right away but he eventually went, got a good job, and had a family. He was there having lunch with his daughter. He always told his kids about Malcolm. He lost track of Malcolm after he went to jail, and eventually he heard about the fire at his barbershop. He asked Malcolm how he was doing now. I guess he didn't know about all of Malcolm's achievements. Malcolm told him that Drew's was rebuilt and it has been there ever since. Malcolm didn't expound on everything else he's been up to. Kent said an emotional *thank you* again to Malcolm for saving his life. We looked at Malcolm who looked at Kent with no real expression. Kent said he knows that most people were afraid of Malcolm and for good reason. But he has always looked up to Malcolm and when Malcolm pointed him in a different direction he felt that Malcolm really cared about him as a person. Malcolm said very dryly that Kent was a nerd and he had no business trying to flex. He said Kent would've gotten himself killed for nothing. Kent asked if it was ok to bring his daughter over to introduce her and then he'd leave us alone. Malcolm told him it was ok, and you could tell he was so proud of his little girl, she was a teenager and you could tell she was a good kid. She bashfully said hello, then she told us that she's heard about Malcolm all her life. Malcolm asked her what her grades were like in school. She said she does ok but not fantastic, when he asked her why not, she shrugged. He told her that her education is the one thing that could never be taken away from her. Then Yussef shared that until Malcolm cracked his whip he wasn't applying himself in school either. He said it's not as hard as she thinks it is to be on top.
When they left Yussef shared his experience growing up with Malcolm. I couldn't help

but feel a little cheated because it felt like Yussef was kept from me. I was quietly listening when Malcolm looked at me and told me that Yussef wasn't kept from me on purpose. Yussef had a goofy look on his face, he leaned and asked me if I felt left out. When I said yes, he said he and his sister did too. Then he said all that matters now is that we're all together. I could tell he was trying to smooth things out. I couldn't understand why Troy never mentioned his kids. Then Malcolm stayed quiet about it so long, I couldn't help but wonder about all the things he could be keeping from me as well. That fast I decided it was stupid to worry about it.

Malcolm said we needed to give my Uncle Dale a go or no go on the house. I exhaled; I really didn't know what I wanted to do. I was explaining to Ms. Laverne how my Nana bought that house for me. I didn't want the house to just sit. Darryl was going to take over Malcolm's house and Andrew was going to rent out his loft. Yussef smiled and said he would gladly take the house off my hands. He said his instant family has out grown his two-bedroom apartment. Malcolm asked him why he wouldn't buy a house within the development with us. Yussef smiled and said that he already has the paperwork in process on a house, but until he was sure about things with his girlfriend and daughters he needed a more low key existence at first. I told Yussef the thought of my house staying in the family made me feel good.

As we finished lunch my Uncle Frank called me. He said he wanted me to come visit him today or tomorrow. I told him I'd come today and that I was finishing up lunch with Malcolm and Yussef. I spent twenty minutes kissing my man's wonderful lips goodbye then I headed out to Walnut Creek. My uncle buzzed me in at the gate and I slowly drove up the hill to his house. No matter how many times I come here I always feel like Uncle Frank's house is huge. When I pulled up to the house I waited in the car until Uncle Jeff came to the door. He met me at the car; I saw one of the dogs looking to make sure everything was ok. I gave my uncle a huge hug and then I followed him into the big living room. Uncle Jeff told me to sit then he sat next to his brother. Uncle Frank was trying to do his casual conversation thing, and I could tell Uncle Jeff wanted to tell him to get to the point. I had no idea of what was going on. "So, Jeffrey and I were talking...."

"Alright Franklin junior!" Suddenly they looked like two big kids.

"We've been over here arguing all morning. So it's perfect that you came today. I think we would've torn this house down trying to wait to talk tomorrow." Uncle Frank said.

"You guys are arguing about me?" I was confused.

"Yes! I feel that we have always had a special bond and Tim would want me to walk you down the aisle."

"And I'm telling him he did too much powder in the 70's. I'm your favorite uncle and I should walk you down." Uncle Jeff responded.

"Uncle Frank you did powder?" I was in shock.

Uncle Jeff started cracking up laughing. Uncle Frank was not laughing. He looked at Uncle Jeff like he was an annoying little brother. "Your uncle likes to spread rumors." He said glaring at him. "Tell him you've chosen me."

"Actually, I don't know what I'm gonna do yet." Both of them looked surprised. "Maybe one of my brothers should do it. Or my sons? I don't know. Now I would feel guilty choosing between you two."

"No! No! No! It has to be me. All the sleepovers at my house. All the time we've spent together. Come on!" Uncle Jeff pleaded. "You know you, Sophia, and Jade were my triplets."

"Yes, but I didn't kill Malcolm when you gave us the news. You could be married to Tag right now if it weren't for me." Then Uncle Frank chuckled.

Uncle Jeff and I looked at him with blank stares. "I would've never allowed that! If he wasn't good enough for Sophia he wasn't good enough for any of them!"

"Amber I love you sweetheart, I think I should have the honor. I knew Malcolm way

before any of you did. I vouched for him, Tim wanted his head." Uncle Frank said.
"True! Your daddy wanted to kill him! But thanks to me he didn't." Uncle Jeff said.
"Daddy wanted to kill Malcolm?"
"Only at first. His fourteen year old daughter just told him she was pregnant, what father who loves his daughter wouldn't want the head of the fool who deflowered his baby girl? As you see they got really close after that." Then he cleared his throat, "thanks to me! When I pointed out how love struck Malcolm was over you, Tim calmed down a lot. You weren't just a conquest to Malcolm. Everything he's ever done has been for you." A tear fell from my eye, hearing all this made me emotional. Thinking about my parents always affects me this way. Mix that with loving sentiments about Malcolm and I was gonna be a blubbering fool. "See! That's why I should be the one to give you away. I got all the background information." Uncle Jeff said proudly.
"I'm the oldest."
"You two sound like my boys. Maybe I should ask Uncle Dale or Uncle Matt."
"NO!" Uncle Jeff yelled.
We all laughed, then I told them that I couldn't choose between the two of them. I told them I felt so loved that they would waste time arguing about my long overdue wedding.

Tracy

"Thursday is show and tell at my school. And it's finally my turn." Andre said.
"What do you want to show?"
"A cake." He said with a big smile.
All I could do was smile, "what kind of cake?"
"I don't know." He put his little finger up to his brain like he was thinking which let me know he knew already. "Peanut butter?"
"You want a peanut butter cake?"
"Yes, and I want it to look like a peanut." Then he laughed.
"Can I ask why?"
Andre started blushing and I immediately knew a girl was involved. "Just cause..." His little ears were red.
He was blushing so hard that I started blushing. Andrew walked in the kitchen; he looked at both of us. "What's going on?"
"Tell your daddy what you told me." I was still blushing.
So Andre told him like he told me, Andrew grinned and asked who the girl is. Andre couldn't stop giggling, as he turned completely red. His giggle was contagious then he told us the little girl's name was Monet and she was his girlfriend. I had to sit down, a girlfriend really? He was barely in kindergarten come this fall. Andrew asked him what he knew about having a girlfriend. Andre said they sit together at lunch, and he chases her around the playground at recess. I told Andre we needed to go to the store to see if we could find a cake mold in the shape of a peanut, and then they needed ingredients. Andrew asked if that was the plan for today? I told him we'd make the tester today. Andrew said he got a call from Will, Toya's husband. He wanted to bring the kids by, if we weren't busy. Immediately I wanted to cry, but I sucked it up. I told Andrew that was fine if he felt up to it. Andrew exhaled and said he was fine. I asked him to tell Will to come around two. I took out a notepad and started writing my shopping list. The boys would eat hot dogs; if the little girl is eating table food she could have a hot dog as well. I put yogurt and apple sauce on the list. Andrew watched me for a minute. He said if today wasn't a good day he could tell him some other time. I exhaled and told him it was fine. Andre needed to know his little brother and sister, and I needed to get over it. Andrew put his arms around me and told me I was amazing for dealing with this. That made me feel better, but I decided to busy myself with a tester cake for Amber while the kids played.

Andre and I went to a few stores looking for a peanut shaped cake mold. We finally found one in the last store we visited. But I also bought other essentials that I needed. Andre was so excited. I asked him what he wanted, a chocolate cake with peanut butter filling, or peanut butter cake with chocolate filling. He thought about it and he said peanut butter cake with peanut butter filling and chocolate icing. I hadn't considered that combination. Then we went to the grocery store and got things for his play date with his little brother and little sister. Normally when they got the kids together I had plans already so I hadn't seen them in months. I kept taking deep breaths.

When we got home Andre and I washed our hands, put on our aprons and then we took everything out. As usual I explained how we were going to create our cake. I told him since the filling was going to be peanut butter as well we needed a light peanut butter flavor in the cake. We made our ganache first. Then our cake, since we were creating this recipe by taste, Andre had to keep reminding me to write down all of my add-ins. We cleaned up while the cake was in the oven and then we made our fondant to cover the cake. Andre kept looking in the oven window at his cake, and he kept giving that goofy laugh at the progress. When his cake was done Andre and I gave each other high-fives. It was beautiful; I told him he could share his cake with his siblings after dinner. I told him to go wash up cause they would be here in a little bit. I took pictures of Andre's cake. I printed the pictures and placed them in my cake book and titled them as *Andre's Peanut Butter Crush*, and then I smiled. As I placed my ingredients for Amber's cake on the counter, the doorbell rang. Andre ran very excitedly to the door behind his father. I took breaths to calm myself. Andre and his little brother Will Jr. came in the kitchen. Andre very proudly told him I was his mommy. Little Will looked like a complete combination of Steve and Toya. He was a little chocolate cutie. He said a very shy hi. I swallowed and said hello. Eve and Cain came to the window to see who was inside. Andre told little Will to come out back with him. My poor puppies saw the boys coming and they ran away. Andrew brought Will and the baby in the family room. Will put the baby on the floor and then came to meet me. Will looked as happy as a broken hearted single dad could look. I offered Will some apple juice while I watched Andrew make his way to the baby. She had a head full of hair. I was impressed that Will had it neatly pulled up into a ponytail on her head. She looked at Andrew like she was trying to figure him out. She allowed him to pick her up, but she was looking at him like she was reading him. Will and I watched them, and then I said she's got a lot of her momma in her. Will said a sad "yea." Then he asked Andrew how he dealt with Toya's mom. Andrew shrugged and said he doesn't. Will said she gives him a hard time for no reason half the time. I could see love for Toya in his eyes, as he convinced himself that her mother was the reason why she led him to believe that the son that carries his name was actually the son of my ex-boyfriend. I could tell Andrew felt bad for him. But I would be lying if I said his interaction with that baby was ok with me. I started feeling bad about it; it makes no sense to be jealous of a baby. I got in my zone creating my cake. Will asked what I was doing when he saw me get the rum. Andrew smiled proudly and told him I was creating. As I finished cleaning up and my cakes were cooling on the racks the baby crawled in the kitchen. Will and Andrew were watching something on the TV not paying attention to her. She pulled herself up and then she moved closer to me. I imagined her looking me up and down like her mother would and then telling me something evil. Instead she gave me the biggest toothless grin as she let go of the cabinet and focused on balancing herself while she smiled at me. Then she raised her arms to me. As if she sensed my hesitation she gave me another toothless smile while keeping her arms out. I exhaled and gave in to her cuteness. If Toya did nothing right in her life, she definitely made gorgeous babies. While the kids ate I called Amber and I told her I was about to assemble her cake and then work on the design. She got really excited and asked if she could come over. I told her she never needed to ask. When I opened the door Amber walked in with Malcolm right behind her. Amber immediately took the baby, when Malcolm asked who's baby, I said Will & Toya's, then he turned on his heels and walked into the family room. Amber smiled at me as we did our best to hold back our laughter. When Malcolm walked in the family room Andre yelled, "Poppa!" Then he hurried out of his chair to hug Malcolm. Andrew had the goofiest grin as he watched his father hug and kiss his grandson. Then Andrew introduced Will to Malcolm. I wished I could read Malcolm's mind in that moment. I could tell he was reading him, but I wanted to know what he read. Amber waved hello to Will and then she excitedly walked in the kitchen with the baby on her hip. She clapped her hands at the cake. I had the tiers filled and iced. Now I needed to decorate it. I rolled out the purple fondant and covered each tier. Amber stood there smiling as she watched me. I placed a gold sash around the top and bottom tier, and my interpretation of a Jade colored sash on the middle tier. Then I took them off. I took a paper towel down and I drew a tree with my edible gold paint with sparkling green leaves. Then I turned it to Amber. I told her that the gold represented her mother and also her roots. And the green leaves were her sister and part of the fruitage of that tree. I told her the tree was underneath a purple sky the canvas and beautiful backdrop. Amber smiled and squealed, she said she loved it. She quietly watched me paint the tree along the side of the cake. When I finished I stepped back, I was satisfied with my cake. Amber clapped and said she loved it. I called the men to come see while Amber moved around taking pictures of the whole thing. Malcolm said nothing while Andrew and Will sang my praises. I thought maybe he didn't like it. Amber was happy enough for the both of them even if he didn't like it. I couldn't read his face. Malcolm told me to come with him, and then he walked into the living room. I looked at Andrew and his face was serious, Amber was still all smiles so I figured I was overreacting. When I sat on the couch across from him, he got up and moved next to me. I felt like I was in trouble. "Tracy those cakes are amazing. Why don't you want to open your bakery?" His voice was low and even deeper than Andrew's.

I opened my hands and closed them. "I'm scared, but Andrew and I talked about it the other day in detail. I'm going to do it, it's a matter of when."

"Good!"

"Malcolm?"

"Yes?"

"Why are we whispering in the living room?"

He looked at me, "I don't know him! Don't trust him! I don't want him in our business!"

Malachi

"Daddy, when I grow up I want to marry a man just like you." My baby girl said to me from her heart.

"Amaya, when you marry I want you to marry someone better. I want him to be worthy of you." Guilt washed over me.

"There's no man better than my daddy!" She cheered.

I smiled but her words stabbed me all over. Denise watched my immediate mood change. "What is it?"

I shook off the bad feeling. "Who could have a more beautiful family?" I said touching her hand. She smiled but she continued to search my face.

"You're taking us to the movies when you come back right?" Amaya confirmed.

"Yes sweetheart, we're going to the movies." The girls cheered quietly at the table.

Jada and Amaya started going over the list of things they were going to ask for when we went out. Whenever I come home from one of my trips, I take the girls wherever they want and they can have whatever they want. Denise normally doesn't go with us because she's such a party pooper telling us that all the sweets will make us sick and stuff like that. Besides it makes me feel great to bask in the love of my girls. "Are you ok?" Denise asked still checking me out.

"I'm fine. I'm going to miss you guys."

Denise rubbed my hand and then she returned to her meal. After dinner Denise and I washed the dishes together chatting about lighthearted things. Then we tucked the girls into their beds. We sang them silly songs then we kissed them goodnight. I followed Denise into the bedroom. She stopped in the middle of the floor and turned to face me. She smiled a nervous smile then she kissed me. I waited for her to speak. She put her hands on my shoulders then she exhaled. I put my arms around her and I waited. She said she wanted to ask me something but she was nervous about my reaction. Then she said she wanted another baby as she braced herself for my reaction. I chuckled and asked her why. Denise exhaled and said she feels empty. She said our plan was always for at least four and she felt it was time to get started on our next two. I asked her if she was sure that that's what she wanted because of my job I travel a lot. Denise's face turned sad and she said she was sure. I asked her what was wrong; I could see the sadness in her eyes. She spaced out for a few minutes, I don't know where she went but she was almost in tears when she came back to our room. I stood there staring at her. I asked her if she was ok. One tear fell as she said she misses her mother. I know the feeling all too well. I hugged her and told her I understood. She told me I didn't understand, I had my father and my siblings when my momma died. I reminded her that she had her sister and she cried harder as she disagreed with me. I let it bounce off of me best I could that she would actually argue that her pain of losing her mother was greater than mine. I also knew that with her being upset like this it was pointless to try to make love to her before I left. I had been looking forward to our farewell sex all day. Instead I rubbed her back until she calmed down then I took a very cold shower. She was fast asleep when I got in the bed. I put my arm around her, and she scooted away from me. I laid there listening to her light snore wondering how we would have a baby with all this distance between us.

I rolled out of bed at the last minute. I put on my travel clothes, grabbed my bag and headed to the Oakland airport. On my flight to LA, I used my pent up frustration to work on my laptop and prepare for work. My wife wants to have more kids, fine. We could have a whole village and I wouldn't care. But I wonder if she remembers that in order to have a baby I have to touch her. When my plane landed, I did the same song and dance I always do when I'm here. I had a four-hour layover, I could call Richard or Sasha and hangout with them until I needed to come back or I could get a room for a few hours and "relax." Since my bags were checked I exhaled and headed to the airport Hilton. I paid upfront for the room in cash and I used my company card for incidentals. I pulled out my prepaid phone and I texted my room number. Then I walked out on the balcony. As usual I told myself this is the last time. I guess she was anticipating my text, I promise thirty minutes didn't go by before she walked in the room. She had the biggest smile on her face. Cora was always so excited to see me when she did. She dropped her bags by the door and she charged me. She threw her arms around my neck and kept kissing me. I couldn't stop laughing; I asked her how she's been. She kept saying, who cares. Who cares! Within one minute she had me undressed and she was putting a condom on me before she took me in to her mouth. It has been awhile since I've seen her and her eagerness told me she was counting the time that passed. I wanted to talk but I guess Cora figured we'd get to that part after.

Drenched in sweat Cora collapsed on top of me and I told my guilt to stay back. "I've missed you!" She said still catching her breath.

"Missed you."

"You've been avoiding me haven't you?" She sat up to look at me.

Beautiful glowing chocolate skin in the morning, is there any better sight? "I had a lot of family stuff come up. It was easier to have Gerald go instead."

"And you see what happens when you send a stand-in. Production is off, projections are not rating high. It's a mess."

"I had to squeeze this trip in. My sister, niece, and nephew are getting married. The family's throwing a big engagement party. I'm going to be running on no energy when I get home. Everyone's gonna need me in each direction."

She exhaled, "meanwhile Cora holds her breath until she gets to see you again." Her eyes danced around the room. "I could move out there to make things easier."

Irritation stole my breath; I pushed her hips to make her move. "We've talked about this! This is the last time Cora. It would be pointless for you to move up north. I wouldn't see you anymore than I already do if at all. You have your life out here, we need to stop anyways."

"Don't get your feathers all ruffled Malachi. I'm not going to confront your wife or anything like that; I hate all this distance between us. I would like the option to see you when the feeling moves us. It's been almost nine months since I've seen you. That's too long!"

I got up irritated, "how is nine months too long when last time was supposed to be the last time?"

She sat there looking at me with a smile. "You always say this time is the last time. Now I only agree to humor you. You love me Malachi, even though you try not to admit it. I know you're not gonna leave your wife. I know you love her to death. You guys have been through a lot together, you've grieved together. You have children, I understand how those bonds work. I get it Malachi, I get it. But I also know that you love me. If you didn't love me, I wouldn't be here right now. If you didn't love me you wouldn't be upset that I'm moving closer to you. The temptation wouldn't bother you. You'd walk out that door and be done with me. But I know you! I know us! You love me, and I love you! I never thought of myself as a second best kind of woman, I've got to be first in everything else. I love everything about you. For you I will settle for being second just so I can have you in my life. You are important enough to me to step to the side for. I will gladly do it in a heartbeat. You are the only man I can submit to, and when you find a man like you. You'd be a fool to let you go!"

"Cora, I don't belong to you. You have nothing to hold on to. I'm in love with my wife! This was a mistake!" I said walking to the bathroom. I flushed both condoms. I got in the shower and washed her smell off of me.

When I walked out of the shower she hadn't moved. "I know you love your wife, and I don't fight you on that. I need you too. I'm stuck out here waiting for you. At least if I could see you I could be ok. Even if we never sleep together again, I still want you in my life any way I can have you. I love you Malachi, I just wanna see you. I'll settle for being a fly on your wall."

"Cora, you stay out here! I'm not playing with you!"

"Fine, but can we discuss it later?"

"What is there to discuss? My family and I live out there, you live out here."

"Malachi!"

"Cora I will walk out of this room and never look back!" I said putting on my clothes.

"Ok! Ok! Fine!" She said faking defeat. I know better than to believe this is the last time she'll bring it up.

I went back to the airport while she was in the shower. Gerald found me in the restaurant having a bite to eat for breakfast. He ordered a shot of patron to help him with his nerves. He hates flying but he has to do it on a regular basis. Cora found us and Gerald went into instant drool mode when he saw Cora. She did look good, beautiful chocolate skin; short haircut that said I run this, wonderfully *big smack-me-booty*. I immediately felt like I wanted to go another round. Gerald invited Cora to sit at our table with us. She said a nonchalant hello to us as she sat. Gerald was doing his best to draw Cora out in conversation; I knew she was sulking from not getting her way. So I sat back and watched them interact. Our waitress asked me if I needed anything else. I jokingly said I could use a drink for my twelve-hour flight to Tokyo, she laughed along with us. Gerald asked Cora if she wanted to order anything, our waitress pretended that she didn't see Cora before. Cora ordered fruit and yogurt. When our waitress came back her attention was on me. She gave Cora her breakfast then she asked me if I needed *anything*. Gerald said he would like some more orange juice. She gave him a courtesy smile then she asked me if I wanted *anything else*. The way her question hung on the air we all knew she was asking about more than breakfast. I massaged my wedding band and told her I was good and I only needed the check. Cora kept her eyes on her food but I could tell she was irritated. Gerald went on and on about how he would be all over that girl if she even winked at him. I humored him and I didn't say anything. Our waitress brought the check and a paper to go cup for me with a lid. I put my company card in the billfold, gave it to her, and then I opened the cup. Sixteen ounces of single malt. I smiled and Gerald asked me what was in the cup. I told him it was a little juice. The waitress came back with a knowing smile and she sat the billfold in front of me. She said, "Malachi please let me know if you need *anything else*." She even wrote me a little note apologizing for her being so forward with me, but she thought I was so handsome *blah, blah, blah*. I left her an incredibly huge tip and then we made our way to our gate. Amaya and Jada called me to wish me good morning and a safe trip. I talked to them for a minute, and then we got off the phone. Gerald asked me to say my girl's names again. Aa-my-aa and Jay-duh, I told him my girls had the same initials as my sisters Amber and Jade whom I love dearly. He asked if I was going to try for a boy. I told him my wife and I plan on having more, Cora looked at me. I told him I didn't care whether we ever had a son; I just wanted my wife to be happy.

Marian was sitting with her laptop staring at the screen like she had X-ray vision. She got excited when she saw me. She waved us over, the whole time Gerald was trying to get in good with Cora. Marian was looking at specs and she had questions. Marian's eyes bounced all over the place, she would not give me eye contact. One time she accused me of being prejudice. In her defense she was drunk, and frustrated cause I wasn't accepting any of her advances. She said I didn't like white people. I told her I am white, what sense does it make to hate myself? I told her I'm white, and I'm black, AND my wife is Dominican. But ever since then she has had a hard time looking me in my face. I don't mention it. That was years ago, she always acts like it was five minutes ago. She's embarrassed so I let it go. Marian is good at what she does, so is Cora. In an industry dominated by mostly men, both of them hold their own, it's impressive. On the flight, I worked, I slept, and I mostly thought about Denise. I don't know if a baby is a good idea for us right now. I want my wife to be happy, but I want her to want me again. This is the first time I've ever left without making love to her. I glanced at Cora who was knocked out; even in her sleep she's beautiful. I could hear my momma saying she looked like her. Then I could hear my dad saying I'm spinning my wheels for nothing with her. How could my dad not be in love with my momma? She was a beautiful, strong, and intelligent black woman. Yes she was crazy, but that part made her even more amazing to me. I loved my moments alone with her. When Amber wasn't driving her crazy, and Timothy wasn't there sucking up all of her attention. My momma would tell me how much she loved me, all her hopes and dreams for me. She said I was more like daddy than Timothy was. Timothy was her first baby so she had a different relationship with him than me. She would always say that I tested limits and until Amber came along, she felt I acted most like her. Then Amber was born, looking like dad and acting like momma. Whoa is all I could say sometimes. When momma came with her belt Amber would automatically run. Nine times out of ten she was coming for her though. I'd try to save her as much as I could. I got beat a few times for interfering. Timothy was the only one who could talk momma out of whooping anybody. Jade was such a good little girl, she played momma to all of us. She gave all of us the hugs and gentle concern that momma couldn't at times. I called Denise to tell her I made it. She was in tears cause she realized that last night was a bust. We had one of the best conversations we've had in years. She was so apologetic; she said she feels like she keeps letting me down. I didn't lie and say it was ok. Cause it's not, I asked her where she went last night. She exhaled and said there were things about her family she'd rather not talk about. I told her I need to understand what's going on with her. I honestly told her that my head is spinning and has been for a long time. She told me she knew and she apologized. I didn't want her to apologize, I wanted my wife back. I miss her so much! Denise suggested that we spend some time alone after I got back. I loved the sound of that.

****

Cora keeps watching me, waiting for me to summon her. But I don't, she wants to move to The Bay. No matter how she tries to spin it, that's too close to Denise for my comfort. I don't want to argue about it cause then she starts talking about love, and I don't want to hear how much she loves me. After dinner Gerald, Cora, and Marian decided they were going out dancing. I bowed out and went back to my room. I called Denise and the girls; the girls got a kick out of the fact that there was almost a day difference in our time zones. I talked to them for a while and I couldn't wait to make my way home in a few days. I virtually kissed everyone and then I got in the bed. Just as I fell asleep there was a knock at my door. I tried to ignore her and act like I wasn't there. Thirty minutes later she was still knocking at the door. I slowly cracked my door and I made sure I gave her the evilest look. "And you wonder why I don't want you moving to The Bay! I don't want to deal with this!"

"Please let me in." Her face was really sad.

"No, aren't you supposed to be out?"

"They think I hooked up, please let me in." She calmly begged.

"I'm sleep!"

"Then I wanna watch you sleep! Please let me in. I'll be good I promise!" She said putting her hands up.

"Cora, I didn't invite you here! I didn't like our last conversation. I'm cool!"

"Malachi, I'm sorry! I will let you be the man. I will wait for you to invite me. Please let me in."

"That's the thing, I didn't invite you here. If I let you in that's a contradiction of what you just said. Go back to your room Cora. Or go find your hookup, I'm done."

"Malachi!" She sighed, "you always say you're done. Then you text me your room number from some random number. You're mad at me fine, I'm mad at you."

"You have no reason to be mad at me."

"You're going to have more kids with your wife? How do you think that makes me feel?"

"You're making my point for me. Goodnight Cora!" I shut my door.

She hit the door and then she walked away.

Episode 4

Amber

"Oh my goodness AMBER!" Jade said with her eyes rolling in her head. "This cake is SO GOOD!" She savored the bite. "Oh! The cake is so moist; the caramel is sweet but not too sweet. OH! And then there's that kick from the rum at the last taste of the cake. How does she do this?"

"GIRL! I don't know, isn't it good! I told her I want my cake exactly like this for the party. She does this all by taste."

"It's a gift Amber!" Jade enjoyed her next bite.

"Alright!" Tony announced walking into Jade's office. "Ok, show me the pictures." I gave him my phone so he could scroll. He oohed and ahh'ed the pictures. "You taste with your eyes first so that was delicious." He picked up the knife and cut a small slice of the cake. "Now let's taste." Jade and I watched his face. His eyes got really big. "I see why your son married her! This is FANTASTIC! If my last girlfriend knew how to bake like this I'd be married, happy, and fat!" We laughed, "shoot if she could boil water I would've been satisfied. I still dream about that Red Velvet she made for your event. I had that and some sweet potato pie. I'm first in line whenever she opens her bakery." He cut a second much larger piece of cake.

"Is she gonna open any time soon?" Jade asked, chair dancing with her cake.

"Malcolm asked her about it, and she said she and Andrew are going to do it. They just don't know when yet." Then Tony gave me my phone back. I scrolled to the next picture. "Oh and check this out. So my little Dre has a girlfriend."

"A what?" Jade was not smiling.

"He and Tracy made this cake for show and tell. He wanted this cake cause he knows she likes peanuts." I showed them the pictures.

"Andrew is ok with this?"

"Oh come on, it's just a little crush."

"I guess, and he did go to his parents with it. These kids today scare me." I didn't like the direction of the conversation. "Do you have your dress for the engagement party yet?"

"Of course, when do I do anything last minute?" She twisted in her chair, "have you decided what you're going to do about Rosalind?"

I exhaled, "I don't have to pick my bridal party just yet. I don't even have a date. I guess we need to talk. I can never pin her down though. She avoids me like the plague. I asked Tanisha why she does that." I could feel the pain in my heart. "It feels like losing Troy all over again every time I think of how I lost her too."

"Just remember that it's not about you. Her way of trying to cope with losing the love of her life was to shut down from everyone. She tried to replace him with that nightmare, she's hurting."

"She shut down, Malcolm shut down." I exhaled like the pain was right there again.

"Troy got babies coming out of nowhere. Who knows if Yussef and Latia were his only kids? History repeats itself and his poor son ends up with trifling females as the mothers of his kids." I looked up at the ceiling, " THE DRAMA!"

"Ok, but when you talk to her you can't do that."

"Do what?"

"Turn the conversation to Troy. Let her do that if she does. That could be why she avoids you. When Sonny dies I don't want everybody bringing him up in conversation."

"When Sonny dies? You know something we don't?" Tony interjected.

Jade smiled, "we have a deal. He has to die before me. He couldn't handle life without me." Then her smile turned evil, "and I won't let him."

"You are crazy!' I laughed, "we are too young to be thinking about death! I could have a baby right now if I wanted to."

"Are you and Malcolm gonna try?" Tony asked.

"Are you kidding? I've got a grandson, another on the way, and whenever Andy and Tracy get to it, a third around the corner. I can spoil them and send them home. I know it's wrong to think this way, but I enjoy looking like I could be the momma even though I'm the Nana. I'm not going backwards, I'll do the hysterectomy myself!"

Chantel

"Hubby and Nicole are coming to our engagement party. How do you feel about their

36

friend Sonya coming?" Derrick asked.

"Did you use to date her or something?" I searched his face for an answer.

He frowned, "No! If anything Nicole tried to hook her up with Drew, and he wasn't going for it. She was at Drew's wedding though. I think she was distracted by you being there. That girl's mouth don't quit."

"She talks a lot?"

"A whole lot!"

"So why is she coming to the engagement party?" I didn't understand what he was asking me.

"She doesn't have to. I was asking if it was ok with you."

I stared at him for a minute the question didn't make sense to me. "I'm changing the subject cause I don't care. Paul and Brandy are coming with Lewis and Latia. I can't wait to see my girl!"

The guest list was huge, but it was also very specific. Security was going to be tight; Derrick was very intolerant about any silly stuff especially while I'm pregnant. Between Derrick and my brother Cyrus my safety was covered.

Derrick smiled, "I'm glad you're excited. There's going to be Wallace's, Latour's, Mason's, and Cardell's under the same roof. Prepare yourself for the fireworks."

"Cardell's?"

"Sasha's family. Richard comes from *interesting* stock as well."

"What do you mean by *interesting*?"

"You'll see. Some of them will be at the party. There will be more at the wedding."

I took Derrick in. Look at my baby's daddy. I smiled to myself. Not bad Chantel, not bad. There's no way in the world I ever thought that someone like him would notice me, or even be into me. I remember drooling at the sight of him, when others were shaking in their boots. I had no idea his heart was as big as it is, and there was so much more to him. I'm thankful that he has been patient enough to pay attention to someone like me. He doesn't like it when I say stuff like that, but it's true. I was the awkward girl in the corner. Sigh! Ok so looking back I didn't have money for fashionable clothes until I got a better paying job. I felt better about myself when I could afford to get my hair done, buy a pair of jeans.

I know that now that I'm this huge celebrity everyone expects me to be this super confident person. But I'm not; every time someone wants to collaborate with me I get a little panicked. What if they don't like me? What if I don't deliver? What if they think I'm an idiot? Aleisha has taken off in her own right. I wish I exuded the confidence that she does. We claim each other as sisters in the business, just like I claim Lewis as my big brother. However since she's white and I've been labeled the Black and Latina spokesperson, I'm sure everyone understands the reference isn't literal. Jesse is the next up and coming artist under Urbane Management. We collaborated on a few songs on my latest project. Two of them will be released on the radio. He's on Aleisha's project, and he has something in the works with Lewis. In addition to working on his own project. Lewis is managed under JoJo as well. Lewis said that signing with Musical Melodies has made his life so much better than being with his former manager Wade. He has a lot more freedom and his final take home is a lot bigger.

I turned to the side to check out my little pregnant pooch. I couldn't believe I was having a baby. Then I looked at Derrick in my mirror and said "**OH YEA!**" Derrick stopped dressing to look at me. He told me I was weird and went back to what he was doing. Derrick is mine and OF COURSE I'm having his baby! I'd be a fool not to. He's the only person I would ever do this with. I worry about becoming like my mother. She wanted the man not the babies. She only had the babies to make him happy. I understand that sort of thinking so much more now than I ever did before. Even though this pregnancy was not planned, I don't know if I would be pregnant right now if Derrick didn't want it.

We walked in through the back door of **The Place Where Jazz is Played**. Gus gave us excited hellos as he greeted us. Gus had Candice escort Cyrus, Sherrell, and I to my table up front. Derrick was playing tonight so I was excited. I've heard him working on a melody sometimes on the piano, or his sax. The Jazz house has been packed ever since that video went viral of Derrick and I performing here. People have flocked to this place in hopes of getting a glimpse of me. Then they come back because Narration the house band, my daddy, my brothers, and sometimes my baby D-Rick rock the house like nobody's business. I perform every once in a blue moon, I mostly come to listen. The line is normally wrapped around the building, and you can hear people outside going crazy as they miss out on what's happening inside. "How's everybody doing tonight?" The audience applauded. "We got a special treat for everyone here tonight. We got Chantel Shaw in the house!' Everyone clapped as the spotlight shined on me. I waved to everyone. "She is the muse for this musical set tonight. So everyone sit back and relax, enjoy the melodious sounds of Narration, Daniel Shaw & Company, and D-Rick!" The regulars applauded louder. My brothers, father, and Derrick took the stage along with the band. They played some of my songs while DJ and Mario took turns singing my songs in very manly ways. I couldn't believe how good they sounded. And I loved that the audience loved it as much as I did. Then my daddy sang a couple songs and he closed with the song he wrote for Cyrus and I. The lighting changed and then D-Rick played a beautiful song for me on his sax. When he came close to me while he played, people in the audience screamed with excitement as I swooned. I LOVE when he does this to me. For his last song he sat at the piano, and he asked me to join him, and he played a new melody. DJ sang Derrick's words of love and gratitude for having me in his life. Overwhelmed with emotion I put my face down as I cried. How did I happen to find someone so perfect for me?

Sasha

"I'm so excited!" I yelled.

"Uh! We can tell." Ava said with the biggest smile.

"We're going to my neck of the woods, what do you want to see first?" I asked Ava and Nathan.

Ava rattled off all the major tourist attractions the Golden Gate Bridge, Alcatraz, Fisherman's Wharf, etc. El smiled as he watched me excitely talk about the places I'd take them to eat, and stuff like that. Nathan reminded me that he's from The Bay Area as well, so he could suggest a few locations. First stop of course was my momma's restaurant as soon as we got off this plane. First thing Ava noticed is that Bay Area traffic was never as horrible as LA traffic. We checked into our hotel, set down our bags and got right back on the freeway to Walnut Creek to see my momma and my little sister Sabrina.

When we got to the restaurant Sabrina and my cousin Emerald were hosting, they said that everyone was in the party room. When we walked in the door I suddenly remembered that Ava and JoJo had dated once upon a time. I wondered if it would be awkward, but Ava excitedly introduced Nathan to my uncles and their women. I love having mature family and friends. I got excited when I saw Travis talking to my Nana, I haven't had a chance to spend time with him since he and my momma got back together. Nor had he had a chance to meet El, I bounced up and down like a goofy teenager as I introduced the best stepfather ever to my soon to be husband. Andrew, Tracy, and Andre walked in the door looking like a magazine family. Too much was happening at the wedding, so I reintroduced Tracy and El. Andrew stood in front of me not budging cause I acknowledged everyone except him. He told me I was such a spoiled little brat. I told him I wasn't too spoiled since he seemed to be able to forget me. He put his arms around me and asked how long was I gonna stay mad? Forever as far as I could tell. I may have been smiling but that smile didn't hide how much he hurt me by forgetting me, and I wasn't going to let it go. He said we needed to sit down and talk after the party so that we could officially clear the air. He said so much was happening before his wedding, but that was still no excuse for hurting me like he did. At least he knew it, Tracy smiled at me. Amber came with Derrick and Chantel, and a few minutes later Malcolm came with Uncle Frank, some of my cousins, and my Poppa. My cousin Tina came with her parents Timothy and Grace. Tina told me again that my man was gorgeous! I thanked her, then she told me when we were away from the family she wanted to introduce me to someone, but it was sort of a secret. I gave her a look, and she reminded me that I knew how her daddy was. I asked her what Lanie thought of him. She clinched her jaw and then she said that they only met once, and that Lanie never likes anyone so go figure. That was true, but Lanie liked El, so I give her reading of people some credit. Say what you want, but it had all the makings of a disaster to me. Before we ate I noticed Tracy and Andre over in the corner praying before their meal. Andrew watched my eyes, and then he smiled at me. I rolled my eyes. Darryl strolled in right as Malcolm asked where he was. He said hi to everyone then he walked over to Malcolm and said something lowly to him. Malcolm nodded to show he heard him. He took one more bite of his food then he excused himself from the table. All the men except for Cyrus, Travis, and El followed them out. El looked at me and I shrugged, I told him the men did that from time to time. They were forever on the clock. Amber showed me pictures of her cake that Tracy was going to make for her. Then she asked me who was making my cake. I told her Carina, the party planner, chose a bakery for me. Carina suggested Tracy at first, but I didn't want my cake to look and taste like she made it. I was very surprised looking at Amber's pictures. The picture was nice, but the taste remained to be proven. When the men returned I asked Andrew what was up, and he said nothing just business. I stared at him that was the obvious part. Then he said later. I got up when Hunter and his wife Lisa walked in. Hunter was my friend from high school; we hadn't spoken much since his wedding. But I felt obligated to invite him when my momma said she ran into him at the store and she told him about my engagement. After all I was in his wedding. Hunter looked confused, when I was in his wedding Yussef escorted me. So I'm sure he thought that's whom I'm marrying. I introduced Hunter and Lisa to El and I offered no explanation. I asked my momma where my Dan-Dan (my father's mother) was. She said my Dan-Dan called at the last minute and said she wasn't going to be able to make it. Instantly I knew it was Richard, I told him I wasn't telling my momma about the baby. I didn't want to be in the middle of that explosion. I have no idea how my momma will respond to it. My parents have been stuck on stupid over each other since they were kids; I am a product of their stupidity. However, they could never seem to get it quite right. Now they're both in separate relationships, which I personally think is for the best. However, my father and his girlfriend are expecting. I know my momma's gonna have some kind of a reaction, I just don't know what. Richard did not respond well when he found out about my little sister, but he eventually got over it. I'd say he looks at Sabrina like she's an extension of my momma and he loves her all the same. I just don't know what to expect from my momma. Sometimes I can't help but wonder how much of my parent's stupidity lives in me. I know I want to be married and I'm the reason why El and I are at this point. Sometimes I feel like I'm forcing the idea to try to prove that I'm not like my parents. I can't believe that sometimes I actually feel like I could be making a mistake. Anyways, I hope they wait until after the party to get into all that. I'm looking forward to a drama free party with my family.

Yussef

"Is an engagement party really a party for kids?" Angela asked.

I hadn't thought of it any other way. "I don't see why they wouldn't come. Drew is bringing Dre. This is a family party."

"I guess," she exhaled.

Since I have the girls every other weekend, last weekend I did everything I could to make our time together as romantic as possible. Angela has seemed wounded ever since our meeting with Melissa and Sylvia. I keep trying to reassure her that they are my past and I only want her, but she keeps getting caught up on their appearances. Meeting Tracy was one thing, and in the end she said she liked her. I know a lot of that has to do with the fact that she feels pretty comfortable that Tracy isn't after me. I don't know if Angela can handle my life and the thought of that saddens me. Two kids with two different women can be too much. I don't know how Roz... Roz, she was my father's girlfriend when he passed away. I need to talk to her. I need help! As far as I know Roz didn't question my father's love for her. I need to know how she handled it. "Let me make a phone call." I said to Angela as I pulled out my phone. Roz picked up on the second ring. She sounds so happy to hear from me every time I call. I asked her if she was busy, and if not could Angela and I come take her out to dinner. I could hear her smile through the phone. I told her we'd be at her house in thirty minutes and she needed to think of where she wanted to go. When I told Angela we were going to get Roz she didn't seem excited but she went along with it. I got a little irritated and then I found myself wondering how Tracy responded to Andre and Toya initially. At least in her case Toya's in jail and Andre is with them 24/7, so maybe she can connect Andre more to Andrew. I don't know, but I need Angela to not fall apart. As we drove to Richmond to pick up Roz my phone rang. Angela took it out of her purse; she exhaled and said it was Melissa. I told her to put it on speaker, "Hello?"

"Your girlfriend finally gave you your phone back?"

"You're on speaker Melissa what do you need?"

She sucked her teeth, "what color dress do you want Yesmina to wear to this party? She has a ton of dresses and I'll do her hair accordingly."

"We already bought both of the girls' dresses. Angela picked out barrettes, you can style it any way you want."

"Why wouldn't you want her mother's opinion on a dress you're buying for her. Is it the same dress as Sydney? Cause they have different body types."

Angela rolled her eyes, "Melissa, they're little girls. I picked them out; I think the girls will look nice. Please don't plant any competitive vibes in my little girl's heart against her sister. They are unbelievably close and I really want them to stay that way. Angela can send you a picture of the dresses when we get home later on tonight. Or we'll send you pictures once they're dressed."

Melissa was quiet for a minute, "I'm gonna need to talk directly to you when you have a spare minute."

"You're talking directly to me now.".

"Without the audience, can we meet somewhere?"

Angela cut her eyes at me, "no, no that's not a good idea. Melissa you need to stay on your side of the pool."

"Yussef! I hate this! I need to talk to you, not her. I am the mother of your first born, don't I deserve a conversation?"

"Melissa you deserve a whole lot of things that my Christian upbringing won't allow," I spit at her. "Go to service, say a prayer cause you're heading in the wrong direction." I exhaled, "what time will Yezzy be ready?"

"Whatever time you need her to be ready. You're going to come get her first right?"

"If she's ready first. I would like to come early so we can have breakfast as a family."

"When are you going back to service? Or have you become too accustom to sinning that you're never coming back?"

"What I do with my life is none of your business. Just worry about keeping yourself on the straight and narrow. I'll come get Yezzy at eight."

"Ok, see you then." Then she hung up.

I exhaled and I looked at Angela who was beyond irritated. I asked her to call Sylvia on speaker. "Sylvia?"

"Yes" she said with a smile in her voice. "I'm glad you got your phone back."

"You're on speaker, I'm going to pick Yezzy up at eight and I will be right over to get Syd directly after."

She hesitated, "I don't have a dress for her for your party."

"I bought the girls dresses already. If you want her hair done a certain way then please do it. She's already taken care of."

Sylvia sound relieved. "Ok," then she hesitated. "Is it pushing it to ask to speak to you privately?"

Angela shook her head. "Sylvia what do you want? This is as private as we're going to get."

"Ok, ok..." She exhaled, I imagined her twisting her hair like she always used to when she was nervous about something. "Angela I mean no disrespect, let me say that first off. I know I said I was sorry before, but I don't feel like I can express how sorry I am. These past few years with Sydney by myself have been such a wakeup call. I know I broke your heart, and I feel so badly about it. You offered me everything and you were so good to me. No man has ever been as good to me as you were. I took you and everything we had for granted. I feel like I owe you whatever you ask of me from now until the day I die. Nothing I can say or do can take back what I did to you. Even though it's messed up, I am happy to have you back in my life even if it has to be like this. I appreciate everything you do for Sydney. She's gone from no father, to a very hands on and loving father. I tell her all kinds of stories about us. I tell her how in love we were. Yussef she's so much happier knowing about you. I've noticed a change in her for the better. And to have her best friend as a sister is amazing. I mean what are the odds? Yussef I love you so much," then she paused. "Respectfully of course Angela." Angela blank stared at me. "I want to say thank you for stepping up. I'm not stressed anymore and I know I owe it to you. I know I don't deserve any of this, but thank you. Sydney and I are going to move to a nicer place and we're getting a two bedroom. I'll be able to afford to take my baby to see movies." She started crying, "it's been really hard trying to do this on my own. I just wanted to say thank you. And Angela thank you for allowing him to be a father to his girls. I know he couldn't do all he's done without your support."

I glanced at Angela and she looked out the window. "Alright, um." I didn't know what to say to all of that. "Ok, so we'll get Syd in the morning a little after eight. Enjoy your weekend Sylvia."

"Ok, you guys too." She said sniffling as she hung up.

Angela growled, "these manipulative females! At least Melissa is up front with her garbage. Sylvia's sitting over there crying beautiful tears trying to pull at your heart."

"What? I don't think she was lying." I said confused by her irritation.

"No, all that she said was probably true. BUT! She's on the same path as Melissa; she's just going about it differently. Her eyes got so big when she saw the amount you're paying her. She wants all the money!"

I was quiet the rest of the way to Roz's what was I supposed to say to that. I asked where Roz wanted to go for dinner, and she said The Dead Fish in Crockett like a big kid. Roz asked Angela what was wrong; Angela twisted in her seat and said nothing. When we got to the restaurant Roz asked Angela again. Angela huffed and then she said she didn't want to unload on her or put her in the middle of our business. Roz looked at me and I told her it was ok. Inside I was screaming at Angela to just get it out. Then Angela went in, she explained that it hasn't even been six months and it's been one thing after another. First she doesn't even know me by the right name, when I finally fess up then I lay the fact that I have a child on her and she doesn't date men with children because of the crazy baby momma factor. I tell her that my baby momma is happily married. Ok so when she warms up to that idea she hasn't even met the one child then I blindside her with another daughter and baby momma. She said it's so obvious that both of them still want me. Roz listened to everything she said and she sympathized with her. Then she looked at me, "looks like you couldn't avoid becoming your father no matter how hard you tried." Her comment wounded me, Angela saw me slump a little in my seat. "Baby, I know it's hard. Look at your man, can't you see how irresistible he is?" I frowned and Angela smiled. "There's always gonna be some female hanging on trying to get to him. Your man is just like his daddy. He's smart, handsome, he has a beautiful heart, and he is a good man. Troy had the worst baby momma's ever. Yussef's momma Shonda and Latia's momma Linda, oh my goodness I don't miss them. That was the package he came with. I've never loved a man like I loved Troy. There wasn't anything I couldn't tell him, nothing I couldn't share with him. Honey I know it's hard, but when you have a good man and he's this FINE females are always gonna want him. They will think they can get him, and try. You have to decide whether you've got the stomach for this roller coaster. Cause at the end of the day children are involved, and if you can't handle it you need to bow out now. Before those girls bond to you and rely on you to love their father." Angela sat back like she was thinking about it. "Yea, Troy didn't always make the right choices. I knew about what happened every time he took you home." She looked at me. "It wasn't ok with me, but there were so many things that your father accepted about me." I wanted to ask but only if she wanted to share. "Like the fact that I was still married to Tanisha's father when we got together. Troy wanted me to get divorced so that we could get married. I was scared," she said as tears started falling out of her eyes. Troy got me to see that Ben was wrong, until Troy I thought the demise of my marriage was my fault. That's the way Ben made me feel, your father was good to me. He was good to my daughter. He didn't handle everything right, and I was constantly on him about you and Latia." She grabbed my hand, "I'm sorry I wasn't there for you when he died." She cried harder.

"Roz! You were there for me. You didn't abandon me if that's what you think. I was always welcomed at your home or at least that's the way I felt even when you were with that fool."

"You're my baby, you're always welcomed where ever I am," Roz said.

Kendra

Being mad at Anton definitely removes any guilt I might've felt about going to this party with Darryl. Ahjanae and I have gone from store to store looking for dresses. By chance Ahjanae found a dressmaker in downtown Oakland. Her shop was small and she looked like a hippie from Berkeley, her style was very eclectic. We liked her sample dresses and pictures of other dresses she's done. I explained that I only wear pants and the last dress I wore was very sexy. She asked if I wanted to stick with the sexy theme and Ahjanae and I smiled very big as we said yes. I showed her a picture of my previous dress. Then she started sketching. The dress was going to be long and see through. The bodice was a box shaped sweetheart neckline and solid underneath the see through material. The skirt was short and the see through lace over it was long. I loved it. Then she asked what color I wanted. I decided on a chocolate brown. Then she designed Ahjanae's dress. It was long with a split up the thigh and the back out, the straps drew attention to her back. She kept saying she wanted to be sexy but respectful of the fact that she had two kids. She asked if

I thought Ryder would like her dress. I told her he was going to love it. We told the girl if everything worked out that Ahjanae would be back for three more dresses. The dressmaker told us to come back this weekend and she'd have us try on our almost finished dresses. I couldn't believe she was going to have them almost ready in a week. Anton is still running from that girl and now I wonder how much of his story was true. Did she leave like he said she did? I've been going to his place and waiting for her to pop up. I call Anton randomly and he always answers. I keep asking what the problem is with this girl and he shuts down. I'm tempted to call her myself but I'm trying to be patient and let him work this out on his own.

"What are you going to do with your hair?" Ahjanae asked.

"I like the cut, I'm just going to get it freshened up." Ahjanae smiled. "What?" I knew whatever she was about to say was going to annoy me.

"You ever notice how when you're all into Anton your hair has to be long? But when you're into Darryl your hair gets short."

I rolled my eyes, "so I would say my asymmetrical bob puts me in the middle of both worlds."

She shook her head no, "Anton likes your hair long down your back. Darryl likes whatever you like."

"So you're saying I'm into Darryl right now while I'm engaged to Anton?"

"Stranger things have happened. Don't beat yourself up about it. I think you should call off your engagement."

"Good thing I wasn't asking you what you thought. What sense does it make to give up a good guy for a playboy? A playboy who will never give me what I want at that."

"Is my life lacking because Ryder and I aren't married? We have a beautiful family, I have everything I need."

"I need the commitment."

"Ryder and I are committed. He can't leave me, and I would never leave him. We changed Erin's name and everything. It's just paper Kendra."

"You changed Erin's on paper and not yours?" I raised an eyebrow.

"We're not married."

"I NEED THE PAPER!" I said getting angry.

"Don't get mad at me for asking you why you need it. It's a valid question."

"I need a man who will walk to the ends of the earth and back for me. I need to know that man is as committed as I am."

"Just because you have paper isn't a guarantee that the commitment will be any stronger." I looked at Ahjanae irritated. I didn't want to go here but she brought this on herself.

"That's true, so tell me again why you and Ryder aren't getting married?"

"Because we don't need the paper," she said plainly.

"You don't need the paper or Ryder doesn't? I do recall that until Ryder you looked forward to getting married as well."

Ahjanae shifted in her seat. "I did, but I've never had the security in a relationship that I have with Ryder."

"Oh that's right because before Ryder you had so many relationships? Oh wait! Before Ryder you only dated one other person." Ahjanae stared at me. "Don't sit up here and act like I'm wrong for standing up for what I need. I know you! I know you still want marriage the whole nine yards. You're too afraid to stand up and demand it for yourself so you're trying to shame me for being true to myself. Instead of making Ryder put up or shut up you chickened out and had his baby instead. Trying to convince yourself that a baby is the same commitment. You know as well as I do that it's not. I don't want a permanent boyfriend, I need someone who wants me and loves me enough to put it on paper."

Ahjanae was quiet for a minute like she was reviewing what I said. "At least I wouldn't

stoop to marrying someone I didn't love just to say I've stuck to my guns and someone loved me enough to do it. I compromised for the love of my life. You're settling for a mediocre life. You're so in love with Darryl that it's pathetic! Weren't you planning your own baby sabotage with Darryl before his indiscretions came to the light? And then when he calls you on it you go running to your daddy! Why don't the rules apply to Kendra? Didn't you cheat on Omar with Darryl? Oh but that don't count huh? You're so much better than everyone else that even your dirt is above reproach? Stop stringing Anton a long and get back with Darryl! It's funny how you can forgive everyone except **Darryl**!"
I did not see that backfiring on me. "Put your foot down with Ryder!"
"Break up with Anton!"
"No! Anton is a good guy."
"He's not Darryl!"
"And that's one of the things I love about him."
"Please Anton is boring! I bet you the sex is boring too!" I refused to answer that. She laughed. "I was on the other side of the wall, I know how you and Darryl got down. And don't let you guys drink!"
I sunk in my seat, "SHUT UP! I HATE YOU SO MUCH!"
Ahjanae kissed at me, "I love you too boo!"

Malachi

The dramatic highlight of my trip happened when we were leaving our final meeting just before our long flight home. Cora turned and looked at me and says, "so I guess we're done Malachi?"
Knowing that she was talking about our relationship I agreed with her, "you're correct. We're done!"
Cora said ok, and then she turned on her heels and started talking to the other members. I knew better than to think she'd gonna give up just like that. She's never been this persistent before. As I walked out the door, Gerald and Marian advised that their flights weren't until later so it was Cora and I alone in our taxi. Cora wasted no time; as soon as the car door closed she was on. She was screaming at me asking me how I could drop her like a bad habit. I told her I needed to focus on making my marriage work, and all we were doing was making things worse. She said things weren't worse for her, worse for her would be living without me. I asked her if she loved me, and she asked me how I could ask her that. She said of course she does and that was what all this was about. I asked her if she loved herself or me more. She got angry, I told her I needed to let her go. She looked me in my eyes and said she could see in my eyes that I didn't want to let her go. I exhaled in pure exhaustion. I told her the moment she threatens to jeopardize my family I can't continue. Cora started crying and telling me that she couldn't give up on me. I told her she wasn't submitting by fighting me. After I couldn't bare her tears I hugged her and told her she needed to give me time to sort things out. That hug turned into a kiss, that kiss turned into passion, next thing I know we're in the family bathroom going at it. We were sitting next to each other on the plane, and I found myself promising to call her and to do a better job about keeping in touch with her. She kept trying to get me to come back to her place during my layover in LA, but I called Richard, Sasha's father instead. He met me for a drink and a light meal, I was anxious to see my wife and children.
My heart started pounding as soon as we started to descend into Oakland. I reminded myself that I needed to take a shower immediately. I couldn't risk that Cora's smell might be all over me. I stopped at a Motel by the airport, I paid for a room in cash. I showered and decided I didn't need the clothes I was wearing anymore. I put them in the trash, I took a deep breath. Then I drove to our home in Fremont. Denise and the girls excitedly

greeted me at the garage door. I hugged my girls; there was no better feeling than the feeling of being loved by the women in your life. Denise gave me the biggest kiss and she told me she missed me. My heart burned for her right in that moment. Denise took my bags and told us to go have a ball. Then she kissed me and told me she was going to wait for me, her devilish smile made me almost forget about my girls. Their calls for their daddy brought me back to the moment. Even though I was completely tired and could've used a nap, my girl's anxious smiles told me they had been bubbling over waiting for me. I couldn't disappoint them. I took them out to dinner where we ate burgers, fries, and milkshakes. Then we went to the movies, they were so excited about this movie that was completely goofy. The biggest popcorn, boxes of candy, ice cream, and large sodas were in our arsenal for this movie. We laughed so hard at the silliness of this film; we all came out with smiles. The girls were amped up on sugar and giggling harder than I'd ever heard them. By the time I pulled into our garage they were knocked out. Anticipating their sugar comas Denise met us in the garage. I picked up Jada our oldest, and Denise picked up Amaya. We undressed the girls and put them in their beds. I noticed Denise's robe and I hoped that meant she was waiting for me in a manner worthy of a husband who hasn't touched his wife in too long. I followed Denise into our bedroom; she sat in front of the computer. She had a big smile on her face. She said she's been doing research, she said she was trying to think of somewhere romantic to go. I massaged her shoulders and I told her we could stay in our bedroom and that would be all the romance that I needed. She tensed up and got irritated with me, "why would I be excited about staying in this bedroom? I'm here every night!"

Trying to deflect her irritation I smiled at her, and then I took a step back. "Because I'm here!" She wasn't expecting me to hit her with my smile. I saw her completely weaken. I took her hand, "baby! I don't care where we go. You just tell me where and I'll give you the dates. I don't care about any of that right now. I miss my wife! I need to spend the night with you! I know you're probably tired, but I'm begging you not to deny me tonight. I'll die Denise! I'll die! I need you baby!" The expression on her face was like my frankness caught her off guard. I kissed her.

"You need me?" She had tears in her eyes.

"I'm about to burst!" I said honestly, and then I pulled her to stand up. I opened her robe and she had on a satin nightgown. Nothing fancy but you could've sworn it was the most erotic attire by my reaction. I told her she looked beautiful and she relaxed even more. I kept kissing her and telling her how much I loved and needed her. My baby came alive and whatever was holding her back from me melted in that moment. We spent the night entangled in each other. YES! My wife is back!

Lanie

Donzae looked at me with her mouth opened as I told her my story. I blew air in complete frustration. "I just can't believe you're still a virgin after all this time. Might explain why you're so crazy though. All that pent up frustration."

"I know! I know! Feel my pain Gurl! AND THEN! D keep trying to tell me that Yussef and I are related. I shook my family tree, ain't no blood link between us! He needs to go somewhere with that. "

"Go somewhere with what?" Ryder said suddenly behind me.

"Hi!" Donzae said waiving at him with a goofy smile.

"Cousin, don't look at my cousin like that!" I stood to hug Ryder.

"Like you said, ain't no blood link between us."

I caught the snarls of a couple of brothas in our direction. "Boo!" Both of them looked surprised at my response to them. To say they were pissed would be an understatement. They kept staring in our direction as if they were waiting for their moment to say something.

"They're stupid, leave them alone Lanie." Ryder's voice slightly rumbled the table.

"Where's your girlfriend at, you need someone you can actually boss around. You should already know, I'm not hearing you." Another guy walked to the table with his friends. He was smiling until he asked them what was wrong. I couldn't hear what they were saying, but his eyes darted across the food court to us. The third guy looked at me with recognition. He turned quickly to his friends and one of them turned pale. I guess they were no longer hungry cause they quickly got up, threw their food away, and walked away.

"Which name you think he dropped Wallace or Latour?" Donzae asked.

"Don't matter either way we are all crazy peas out of the same pod."

"Ladies, if you are done. I've got to go back to work. Lanie can you pick Erin up for me today?"

"Of course! Can we get mani's and pedi's before I return her?"

"My little girl don't need all that womanly stuff." He frowned.

"It's our rite of passage as women. You know what forget I asked you, I'll call Jen myself." I clapped my hands together with excitement.

Ryder sighed in defeat, "it's fine Lanie. Try not to rub off too much on my highly impressionable sweetheart. Pull back as much of Nana's fire as you can."

"I make no promises! Sometimes people get shot, and sometimes you the one who gotta do the shooting."

"As long as you teach her to shoot responsibly." He hugged me and kissed me again.

"Thanks for helping me out."

"What time she get out?"

Ryder looked at his watch, "an hour. The password is zither."

I frowned, "why you gotta come to me on the hard word day? Text me the password, I'm not going to remember that."

"You can and you will, zither." Then he walked away.

"The nerve of him, he acts like he's forgetting that he's asking me for a favor."

Donzae and I finished our lunch and then I went to pick up my little cousin. She smiled big as she walked towards me holding her straps. "Lanie."

"Erin," I smiled.

She stopped far enough away from me to run if she needed to, the whole time she's smiling from ear to ear. "The password?" Demanding an answer gave her a sense of power.

"Zither," I rolled my eyes. Erin smiled bigger and gave me the biggest hug. "Who came up with that one?"

"Dad of course."

"Did he tell you what it meant?"

"You use it to make music."

I could've cared less, "guess what we're going to do next?"

"SOMETHING AMAZING!" She cheered.

"Of course, everything with me is amazing!" She shook her head yes. "Can you say Manicures?"

"Is Janell coming with us?"

She was talking about EJ's daughter. "No baby, her daddy won't let her get her nails done."

"BUT SHE'S BIGGER THAN ME!"

I nodded in agreement. My brother in his control issues sometimes. Shelby was fine with it, but EJ just doesn't want his daughter growing up. We put on our shades and rode in style to the shop my Grammy owns. Grammy turned her shop into an all-out salon and you could get everything done here. Grammy still has a handful of clients that she waits on personally. Like her daughter in-laws, and granddaughters, and her regulars from a simpler time. Now you can get massages, facials, manicures, pedicures, the works. Erin and I breezed in the door sporting our shades and diva style. The receptionist squeezed Erin and I in, then we took our seats in the throne chairs to receive our awesome treatments. You could see the excitement amongst the staff to know who was going to get us today. Since I didn't pay for my service, I always tipped the person the cost of my service and if they exceeded expectations, I'd tip them above that. Everyone wanted to work on me whenever I came. As we let our feet soak in the colorful heated sauna for our feet, I asked Erin how her day was. She went on and on about nothingness. No matter what you asked Erin she somehow went back to her little brother and something cute he said or did recently. She's such a good big sister. I know there's a reason I was born last. I doubt any sibling would've survived under my care.

I did a double take as I saw Frank walking through the floor towards my Grammy's office. He had a large bouquet of flowers in his hand. "Frank?" I called out.

He looked at me like he knew I was here, "one moment." Then he continued walking towards the office. A few of the staff members looked at each other and smiled like there was some kind of inside conversation going on.

Frank was in Grammy's office for a minute then they came out together. Grammy was smiling and Frank was Frank. "Hello baby." Grammy said giving me a hug. Then she turned to Erin to do the same. "You two having girl time I see."

"Why are you bringing my Grammy flowers?" I asked Frank.

"Mind your own business little girl." Grammy said.

I looked at Frank and he only looked at me. "Do you come here a lot?" Grammy cut her eyes at me like she was going to get me. "What? I don't understand what's going on. You know if I don't ask Zoey will."

"Why would Zoey ask me questions about something she knows nothing about?" Grammy crossed her arms.

"Cause I'm going to call her as soon as I leave, or I'll see her tonight. One way or the other she's going to know."

"Grow up Lanie," then she turned her back to me. I could hear the smile in her voice. "Thank you for the flowers, I'll call you later."

"It was nice chatting with you Frank, you're a regular chatter box as usual."

Frank hugged Erin, then he pushed my head as he walked out. I raised my eyebrows at my Grammy who looked like she was blushing.

We got to Ryder's place at the same time as Jen. Erin happily showed off her hands and feet. I hugged Jen and chatted for a little bit. The whole time I'm thinking about Dorian's distance lately and how it's getting on my nerves. We should be moving forward not standing stagnant and arguing about petty stuff.

Erica and Zoey said they think our Grammy and Frank are getting back together. She said he's been hanging around the salon a lot more these days, and they've left for the evening together without saying a word to anyone. We faked disgust as we laughed at them. Even my Grammy is getting *some*!

****

"Oh my goodness Lanie you're so funny." April said laughing too hard at my sarcasm that was not meant for her enjoyment.

"Ha! Ha!" I wasn't laughing.

I watched Dorian approach our group to play all mighty leader and director. He knows the only reason I'm here is because he hasn't answered any of my calls. I really hope for his safety he doesn't think we broke up. Dorian told everyone that since Yoshi's was just around the corner we could walk unless someone needed to move their car. April watched us as everyone started walking and I hung back to talk to Dorian. I bucked my eyes at her and she smiled as she started to walk behind the group. "This is not the time

47

Lanie." Dorian put his hands in his pockets as he looked down at me.

"You tell me when is the right time then? I've been calling you. You've been sending me to voicemail! ME!"

"There's nothing left to say."

"Nothing?"

"I told you what I need and you can't give me that. What else is there to say? You're only trying to complicate things now."

"Dorian, I love you. You just don't understand! You're trying to change me into someone I'm not. What happened to us accepting each other for who we are?"

"Trust me, I am accepting everything about you. You're a spoiled brat who doesn't know how to accept no for an answer. You have a wicked temper, you're blunt, and rude."

"Those all sound like pluses to me. Yes I know I'm awesome, but where's the problem?"

"I NEED a wife who worships with me. I'll compromise on everything else."

"Compromise? Being with me is an upgrade for you. All those girls are boring! You know you'd be bored stupid without me in your life."

He put his hands out to weigh the differences. "Bored or spiritually alone. I'd rather be bored than have to worship alone. And I'd be able to share spiritual truths with them."

My chest burned, is this what rejection feels like? "You're seriously breaking up with me? You sure you want to do that?"

He was trying to keep emotion off his face. "I'm in love with you Lanie. I don't want to break up with you. We have so much history; my days and nights are filled with visions of you. I can't ignore what I need in order to feel complete in my life. The stunt you pulled the other night was not cool. I've been waiting for you all this time and you tried to reduce us to a cheap level of nothing."

I clinched my teeth, "are you breaking up with me?" I looked at the group far ahead of us.

He stopped walking. "I don't want to, but you're not leaving me with a choice."

"Yes or No Dorian! Be a man for once in your life!"

I could see the smoke above his head. "What would you know about a real man? If it ain't thuggish you can't relate. I am more man than you will ever know. Yes, I am breaking up with you. There's no point in prolonging this."

"You don't love me anymore?" I felt like I couldn't breathe.

"I could never love anyone more than I love you. You just aren't what I need."

I kicked him in his leg. He stood there like it didn't hurt. I reached up to slap him and he grabbed my wrist. "You're so full of it! Go on and get with one of those boring females. When your soul starts burning for me remember that you brought this on yourself!" I snatched my hand away from him. I was not giving him the satisfaction of one tear. I turned around and started walking towards my car. Dorian was walking behind me. "Don't follow me!"

"I'm making sure you make it to your car safely."

"Please! I'm more protection for you than you could ever be for me. I got my gun at all times!"

"I'm leaving too, I'm not in the mood for the concert."

"What you gonna do, go home and cry? Cry cause you're too much of a punk. You have me! Who rejects someone like me over petty differences?"

He shook his head, "you don't get it. We're not evenly yoked. It can't work."

"You're making it harder than it has to be. My parents make it work, you just don't want to."

"I guess I'm not as strong as your mother then."

"Clearly! You better not call me later! I don't want to hear it!" I took out my phone and I called Oneika. "I'm leaving cause this punk and sorry excuse for a man has decided to break my heart!"

"Whoa! Where's Dorian?"

"He's going to go cry in a corner somewhere. He'll be back to give in to April and have a boring marriage and a boring life!" Dorian was mad, ask me if I care.

"Ok, I'll tell the others he won't be back either. Where you going?"

"OUT TO FIND A REAL MAN!" I screamed at Dorian. Then I hung up. "My real man is going to come back and kick your butt for being so stupid!" I could see him getting madder and madder but I didn't care. "Then I'm going to break into your house and have sex with my real man in your bed! ON YOUR PILLOW!"

"Shut up Lanie!"

"YEP! I'm going to go get me some thug passion and I'm not looking back! You on the other hand will be crying from your soul because you miss me!"

"Shut up Lanie!" He yelled as he walked towards me with his hands in his pockets.

"I'm never going to service again! All you square idiots turn to religion when you know that's the only way to have a herd of females pining after you, pumping your head up cause that's the ONLY way a woman would want you!"

He stood in my face. "But you want me! Why are you trying to hurt me? This is painful enough." The calmness of his voice did not reflect the anger on his face.

"Because you're killing me!"

"Baby I'm dying too!" He kept his hands in his pockets.

"Then don't do this!"

"Come on Lanie. Come to service on Sunday's and Tuesday's. It's just a couple of hours a week. That's all I'm begging you to do. Please do this for us. I promise I will spend my life making up for it. I'm begging for this one thing. Then we can go get married, we'll have everything like we planned all our lives for. Please Lanie!"

"It sounds simpler than it is. It's hard to walk in there with all those people judging me."

"Forget them! It's just you, God, and me. Lanie please! I don't want to breakup, but if we can't have this we have nothing."

"Dorian! We'll still have each other. My parents make it work, why can't we?"

"Cause I don't want to worship alone." He put his hands on my face. Then he kissed me so deeply, I threw my arms around his neck and my leg up on his hip. "We broke up because of you not me. I didn't change the plan. You did." Then he released me and walked back to his car. He waited for me to drive away then he went in the direction of his house.

All those years of self-control that he promised were going to lead somewhere left me nowhere. We promised to be each other's first! He owes me his virginity at least. I'll try to be civil about everything else, but his virginity is mine!

I went to the store and I stared at the condoms. I looked at my hand trying to remember how much was outside of my hand to decide if I needed regular sized or magnums. An employee walked past my aisle with her red shirt and khaki uniform. "Excuse me can you help me?" I called out.

She came back with a smile. "Sure, how can I help you?"

"Are you a virgin?"

The girl gasped and started laughing, "um..."

"If you're a virgin you can't help me."

She cleared her throat as she cheesed. "No."

"Ok, good!" I put my hand out like it was when I was holding him. "My boyfriend and I are virgins. I've decided that tonight he's giving it up. When I held him this much was over my hand. Does that make him huge or average?"

The girl laughed as she used imaginary measuring tape to measure what we're dealing with. "I'd say he's average, but definitely a GOOD average."

Then I looked at the wall of condoms, "which brand do you recommend?"

"Most of this stuff is for later when you know to be more specific. Tonight you only need

the basics. If you're lucky you'll use more than one."
"Thank you, I hope you're right."
I bought the condoms and then I went to the liquor store. Dorian was inside and I drank my courage juice in the car, and I put condoms in my bra. When I knocked on his front door Dorian stared at me. He wasn't surprised to see me; he said nothing's left to say. When a tear fell from my eye he jumped hard. I put my purse on the couch then I went in the bathroom. I put my panties in my pocket, then I smoothed out my skirt. I splashed water on my face and I took a deep breath. When I came out the bathroom he was putting away the evidence that he had been drinking as well. He sat on the couch looking completely sexy and angelic in his sweats and no shirt. I walked up to him and kissed him in the middle of his chest remembering how much he likes when I do that. I kissed his neck and then his mouth. He tasted like liquor. His eyes were droopy and sad looking. I told him I loved him so much and we needed to say goodbye properly. He said he didn't want to say goodbye. He didn't notice when I took the condom out of my bra. I told myself to focus, I had a small window before he tried to stop me and I was trying to get to the point of no return. He let me move his sweats down and he asked me what I was doing. I got so excited as I slid the condom on him. He asked me again what I was doing. I took another deep breath then I watched his eyes as I slowly worked him inside of me. Dorian was a lot tipsier than I realize cause he didn't stop me he moaned out loud then he asked me what I was doing. Now that I had him in I didn't know what else to do and I was a little uncomfortable. Dorian's moan as he put his hands on my hips made my body contract. He moved a little then he rolled us on the floor. He went back in and then he took over moving and I opened my eyes cause this was real. Dorian was really inside of me. This was really happening. Dorian kept moaning and kissing me. Then he stiffened, and slightly yelled. Then he collapsed on me. He rolled over and I took the condom off of him. I went to the bathroom and flushed his baby makers down the toilet. I went in the living room and he was laying on the floor with his sweats half down. I sat next to him and he sat up. He kissed me and started undressing me; he didn't notice the condoms that fell out of my bra. He took off his sweats then he picked me up and took me to his bed. The memory of his moans excited me and surpassed my throbbing as he entered me again. This time he was smoother and warmer. My leg started shaking as he moaned in my ear and the best feeling came over me as he slightly yelled again. He laid on me again as he pushed my hair back. He said this is the best dream ever, and then I could hear him trying to gain some sobriety. Immediately I realized how drunk he was and I felt guilty. He started moving again and the feeling was back. This time he moved harder which was uncomfortable but I didn't say anything cause it still felt good. I accidentally scratched his arm as he released again. He kept kissing me until he fell asleep hard. I looked at him laying naked on the bed then I got up. When I went to the bathroom and wiped myself there was a little blood. Immediately I thought about the bed and I cringed at the thought of him discovering that in the morning. As I picked up my condoms I realized none were used in the bedroom. I cursed as I put on my clothes! All my stupid scheming! I removed any evidence of me. I brought a bottle of liquor in his room and I put it by the bed. My guilty conscience wanted him to think tonight was truly a dream.

****

Dorian was in the lobby as I exited the elevator. He was beyond pissed off. He grabbed my arm and rushed out the lobby. "Lanie are you ok?" A staff member asked me.
"Yes," I said trying to push past my guilt.
"HOW COULD YOU?" Dorian was the angriest I've ever seen him.
"What are you talking about?" I tried to play dumb.
"You took advantage of me!"
I lowered my eyes, "do you have any idea how dumb you sound? I don't know what you're talking about."

"You know exactly what I'm talking about." He pulled up his sleeve and revealed the healing scratch on his arm. "How could you do this to me?"

"I don't know what you're talking about." I couldn't look at him.

"You know exactly what I'm talking about. You've ruined me! I hope you're happy with yourself! STAY AWAY FROM ME!" Then he walked away angry.

****

A day late doesn't mean anything. It could be the stress and depression right? Dorian won't talk to me; I think I officially pushed him away this time. My momma and Erica came home last week saying that Dorian stepped down from his responsibilities in the congregation. My momma asked me what I did and I gave her a guilty *nothing* while my daddy stared through me. I slinked away up the stairs and Zoey followed me. She asked me what happened and I told her nothing happened. She didn't believe me anymore than anyone else. I sat at my desk thinking about what it would mean if I was pregnant. I mean Dorian would be upset at first but he'd have to marry me. We'd be starting our family like we always talked about. Dorian is so good to me he'd have to be a good father, he has a good job. Besides I make more than enough to support all of us. I've always acted like I made a little chump change. I like when he pays for us. I like when he buys me things with his hard earned money. I don't think he'd let me pay even if he knew how much money I make and how much money I have in the bank. Oh! Dorian would have to give in to his love for me. He'd have to stop ignoring me; he'd have to give me all of him. I sat at my desk falling in love with the idea of being pregnant with Dorian's baby. I love this man so much and there will never be another person who means as much to me as he does. I looked at the clock, it was time to clock out and meet my sisters for our Wednesday night sister's dinner. Even though all three of us were at home with our parents it was still hit or miss when we saw each other. We all (all my siblings and Uncle Dito's kids) work for different divisions of my grandfather's businesses. My grandfather refused for us to work for anyone other than him or ourselves. A lot of our business functions cross over with Malcolm's businesses in different ways. Between Malcolm and my grandfather they've got this country locked up in one way or another.

I drove to our spot for every third Wednesday of the month. We have a spot for the first, second, third, and fourth Wednesday. On rare occasions there was a fifth and then we'd pick somewhere random. I couldn't stop rubbing my stomach, life was growing inside of me, and I couldn't be more excited. Erica was there first and she was already working on her first cocktail, I asked for lemonade. Erica was telling me about her day when Zoey hurried in. "Sorry I'm late! I was arguing with my last mistake, telling him why he's FIRED! He wants to try to act like he don't understand it." She touched the happy hour menu, "what's with her?" She asked Erica like I wasn't sitting here.

Erica frowned, "yea. What's with the lemonade?"

I might as well share with my sisters. "I'm a day late." Then I covered my mouth.

Both of them stared at me. "Ooh! I knew it was you!" Erica said shaking her finger at me.

Zoey squinted, "are you sure? We're on the same schedule and I'm not due for another week."

"I counted like five times."

"Yeah, but you never write it down." Zoey pulled out her phone. She pulled up her calendar, "see. The first day of my last period was on the 21st. It's not even the 13th."

"How do you know we started on the same day?"

"Remember you were cramping real bad and you came and got in my bed after you raided my Midol."

Irritation filled me, "maybe you're right. It could still not come."

"Are you trying to get pregnant? I thought you guys broke up?"

"Yeah, backup start from the beginning. How did all this happen? I didn't think Dorian would give in."

51

"How you know he didn't come at me?" Erica and Zoey looked at each other and started cracking up. "Shut up! You guys just think you know something." I explained the night to them. Zoey smiled while Erica looked horrified.

"That's not the way you'd want to start your marriage. Dorian sounds mad." Erica said.

"Yeah, but he'd get over it, and then we'd be a happy family as originally planned."

"Lanie! Lanie! Lanie! Baby girl nothing good comes from scheming like this. You want him to choose you. I thought a baby with Darnel would've been wonderful too. You see we're not together."

"That was your story. Darnel could come back anyways. You never know."

"Lanie, you're being too idealistic. Z is right; you're not listening to what he told you. Now you've crossed a line, you may have lost him forever, pregnant or not."

Next week as schedule my period came. I was devastated.

Episode 5

Tracy

"Mommy if you put this strap like this," Andre said putting the Velcro strap across the middle box. "Then this one won't move and it won't let the others move either." He smiled real big.

I stood there in amazement. "Baby you have no idea how long I've been trying to figure out how to secure these boxes. You are so smart Andre. When I grow up I wanna be just like you." Andre giggled at me.

"Alright, we ready?" Andrew said coming out to the car.

"I still think we should take separate cars. You take way longer at that barber shop then I do at the shop."

"Then you take the car and pick us up when you're done."

"Oh just like that? You and your son are full of solutions today." He looked at me confused then he shrugged at Andre like I was tripping. Maybe I was, but they were getting on my nerves with their simple solutions to the things that were frustrating me cause I couldn't see past them.

We went to the reception hall to put the cakes in the back of the refrigerators. Sasha's cake was arriving at the same time. Her cake was very pretty. Carina was there directing the deliveries. She had specific space saved for my cakes. I was going to assemble them just before the party. I snapped a couple of pictures of the reception hall in its original state; I knew it was going to be completely transformed by the time of the party. The space had high theater like ceilings, a stage, and red carpet. There was no dance floor. I imagined this space being used regularly for dinner theater of sorts. A lot of the fixtures had an old antique look, I'm sure the facility could stand an update. I was curious to see the final product cause I know Carina could make anything happen. I had a few minutes to kill before I headed over to Hilltop for my hair appointment, so I went inside with Andrew and Andre. The woman at the receptionist desk got up quickly and came to hug the boys, and then she hugged me as well. Andrew reminded me that this was his cousin Tiffany; I met her at the wedding and at Renee's house. Tiffany told me not to worry she knows there were too many people there for me to keep it all-straight. It was just after eight in the morning and the barbershop was already humming. Women and men were getting their hair braided, loc'ed and cut. An average height man came out the back office, and he lit up when he saw Andrew. "Drew! How you doing man!" He said coming in with a strong handshake and half body hug. Then he looked at me, "it's good to see you again Tracy, how are you?"

"I'm good," I said embarrassed cause again I had no idea who he was.

"Hey Andre! How's it going?"

Andre mimicked the way his father shook this man's hand. It was too cute. "Hey Jason!"

"I got you guys on the books this morning?"

"You know it!" Andrew said looking around. "You got a new guy I see."

"Yea, I put him on the books two weeks ago. You didn't see the report?"

"Malcolm's nose is all open, he's been slipping."

Jason laughed, "Well it's about time isn't it? I was here when you were just a little fella following your parents around."

"I guess," Andrew said running his hand across his head. I know he was still adjusting to the idea of his parents. He's been telling me little things here and there about them. It's still hard for him. And I appreciate that he's opening up about his past, he still gets uneasy some times. But I've noticed that he's trying to talk to me more about his family and I appreciate the effort.

I kissed Andrew and Andre then I ran to the shop to get my hair done. An hour and a half later my hair was bouncing and behaving. When I got back to the shop Andre was in Jason's chair as he was finishing him up. We grabbed lunch on the way home. I looked forward to having a good time tonight. I packed my dress and everything I needed then I made sure Andre had his things, and then we made our way back to the reception hall. The workers looked like ants with the constant stream of people coming in and out. I knew I was walking into greatness! I took my camera out and I started snapping pictures from the doorway. The walls were covered with white draping, all the antique and old and run down look were covered. There was a dance floor now. She had specific lighting as the backdrop. The color theme for tonight was purple, burgundy, and turquoise. I never would've thought of putting the colors together, but since I knew the purple was Amber's color I assume the others were Chantel and Sasha. On the stage there was a main table and the centerpiece for that table was the most elaborate and then a table on either side with equally nice centerpieces. The middle table was purple, and the other two had either turquoise, or black and silver with little burgundy accents. It was gorgeous. Carina had a photographer capturing everything; it wasn't until she took the camera off of her face that I realized it was Angela, Yussef's girlfriend. I very excitedly gave her a hug, and it wasn't until I was hugging her that the thought occurred to me that maybe she might not have had a warm and fuzzy feeling about me. I know Yussef's a good guy, I think he would've told her about me but I wasn't sure. I was just so happy to see her, but that also meant at some point I would see Yussef. And at that point I was going to have to be on guard to make sure everything I did in his direction was appropriate, cause the last thing I needed was for Andrew to be upset.

Just as I was about to call Joy to see where she was, she was walking in and declaring how much she loved what Carina did with the space. I introduced Angela and Joy and then Angela went back to taking her pictures. Joy and I walked around taking in even the smallest details. Once we were finished with our drool over the space, we went over to Amber's cake table to dress it. I took a picture of the empty table; I told Joy this is the beginning. Carina came out and she said she was happy we were starting cause the lighting guys had instructions about how to highlight my table that she needed to make sure were perfect. While Joy and I worked on the table Sasha and Chantel's cakes came out. I asked Carina what kind of cakes they were and where they got them. She told me, and then she asked what kind of cake Amber had. When I told her she smiled and said she knew I hit it out of the park and that she had no doubt about that. I gave Joy a panicked look and she told me to cut it out cause I knew my cake was gonna be delicious, I hoped she was right. When we had the cake setup I looked at my cake compared to the other two and I thought my cake looked pretty good. All three cakes looked professionally made to me. Once the lighting was adjusted on my cake the gold tree seemed like it sparkled, and the sparkles made it seem like it was dancing. I stood back and exhaled a satisfied sigh of relief. Now for the public opinion, the part that made me nervous and curious all at the same time. Andrew came and told me it was time to get dressed, Rosalind and Tanisha were on their way. Rosalind was doing my makeup, I thanked Joy for coming then I went with Andrew.

Sasha

"Good morning, I'm Sasha Wallace I'm here to pick up my dress and shoes." I said to the girl sitting at the receptionist desk.

"Good morning Ms. Wallace, please have a seat your consultant will be with you in just a minute." The girl at the desk said. When I sat down she smiled, "so I wanna know." She almost whispered as if she was breaking character. "Who is this guy that you hooked Tia up with and do you have anymore?"

I had a stuck look as I looked at her. This girl was only familiar to me from my previous visit. "Tia?"

She smiled, "yes Tracy's sister Tia. Tara and I talk on a regular basis and she told me how Tia met someone through you. I'm Dafina, Cassondra's youngest daughter."

"Oh!" I chuckled, "I was stuck for a minute. He's a friend of my fiancé's. Brody's a good guy. So things are going well?" Mrs. Parsons and I leaned in to hear.

"It's still new, but so far so good." She smiled.

My consultant Nihjia walked down the stairs, she greeted us with hugs and then she took Mrs. Parsons, Ava, and I down to the alterations area. Nihjia said that they were so excited about the party tonight. I guess I didn't think about the fact that they would be there, but Amber, my momma, Rosalind, and Cassondra go all the way back to middle school. When I put on my turquoise dress it hugged my body even better than I remembered that they said it would after alterations. I put on my shoes and jewelry then I walked out. Mrs. Parsons smiled really big and she told me she loved my figure. I thanked her and then I gathered my hair and asked Ava what she was going to do with it. Ava tilted her head from side to side. She suggested a half up and half down style. That way I could keep my bridal softness, and have the complexity of an up do. I told her my hair was her canvas to create on. Mrs. Parsons was eyeing a cola colored dress over to the side, but I knew she'd never say anything. She was too sweet and modest. So I asked her what she was wearing tonight. She told me about the dress she brought, but there was no excitement in her tone about it. I asked her if she would do me a huge favor and try on the dress. She looked surprised and embarrassed. I pleaded with her like only I can. Nihjia put her in a dressing room, and when she came out she had the biggest smile. The dress didn't quite fit, so I asked Nihjia if they had that dress in a size smaller on the for sale rack. Nihjia ran up the stairs. Mrs. Parsons looked at the price tag and she said she didn't want to try on anymore. I put my garment bag on the rack and I gently pleaded with her to let me do this for her. She still said it was too much money on one dress for one night. I leaned in and whispered that we got a discount, I lied. Well kind of, cause Cassondra wanted to give me a discount and I wouldn't hear of it. Then I told her to imagine Mr. Parsons' eyes when he saw her in that dress tonight. She very shyly giggled at the thought of it. Then Ava chimed in on the ideas she had for her hair. Mrs. Parsons agreed in blissful defeat to allow us to make her over. Nihjia came down with three dress options in Mrs. Parsons' size. She liked the first dress and then we found shoes, a purse, earrings, a necklace, and a pretty barrette. I told Mrs. Parsons' to look away as the total kept building at the register. I gave Nihjia my credit card and I didn't look back. I told the girls we'd see them tonight, and then we took Mrs. Parsons' dress back to our hotel and asked them to press it for us. Normally the store would do it, but since we were running short on time it made sense to have it all done in one spot and to get out of the city while the getting was good. As we were having breakfast Richard called me, and my suspicions were correct, he told my Dan-Dan about the baby as she was meeting Erica. I begged him not to tell my momma tonight, I didn't want any drama. He agreed, and then he told me he'd see me tonight. When we finished eating we went straight up to Ava's room. The men were out getting haircuts at Drew's. I told Ava and Mrs. Parson's that it would be awhile before we saw them cause the men seem to get sucked into Drew's and then eventually spit out. I loved Mrs. Parsons' hair when Ava was done. It was a simple French roll up-do but her facial features seem to pop out, and I could see a lot of her in El's face. She cried happy tears and thanked us as she looked in the mirror. Mrs. Parsons was so thankful, and while Ava and I worked on her she told us stuff about El and Zoila his first wife. She said Zoila had sweet moments, in the end she was horrible, and her heart broke for her son. She said she knew that the personality Zoila morphed into or finally showed her true person was not the woman that El signed up for. I told her I had my diva moments, and Mrs. Parsons assured me that we were not talking about the same things. She said El was so much happier with me and content with life. Zoila had him bending over backwards for nonsense and she put unnecessary strain on their relationship when the things they went through were bad enough. She said she was so relieved when they broke up, but then she worried about how El was going to handle everything. She asked me how he approached me. I told her how I had just suffered a devastating loss of my own right after meeting El. I told her how we started off as friends. I was used to people demanding and expecting me to be this 24/7 vixen, but El never responded to me when I would put that costume on. He always made me relax and encouraged me to. I told her that I loved how I could be myself with him for better and for worse and he worked with me. Sometimes we clashed and everybody watch out when we do, BUT he was my best friend and we always ended up working things out no matter what. I told her I was so happy that my mother in-law was so sweet and loving, cause I rarely get along with other females for one reason or another. She said it was because I was confident in my appearance and most females couldn't handle that especially when they were insecure in their own.

Mrs. Parsons and I went to our rooms to get ready and wait for the men. El walked in our room as I was putting lotion on. He stood there staring at me for a minute not saying anything. I smiled and asked him what was going on. "You are so beautiful! I'm so honored that you said yes."

Butterflies struck my stomach. "Un un! El! Stop it! If you keep talking to me like that we may never leave this room. And I've waited a long time for this party." He smiled at me and then he grabbed his suit. My eyes danced all over his body, "but!" He gave me a knowing smile. "When we get back, it's on!"

"If we even make it to the room." He chimed in.

"Uh we kind of have to. I'm sure your parents nor Ava and Nathan wanna see me working you over."

We started laughing as we gave our spins on how the night would end if we did something like that. I waited until we were walking out the door to put my dress on. El smiled big as he gave me his approval of my overall look. Our limo was downstairs; I took a deep breath, it was time to celebrate with my family.

Yussef

"Yesmina, give me a hug and kiss goodbye. Don't just walk out of here like that." Melissa demanded. Yezzy turned around and hugged her, and then she excitedly grabbed my hand then she turned towards the car. Melissa looked over to the car where Angela was waiting inside and Yesmina was running to hug her. "Yussef, seriously. I need a moment alone with you." She said like she was bubbling over inside.

"No Melissa, last time I was alone with you, you *ambushed* me. You're married and I have a girlfriend. What was the agreement? You give me space in my relationship. Your thinly veiled jealousy isn't cool. I don't like it, do a better job of keeping it together."

Melissa looked angry, "what am I supposed to do? I hate seeing you with anyone who isn't me. And knowing you put me in the same category as that tramp Sylvia is insulting."

"Melissa I'm not going to do this with you. Have a good weekend, I'll bring Yezzy home tomorrow night." Angela was looking.

Yezzy talked our ears off as we drove to the other side of San Leandro to pick up Syd. Yezzy said at school she and Syd talked about their dresses and how excited they were to go out looking like twins. I asked her if they considered themselves twins and Yezzy said yes as if that was a ridiculous question.

Yezzy was born on the 10th and Syd was born the next day on the 11th. Even though I was in a relationship with Sylvia the night they were both conceived was the night that Sylvia and I broke up. Sylvia and I hadn't touched each other in a while then we had sex that evening, and I ran to Melissa's when we broke up. The only reason I got a DNA test for Yesmina was to have it on paper that she was mine. I knew Melissa although engaged was not sleeping with her fiancé. I remembered giving her everything in me that night; I did make love to her. But I was making love earlier that day to Sylvia, I loved her so much. Either way, both of my girls were conceived in love, at least on my part.

Yezzy and I walked inside the courtyard of Sylvia's building. Her place was really small; she had a studio apartment that she and Syd shared. They had the bare essentials, nothing fancy. How could I see that my daughter was living like this and not feel compelled to do something about it. Sylvia may have been a gold digging diva when we were together, but today she was living on the bare minimum. Sylvia opened the door and she and Syd had huge smiles. She invited us in. Sylvia and Sydney shared a futon, when I say they barely had, they barely had. Yezzy and Syd exchanged excited hugs. Sylvia asked where Angela was, and I told her she was in the car. She said she would walk us out. I looked around their too small for one-person apartment and I exhaled. I opened the door to walk out and a guy was at the door. It was just after eight and he reeked of alcohol. "Who are you?" The guy said.

"Yussef," I said immediately not liking him. I looked at Syd and fear was on her face. "Who are you?"

"Brian, I own the building," he said swaying.

"What do you want Brian? I told you not to come to my apartment, I'm gonna call the police again!" Sylvia yelled.

"This is your landlord?"

"Yes," she said sadly.

"Yea, but I told you, you don't have to pay rent if you would just put out."

I saw red, if this is how he talks to Sylvia fine. But not in front of my daughter. And I wasn't liking Syd's reaction to this guy. "You need to leave!"

He put his hands up, "are you her man or something? No disrespect!"

"All you need to know is that they're moving! When you sober up the paperwork will be served. Sylvia pack up your stuff. Matter of fact just a minute." I told the girls to come with me. I closed the door behind me. I put the girls in the car with Angela and I told her I would be right back. I called Juan on my cell. I gave him Sylvia's address and I told him I needed someone on the apartment. I took a picture of Brian with my phone then I sent it to him. Brian started wandering around the courtyard; at least he was bugging everybody. I told Sylvia she needed to move today. Her eyes got sad and she said she needed to save the child support money for a couple months to afford it. I told her she had until two-thirty no later than three to find a place that she could get the keys to today. I told her to tell me how much the move-in would be and I would pay it. Sylvia was shocked and then she started crying. I told her to stop wasting time crying and get going. I told her I would help her move the few things she had tomorrow. I told her to bring her child support paperwork to show as income. She grabbed her jacket and keys and walked out with me. I could tell Angela wanted to know what was going on; when we got to the restaurant I whispered to Angela everything that happened. I could tell she didn't like it, but she knew that it had to happen. You didn't get a warm and fuzzy feeling looking at the building from outside. After breakfast Angela packed up her dress for tonight, and her camera, then the girls and I dropped her off at the reception hall. Carina hired Angela as our photographer for the night, so she needed to get there early and photograph everything from development through the evening. Sylvia called as we were pulling away. She told me where she was and the girls and I went over. I exhaled and relaxed a little driving up to the nice looking apartment community. An added plus is that it wasn't far from Melissa so the girls would still be in school together. I wanted to go get the cashier's check but Sylvia asked me to come in. The person in the leasing office was saying since Sylvia didn't have any credit, someone else needed to sign on her lease. I knew Angela would not go for that. I took a step back, there had to be another way. I called Malcolm, he said he had already spoken to Juan and he knew I was going to be calling. He said Amber had a unit available in her building. He told me to come get the keys from him at Amber's house, I asked him if he could meet me there. He sighed and then he agreed.

Sylvia was going to follow me but her car wouldn't start. I knew the sound of that cough, her car just died on her. Sylvia screamed in frustration, Syd started to cry seeing her mother so upset. Yezzy comforted Syd and she told her it was going to be ok. I walked close, and I told myself don't hug her. I told Sylvia it was going to be ok. I told her all this was just payback for hurting me like she did, then I smiled. She cried harder. I put my arm around her shoulder and I told her to suck it up. What's done is done, I told her it could only get better from here. She got in my car and we drove a few blocks over to Amber's apartment building. It was nice and neat, nothing over the top or too fancy. It gave Sylvia everything she needed. Malcolm pulled up and handed me keys. "Hi Uncle Malcolm!" Yezzy said very excited as she explained to Syd that he was their uncle. Malcolm looked at the girls, said hello, and then he looked at me and said wow! I knew he meant they were definitely my girls, I shook my head. Then he looked at Sylvia, he told her that I would give her the lease agreement to sign. Sylvia said a very nervous ok, and then Malcolm drove away. I pointed out her garage, and then we went inside. Sylvia cried AGAIN and Syd was in love. She couldn't believe she was getting her own room. This place was a lot smaller and not as fancy as mine, but to her she should feel like this place was gigantic. I gave Sylvia the keys to my nice car, and I told her I would have her car towed to the junkyard. Again Syd got really happy and she said thank you. Yezzy asked me if I was going to give her mom a car too. I told her that her mom didn't need a car and if she did Jackson could buy her any kind of car she wanted. I told her that Sylvia doesn't have anyone to help her and Syd so I needed to pitch in and help them. Yezzy was quiet then she looked at her sister and told her she was happy she was going to get her own room, and a car. Just like that they were over it. I had a feeling that it wasn't going to be that easy to explain this to Angela, and Melissa was going to have a cow. I thought about telling Yezzy not to say anything but I didn't want to tell her to keep secrets from her mother. When we got back to my place I told them to go and help each other get ready. I was feeling exhausted and we hadn't even gotten to the party yet. When my girls walked out proudly in the same dress they looked like little angels. I could feel my heart beating with pride and love for them. I picked up one in each arm and then I took them to the couch. They were giggling so loud. Both of them sat on my lap looking at me with my grandmother's eyes. I told them I loved them more than they could ever understand, and I told them that I was so proud to be their daddy. I told them no matter what anyone says or does they are sisters and I am their father, then I told them I had the paperwork to prove it too. I told them to never let ANYONE come between them as sisters, cause sometimes your siblings may be all you have. I told them how I was just like them and I didn't know I had a sister until my father died. I told them how happy it made me not to feel alone. I told them now that they had each other they would never be alone either. The girls giggled with the same laugh just like Latia's and then they smothered me with kisses. I placed this moment on my heart, as long as I have my girls I can't exactly worry about someone else leaving me. I told the girls to get ready to go cause we had a party to go to.

Malachi

"I love you so much!" Denise said kissing my neck
"And still, I love you more!" I kissed her cheek.
"It's been too long since we've done that. I feel so good!" She said stretching and yawning. I didn't say anything to that, what could I say? "So about the baby," I braced myself. "Would it matter to you if we only had girls?"
"As long as the baby is healthy I don't care." Then I swallowed, "do you think right now is the right time?" I needed to choose my words; I didn't want to hurt her. But I also didn't want things to get too complicated to see our way out.
"What do you mean, right time? Why wouldn't now be the right time?"
"Last night was the first time in how long that we've shared each other. Shouldn't we address that before we throw a baby in the mix?"
"Oh Mali please don't do this. I stopped taking my birth control." Her body tensed up and she pulled away from me.
"Why are you pulling away from me? I'm just trying to talk to you. Come back."
Of course she wouldn't, "why would you wait until we make love to bring this up? You could've gone to the store and got some condoms."
I looked at her, "condoms? Really? Who uses condoms with their wife?"
"A Husband who's on the fence about pregnancy!" She threw herself to her feet.
"Denise! Don't do this I'm just trying to talk to you. We have bigger issues than a baby right now."
"What issues?" She walked into the bathroom and left the door open while she peed.
"We're happy Malachi, or at least I thought we were. I figured a baby would only enhance that" She washed her hands then she started the water for a shower. "Ok so maybe we're not having sex every other day like we did when we were kids. But that was a long time ago."
"Denise tell me before last night when the last time was." I sat there waiting for her to tell me. Cause I knew, and it was more or less the fact that I had a dream about my momma and I needed comfort. One of the worse feelings is when you're having sex and the other person involved would rather be anywhere but with you at that moment. Last night was amazing she was into it. She was responding and she kept wanting more. The way we used to be.
She stood there thinking for a minute, she got frustrated when she couldn't remember.
"So what? I'm unworthy of your seed because I wasn't paying attention?"
"Denise please come sit down and talk to me." I patted the bed.
"No! I'm so tired of you!"
Fire turned in my stomach. "Denise!" I heard my voice bounce off the walls. I walked into the bathroom where she was standing. I turned off the shower water. "Go sit your happy go lucky tail down and talk to me like you got some sense!" Denise did as she was told; I took a minute to calm myself. Then I walked out of the bathroom. "Woman what is wrong with you? I ask a simple question and you took that and ran with it. If you don't stop this nonsense and talk to me!"
Denise started crying and then she apologized. She said she feels so broken right now. She said she knows she's been letting me down, but she feels a baby would fix that. I told

her I don't need a baby and all I need is her. She cried harder, and then she said I was too good to her and she didn't deserve me. Overcome with guilt I felt the need to burst her bubble but Jada was at the door knocking. She was crying about a mosquito bite that was driving her crazy. I guess to a little girl that was a life drama worthy of interrupting her parent's conversation for. Denise instantly went into loving mother mode, giving away the love I was supposed to be getting. I packed my suit, Denise and the girl's dresses in my garment bag. I made sure we had everything we needed for tonight and then I put myself in the shower. I let the water beat me in the face. I was frustrated and I kept telling myself this is just a phase we're going through. My wife loves me and she's gonna come back to me.

When we got in the car I asked the girls who wanted huervos rancheros, and the girls cheered saying they did. I texted my brother Timothy and told him we were on our way. We were meeting at Gonzalez's for breakfast, and then we were going to hang out with them until the party later. Denise kept whispering that she was sorry, I accepted her apology but it didn't mean anything to me. It wasn't changing anything. I found myself wrestling with a bad mood. When we got to the restaurant Timothy and Grace were cuddling into each other and immediately I was jealous. Then Ethan and Jenise walked in right behind us on the same level. I told myself to get it together. Out of the corner of my eye a woman looked at me like she recognized me. She looked a lot older than I'm sure she was, but her face did not ring a bell so I said hello to my big brother, sister-in-law, and cousins and then we took our seats. The woman kept looking at me so I stared at her and took her in, she became a little familiar but I couldn't place her. Timothy saw me trying to figure her out and he shrugged at me, I shrugged back. When she stood up with the other woman at her table **her hair**! Her hair took me back to my youth. Back when I was young and running the streets, she was the woman I used to smash. Tammy! I was a minor and she was over twenty-one when we started hooking up. When I went away to college we drifted apart, when I came back Amber told me she was strung out. I only saw her one time after that and it was true she was promising me anything I wanted for some money. "Tammy?"

She smiled an embarrassed smile showing a few missing teeth on either side of her mouth. "How are you doing Malachi? Is this your family?" She motioned to the table. "Yes, this is my wife Denise and our girls. That's my brother Timothy and my sister in-law Grace. My cousin Ethan and his wife Jenise. How are you?" I said rising to hug her. "I'm seven years clean. This is my cousin Monica." Monica and I waved hello, "I just wanted to say hello. You look really good Malachi. I'm happy life has treated you well. How's your sisters, and your nephew?" She snapped her fingers trying to remember his name.

"Andrew."

"Yes! That's his name, how are they?"

"Jade is married and has three kids, she's doing really well. Andrew got married a couple months ago, and he has a son. Amber and Malcolm are finally engaged and we're going to their engagement party tonight."

She bucked her eyes, "just now? I guess it's better late than never. Malcolm is ok?" Her eyes got really sad, she thought about what happened to Troy, I could see it in her eyes. "He'll never be the same, but he's surviving."

Tears came to Tammy's eyes, "well I didn't want to keep you. I wanted to say hello." Then she looked at Denise, "you've got yourself a *GOOD* man right here! Never take that for granted." When she put emphasis on the "*GOOD*" Jenise and Grace sat up. If Grace didn't flash Jenise a momma look I don't know what crazy looks like.

"Who is she?" Grace interrupted loudly.

I waved to Tammy to leave; she was about to be in trouble. I talked slowly as Tammy and her cousin walked out. "We kind of dated when I was a kid."

"No she didn't!" Grace said standing up and looking around through the glass to see which way they went.

"Dated, dated? She has to be older than Timothy." Denise asked.

"It wasn't exactly legal, but it was a long time ago." I smiled.

Denise's mouth fell open, Grace looked at Timothy. He put his hands up, "I was across the Bay with you. I never met her."

"I wish one of your ex's would walk in here telling me I got a **GOOD** man!" Grace blew air, "I bet you she would be picking it up right now!"

"Good Lord Timothy! You married momma!" I laughed.

Grace smiled, "thank you for the compliment. But I'm not kidding!"

"I know that's the part I love about you." Timothy said giving Grace another kiss.

"Well Timothy ain't Dad! I'm closer to dad than he will ever be." I said changing the subject cause their mutual affection for each other hurt me.

"You got that right, your name should be Timothy instead of mine."

"I don't remind you of your mother?" Denise asked, I guess she was feeling the jealousy too.

"No," I said flatly.

Timothy changed the subject immediately.

Lanie

I sat in my car trying to decide whether I should run Dorian over or not when he came out of his apartment. HOW DARE HIM! He changed his number and then he up and moved all the way from Berkeley to El Sobrante. As if I wouldn't find him. I mean if he was trying to hurt me, I'm hurt. I didn't mean to ruin his life. I wasn't trying to hurt him. I just…. I just… HE WAS HURTING ME! All his talk about breaking up scared me. Now he acts like that breakup was real, like he could really live without me. I want to run him over for thinking that he could even try this mess. Like there would ever be anywhere he could run from me. I sat there waiting and waiting for him to come out. I looked at the clock, I didn't have time for him to keep lingering inside, I had to go to my Grammy's to get my hair done for tonight. UGH! Dorian plays too much! Then a little red two door Honda civic pulled up like it was summoned. The girl who got out had drive-thru breakfast in her hands, and she looked too happy for my liking. I watched her walk disobeying every dare I forbid her to take as she got closer to his front door. Dorian opened the door with **NO SHIRT** on, hugged her, and then he invited her in. I hit the steering wheel as I sat there counting backwards from a thousand. WHO WAS THAT? That sure in the heck wasn't April! Who is she? Who is she? Who is she? I got out the car and walked around the back to the hillside. Stupid Dorian had all his blinds open. Probably cause he didn't think anyone would be crazy enough to scale this hill just to look inside his apartment, and then enters *Lanie*. They were sitting at his table and he now had a t-shirt on. He was smiling at her while she talked. I moved my binoculars around looking inside his nice apartment. Everything was set up the same as it was in the last apartment. I hated it; each space deserves its own look. I've told him this time and time again! They talked for a little while then they stood. They hugged then he walked her out to her car. Oh so he's not afraid of being seen anymore? I CAN'T STAND HIM! I waited until he went back upstairs then I quickly walked to my car. I sped up until I caught up to little miss civic. I followed her to Hercules. She parked at the park on Refugio Valley and then she took her mat and weights out of her car to join the group of people assembling for a workout boot camp. I'm sure the drive thru breakfast went against everything she was about to do here. I got of out my car walked a few circles around her car, then I snapped pictures. I got her license plate, her VIN, and then I kicked one of the tail lights out. I couldn't help it, I was mad. I uploaded the pictures and I put the request for information in. I looked at the time. I had to get going.

When I got to Grammy's, Zoey and Grammy asked me what I did. Zoey said I had rage all over my face. So I told them about my morning. "Why are you stalking Dorian? Did you two breakup again?"

"Grammy this time is different. He changed his number and moved without sending me a forwarding address. As if he could ever do something like that to me and get away with it."

"Lanie, you can't make that boy be with you."

I started laughing, "yes I can."

"Mom's right something is wrong with you," Zoey said.

"Nothing is wrong with me. If something is wrong with me then there's something wrong with the twins too. Just because they're boys it's different?"

"Yes! Now get over it. You can't go trying to overpower a man and then think he's supposed to choose you. Only a weakling does that and who wants a weakling? You've got to let a man be a man, let him feel like he's beating his chest a little. Play nice Lanie."

"Oh you mean act all sugary sweet and say *whatever kind of food you like...* Stuff like that?" Grammy looked at me in the mirror while Zoey smiled at me. "I'm not that kind of woman! I'm strong and I demand to be appreciated for my strength. Zoey's the same way. How come you never tell her to tone it down?"

"Yes I do, wasn't I just telling you to get it together?" She looked down at Zoey through the mirror.

"Yes ma'am! She was, it's true Lanie. We are too much for these sorry excuses for men. The difference between you and me is I do turn off the strong every now and then. You're on 24/7."

"And every time you turn off the strong you come crying to me because you're mad for letting another simpleton get over. Dorian is going to come back begging me. You know what it doesn't even matter. Tonight I'm going to be looking amazing in my oh so sexy dress. Yussef is going to be there looking delicious!" I shook my head at the thought.

"Even if tonight isn't the night I make him mine, it's going to look like it all over social media. I'm going to post my pictures and then all my friends are going to post them so no matter what Dorian's going to see the HOTT pictures of me looking like a million bucks on the arm of someone who's better than HIM!"

"Did you miss that he has a girlfriend?"

"What in the world is she supposed to mean to me? That girl is barely cute, Yussef needs to quit playing. That's not his future wife!"

Chantel

"Baby I don't need all these fancy things. Today is your day." Grandma Rosa said patting my hands.

"I can't believe you never had crepes, they happen to be a specialty of mine. Brandy these preserves your aunt makes are the perfect compliment!"

"GURL! Who you telling?" Brandy said sharing her plate with her son who was tearing everything up like the rest of us.

Marion Berry Preserves with crepes, eggs and bacon. Breakfast of champions and the baby was enjoying breakfast thank goodness. "Grandma I need your help."

Grandma Rosa stopped eating and gave me her undivided attention. "What's up baby?"

"Sherrell and I were talking," Sherrell's eyes got big as she swallowed and listened. "I really want Cyrus to give me away at my wedding but I don't know how to break the news to my daddy. Sherrell said I should barter something he really wants in hopes that he will choose that over walking me down. But I don't know what."

"Oh dear honey." Grandma wringed her hands together for a bit. "Is that what you really want?"

"You know how much I love my brother, and it would mean so much more to me if he did it. Cyrus has always had my back. I know it's not his fault that he wasn't around." Then I felt a little angry. "Well not his fault completely, but I want Cyrus to do it."

"Is he already performing?" She asked.

"Now you know there's going to be a crowd, he's already working on his set."

The idea came to her, "I got it." Then she looked at me, "it's gonna cost you." I didn't know what she meant but we were all sitting on the edge of our seats waiting for her to say. "I KNOW you had no intentions of inviting your aunties, right?" I froze, "tell him to choose which one he wants. His sisters or walking you down. Whichever one he chooses you've gotta live with."

"No! No! Isn't there something else? ANYTHING ELSE?"

Brandy started cracking up laughing, "are they still that bad?"

Everybody looked at her, "Yes!"

I felt stressed thinking about that. Either way I just screwed myself. But she was right that was my only fifty-fifty chance to get out of this. I sat there pouting when Derrick, Paul, Cyrus, Latia, and Lewis walked in. We said our hellos and then I made Derrick's plate even though he protested telling me he could do it.

Around three my father, stepmother, brothers and sister arrived. Derrick told me that Sonya was running late and she didn't have Carina's number. I asked Derrick if she still needed to come if she couldn't even get there on time to help out. I know she wanted to party, she didn't want to help out if she could avoid it. Derrick told me to ask Carina. When I called her she said she could still use the help. So I gave her Sonya's number and I asked her to call her directly and let her know. I did not want to be bothered with all those minor details. My father and his family went to Cyrus' house to get ready. Brandy and I giggled over Latia's ring. I was so happy she finally said yes. I asked her what made her change her mind, cause she had been telling him no for years. She said she decided not to let her father's bad choices and her past stop her from moving forward. Then she said besides her brother Yussef has two kids and she started to get that itch for a family of her own. I asked her how he was doing with all of that and she said so far so good. Latia asked if I had my bridal party pinned down yet. I told her Derrick wants his brothers, which includes his technical uncles, cousins, and Yussef. I want my brothers, so it was huge already. Ask me if I care, cause I told him that Dude HAD to be in our wedding as well. And if Dude was gonna be in it then Hubby had to be in it. I told her my wedding party was huge. They got all sentimental when I told them that Derrick was going to ask Malcolm to be his best man. I guess that was pretty sweet, but he has his own wedding to plan for. We bumped around the house getting ready for the night. When I came out the bathroom in my burgundy dress Derrick said you couldn't even see my stomach in my dress. That's what I liked; I didn't want to feel pregnant tonight. I wanted to enjoy the party and have a good time with my man.

As we were walking out the door my phone rang it was Pearla. "Is Sonya really gonna be there tonight?" No hello, how are you or anything like that, so I knew that meant she was upset.

"Yes, she should be there helping Carina right now."

Pearla cursed in the background, Derrick heard her yelling. "Ok! Ok! I'm just letting you know right now, if her mouth is going a thousand miles a minute I'm on her!"

"Are you guys funking?"

"No, but her mouth preludes her. I just wanted to give you guys a head's up." Then as if she wasn't just fussing, her voice got all happy and cheery. "Ok love you guys can't wait to see you!" I laughed and said ditto.

Amber

"What time is it?" I looked at the clock

"Time for round four," Malcolm said matter of factly.

Even though the thought of it made me tingle I was supposed to be meeting Sophia and Jade at Sophia's to help out for tonight. "As appealing as that sounds, I can't stay in this bed with you Malcolm."

"And why not? Did I put a ring on your finger?"

I sighed, "yes Malcolm."

"Isn't that ring what you've been asking for all this time?"

"Yes Malcolm."

"So if I wake up feeling some kind of way this morning, it's my right to demand that my wife stays in bed with me until we have to leave it."

Hearing him refer to me as his wife made me go right back into the orgasm that knocked me out. "You ok?" I checked my tingles at the door.

He exhaled, "who's gonna be my best man?" His eyes pierced me. He exhaled hard, "I swear if it wasn't for you I wouldn't bother. I hate feeling like this!"

I put my arms around him, "Malcolm I love you so much! Thank you for loving me enough to go through this. Thank you for understanding that I need this."

"I always knew it would be me and Troy." His body tensed, then he exhaled. "Then I thought it would be Tim," and his body tensed again. He exhaled, how do I choose one of my boys without offending the other? Why we got so many kids Amber?" He smiled. "I think Derrick and Darryl would understand if I had the closest thing to Troy stand next to me, but Andrew won't get it. So it's down to Malachi, Ethan, or Juan. Because my first choice isn't here." His body tensed again.

I kissed him, "what about Fuzzy?"

He sucked his teeth, "get real! I'd have Bernadette before I had him. He'd be up there crying like a baby." We laughed.

"I'm on the fence about asking Rosalind."

"Were you going to have Cassondra?"

"I was thinking about it."

"Then you gotta have Rosalind, she's your oldest friend." He said matter of factly.

"Unless we have one person each and call it a day."

"That won't work."

"Why won't it?"

He laughed, "who you gonna pick Jade or Sophia?" I made a wounded sound, "exactly and then we end up right back here." Then he turned to me, "which is why I'd rather stay in the bed making love to the woman who had me on severe lockdown for too long!"

"Who's fault is that?"

"Yours!" We said at the same time, and then we laughed.

"Malcolm you're a beast you know exactly why you were on lockdown."

He growled at me and then he kissed me. Even his kiss sent me spinning. While we were at it I could hear my phone going off, probably Sophia checking to see where I was. Then we heard Malcolm's phone. Then she called the house phone, and her voicemail played over the speakerphone, "Uh! Amber! and Malcolm! If you guys could come up for air, we're trying to get your party together. I know the big dick is good, but dang! Malcolm ain't going nowhere. You gonna end up chaffing and walking funny all night." Malcolm and I laughed for a second and then we went back to pleasuring each other. When I looked at the clock it was now ten-thirty and we were supposed to meet at Sophia's at seven. I felt like I had been drugged, "Hello?" I said with a mouth completely dry.

"I HATE YOU! I HATE YOU! Don't you think I want to be in bed under my man right now? Travis was showing me something early this morning and I wanted more, but NO!

I'm an adult and I left my warm bed with my man looking too good in it to come out here for you! Now I'm pent up and you're probably still at it while I'm fussing." I laughed.
"AND THEN YOU LAUGH AT ME! You better be happy I love you! Get your butt out of the bed, tell Malcolm you'll be right back and get over here!"
"Ok! Ok!" I said feeling like a kid. Malcolm was in the bathroom, but I didn't feel him get up. Shows how knocked out I was.
Malcolm came out and sat on the bed, "do you have any vacancies in your building?"
"You gotta be more specific which one?"
"Nana's."
"My old unit, what's up?"
"Juan called, Yussef's baby momma needs a place to move to immediately. He hasn't called me yet, but I know he's going to."
"The spare keys are in the safe." I got up. "Just give me a copy of the paperwork."
When I got to Sophia's Sophia gave me a hard time, Jade kept laughing. She said there was nothing left to say cause Sophia said it all. They didn't even need me there, Sophia was just mad cause I was getting some and she had to work. When I got home Malcolm was gone, and then Darryl pulled up a few minutes later. He was extremely excited about tonight. Then he told me he was bringing a date. I leaned in and asked what this meant, Darryl never brings girls around except for that one girl YEARS ago at his graduation. Darryl blushed and told me not to get too excited cause it wasn't real yet, but he figured he should bring a girl around soon before everyone started asking questions. I told him like any one would care. Then Malcolm walked in the door. Darryl looked at Malcolm like he was crazy, "oh it's like that? You guys go from zero to sixty in no time flat!" Malcolm asked him what he was talking about. And he mentioned Malcolm's key. Malcolm didn't look amused, he told him I have keys to his everything as well. Darryl nodded and said he liked the sound of that.
I went upstairs to get ready. I could hear them downstairs carrying on. When Malcolm walked in the room he closed the door and stood there with his eyes analyzing me in my dress. I smiled at him, "you like?"
"I LOVE!" Darryl called up and said he'd see us there and he was leaving. Malcolm kept stopping what he was doing to look at me. Then he chuckled, "you have no idea how many fights me and Troy used to get into cause he would tell me I was sprung and I would try to act like it wasn't so. I never had to ask him, he was always on point when it came to you. I don't even truly buy that he didn't know about Derrick."
"I don't know, I was pretty good about covering myself."
"Troy was watching you like a hawk. How could he have missed such an important detail? I knew he knew, or had a feeling, but he knew me better than I knew myself." He exhaled, "after all this time I still can't believe he's gone."
"Me neither," I could feel the sadness wash over me. "Seems like I lost him and then everybody else with him." I sat on the bed feeling depressed. "Nana wouldn't let me take your crap. She empowered me to get my body back or I'd probably still be fat and depressed. If she wouldn't have given me that apartment exactly when she did, Andrew and I would be dead. If she wouldn't have bought me this house…." I saw David's face clearly and it pained me.
Malcolm watched me for a minute, "and this is when we should stop talking cause I'm getting angry."
That snapped me out of my trance, "what? Why?"
Malcolm's eyes shot bullets at me through the mirror he was facing. "Honestly if you're feeling anything other than relief that he's gone. I don't want to hear about it." I didn't say anything I just blank stared at him. What was I supposed to say to that?

Kendra

As I pulled up to the shop I saw Andrew's wife walk out the door. She looked really happy. I imagined her satisfaction with each step knowing that her man loved her enough to put it on paper.

When I tried my dress on last night I couldn't stop imagining Darryl's reaction to me in my dress. When my hair and makeup were done, I sat there taking myself in. Most days I consider myself pretty cute. But today I'm breathtaking, and I'm not saying that because it's me. I was appreciating my appearance like I do from time to time. I'm not as bad as Darryl who knows for a fact that he's sexy and he won't let you try to minimize him to anything less.

As I got in the car Anton called, "what do you want for dinner tonight?"

"Anton I told you, my family is going to an engagement party tonight."

"A wedding, now an engagement party? All without me."

"What are you saying?"

"What I just said. Why do you keep going to these events without me?"

"Only my family was invited."

"I'm your family, who excludes the fiancé to something like that?"

I exhaled, "are you trying to pick a fight?"

"If a fight is what it takes for you to pay me some attention. I need you Kendra."

"You could've fooled me. I've been at your house every night, where have you been?"

"You know where I've been. Why can't we stay at your house for a while?"

"Anton I will not be your accomplice in your efforts to punk out and run from your ex."

"Punk out?"

"You're the one running from a girl." I sarcastically laughed at him.

Anton's breathing doubled then he hung up in my face. When he called me back we got in to the biggest argument. In the end I told him I didn't care what he did, and I had to go. When he kept talking I hung up in his face. I paced a little while until my body cooled down. Then I carefully put on my dress. I couldn't reach my zipper anymore when it got to the middle of my back. Like clockwork Darryl rang my doorbell thirty minutes early. I opened the door then I backed away so he could come in. "KB! KB! K... B! I don't know if my heart can handle you turning around." He crossed his arms looked me up and down shaking his head in agreement. He put his hand over his mouth. "Ok, ok! I think I can handle it. Spin around for me." When I turned around he gasped in appreciation. "I'm walking behind you ALL NIGHT!" He smiled, "let me help you with your zipper." He stepped into my personal space. "KB, when we dance, you gonna back that thang up on me? You know for old times' sake."

"No!" I laughed, "I'm going by blackmail remember?"

"You gonna let a little blackmail get in the way of our fun tonight?"

"Yes!" I picked up my purse and Darryl watched me walk with a smile.

Episode 6

Yussef

The girls and I were amongst the first to arrive. When we walked in the door Tracy was walking past. She looked really pretty in her dress, and she smiled really big when she saw us. She said hello to the girls and they bashfully said hello back. I saw her eyes look me over; she said she liked my hair. I ran my hand over my head I told her I'm still getting used to it. She said it looked good then she exhaled and looked around. I told her I would see her later.

When I walked further into the auditorium Angela was taking pictures of the cakes. I walked over and I gave her a kiss, I asked her which one was Tracy's. And she told me to guess, I looked at each cake, and although all three of them were beautiful. I thought about the heart and soul of the middle cake. The way the tree stood out, it had to be that one. But since I was the idiot who started this little trivia moment I knew I had to pick the wrong one. I pointed to the turquoise cake, "this is Tracy's cake." Angela asked me why I thought so. So I explained the details and some stupid way. Angela looked at me and said that I knew Amber's favorite color was purple and I was the one who told her that Tracy was making Amber's cake. Yea, I felt dumb. Angela handed me her camera and said she'd be back; she needed to change into her dress.

I stood there feeling like the fool that I am. I pointed the camera at a few things and clicked. Sonya came in talking to Carina; she was apologizing for being late. Carina pointed out the table that she was going to be sitting at so she could put her stuff down. Sonya looked pretty. Carina told her she was going to be assisting Angela while she took pictures of everything. Sonya smiled at me and came over and gave me a big hug. I asked her where her man was and she said he had a prior engagement so he couldn't make it. She had a huge so happy to be here look on her face. Then she spotted my girls who were walking around the auditorium with Andre. They were having their own kid conversation when Sonya asked me who my girls were. I told her they were my girls and she looked like she was processing the information. She was about to ask me a question when Carina and Angela came out of the back. Angela looked beautiful and she smiled at my smile as they approached. Carina introduced Sonya and Angela while I went in for a kiss, I whispered in Angela's ear that she looked beautiful. Angela blushed and thanked me. Andrew walked over with Tracy in tow. He was coming to ask Carina something, when Sonya interrupted him to say hello. Andrew looked at Sonya and asked why she was there as she and Tracy hugged hello. Carina explained that Sonya was going to be assisting Angela. Andrew looked at me; he asked me if I was ok with that. He reminded me that her mouth don't quit, Sonya frowned and told Andrew he was being mean to her for no reason. He looked at her like she had to be kidding. Then he looked at her and said as long as she didn't start no mess she could stay. The way he spoke to her was like he could see potential drama.

Guest started arriving and Angela was clicking pictures of each guest as they were cleared by security at the door. Sonya was fixing collars, stuff like that before Angela took their pictures. When Randi and Jeff arrived I gave Randi a hug and Jeff. I pointed out my girls who were now walking around with Andre and a cousin; I just didn't remember which one. You could see the excitement in Sonya when JoJo arrived with Aleisha. If Sonya could've found an excuse to leave Angela she would've. Aleisha gave me an excited hello hug and kiss on the cheek. I've known her since she was just the girl who sang at Andrew's club, it's a trip seeing her on TV doing what she was born to do. When Sophia arrived she wanted to check out the kitchen, but she stopped when she saw Sonya. She asked her why she was here. Sonya said she was helping Angela; Sophia put fingers up to her eyes to tell her she was watching her.

Andrew and Roz came from the back, she looked really beautiful. I hadn't seen her look so done up in a long time. I thanked her so much for all that she said last night. I told her that she really helped me out. She said she was only telling the truth. I thanked her for being honest. Sonya was talking to Angela and I saw her head nod over to Andrew and Tanisha who were talking. Angela had a confused look, but she was taking whatever Sonya was saying in. I looked at Tanisha and Andrew; they couldn't have been talking about anything serious. Andrew was animated and Tanisha as always was listening to whatever he was saying. I looked at Tanisha's pants and button up shirt. I wondered if that was supposed to be considered dressing up? I have on a suit for crying out loud. But no matter what Tanisha was always gonna be Tanisha I guess. I spoke to different ones as they arrived. When Frank arrived he put his hand up to Angela and told her not to take his picture, there was no smile on his face. He came over to me and asked how things were going. We chatted for a while, as the reception hall filled up Latia and Lewis arrived and I gave my sister and soon to be brother in-law hugs. Carina asked everyone to find their table as the guest of honor arrived. Derrick and Chantel arrived first and everyone was going crazy cheering for them. Then Sasha and her fiancé walked in. I told myself not to have a reaction but she was beautiful, I reminded myself that I did the right thing by walking away from her. Then the whole house roared as Amber and Malcolm walked in. Amber had the biggest smile as she enjoyed every second of their moment while Malcolm was not amused. I could tell he was doing this for her; cause stuff like this wasn't his scene. Malcolm doesn't ever strive to stand out. The couples went up to the stage and took their seats. As everyone settled down, I saw Alexa slip in and my stomach bubbled over when I saw she came with the pretty boy as her date.

Malachi

I helped the girls dress while Denise sulked and hung out with Grace. Don't ask questions you can't handle the answer to. Even if you don't like the answer, be happy I told the truth and didn't lie. Denise has small moments when she reminds me of my momma. But they're so far and in-between, and it's not like it matters anyways. Timothy asked me to go out in the backyard once I was dressed. He handed me a drink then he asked me what was going on with me. I told him I didn't understand what he meant. He said it was obvious that I was upset about something he was asking what it was. I asked him why he only had two kids. He said that they didn't want to be outnumbered by their kids, and then he laughed. When I didn't, he said it was too hard on Grace. He said they always planned for a big family, but she had too many complications during both pregnancies so they decided that two kids were more than enough. His kids were good kids, but you could see that desire for the Wallace life unlike anything they were shown growing up in his daughter Tina especially. Timothy said its hard sometimes cause his kids have no idea who he is or who they are in that regard. But he never really broke everything down to Grace either. He said dad told him to raise his kids with awareness but they didn't need to know life like we know it. I told him his son would probably piss his pants if he saw a gun. He said not exactly piss his pants, but he asked me not to show his son my gun cause he knew I was packing. I smiled and we said, "you never know where the night could lead us!" Dad used to always say that when we went out. I told him that Denise wants to have another baby and I don't have a problem with that but our relationship sucked right now, and I'd rather exert the energy working on us first. Denise starts freaking out the moment it sounds like she's not getting her way. Timothy asked if she normally gets her way. I said when it was important to her she did. I told him I don't mind having another kid, I just want my wife back. Grace popped her head out and said it was time to go. Tina and Tim were inside, I hugged my nephew and my beautiful niece then we went to the reception hall.

There was a small line in front of the door. I grabbed Jada's hand while Denise picked up Amaya and we walked. The girls at the door stopped us for a picture. I picked up Jada and put my other arm around Denise. I hit them with my smile and both of the girls blushed and welcomed us to the party. I pointed out Andre and the rest of the kids and the girls went over. Denise and I hugged family member after family member as we found our table and where we were sitting.

I almost didn't recognize Yussef, he cut his hair off. If a son ever looked, sound, and carried his-self like his father. I told myself he has to have heard it his whole life, he was Troy. When Sonny saw me he started reading me. I gave my best friend who I hadn't talked to in forever a hug. Immediately he asked me what was up. I told him we'd talk about it later. I asked him how things were with him and he said they were good. My sister Jade gave me a hug and kiss then she asked Sonny to get something out of their car for them. When she was out of sight he called his son Emmanuel over and reassigned the task. We shared a laugh as he said he didn't feel like going outside any more than she did which was why she asked him to go. As we were talking Malcolm's cousin Pearla came over to us. This little girl has always had a crush on me, I know. She has to know that I would always see her as a little girl. She gave me a hug, Paulette and Liz came over and I hugged them as well. Forever little girls they got all giggly about me hugging them. I kind of felt like I was a little celebrity. These little girls definitely put me in a better mood. I guess they lingered too long cause Denise came over to say hi, and all three of them said deflated hellos. Sonny and I cracked up laughing, we couldn't help it. When they walked away Denise told me not to tease the children. I smiled at her and said I was only being nice. I liked seeing her be a little jealous.

Cassondra walked over with her husband Xavier in tow. I gave her a hug, seeing her took me back to high school again. Cassondra was Jade and Amber's little friend, but I knew she liked me. We almost kissed one time when I took her home after she visited with Amber, but I knew I was a knucklehead and she was a good girl. I didn't want to turn her out and have my sisters mad at me, and since Amber nor Jade ever looped around to curse me out I figured she never said anything either. Her husband seemed cool, definitely square like her, but that was what she needed, I would've been too fast for her. Maybe if I would've been with her I could've had some chocolate thunder in my life. But I would've had to marry her a lot sooner than I was ready to. That would've been a disaster. Cassondra introduced us to her granddaughters. Cassondra is Amber's age and she's a grandmother already. Am I too old to be having babies? I guess as long as Denise is younger than me, shoot she's younger than Amber it doesn't matter.

I made my rounds saying hello to everybody, Derrick's family was here too. I said hello to his uncle, gave his aunt and grandmother a hug and kiss hello. I helped them find their seats. Richard and I exchanged excited hellos and he introduced me to his lady, she was glowing and very happy. I could tell she was meeting so many people that she wouldn't remember me. Richard exhaled a satisfied breath as he took in the scene, he was a proud father.

Darryl came in the door calmly not in his normal loud fashion with a pretty little thing on his arm. The kids all screamed DARRYL! And ran to him when he got to my table. He was beaming with pride as he introduced each child to his friend. She looked familiar, and then Darryl introduced her as Kendra. He said she was at his high school graduation party, and Andrew's wedding. I told her it was nice to meet her. I was talking to my cousin Sharon and Sophia's man Travis when Carina asked everyone to find their seats. All the couples looked so happy together, I couldn't stop laughing at Malcolm though. This standing in front of everybody without it being business was not his scene. I could tell he wanted this over sooner rather than later. Late comers came trying to slide in but a lot of people's heads were turning. When I saw it was Alexa I figured they were just star struck. When I saw that Dwayne was her date, RED ALERT went off in my mind. His expression said he didn't know he was coming here. **CRAP!**

Tracy

Sonya was hurrying from the parking lot and I gave her a hug. I didn't expect to see her here. She said she begged Nicole to get her invited, but instead she was assigned to work. She said next time she'd ask herself. I asked her what was so important about being here. And she said there were going to be celebrities here, and she wanted to be able to say that she partied with them. I sucked my teeth, I told her she should only want to be here to be here for the couples. Today was about them not who came to support them. She rolled her eyes and said yea right. Then she asked me what I knew about Yussef's girlfriend. I told her we just met, and that she seemed nice enough. Sonya said she wondered how she was dealing with Yussef having two-baby momma's. I know I shouldn't have listened to her

gossip, but shoot she was the only one to give me a real heads up on Toya. The way she described his ex's she said one was beautiful and one was just all right. Looking at his girls I know they both have to be equally pretty but I didn't say anything cause I never met them. Then she said, "Yea I didn't know what to think when they thought the light skinned baby could've been Yussef's or Drew's." She said that so matter of factly.
My face turned serious, "say that again?"
Sonya leaned in, "don't repeat this, but that's why Yussef and Drew haven't been talking all these years. They got into it over that little girl's momma."
Ok! Ok! Clearly she doesn't have all her facts right, cause they were still close when Andrew had Yussef over my security detail. Now I wanted to know the actual story. How much of this was truth, and how much of it was gossip. Until today I assumed that the girls were his girlfriend's kids. I didn't look at them close enough to see that they looked like him. I started to ask her for the whole story, but Rosalind needed to get something from me to put a couple of last touches on Angela's makeup. I stood there telling myself to calm down. It's in the past; maybe she was lying or had the facts confused.
When Nicole and Hubby walked in the door, Nicole immediately asked me what was wrong. Hubby looked at my face and then he heard me say Sonya to Nicole and he disappeared. Andrew and Hubby walked out. There was no friendliness in his face. Hubby gave me a hug and said hello while Andrew walked past us and into the dining room, I followed Andrew, I was curious to hear what he was going to say. Tanisha asked what happened, I felt stupid for repeating it so I said that Sonya was telling me some crazy story about Andrew's past and it was kind of upsetting. Tanisha frowned and looked at Nicole, she asked her what was wrong with her friend? I could tell she felt guilty, so I rubbed her back telling her Sonya is grown and she's not responsible for her. She thanked me.
I was completely surprised when I saw my sisters walk in. Apparently Sasha invited them, and they decided to surprise me. I told them I couldn't believe they got mom to keep their arrival a secret. Tia's face turned bashful as she said she wanted me to meet her friend. I was wondering why this guy was standing close by. I guess I would've expected Tara to come with a guy before Tia. Last I knew she was drawing closer to God and things like that. Tara shot me a look telling me she'd fill me in later. Brody was nice though; I didn't get any creepy vibes from him. He seems to really like Tia so if she likes him I love him. We made plans to have breakfast tomorrow together.
As different family members arrived they kept telling me how much they enjoyed the wedding and stuff like that. When I saw Andrew's Uncle Frank coming I knew he was coming for answers. "Hello Tracy."
"Hello, should I call you Uncle too?"
"I think you should we're family now." Then he put his arm around my shoulder. "Let me show you something." He took me to the cake tables. "I see a very talented person's work. This is amazing! You created this all without any formal training."
"Uncle Frank can I ask you why everyone is pushing for me to open a bakery? The idea of stepping out on my own scares me."
"The most important reason is so we won't feel selfish for requesting cakes all the time." He smiled at me. "But why should you work for someone else? Make money for someone else when you could write your own ticket? I own several businesses of my own. Most of my siblings do too, and we try to pass that thought process down. When you work for someone else you're limited to what they want for their product or service."
"Andrew works for someone else though."
"That's different, one day he'll explain, however he still has so many businesses outside of his nine to five."
"Uncle Frank we're going to do it. We haven't set a date yet."
He smiled, "you are? That makes me happy."

"I see, you're actually smiling."

"I've been known to do that from time to time. So...." He closed his eyes while he thought about it. "Where do you want to set up shop?"

"I have no idea, somewhere close to home I guess."

"This is off the top of my head, but somewhere close to the college. But easily accessible from the freeway. Ooh! I think you should open your shop over by the Rockridge shopping center, and then have a little kiosk by the college. You need to prey on those poor starving students who have no choice but to drown their sorrows in cakes and pies." I looked at him in amazement. How did he come up with that on the fly like that? "That sounds wonderful." My head was spinning.

"We'll go over the details more later. Tell Malcolm it's a go, we're gonna kick this into high gear." He said with a smile in his voice.

"Ok" I smiled back.

When Carina asked everyone to take their seats Andrew was smiling big until he looked at me then he asked me what was wrong and I forced a smile. I was looking at Andre who was talking with his hands across the room to a cousin when Andrew grabbed my arm. I turned to see who he was looking at. It was Alexa the singer, she was sliding in and she looked gorgeous. I looked at Andrew trying to understand what the problem was. I wondered if he was going to tell me he dated her too. She was with Dwayne Reed; he was looking normal until he looked at the stage. Andrew, followed by Darryl, Yussef, and Uncle Malachi walked towards him.

Lanie

"Smile!" Angela said with her little rinky-dink camera.

Shoot if I knew they were desperate for a photographer I would've volunteered. I did not smile at this girl who was an afterthought to me. Zoey smiled for the both of us, when I gave this irrelevant to me girl "FACE!"

"Elaine right?" The girl with her said.

Zoey shook her head like she was hoping I went easy on this girl. "Who's asking?"

"I'm Sonya and I'm assisting Angela tonight."

"Sonya all you need to know is that I'm a Wallace and I belong here. You on the other hand better find out what name you should be addressing me as and then bow down!"

Sonya looked surprised and shocked. "What is wrong with you? You obviously don't know me, but you're trying to act like you know everybody in here on a first name basis. They need to fire your behind cause you just pissed me off and I ain't even got in the door good!"

"Lanie, please. Can we please go find our seats?" Erica pleaded.

"It's not my fault, I'm trying to be peaceable and she gonna set me off before I get in the door good."

"Hi Lanie!" Little Andre said like he was too excited to see me.

I got excited and hurried over to my baby. "Hey Dre! What's going on? You are looking sharp! Let me see the pose." Andre hit the little man pose that we practiced at the wedding. "Dre! You are sizzling!" Then I looked at the little girls. "Ok so we haven't met yet. What are your names?"

"I'm Yesmina."

"And I'm Sydney."

"Come on, do I look like a grown up?"

"Yes!" Andre laughed.

"Shut up Dre! No I don't, I'm trying to get in good with my little friends here. What are your nicknames?"

"That's Yezzy and that's Syd."

"Nice to meet you ladies, where is your daddy?" They pointed him out across the room talking to Jeff. I told them I wanted to dance with them later on when they opened the dance floor. I took out my phone and gave it to Zoey. I marched right up to them. "Gentlemen aren't we looking dapper tonight?"

"Hey cousin, look at you." Jeff said going in for a hug.

"Yes! Yes! Look at me!" I smiled. "I need pictures." I put my arms out and then I sandwiched myself in between them. "Say Lanie!" I smiled again. Jeff and Yussef smiled as they said my name. I told myself to keep my composure. Then I took a couple snaps with my big cousin Jeff. I tried to control inner excitement as I took quite a few snaps in Yussef's arms. Yeah they may have seemed innocent to him. Wait until I caption them.

"Ahem," that was Darryl. "Lanie what are you doing?" He smiled real big at me.

"Taking pictures." I told him to shut up with my eyes.

"Ooh! We're taking cousin pictures, I want some too! Where's mine?"

"Your name is not Yussef or Jeff. Where's JoJo as a matter of fact anybody but you."

"Aw Lanie, don't be like that." Darryl said following me as I retreated. "How you doing cousin?" He said giving Zoey a hug and kiss. Then Darryl put his arm around me. "Your crush on your cousin is ridiculous. You really need to stop."

"He's not my cousin D, I could have his babies and they'll come ninety-five percent fine."

He smiled at me, "and the other five percent?"

"Completely and totally AWESOME! Don't act like you didn't know!"

Darryl laughed, "you wanna be like me so badly it hurts doesn't it?" He sighed as he looked off into the distance. "The world couldn't handle two of me."

"Um! I do believe I am technically older than you. So you're striving to be like me."

"Those few months don't count. Watch tonight my awesomeness is going to shine so bright your girl," he pointed to Kendra. "Is gonna finely get some act right."

Who cares what he was talking about I hurried over to Kendra and we hugged. "So what does this mean? You getting back with my cousin? Did that flower boy cry when you kicked him to the curb?"

Kendra laughed, then she told me that Darryl blackmailed her into coming here tonight. She was trying to act like she wasn't excited to be here and on D's arm. My momma didn't raise no fool, I knew better than to believe her. It was written all over her face. D came and told her he wanted her to meet some more people, I told my girl we would talk later. Zoey and I found Erica talking to our grandfather and some cousins. Even though we just saw everybody at Drew's wedding you would've sworn this was the first time we saw each other in years. When they told us to find our seats, I gasped when I saw Dwayne…. Someone light the fuse I was waiting for the fireworks.

Sasha

The auditorium was packed. I heard Carina ask everyone to find their seats. I excitedly held El's hand. When Derrick and Chantel walked in everyone went crazy. Then Carina told us to come and just like I dreamed it was a room full of people excited for me. As we made our way to the stage, I glanced around the room. Everyone was smiling at us and I felt great. Then I saw him, at first I didn't think it was him. Yussef has dreads! That's definitely him! Oh my goodness! I swallowed and continued walking with El. Richard was smiling and clapping. My Dan-Dan was smiling and clapping. SYSTEM OVERLOAD! Richard's father is here! I've only seen him a few times in my lifetime mostly at funerals, but he's here. My aunties and uncles on the Cardell side were blending with my Wallace side. My eyes kept scanning the room; some people I didn't recognize but for the most part I knew everyone there. When we got to the table and everyone was focused on Malcolm and Amber, El leaned in. He motioned towards Yussef and asked if that was him, I guess I looked harder than I thought I did. I smiled and said yes, then I looked at Malcolm who's eyes looked like they fixed on someone in the audience. I saw Andrew and Malachi moving towards the back. I didn't even see Yussef move but he was talking to Dwayne. How in the world did that happen? I couldn't tell if Malcolm was upset or not, he was looking with a smirk on his face and his arm around Amber. Amber wasn't paying attention, she was still waving hello to everyone. Yussef and Malachi were talking to Dwayne who moved to the very back of the room. Malcolm took Amber's hand they walked down the stairs on the side of the stage on to the dance floor. Michael Jackson's music started to play as Amber melted into Malcolm's arms. I could tell Amber was on cloud nine unaware that anything was going on. El and I watched as Dwayne's body rejected what he was seeing and walked out. Alexa came up with sad eyes; Chantel went down and hugged her. They said something to each other. I didn't understand why Chantel would invite her knowing that they were "dating" or whatever the celebrity version of kicking it is. Derrick's eyes were glued to them the entire time they were talking. It seemed like they were talking forever but since we had only gotten to the bridge of the song I know it only seemed longer in my mind. Alexa sucked it up and walked out. Derrick did not look happy when Chantel sat down. She started whispering to him and then he returned his attention back to his parents. When Malcolm dipped Amber I thought they were going to go at it right there on the dance floor. As the song was finishing servers were serving salads to everyone. Our salads were served first then the guests. El looked at his parents and smiled, they looked like they were enjoying their conversation at the table with my Dan-Dan, my Grandfather Victor, and Richard. I caught my momma looking Richard's girlfriend up and down. She exhaled and returned her attention to Travis and her table. I exhaled it was going to be a good night. El kept flirting with me and I was eating it all up. Just after the salad Derrick led Chantel to the dance floor. Chantel got all choked up when the music started playing. Teddy P was singing, "I've been so many places, I've seen so many things, but none quite as lovely as you! More beautiful than the Mona Lisa, worth more than gold, and my eyes have the pleasure to behold...." Aw! The song was so pretty and Chantel cried as Derrick held on to her. Darryl and Ryder were fake crying at them making everybody crack up. Malcolm was actually smiling at his son and soon to be daughter in-law. As they were finishing soup was served to everyone, cauliflower soup yum! When I finished my soup, El said it was our turn. As soon as I heard the music I buried my head in his chest. Aaliyah started singing, "Let me know! Let me know! When you feel, what you feel! Sometimes it's hard to tell you so..." I guess I missed that each song was special to each couple. I didn't want to mess up my makeup, but El wasn't fighting fair! He was singing the song quietly to me, and although my baby didn't have any fancy moves like Malcolm or Derrick I felt myself melting to the sound of his voice. When we finished our dance El led me back to our table. When I sat down I had to fan myself. As our food was served I caught Hubby staring. He looked away when I caught him. Yussef wasn't looking in our direction. I guess that's his girlfriend and her girls. I could totally see him being an excellent step dad.

We ate our meal then Carina brought the microphone to Richard. "Hello everyone, I hope you're enjoying your evening. I wanted to thank everyone who could make it tonight. That's my baby girl up there." He pointed to me. "Sasha, I am so proud of you. You held out and made sure you found a true prince. No matter how many ways or times I threaten this guy he doesn't flinch! That's alright in my book." Everyone laughed, "you guys know me." He shrugged, "welcome to the family Eldridge."

Then Carina took the microphone to an older lady. The man next to her reached for it, and she popped his hand. Everyone laughed again, "hello. My name is Rosa Shaw and I'm Chantel's grandmother. I just wanted to say that I am happy for my grand baby. I think I can safely say Derrick has bent over backwards for my baby all these years. It takes a special kind of man to love a Shaw woman and especially with the tenacity that he always has. I love you Derrick, and you're stuck with us now!"

Carina was walking to Andrew but Darryl intercepted her before she could give him the mic. "There's no introduction needed. For those of you who don't know who I am by now you will by the end of the night." He smiled real big, "that's my momma right there. Sitting next to my natural father. I don't care what anyone says, no one can be more relieved than me that this time is FINALLY here! Look at me I'm grown. I'm happy that you took your time to do it right. I've got a song for those two, but we're gonna play that in a minute. I wanna thank you guys for taking your time to do this right. You can't rush perfection and you two are perfect for each other especially now. It does my heart good to look up at the two of you sitting there looking at each other with so much love and adoration. Congratulations momma and Malcolm! Now the other son can speak."

Andrew snatched the mic from Darryl. "Chantel you were just this skinny little hard worker in the office. And my brother took one look at you and said you were priceless. You guys grew up together, I'm happy for you. Congratulations!" He exhaled and looked at me and El. "My twin! I know you're still mad at me, as long as you're mad that means you still love me enough to act a fool over me. I pretend like I can't handle it but you know the truth. El, one sentence from you helped me put the proper perspective on my future. I don't think I ever looped back around and thanked you for that. Looking at my twin I can see that she's truly happy. Sasha wears jeans and T-shirts now. For those of you who know her, and knew her when, you understand what that means. I love you and congratulations El!" He exhaled when he looked at his parents. "Malcolm for somebody who is normally decisive. Ring shopping with you was exhausting!" Everyone chuckled. "I think it's nice that the only vulnerability you have is my momma." He looked at Tracy, "I think that position should always belong to your woman. We've bumped heads so much over the years and I look forward to clashing with you in the future. The two of you together is just..." Andrew paused.

"YOU BETTER NOT!" Darryl said loud enough for everybody to hear. "IF YOU SHED ONE TEAR I'M NEVER LETTING YOU LIVE IT DOWN! DO IT!" Darryl said daring him.

Everyone laughed, and Andrew handed the mic back to Carina then he went up to the stage and hugged Amber ever so gently. He gave Malcolm a pound, he pushed the back of my head, and then he kissed my cheek. He gave El a pound then he did the same with Chantel and Derrick. Then my momma told everybody it was time to dance. Different people came and told all of us congratulations. The dance floor filled up quickly, I got so tickled seeing little Andre breaking it down on the dance floor. He was definitely a chip off the old block. El asked me if that's what our son was gonna be like, and I told him as long as I had something to do with it he would. Sabrina and Emerald kept trying to get Amber to dance. She told them she was shy, and everybody laughed at her on that one. I saw Hubby continuing to stare in my direction whenever his wife wasn't looking. I don't know why that would make me look at Yussef who was not paying me any real attention. I didn't know what Hubby's problem was, but I wasn't in the mood for him. Everybody says he's so in love with his wife, well if he's so in love why is he looking so hard? His brother Dude purposely bumped me on the dance floor. "I know you're not technically my sister in-law anymore but don't I get a brother introduction?"

"El this is Carlos, but we've always called him Dude. He's Hubby's big brother. Dude, this is my fiancé El."

They shook hands, "El like that light skinned cat who sings?"

"No, El as in Eldridge." El said not laughing.

"Oh my bad! Well it's nice to meet you. I always thought Sasha was gonna be my sister in-law, sometimes you just never know how things are going to work out. I get locked up and it seems like the whole world stood on its head."

73

"Maybe if you…" I caught myself. El looked at me like he was daring me to finish that statement. "Dude you gotta go away. You're getting me in trouble." I said through a fake laugh while I freaked out inside. I didn't mean to almost say that maybe if he didn't go away Hubby and I would still be together. It was completely a slip of the tongue.

I was apologizing when I saw the black curly mostly wavy hair make its way through the crowd, that clay like skin. I immediately started looking for Tanisha. When my eyes landed on her, she was standing over to the side watching with the biggest stuck look on her face. He walked up to Malcolm and grabbed his hand so hard it sound like he slapped hands with him. Both of them were smiling. I excused myself and I made a beeline to Tanisha, she sat down while her mouth was literally hanging open. I asked her where her momma was and she shrugged. She was no help, I didn't know if Rosalind was gonna be happy to see him or what. Rosalind was kind of hiding behind Yussef with the same stuck look on her face as Tanisha. He spotted Tanisha and he came straight to her with a small smile on his face. "How you doing?" Tanisha's father Benjamin asked her. I hadn't seen him since we were kids.

Tanisha frowned, "why are you here?"

"My friends since middle school are engaged, why wouldn't I be here?" He asked, "besides I wanted to see you. It seems like it's almost impossible to get a hold of you these days. I've been leaving you messages. Maybe if you would've listened to one of them you would've heard me say that I was going to be here." Then he looked around, "where's your mother?" The look on his face when he saw her, "aren't you a sight for sore eyes! Rosalind you're still beautiful!" He said. Tanisha sucked her teeth and walked away.

Yussef inserted himself in front of Benjamin's view of Rosalind, "I'm her son Yussef. And you are?"

"Her husband," he said matter of factly.

"Ex-husband," Rosalind volunteered. "We are at my friend's party. I would appreciate it, if you didn't talk to me." She said then she walked away in the same direction that her daughter went in.

"Ben!" Malcolm was calling him back with a smile.

"I'll go check on them." Yussef said taking off in the direction of Rosalind.

Leaving his girlfriend and I standing there awkwardly. "Hi I'm Angela."

"Sasha."

"So you're THE Sasha!" A girl I didn't recognize said. Angela and I tilted our heads at her.

"Who are you?"

"Sonya, Nicole and I are good friends."

I didn't like her tone, as far as I knew Nicole didn't know about Hubby and I. "Ok"

"Nicole, Hubby's wife." She said clarifying…

I shook my head, "good to know. Why are you here?"

"She's supposed to be assisting me." Angela said. She looked irritated with her.

"Have you met Nicole?"

"Yes, I have. Have you met my man?" I said with all assertiveness. If she saw my man why would she think I was concerned with Hubby? "You do realize this is my house! Are you really that dumb to step to me like this?"

Angela looked between the two of us. Sonya backed down like she better had! Lanie was looking and I pointed at this Sonya girl like someone better get her. Andrew went out the door to check on Tanisha, I decided to follow cause this chick was gonna make me hurt her. Yussef was hugging Rosalind, and Tanisha was standing there refusing to let anyone touch her. Carina was trying to comfort her but Tanisha kept snapping at her. Andrew stood to the side with his hands in his pockets, looking directly at Tanisha. "Why is he here?" Tanisha yelled, I stood next to Andrew.

"Baby he's friends with Malcolm. I guess it's only fair that he's here." Rosalind said trying to fix her mood.

"Whatever! Don't be weak!" She barked at her momma.

"Excuse you?"

"Momma you're always weak when it comes to him. He expects that. Don't do it!"

"Tanisha, cut your mom some slack, they go..."

"Shut up Drew! What would you know about it? You gonna forever get tripped up over Toya? Is that what you're trying to tell us?"

I looked at Andrew to see how he was going to respond. He didn't look mad, "Toya wasn't my first. Your parents have so much history. Don't fault your momma for feeling something. Everybody can't be as cold and standoffish as you!" He spit back.

"So you came out here to argue with me?"

"Nope, came to offer some comfort, but you know how you are."

"Tanisha baby I'm fine. Here's what we're going to do. We're going to have the time of our lives out here tonight. He needs to know that we don't fall apart just because of him." She walked up to Tanisha and put her hands on her face. "Baby, we're ok. Ok?"

Tanisha was angry, Yussef and I exchanged looks. Andrew was the only one to ever be dumb enough to say anything to her when she's in that space. Tanisha exhaled and reluctantly agreed. As she was calming down, Andrew cleared his throat. "Since when you think it's ok to tell me to shut up?"

Tanisha smiled, "when you stick your nose in my business that's what happens." Then she walked back inside.

I squinted my eyes at Andrew. "What?" He said shrugging.

"Cut it out!"

"Cut what out?" He smiled and then he walked back inside.

"Roz are you gonna be ok?" Yussef asked completely concerned.

"Yes baby thank you. I think I'll go dance with the girls."

"Your step daughters are really cute," I said.

"Thank you but they're mine. It's a long story." Then he started walking inside with Rosalind.

I thought I heard him wrong, but when I walked into the auditorium I looked both of the girls in their faces. I looked at his sister who was on the dance floor having a good time with Shameless the rapper. They looked just like her. The room spun.

Kendra

Darryl was proudly introducing me to everybody. When they told us to take our seats, we were sitting with Ryder and Ahjanae, my parents, and Darryl's Auntie Lorraine, her husband, and Grandmother. As the happy couples filled into the banquet hall I felt like someone was looking at me. I looked around the room until I saw Nathan staring at me. I frowned at him, and then I rolled my eyes. Darryl looked at my face then he looked around the room. He spotted Nathan then he said something to Ryder. Both of them looked at Nathan with smiles on their faces. What is he doing here? We watched the happy couples dance as we ate. Each couple danced to specific songs and you could tell each song had sentimental meaning to them and their relationships.

After dinner and the well wishes everyone went out on the dance floor. Darryl kept smiling at me and telling me to do it, I shook my head no. We were in a room full of his family and he wanted to act like we were in a club, I wasn't going to do it. Darryl's momma came over and thanked me for coming. She was glowing from her happiness and excitement. We chatted for a little bit. Then I heard Darryl's voice on the DJ's microphone and I said oh no. His momma laughed at my reaction as we listened for what he was going to say. "KB! This song is for us." When I heard the music I looked at

Ahjanae and Kalani and we started cracking up. Darryl danced up to me and rapped Positive K's part. "A-yo sweetie, you're looking kinda pretty what's a girl like you doing in this rough city...." I was cracking up. I had to sing my part. "No it's not that see you don't understand how should I put it? I got a man?"
Darryl: "what's your man gotta do with me?"
Me: "I told ya."
We had a good time clowning around on the dance floor. Darryl had me in his arms while we danced when fussing broke our concentration. We looked to our right and his cousin Sasha punched another girl in her face and she went flying. Sasha was going in to finish what she started when security picked the girl up off the floor and people held Sasha back. Lanie was telling them to let Sasha go cause she didn't like the girl. I asked her why, and she said the girl was trying to act too familiar too quick. Darryl was cracking up, he said Sasha was crazy. I asked him if he needed to check on her. He said she was covered, but then another girl started going off and then Darryl said he'd be back as he and Ryder walked towards the commotion. Kaleah came over to us with a smile that said she had the juice. We moved off the dance floor to the side Ahjanae, Kalani, and I moved in close so we could hear. Kaleah said the girl who got hit name is Sonya, and she has been running her mouth all night. Apparently, then she pointed out Hubby, Hubby and Sasha used to date, but his wife didn't know that. Sonya felt the need to tell everybody about it right now. Hubby's wife was upset of course because she had no idea. Sasha was mad about the way Sonya did it. Kaleah said she didn't expect Sasha to knock Sonya like that. She said when she hit her you heard it. We looked around and people were moving around like normal they weren't too choked up about what just happened. Everybody was back to dancing and not phased at all. "This family is a trip." Ahjanae said.
"Ok! Ok! I'm getting a dance with the cutie tonight!" Kalani tried to muster the courage. We laughed at her, cause she said the same thing at Drew's wedding and she didn't utter a word to Darryl's cousin. She said he was too cute, but this time she was going to do it. Darryl came back and took me back on the dance floor. "KB! Why you holding back?"
"Holding back?"
"You being stiff in the hips, and you know that dress deserves you to drop it at least once."
"Um, I don't feel comfortable dropping it in front of your momma."
"KB! You don't know my momma." Then he smiled, "you down to come to E.A. tonight for the after party?"
"Sure," I wasn't not thinking much of it.
"Your boy over there all sad, you want him to apologize or is it water under the bridge?" Darryl was referring to Nathan.
"It's water under the bridge, it was so long ago."
"Ok," Darryl said shrugging it off.
The kids, under aged cuties were taken away in a limo; the party poopers went home as well. Then we caravanned to E.A. We were so deep as we filled into the club's VIP section. One booth was like a coat and purse station cause that's where we put them. Someone stood posted by our things then we flooded the dance floor. Lanie, her sisters, Darryl's parents, his cousin Sophia and her man, his cousins and their women, everybody was on the dance floor. Darryl almost fell on the ground laughing at me when my mouth fell open as I watched his momma throw her leg up on his father's side and freak him. They were in their own world not worried about nobody. I didn't know his momma could dance like that or that she would. Drew and his bride were in their own world too. Darryl told me I don't know his family. Ok, ok so then I let my hair down. I forgot how much fun and stimulating it is to dance with Darryl. Mix that with alcohol and yeah, it was like Anton who? The music was pumping, I don't know how many drinks I had but I was feeling good. Darryl looked at me and smiled, and then he told me to kiss him. When I

did, I melted into him. When he told me I was spending the night with him I didn't object. I was feeling good and I didn't want the night to end. As we poured out of the club everyone said their goodbyes, I asked him if he was ok to drive cause I wasn't. He looked at me and said he'd never endanger my life. I think he thought at any given moment I was going to come to my senses cause he wasn't jumping right in. He was moving slower than he ever had before. He laughed a goofy laugh as he unzipped my dress. Then he looked at me, "KB!" He shook his head. "Kendra! You're still beautiful!" Then he kissed me and thanked me for coming here with him tonight. I wasn't so drunk that it went unnoticed that we didn't use one condom. He made sure I stayed breathless; I gave up on trying to remember to ask.

Episode 7

Yussef

"If I had a pickup we could've done this faster." I signed the papers for the small rental truck. "Ladies are you riding with me?" I said to my girls.

"Yes!" They said excitedly.

"We'll meet you two at the old place." I said to Sylvia and Angela. I was praying that they got along long enough for us to get Syd and Sylvia situated.

Angela was not happy last night when I told her I gave Sylvia my nice car cause hers died. But what was I supposed to do? My child needs a way to school, the grocery store, or wherever. I had a flashback of catching the bus with my momma when we went grocery shopping. It was always a headache. I don't want that for my daughter. It's bad enough that her clothes are all old and very worn. Yezzy has nice clothes and lives the way I imagine my daughter should. Jackson takes very good care of his family even though he's sickly and in and out of the hospital. I imagine that half the appeal with Jackson was that she wouldn't have to work unless she wanted to. Where Sylvia although she was taking classes at Laney College has no real employable skills. She probably thought her beauty was always going to carry her. I don't know why her family doesn't help her. When she stopped chasing the money she probably was of no use to them.

I held the door open for the girls. Then I got in on the driver's side. I put the key in the ignition and then I turned to my beautiful girls. "So I have a question, I need to know what you guys think." Both of them looked at me with smiles. "I was thinking we should give Syd the furniture in your room. Syd doesn't have her own bed and we don't want her sleeping on the floor do we?" Syd looked embarrassed as she looked at Yezzy.

Yezzy smiled and asked me, "does that mean we get to go shopping for new stuff for our room?"

Syd's face lit up as she looked at me waiting for me to answer. I laughed, "girls love to shop! Here's the thing. We're gonna be moving in a bit. I want to wait until we're in our new place before we refurnish your room. I'll get an air mattress for you guys for now. What do you say?"

"Of course! I don't want my twin sleeping on the floor." Yezzy said making her sister laugh.

We moved all of Sylvia's things real easy. She didn't have much to move. I told her we were moving the girl's furniture into Syd's room. Sylvia went with us to my place. She stood by the door like a visitor until Angela gave her a job to do. We packed the girl's room quickly, and I sent all the clothes that Angela picked out for the girls home with them. Melissa might throw a fit, but Sylvia was grateful. Angela asked me when I was going to go shopping for new furniture, and the girls volunteered that we were moving. Angela didn't say anything else, but I knew she didn't appreciate hearing that news from the girls. The bunk beds, etc. looked great in Syd's new room. The girls should've been exhausted but they were playing and having a good time. I asked Angela if it was ok with her if we took everyone out to eat. I made sure I asked her when it was just she and I in case she said no. She exhaled and then she agreed reluctantly. I asked the girls what they wanted to eat. When the girls said Chinese food Angela and I looked at each other The Palace Golden was the only acceptable answer. Sylvia looked surprised when Angela told her she was invited as well. We took the rental truck back, and then Sylvia drove us to Richmond. I smiled to myself as Sylvia pretended she didn't know where she was going. I used to bring Sylvia here all the time. She almost got away with it until our waitress came with a confused look on her face. I was sitting in the booth between Yezzy and Syd with Angela and Sylvia on the ends. "I know it none my business." She said with her thick accent. "Are you here with her or her?" She pointed between Angela and Sylvia. "You come in here all time with her, long time ago." She said pointing at Sylvia. "Now I see you with her." She said pointing at Angela.

Angela cut her eyes at me. I smiled, "these are my girls. We're having a family meal. I would like to order three orders of prawns, pork fried rice, chicken chow mien, shrimp egg foo yung, and an order of glass noodles. Did anybody want anything else?"

Sylvia turned her head, "you always eat weird stuff."

"Why are you eating glass?" Yezzy asked.

"It's not really glass, it's jellyfish."

"JELLYFISH?" They screamed together. "Eeewwllll!"

"It's good. Try it when I get it." Yezzy agreed, but Syd said no thanks.

Angela and Sylvia sat quietly for the most part. I ignored them both and enjoyed my girls. Yezzy tried the jellyfish and decided she liked it. After about twenty minutes of convincing we got Syd to try it. She said it wasn't nasty but she didn't want anymore. I couldn't think of any other reason to prolong the day so I asked Sylvia to drive us to Yezzy's house. No one was home, then Melissa and family pulled up. Melissa looked really pretty as she glided out of the car. They were dressed in their Sunday best; it looked like they were coming from Service. Yezzy and I got out, and Melissa's eyes scanned the car. Her entire body jerked when she saw Sylvia in the driver's seat of my car. "What's going on?"

I hugged Yezzy and told her I'd see her on Tuesday, I waved bye to Jackson and little Jack and then I got back in the back seat with Syd. "Why does she act mad all the time? Yesmina's mom used to be so nice to me. Now she looks at me like she's mad at me."

I put my arm around her, "Sydney don't pay her looks any attention. She looks at everybody like that these days. I want my twins to always love each other and take care of each other. Can you do that for me?"

"Yes daddy," she said smiling back at me.

Sylvia dropped Angela and I off at my place. She thanked me ten thousand times for everything. I told her we would transfer the pink slip, etc. over to her name tomorrow. I could tell Angela was upset when we walked inside. I was thankful we made it inside the apartment before she blew. "So you're moving?"

"Eventually, Malcolm and Amber are having a house built. Once they move in then I'm taking over one of their houses." I sat on the couch.

"Why didn't you tell me? Why did I have to find out from your girls?"

"I was going to tell you, but it slipped my mind. It's not anything pressing at the moment."

"You dated Brandy?"

"Who?" I looked at her like she was crazy.

"Chantel's friend."

"No, she...." I caught myself. "You don't believe that you're the first woman that I've dated, cause if you do we need to talk." I was trying to be funny.

"Why didn't you tell me about Sasha?"

"Cause there was nothing to tell. We were never together."

"I saw the way she kept looking at you."

"Then you also saw how in love she is with her fiancé. I'm not checking for her and she's not checking for me."

"Yussef your world is crazy, I don't know if I can do this. I don't have it in me to do the whole baby momma scene. I hated sitting in the passenger seat of my man's car being driven by his ex. You've already got two kids do you even want to have any more?"

"Of course I do! I didn't get to hold or know either of my girls when they were babies. We're just now meeting. I want the pregnancy, the delivery, the sleepless nights. I want a baby, just not right now."

"How do you think it's going to make your girls feel when you have another baby?"

"They should be happy to have another sibling duh!"

"I don't know if I can do this." She said in a defeated tone.

I was too tired to argue with her. "Fine! I'm not going to beg you to stay Angela. You stay because you want to, not because I begged you. It sucks though, cause we never got a chance to see what we could be together. You're right; this is a lot to take in all at once. I go from single to a single parent overnight basically. I don't want you to go; I think we could figure out how to make this work. You gotta want it to work, instead of getting your feathers all ruffled behind two females who each had me. And had me dying to be with them at some point and who both of them broke my heart in different unforgiveable ways. I could tell you until I'm blue in the face that I don't want either one of them, but you won't believe me so what would we have at that point? We haven't even had a chance to dive into your drama yet. I guess it's good that this happens now before I was thinking about proposing to you, or you find out you're pregnant too. You want me to pack your stuff for you?"

"What?" She looked confused.

"I'm tired Angela! I'm tired of fighting for someone to love me just for it not to work out. I have my girls, my unconditional love. That's all I've ever wanted. I don't want to fight with you to love me. You have no idea the HELL I went through behind both of those women! Or anyone! It doesn't matter cause you don't date men with kids, it's too much for you. Fine! I'm done with insecure females. If a man tells you and then shows you he wants you, why would you care about what the next female is doing? I want you, but I'm done fighting. If you can't see me, then oh well." I stood up, "call me if you change your mind. Hopefully I'm single at that point and there's something left to salvage. I'm gonna take a shower."

"Jere…" she exhaled. "Yussef, I'm not secure enough with myself to be in a relationship with four other women."

"Fine! Whatever, I can't even care. Leave your keys on the way out."

"Just like that? You're ready to be done with me?" She asked crying.

"I just told you. What do you want from me? You want me to beg and plead with you not to go? I just told you I don't have it in me to be that way. Maybe I need to be alone while I figure this whole thing with my girls out. I don't want you to go; I honestly feel we could have something special. But I lied to you from the beginning. Part of it I didn't know I was lying but that doesn't change the fact that I lied about my name. I lied about having no kids, but in my defense I didn't know I had them. Still you were signing up for something other than what you got. I'm not mad at you Angela, I'm just tired. I'm tired of this game. You're gonna walk away from me because of this situation, then sometime will pass and you'll say Yussef was actually a great guy. I want him back! And then even though it's not convenient for me you'll want me back. Then you'll start acting crazy, bringing me more drama. When can I find someone who wants me for me when I want them?" I exhaled, "oh and one more thing. When you leave stay gone. Please don't come back. If you aren't sure about leaving suck it up and stay. I'm not gonna beg you to stay. You have every right to leave and never come back. The choice is yours."

Angela stood there shifting her weight from leg to leg as she thought about it. "I don't know what to do! You're a good man. I can see that, but I know me. I have to be first!"
"You are first!"
"No I'm not. Your girls are first which kind of makes their mothers first."
"That's according to you."
"I am so happy for your girls. I'm sure I'd be a different person if my father cared even a smidgen as you do for yours. Honestly Yussef I can't. I'm being honest, I'm not secure enough with myself to be with someone in a relationship like this."
"Fine!" She walked out the living room. I heard what I assume were my keys being put on the counter. I growled to myself, and then I turned on the shower. I didn't hear the door so I knew she was still inside, probably pacing in the living room. She came in the bathroom while I was in the shower. She sat on the counter and started rambling. She said we're trying to move too fast. I didn't think so but I listened. She said she knows it's selfish but she wasn't ready to share me. BUT! She'd be a fool to walk away from me. So she said she needed to go home at nights and refocus her energy. We weren't breaking up, but slowing down. It sounds ridiculous to me, but if it made her happy then fine!

****

"Sydney loves this car. She said sometimes you take them out in it with the top down, and Angela bought them scarves and shades to wear for those occasions." Hearing her mention Angela hurt, but I nodded in agreement. "You're the man of very little words today."
"So," I shrugged.
"Do you realize this is the first time we've been alone since we were together all those years ago?" I gave her a look that said so what. "There's so much I want to say to you. I feel like I only have a small window to say it in."
"We're going to go to the DMV in Concord because the wait time should be a lot shorter." I said trying to show her I didn't care.
"Ok," her eyes bounced around. "I hope I don't keep sounding like a broken record to you. But I am so grateful for everything you've done for Sydney. She's so much happier now that you're here."
"That's good. She deserves to be happy."
Then her phone rang. When she said it was her job I turned the radio off so she could hear. I guess she was talking to her supervisor. She exhaled hard and looked sad, she said she understood and she'd have to call her back. She didn't wait for me to ask, "on the weeknights and weekends when you have Sydney I work overtime. My boss said if I take today off, Saturday won't count as overtime. She suggested that I come in late but still put in my eight hours so I don't lose any money. Do you mind keeping Sydney until I get off? Will Angela be mad?"
"Why would I mind? That's perfectly fine. She can see where I work." Sylvia said thank you then she got quiet.
"What?" I said knowing I was going to regret asking in a minute.
"You have no idea how much I love you right now."
I exhaled, "of course I do. You're like everybody else. You don't truly appreciate me until you can't have me." I could tell my comment wounded her, but I was in a place where I didn't care. It's not like I lied. The Concord DMV moved its line like no other DMV I've ever gone to. We were in and out in no time; we registered the car under her name, etc. On the car ride back to her place she was still quiet. "Why do you need to work so much overtime?"
"The money you're paying is for Sydney. I've acquired a huge amount of debt that until now I had no way of paying off. Whenever you have Sydney I work longer hours. Every bit of that overtime goes towards those bills."
"Do you need me to take her more often?"

She slouched, "every other weekend is still fine. But if you could get her after school. My call center closes at eight, it would help me out a lot."
I got a little excited; "I get to have my baby girl every day after school?"
"Only if it's not a burden."
"My child would never be a burden to me. You could be, but never my girls."

I saw Melissa's car driving away as I pulled up to the school. Sydney bolted up to the car screaming "DADDY!" She was my first real sense of happiness all day. I got out of the car and opened her door for her. She was so excited when she got in. I asked her if it was ok with her if she hung out with her old man for a few hours. She smiled the biggest smile as she said yes.
When we got back to the office Ms. Laverne said Sydney was even prettier in person than in her pictures. Sydney naturally embraced Ms. Laverne like everyone did. I had her sit at the table and do her homework while I finished up my work for the day. Sydney started getting frustrated with her work. When I asked her what was wrong, she said schoolwork was very easy for Yesmina, while it frustrated her. She said Yesmina always helps her understand. I smiled when I thought about Latia and I. How she helped me to be better. Sydney sat there wide eyed as I helped her with her multiplication tables, etc. She wasn't a bad student; I think she's more like me. I needed that one on one attention until I got it. Then once I got it watch out. I asked Syd if we should cook or go out to dinner. We went out to dinner just she and I, she was so cute rambling on and on about nothing. I kept thinking this beautiful creature came from me, and I couldn't believe it. We bought a bunch of fruits, and then we had fruit salad for dessert. Sydney dozed off by the time Sylvia buzzed at the door. I carried Sydney down with her things and I put her in the car. I gave her a kiss on her forehead and I told her I couldn't wait to see her tomorrow.
****
"Ok ladies, here's today's mission. Since Daddy doesn't have a nice car anymore, I need to replace it."
"But you still have Granddad's car, you could drive that." Yezzy said.
"Yes, and I will. But Granddad's car is mostly for special occasions. I want to keep that car nice because it has special meaning to me." Then I touched Yezzy's nose. "So, we need a newer and nicer car than the one we had before. I need my ladies to sign off on the car before I buy it. So tell me which one you agree on and then we'll go from there. Got it?"
"Got it!" They smiled.
We caught a cab over to Broadway Street in downtown Oakland and then we walked past each dealership. It took the longest time for us to agree on the dealership that we wanted to look around in. My girls took their job seriously and rejected cars because they didn't like the way the lights looked, stuff I could've cared less about, but apparently it was important to them. Each time the girls folded their arms that was a wrap for that dealership. The sales woman came over with a smile and asked us if she could help us with anything. Yesmina spoke up, "we are looking for a new car for our daddy."
The lady smiled, "did you have anything in mind?"
"Yes, he needs a black car." Yezzy said.
"Oh I do?" I laughed.
"Yes, cause we like your bike and it's black. Your car should match your bike." Syd said.
"What about a SUV?" The woman asked.
Both of the girls gave her thumbs down, "our daddy is not big. He needs a car like him." Yezzy said.
"What am I like?" I said completely tickled.
"A cat!" Syd blurted out.
"A cat?" I was cracking up.

"YES! The way you walk real quiet is like a cat. My dad, I mean my stepdad Jackson always makes a lot of noise when he walks. We never hear you coming."

"Yes, you are like a big black cat!" Syd said laughing.

"So I take it you guys have discussed this before?"

"Yep!" They said in unison.

I looked at the saleswoman, "do you have a black cat daddy car in your inventory?"

"What is your price range?" As she mentally went over the inventory.

"If we like it, I'm getting it." I said.

She took us to a low-end car, and the girls said no. I didn't like it either. Mid-range, Syd liked it, but Yezzy said it wasn't cat like enough. Then she took us to a high-end model. Both of the girl's eyes lit up when they saw it. It was black on black, Syd got excited then Yezzy told her to hold on for a minute. They held hands whispering about the car as they walked around it. The saleswoman said she felt sorry for me when they grew up. They opened the door and took turns sitting in the driver's seat. Then Syd reminded Yezzy that they needed to look in the trunk. Yezzy asked Syd what she thought, and Syd nodded her head in approval. Then Yezzy informed us that they agreed on this car. The sales woman brought the car around to the front. This car glided down the street like it was lava gliding down a mountain. The girls sat in the back with mile wide grins on their faces. At the end of our test drive I asked the girls what they thought, and they gave the car two thumbs up each. I looked at the asking price; expensive taste my girls have that honestly. I told the saleswoman to have her manager come out. When he came out I told him I didn't want to do the back and forth because I needed to take my girls out to dinner before it got too late. I told him I would pay so much for the car in cash, and if they couldn't do it or thought he could get a better price then we would go somewhere else. He took my offer to the back and of course he tried to counter but when I told the girls we were leaving he said ok. We caught my bank just before it closed. I got a cashier's check for the total agreed upon price after all the extras were added. I thanked the saleswoman and then my girls and I went to Piedmont to have dinner and ice cream at Fenton's.

****

"So what kind of wedding are you going to have?" My grandma asked Latia.

"I don't want anything too big." She exhaled, "Yussef I have a problem. Lewis and Dwayne are close; he wants Dwayne to be his best man. I wanted to ask Malcolm to walk me down the aisle." Tears came to her eyes, "do you think he might not come because of Dwayne?"

I laughed, "Malcolm's not gonna punk out because the pretty boy is there. Malcolm would be there and taunt him with Amber all night. You should make sure the pretty boy could handle it."

Latia looked relieved, "and the girls are still my flower girls? Jackson is going to be my ring bearer."

That was her way of saying Melissa and family were going to be there. Then there was a knock at the door. Arthur went to answer it, the panic that flashed across all of our faces as we heard my momma's voice. We gathered all the papers, stuffed them in the folder, and threw everything in the oven. Then we all tried to sit there like we were casually sitting at the table in the kitchen just shooting the breeze. "Is that your new car out front?"

"Hi momma how are you?" I said raising to hug her.

"Hi baby!" She said checking herself, and hugging me back. "Is it?"

"Yes" I said exhaustedly.

"So the temping game must be going pretty well!" Her husband Jarvis said walking in the kitchen behind her. "That, or you're the fool that spends all his money on a car. But can't afford to eat come dinner. You need some lunch money sonny boy?" He said laughing.

"Jarvis! Don't come in my house disrespecting my grandson like this. His financial affairs are none of your business. Leave him alone!" Arthur said with bass in his voice. My grandma was smiling so proudly at her husband. I was touched that he referred to me as his grandson. They've been married a little while now, and I've grown fond of him as well. I'm glad to know the feeling is mutual.

"Goodness Arthur! I was just having a little afternoon fun. You wanna shelter the boy fine." He said surrendering in defeat.

"Anyways I have a bone to pick with you!" My momma said pointing at me.

"What now?"

She marched out of the kitchen and came back with the picture of me and my girls that Angela took and framed for my grandma's wall. "Who is this?" She said pointing to Sydney.

I exhaled again, "my daughter Sydney."

"WHAT???" She screamed grabbing her chest. "You mean I have two grandbabies and I've only barely met one of them?"

"Yes."

"Yussef! I wanna meet them! I want them to know me! I always wanted a little girl and now there are two of them. Why wouldn't you tell me?"

"It slipped my mind. You know how you are. I don't want drama around them anymore than it has to be."

"Hold on, you can't talk to my wife like that!" Jarvis said.

"This is between me and my momma! You need to sit there and shut up!"

"Oh so the little temp boy thinks he can get at a man!"

I stood up, "let's go! Out back!"

Jarvis laughed, "little boy you don't want none. Your friend isn't here to sucker punch me this time."

I walked out the kitchen door. I was angry but calmly angry. This fool needed to recognize that he needed to back down. I was tired of him. Jarvis was tall and thin but that meant nothing, I was tall and solid. Everyone stood watching from the doorway. The way Jarvis approached me I could tell he could handle himself, didn't matter. He underestimated me, when he woke up he was completely surprised. I got in my momma's face and I told her to get her man in line. I told her I didn't want my girls seeing her as an example for what a real woman should be. She promised to be on best behavior, she just wanted to meet them.

I told Latia to call me later. I looked at Jarvis who was sitting on the ground embarrassed. I decided to leave so he wouldn't have to apologize right away. Arthur smiled real big at me and then he walked with me out the door. He kept grinning at me looking very proud. I tried to drive casually, but I was anxious to see Angela. I hadn't seen her all week, I was killing time at my grandma's but Jarvis and my momma killed my attempt to cool any further. Renee was taking out the trash when I pulled up. I begged her to let me do it for her. She smiled at the car, she said it was pretty. I told her to take it for a spin. Her eyes got really big; she asked if I was sure. When I said I was she said she wanted to check out a store in Pleasanton, and she asked if we could go. Angela was in the window listening. I told her to take my car and Angela and I would hang out at the house. Renee was so shocked; Angela sat in the window smiling. Renee said she had to put on something nicer than what she was wearing to ride in my car. Angela and her mother giggled in her mother's room getting her dressed. I asked Angela for an envelope, she gave it to me and then she hurried back to her mother. I put a few hundred dollars in the envelope, then I wrote "For Renee's shopping trip" on the front. I set it on the passenger front seat. She looked nice in her dress and heels. I told her she couldn't open the envelope until she got to Pleasanton. She agreed and then Angela and I watched her drive away. Angela said it was really sweet of me to do that for her mother. I told her I did it so we could have time alone. Angela blushed and I hurried her inside. The door barely closed before I had her entangled in a kiss. Angela backed away from me trying to catch her breath. She grabbed my hand and told me to come upstairs. As she erupted in ecstasy I asked her how she could go a week without seeing me. I knew what I was doing! Yussef would forever be etched upon her brain! Whether we stayed together or not.

Kendra

When I sat up there was that hangover headache. I grabbed my head as I tried to focus on the room. Darryl had water and pills. He told me breakfast would be ready by the time the pills started working. He told me to drink all of the water and I sucked my teeth. This cup was huge, "how you gonna give me the King Kong cup of water and then tell me to finish it?"

Darryl smiled and walked towards the kitchen. "Just do it."

Once my headache lifted, I pulled open a drawer in his dresser. Everything was neatly folded and in its place. I exhaled; Anton's drawers were a joke. When I found his shirt drawer I picked a T-shirt. It had a Tasmanian Devil on the front. I picked up our clothes and made the bed, and then I tip-toed down the hallway. Darryl was watching the corner waiting for me to arrive. His face lit up when he looked at me. "You heard me?"

"Of course! Nobody can out creep me." Then he smiled at me. "It's amazing that you picked that shirt."

I looked at it, "what's special about this shirt?" I was clueless.

He motioned for me to come sit on the stool at the counter. "Remember when we met, you spun around just like Taz!" Then he started cracking up laughing.

I frowned as I chuckled, "you're rude!"

"Make sure you get your smell all in that shirt. I'm never washing it again!"

"You're silly. It smells delicious in here."

He paused and posed in front of the stove. "A nigga got gifts! Could've been a chef, but then I might've killed a complaining customer."

He put my plate in front of me, and the smell slapped me in the mouth. I didn't realize I was hungry until I was looking at my plate. "Potatoes and a biscuit, you trying to make me fat?"

He shrugged, "I'd rather you'd be happy and satisfied. Then skinny and mean cause you hungry. As long as I'm the one who makes you fat I don't care."

"So you say now."

"If that booty gets bigger so does my love for you. If that booty goes away so does my love. Take that to the bank." He started washing dishes.

"You are so silly." I enjoyed my plate.

When he finished the dishes he brought his plate next to mine. He exhaled real loud. "I said I wasn't going to, but it feels like I have to." He looked at me, "you staying?"

"What do you mean by staying?"

"Why you always gotta make me be the female?" I frowned while smiling. Darryl flipped his imaginary hair. "So like last night? Was that just a booty call?" He was using a valley girl accent. "Or was that like your way of telling me you want me back?"

I shifted in my seat, "I don't know. I honestly expected to wake up in my bed this morning."

"So call that loser and stay with me!"

"It's not that simple, he's my fiancé."

Darryl's face turned angry, it startled me. "So now you're playing games!"

"No I'm not."

"So what do you call last night?"

"I got caught up, you made me come."

"I didn't force you to cum, I invited you and you did. Over and over again!" He threw my hands away from him. He was completely pissed off. "When do you understand I don't do this for everybody?"

"I'm supposed to drop everything because you go outside of your comfort zone? YOU ALWAYS GOT ME CHEATING ON SOMEONE FOR YOU! I DON'T DO THAT EITHER!"

He shook his head, "whatever Kendra!"

Suddenly I didn't like the way my name sound coming off his lips. "WHATEVER? WHATEVER!" I pushed his head. "Take me home!" I stood up.

"When I'm finished eating." He said with no emotion in his face as he put one potato from his mountain of potatoes on his plate in his mouth and chewed it slowly.

"Forget your food! I want to go home now!"

"You can wait, or you can walk. You have choices." He said picking up another potato.

"YOU MAKE ME SICK!" I pushed his back.

"Keep your hands to yourself, that's the last time I'm gonna warn you!" NO HE DIDN'T THINK HE COULD THREATEN ME! I pushed him again as hard as I could, then I ran. He threw his spoon and it hit the wall by my head real hard. "Next time I won't miss."

I wasn't waiting on him! I took a pair of his sweats, socks, and flip-flops. He better be happy I wasn't gonna call Jason! How could I explain my walk of shame without being as equally in trouble? I folded my dress, and gathered everything in my arms. I went in the kitchen and searched the drawers until I found a plastic bag to put my things in. Darryl was still sitting at the counter eating his potatoes one by one. When he finally looked at me he shook his head, saying I couldn't take that shirt. I told him too bad, I was wearing it. Darryl exhaled and hopped off his stool. He walked out the kitchen, I heard something lock on the front door then he went in his room. I heard him open a drawer as I tried to open the door. No matter which way I turned the locks the door would not open. Frustrated I went in the living room and opened the window, I kicked the screen out, and then I was almost out the window when he grabbed my leg and pulled me back inside. His hands were locked on me and I wasn't going anywhere other than where he led me. I told him to let me go and I kept swinging at him. He acted like I was an unruly child. He sat me down and took his shirt off of me. Then he threw the white T-shirt in my face. He went back to the door did something, and then went back to his food. I got off the couch and charged him. He looked at me when I was running at him with a look like I was annoying or something. When I got close he grabbed my wrist and spun me around. He pushed me in the opposite direction. He said he was tired of playing with me; I was never going to appreciate anything that he does for me so he was done trying. "Thanks for the raw pussy last night. It was," he smelled his fingers. "Fun? For the lack of a better word." He said coldly.

"I hate you!"

"Good! Cause, at least we're on the same page. I hate you too! I hate that I ever cared about you, or even went out of my way for you. Thanks for letting me off the hook; I can't see being stuck with you for the rest of my life. Get out of my house Kendra! I'm done!" There was no emotion in his voice. I was standing there looking at him like he was a stranger. "Do you need something? Or did you think I'd chase you for the rest of my life? You've had too many chances to reject me. You can play that game with the guy who can't even pay the bill! I got what I wanted, I'm good!" Then he went back to eating one potato at a time.

I just knew he'd eventually follow me. When the cab pulled up to my house and he never showed up I finally let myself cry about it. I cried myself to sleep.

****

"I told you to get back with him, not to do this!" Ahjanae said.

I was sitting in the middle of my bed crying from my heart. "He let you walk all the way home?" Kalani said with her mouth open.

"Break up with Anton and go apologize!" I shook my head no. "Now is not the time to be stubborn." I kept crying. "You don't love Anton!"

"Yes I do!"

Ahjanae sucked her teeth, "it's your life Kendra. You're messing up though."

"I did not ask Ahjanae for her opinion on my life!"

Ahjanae rolled her eyes. "Call me when you've come back to your senses."

"I haven't lost my senses."

"You have if you honestly think Darryl is supposed to sit back and chase you for the rest of his life. He's got feelings too." She grabbed her purse and walked out the door.

Kalani sat there with big eyes. "You guys are really fighting?"

I cried harder, "she doesn't understand." Kalani watched me wide eyed. "He doesn't want to marry me. He wants to play boyfriend and girlfriend forever. Even with that, is he faithful to me? You know about that Nellie stuff. He won't even say vows, act like I'm first, but I'm supposed to give in and give him what he wants?"

"Do you love Anton? For real?"

"I love him, I'm not in love with him."

"Don't marry him, call off this sorry excuse for an engagement. He was your rebound from Darryl. You don't marry the rebound guy."

I cried and hugged my sister.

****

I pulled up to Anton's house. That rental car was in his driveway blocking his truck in. I exhaled cause I didn't know what I was walking in on.

I could hear them fussing on the other side of the door. I put my key in fast; Megan fell on the floor trying to stand too fast. Anton looked guilty with his clothes all wrinkled.

"Kendra!" He put his hands out, "baby I can explain."

I looked at Megan, "did you have his baby?"

She looked confused, "we have a son." Then she looked at Anton like she didn't understand.

"How did you get this address?"

She turned red and looked at Anton. "Court documents. We established, child support and visitation. We've been talking over the phone for months."

I took my ring off, "you proposed to me after you knew all this didn't you?" When he didn't respond, I threw the ring at him. I went in his room; I put all my stuff in his suitcase as she screamed at him. I realized that I felt relieved.

Episode 8

Tracy

I looked at Sasha and her fiancé they looked like they got pulled into this whole setup without knowing what they were truly signing up for. Andrew kept smiling at Sasha and she kept rolling her eyes at him. Even I chuckled at Sasha a little. I understand why she's upset with Andrew I would be too. But the truth of the matter is she wouldn't be in my house of worship if she didn't care about Drew. I guess she was truly his introduction into dealing with females.

After service Joy and Anthony came over to say their hellos. We got quiet as my dad sized up Brody. It was an awkward moment, and then my dad announced that we were going out to brunch. Ignoring my dad's glare Tia asked if we were going to Berkeley. When he said yes I asked if Joy and Anthony could come. He said of course as if we should've known they were included. Andre and little Anthony high-fived. Immediately they started talking about what they were going to eat.

When we got to the hotel my dad told Brody to step outside with him. Andrew started to laugh and then my dad said he and Anthony needed to come too. Andrew chuckled and said he remembered this conversation. Tia gave me a nervous look, and I told her not to worry. I told her that dad did the same thing to Andrew when they met for the first time. That didn't take her nervous look away, but dad was only doing his job as a father. Breakfast was nice and Sasha was trying her best to continue with the cold shoulder act, but she kept slipping into conversation and then catching herself. Andrew informed Sasha that he was going back to the hotel with them. Sasha rolled her eyes but it was so obvious that she was happy he was coming. I decided to give them some space to work out their stuff so I asked my mom if I could come by. Plus it would give me a chance to get a better look at this Brody guy. It was obvious that he was quite taken with Tia, but I didn't know him. He was a friend of Sasha's man that meant nothing really to me.

Tara rode with me and she was going on and on about how FINE Yussef was. She said she had no idea that was the voice on the other end of that phone call when she and I ran away together. She said no wonder I was caught up. I laughed and told her he wasn't finer than my man, and she said that was a matter of opinion. She said Andrew was handsome, but Yussef was WOW! We laughed, I reminded her that if for some strange reason he and his girlfriend broke up they couldn't date. It would be too weird for me. She said that would be against the sister code, although he was tempting. I laughed and then I asked her about Brody. She said he was a good guy; he's even started going to service with Tia. I smiled at her and asked if he was spending the night yet. She laughed, she said she thought Tia was gonna do it and hold out, but just before they came out he was in the bathroom one morning. I laughed and told her I understood the dilemma. Tara said she was so happy Tia was getting some now though cause she was mellowing out. She was a bit stuck up there for a minute, and it's nothing like a good man laying it down to mellow you out. Tara said they were perfectly matched. And she could see them going all the way, which was good to hear. I asked Tara about her love life, and she said she was too young to be worried about it. She was still having fun and enjoying everything and everyone.

"How did it go last night? Did everyone love the cake?" My mom asked.

"Yes, people were fighting over my crumbs. It was hilarious."

"That's good," she smiled.

"Andrew and I were talking and we're going to open the bakery. His family really wants us to do it."

"Do you want to do it?" My mom watched my face.

"I'm just scared. But Andrew said this way whenever I end up pregnant we can set my own schedule." My mom rubbed my hand. "Why aren't I pregnant mom?"

She hugged me and rubbed my back. "It's not as easy as it seems to get pregnant. So many things have to happen at the right time. It took us a couple of years to get pregnant with Terrence. Don't worry about that right now. You finally get to enjoy your husband guilt free. Just enjoy him and the baby will happen when your body is ready."

I hugged her back, "thanks mom."

I sucked it up as my sisters and everyone minus my dad and Andre and little Anthony came in the living room. We entertained Brody with embarrassing stories about Tia when we were growing up. Tia was always the good girl and Tara and I were always talking her into mischief. Terrence shared how we always ganged up on him. He said he was so happy that Andrew and Andre came along, cause now he had allies whenever our dramatics started mounting up. I didn't realize my brother considered me to be a drama queen as well. He said that was one of the first conversations he had with Andrew was warning him about how dramatic I could get, but once I calmed down I was good again. I frowned at my big brother for talking against me. I told him he should've only told Andrew how sweet and loving I am. He said he did all that but he had to tell the truth too. Everyone laughed but me.

Then we went in my dad's train room. He had a room where he had his train set setup. He was letting Andre and little Anthony run the trains. He had a little train depot with people waiting for the train. A tunnel through a mountain for his train, it was definitely a room dedicated to the kid in my dad, and the boys were eating it up. They were having a blast. When I got to Joy's house to drop little Anthony off, I told her about the bakery as well. Immediately she started thinking of design concepts, logos, and business trademarks. I told her Amber suggested "Tracy's Tasty Treats" and I liked that name.

Amber

"MMMMMOOOOOOMMMMMMMMMA!" Darryl whined coming in the front door.
Malcolm shook his head looking down at his plate, "we're in here baby."
Darryl came in the kitchen and hugged me. "MOMMA! MOMMA! MOMMA! MOMMA! MOMMA!" He said rocking me in his arms with his head on my shoulder.
"What's wrong baby?" I stroked his curls.
He looked at Malcolm who looked completely annoyed. Malcolm sucked his teeth, and then he got up, put his plate in the sink, and mumbled on his way out the kitchen. "I wanna cry! I mean I really wanna cry, but no tears will come out. I think they're stuck! Help me get them unstuck momma."
"What happened baby, what's going on?"
Darryl dramatically plopped in the seat. "I need to tell you a secret." He exhaled.
"Go ahead," I waited for him to spill it.
"Don't tell nobody and I mean nobody, cause I will deny it if you ever tell momma."
"Ok," I said smiling at his dramatics.
"I'm in love momma!" He said like it pained him.
"PUNK!" Malcolm's deep voice called out from the other room.
"Malcolm? Daddy? How could you tease me right now? I'm in the thick of it." Darryl said shaking his head, "you wanna kick a brotha when he's down." He looked at the floor. "She's engaged to someone else."
"PUNK!" Malcolm called out again.
"Man! Momma can we go somewhere where he's not throwing shade on me? It's your fault I'm in this situation in the first place!" He said to Malcolm. "You wanna wait until I'm grown to say this is what love looks like. I don't want marriage behind watching you guys and then you gonna change the script on me!"
Malcolm walked back in the kitchen. "Be a man! If you want her, go get her. If not, shut up whining about it cause don't nobody want to hear all that noise."
"It's not that simple, she's engaged to someone else." Darryl said in defeat.
"She's only engaged to him because you wouldn't do it. She's not going to marry that guy. He couldn't even pay the check." Malcolm said matter of factly.
Darryl hopped out of his chair and spun around. "I'm saying! She keeps trying to act like that square is better than me though."
Malcolm cut his eyes at me, "they do that sometimes. Doesn't mean she stopped loving you. That just means he's offering her the one thing you couldn't or wouldn't."
"I'm done with her!" Darryl said sinking in his seat.
Malcolm shrugged, "suit yourself. I felt the same way about your momma at times. Give the girl some space." Then he looked at me. "Not too much space, cause women are just as goofy as men."
"What happened? You guys seemed like you were having a good time last night."
"The morning! I shouldn't have asked momma! But I had to ask momma! Momma! I'm feeling things! Momma! Oh momma! I feel..." He scratched his head, "disappointment? No, is this what rejection feels like?"
"You've been rejected before." I tried to hold back my smile.
"Not until Kendra." He shook his head like he was confused. "I am a lovable sexy guy! All the ladies love me! Then she takes me in and spits me out."
I started feeling irritated for my son. "If you put yourself on the line for her and she

rejects you, then you move on. There are other girls!"

"Amber, he's not giving you the full picture." Malcolm said trying to calm my irritation.

"Tell your momma what you did."

Darryl slouched, "what did you do?" I eyed him.

"I was young and not seeing the full picture momma. I got caught up"

"What did you do?"

Darryl put his hands out, "momma I feel the winds of change coming. I want you on my side, it's her fault. I'm your innocent favorite baby." He tried to make his face pitiful.

Malcolm folded his arms and looked at me. "Darryl?"

"Malcolm! Why you gotta be like that with your nonverbal cues? I feel like you guys are double teaming me. I don't want to have this conversation anymore." Darryl shook his head.

"Darryl!"

He put his head down, "I had smashed this girl she knew."

"DARRYL!"

"For a long time." He cringed.

"DARRYL!"

"And they used to be best friends." He cringed harder.

I smacked him upside the head. "Get out of my kitchen!" I yelled at him.

"But momma...."

I could feel my anger bubbling forward. "I did not raise you to be so disrespectful! You've got the nerve to be in my kitchen complaining about anything! I don't know how she could stomach you last night! You know my life! You know my pains! And you HAVE THE NERVE to think I should feel sympathy for you cause you feel something after doing something so horrible! Hopefully she will learn not to be a slave to her love for you." I looked at Malcolm, "someone should be able to escape this life!"

Malcolm looked at Darryl, "you boys always getting me in trouble. Amber I didn't do anything remotely that disrespectful."

"You've done enough!" I went completely off, I smack Darryl upside the head a few times for good measure, before Malcolm rescued him and took him in his office. When I finally calmed down I eavesdropped on their conversation. Malcolm asked Darryl if he still loved her, and Darryl said a defeated yes. He told him to give her a measure of space. If she loved him she wouldn't go too far away. Then he told him to stop bringing his drama to the house.

Sasha

"Let's have it out once and for all. We got so many other important things to do." Drew said to me.

"I am so hurt Drew, stop calling me twin. Just call me your cousin and distant cousin at that."

"I'm not gonna do that, you are my twin. You've always been a factor in my life. I messed up; Tracy and I's relationship has been so crazy. She and I have been fine, but there was so much going on around that."

"What could be so tumultuous that you could forget me?" I didn't believing him.

Andrew shook his Hennessy around his glass, he took a deep breath and then he told me. He told me about how crazy and jealous Toya became. Then he told me about Tracy's ex. It was literally one drama after another. Then he exhaled and said that the hardest part was dealing with the Yussef aspect of the situation. I tried not to show a physical reaction and I waited for him to tell it. I was dumbfounded, "see I told you. It's been a lot going on. I wasn't trying to purposely leave you out." Down to the night before his wedding the drama just kept going. "See! I had a lot on my plate with all the madness. It's no excuse of course, but I was emotionally exhausted at points. I still haven't explained much about us to her. She knows what she needs to know and I'm working my way up to the rest."

"I guess I can understand that. El doesn't understand the gravity of half the things he sees. But I think it's easier for me to get away with since I'm a girl you know."

"Don't I know it! You guys get away with highway robbery." Then he looked at me, "so why did you hit Sonya?"

I exhaled, "she runs her mouth too much! Nicole didn't even know that Hubby and I used to date. And she was running her mouth spouting out assumptions, but some of them were true."

His eyes pointed at me, "like?"

I took a swallow of my Hennessy, "it's in the past Drew let it go!" I waved him off.

"No, un un. It sounds like my best friend dipped his hand in the Sasha jar and I can recall threatening his life if things ever went that far."

I smiled, "you did that? That's so sweet!"

"Whatever Sasha spill it!"

"No Andrew! It's in the past, you were always swearing people to secrecy about stuff. I don't want to discuss it."

"Like who? Like what?" He said like there was nothing he held back from me.

"The fact that all those little so-called friends of mine who were only trying to befriend Tanisha and I to get closer to you. All you guys, Jeff, JoJo, Eric, EJ, YOU! You guys successfully dug out all my friends and then had the nerve to tell them not to tell me like they would ever keep that secret. They all sang like canaries, some of them were even pretty scared."

"Why?" He frowned.

"Rumor has it you're pretty hung my friend. A lot of them girls never walked the same." We laughed, "just so you know. I know about you and Tanisha."

Andrew froze with a busted look on his face, "huh?" Then he started laughing.

"Come on! Tanisha and I are sisters, no matter what's going on with her I know about it. Did you honestly think she didn't tell me? Or actually I figured it out, she had the nerve to act like she wasn't gonna tell me. I KNOW Drew!"

Drew kept laughing probably because he was in shock, "I don't know what you're talking about." He was trying to hold on to his cover.

"The first time it happened you said you were going with Hubby to the movies when you were supposed to be coming over my house. Tanisha was all of a sudden staying home after you said you weren't coming. You guys were so bashful around each other after that. But if the three of us were supposed to be doing something together and then you two came up with stupid excuses for why you couldn't but everyone still thought the three of us were together, I mean come on! Then Tanisha started getting really jealous, it's not rocket science. I confronted her about it right away. And to torture you I kept making your life difficult." Andrew started laughing, "if you were going to Gonzalez's I wanted a burrito. If you were going to the library I needed you to return my books, or check a book out for me."

Drew faked mad, "you were so wrong. Had me tearing the library apart for their one copy of that book that you already had. I haven't forgiven you for that!"

"You should've told me! But no you wanted the whole thrill of the secret."

"I really didn't. She threatened my life if I told anyone. And you know Tanisha." He looked off into the distance.

"Which is why I told you to cut it out last night talking about Toya wasn't your first. Were you trying to tell her you still love her? Why is that relevant when you're married to Tracy?"

"Tanisha was the reason we weren't together, not me. I know how her father forgetting her devastated her. I don't want her thinking that I forgot her too. I love my wife and in the end I know it's the best thing that I'm married to Tracy. I just don't want Tanisha hurting she's been through enough you know."

"I guess, but if the shoe were on the other foot, how would you respond to me saying something like that to Hubby?"

He shook his head, "I can't believe you let Hubby in! And that he actually risked his life for you." Then his face got serious, "who broke up with whom?"

I laughed, "I broke up with him. The distance was too much, we were too young."

"His devastation takes on a whole new meaning. That fool was so hurt, I think that's why he latched onto Nicole even harder than he was initially planning to."

"Is it true that he's sprung off of her?"

"Very sprung! Anyone trying to come between him and his lady gets the automatic smack down."

"Drew so that the air is completely clear... what's said here today stays between me and you right? And this is a safe space?"

He pointed his eyes at me again, "WHAT?"

"Just agree first ok!"

He grumbled then he looked at me, "what Sasha?"

"I'm over it now, but I feel like I should tell you. El already knows, he knows about everything we've talked about."

"So I'm the last to know about everything? Spill it Sasha!"

"Would you like another round?" The bartender asked.

"YES! And can you make both of them doubles, pronto!"

"What Sasha?" He said not taking his eyes off of me.

"Hold on! Hold on!" I said stalling until our drinks came. "Thank you and we'll take another, singles this time." I said taking our drinks from the bartender. "Drink Drew!"

"I'm not thirsty!" He stared....

"I don't speak until you've drinken...." I taunted. He took the double straight to the head then he looked at me. I took a swallow of my drink. "I was kind of a little bit in love with Yussef!" I braced myself.

"SASHA! YOU TOO???? What is it about that Fool! Got all ya'll females tripping! You slept with him too?"

I was embarrassed people in the bar were looking at us. I spoke through clinched teeth, "if you don't sit down and stop putting my business out there for everybody!" Drew sat down but he was mad, "I did not sleep with him. Although I would have loved to, he wouldn't let me get to him beyond my kissing ambushes. I tried, believe me I did. He wouldn't do it."

"Sasha!"

"I'm just telling you the truth. I didn't know about Tracy, but I understand the temptation. Knowing him like I do though, if he could walk away from me. I know he wasn't trying to steal your woman."

"Please explain this to me, cause I don't get it. What's great about him?"

"He's a gentleman, and there aren't very many of those today. He tells you the truth without hurling it at you. When you're with him you have his undivided attention. He makes you feel like you're the only person in the world that matters in that moment. And the fact that he doesn't push the limits when everyone else does... Absolute turn on! Add to it that he's FINE! He could've had me any way he wanted me and he wouldn't do it. Then out of his love and respect for you. From the sounds of it, he was a better friend to you than you were to him."

Drew exhaled, my comment wounded him. "I didn't.... I was drunk! I know that's no excuse, but my momma and Malcolm had just had that blow out. All of us thought that was it! I heard him call her his wife, we leave with you and JoJo and then everything stood on its head. I apologized and he didn't bring it up again, I still feel like dirt about it.

And I didn't know he was family!"

"Like that should matter!"

He sunk in his chair, "I know!" He stared out the window. "I have never loved anyone like I do Tracy! I imagine this is how he felt about that girl. Or maybe there was something going on in the back of his mind, cause they were together a long time before I met her. I know if the shoe were on the other foot, feeling like I do, he'd be dead!" He said with a cold look on his face.

We were quiet for a few minutes. Then Tina rounded the corner, she was with a guy. She stopped in her tracks when she saw Drew. I forgot she was coming. She shot me a look and then she grabbed the guy's hand and came to us. "Um, why is Drew here?"

"We needed to talk." I was starting to feel my drink a little bit.

"Who is this?" Drew said standing up and looking the guy up and down.

"Drew, calm down. This is my boyfriend Luke. Luke these are my cousins Sasha and Drew." Tina said dismissively.

I could tell by Drew's demeanor that we were on the same page. I didn't like him either and he hadn't even said hello. Luke was tall like Andrew but not as solid. He was a little lighter skinned than Drew. He was cute in his own right, but a bad boy. He looked like he didn't respect limits, and I saw meanness in his eyes. He had a childlike kind of look to him too, but I could tell he played on that. I didn't understand what Tina was doing with this clown. "Does your daddy know about him?" Drew said snapping a picture so fast I didn't even see him pick up his phone.

"Wait a minute! I don't like having my picture taken!" He said with his temper flaring.

"I don't like you so we're even." Drew said like he didn't care.

"Drew, you don't even know him!"

"Don't need to, and you need to get rid of him before he starts going upside your head." Drew sent the picture off. "Luke what? What's your last name?"

He smirked, "for you I don't have one. Just call me Luke."

Drew was mad, he walked away.

"Why would you have him here? You know how they act!" Tina said annoyed with Drew.

"What makes you think I would act any different?" I said cutting my eyes at Luke.

"Excuse you, can I have my clothes back!" This fool had the nerve to be drooling. I could feel his hands all over me through his eyes and I was immediately pissed. This fool was so disrespectful!

"Tina you come from GOOD genes!" He said still looking me up and down.

"Tina!" I said.

"Hold on! Hold on! Luke stop playing! Sasha thinks you're serious." She grabbed my arm cause I was leaving.

He chuckled. "I was just playing, all jokes aside Tina talks about you all the time. It's nice to finally meet you."

I looked at Tina, "you know there's truth in a person's joke. I don't like him, I don't trust him, dump him!"

"Oh come on Miss Sasha, I'm not that bad."

Drew came back looking at his phone. "So Luke Brown, you just appeared out of thin air huh?"

He frowned, "how did you find me?"

"Don't worry about that. You're on my radar now. I'll know your whole life story by end of day tomorrow. You might want to duck out now while you still have a chance to get away."

"See! This is exactly why I never bring anyone home to you guys. Look at how you act!"

"And I'm telling your daddy!" Drew smiled at her.

"WHY?" Tina spun around like the true brat she is.

"Why does that matter? You're a grown woman!" Luke said.

"Who still lives at home with her parents; but that's beside the point. Anyone around anyone in our family is a family affair."

Luke laughed, "ain't nobody scared of you fool! You obviously don't know who you're dealing with. I don't play!"

Drew looked at Tina, "this is what happens when you don't know who you are. You need to go home and have a long talk with your dad. Matter of fact, when Tracy picks us up, we'll talk to him together.

"I'm leaving with Luke!" She tried to say with attitude.

Drew walked in her face, "Tina you are leaving with me. Send this little punk on his merry little way or I'll do it for you. You won't like what happens to him. And so help me if you run from me it will suck to be you!"

Tina looked at me wide eyed like she didn't know if he was for real or not. When I assured her that he was, she huffed and told Luke she'd walk him out.

When she came back no matter how we tried to explain it to her, Tina wasn't getting it. All she could see is that we were controlling her. When Tracy came I walked them out of the hotel to the car. I said bye to Tracy and Andre, then I told Drew to call me when he got home.

I went up to our room and El said his parents made it home. Their flight left early this morning. I asked him if Ava and Nathan had come up for air yet and he said he hadn't heard anything from them. When he kissed me he asked me how much I had to drink down at the bar. I told him I needed a double before I told Drew about Yussef. He smiled; he asked how he took it. I told him he took it a lot better than I thought he would.

That night Drew called me; he said Uncle Timothy hit the roof! Drew said he had to calm down so that he didn't encourage Uncle Timothy to keep going off like he was. He said he could tell Tina nor Grace had ever seen him like that. He said Uncle wants a full detail on Tina now. She has no idea what has just happened to her world.

****

Ok, that same car has been following us all day. I don't know if El has noticed, but it's starting to bug me. El pulled into a parking space in the garage and Tara pulled up next to us. I looked at the mystery car as it looked for a spot to park. I could see that the driver was chocolate and bald, grey shirt, and a silver watch. I smiled at El, and then I casually encouraged our group to walk on before he got out of his car.

We stood on Fisherman's Wharf trying to decide where to have dinner for our last night in The Bay. El and I met with Carina and Tanisha earlier to give them our wish list of things we would like for our wedding venue. I asked Tanisha if she was ok, I know seeing her father this weekend rocked her to the core. She said she was, but she was trying her best to appear to be unfazed. I know her better than that. I could see the guy crossing the street as Tia said that the restaurant in front of us looked promising. As everyone started in I told El I would be right in, I wanted to ask the host about their wine list. He wasn't completely buying my excuse but he said ok. I stood over to the side and I watched the chocolate drop walk inside analyzing my group. He didn't see me so I stepped to him from behind. "Why are you following us?"

He smiled, and then he held up a badge. "Detective Turan!" He revealed pretty, straight, pearly whites.

"So! Doesn't explain why you're following us."

"Your family has been under observation for some years now, surely you know that?" He said letting his eyes dance all over me.

"Still doesn't explain why you're following us."

"Not them, just you." Then he put his hands in his pockets. "When will you be back in town? I think I'll need to bring you in for questioning."

His eyes said he wants me, "questioning for what?"

"Questions about your family. Or maybe I'll come out your way to do that."

"You don't care about what my family does. You're obsessed with Amber."

"And now you, Zoey, Erica, Lanie, and Tina, your family does have some gorgeous women."

"Why wouldn't you protect us instead of harass us?"

"I've protected you to a point. See I don't like Malcolm, so I can't work in harmony with his endeavors. As soon as he's out the way…." He smiled, "well I was going to step to Amber. I think Tina might be the most willing. Especially since she's the most clueless one in your bunch. She wants a bad boy so bad that she's not even falling for a good one. I've protected her plenty; she's so clueless she doesn't see it. Now that I'm standing here talking to you. I don't know who I'd pick."

"You're delusional!"

"Does the name Phineas Cobb ring any bells?"

The upstate New York conference room for the temping agency that Mitigated acquired some years ago flashed across my mind. Phineas was upset when Malcolm told them that he was in charge and then shortly after that, that building went up in flames. "Vaguely, what about him?"

Detective Turan smiled again, "he's waging an all-out war with Malcolm. Malcolm's been doing a good job of keeping their little tiff from you guys. All of you are about to feel the boom!"

"Who are you?" El said walking up on us.

"Detective Turan, you're the little fiancé right?"

"Little?" El looked him up and down.

"Official police business, step back." He said holding his badge out.

"So! That's my wife!" El put me behind him.

"You're not married yet!"

"As far as you know!"

El was angry that I went out there to talk to the Detective alone. He told me to never do that again. At dinner I was texting Richard like crazy telling him everything that happened. I wasn't going to go home, but he reminded me that Chantel was coming in a few days to stay with me, so I needed to be there at least for that.

Chantel

"I'm so sorry! I didn't realize you're marrying Amber's son. I didn't put it all together. I hope I didn't cause too much trouble." Alexa said.

"Gurl naw! I think everyone was surprised."

"He stayed upset the rest of the night, and all day Sunday. I had to leave him in the hotel this morning cause he hasn't calmed down." Her eyes moved around the room. "At least now I know what the deal is with him."

"What do you mean?"

"He's still in love with her. I thought it was his ex-wife, but I stand corrected."

"What does that mean for you guys?"

"I don't know. He's a lot older than me anyways. Maybe we go our separate ways. He doesn't want any more kids and I want children of my own. Besides his girls don't like me, so…" She exhaled, "I guess this is the end of the road for us. Kind of sucks cause I really did like him."

"Maybe you guys will get past it and have a happily ever after."

"I don't know, let's get back to business." She took out the song she wrote for me. She played it on Derrick's piano, it was really pretty.

I asked her why she didn't want to keep it for herself, and she said when she wrote it she always heard my voice in her head. I was honored; we practiced the song over and over again. Brandy and Sherrell came around trying to give us space, but they were being nosey. We went in the home studio and recorded our practice. I called Cyrus and we went over scheduling for studio time, etc. I was going to be in LA in a few days for a week. I was cramming to get everything in before the wedding. Now that the party is over, Carina is coming over so that we could block off time for my wedding, delivery, and bonding time with the baby. But that means that I'm going to be cramming interview after interview in. I've got a few songs coming up in soundtracks that I'm going to have to skip the premieres for. I just can't burn the candle at both ends anymore. My doctor and Derrick have been on me about getting my rest. Derrick has even arranged his schedule a few times to come with me and make sure I'm taking it easy and that Bruce has my security on point. Although Derrick doesn't say anything, I get the impression that the coast isn't exactly clear. That's nerve-racking cause I didn't sign up for haters coming out of the wood works left and right.

Yussef knocked on the door, his eyes looked sad. I didn't ask him what was going on. Alexa cleared her throat as Yussef was getting ready to walk away and I hadn't introduced her. I introduced them, Yussef dropped by looking for Derrick. As soon as Yussef left the room Alexa started drilling me with questions. I smiled and told her he was family and had a girlfriend. Then I teased her saying her relationship wasn't even cold and she was moving on. She smiled really big.

Tracy

"Andrew is so wrong for keeping you from us. What he think we were gonna do? Corrupt you?" Pearla said

"I don't know, I think the timing and drama kept us in our own world." I said in my husband's defense.

"Ok so cousin it's important that you remember me. I'm Pearla, and the most important cousin in the Latour family." Then she laughed, "self-proclaimed anyways."

In a lot of ways Pearla reminded me of Darryl. You could tell they were family. I told Pearla and Sherrell to come to my office in business casual clothes and then I could put us in a conference room. I liked the way Sherrell conducted business. She said Chantel wasn't too picky about the design as long as it looked professional. So she said she and Pearla came up with some ideas of their own. They said music was a big part of Derrick and Chantel's relationship. Pearla started telling us stories about how Derrick has always been musically inclined and all the music recitals they would go to at The Center in Richmond the school that Amber collaborates her dance school with. So we decided on white fondant with a black fondant sash like band around each layer with silver music notes and red flowers. Sherrell sketched out my thoughts perfectly. Then we threw around flavor ideas. I suggested that they come over for a cake tasting. I wanted them to taste my idea for a peach Bellini cake. Champagne cake with a peach Bellini filling and champagne icing. And a red and black marble cake with a caramel custard filling. And finally a white cake with a raspberry cream filling. When we were done Sherrell asked if I wanted to have lunch with them. As we walked out of the conference room Neil was hovering over my cube. I introduced him, and then Pearla invited him to lunch with us. Sherrell and I exchanged goofy looks. Lunch was interesting; Pearla and Neil had a blast.

When I got home Andrew and Andre were waiting for me in the driveway. Andre excitedly waved a scarf around as he told me we were going on a surprise trip. I looked at the scarf and asked Andrew if I could close my eyes and I promised not to peek. He said no because we both knew I was lying. I told him he better not let me fall. He knows how clumsy I am. So of course I banged my leg getting in Andrew's stupid car. He laughed at me and said *oops*! I wanted to smack him, but I couldn't see him. Andre excitedly rambled on and on. We were only in the car for a couple minutes. I could hear footsteps moving around me. And excited breaths, Andrew let my arm go and a stronger hand guided me and positioned me. Then they put their hands on the blindfold. My heart was pounding; I guess Andrew wanted to show me something. When the blindfold was removed I was standing next to Malcolm who actually had a smile on his face. Everyone said "*SURPRISE*!" Pointing towards an office space. My mom and dad were there, my cousin Marie, Terence and Amy, Joy and Anthony, Veronica and little Anthony, Amber and Darryl, Derrick and Uncle Frank, Yussef and his girls, and Pearla and Sherrell and her little girl. They said if I liked it the space was mine. As discussed it was office space in the Rockridge Shopping center. The office space was on the bottom level and easily accessible from the parking lot and people walking by. My store would be one of the first stores you'd see when you enter the shopping center. I loved it! I threw my arms around Malcolm and as usual he froze in place. I said a huge thank you while everyone laughed at us. Carina walked up with Jeff and his wife Randi. Carina pointed out her office space that was still under construction a few spaces over. Then Uncle Frank invited us to have dinner at his restaurant on the other side of the lot. I excitedly grabbed Andrew's hand I couldn't believe everything was coming together. I asked Andrew why we had never been here, especially since it was so close to the house. He shrugged and changed the subject. Then the thought occurred to me to ask who owned this property. Uncle Frank said they would explain everything when we met. Even though he was smiling I kind of got a sinking feeling. As if he could read my mind Yussef told me to relax from across the table. When I looked embarrassed he got Andrew's attention and pointed at me. Andrew asked me what was wrong, and I said nothing. Then Yussef told him to ask me again later. Andrew looked a little annoyed. Amber asked Yussef when he was going to sign his girls up for classes at her school. I thanked her with my eyes for changing the subject. When we got home Andrew went to Andre's room. Andre showered and then Andrew tucked him in. I was trying to wrap my mind around my feelings to express them properly.

Andrew asked me what was wrong. I told him that there was so much about his family that I didn't understand. Like who is Uncle Frank, who is Malcolm. I touched his arm tenderly as I reminded him that he still hadn't shared with me about his stepfather. I told him his family feels like I was kept away from them. He point blankly said that I was kept separate from everyone. I asked him why and he said I'm too sensitive to handle everything. I frowned at him, then I figured now was as good a time as any. "So the other night Sonya," he rolled his eyes. "She said something about you and Yussef fighting over a girl."

"You mean you?" He snapped, "I don't like that he thinks he knows you better than I do."

"I think she meant before me."

He exhaled, "Yussef's girl was checking for me. When he found out about it he kicked her to the curb. Yussef and I talked it out. It's done! She runs her mouth too much! That's why I was never interested."

"What do you mean?"

"Nicole tried to hook me up with her, but I was insulted. That girl's mouth don't quit."

"What? When was this? Where was I? Why would she bring Sonya to you over me?"

"I DON'T KNOW! Imagine how much sooner we could've started and been happy if Nicole wouldn't have held back the good stuff!" He halfway smiled.

Then I started laughing, "I don't think I would've been ready for the Beast any sooner than he showed up though. I might've ran from you."

"That's ok, I would've chased you." Then he put his arms around me. "I love you!"

"I love you daddy!" I kissed his cheek.

He growled in my ear, "call me daddy one more time!"

I smiled, "yes daddy!"

****

"There you have it. You have any more questions?" Malcolm said dryly.

"This plan is amazing! Do you really project earnings like this in my first year?"

"Yes! You will provide the desserts for North Star's charity and Investor functions, for Sophia's in Walnut Creek, and once she expands back to Piedmont, that location as well, Shylight, the list goes on and on. The Meridian Marketing Company is going to handle your promotions. This firm has handled the marketing for so many of my endeavors, with this firm alone you're guaranteed to have a name out there for yourself. These projections are on the low end of the pool, I see you going much bigger. You should figure out whom you want on your staff and figure out how you're going to allocate your salary budget for them. For the first year, let's see how you do with the two locations. Next year let's talk about expanding."

My eyes watered up, "Malcolm do you really think I can do all this?"

He looked annoyed, "why are you looking like you're going to cry?"

"This is all very overwhelming and happening so fast. I can't believe you can see all of this happening for me, and then you're making it happen." Tears started trickling out of my eyes.

"I still don't see why that's a reason to cry. All of this is based upon how you perform. I have no tolerance for lazy and useless people. Fortunately neither of my sons have picked women like that and I'm proud. You gotta stop crying, I hate that!" He sounded like my tears weakened him.

That only made me cry harder, "I'm sorry! I guess all of this means you really do like me. Amber said you did, but I thought she was being nice. I didn't think you did." Malcolm rolled his eyes and looked at the ceiling. "I'm so relieved that you do."

"Are you pregnant or something? Why all the water works?"

"Not that I know of," I said trying to pull back my tears that were forcing their way to erupt. "I'm sorry for making you uncomfortable, it means a lot to me that you think so highly of me."

He sat back in his chair, "the sooner we get you out of here the better. Do you even know who your new assistant is?"

I frowned, "what's wrong with Neil?"

"I don't know him, but his father is very slimy. The sooner you get away from his son the better."

"He doesn't even like his dad." I said in his defense.

Malcolm's cold eyes stared at me. "It's stuff like that. Why would he share something so personal with a stranger? You were with Drew for how long before he said anything about me?"

"Well over a year."

"Right! Over a year, think about it Tracy. There are games going on all around you. You gotta pay more attention, otherwise someone will try to use you as a pawn in their game. Prepare your resignation letter. The plans are almost approved for the construction on your space."

"When do you think I should quit?"

"If it were up to me I'd tell you to do it today. But discuss it with Drew. I'm gonna tell him about your little assistant."

"Is his father really that bad?"

"I don't like him, but I don't like too many people so...."

Then I smiled real big, "but you like me."

"Bye Tracy!" He stood up. "Before I forget, when are you gonna make another pot roast?"

I smiled, "you liked that?"

"Maybe," he said picking up his papers to put them in his briefcase.

"Did you like that Caramel Rum cake?"

"Yes, it was very good. However, when are you going to make a pineapple upside down cake?"

"I guess the same day I make a pot roast. I was thinking about making that on Saturday. Do you and Amber have plans?"

"I'll have to check, Amber gets back Friday night. Tell Drew to call me." Then he walked out the door of the conference room.

I smiled all the way back to my cubical. Danielle came in and asked who Malcolm was, she was whispering while she foamed at the mouth. I told her that was my father in-law. She plopped down in my extra chair in my cubical, and asked how that was possible. I told her he was a young dad, and she agreed he had to be a baby.

That night I told Andrew about my visit with Malcolm. He made me tell him about Malcolm's reaction to my tears twice as he cracked up laughing. I didn't get why that was so funny but apparently it was a knee slapper to Andrew and Andre followed suit. I looked at Eve and she blank stared back at them with me. I changed the subject by asking if Andrew had plans on Saturday. He said the normal business rounds in the morning and then he was free in the afternoon. I asked him if he thought it was a good idea to have his parents over. He said as long as I felt up to it. I told him to tell his father that we were on board and to make sure they were. Andrew said ok and then he smacked my butt, then he stopped in his tracks and looked at my butt. I thought something was on my dress. He smiled and told Andre we'd be right back. He gave me a devilish grin as he led me up the stairs not answering me as I asked him what was up. The door barely closed when he said he had to have me! I was caught off guard and loving every moment of it. Afterwards, he told me I should take a test. I told him that would be a waste cause I just had my period two weeks ago. "Woman! Just do it! What's it to you if you waste a test to appease me?" I huffed cause it was a stupid waste of a test in my opinion. Andrew stood there watching me pee on the stick, no privacy. I put the cover on it and handed it to him. As I washed my hands his smile got big. "What?" I said feeling stuck.

"I'm so good I amaze myself! Congratulations baby! You're gonna be a mommy!" He said holding the positive test for me to see. I screamed and ran in the bedroom. Andrew couldn't breathe he was laughing so hard. "Who are you running from? Where are you running to?"

My heart was pounding, "I don't know! I don't know! What should we do?" I asked feeling panicked.

Andrew couldn't stop laughing. Andre knocked on the door, "I heard mommy scream, is it a spider?"

Andrew opened the door still laughing, "you're mommy is so silly. She's ok."

Andre looked around the room, "why did she scream?"

"Go ahead and finish your dinner, we'll be down to talk to you in a minute."

"Ok," Andre said looking his dad up and down.

My heart wouldn't stop pounding. "What if I took it wrong? What if that test is defective? Before I get excited I want to be sure. I mean I just had a period two weeks ago."

"Was it normal?"

"Now that I think about it, it was lighter than usual. And it was over faster than normal. I was so disappointed that it came that I stopped taking notes." My heart started pounding again, "I want a blood test before we tell people."

Andrew groaned, "every time my momma was pregnant it had to be this big ole secret. Do you know what kind of torture that is on a kid? Imagine Andre having to keep a secret that big!"

"I don't think he can."

"Right, and he shouldn't have to. When can you get the blood test?"

"I can probably get one in the morning before work. And then I should have the results no later than the following day."

"It seems pretty silly if this test taken in the evening says you are." He shook his head.

"It serves dual purpose, I can get confirmation and then my doctor will have proof."

Excitement hit my stomach like lightning. "Why did you make me take the test?"

Andrew laughed, "your butt got bigger. I wasn't gonna say anything if you weren't cause you'd start throwing away the ice cream I just bought, etc." He laughed.

I turned to look at my butt, "it did?"

"Not by much, but I know your body. Let's go tell Andre, and I don't think this needs to be a secret. You are and we're happy."

"Andrew! I'm gonna give birth!" I lost my air, "things just got real. I'm going to be even more emotional than now? I don't want to live with me through that!" I laughed, but Andrew laughed harder, which made me stop laughing.

We sat Andre down on the couch, and I expected Andrew to go into this whole speech about how much we loved him and our family was going to increase. "Andre, you're going to be a big brother." Andrew said with a smile.

"I already am." Andre said matter of factly.

"Yes, but now Tracy's going to have a baby."

Andre's face lit up, "really? I get to have a baby that will live with me and not go home?"

"Yep!"

"Thank you mommy!" Andre said giving me a big hug. I started crying again.

****

"Why are we making a cake in the pan?" Andre asked.

"This is a cast iron skillet. We're going to caramelize the pineapples in here and set them the way we want them to sit on the cake." Andre was taking everything I said in and dedicating it to memory. "Then we're going to pour the cake batter over it and bake it in the oven. The caramelized butter and sugar mixed with the pineapple sauce is going to create a tasty coating. An icing of sorts. Got it?"

"Got it!" Andre stood on the stool helping me. "Mommy are you scared?"

"Of what baby?"

"Of the baby coming out. Titus said when his mommy had his little brother she screamed so loud cause it hurt so bad. I don't want you to do it if it's going to hurt you."

I smiled and I gave him a hug. Andre's eyes were completely concerned for me and what I was going to go through. "I'm a little nervous, but I wouldn't change it for anything in the world. You were a little baby when your daddy and I got together. This pregnancy is the only part of the motherhood experience I haven't had. Don't worry about it baby, we're going to have a little baby who looks and acts just like you. Do you think your Nana and Poppa will be surprised?"

"Yes! They can't wait for you to have a baby."

"How do you know?"

"I hear Nana saying it to Auntie Sophia all the time. She says she has a grandson, and a baby on the way from Uncle D-Rick, and then whenever you have a baby and she still gets to look young. Mommy how old is Nana?"

"I don't know exactly." I said not wanting to do the math and then admit that I knew. But it wasn't hard to figure out. She's only fifteen years older than Andrew.

"Kids at school always think she's my mommy. But then their mommy's look older than my Nana."

"Your Nana looks very good! If I didn't know for a fact that she was your Nana I would think she was your mommy too."

"Does that mean when I'm a Poppa I will look like the daddy?"

"Possibly. Your parents are very good looking people, you had no choice but to be irresistibly handsome." Then I tickled his side.

Andre laughed then he got quiet, "do you think she thinks about me?"
"Who Toya?"
"Yea."
"Of course she does baby. I didn't give birth to you and I think about you nonstop."
"Why doesn't she write me letters? Or do anything that says she's thinking about me."
My heart burned, "I don't know baby. Maybe she's afraid that you will be mad at her."
Tears came to my eyes immediately.
Andrew came around the corner and the look on his face said he was listening to our
conversation, I just don't know how much he heard. "What's up Dre?"
Andre tried to suck up his mood change. "Do you think she thinks about me?"
"Of course she does, you're her son."
"Why doesn't she write me letters?"
"Maybe she doesn't know what to say to you. When Poppa was in jail he didn't write me
letters either."
Andre and I's eyes got big, "Poppa was in jail?" Andre asked and I stood there waiting for
his answer.
Andrew exhaled, "yep. I was about your age when he got out. Poppa thought about me all
the time, and he made plans for me for when he got out. He took me to a football game,
the movies, it wasn't all the time but he did it when he could. I highly doubt your mother
is going to get out. But if she ever does, she's going to want to see you."
Andre's face lit up, "she is?"
I started crying, I wished Andrew wouldn't build his hopes up like that. She wasn't
concerned with him before she went in. Why would she come out this changed person?
"Yep, meanwhile you got a mommy and a daddy who love you very much and we always
want you with us. Does mommy go anywhere without you?"
"Nope, she always asks me to go to the store with her."
"Right and anywhere else." Then he put his hand up to his mouth like he was whispering,
"except when she does girlie stuff with her family and friends. We don't want anything to
do with that no how. Right?"
Andre laughed, "right!"
"Ok, hit the switch." I told Andre for the mixer.
When we put the cake in the oven Andre ran upstairs to get his art supplies. When I could
hear him bumping around up there I looked at Andrew who was waiting for me to say
what was on my mind. "I don't think you should build his expectations that Toya will
want to see him if she ever gets out. He'll be devastated if she gets out and doesn't come
for him."
"If she ever gets out she will come for Andre." He was so sure of himself.
"How do you know?"
"She'll come out looking for me, and the only way to see me is to see her son."
I didn't like the thought of that, but he was telling the truth. "Why was Malcolm in jail?"
Andrew cut his eyes at me. "I can't do this right now," he said like the thought of it took
him somewhere he was trying not to go.
Amber and Malcolm came during the last thirty minutes of the timer for the roast. Amber
was quieter than normal, and well Malcolm was always quiet unless you got him talking
about something good. Andrew kept looking at his mom like he was reading her. Andre
came in the room so excited, "Can I tell them now?"
"Go ahead son," Andrew put his arm around me as I snuggled into him on the couch.
"We're going to have a baby!" Andre said so excited.
Malcolm smiled for the third or fourth time ever, and Amber jumped up excited like she
just got a second wind. "You are! I didn't know you were married Andre!" She smiled at
him.
Andre giggled, "no our family is going to have a baby." He said blushing.

"CONGRATULATIONS!" Amber gave us both hugs.

"Congratulations!" Malcolm said from his seat.

"Seriously Malcolm? Get up and give your son a hug!"

"Amber, he doesn't want me to hug him." He said returning to his normal stern face.

"Actually daddy," Andrew tried to make his voice sound little and small. "I do!" Then he smiled.

Malcolm sighed, "you've spent too much time with your mother!" Malcolm grumbled as he got up and walked over to Andrew who was now standing with his arms extended. "Congratulations!" Malcolm said like he was forced.

"What about me? I want one!" I said as I stood up, "I mean since you're passing them out. This may be my only chance to get one."

Malcolm hugged me and kissed my forehead, "congratulations!"

"Hey! How come she gets a kiss and I didn't?" Andrew teased.

Malcolm pointed his eyes at Andrew, "I'm not going to kiss you!" Then he gave Andre a congratulatory hug.

That night as we laid in the dark having our normal pillow talk, Andrew told me a story. He told me about how men came to kill him and his mother, but they happened to not follow their routine that night so they weren't home. He said Malcolm went to jail, for involuntary manslaughter. He served time because he wouldn't tell the court who helped him. My heart was pounding as Andrew told me the story. I held on to him as he spoke. He said he knows Toya isn't right, but the fact that she was upset about Andre calling me mommy means she cares even if it's only a little bit.

Chantel

"I think you're going to love this idea." Carina smiled really big taking her laptop out "This hotel is on the cliff of an ocean beach. It's available within your block of time, we need to book it now though if you're interested." She brought up the website and I melted. The pictures were completely romantic; there was a white gazebo and white chairs and runners. The pictures all highlighted ceremonies by sunset, and that's what I wanted. Derrick came in the room at the tail end of my excitement. I told him we had to get married in Half Moon Bay by the water. We had to do it! Derrick liked my enthusiasm but he was still analyzing everything. He had concerns about securing the site. After I whined for ten seconds (the maximum whine he could stand without snapping) he exhaled and told Carina to book it. I got excited and hugged him. Carina said we were limited to three hundred guests with this venue. Her fingers glided lightning fast over the keyboard. Her phone rang and she answered in a very business tone. "This is Carina... Yes... We want the date......... we want the block of rooms...........
Yes.............. This will be a celebrity event so we will need non-disclosure commitments from your entire staff before we will commit to the location...." I liked listening to her handle her business. I felt like we were being handled the way we should. When Carina asked about budget again, Derrick sighed, they went over numbers. I told Derrick I could pitch in and he told me the money wasn't the issue. Carina told me I was going to need a guest list and wedding party list as soon as possible. Since I didn't have time to worry about the bridesmaids dresses we went to Cassondra's website and I picked four styles of black dresses that I liked. Our wedding colors are going to be Black, Red, and Silver. And I told her I'd prefer a burgundy whenever possible rather than a vague red.

That night as I packed my bags Derrick and I went back and forth about the wedding party. He took a deep breath and he called his father on speaker. "Derrick" Malcolm said as he answered the phone.

I expected this grand emotional conversation where Derrick explained how much

Malcolm has meant to him, and that they'd get really emotional. Instead, "Malcolm will you be my best man?" Derrick said matter of factly.

"You sure you don't want Drew or EJ?"

"I'm sure."

"Ok."

"Alright talk to you later." Then Derrick hung up satisfied with himself.

I blank stared at him. "THAT'S it?"

"Yea," Derrick said like he didn't understand what the issue was.

I told him to watch the difference. I dialed Sherrell, when she picked up I asked her to hold and then I conferenced Pearla on the line. I could feel the emotion as I tried to pull it back. Through tears I said, "I love you guys so much! Both of you are the closest things to sisters that I have. I can't pick one over the other I need you both as my matron and maid of honor." I sobbed.

Sherrell and Pearla gave way to tears and we cried over the phone together. I told them I'd give Carina their phone numbers to be my point people for all questions. We cried a little longer, and then we got off the phone. As I pulled myself together Derrick stood there in disbelief. He said he had to try it, he needed an emotional male.

He dialed the number and put it on speaker. "D-Rick!"

"Drew!"

"What's up?"

Then he mimicked my tone, "I just wanted to tell you how much you mean to me." Drew said nothing. "You've been the best big brother a guy could ever have!"

"What?"

"I love you, and I need a second best man cause Chantel is having two."

"Man! I don't have time for this Tracy is waiting for me to lay it down. I just got married ask Darryl; he'll be too juiced! I'm out!"

Derrick started laughing, "I knew you'd say that. Don't say I didn't ask. Later!" Then he dialed Darryl. "Be my second best man!" No hello hi or anything.

"Who's the first?"

"Malcolm of course."

"Alright! Later!"

"Later!" Derrick looked at me. "Ya'll females be too emotional."

****

I liked the way this outfit felt. It was soft and flowing. It was definitely a maternity dress but it didn't look like one. Leslie was going on and on about how fortunate I was that I hadn't turned ugly yet. As if my pregnancy was going to turn me into a creature. When Leslie turned me to face the mirror, I clapped to show my appreciation. Cyrus told him he did excellent work. As Cyrus and I walked down the hallway, I told him about my master plan with our father. He laughed and wished me luck. I swallowed hard when we walked into the studio and Gerard was my photographer. As usual his eyes went all over my body. Cyrus looked at my expression and instantly started frowning. Gerard came in for a hug, so I gave him a church hug back. He said it was so good to see me, and then he looked at my hand. His face and demeanor changed, "you're engaged?"

I laughed a nervous laugh; "I guess you don't follow my interviews then."

Then he started looking around, "where's your other assistant?"

"What do you need?" Cyrus asked him in an annoyed tone.

Gerard was thinking for a minute. "Caprice! Yea, that's her name where is she?"

"She was fired a long time ago." I said not wanting to get into it.

"Fired?" Gerard frowned.

"Can we get to the photo-shoot?" Cyrus said, "we've got a schedule to keep."

"I guess I'll call her later." Gerard said in defeat.

I looked at Cyrus and he was trying to keep a straight face, but I could tell hearing

Caprice's name bothered him. Gerard did his photography thing, but I could tell he was bothered too. I had no idea that he and Caprice ever talked outside of little conversations during my appointments. Derrick said she steered me towards him and I guess it had to be true if he said it. I guess he wasn't woven too deeply in the whole scheme of things cause he's still here. I stopped asking questions anymore, there were people who were a part of my team that suddenly no longer were when all that drama happened before.

At the end of my shoot Gerard said that pregnancy suited me and he was happy for me. I didn't know how much of that was actually true but I thanked him anyways. He didn't seem too happy for me. I had an interview directly after the shoot, I changed clothes and then we hurried over. They had these people from baby magazines, etc. there as well. All of them wanted me to endorse their maternity lines and products. Some of them sounded really good to me, but I pointed them all to Cyrus. He took all their information and he told them we'd call them back in a few hours. We made our way to Sasha's house in the HOT L.A. sun and traffic. El buzzed us in and greeted us at the door. He said the dining room was setup for us. I was thankful for the tons of water, fruit, veggie platter, and sandwiches. I didn't realize I was as hungry as I was until I saw the food. Cyrus dialed the conference line while I ran to the bathroom and then when I came back I took a huge bite of my sandwich. One thing about pregnancy I was always thirsty and food never tasted SO GOOD! The radio station came on to confirm I was on the line before the on the air interview started. Fortunately the interview was brief, but I had to do the same thing for the sister stations across the states. Fortunately they went smoothly as well. After the interviews where I would've been done for the day, now we had those companies from earlier. I stuffed my face with my sandwich while Cyrus did most of the talking. One company wanted to meet with me tonight for a photo shoot in their maternity clothes. Cyrus said no and would not budge. He told them I needed some rest and today had already gone longer than anticipated. I smiled at my big brother; he's always taken such good care of me.

Sasha came home while we were on the phone. She peeked her head in the dining room and then she went upstairs with El. Now that my schedule was completely rearranged I watched Cyrus put everything together while I sucked on pineapples and strawberries. He was looking at contract proposals and sending them for legal review and approval before having me look at them and provide electronic signatures. When Cyrus said my part was done as he continued to work on his computer I snuck away. I went upstairs to my usual room and I laid on the bed with the door open. I was just about to fall asleep when I realized Sasha was in the doorway. I didn't hear her coming so she halfway scared me. She apologized for scaring me, but she had an interesting look on her face. I patted the bed and told her to come. She was looking like Derrick does when he's trying to choose his words. She exhaled and then she asked me why I would have Alexa come to the engagement party when I knew she was dating Dwayne? I told her I didn't know she was dating him, and Alexa said she didn't realize that I was marrying Amber's son. I explained how the whole thing was a misunderstanding. Sasha was really upset about it, but she said it was over and she wanted to talk to me directly about it. I told her that Alexa and Dwayne broke up so Alexa would be at my wedding. We talked about that night and how crazy it was. I asked her why she hit Sonya, and Sasha got mad all over again. It was kind of funny watching her temper rage like it did. She said that girl was running her mouth, and she better be happy she only hit her once.

She brought in her laptop and I showed her my venue for Derrick and I's wedding. She said it was beautiful and she wished she would've found that place first. She said she's getting married in The Bay as well. I told her she had to stay with Derrick and I when she comes out. She said that she'd have to split her time between my house and Drew's. I asked her what she thought of Tracy's cake. Sasha gave me an embarrassed look, she said she thought Tracy's cake would look and taste like it came out of a box. We sat there drooling over the memory of her cake. I told her that I knew Tracy's cakes were good, I just didn't know what they would look like. Sasha said she was completely surprised all the way around. I told her since I was so busy I left the cake decision up to my matron and maid of honor. Then I swallowed, I told her I knew it was completely selfish and she could say no, but I wanted her to be in my wedding even though hers was coming up right after. Sasha got so excited and she hugged me. She said she wanted to be but she didn't want to ask me about it. We were sad that I would be too pregnant to be in her wedding. I promised to sing a song for her first dance as long as the baby didn't have me out for the count.

I put my hand on my stomach cause the baby was moving. Sasha talked to the baby, and then she asked me what I was hoping for. I told her a little boy of course; I wanted a little Derrick to hold on to. Then she asked me a question I hadn't thought of. Who was going to care for the baby once I went back to work. She said with my line of work I was going to need a nanny. I hadn't thought of it, I told her I wasn't going back to work right away, so I had time to figure it out. I told her Derrick and I would find out the sex of the baby at my next appointment. She said I had to call her directly after so she would know what to bring to my baby shower slash bridal shower.

For the rest of the week, Cyrus pointed me in the right direction and I went. The rest of our time out in LA was full of interviews, photo shoots, and studio time. In between each appointment I slept best I could. I talked to Derrick regularly, and sometimes he'd tell me to stop what I was doing and rest because I sounded beyond tired. And every time he said that I had no argument because I was. I was so happy to be going home. I wanted to know who was in there, although I knew it was a boy I couldn't wait for confirmation.

****

"Did you want to know the sex of the baby?" The technician said as she captured pictures of the baby and measurements.

"Yes."

Derrick was looking at the screen like he was analyzing everything. He smiled his biggest smile yet. "It's a girl." He gripped my hand.

"A WHAT?" I knew I heard him wrong.

"You are good mister Mason, that's right it's a girl."

"Are you sure? Couldn't you be wrong?" I said not wanting to accept their answer.

The technician pointed out the genitals on the baby, "that's her labia."

I looked at Derrick I was completely disappointed, but his smile was huge and he looked completely excited. "You're not disappointed?"

"I'm excited! I got what I wanted." He kissed my forehead

"You wanted a girl? I thought you wanted a son?"

"You wanted a boy. I've always wanted a little you. Besides there's so many guys in my family, it's about time we add some girls." Derrick smiled real big, "my momma's gonna be so excited! Everybody is! Thank you baby! You make me so happy!"

And with that I was perfectly ok with having a girl. In the car I was watching Derrick call his mother, his auntie, his cousin EJ, and then Yussef. He excitedly told each one of them that it was a girl. Then I called Sasha and I told her, she asked me if I was ok with it being a girl, and I explained how excited Derrick is so I was fine.

I exhaled and then I told Derrick it was time to go to my father's house. Derrick asked me if I was sure, and I said yes. I kept going over what I was going to say in my head. When we got to the house my father was feeding the twins lunch. My little brother came running while my little sister was still wobbly. My father was very excited to see us, since he knew we just found out the sex of the baby. He anxiously sat on the couch waiting for the news. When I said it was a girl, he got excited and said I was going to have a mini-me. I smiled then I swallowed, Derrick sat on the floor playing with the babies and they were having a blast. "Daddy there's going to be limited space at our wedding."

"Ok" he said not knowing where I was going with my comment.

"I know you weren't at Derrick's brother Andrew's wedding not too long ago, but they had over five hundred people there and I think they're still finding out that some people were left off the list."

"Ok... what are you saying?"

"That I don't want to invite your sisters to my wedding." I braced myself for his dramatic reaction.

And sure enough Daniel Shaw doesn't disappoint, "WHAT? Chantel No! They have to be there! They are my sisters! Derrick tell her how important family is during times like this."

Derrick put his hands up, "this is between you two."

"Chantel baby it's not like I'm asking that all my family is there. Both of my parents come from big families and you haven't even begun to meet all the family that you need to meet. I need my sisters there for your special day. Please reconsider."

"Daddy your sisters are disrespectful opportunist! I really don't like Tania there isn't a day that goes by that I don't wish I would've kept going upside her head." I could feel myself getting angry all over again.

"Chantel, calm down." Derrick said and I took deep breaths to calm myself.

"Daddy, I don't like your sisters and they don't like me, so I don't see why they have to be at my wedding."

"Because they're your aunt's and they do love you. They have their own way of showing it though. Please Chantel, please!"

"I really don't want them there! I don't think it would make or break you if they were or not."

"Are you kidding? I would be devastated if they weren't there! These are my sisters, the way you feel for Cyrus is how I feel about Deborah and Tania."

"It means that much to you to have them there?"

"Yes it does!"

I looked up at the ceiling my heart was pounding, it was now or never. "Let's see how much it means to you." I looked at him and he shook his head ok as he repositioned himself on the couch. I could see Derrick holding back a smile out the corner of my eye. "The choice is yours daddy, you choose. If you want your sisters there then you have to be responsible for them the entire time and especially during the ceremony. So..." I swallowed, "that would mean Cyrus would have to give me away so that you could be with them. OR! We can stick to the original plan and you give me away and they're not invited. This is not up for negotiation it's one or the other. Which one do you choose?"

My father's face looked stuck, "CHANTEL!" He yelled and the babies jumped and looked at him. "This is utterly ridiculous! Of course I'm giving you away! Derrick please talk some sense into this girl."

Derrick put his hands up again, "I'm not in this. Chantel you're cold though!" Then he winked at me.

My father got up and started pacing the floor. "How you gonna do me like this?" I almost felt sorry for him, ALMOST! "Seriously? This is your ultimatum?"

"Yes daddy! I know you're going to choose walking me so I think we can lay this issue to rest. I really don't want them there." And that was no lie. My aunts especially my Auntie Tania was so disrespectful and rude. We've had more than one physical fight even. She's a bully and I never have to have her anywhere I am.

He was still pacing, "this is the ONLY way I can get them there? Maria could watch over them while I walk you."

"Oh come on, Maria is too sweet! You know she's not going to control them. I want them controlled and subdued." I sat there waiting for him to come to the natural conclusion.

"Just agree that they're not coming and lets be done with this!"

"Chantel baby I couldn't bare the idea of them not being there." Although ultimately I was getting what I wanted, I hated that it meant that I had to deal with something I didn't want. "I need my sisters there. Cyrus will have to walk you down."

"Daddy!" I said a little irritated.

"Chantel, your dad has chosen his sisters, let it go." Derrick said.

Episode 9

Sasha

"Sasha!"

"Hey Drew-Drew! What's up?"

He was extremely excited, "tell me why I'm calling! Tell me why I'm excited!"

"You just save hundreds on your car insurance?" I laughed.

He laughed, "that too. But why else! I'm using my twin powers to tell you. Am I coming in clear?"

I sat there quiet for a minute. I was getting ready for work and I had him on speaker. El started laughing at me. "Drew you should see her, she looks like she's trying to pull the answer out of the air."

He was excited and it sound like he was on his way to work. What could he be this happy about this early in the morning? "Who else is involved?"

"Tracy and me!"

I started jumping up and down. "Ooh! Ooh! She's pregnant?"

"Yes! You won this round of twin telepathy! Tell her what she's won El!"

"She's won a kiss from me!" El joined right in our silliness, and then he gave me a congratulatory kiss.

"You're the first person that I've told, we found out last night. My momma and Malcolm are coming over this weekend and we'll tell them then. So don't tell your momma until you talk to her on Sunday."

"Is Andre excited?"

"Of course! Tracy wanted to wait to tell people, but I don't want to. She's too paranoid sometimes."

"Technically you're supposed to wait until you're out of your first trimester to tell people because anything could happen."

He was thoughtful, "yea and she has miscarried before."

"WHAT! You were pregnant before and didn't tell me?" I was getting angry.

"No, not with me. Maybe that's why she was saying that last night. I didn't even think of that." He was quiet for a minute. "Ok, besides all of her normal dramatics I could see her being scared. We've been waiting for this since our wedding night."

"It hasn't even been six months yet."

"Sasha! This girl was so scared of getting knocked up before the wedding she had me on lock down. Our wedding kiss should've knocked her up, I was so backed up."

"TMI Drew!"

"I'm just saying, I didn't think about her past. That just means that she's freaking out more than I thought about. How will I know that everything's ok though? I don't know that I could handle a miscarry either."

El put his hand on my shoulder to ask my permission to speak. I rubbed his hand and smiled. "Andrew?"

"Yea man?"

"Go with her to her doctor's appointment. Have a list of questions and make sure you ask them all. Unfortunately it's not uncommon to miscarry in the first three months and a lot of the times there's no real reason why. But don't let the possibility stop your excitement

the fact that you guys are pregnant says that everything is working. Just hang in there in a little while you're gonna have a little bundle of your love to care for."
I looked at El and he had a half smile. His tattoo on his chest jumped out at me in that moment. "That is a good suggestion baby thank you." I gave him a kiss.
"Good suggestion." Drew said like he was thinking.
I laughed, "how much work are you going to get done today?"
"Probably none."
"Don't get on the internet and drive yourself crazy with all the worst case scenarios. Just do like El said and go to the doctor with her."
"Ok, I will."
"I'm coming out in a week. Am I staying with you or D-Rick?"
"Me of course. What do I owe the pleasure to?"
"Wedding planning and business stuff. Mainly the wedding. Now that Derrick and Chantel have a date I need to set mine."
"And you're coming to check on Tina too." He said knowingly.
"I'm worried about her Drew! She's so clueless. That detective said he has protected her, from what? How come we're just now paying attention to her?"
"I guess the assumption was that Timothy's kids were cool. With everything that's been happening I don't know how Malcolm's kept everything straight. From the sound of things, if she don't shape up Uncle Frank is going to step in."
"Crap! Sucks to be her if that happens. She thinks Malcolm is scary, but Uncle Frank…"
I whistled.
"He's no worse than Malcolm." Drew said.
"Yea, and he's no better either."

Amber

"Now let me see it again, get it right and then we can knock off for the night." The dancers cheered with excitement. I know I was tired and they should be. "5, 6, 7, 8!"
They put everything they had into it, and I was pleased with the results. Corey nodded to me that he was happy with their work. "And that's a wrap everybody. See you in the morning at eight o'clock." They cheered with excitement because sometimes we have to start as early as six. I told Corey I'd see him in the morning. When I got to the condo, I showered then I got ready to pass out. "Good evening," I said when Malcolm answered the phone.
"Good evening."
"So… I was thinking about Mexico. We don't have to be gone for a long time. At least three days."
"Amber it's not a good time right now."
"So, it's never a good time. But I say we do it any ways."
"I've got a lot of balls in the air right now. Dropping one could unravel everything."
I took a deep breath to calm myself. "So the plan is to get married and then go back to work on Monday?"
Malcolm exhaled exhausted air, "Amber what do you expect? This wedding thing is already outside of my comfort zone. That's not good enough, now you want a honeymoon and a practice honeymoon? Come on!"
"I'll never understand why everything has to be a battle with you. This is what I want so stop trying to fight me on it and just do it, ok. Make both of our lives a little easier."
"You're the one making things difficult! What am I supposed to do?"
"Come away with me! Relax with me! You're always working, always taking care of business. The only vacation you've ever taken with us was for Poppa's camping trip. You can't tell me it didn't feel good to unplug. That it didn't feel good to just be away. I want

to do that again and I know you're overdue."

"It's just not a good time right now."

"You don't even know when. I never said when, you just don't want to do it. Malcolm if you keep going like this, never stopping to smell the flowers you're going to kill over and die. We're too young to be living like old people."

"We are young…"

I got excited feeling as if I was getting my way. "Yes we are! And I think we should live like it!"

"Yea, like having a baby."

I lost my air, "what?"

"Like having a baby, we could still try."

"Malcolm! Stop playing!"

"I'm not!" His voice was deep with no joking tone to it.

"EEEWWLLLL! Malcolm come on! We have a grandson and another baby on the way. That ship has sailed."

"You're the one pointing out how young we are, but when I draw on that you back pedal. You want me all outside of my comfort zone, but you're refusing to compromise."

"I'm not being unreasonable to get out of something I don't want to do. You are so wrong Malcolm! You know it is not baby making time for us. You're just trying to make me back down. I'm not falling for it buddy! Nope not gonna do it!"

"Is that what I'm trying to do?" He said with a smile in his voice.

"YES! And I don't appreciate it. I wanna make love to you in another country. Mexico is right there. We go, hump like CRAZY and then we come home satisfied. It's simple, stop fighting me Malcolm. Trust me, you want to take this trip with me. Plus we can gauge what kind of honeymoon we want to take from this trip."

He exhaled, I could tell I was wearing him down. "I'll think about it." He was still smiling in his voice. "You miss me?"

"Like crazy! I can't wait to get home."

"Saturday did you have plans?"

"Not really, what's up?"

"Tracy's gonna cook, I asked her when she was going to make pot roast again and she said Saturday."

I smiled, "sounds good to me. So you guys have been getting to know each other." He exhaled, "quit it!"

I smiled bigger, "all these little girls infiltrating your heart. Look at you becoming a softer cuddly Malcolm."

Malcolm and I talked a little longer and then I went to bed to get ready for the next day.

****

Malcolm picked me up at the gate when I exited the plane. I immediately started in on him about our vacation. He kept kissing me to shut me up. Which was fine at first but all I could think about was being away with Malcolm and enjoying ourselves. After we pleasured each other and I woke up, I went right back to where I left off. Malcolm got irritated and that's when the argument began. He said he has an empire to run and he needed to be present to make sure he was on top of everything. I asked him what was the point of working so hard, if he never took time out to enjoy life. He said there was so much going on right now, that I didn't understand and something's I couldn't understand. Of course I didn't let up until he agreed to give me a date by midday Monday. Malcolm didn't seem excited about the idea of having me all to himself, which was annoying. Why wouldn't the thought of a romantic get away with me automatically turn him on? I asked him what kind of honeymoon did he picture us having. And he said he hadn't thought of it. Annoyed with the topic I stopped talking altogether. When we got to Andy's he was extremely excited about something until he saw my face. Then he sat there reading me like his daddy. I didn't want to think about it, I want to have a nice evening with my son. We were barely sitting down when Andre came in and asked his daddy if he could tell us. Suddenly I had a deja vu moment. Andre looking just like his father excitedly said that his mommy was going to have a baby. Suddenly I was in my living room and Andy was excitedly telling David I was pregnant with Darryl. I shook off the feeling and gave my son who was too excited a congratulatory hug. I even made Malcolm do the same. I could see excitement and fear all over Tracy's face. When Tracy took the delicious smelling roast out of the oven I asked her how she was holding up? She said she was scared out of her mind. I told her not to worry, and to remember that each pregnancy was different. She tried to find comfort in that thought but I know she was scared. She said even though they had a little bit of time before the bakery opened she and Andrew decided to put in her resignation last week and she was going to take some time to wrap her head around everything. I told her that was a good idea.

****

"Hello?"

"Sasha told me about the baby, congratulations." Sophia said sounding upset.

I looked at the clock and it was just after eight on a Sunday morning. "Why are you up so early? And at the restaurant at that?"

Sophia exhaled, "I…" she tried to find her words.

"I'm on my way." I hung up on her.

Malcolm shot me a look, "what's going on?"

"I don't know, but she needs me so I'm going."

"I need you." He said sounding petty.

"Yea, yea. You need me in this bed and for kicks we could go to your place for a change of scenery." Malcolm stared at me and I continued to get up and ready. I took a quick shower, brushed my teeth. And I told Malcolm I'd catch up to him later. When I got to the restaurant Sophia was in her office crying broken hearted tears. Tears like this had to be associated with a man. I rubbed her back and then I had her come sit with me on the couch.

"It's over!" She said very heartbrokenly.

"Travis?" I asked gently.

"Richard! His girlfriend is pregnant! I thought that heifer looked a little juicy in the middle!" I didn't say anything, I imagined how heartbroken I would be if Malcolm ever had a child with someone else. "He seemed distracted at Andy's wedding, but so was I. I guess I know why."

"It's going to be ok, you didn't want any more kids anyways."

"I know, but I can't believe this!"

"Are you happy with Travis?"

"Very happy, Travis has been good to me you know that, he's just white." Then we laughed.

"Again, what's wrong with a white man? Our daddy's are white."

"Nothing, it's just different. I've always envisioned myself with Richard or someone just like him."

"You love who you love," I thought of my momma. Her momma used to give her such a hard time because my daddy was white. She would say that she couldn't help who she fell in love with, but her racist momma didn't care. If he wasn't black it was wrong. "You gonna be ok?"

"NO! He knows what this means! This is the end of the road for he and I! We got together just after you and Malcolm, can you imagine life without Malcolm?"

"You know I can't, but I was going to if he didn't propose. Now I can't get him to take a vacation with me for nothing."

"Vacation?"

"I want to take a mini vacation before our honeymoon."

"Malcolm on vacation though? When has he ever done that? Wasn't that a you and Dwayne thing?"

"True, as long as it was after the season he'd go anywhere I wanted."

"I bet you he was wishing for a vacation after seeing you and Malcolm like that."

"Like what?"

"He made a cameo at your engagement party, you didn't know?"

I pointed to my face, "this is the face of a person in the know."

"Malcolm saw him though."

I guess it figured that he wouldn't say anything if I saw one of his ex's somewhere, I wouldn't say anything either. "When was he there?"

"He came with Alexa, Sasha said it was an honest mistake that he ended up there. So I guess he knows now if he didn't before that you are moving forward with Malcolm. Maybe he can finally let it go and move on with his life. He can stop looking for space fillers that remind him of you." Then she laughed, "you must've put some number on him cause he only dates women who remind him of you. Even Malcolm had variety in his day."

"Dwayne was good to me. I don't wish him any harm." I felt bad for him.

"He better not get any ideas, Malcolm has no patience when it comes to him."

"Malcolm has no patience for anyone trying to get my attention."

"Right so how is he going to handle Latia's wedding? You know Dwayne and Ramell at least are going to be there."

I blank stared at her, "how Malcolm is going to handle it, or how they are going to handle it? You know he don't care as long as they stand down."

She smiled, "yea. I guess this is how he felt when I had Sabrina huh." She said changing the subject.

"Um! Didn't he call you going off?"

"He told me off so badly my ears still ring. I guess it's for the best, cause I'm not having any more babies. Sasha will be having her own soon. I'm not about to be like my momma!"

"Not your mom's fault you had a baby at fifteen."

"Yours either," she shot back.

I frowned, "get out of my business!" We laughed.

****

"Ms. Amber you're teaching the class today???" One of the students asked while all the others watched with big eyes.

"Yes I am." I smiled, "and! We have three new students. Everybody say hello to Yesmina, Sydney, and Desiree." All the kids yelled hello. I told the girls to find empty x's on the floor to sit on like the rest of the children. "This class is going to have a new teacher next week. I know we were sad to see Ms. Ada go, but she received a wonderful opportunity in New York that she could not pass up. So for today how about we have some fun?" All the kids cheered, "everybody stand up." They did, I turned on music.

"Now I wanna see everybody move, Emerald and I are gonna observe you for a little bit." All the kids started dancing and having a good time. Desiree stood out like a sore thumb. She had no rhythm and she was so uncomfortable. She looked like she was going to cry, I gently grabbed her hands and I moved her body to the sound of the music. I told her to close her eyes and relax. She did as she was told and she got a lot better. I rubbed her shoulder and told her she did good. She just needed to practice. Her smile got really big and she kept going.

We separated the kids into three groups. Each group had an equal amount of strong to new dancers.

I gave them a simple routine and then they practiced. I told them to ask Emerald if they had any questions. I walked down the hall to the main lobby. Tony was at the front desk on the phone and little Sonny was filing paperwork. I knocked on Jade's door; I was surprised when I saw Yussef in the office with her. He was clicking away on a laptop, and Jade was giving him information. Both of their faces were serious and there was tension in the air. Jade told me to sit down. I sat next to Yussef who had multiple screens going on his laptop and a picture of our new hire was up. Jade reminded me that there was something Ginger was holding back when she met her. I didn't know what to make of it. Yussef explained that she is a mole; they were /trying to figure out for whom. My body temperature went up. I hated stuff like this. I reminded Yussef that my school was clean. He said Phineas has been attacking the electric fence sort of speak for a while, and he's been trying to find a weak spot. Jade's desk phone rang and she answered it on speaker, it was Malcolm. He gave Yussef information then he told him to cross-reference with Derrick. I asked Malcolm if we were still bringing Ginger on. I could hear the smile in his voice as he said yes. He said that we couldn't let on that we know, and we need confirmation of whom she was working for. She could be undercover working for Phineas. I asked if this was out of the blue? Yussef shook his head no as he said "we're always on defense, but we try to keep stuff like this away from the women." Then Malcolm said Poppa wanted the women to always maintain their sanity as much as possible.

I went back to my class, watching all the kids work together put a big smile on my face. At the last few minutes of the class Yussef came over to watch. He sat there so proud of his girls as they perfectly blended in with the class. He blushed so hard when I told him that they both showed natural abilities and if they wanted to dance in the future they could. Both of the girls smiled really big and thanked me, it looked like Yesmina was in deep thought about my comment though. I hugged and kissed them, then I reminded them to say bye to their big cousin Emerald. Yussef caught Desiree watching us, and he asked who she was. I told him she was a new student. He asked me if her information was on file, and I told him it should be. Then he returned to being a proud father. Out of all the students in this class I wondered why he zoned in on Desiree. She looked like an ordinary child to me. I thanked each child for coming and I told them that they did a good job. When I got to Desiree I asked her if she was leaning towards this hip-hop dance class or another dance expression. She said she liked this class after I helped her. She was kind of shy, and definitely not comfortable in her own skin. She had that same withdrawn look in her face that Jade used to have when she stopped talking. I gave Desiree a hug and she squeezed me tight thanking me for everything. When Jade, Emerald, Little Sonny, and I walked out to our cars Yussef was still in the parking lot. We were talking to him when Desiree came out of the school. Yussef told all of us to move in close for a picture. He snapped a picture of us then he said one more and he took like three of Desiree. I looked at him funny, and he said it was *research*. He took more pictures of the car that came to pick her up. Then we got in our cars and left.

That night I tried to ask Malcolm tons of questions but he was focused on making me dinner. I get a kick out of watching him in the kitchen, because this is a new feature. He's still new to the kitchen, but my big cousin Ethan has been showing him some things. "Malcolm, what's going on?"

He brought a spoon, "taste my sauce it's missing something."

"It needs a little garlic and then it's good. Malcolm."

"Hold on, hold on." He moved around the kitchen quickly. In his true OCD manner he cleaned everything immediately. He put our plates on the table then he put the bottle of wine he opened to breathe on the table. I sat down staring at him. "You know about the detectives, they're still on us. Some things don't change. They thought they had me with Toya, and they've been scrambling to find someone to fill that void. Then there's this guy Phineas Cobb. I had no idea that he would take business so personal. I absorbed his company when we expanded to the east coast. He's mad about it so he's been striking at Latour Enterprises ever since. I'm always battling somebody, if it's not in the streets it's in the courts." Then he looked at me, "you're safe Amber. You don't ever have to worry about that."

"Yea but our family is growing." I said eating some salad. His dressing was delicious. "This is so good!"

He smiled, "glad you like it." He chewed for a minute. "Before I forget, I need you to try to talk some sense into your niece."

I frowned, "which one?"

"Tina, no one's told you?" I shook my head no. "She's a sheltered little brat! I told Timothy she has a choice in how she lives, she is technically grown. But she doesn't understand who she is. Wallace is just a name to her. It might be a little too late for her, but for your sake I'll give it one more try."

"What happened?"

Malcolm told me what he's found so far. I felt bad for my brother, he was always so protective of me growing up, I can imagine how tore up he is about all that's happened. Tina has been hanging on like a groupie and partying and she's hooked up with some guy that they're still trying to make sense of. Malcolm said my friend Detective Turan spilled his guts to Sasha. I frowned cause he wasn't my friend, we've flirted from time to time, but that was before Malcolm and I got back together. I rolled my eyes at him. Then Malcolm exhaled, "about this trip."

My heart fluttered, "yes Malcolm?"

"You're right, I do need to get away. Being honest I don't like the idea of leaving especially with everything that's going on. But I think it will be good for us to be alone. Just me and you like it used to be. Before you made me get you pregnant." He smiled.

****

"Hey Amber how you doing?" Sharon said meeting me at my car and giving me a hug. "I'm good how are you?"

"Your brother and my daddy are at your house right now. I'll walk you over." Sharon was telling me about Darryl and her son Ryder's latest adventure. She said they were two coo-coo nuts in a pod.

Timothy and Uncle Dale were discussing something about the plans. As if he knew I was here to talk to Timothy, Uncle Dale kissed me and then he walked away with Sharon.

"Hey chipmunk," Timothy said giving me a deflated hug and kiss. "This house is beautiful. It's what I always wanted for you." He exhaled, "I'm happy for you."

"How's Malachi's house coming along?"

"Good, it should be done pretty soon actually. Next month Denise will pick out colors, stuff like that." He exhaled again. "You talked to Malcolm I take it?" I nodded my head yes. He exhaled, "when did it become a bad thing to want better for my children?"

"I don't understand?"

"Malcolm faults me for not letting my children know who we are. I wanted something different for them. Dad said I was doing the right thing."

"But we also know who we are."

"Amber you nor Jade knew until you popped up pregnant."

"Right! My whole world turned upside down. I never hid who we are from my boys. I couldn't even if I wanted to, can you imagine them bumping around the Bay not knowing. It's time to rip the band aid off sort of speak. She needs to see that she has to be careful with herself before all of this gets way out of hand. Can I have her for a little bit?"

"What do you mean have her?"

"Take her with me for a while. Malcolm and I are going on vacation but when I come back, I wanna spend a little time with my niece. Don't tell her, she might try to run away." I laughed.

"I don't know Amber, her mouth!"

I smiled, "she'll have to see my Annette side."

He frowned, "don't put bruises on my child like momma used to do you."

I put my hands up, "let's just see where the day takes us. I can't make no promises if she tries to jump bad with me." He looked like he was thinking about it. "You could choose Jade but you know she's crazy! She'll bop her and then use her psychology talk on her. Poor thing wouldn't know which way is up."

He took a deep breath. "True."

We talked for a while longer and then we walked over to Malachi's house. He was trying to explain an aspect of the design that I didn't comprehend. Denise pulled up while we were standing outside talking. She said hello, but it was a flat hello. Timothy asked her if she was ok, and she said she was fine. Timothy looked at me and then he walked away. I asked her if she had lunch yet, and she hadn't. She was coming to look at the house for inspiration as she went to look at furniture. I asked her about the furniture they have and she said she was keeping that but she wanted to add pieces. I asked her to come have lunch with me; I was heading over to Sophia's. She agreed, we left her car in front of her house, and she rode with me. I asked her how she was doing, and she said ok she guessed, but she wasn't ready to talk about it. So I said ok as if I was really going to leave it alone.

I knocked on Sophia's door to her office, and I told her to look who I had with me. She got excited and gave Denise an excited hug. Denise relaxed some when Sophia greeted her that way. I told Sophia we were hungry, and Sophia said we were in luck cause she had a room with a stove and everything next door. I ignored the smart comment as I looked over the menu. Sophia said she didn't know why I pretended like I was going to get something else. I came for a meatball sandwich so I needed to stop playing. I told her she didn't know me that well, today I could've come for something different. When Denise said she was going to have the chicken parm, Sophia looked at me knowing what I was going to say. I handed her the menu as I looked away. She snatched the menu as she laughed at me. I hollered extra cheese as she disappeared. Denise relaxed a little more. Sophia said it would be a few minutes before our food was ready. "Um! I called you last night!" Sophia said.

"Yea, Um! I was busy!" I rolled my eyes.

Sophia exhaled, "can you guys give me the schedule so I can know when is a good time to call you? I swear you guys weren't this bad when you were kids."

"I guess we're making up for lost time, I don't know. BUT I'M NOT COMPLAINING!"

"OK!" Sophia and I high-fived.

"And you're one to talk, at least I don't answer the phone like some people I know!"

Sophia turned red, "I don't know. You could be dying or something. Once I know you're ok, I call you back later."

We were cracking up, and Denise was politely smiling, part of me forgot we had an audience. "Denise, it's ok. What's said in here stays in here. Just don't say *your brother* and we're good." I smiled.

Denise swallowed, "Malachi and I...." she adjusted in her chair. " Well we don't...."

I frowned, "you don't what? I know what kind of parents we had. My momma was getting her back blown out until the end."

She crossed her ankles and turned to the side in her chair, "we're in a slump."

"Malachi is? Or you are?" Sophia asked.

"I am, my mother being sick took a lot out of me. Poor Malachi has taken it and not really complained. I don't feel very sexy! I don't feel like he should want me! I feel horrible! I don't want him to look at me."

"Why don't you want him to look at you?" Sophia asked.

"Cause he'll say something like I'm beautiful, or whatever. I want to believe him, but I know what he sees when he sees me. I'm still that dork from high school who could never have a man as gorgeous as Malachi."

One of the servers knocked on the door, he was bringing our food. "Here you go Amber," he said handing me my peach Italian soda. I loved this stuff! It was the perfect compliment to my sandwich.

As soon as he stepped out the door Sophia went in. "Why do you have to be you?" I smiled cause I knew exactly what she meant, Denise had no idea. "There are going to be times when you don't feel sexy. But you still need to get some." Denise had a confused look on her face. "There's a reason why both of my baby daddy's is sprung stupid!" Denise leaned in, I laughed. Sophia sat at her desk and pulled up her favorite online costume shop. "Come here baby." She called Denise over. I stood on the other side of her shoulder. She had a schoolgirl uniform up, "when I wear this my name is Felicity and I'm a good girl who's been very bad!" She said making her voice sound all baby girl like. Then she showed us a lot of Felicity's costumes. "But when I wear this," a police officer costume on the screen. "Then my name is Robin!" She made her voice deeper, "Robin takes charge!"

Denise couldn't stop laughing. "You do this too?" She asked me.

"I haven't in years, Malcolm and I just got back together. The one time I did, it was well received. I mostly give Malcolm private shows. But again, I haven't done that in a long time either."

"Private show?"

"Lap dance, private show, potato, potat-to!" I laughed.

Denise's eyes got big, "I always wanted to try that but I wouldn't know what to do?"

"Honey being a stripper for your man ain't hard. You already know what he likes so you do your little dance; tease the life out of him. When he or you can't take it anymore, whatever *cums* first you go for it. There are no rules! If you've never done it before you could start with some pretty lingerie and some heels. Do a little two step while you take it all off, and your man will be SPRUNG!" I laughed.

"You say that cause you're a dancer." Denise said.

"Yea Amber, why don't you give us a private strip lesson!" Sophia said winking at me.

"Alright! Tomorrow's schedule what you guys got?"

"Name the time and where, and I'm there!" Sophia said egging us on.

"I can come after I drop the girls off at school."

"Ok, nine-thirty at the school. Come dressed to exercise. Make sure you bring your highest heels. Red bottom CFM's if you got them."

"CFM's?" Denise asked embarrassed.

"Oh my goodness! Amber! We're gonna turn the poor child out." Sophia said pretending to feel guilty.

"No! I need to know these things; no one's ever said anything. They kind of put you out there and expect you to know it all."

"My momma overloaded me with information when I got married. I still haven't recovered." Sophia shuddered at the memory.

"When Jade got married my momma did the same thing. I guess she was waiting for me to get married. After three kids she probably figured I had experienced something."

"My mother was a prude, and she would say that Malachi was too pretty to ever be good to me. Her voice stays in my head now that she's gone."

Sophia and I sat there quiet for a minute. "You know that old school way of thinking and dealing with things. They would tell us to force the freak out of our system, and then when you get married you're supposed to know what to do with all of your husband's demands. I understand what you mean." Sophia said.

"You do?" Denise's eyes watered up and then tears fell.

"Of course I do! You're not alone, you have a family full of people who love you and

have been through similar things." Sophia stood and hugged Denise.
"Yea, you've been a part of this family for so long. You better not feel like you're alone."
I demanded.
"Stop crying it's contagious!" Sophia wiped tears from her eyes."
"Nine-thirty?" I asked.
"Nine-thirty!"

I got to the school at eight-thirty and I blocked off the small room for the day. Jade told
Tony to call her cell if he needed her she was coming to my class as well. Tony wanted to
know what we were going to be doing in the class, and I told him it was none of his
business. When we went in the classroom Jade said she locked her office and turned off
the camera in there. Sophia and Denise walked in together. "Ok so, I think we should
come up with stripper names for our class." I smiled, "it'll help us get into character."
"I'm Jewel!" Jade said right away.
"That doesn't sound like a name you pulled out of the air." I teased.
"I've been married to the same man since college and I have three kids. Me and my man
know how to have fun is all I got to say!" Jade wiggled her neck.
"Ok, ok how about Sparkle?" Sophia announced.
"If you like it I love it."
"I don't know you go Amber." Denise said.
I was thinking and thinking, "I don't know. I guess us newbies need to put more thought
into it." I teased.
"I got it, Cinnamon," Denise blushed again.
"Good one! Crap! Let me think!" I was racking my brain. "Nothing sounds good to me."
"Seriously Amber it's not that hard. Jewel, Sparkle, and Cinnamon don't have all day."
Jade said trying to hurry me up.
"Buttercup!"
Sophia frowned, "I like Blossom better!"
"Ooh! Ooh! Me too! Yea, that!" Then I went down in the splits.
Denise's mouth dropped, "can you all do them?"
Only front ways, Blossom cheats and does them either way."
"Come on Cinnamon, all you gotta do is stretch daily like this and in no time you will at
least hit them like them." I showed her how to stretch. Once we were good and stretched
I put on music. We had so much fun, once Denise relaxed her island flavor started to
show. I was happy to see another side to my sister in-law. We agreed that we needed to
do this once a month at least.

Episode 10

Malachi

She tiptoed in the bathroom. I could hear her unwrapping the test. She peed and then she
washed her hands and waited. Then I heard her aggravated sigh and she tossed the test in
the trash. I exhaled, one less crazy thing for us. I could hear her in the bathroom trying to
quietly cry to herself. I laid there feeling conflicted, I knew her tears meant she wasn't
pregnant. I was relieved, but I know she really thinks having a baby will fix us. I've
stopped trying to talk to her about this whole thing; we end up arguing about anything
other than talking about what's really wrong. So when my job said they needed me to go
to Southern California to Torrance, I didn't fight it. I packed my bags and prepared for
my trip.
Denise plopped in the bed, exhaling loudly. If she wanted me to wake up she was going
to have to try harder. She backed up into me when I didn't turn over and off my back to
spoon her like I normally would she exhaled again. Then she disappeared under the

covers. The warmth of her mouth grabbed my attention. Well alright! I like this action; once I was at full salute she came up. "Hi."

"Hello!" I smiled back. I was about to get my good send off. I was excited.

The worst thing you could EVER do to yourself during sex is to think. Sex is for love, release, and endorphins! Not thinking! If I reach for a condom she's gonna shut down, and she probably won't let me back in. We'll argue and I don't want to leave on that note. I went in on her, thought about everything to keep me from blowing my top. When she finished, I pretended like I was finishing too which stung like you wouldn't believe. Even if it was a lie, I enjoyed the moment when she let me hold her like I used to. She gave me a real kiss, and then she asked if I was up for round two. Fortunately I didn't have time and Amaya was at the door with her breakfast order. While she busied herself with the kids I relieved myself in the shower. I chewed back my bad mood as I prepared my girls so that I could take them to school. I kissed my wife goodbye as her happiness saddened me. I couldn't tell her I tricked her, but this morning was the first time since the party. I bought a big Costco sized box of condoms and I put them on the nightstand next to the bed. That started an argument where she ended up sleeping in the guest room cause I refused to leave our bed. How she think she gonna tell me to sleep outside the bedroom I pay for! Please! She had me confused with some little boy who didn't know better. And two nights of that was all I could stand. I told her to stop playing and come back to our bed. We weren't comfy cozy, but at least my girls wouldn't see that something was wrong.

In the car the girls said they wanted to do something with all their cousins when I came back. I knew they were referring to Drew's little boy, EJ's kids, Ryder and Yussef's girls. Simple enough, I told them I would set it up. I kissed my girls goodbye then I caught my flight out of San Jose airport. I got a rental car and headed over to the office. I laughed as I imagined Cora's reaction when she saw me. I didn't tell her I was coming. I got my security badge and then I went up to Larry's office. He smiled and looked at his watch. He had to be one of the few people who still wore one. He said I was always on time, I smiled but we both knew his amazement was a backwards compliment against the whole CPT idea. We went to the conference room early and waited for the rest of the team to arrive. He asked how my wife and kids were; I gave the standard that they were *good* statement. As people filled in Heidi walked in. "MALACHI?" She blurted as she looked surprised and embarrassed that she showed a reaction. I nodded hello, it was sweet of her to notice me. Heidi changed directions and sat across from me at the table. I told Cora about being late, but last and certainly not least was Cora. If she knew I was coming she would've been early. The only reaction she had was that she bucked her eyes at me. Then she eyed Heidi and sat next to her. Everyone over the phone line announced their presence as I closed the door. My call went smoothly, we mapped out the plan of attack while I was out here.

At the end of the day Larry convinced me to have dinner with him and his wife, and in his way of being funny he invited Heidi as well. I guess it didn't take a genius to know that she liked me. Cora walked by, the way she cut her eyes at me, I knew she was upset. After dinner I drove to Cora's condo. She already had a parking pass waiting for me at the gate. The door was unlocked when I checked it. I always get on her about locking her door. Just because she's in a gated community doesn't mean she's safe. I keep trying to explain this to her but she never listens. I can always count on her door being open. Her doors, windows, car... You name it. I slowly pushed the door open. Cora was bumping around in the kitchen, her balcony door was open and she didn't notice the pressure change when I opened or closed the door. I stood tall in her living room waiting for her to discover me. She was humming a song, and then she remembered something in another room. She darted out the kitchen and when she saw me standing there she screamed a blood-curdling scream at the top of her lungs while she waved her hands like she was going to fly away. I fell to the ground laughing! "MALACHI THAT'S NOT FUNNY! WHY WOULD YOU SCARE ME LIKE THAT?" She held her chest trying to catch her breath.

Once I stopped laughing I looked at her, "I told you about the locks! You don't listen!"

"I was going to get my phone to see if you called me. I know you ate."

"I did." I said going in for a hug.

"Did Heidi throw herself at you?" She asked watching my eyes.

"Yep! Lap dance right there in the middle of the restaurant."

"Don't play! She likes you!"

"So!"

She rolled her eyes as she walked back in the kitchen. I hung out for a while, we didn't do anything wrong. I was a good boy tonight. I left when Denise called with my girls to say goodnight.

****

"Malachi I didn't do this!" Cora pleaded with her eyes.

I took a deep breath to calm myself, and then I took the intercom off mute. "Do you really think that's necessary? From a logistical perspective wouldn't it make sense to keep everyone where they are?"

"This is a temporary move. Cora if you can't relocate to the Fremont office for the duration of this project we'll have to find someone who can." My bosses' bosses boss said.

"I can manage it sir." She tried to hold back her excitement for my sake.

"We'll send out the package information for you. But basically you'll have a corporate apartment and a car. This project will only run a maximum of two years, but it could be as short as six months so don't get too comfortable."

"Yes sir, I understand." She didn't take her eyes off me.

"Malachi you should be excited to have your dream team hands on for this high profile project. We look forward to seeing your results."

"Alright, I'll touch base with you later. " I couldn't think of anything else to say to them. When they hung up the phone I stared at Cora.

She put her hands up, "I'm just as surprised as you are. I had no idea."

"Cora!" I scooted my chair back. "If you try to pull one stunt and I do mean one! I will break your neck and not think twice about it!"

She frowned, "I'm not coming to bring you any drama, Malachi."

"I'm not playing with you!" I said trying to take some of the bass out of my voice cause I was really pissed off. She was right, this decision was beyond her.

There was a knock at the door and Larry pushed in. "So it looks like we're going to be neighbors." Larry said with a smile. "Unless you live in the ghetto, then I guess I'll only see you in the office."

"Larry! You say some of the dumbest off color stuff. You don't hear me saying hey little dick! Come back another day, I've got too much on my plate to deal with you and your racist remarks today."

Larry turned beet red, and Cora covered her mouth as she looked away. "Ok fine, somebody's got their panties in a bunch today!" Then he walked out.

I looked at Cora, "I'm not playing with you!"

****

"There they go!" I said pointing to Andre, Erin Ryder's little girl, and one of Yussef's daughters. Jada grabbed Amaya's hand and they took off very excitedly towards their cousins in the play area. Andrew and Yussef stood up when they saw me approaching, Darryl and Ryder were laughing about something as usual. "I thought you had two?" I said to Yussef as we shook hands.

"Yezzy's with her mom. It's not my weekend, and it would've required more talking than

I wanted to do to ask for Yezzy. Next time we can plan around when I'll have both of them."

"EJ couldn't make it either, he said to hit him up next time." Darryl chimed in.

We sat down, "so what's new?"

Drew smiled, "I have news actually. Tracy's pregnant."

Yussef's head whipped to Drew, "that was fast."

"I don't waste time." Drew shot back.

"This is happening so fast, seems like we keep multiplying." Darryl twirled his finger around in a circle.

"Congratulations nephew! Your auntie is getting that itch herself." I said.

"Jen and I are going to get started on another one soon."

"See!" Darryl said.

"Early congratulations!" Yussef said, "congratulations Drew."

"Thanks man!" Drew smiled.

We sat there watching the kids play their little hearts out. Denise basically pushed us out the door. I barely saw her, but ok. She's been stuck at home with the kids all week; she probably wanted some peace and quiet. I doubt she's going to be open to anything tonight, especially since she may think that we planted the seed last time. I didn't feel up to begging her for anything. If she didn't want me to touch her fine. The kids played until their arms were about to fall off. When I got to the house Denise didn't come out to help me like she normally does. It was ok though, Jada was barely awake and I carried Amaya. I put them in their PJ's and then I put them in their beds, I kissed them goodnight, and then I went to the bedroom. When I opened the door the lights were off but there were candles around the room and a folding chair in the middle of the floor. Completely surprised, I did as the note in the seat said. It said, "**SIT**!" I couldn't stop smiling, what was all this? Then music started, I got excited and leaned forward. My baby came out of the bathroom in a cheerleader's uniform and pom-poms. She blushed a little bit at first and then she got into character. Her little dance was cute, and then she sat in my lap. Ok! Ok! Whatever she wanted she could have. I tried to remember if she crashed her car or something, but I would've noticed. I couldn't think of anything she wanted, besides my seed. This little song and dance got her everything.

****

"I want everyone to come out to dinner with us tonight, bring your spouses. Call a sitter, it's mandatory!" The big boss said.

I know his heart was in the right place, but he was killing me! I shot Cora daggers when I eventually looked at her. This was not good, my life started to flash before my eyes. I was hoping the girls or Denise weren't feeling well when I called. Nothing too bad of course, like maybe a little nausea, or exhaustion that would cause them to have to stay home. Alas, Denise and my girls were as healthy as oxen, and Denise knew who to call to babysit for us. Things have been going so well between us, I was getting served on the regular. And not pity sex, the good stuff! Cora was going to look one time too many in my direction and Denise was gonna lose it.

Once the babysitters Sabrina and Emerald were situated Denise and I left to the restaurant. They had a long table for our party of twenty; Martha, Larry's wife, made a beeline for Denise. She told her about me sharing her picture with her and how beautiful she thinks she is. Denise blushed and thanked her. Since Cora arrived late she had to take the only seat available, which was directly across from us. I couldn't look at Cora any more, my stomach was in knots.

Cora was quiet at first, and then Denise complimented her dress. She thanked her and gave the same compliment back. Heidi kept watching from the front of the table. Since we were the only three people of color at the table it seemed like Cora and Denise couldn't help but continue to talk to each other. I got a sinking feeling as they appeared to hit it off. They even went to the bathroom together that's when I knew I was dead. I wanted to snatch Cora up like I've never snatched a woman up before. I couldn't believe how violent I felt in that moment. "Malachi has always said how sweet you are. But I had no idea!" Cora offered.

"Really? What else has Mr. Wallace said?" Denise said smiling at me with nothing but love in her eyes for me.

"A man's love for his wife has never been more evident." Martha butted in their conversation.

"You are his heart." Cora said smiling a painful smile.

"Aw! Thank you, when your spouse travels, as much as ours do. Sometimes you wonder what they tell their teammates about you."

"Malachi is always no nonsense, goes to work, he may go out to dinner, but he's not going out dancing with us. He's always on best behavior" Marian said.

I guess you can fool most of the people most of the time.

****

"I don't know what to do. I already told her that I only have a cousin out in this area. So it's gonna look like I'm avoiding her."

"I CANNOT BELIEVE THIS IS HAPPENING!" I growled. Denise was loved and adored by everyone at the dinner. Quite naturally she's lovable and her full personality was on that night. Everyone said we are such a compatible couple. Denise picked up on Marian and Heidi's gazes and I guess the things they said. She asked me what the stories were, so I told her about Marian's drunken advances and then comment about me being prejudice. Then I told her about the dinner with Heidi, Larry, and Martha. Then she asked me what I thought of Marian and Heidi. I told her they were colleagues and that was it. She told me to keep an eye on them since I'm aware that they're attracted to me, I couldn't be overly friendly with them. Things I already knew, but then she starts going on and on about how much she likes Cora. I laid there feeling like the biggest phony alive while Denise talked about her new friend connection. This whole thing keeps getting worse and worse. "So you're going to go?"

"I don't see a way out, please Malachi if you can think of anything please, tell me and I'll use it."

"You are becoming a real PAIN!" I growled.

"What did I do? I didn't ask to move out here. I tried to get out of dinner until they said it was mandatory. If I would've had an attitude out of nowhere with your wife that would've raised suspicion. I'm trying to be cool; I don't want to hurt her any more than you do. I understand why you love her. Denise is a good woman, I don't want to hurt her anymore either."

"At least we're in agreement there." I ran my hand through my hair. "So we're clear? We're done!"

"Yes Malachi, we are done!"

Her agreement hit me some kind of way cause she hasn't agreed with me to end, since her divorce. I took a deep breath, "Cora please don't think about crossing me. You don't wanna play that game with me."

"Right, well me neither."

Kendra

"Hello pretty ladies I'm Jude." He introduced himself.

"Nice to meet you Kalani."

"And you are?" He looked at me.

"Kendra."

"Are you out celebrating?"

119

"The end of the week if that counts." Kalani volunteered.

Lately downtown Oakland after dark has become our Friday night playground. Sometimes we hit a few lounges before we land on our sweet spot for the evening. We've become regulars all over the place to the point where people recognize us all the time. I've seen this guy before; I guess he finally found the courage to step to us. When his friend came to join him, he gave him a pound in agreement of his choice for the evening.

"What are you drinking? I'll buy the next round." Jude volunteered.

Kalani pointed to our glasses and said *Adios* Jude smiled and said ok.

"I'm Raphael," his friend volunteers sticking his hand out to shake ours.

Raphael was cute average height shoulder length dreads, nicely trimmed goatee, and medium build. "Kendra, and this is my sister Kalani."

"Nice to meet you ladies, are we celebrating tonight?" He asked looking between the both of us.

"Not really, how about you and your friend?"

Raphael smiled and said he guessed so. Jude came back with drinks for all of us. Raphael told him that I asked if they were celebrating anything and Jude smiled a pained smile as he said his divorce. I looked at Jude again trying to figure out how old he is to have married and now divorced. As the evening progressed Jude shared that he was married two years no kids and now divorced. I told Raphael that I was going to call him Raffy, cause calling him by his name made me think of the turtles. Again Raffy laughed at me, apparently he understands my humor and was cracking up all night. When it got late, Kalani and I stood to leave. Raffy and Jude volunteered to walk us out to our car. We thanked them for the gentlemanly gesture and then we left. "Jude is annoying! No wonder his wife wanted to be free!" Kalani said as we were driving away.

****

Next Friday night, in a different lounge who do we see? Our friends Raffy and Jude. This continued to happen for the next three to four weeks, until Raffy finally asked for my number. Raffy asked me if he could take me out on a real date and I said that's fine, but I wanted to meet him wherever he'd like to go. When he asked me why he couldn't pick me up, I told him I don't know him and I don't want some stranger knowing where I live. He agreed by defeat. Since I live in Richmond and Raffy lives in San Leandro, we agreed that Emeryville and Oakland were nice halfway points. I didn't like the idea of being in Darryl's backyard, but since he's done with me I guess it really doesn't matter. I met Raffy at the Jamaican Food restaurant in downtown Oakland right around the corner from Kalani and I's playground. She said she was going to play in our playground and if the date turned out to be a bust to come join her and her friends. Our plan was to meet at 7:30, at 7:45 I was starting my car to drive around the corner when Raffy pulled up. He looked surprised and confused when I said I was leaving. I told him our date was for 7:30 at 7:32 he was late and that was unacceptable. Raffy smiled a killer but embarrassed smile. He said punctuality is not one of his strong suits. I told him if he wanted to be my friend he was going to have to master timeliness cause I have no tolerance for constant tardiness. Raffy looked me up and down like he was thinking about leaving. "You better be happy I got a taste for some jerk chicken. I don't let females talk to me like that." He said calming himself and relaxing.

"Whatever, I will not wait on you again. Respect my time!"

"Respect me and watch your mouth!"

"Whatever!" I rolled my eyes.

"Whatever!" He said holding the door open for me. At least he knew to do that.

When we sat down at our table you could cut the tension with a knife. Ask me if I cared though. Its rude to have people waiting on you when you know they're here to see you. When the waitress came to take our drink order Raffy told her to bring us two rum punches IMMEDIATELY! I looked at him like no he didn't just order for me. When I leaned in to tell him about his self he countered my obvious mood by saying how pretty I looked. I wasn't going to fall for that at first. He kept going until he had me laughing and in a better mood. The rum punch was good, so I had a few of them. Dinner was delicious and then I told him that Kalani was around the corner at the Sake bar. He asked me if I wanted to walk over which was fine with me. As we walked he took something out of his jacket and lit it. He hit it then he asked me if I wanted some. I told him no, as I felt completely square. I had only ever smoked with Darryl before and he had me so nerved up about knowing where it came from. Seeing it rolled that I don't think I could trust anyone. That was years ago, Darryl stopped smoking because he said he had to be on point cause too much was happening for him to be caught slipping. So when he stopped, I stopped. Raffy was cool, but I didn't know him like that to be that open around him. When we got to the Saki bar, Jude was at the table with Kalani and her friends. Raffy and Jude went outside and then they came back relaxed. We had a good time in the bar, and then Raffy walked me back to my car. He told me next time we go out I can't start the date off fussing at him, that ruined the vibe. I told him he needed to be considerate of my time. I told him I'd rather he cancel on me, than to have me waiting. He said my point was received and he'd do better next time. I asked him what made him so sure there would be a next time. He gave me a knowing smile, and then he kissed me. This kiss was so juicy and good; I grabbed his jacket in order to save myself. I wasn't expecting his kiss to be that good. Anton could never kiss me like this. I looked at him wide eyed and he smiled. He said we were going out again next Friday.

****

"So," I looked down at the paper. "Reva tell me about yourself." This was my last interview of the day. Kalani and I were filling spaces for our evening nighttime staff. Business has picked up so much since we joined forces with Mitigated, and I loved being able to lean on them for staffing assistance. If we brought someone on as a temp and we didn't like him or her, we could call the agency and tell them to send someone else. Mitigated sent us all kinds of jobs as well. Evening and Night time Janitorial jobs, housekeeping, and apartment complex cleanings. You name it, our books stayed full these days. Since Ahjanae has to keep up with Erin and little Justin she runs the office and keeps the books. Tamille still works in the office but now she assists Ahjanae with a lot of the front line work. I still meet directly with our vendors and providers, however Kalani and I like to meet all of our new clients first and get a feel for the project before we let someone else handle them, and then it depends on the client if we turn them over. Kalani and I still personally service our elderly clients who were our original clients. When the interview was over, I gave Reva's information to Ahjanae. I told her I was going to the Parker-Pelayo house and then I was done for the day.

I took a deep breath when I saw Anton's truck parked in the driveway. I figured he probably decided the only way we'd cross paths again was to somehow be over here to Nellie's house and *work* on their backyard. Jason won't let Anton near my house; he hired a gardener to keep my front and back yard. One time he tried to pop up at my house and Jason's *friends* made him leave. I think the whole scene spooked Anton cause he didn't pay attention to the fact that there's always someone watching Kalani and I's house, which is right next-door.

I got my cleaning supplies out the back of my car and then I walked towards the house. Nellie opened the door with the goofiest look. I could tell by the look on her face he told her we broke up. When she asked about him before I've said he was fine, but I didn't go into it. What's hilarious to me is that she pays me to come to her house every two weeks to clean it. She follows me around the entire time cleaning with me. I know she could do all of this on her own, but she says I'm her only friend so I guess this is her way of trying to keep me around. "He says you guys broke up?" Her voice lingered to imply her question. "BUT! He wants you back."

"Yes, we broke up and no he can't get back with me. I'm done it's over. That's that."
Nellie's eyes begged me to tell her what happened. "Kendra?"
"He's still in love with his baby momma. I think he was with me to prove to his momma
he could date a black girl."
"Dating you doesn't mean he had to propose to you."
I shrugged, "I guess he got caught up. Either way he's still in love with her, and I don't
share." Nellie was quiet I could tell she didn't want to say anything to make me think
about our history. "How's design school going?"
"Good," she smiled excitedly. "Can I show you my latest design?"
"Of course!" I said standing up cause the bathroom now sparkled.
She motioned for me to follow her to the office that they both used for Marquez's after
hours work and Nellie's creations. She showed me her mannequin that had a pinned
blazer over a sheath dress. The dress material was white with a green and pink floral
pattern. The blazer was a soft pink to compliment the dress. I told her she will always try
to put pink in everything she does, she smiled. She was showing me some of her other
things from school, and telling me about the advancements she made with the help of her
sorority sisters, when Anton walked in the room. He had his big *I'm sorry* eyes on as he
looked at me. I smiled at him and said hello just like I would to any stranger on the street.
He asked me if he could talk to me, and I told him there was nothing that he needed to
say to me. I told him I was working and if he harassed me on my job I would have to
cancel this job altogether to avoid him. That's when Nellie told him to get out and she
restricted him to the outside, she said he couldn't come back inside. I tried to hold back
my laugh, but it came out anyways. She would not tolerate him causing her to lose her
only connection with me.
"Hey, guess who I saw?"
Nellie's eyes got big, "who?"
"Nathan. It's a small world; he's married to Darryl's cousin's best friend. I've been
meaning to ask you about that but it kept slipping my mind."
"Wow! It is a small world" She looked around the room. "So... you and Anton broke
up..."
I cut my eyes at her cause I knew she knew better than to open her mouth to ask me about
Darryl, but she was hoping I'd say. I let her invisible question ride on the air.

****

"This is Kendra, Kendra this is my cousin Sonya and her boyfriend Philip." Jude said.
"My man Philip!" She corrected him, and then she looked at me. "You look familiar,
have we met before?"
Inside I was dying, no we weren't introduced. How could I forget the female that Sasha
laid out with one punch? "I don't think we ever met. Nice to meet you." I said shaking
her hand. Kalani pressed her leg against my thigh and I smiled and shook my head yes to
tell her I remembered her. Raffy grabbed my hand and told me to come on. He wanted an
excuse to admire my African print jumper suit some more. It was really cute if I say so
myself. It was comfortable and gathered at the waist showing off my assets without
clinging to me. I loved the way it went with my braids and whole look. Raffy loved it and
he kept telling me how good I looked. We danced to a few songs then we went back to
our table for a drink.
"You were with Darryl!" Sonya said before I could sit down.
Kalani and I looked at her like she was crazy. "Didn't Sasha blacken your eye for running
your mouth? Some females never learn."
Kalani's comment upset her, but she had no come back for it. "Who's Darryl?" Raffy
asked nonchalantly.
"My ex."
Sonya laughed, "something funny?" Raffy asked looking at Sonya.

122

"You don't breakup with a Wallace, you may be on time out for a while, but they don't let people into their family and then let them leave whenever they want. It's cute that you would think it's over though."

Raffy looked at Jude, "she always running her mouth!" Then he looked at me, "so who's he supposed to be? Some big deal Richmond guy?" He said like it was a joke.

"Not just Richmond, mostly in Oakland! He got family and *people* everywhere. You two should call this off right now!" She said like she was warning us.

"First of all, I don't recall asking your opinion about nothing that goes on in my life. You need to shut up and mind your own business."

"And if you can't do that I'm sure I can find a way to help you with that!" Kalani said.

"Little girl, let me explain how adults handle things. You still young with the similac dripping from your lips. When we don't like something that someone says we use our words. Hitting is for children."

"So what words did you use when Sasha hit you in your eye?" Kalani put her hand up to her ear like she was listening for her answer. "Right! Like I thought! You didn't have anything to say when Sasha laid you out. Keep running your mouth about my sister and it's gonna be me and you!"

"Hey hey Kalani," Jude tried to say.

"Don't Kalani me, get your cousin. We were having a good time until she came running her mouth."

Sonya stood up and then she pointed to an open table for her and her man to go to.

"Whatever little girl, all I'm saying is don't be stupid. You don't mess with the Wallace's and don't be surprised when...."

Darryl glided through the doors; Sonya stopped talking and smiled like her point had been made. She got excited like she was heading to her seat to watch the show. Darryl was with that same girl from before. Sonya now had me wondering if it was a coincidence that he was here. Darryl and his girl were the only people I recognized in his group. They sat at a table reserved for them, as soon as Darryl sat down he looked directly at me, and my insides screamed. He didn't smile or frown he just looked at me. Raffy looked at Darryl then he shrugged him off. Raffy told me to come dance with him again. On the second song, Darryl walked up to us on the dance floor. No pretense of dancing or an excuse to speak he just stood there. I rolled my eyes at Darryl, Kalani came over. "What's up Darryl?" She said giving him a hug.

Raphael stood there locked in a stare down with Darryl. "Who's the foot soldier?" Darryl asked me.

"Foot soldier?" I crossed my arms.

"Oh my bad he probably hasn't told you what he does for a living." Then he looked me up and down, "that's a nice onesie! You get that at Babies R Us?"

"Look! I don't know who you are, but you have no idea who I am. I suggest you run back over there to your little group before you get your feelings hurt. She's here with me." Raphael said at the bottom of his voice.

Darryl looked at me, "look here RUNNER! You in MY HOUSE! Buck up at me again and I will kill you!" Then Darryl looked back at his table, "Q! Ain't this your guy? Somebody needs to tell him!"

Whoever Q is called Raphael over to Darryl's table. You could tell he didn't see the guy before and he didn't want to go but he knew he had to. Darryl looked at me and smiled.

"You got a taste for Thug Passion don't you?" I turned on my heels and walked back to the table. Darryl stood there on the dance floor watching me walk. Sonya was hanging on the edge of her seat watching everything like we were on TV and the drama was unfolding. I told Kalani I was leaving; she grabbed her purse as well. As we passed the table where Raffy was talking to the guy. I heard Raffy tell the guy he wanted to walk us out, and the guy told him he couldn't leave until he was done talking. Raffy looked pissed

123

but not crazy. Darryl took his seat next to the girl who looked irritated as usual by the whole scene, he told two of the guys with him to make sure Kalani and I got in our car safely.

The guys walked casually behind us while I went off about Darryl's little scene. He had the nerve to look good and then command the whole scene like that. Raffy called on our way home, he was apologizing for everything. He said that Q was his boss and everything got out of control.

Lanie

"She's nobody!" I said feeling relieved.

"Trouble in paradise?" Yussef watched me.

I took a deep breath then I got up and closed the door. "I'm going to be straight with you. I like you, I want you. I think we would be good together."

Yussef smiled at me, "so you're single?"

"Only if you're interested. You know, I'm not a virgin anymore and if you're down so am I."

"Your family is my family." He said as his eyes wandered all over my body.

"And you and I are about to be one." I walked over to him. I took him in my arms, touched his locs, and right as I was about to kiss him. The loud banging noise on my door jolted me out of my sleep.

"WAKE UP SLEEPY HEAD!" Eric said as he entered my room.

"Dang it Eric! You always do this to me. Can I at least get some in my dreams?"

"EEEWWLLLL! Lanie!" He shuddered. "You're the one who said you needed to go with me. Are you coming or not?"

The smell of deliciousness hit my nose, "is that what I think it is?"

"I guess you gonna have to get up and find out."

Part of me wanted to go back to sleep and see if I could pick up where my mind left off. I should've known I was dreaming when Yussef still had his locs. I got up, got my shower, and then I dressed and went downstairs. Hennessey caramel French toast, bacon, and eggs breakfast fit for a queen. Eric always spoils me, EJ too, but never as much as Eric. Eric watched me eat and I knew by the look on his face he was going to ask me about Dorian. I shook my head no at him, Eric asked me what was going on and I told him it was a little tiff and that Dorian and I would get back together, unless I could find a way to make Yussef come to his senses. Eric said that Yussef wasn't crazy, and then he kept asking me what happened with Dorian. When I kept saying nothing he looked at my hair like he was going to touch it. I picked up my fork and I told him I would stab him. He smiled at me and asked me again what happened. I told him that Dorian said we had to move forward or breakup and when I wouldn't agree to sit in service like a good girl every Sunday and Tuesday he thinks he broke up with me. "If that's all the man is asking for why wouldn't you just go?"

I shrugged, "what am I supposed to do? Lie and say I'll be there, pretend like that's what I'm going to do and then when we get married fall off?"

"Or just do it."

"If it's so easy how come you don't go?"

"I'm not exactly living right, you have no excuse. You and Dorian have been good and respectable."

"Right, double standards. I don't understand why it's got to be so hard. Momma and Daddy make it work."

"Dad goes more often than he doesn't. You have to learn how to compromise."

"Why I gotta do all the compromising. The man has to enter me, that's a compromise if I've ever seen one."

"Here we go, and he's giving you life when you compromise. What you do with it is up to you. You don't think Dorian's compromising to be with you? You think you fulfill his dreams in every way possible?"

"Yes I do. He's even told me that I was better than any woman he could ever dream of for himself."

"So if you were fulfilling everything why aren't you together right now?"

Anger turned in my stomach while Eric stood there smiling with his stupid smug face. "You get on my nerves."

In the car I was quiet, suddenly the tears I only allowed while I laid on my pillow wouldn't listen to me and back off. I turned my body to the door and I put on my shades as I battled my tears to try to make them obey. Dorian was almost completely happy with me. The only thing April had on me was that she went to service on a regular basis. She could never be as pretty as me, or as smart as me, my body is **WAY** better than hers, and she's a punk. I bet she can't even fight. I made Dorian laugh, and we always had fun even if we were hiding away in his apartment. So maybe I know that all those girls have crushes on him, and his honest love for God is one of the things I love most about him. He always did the right thing even when it didn't come naturally. He had a point when he said those girls come from all over trying to get his attention. It's not like all of them would've backed down just because he was married. I just didn't want to feel like I had to be there. There's no good reason why I didn't want to be there other than to argue. ERIC GETS ON MY NERVES! I texted Oneika and I told her we were going out tonight. I needed to think about something else as I tried to figure out how to apologize to Dorian.

"Thank you for calling Ace Trucking how may I direct your call?" The receptionist said as she mouthed one minute to Eric and I.

"Mr. Wallace and Ms. Wallace, Mr. Wallace will see you now." Tim's secretary said to us as she led us to the back.

She showed us into Tim's office and then we sat as we waited for him. "Sorry about that. I just got off a call and I had to pee like you wouldn't believe." Tim smiled.

"No problem, I noticed you took down your pictures of Stacy. You two didn't breakup?" I faked surprise.

"Lanie you are so rude. You know you never liked her."

"I really didn't. She was fake and phony. Do you have to approach everything so gingerly?"

He frowned at me then he looked at Eric, "is she trying to call me a punk?"

"I think she just did."

"The word is *gingerly*, look it up mister top of your class. Book smart but, I don't know about too much else."

"I understand what you mean Lanie. Just because you've got some fantasy of living thug'tastically does not mean that I'm soft. I'm getting tired of you referring to me that way."

"I'm getting tired of you referring to me that way." I mimicked him, "can you try that again with some bass? Say it like this," I cleared my throat. "I'm 'bout tired of you. Say one more thing and I'ma git wit cha!"

Tim cracked up laughing. "This is what you came for. A lesson in ghetto'isms?"

"You know I like messing with you."

"I do, you've been on me since we moved out here."

"I thought Chi-town kicked out my caliber of men as well. What part you from?"

"Dad kept my nose in books, sports, and everything else. I didn't have time to hang out and try to work on my blackness."

"Your momma's blacker than you!"

We all laughed, "my momma is blacker than everybody."

"Tina coming in to work today?" Eric asked looking across the hallway at her dark office.

"Who knows, I'm not my sister's keeper. Let's discuss business…"
We had a conference call with his father, Malachi, Malcolm, and Jade. Ace Trucking is one of the largest shipping and distribution companies period. Business went well, and then Eric and I had lunch with Tim. I told him I was going out with my friend Oneika tonight and that he should come. Tim kept hesitating but you knew he wanted to go, as soon as Eric invited himself then Tim agreed to go. On the car ride home I told Eric I guessed he wasn't going to service tonight and he smiled and said no. Eric volunteered his house as our meet up spot. Oneika met me at my job and we went directly to my house. I grabbed clothes for tonight and then we went to Eric's too big for just him house. As college graduation presents we each were given homes not too far from my parent's house in Berkeley. Erica, Zoey, and I rent ours out, while EJ moved his family in and Eric moved into his, which wasn't too far from EJ. Their houses were in walking distance to Solano Ave, which was on the Albany and Berkeley boarder. So sometimes we go to their houses and then walk to Solano and then have dinner wherever we choose. Tonight I needed to get to Eric's early so momma wouldn't ask me if I was going to service tonight. I know she means well, but service is the last place I'm thinking of. Besides Erica says it's hit or miss if Dorian shows up these days. She said when she does see him he's gone by the time the closing prayer is over.
When I asked Eric where we were going, he said tonight we were keeping it simple and going to EA. I wanted to go somewhere different, but I was over ruled by our group. Tuesday night clubbing is not the same as Friday night or over the weekend. It wasn't as crowded and most of the people there were looking to unwind after a heavy day or enjoy the performance. I couldn't stop thinking about Dorian. Maybe it was my cousin's very white-collar ways that made me think about my man. By the end of the night I felt like I was going to explode. When I took Oneika home, I drove to El Sobrante to look in Dorian's window. When I pulled up to his building he wasn't home, his car was missing. I walked towards the hill to see if I saw any lights, and there was no sign of life inside his place. As I walked back towards my car, I saw headlights and when the car turned the corner I knew it was Dorian's. I walked back up on the hill. I just wanted a quick look at him and then I was going to go home. Time stopped moving when I realized he wasn't alone. As soon as the door closed he was all over her. I can't believe this fool has got me standing on the side of a hill staring into his window while he kisses some other girl. At any minute he's going to stop, pull back, and then I will leave when he takes her home. My heart sank as he took all of her clothes off and did the same with his own. I felt sick when I watched him put the condom on. I weakly walked to my car, as I knew he was not turning back at that point. So what happened, I got him and I opened the floodgates? Now he's passing out what's mine to everyone but me?

****

"Where's your ring?" I asked staring at Kendra's ring tanned finger.
"We broke up." She looked embarrassed.
"Why on earth would you wait until the end of our lunch to tell me that? You should've led with that. Did Darryl cry when you guys got back together?"
Kendra exhaled and looked away, "you see. What had happened was."
"What had happened? WHAT HAD HAPPENED? Don't make me cut you! Why do you insist on playing with my emotions like this? Give my cousin a break!"
"Your cousin happens to get on my nerves, and drives me completely insane."
I smiled, "that's because he gives you fever. You know you feigning for some thug loving right about now. Say it with me THUG PASSION!"
"What would you know about it?"
"Hey, I'm the thug in my relationship. Look at the successful relationships of time. There's a square and there's a thug. They balance each other that way. Name one relationship where two thugs came together."

126

"Bonnie and Clyde." She said like she was so proud.

"And they died! Next!"

She thought for a minute, "Caine and Ronnie!"

"WHO?"

She tried to hold back her laugh, "Menace to Society."

"HE DIED YOU FOOL!" I threw my French fry at her.

She laughed as she thought about it some more. "I got it! Heathcliff and Claire Huxtable!"

Kendra and I laughed for a long time not speaking. "Who was the thug in their relationship?"

"Claire was absolutely a thug! You see the way she broke people down. She was always on point."

"Kendra you're proving my point, one thug and one non thug."

"Cliff was her supplier and she handled the criminals. They were both thugs on some old Wallace higher education stuff."

We laughed until I thought about it, "is that what you think? Everything we do is a cover up for illegal activity?"

Kendra stopped laughing, "that's not what I said."

"There's a such thing as a legal thug." I watched her.

"Ok."

"Even though I don't think it's exactly legal for me to go around shooting people. I'm not a criminal." Kendra twisted her head at me, "nothing's ever been proven in a court of law."

"Your cousin is mad at me, so I'm mad at him."

I blew air. "You guys need to grow up. You love him, he loves you. He was the first one to tap that nerve and you are forever sprung. Stop playing hard to get."

"So then you and Dorian must finally be getting married?"

"I HATE YOU!"

"Yes, Ms. Lanie let's dig into your love life."

"Ok, ok. Dorian and I broke-up."

Kendra gasped sarcastically, "no. What are you going to do about this? We can't have you two apart."

I surprised myself when I started crying. "He changed his number and moved across town. He hasn't reached out to me once. He's been screwing random females all over the place. He's not even acting like the man I fell in love with. He's got me over here crying to myself like my tears are ever shed without consequences."

"I'm sorry, I was only teasing." She came and hugged me, "I gotta tell you. It is scary seeing you go all female. You're like the last person I'd expect to fall victim to such emotions."

"Yeah, yeah... When are we going out?"

"Tonight sounds good to me, how about you?"

I wiped my eyes and tried to pull my emotions in check. "I'll come to your house to get ready."

Kendra was getting ready as I put the finishing touches on my makeup. I didn't know if my tears were going to surprise me and come bubbling forth again so I didn't go too heavy on my makeup. I took a step back. My black slacks, lime green cami that stopped just above my belly button showed off my chocolate cleavage nicely. I had lime green shoes and accessories, and a little black bolero jacket. My curves were nicely represented without looking like I was trying to display everything to the highest bidder like most of these little girls around here do. When Darryl texted me I knew he wanted to know where we were going. I told him I didn't know, and I asked him to give us space. He responded with a blank face emoticon and I imagined him throwing a fit. I told him I needed a girl's night with my girl, and he could pop up any other night. I knew Darryl wasn't happy, but I didn't want to sit on the side and watch him get at Kendra all night when I needed to get out of my head.

We went to Rodeo and over this little bridge by the waterfront to a karaoke spot. At first I looked at Kendra and Kalani like they had to be kidding. I could've come in jeans and a T-shirt. We ordered food and I ordered a beautiful as I silently asked what I was doing here. As we ate the music started pumping, a guy asked Kalani to dance as soon as we finished eating and it seemed like people started pouring in. So much for this little hole in the wall being a bust. I kept getting asked to dance and I was having so much fun. I finally told the guy I was dancing with I needed to sit down. I needed another drink. When I sat the waitress brought me another beautiful just when I was going to go get one. I asked her who sent it, and she pointed as she smiled. She said he told her I was the only girl who do this drink any justice. It was Dorian and my heart exploded. The guy who followed me was ok, but I told him it was time for him to move on cause he was barking up the wrong tree. Dorian smiled when he saw me send the guy away. He didn't sit or even say hello, he walked up to me and kissed me. He kissed me so deeply I thought I was going to explode. When I started to say something he told me to finish my drink so we could dance. I ate my cherries and then I tossed the rest of the drink back. Dorian asked me if I wanted another and I said yes. He smiled then he disappeared and came back with another drink for me and something else for him. When I started to say something he told me to drink and relax. I told him it seemed like he was trying to get me drunk, he smiled and said maybe. I got butterflies in my stomach. Then he took me out on the dance floor. We bumped and we grinded, I love dancing with him. In between songs he bought me more Beautifuls. Kendra said hello to Dorian and then she smiled at me and said she'd catch up with me later. Dorian told me to give him my keys. I asked him how many drinks had he had; I told him we could take a cab. He said the drink he had with me was the only one he had and he sweated that out a long time ago. I gave him my keys, when we got in my car I asked him how he got here. He smiled and said it didn't matter cause he was leaving with me. I kept trying to talk to him and he would turn up the radio or sing over my words. He better be happy I was drunk cause I would've punched him for that if I was sober. When we pulled up to his place I asked him where we were. He helped me out of the car but he didn't answer me. Drunk or not I knew better than to act like I knew where I was. As soon as he closed the door, he said we were going to do this right this time. I smiled at him loving this side of him. He took me by the hand and led me to the bedroom. He never takes a girl in here; they never get any further than his couch. He has sex with them all over his living room and then he sends them home. He took me to his bed. He kept kissing my stomach then he unbuttoned my pants. He smiled at my underwear and he told me that he liked that no matter what I always wore pretty underwear. I liked that about myself as well, so I smiled. He took off my cami and jacket and he kept smiling and kissing me everywhere, telling me how beautiful I was. I loved this whole scene. This is all I wanted, for him to love me despite everything else. He laid me down and then he took everything off of me. He undressed and then he got in the bed with me. He was trying to go right in and I backed up, um it was still uncomfortable. He smiled at me and said he was happy I waited for him. I smiled an embarrassed smile and then he went slow until he was all the way in. This was so much better than the first time; I watched his face as he tried to keep it together. He asked me if he was hurting me as my body tingled over. I shook my head no and he went in deeper. All night long he kept waking me up and going back in. I told him I loved him that made him lose it even more. I could definitely get used to this forever, I knew he would be good. In the morning I slowly walked to the kitchen and I made us breakfast. When I turned the fire off on the eggs Dorian put his arms around me and started sucking on my ear, I melted. He took me again in the kitchen. As Dorian ate his breakfast he looked at me and forced a smile.

"What's wrong?"

"Last night was good?"

"And this morning."

"This is what you wanted for us?" He blank stared at me.

"Um, not exactly, but kind of I guess."

"Well I'm glad this works for you, and that you finally got what you wanted. I hate this!" His sudden anger caught me off guard. "You hate this?"

"Look at you! Sitting over there perfectly fine with sinning like this. I'd expect a female who didn't grow up like us to be perfectly fine with this moment. I expect more from you!"

"More like what Dorian?"

"Remorse! This isn't the way it's supposed to be. Why am I the only person feeling guilty about any of this? This is ok with you? You'd want to exist like this with me?"

"Dorian please calm down." I felt horrible. Weren't we supposed to be in sexual bliss? Weren't we supposed to be declaring how last night and this morning made our love for each other stronger? I'm sitting here so sprung I can't do anything but cry and that's not me. I'm not the girl who sits and cries cause he hurt my feelings. I sat there watching Dorian go completely off. I couldn't say anything, I cried. And not pretty singular tears. Tears from the bottom of me.

Dorian wasn't letting up on his rant; I got up and put my clothes on. I get it now, he hates me. I pushed him too far thinking my way was the best way like I always do. "Where are you going?"

"Dorian I'm sorry for all of this. It's not until right now that I get it. You wanted something more for us. And I thought you were trying to control me. I've taken you outside of yourself. I understand it now. I'm sorry."

"Where are you going?"

"I'm leaving. You don't want me here. I wouldn't want me here either."

"NOW YOU'RE PLAYING THE VICTIM?"

"I'm not Dorian. You're really angry with me, I get it. I know what I did, and I know I don't deserve someone like you in my life."

"You're just going to leave?"

"If I stay, you'll really start to hate me. You aren't beyond repentance right now Dorian. You can go back and make someone a good husband one day. Every time you see me you're going to feel this." I cried harder, "I have to live with you hating me. I did this to us."

"Lanie!"

"Go ahead and tell me Dorian. Tell me how much you hate me. I took you to all of this nonsense."

"You're trying to make me feel guilty?"

"No!" I hated how weak I was being, and I couldn't blame him for not knowing how to respond to me. He's never seen me like this. BUT! I have NEVER in my life felt this horrible about anything that I've ever done to anyone. I mean anyone I've shot deserved it. Anyone I've beaten deserved it as well. It's very rare that I feel remorse for something I've done. "I know this is all my fault. I'm sorry Dorian." I opened the door, and he slammed it shut.

"Where are you going?"

"Home I guess."

"You are trying to make me feel guilty!"

"No! Baby I'm not. I am so sorry."

"Cut it out Lanie!"

"What do you want from me? You want me to scream at you so you don't feel anything for making me leave your place like you send the rest of the girls away. I know what's been happening here. All your practice, every time it's a new face. I know you're over here drowning your sorrows in new faces and hating yourself afterwards. This isn't you Dorian and you don't even like living like this. I get it, cause in this moment I can't stand for you to look at me. You may be angry, but you're only angry because I hurt you. I pushed you too far, I did this to both of us. You will recover from this because your relationship with God is real to you. I'm not what you need in your life."

"When do you ever give in?"

"When I hurt you!" Then I jerked the door open and pushed him out of my way.

When I got home no one was home thank goodness. I showered then I got in the bed. I cried my eyes out until I fell asleep.

****

Knock, knock, knock…. "Lanie." My daddy opened my door.

I said an exhausted, "yeah dad."

"Get your shoes and meet me at my car." Then he walked out.

If my daddy wasn't always a man of little words it would make me nervous. This is who he is. My momma watched me walk down the stairs and get in the car; she didn't say anything to me. I should've known I was in trouble. "Yes daddy?" I said as I sat in my seat.

"Where's Dorian?"

"I don't know. We broke up."

"What did you do?"

"You really don't want to know daddy."

"Are you pregnant?" His foot got a little heavier on the gas.

"No?"

"Would you tell me if you were?"

"Only after I had momma on my side and in front of me as a barrier."

"Why?"

"I don't know what you would do."

"Why wouldn't my reaction stop you from doing anything that would anger me?"

"I don't know."

"Lanie, I need you to think about things before you do them. I ran around for a minute doing whatever I wanted and then I spent the next twenty plus years trying to make right all that I did wrong. I don't want that for any of my kids especially you. Guilt is a heavy burden for anyone to bare."

Great! Now he tells me. "Daddy?" My hands immediately turned sweaty. "I am a little late, but it could be stress."

His breathing doubled and he gripped the steering wheel. "I can't! I can't do this! You gotta talk to your momma. Cause if you say one more thing Dorian is going to die."

My dad drove me back to the house and then he left. When I walked in the door my momma's eyes were big and locked on me. "Momma." I said with tears rolling down my face.

She put her arms out and I ran to her and buried my head into her arms. "Are you?"

"I think so, but he hates me momma. I forced him. This wasn't the plan he had for us. I messed everything up."

"What do you mean, how could you force him?"

"You know me, I rarely take no for an answer."

Erica came downstairs, "what's going on?"

"Nothing baby, Lanie and I will be back." Momma led me by the hand to her purse in the kitchen and then we got in her car. I couldn't stop crying. Momma took us to the bakery on Merritt for pie and ice cream. "When I met your daddy in college he seemed so unhappy. He was in the corner watching everybody and coming up with observations. I forced myself on him as a friend."

"What does that mean?"

"Kind of like you did with Dorian. I noticed your father and I made him be my best friend, he didn't really have a choice in the matter. He probably never would've kissed me if I didn't make him. I found out later that when he kissed me that was the first time he'd ever kissed anyone."

"I did more than make Dorian kiss me." I sunk in my seat embarrassed.

"I kind of forced that too." She sunk in her seat just like I did.

"MOMMA! Are you my twin soul?"

"No! There is clearly something wrong with you." She laughed, "in a lot of ways we are twin souls. The difference between me and you is that you don't care about hurting people's feelings and I spent most of my life in fear of doing that. You came out stronger than me. You've always been different, but that's always been a good thing. Does Dorian know?"

"No, he already hates me. This will just make things worse."

"Stop running. First thing's first. Let's confirm that you are in fact pregnant. As soon as we know you're going to talk to him and cut all this nonsense out you hear me."

"Yes momma."

Yussef

"WHY IS THAT SKANK DRIVING YOUR CAR!" Melissa blasted me as she opened the door.

I clinched my teeth, Jackson couldn't have been here if she was being this loud. I stood there looking at her telling myself to breathe. "Where's Yezzy?"

"Right here daddy." Yezzy said with sad eyes.

"Let's go!" I said reaching out for her hand.

Melissa slapped my hand, "DON'T IGNORE ME!"

Yezzy jumped when she did it and she looked at me wide eyed, to see what I was going to do. I wanted to choke Melissa up; I'm not a child! But at the same time I had to think about the example I was setting for my daughter. I grabbed her wrist extremely tight to the point where her hand turned red. "Melissa don't you ever in your life touch me like that again! You have completely lost your mind. Yesmina go get in the car with your sister." Yezzy did as she was told. Little Jackson was in the window looking completely wide eyed, but he couldn't see my death grip on his momma's wrist. "Melissa your jealous act is too much!"

"Act! Act? Who's acting? Why do you think I kept you so far away? I knew I couldn't handle this. How am I supposed to be?"

"I told you to control yourself, and you act like a crazy person. Touch me again and I will break my foot off so smooth…"

"I'm sorry. It's just that I've seen her driving your car, and then Yesmina says that Sydney has been coming over your house every day after school and on the Saturdays that she doesn't come. What's going on?"

"It's none of your business what's happening with me and Sydney. You don't ask me questions!" Then I turned to walk away.

"Why can't you see, it's all a game?"

"That you're playing!"

She walked close to me so her son wouldn't hear from the window. "I'm genuinely in love with you. I would do anything for you. She's after the money she hasn't changed."

"I'd believe you if you didn't keep my daughter away from me until you couldn't anymore. Anything for me as long as it doesn't inconvenience you! Even now, you can't let this time be about me and my daughter. You have to keep inserting yourself in whenever you can. All this drama is about what you feel, what you're going through.

What about what I feel? What I'm going through? You're acting just like Shonda these days and it's sickening." My comparison to my momma wounded her. "Since I've met you, you've been hollering I LOVE YOU YUSSEF! You're a good man! You're this... and You're that.... But if I'm so GOOD why did you do me so dirty? There was always something about you. Something that made me hold back with you. I didn't come out the gate spouting love, you did! But if you loved me so much who was calling you at all booty-call hours of the night? It was always little stuff like that, that made me not trust you completely. Then here I am like a fool thinking that the moment you're free I'm gonna sweep you off your feet and never let you go again. And then Boom here's your secret! You had my baby and didn't even have the decency to tell me I have a child, A PART OF ME! Existing in this world! She has my father's eyes, my sister's laugh! My blood flowing through her veins! You want me to be concerned with how any of this affects you? Stand down Melissa! Don't make me hate you any more than I already do! Stop mugging my daughter; Syd hasn't done anything to you! How you treat my child is a reflection of how you treat me!" Tears fell from Melissa's eyes as she turned on her heels and walked inside. My girls were looking with big eyes as I walked to the car. I said a quick prayer to calm myself then I got in the car with a big smile and drove. I listened to the girls talk about their girlie things. Yezzy was telling Syd how much fun they were going to have at their Auntie Latia's. When we got to Latia's house Syd stayed by my side, when Yezzy took off excited to see her aunt who was waiting at the front door. Latia told Yezzy to show Syd around and to show her where to put her things. The girls were going to spend the night with Latia so she could bond with Sydney as well. Latia stared at me for a minute, "it's a trip seeing you with short hair. Can you believe how much you look like him?"

"No, I wonder though. If we shave your head would you get the same reaction?" I smiled. "I happen to love my locs, I have no intentions to shave them. I may cut them shorter, but never completely off."

"How's the wedding planning coming?"

"Ok, I guess. Did I tell you the venue is going to be in New York? His family is huge and for those that I'd actually know to invite we can all fly out together."

"Good to know."

"Where's Angela?"

"She's not feeling the step mom roll so we see each other basically every other weekend."

Latia lowered her voice, "she doesn't like the girls?"

"I think if it were just the girls, she'd be fine. The baby mommas, she's not feeling that."

"You need special skin to deal with them that's for sure."

We talked for a while then we went out to dinner. By the end of dinner Latia had two little bear cubs cuddling up to her. She was in heaven, but so were they. I kissed my girls goodnight and I told them I would see them Sunday. I threw a little bit of a brat fit when Latia asked for my weekend with the girls. I agreed to bring them Friday night so they would have almost a complete weekend to bond. Jeff invited me out for a drink stating that we hadn't hung out in a while. Which was true. We met at a karaoke bar in Emeryville. Once we were talking and relaxing I realized how much I missed adult conversation. I have been so caught up in my girls and putting it on Angela, that I hadn't had time for much else. After we were good and relaxed our waitress put song request papers and a pencil on our table. She kept egging us on to get up and perform. Finally Jeff gave in and asked for the catalog. I told him I wasn't a singer, and he said we could rap. But I wasn't an amazing lyricist outside of my poetry. But when he landed on Heavy D, "We Got Our Own Thing!" It had to happen. As we were walking to the front to perform, I saw Sylvia walking towards the front door with a friend. I rolled my eyes and kept moving. I was the hype man and Jeff knew all the words he didn't need the projector. When someone yelled, "GO WHITE BOY! GO WHITE BOY! GO!" Jeff looked behind himself like they were talking to someone else. Everyone laughed and he continued on with his song. Until that person said it, I forgot that he was white. When we finally took our seats after we did two more songs our waitress came over to give us our salute and a drink on the house for livening up the atmosphere in the bar. Sylvia was staring, so I looked at her. She waited for me to say it was ok for her to come over. I was feeling good so I waved her and her friend over. She asked Jeff if he and Randi were still together. He proudly held up his left hand to show off his band. She told him congratulations and she asked him to give them to Randi for her. Her friend was trying to place our faces. When I reminded her that I met her at Jeff's house when Randi was trying to fix us up, Mandie gasped as it all came back to her. Then she looked confused when she asked Sylvia how I was Sydney's father. Sylvia explained how we didn't know until recently when we had Sydney DNA tested. Mandie made a face like the whole thing was as clear as mud. When they called Sylvia up to the stage cause it was her turn, she looked embarrassed. She got up there and sang "Her hips don't lie." I forgot how good her voice is, she had the whole house rocking as she did her little dance as she got into the song. During her song Mandie's phone started blowing up, obviously someone wanted to speak with her urgently, but she was trying her best to act unaffected by it. Eventually she walked away from the table to take the call. Jeff gave Sylvia a high five and told her she was really good. She thanked him, as she looked around for Mandie. When Mandie came back she said they had to go, and that her man was tripping. Sylvia went up to the front to tell them to cancel her other song she had on the list. I asked Jeff if he was ready to go, Jeff said we were getting old cause he was ready for bed and it was only a little after ten. I told the ladies we'd walk them out. Jeff got directly in his car and left. When Sylvia became chatty-Cathy, I told Mandie who was trying to be patient to go ahead and go to her man, and I would take Sylvia home. Sylvia didn't try to mask her excitement, I don't know what she thought was about to happen. Mandie thanked me and she took off in the opposite direction of Sylvia's place. Sylvia was pulling all the good memories out of her hat, all the good times we had together. She said she told Sydney all the clean stories, and then she looked out the window. She asked where Angela was, and I told her she was around, just not as much while my girls were with me. She started to say something, but I cut her off. "Melissa and Angela seem to think you're only after money." I glanced at her.

"Before money was a factor in everything I did. Now Sydney is."

"So you're trying to find her a daddy?"

"Sydney has a daddy," she smiled really big.

When we pulled in front of her place she asked me if I wanted to come in and see pictures of Sydney when she was a baby. Of course I did! I could tell she was excited that I was coming inside; I normally stayed at the door. When I stepped in the door Sylvia had the place decorated nicely. She definitely made this small apartment a home. The old futon was still there but it was now part of the decor of the room. She invited me to have a seat and then she ran up the stairs. She came back down the stairs with three big photo albums; she set them on the couch next to me. She put one in my hands and told me to start with that one. Then she asked me if I wanted something to drink? I asked for water and she frowned at me. So I repeated my request, then I opened my book. The first set of pictures were of her when she was pregnant. Her hair was longer then, even though she's been growing her hair long again, I like it best on her when it was long like it was when we were together. She brought me a tall glass of water and then a short glass of something brown. When I looked at her, she said it was in case I changed my mind. She sat next to me on the couch, making sure that her breast touched me while I looked at the book. I scooted away from her to give myself some space, I was being nice. I didn't want that to be mistaken for stupid. Her family was in Sydney's pictures for the first two years of her life. My baby girl was adorable, same face just unbelievably smaller. She was a little fat baby, until she started walking. I admired my little girl with every turn. In the last album she had pictures of the girls together. And there it was as clear as day Sydney and Yesmina my project twins looking so much alike that they could be fraternal twins. I smiled at all the pictures she had of them together. They were all of the girls at school, and obviously before I came on the scene. Sylvia said she needed pictures of me and the girls. I told her I'd send some with Sydney cause Angela had taken a bunch of them. When I gestured like I was going to stand Sylvia started talking fast to try to keep me sitting. She told me she owed me everything and she was thankful that I was back. I didn't say anything I stared at her; she honestly thought she was getting some tonight. I didn't come in here with any intentions of smashing her, plus I didn't want to complicate things, I could never feel what I felt for her before. Looking at those pictures it was easy to remember the way it used to be. How in love with her I was, I was so gone that it took us breaking up for me to hear and know that she had cheated on me. My glare made her nervous, and she started twisting her hair. She poured out her heart to me, apologizing for the millionth time. So I sat back and I let her get it out, say all the apology she needed to say. When she started to repeat what she said ten minutes ago I told her she keeps apologizing, I asked if there was a reaction she was looking for from me when she did that. She said she was looking for forgiveness. I asked her how she knew I hadn't forgiven her. She said it was in the way I looked at her, the way I spoke to her, and how I disregarded her. I told her she was holding on to the way I acted when I was in love with her. I told her that ship has sailed. She asked me if that meant I could never forgive her? I told her I've gotten past it as much as I could so that we could be cool for our daughter's sake. Then I stood up to leave, she sighed disappointedly and walked behind me to the door. She asked me for a hug at least and when I stopped to hug her she kissed and gently sucked on my neck like she used to. That sent electricity to my toes; all the memories of her constantly serving me up came rushing back to me. Sex with Sylvia was always great; she put everything she had into it. That was also before I learned a few more tricks of my own. If I smashed her right now she'd be sprung for life. She'd have that same cross-eyed look Angela has whenever I've ripped into her. I also knew that I was half way still mad at Sylvia so if I smashed her right now not only would she be sprung, but she'd be walking funny for at least a week. I told myself to get out of there cause I deserve better than an angry bang with my baby momma right now. I looked at Sylvia I nodded my head then I walked out the door. I called Angela from the car. I felt a little weak in that moment. Angela was mad that I woke her up cause she had to go to work in the morning. I tried to talk to her anyways, but she wasn't going for it. I put my key in the ignition and Sylvia walked out to my car. She said she saw that I was still here and she was making sure I was ok. I told her I was fine, she nervously asked me if I wanted to come back in. I sat there looking at her for a minute. What difference did it make? Angela was hanging on the edge of this relationship. I always do the right thing and here I sit? What difference does it make? Sylvia's eyes got big when I got out of the car. I guess she expected me to say no. When we got inside I had second thoughts and I stood in the doorway for a minute arguing with myself. She put on a movie and said she'd be right back. She ran up those stairs so excitedly fast. I laid down the futon as I heard her turn on the shower. I laid down and closed my eyes when I heard her coming. She called my name and I didn't move. She kissed my cheek and I didn't move. I only moved to tell her to leave me alone. She exhaled disappointedly and then she grabbed a blanket for us. She turned off the TV then she took her robe off and laid next to me under the blanket. She put her body against me and her arm around me. Then she whispered,"Mi amor! Las palabras no pueden expresar cuanto lamento haberte danado como lo hice! Se que eres sigue enojado conmigo. Ojala que pudiera volver atras en el tiempo para borrar el dolor que te cause. Te amo y estoy aqui para ti de ninguna manera que me necesita. Le debo todo. Hare cualquier cosa que quieres. (My love! Words cannot express how sorry I am for hurting you like I did! I know you're still mad at me. I wish I could go back in time to erase the pain I've caused you. I love you and I am here for you in any way you need me to be. I owe you everything. I will do anything you want me to.)" Then she kissed the back of my neck. I used to love when she spoke to me in Spanish. It was an automatic turn on. Now I wondered what she said. I knew I should've taken those Spanish classes when I had the chance.

In the morning I looked at her sleeping, she was almost smiling in her sleep. I went to the bathroom took a deep breath. When I came out the bathroom she was running down the stairs and I could smell her toothpaste. She asked me if I was hungry, I told her to get dressed and I would be back to take her out to breakfast.

Sylvia lost all color when I returned on my bike. When we were dating she refused to ride with me. I held out her helmet and I asked her if she was coming or not. Sylvia said a little prayer and then she took the helmet. I couldn't believe she was getting on my bike. I knew she was scared and she squeezed the life out of me once she got on. I could feel her body trembling; I reached back and patted her leg. I told her she was safe, and to relax. This was my first time on my bike without my dreads, my helmet even fit differently. After an hour on my bike Sylvia finally relaxed some. Right before we got on highway one I stopped to fill up. Sylvia took her helmet off and tried to wipe the tears off her face before I saw them but her eyes were red. I smiled at her and asked her why she was that scared of my bike. She said she's always thought of motorcycles as death on wheels. Then she thanked me for not doing anything to scare her. You could smell the ocean air. She asked where we were going, and I told her we were going to Bodega Bay to have breakfast and spend the day. She smiled then she asked me to open the box so she could call in and let her boss know she wasn't coming in today. Then she asked me how I ever heard of a place so far away? I blank stared at her, "you've never seen that movie *The Birds*?" She shook her head no, I explained the movie the best I could and how the birds started attacking the people in this town. Her eyes got big and she asked me why would I take her to be eaten by birds? She said she knew I hated her, but she never thought I would use her as bird food. I let her comment about me hating her ride on the air. I told her to get back on the bike. I told her the seafood here was really fresh, plus I liked the idea of being away from home without being too far away. We stopped at a cafe on the water. There was a pier right outside and some fishermen were going out on their boats. Sylvia smiled taking it all in, she said its beautiful out here. I nodded in agreement as I stared out at the water. Sylvia asked me what I was going to have bringing my attention back to the cafe. Breakfast was nice but Sylvia was waiting to hear why I brought her here. We drove up the coastline a little and there was a park nearby. I asked Sylvia if she wanted to go horseback riding. Sylvia nervously said she'd do it if I wanted her to. I parked on the beach and then I sat on the sand. Sylvia sat next to me and she picked up sand in her hand and let it slip through her fingers. We were quiet for a long time, and then she apologized again. I told her normally I would tell someone to stop apologizing as soon as they uttered the second apology, but in her case she owed every single apology she could utter. She kept her head low as she accepted every direct statement from me. No sugar coating or yielding for her feelings. She took it all and I could see the weight of it all on her. I asked her point blank if she was offering herself to me in hopes that she'd have access to my pockets again. She looked at me and said that she had Sydney and as long as she had her she had access to my pockets, but that's not why she invited me in. I couldn't argue that, she said at the mediation office when Sydney was a baby and they read the paternity results she said the weight of what she did was visible in me. She said I had lost weight and even though I was happy when they said I was not the father I looked sad. When I looked at her all she saw was hatred and that was a hard pill to swallow when just a short while ago we were in love. She said she tried to date, but it was difficult with her daughter watching. She said Sydney's first word was Da-Da, and she didn't know what to tell her. Her family got tired of helping her cause it wasn't benefiting them. She said she tried to stay with her cousin Monica. Even Monica was tired of dealing with her. Then Monica's boyfriend made her uncomfortable with his sudden interest in Sydney. She said she was on welfare for a brief moment and they put her in the program to find her current job. She learned the value of every hard earned dollar. She also learned the difference between when a man loves you and trust you verses all that she experienced after me. She said she has no right to complain but some people were heartless and she didn't want Sydney exposed to any more ridiculousness than she had to be.

I asked her why she cut her hair, she said she was tired of it all, the cat and mouse game. She was tired of being used. So I asked why she keeps offering herself on a platter if she was so tired. She said that was only for me. She said she prepared herself to be celibate the rest of her life. I looped back around to this boyfriend who was paying attention to Sydney, and I asked her what happened. She said they got out of there before anything *bad* happened. But she said Sydney was always scared of him and stayed stuck to her side whenever he came around.

I told her that I was impressed that she got on the bike. She swallowed and said it still wasn't her cup of tea, but she'd do anything for me. I told her I was still hurt, but not as much anymore. I told her about Drew being married, she looked surprised. She said she didn't see him as the marrying type. I told her he's married and faithfully married to a good girl. I told her everyone was either married or on their way to being married except for me. She asked me about Angela, and I exhaled exhausted air. I told her she doesn't make complete sense to me. Then again I understood. I thanked her for trying to be cool as far as my relationship is concerned, but Melissa was a trip. Then Sylvia asked me where Melissa came from and how did she get pregnant? I told her the whole story, how Melissa and I were spending time as friends, and that I threw us over that friend line. She smiled a pained smile and said she thought she didn't let me leave the house with any more fuel in the tank. I reminded her that she had been slipping on her job at that point. "So now what?"

I exhaled, "Angela's asking for time but I guess I can't work that way. Seeing her one-day every two weeks seems to suit her fine, but it's not working for me. I love her, but it's not working."

"I guess throwing myself at you doesn't help huh?"

"Nope!" I said grabbing the sand. "It feels like a trick, but I don't get that impression when I look in your eyes." Then I exhaled, "but maybe you're that one person I can't read."

"That or you don't want to."

"Why wouldn't I want to?"

"Cause you'd see the truth and sincerity in my eyes and you don't want to forgive me."

"I don't! Forgiving you feels like being taken in by my momma and all her games. I could kill you if I let you in to hurt me again."

She put her head on my shoulder, "as long as there's breath in my body. I won't be the source of any intentional pain in your life. I'll do whatever you want me to, and I won't complain."

I smiled, "even eat jellyfish with me?"

She popped up, "please no!" Then she swallowed, "whatever means whatever."

"I don't know what I'm going to do with Angela yet. I love her and I want to be with her."

"I'm not going anywhere, I'm waiting on you."

I inhaled, the air smelled fresher in that moment.

"So if things continue on their current course. I'm going to need a date for my sister's wedding. If I don't invite Angela will you go with me?"

She swallowed, "will your sister be mad? She didn't like me."

"If I officially invite you then she is ok with it."

"Yussef?" I looked at her, "can I kiss you?"

"Not at this moment." I said wrestling with myself.

We spent the rest of the day walking around the nearby state park looking at everything God provided for our enjoyment. One of the things I missed about Melissa and Tracy was having bible discussions. We'd discuss everything about the bible and Melissa would ask me why I hadn't come back to service. Tracy understood the conflict and knowing that we weren't living exactly right, but she would encourage me to go anyways. Sylvia was listening to me unlike the way she used to. Most of the things I was saying seemed like new information to her. Which also led to questions and then more information. On our way back I decided to stop by my grandma's house. Sylvia's eyes got big when my grandma stepped out on the porch. My grandma didn't smile when she saw Sylvia, but she didn't frown either. She invited Sylvia in, very nervously she walked behind me. I cringed when I heard my momma's laugh.

"Yussef I thought I told you that I wanted to meet my grandbabies!" She barked as I walked in the door. She was sitting under Jarvis' arm smiling from ear to ear. Her eyes darted to Sylvia, "who's that? Cause I could've sworn my momma said your girlfriend and I could use the same comb!"

"I bet he met her on one of his temping assignments." Jarvis chimed in. I shot him a look and he got irritated.

I looked at Sylvia, "you remember my grandma?"

"Yes, hello. Nice to see you again."

"And this is the infamous Shonda, also known as my momma."

"Nice to meet you, Sylvia."

"Where's the black girl?" My momma said not even acknowledging Sylvia's hello.

"Shonda why do you have to be so rude?" Grandma said.

"Yussef nothing about this girl reminds me of me. Why would you come home with such a girl?"

"Why on earth would I EVER want a female who reminds me of you?" Jarvis acted like he was going to say something in my momma's defense, but he shut up when I looked at him. "You know you were raised to be loving of everybody, and this is how you act? Why would I introduce my daughters to you when you act so ugly? This is Sydney's mother. So next time you want to ask me why you don't know them just remember this right here."

"I didn't know that's why the baby is light skinned. I'm sorry." She said as if she didn't care.

"Shonda get out!" My grandma said.

"What?" She said like my grandmother's demand was unwarranted.

"You heard me! Get out and don't come back until you have a better sense of act right!"

"Momma!"

Grandma reached and took her shoe off, "don't make me tell you again. I'll have Yussef put you over my knee!"

My momma huffed then she and her husband left. My grandma exhaled, then she looked at Sylvia. "Hello again." She looked like she was trying to read Sylvia.

"Hello," Sylvia said completely embarrassed.

"Well didn't you grow up nicely." Then she looked at me, "what are you doing?" She cut her eyes at me.

"The girls are with Latia, I ran into her last night. We went for a ride this morning. That's all."

She looked me up and down, "un huh. Where's Angela?" She said walking in the kitchen. We followed her and she told Sylvia to sit at the table. "I called her last night and she got mad cause it was late and she had to get up early."

"Did she call you back?"

I shrugged, "yea."

My grandma exhaled, "boy! Why you gotta be so hard headed?"

"Grandma what am I supposed to do? She doesn't want my life. I gave her some space and she likes it. She likes it too much. It's a waste of energy if you ask me. I didn't know I had kids when I met her. If you love someone you accept the good and the bad. If the bad is too much you walk away. You don't keep the person in limbo like this. I didn't do this on purpose." I said frustrated.

"Meanwhile what are you doing with Sylvia?"

"We talked."

"About?"

I looked at Sylvia, "she apologized for the whatever time, and then we got caught up. She showed me baby pictures of my baby, it's been completely innocent."

"Un huh!" She said turning her attention to the stove. "So Sylvia, what's new? I like the new look. It looks like you've been humbled."

"Yes I have. I'm not trying to cause Yussef any problems." Sylvia explained.

"I know baby, I can see that. What a difference single parenthood can make in a person's life huh."

"Oh yes, I love my baby. But now she exudes love with her father in her life. It's like she's a new person. I'm so grateful for everything he's done for Sydney."

"What about you?" She asked, Sylvia looked quizzical. "What has he done for you?"

"Everything he's done for me has been for Sydney's benefit."

"Even today?"

Sylvia blushed, "seeing my daughter so happy has given me wind beneath my wings. I feel so much better and my confidence in everything has been coming back. I owe Yussef my life, it's been hard to see any good in me without him."

Grandma turned around, "I wish I would've met this person all those years ago instead of that self-centered little brat."

"I was horrible, wasn't I."

"OH! My momma didn't like you! She was spitting nails!" Sylvia's eyes bounced around the room. "She passed away a few years ago."

"Baby! Did I miss? Shonda? Darn!" Arthur called out sarcastically from the front door. "I see my grandson's bike out front."

My grandma smiled real big, "I remarried." Then she blushed, "Arthur we're in the kitchen." She called out.

Arthur walked in the kitchen, "whoa! Who's this pretty little thing? Hey son!" He said giving me a hug.

"This is Sydney's mother Sylvia. Sylvia this is Arthur my grandfather."

Arthur smiled real big and prideful, "nice to meet you." Then he kissed my grandma.

The four of us sat in the kitchen chatting for a long time. Then Arthur reminded my grandma that they were going over his son's for dinner. As we got on the bike I asked Sylvia if she was hungry for dinner, and she suggested ordering a pizza. She thinks she's slick, she's still trying to keep me around. I'm not gonna lie, it felt good to be wanted around. I just wasn't feeling wanted by Angela. I put my bike in her garage, I checked my phone and I had ten missed calls all from Angela. I called Latia to check on the girls again, and she told me I was interrupting their fun and to stop calling them. We ate pizza and then I found myself laying on her couch like I used to lay on ours and I invited her to lay across me like we used to. So of course I put my hand on her butt like I used to and she giggled. When I started yawning, I told her I was going to go home. Her eyes pleaded with me not to go. I told her at some point I had to answer Angela's call or call her back.

Sylvia said she understood, but then I found myself really *Sleepy* so I pulled out the futon. I told her to control herself and I'd stay.

Episode 11

Yussef

When Sylvia's breathing changed I knew that meant she was awake. I laid there awhile and then she got up ran upstairs. I went to the bathroom under the stairs. Sleeping in my clothes two nights in a row, wasn't my idea of comfort, but I enjoyed my time with Sylvia all the same. I wondered how long before the old Sylvia surfaced or had she been through enough that the old Sylvia was a thing of the past? I washed my hands and passed water through my mouth, nope I needed toothpaste and a brush. Maybe it was a good thing that I spent all my time focused on my girls, but this weekend had been nice. Adult conversation the entire time, and someone who wanted everything for me. I tried to remember when I've been in a relationship where it was all about what I wanted and needed. I shook my head, Angela was gonna flip out on me when I finally talked to her. But oh well, she couldn't possibly think that what we have is going to cut it. We were together almost every day. How does she think cutting back our interactions to once every two weeks would work for me? And she's gotten so used to me making the sex amazing that it seems like we're only seeing each other to hook up. Like she's a booty call, not my woman. I need more than that in my life. I looked at my father's face in the mirror and I asked him what should I do? I asked him if a lap girl could graduate to a woman who belonged in my head? He didn't have an answer for that, which meant I was going to have to talk to Malcolm to sort this all out.

I walked out the bathroom and Sylvia was still upstairs. I laid back down and closed my eyes. Maybe ten minutes later she came back downstairs. I could smell the fresh soap and toothpaste as her morning smell. She rubbed my head and snuggled up to me. I opened my eyes and looked at her, her eyes showed all these loving sentiments. I didn't say anything I just looked at her. When she couldn't gauge if my look was happy or not she backed down and looked a little sad. I told her to get dressed and then we'd go out to breakfast. She looked surprised and then she happily ran up the stairs so fast. It was still very early and her house phone rang. She was in the bathroom, I looked at the Caller ID and it was a man's name. I picked up the phone, "Sylvia's phone."

He hesitated for a minute, "this is Abraham. Can I speak to Sylvia?"

I called up to her, and told her she had a phone call from Abraham. She hurried down the stairs in her robe. She looked surprised that I answered her phone, but she didn't address it. "Hello?...... No, no voy a trabajar hoy. (No, I'm not coming into work today.)...... Soy consciente de cuanto dinero no estoy haciendo por no entrar. (I'm aware of how much money I'm not making by not coming in.)...... Es de su incumbencia quien es el hombre quien respondio a mi telefono. (It's none of your business who the man is who answered my phone.)" She blew irritated air, "Mañana hablare con mi jefe, todo lo que necesitas es que no entrare hoy a trabajar horas extras. Adios Abraham. (I will talk to my boss tomorrow, all you need to know is that I'm not coming in today to work overtime. Goodbye Abraham.)" Then she hung up the phone. Then she explained that during the normal workweek she worked both the English and Spanish queue at her call center. On the weekends they needed her mostly in the Spanish queue. She said the supervisor Abraham looks forward to when she comes in. She said she tolerates him for the most part, but he didn't even give her a chance to call in and say she wasn't coming, probably cause he saw that she didn't work yesterday.

I asked her if she was missing out on a lot of money by not going in this weekend. She said her overtime gets taxed so heavily that it may come out to be the same since she worked overtime during the week. I could tell she wasn't sure, but she seemed happier to be with me than anything else. She said she would be ready to go in a few minutes. While she was upstairs I looked at her neat folder in the kitchen on the counter in the corner away from everything but under the phone. She had notes everywhere and the papers, but they were mostly collections notices and payment arrangements. They were all credit card bills. She was making good progress on them with her payments.

I sat back down on the couch and turned on the TV, after a few minutes she came bouncing down the stairs. She had fear on her face when we got on my bike, but she did it anyways. When we got to my place I figured it was only a matter of time before Angela showed up here. She was going to lose it when she saw Sylvia, but I didn't care. She had no idea why I called her the other night, and she left me hanging. I parked my bike in the garage next to my cars. We went upstairs, I put the television remote in her hand then I went in my room to get dressed. I showered and then as I came out the shower I heard the door buzzer. The sun was coming up so I knew Angela barely got any sleep. I came out of my room in only my towel. Sylvia stopped breathing as her eyes danced all over my body. I buzzed Angela in and then I cracked the door, Sylvia's eyes stayed glued to me. I went in the kitchen and poured a glass of orange juice, I asked Sylvia if she wanted some and she said yes. I poured the second glass. Angela was fussing before she got in the door good. She stopped talking mid-sentence when she saw me in my towel in the kitchen. Her eyes immediately went to the second glass and then she looked through the nook and saw Sylvia sitting on the couch. She started cursing! I gave Sylvia her glass and then I walked in my bedroom with Angela on my heels." Yussef! What is going on? I've been calling you all weekend!"

"When do I call you late at night?" I said removing my towel to put on lotion.

Angela stared at my dick like she wanted to ask it what it had gotten into this weekend. "I was tired Yussef! So from that you stop taking my calls and now you have her here? Where are the girls?"

"You don't care, so why should I? This joke of a relationship isn't working for me. I'm dealing with a lot and you don't seem to want to deal with it."

"So you break up with me without discussing it with me?"

"The day you decided that seeing me once every two weeks was good enough you broke up with me. It took me this long to get it and understand it. My girls aren't going away, and as far as I know there mothers aren't either. I didn't have sex with Sylvia if that's what you're thinking, but the temptation is there. At least she wants to be with me. You are too busy doing whatever it is that you do these days." I snapped my fingers, "oh yea. Work at the used car lot, take pictures, and scrapbooking. I remember now. All those things are more important than me."

"Yussef, I love you!" She sounded defeated.

"You've got a funny way of showing it. I needed you Friday night. Oh well though…. right?"

"Did you almost have sex with her or something?"

I pulled my jeans on, "nothing like me touching her or kissing her happened." She waited for me to say, "we made up."

"What does that mean? Please tell me you're not falling for her game. She only wants your money."

"Everyone comes for something don't they? What do you come for?"

"I don't want your money Yussef."

"You don't want me either."

"Yes I do!"

"If you wanted me how could once every two weeks work for you? That's not a relationship! I can't function like that. I need more."

"So you talk to me about it, you don't do this."

"I called you remember." I said putting on my shirt.

She sat on my bed and cried, "Yussef! Please don't do this!"

"You already did it for us. What do you want me to do Angela?"

She stood up and threw her arms around me while she cried. I held her back, but it was already done in my mind. She kissed my face, and I allowed her. When she started kissing my neck, I looked up at the ceiling. I told her to stop and that this wasn't going to change anything. She went to the nightstand, got a condom and took off her panties from under her dress as she stood in front of me. I took the condom from her, I didn't trust her not to try and rip it. Every thrust was saying goodbye, have a nice life. She started shaking, which made it hard not to blow, I withdrew when I couldn't hold any longer. It didn't feel safe to let one seed drop in the condom in her soil. I flushed and washed up. When I came out the bathroom Angela was gone. I sat on the bed to take a minute to take a breath. I took a deep breath. Three tears in a bucket... I'm tired of these females! They're always acting like they have the market cornered on feelings. Like everything is about what they feel and what they're going through. I'm tired of always doing the right thing, and for what? What thanks do I get? I could feel the evilness stir in my stomach as I sat there. I took a deep breath and I walked out of my room. Sylvia was sitting on the couch with her head almost between her knees and hands clasped. The TV was off and I know she didn't hear me coming. She almost looked like she was praying, but I saw tears dropping to the floor. She looked like she was debating with herself. I stood there watching her; she grabbed her purse like she just convinced herself to leave. She screamed when she saw me, her eyes were red and it looked like she had been crying for a minute. "Where are you going?"

"Yussef!" She wiped her eye with her wrist. I keep causing you problems. I was going to catch the bus or walk home. I'm sorry!"

"What are you talking about?" I watched her eyes; I was looking for a put on. She never did the sugary sweet voice thing like my momma. So I listened for the tone she used to use, which was just a version of the sugary sweet tone I wasn't familiar with, but her tears seemed genuine.

"I know you guys were arguing about me. I'm not trying to cause you problems. I only want to make things easier for you. Not worse, and it seems like I'm only making them worse. Your mother was not happy to see a Mexican riding with her son. And then you and Angela, I saw how upset she was when she left. You didn't hear her screaming at me?"

"No, what did she say?"

"After she cursed me out, she called me a money hungry, manipulative, back-stabbing, such-and-such."

"I told you that's what they keep saying." I turned a chair from the table around and faced it towards her, and then I sat down. "So let's be real. In this moment I need you to be the most honest that you have ever been with anyone. What do you want from me?"

"I want you to honestly forgive me! I will do whatever it takes to continue to prove how sorry I am to you."

"So say I said I was going to marry Angela and I needed you to disappear, would you do it?"

She looked confused, "if that's what you wanted. How would that work?"

"Give me Sydney. You go your way and we'll go ours. I'll get her a cell phone so she can call you when she wants to talk to you. Any parental communication would go through Angela, but she really doesn't want to talk to you. So you'd have to limit that to minimal communication really."

Her body slumped, she thought about it for a minute. "If that's what you really want. What if Sydney wants to be with me?"

"Convince her that being with her father is best for her." I said watching her eyes.

She cried harder, "ok. If that's what you want."

"Seriously? You'll do it?" I said still watching her eyes.

"Yes."

I picked up my phone and I dialed. "What's up?"

"Hey man, I need you to notarize a document for me." I said.

"How many signatures?" Hubby asked.

"What's your baseline?"

"Let me know what you need, I got you."

"Cool, what time can we come by?"

"Any time after two." He said

"See you then." I said, I told Sylvia to come on. She was crying silent tears to herself, but she came. We went to my office in the Oakland Kiosk for Mitigated. I found a custody agreement online. I typed everything up stating that Sylvia was signing away her parental rights, waiving child support, and would maintain contact with Sydney only through Sydney's cellphone and she would not try to contact me directly ever. I printed everything out, and then we went to the Sprint store and we picked out cellphones for the girls. Sylvia held Syd's phone in her hand and she kept stroking it. I asked Sylvia if she wanted something to eat, but she wasn't hungry. So we sat outside of Hubby and Nicole's house waiting for two o'clock. I expected Sylvia to try to protest or try to defend herself in some way, but she didn't. I wondered if she would get down to the last minute and then try and weasel her way out of it. If I had Syd, there would be no more child support. If I had Syd the way I had it mapped out on this paperwork she'd never really see me again, and she'd be the visitor in her daughter's life.

Hubby opened his door and told us to come in when he saw us outside. "Oh my GOD! Sylvia?" Hubby said as we approached the house.

"WHAT?" Nicole called out from the kitchen.

"Yes, how are you?" She said trying to make her voice sound happier than she felt.

"I'm good, but what the heck is going on?" Hubby asked directly.

"She's waiving her parental rights. I'll need copies for each of us and for my lawyers in case she tries to fight it later."

Sylvia shook her head, "I won't fight you Yussef I told you that. I'll sign whatever you want."

"Wait a minute! Why would you sign? You don't want your daughter anymore?" Nicole said butting into our conversation.

"Of course I do! I love Sydney with everything in me. I also know what I've done. I'll still talk to her from time to time, but it's probably for the best that she's with her father. Yussef has a better grasp on God than I do. That's a good foundation to have; he has a better grasp on loving someone than I do as well. I know how much he loves her, and I know she'd be safe with him. I don't know what I'm going to do without her, I guess I'll just live for the moments when I do get to see her."

"Why are you taking her daughter?" Nicole said with fire in her eyes.

"I'm her father, and I want her with me. Angela has a problem with the women not the girls. One down and one more to go."

"YUSSEF! I can't believe you could be this cold! Hubby talk to him!"

"Woman, this is between them, be quiet."

"CONRAD!"

"WOMAN! Do not call me that! Call me DADDY if you got to find another name to call me other than Hubby." He demanded, "Nicole please leave us to handle business. I cannot have an emotional tie to this, this is business."

"But, it's not right!"

"What's not right? It's not right that I got two-baby momma's when I didn't ask for one! It's not fair, that I got three different women pulling at me when all I ever wanted was a wife and family of my own! It's not right that this woman broke my heart when all I wanted to do was finish school, marry her, and have a truckload of kids with her. Now she wanna tell me she loves me and actually look like she means it. Now she wanna tell me she'd do anything to make me happy! That little girl is here because I was trying to make her happy. Trying to feel loved, because NOBODY had love for me! There's a lot of things that aren't right in this world, at least one thing will be right. My girls will know how much I love them and how much they come first to me." Then I looked at Sylvia, "if everything you've said has been genuine then sign!"

She took the pen in her hand and signed and initialed everywhere she was supposed to, and I did as well. Sylvia started crying when it was all said and done. Nicole hugged her and cried with her as well. Hubby brought back four copies for me, plus the originals. I over paid him for his services, and then Sylvia and I left. I told her we should tell Sydney tonight, and she agreed. I told her when I dropped off Yezzy we'd come by and then we could tell Syd together. She said ok, I dropped her off at home. Then I took my copies to my office. I planned to put a copy in my safe, send a copy to my lawyer, and a copy in my safe deposit box. Then I sat there taking it all in. I called Malcolm from the office and we talked it out. I could hear the smile in his voice when I told him she signed the paperwork.

When I went to Latia's the girls were having a blast still. All three of them were sad when they saw me. I felt rejected until they made it up to me by smothering me with kisses, I love all three of my girls! Then Latia and I went in her room, I told her about my weekend. Her eyes got so big when I told her Sylvia signed. She said she had such a good time with the girls and she couldn't wait to spend more time with them once this was all said and done. I gave the girls their phones, and they were so excited. Latia exhaled and said, "you know this is going to be explosive! Melissa is going to be livid!"

"Melissa is crazy! I can't let her craziness get in my way of doing anything. She needs to put her husband first and get a grip. Jackson may be sickly, but he's not going anywhere. She needs to be thankful that a good man loves her and takes good care of her, when he knows firsthand how trifling she is." I said.

We went out to dinner, and the girls excitedly told me about all the fun they had with their Aunty this weekend. Latia was so proud and happy that the girls enjoyed their time as much as she did. "See! I told you guys I'm a great Aunty!" She said to me, "next weekend little Jackson and I are going to spend some time together as well. I can't have my baby feeling left out."

When I dropped Yezzy off, Melissa came to the door. I asked her where Jackson was, he was in earshot and came to the door and stood next to his wife. I directed my conversation to Jackson; "I bought Yezzy a phone so she can call me whenever she wants. I have every parental lock possible on it. I would prefer to discuss any parental issues or questions with you so that there's no confusion as to what's going on here." I gave Jackson my number; "please call me if there's anything we need to discuss. Your wife has been acting irrational and extremely jealous. Did she tell you she hit me the other day like I was one of the kids?" Jackson looked at his wife with nothing but irritation on his face. "I don't know how you deal with her, but I wanted to choke the life out of her!" I took a breath to calm myself. "I know you have a family structure over here, and I don't want to disturb that. However there are going to be some changes in my life and I don't want Yezzy feeling like she's getting left behind. I would at least like to be able to pick her up for school daily and take her to school so that she and I can have our alone time, since I pick up Syd every day after school."

"That should be fine, I work from home most days."

"Even better!" I said, "and if you can spare any extra evening time or time period, I would appreciate it."

"What changes are you getting ready to make?" Melissa asked.

I continued to ignore her and talk to Jackson, "maybe it would be better if we talked

143

another time and then you can tell your wife how things are going to go."

"Sounds good to me."

"I AM...." Melissa was about to act ugly.

"Melissa! A wife is supposed to have deep respect for her husband. One of the things I admired about you is how well you applied the scriptures to your life and you found pleasure in it. Please stop disrespecting your husband and me by acting as crazy as you have been. You are not setting a very good example for the children, and you are making my life more difficult than it has to be. If you ever loved me please stop all this nonsense and focus on your relationship with God and your family. Call me Jackson, and we can talk this whole thing out." I said then I gave Yezzy a hug and a kiss. I told her I would see her in the morning at seven.

In the car I asked Syd if she had a good time, and she became very excited and exclaimed how much she loves her aunty. She said she loved all the family that she never knew she had, and that she loved her sister most. That made me smile. When we got to Sylvia's apartment, her eyes were sad but she did her best to be upbeat. Syd showed her the new phone she had then she went over her weekend with her mother. As Sylvia prepared herself to talk to Syd, I told her we should have an exact plan of attack before she told her. Confused, Sylvia told Syd to go wash up for bed and then she'd come up to tuck her in. Syd gave me a huge hug goodnight and then she happily ran up the stairs. Sylvia kept saying this is for the best, as if she was trying to convince herself that everyday life without her daughter was for the best. I needed to push her buttons, so I asked her how she could just give up on her daughter like this. Stunned and completely in defense mode she explained that she signed my document because it was within Sydney and my best interest. She got mad and told me she didn't want to let her daughter go. She said Sydney has been her only motivation and family these days. She said she wasn't giving up on her daughter. I accused her of wanting to get rid of Sydney so she could start over. The fire in her eyes, tone, and words proved that wasn't true. I sat there not knowing what else I could do to prove where she stood. Then I thought of, one final test.

I called her to the couch, she didn't want to sit but she did on the opposite end away from me. "Angela said you're manipulating me, and you're after money. I know I keep saying that, but it's what they keep saying. Then we broke up." I watched her face for a reaction and she looked confused. "We're not going to enforce this document right now, but I'm sending it to my lawyer to file with the courts. I talked to Latia and she wants to get a good look at you, but plan on being my date for my sister's wedding. A heads up, Melissa will be there, that is if you still want to go?"

"This was a test?"

"Kind of. The documents are real and they will be filed come end of day tomorrow."

"Did I pass?" she asked still looking confused.

"So far!"

Chantel

A girl! Derrick is so excited and it's so cute. He says she's going to be a little me, and I wonder what a little me with two loving parents would be like. Brooklyn's mother called Derrick when she found out about our engagement. I guess they felt some kind of way about it, but ask me if I care. They need to accept that Derrick has moved on and he's happy. I felt the need to make it clear that I didn't want Brooklyn and her family at our wedding. Even if he doesn't acknowledge it I saw how awkward it was for his family seeing Amber with Malcolm. His aunt didn't say anything cause she's too sweet to say anything and really what could she say?

"AW! CHANTEL! I love it!" Grandma Rosa said when I came out.

I smiled, "you really like it? I love it too!" I stood in the mirror taking myself in. "I think this is it."

"We'll hem the dress the week of your wedding that way we'll have a better gauge of how it should fit." Cassondra explained.

"Ok, sounds good. Grandma I'm gonna take my dress off and then I need to see you in yours."

"I've been meaning to ask you why my dress isn't black."

"My grandmother and mother of the bride dresses are silver, you don't like it?"

"Oh honey Laverne and I love them. We just wondered why they were a different color."

"They're going to look really pretty in the pictures."

After I finished in the dress shop Grandma Rosa and I went out for lunch, I needed to talk to her. "If you don't stop beating around the bush."

"What?"

"Whatever it is, you need to spill it. Get it out. I'm not scary, you can talk to me about anything."

"I need to ask you for something and if you said no I don't know what I'd do cause I've already set my heart on it."

 She frowned, "what is it?"

"When I go back to work, I'm going to need someone to watch the baby..."

She cut me off, "oh! Is that all? I thought it was something bad. I had thought of the same thing already."

"Really?"

"Me or Laverne right?"

Ms. Laverne is my technical mom; she was the first woman to show me motherly affection.

Grandma Rosa and I made plans for when the baby comes. My wedding was right around the corner and I was ready to get this over with.

Tracy

I was showing my mom and my cousin Marie the latest updates on the bakery, and campus kiosk. They were so excited for me. My mom said she's told everyone she knows about the bakery. She said family is telling family and friends she said my Grand Opening is going to be great. When I didn't smile completely my mom asked me what was wrong. I told her the uncertainty of everything in my life right now was a little unnerving. My mom and Marie hugged me and told me to relax, they told me everything would work out just as it should.

****

"Mr. & Mrs. Wallace please keep in mind that each pregnancy is different. However, I've ordered an ultrasound as well as lab work today." My doctor said, "do you have any questions?"

"How do we get a female doctor," Andrew asked.

My doctor laughed, "you can go online at any time and switch doctors. But you need to do it soon. Any other questions?"

Andrew looked at his list of questions, "based upon Tracy's medical history. At a cursory glance do you think this pregnancy will be hard on her? And if so what can I do to make things easier on her?"

"Depending on your lab work today we may have to be more aggressive about your iron intake. Health wise you are a lot healthier than you were when you miscarried. I can't give you more details until we run some more test. Meanwhile, I might as well give you this pamphlet to read." Andrew added that one to the six he already had. "Don't forget to take your prenatal vitamins daily, and read that pamphlet on diet and exercise. Go next door and have your ultrasound and then downstairs to the lab. I'll call you if there's any cause for alarm. Otherwise you will see your results online. If you decide to go with another doctor I would like to say it was nice to meet you two. You're going to be great parents."

I don't know who's more nervous Andrew or me. After he talked to Sasha and El it seems like he's gotten more and more concerned. I appreciated that he seemed to pay attention more now, instead of just knowing everything was going to be ok. His list of questions was longer than mine, and we had duplicate questions mostly, so we worked from his list once I realized this. Andrew held my hand firmly as he guided me to the ultrasound technician. He seemed more nervous than I was. The technician took pictures of our little jellybean and gave us a picture of it. The technician guy kept looking at Andrew, and eventually he told him they went to school together. Andrew was so focused on me that he didn't pay the guy any attention until he said that. Andrew's face didn't turn friendly. He looked at the guy for a minute then he said his name. The guy nervously smiled and confirmed that was who he was. Andrew kept looking at him, but he wasn't saying anything. It was like he was reading him. As we walked to the lab Andrew continued to lead me with a firm grip, but he was completely silent. After my blood work was done Andrew then led me to the car and silently drove to a little cafe in Pinole called Tina's, he said their breakfast was really good. After we ordered I touched his hand. "What is it?"

"All of a sudden I'm scared! I can't control this and I'm freaking out. My heart is set on the baby, and it's too early to know."

I squeezed his hands, "I love you! I'm glad we're on the same page. I'm terrified! But we have to relax, we don't want a child who's stressed and tense about everything."

"No, one of you is enough." He smiled.

"So who was that guy?"

His smile dropped. He was quiet for a minute. He adjusted in his chair, "it's stupid." Our waitress set our plates in front of us. When she went away, he explained the dumb fight they had in middle school. He said he hurt that guy pretty bad.

"Why were you fighting?"

"Toya," then he put food in his mouth. I rolled my eyes, I should've known.

My food was so good! I asked Andrew how he ended up with Toya. He exhaled and said sometimes he wonders the same thing.

Sasha

"Going on a road trip! Road trip! Roooaddd TRIP AAH!" I sang to the top of my lungs for the tenth time.

El blank stared at me. "Why Sasha? Why?"

"El baby, do you ever just have a song in your heart that you gotta belt out at the top of your lungs?"

"I got something for you if you feel like hollering, but you're killing me with that song!" That was his nice way of telling me to shut up! "Why aren't you more excited? We're going to set the date for when I become Sasha Wallace-Parsons! You should be more excited!"

He frowned, "why wouldn't you drop Wallace altogether?"

"I'm proud to be a Wallace, if my name was Cardell, it would be a totally different story. Sasha Wallace is an important piece to my puzzle. Without Wallace you can't see the whole picture. You follow me?"

"As long as you don't try to hyphenate our kids names." I blank stared at him. He glanced at me, "NO SASHA! That's where I draw the line! My children's last names will be Parsons."

"Fine!" I said thinking of loopholes.

"You're plotting on me I can feel it!" He laughed.

"You know me too well."

"What's with all the heavy artillery?" He was referencing the special packing I did.

"Drew and Derrick want me to come set up my rooms in their houses. These are just safety precautions, nothing to worry your pretty little head about."

"Are you guys anticipating a war?"

I smiled and spoke in my best Malcolm voice. "We're always at war! The moment you're caught slipping is the moment you DIE!" I yelled.

"Did you eat sugar today? Seriously Sasha!" He said laughing.

"All jokes aside, let's talk." El agreed and he sat up straight while still focusing on the road. "I was thinking. Maybe we should buy a condo, and some property in the bay. Kind of like how Amber and Malcolm have their own spot in Beverly Hills, but they live out there. And I wanna invest in some rental properties out there as well as something for us."

"But we have properties in LA."

"I know, but there's no law that says we have to only buy around our primary residence. My family collectively owns property all over the country. Amber has had a lot of shoots in Miami lately, so she's gonna get a spot out there. Hotels get old."

"That's fine! You gonna booby-trap that place too?"

"Of course! Each location needs at least one breadbox. The condo in New York is setup as well."

"WHAT? How? We've always flown out there."

"I can be slippery when I need to be. Plus I needed you to be cool, it worked." Then I inhaled, "my baby D-Rick is getting married! At least he didn't forget me."

El changed the subject cause I was beating a dead horse. Drew agreed to provide all the first class transportation for my guests. I know I shouldn't look a gift horse in the mouth, but he owns Regal Rendezvous the limo company so how hard is it to direct his staff in our direction? But I know how excited my Dan-Dan and everyone on the Cardell side of my family will be to ride in luxury so I know I shouldn't complain.

We got to Drew's house a little after one in the afternoon. He introduced us to his puppies Cain and Eve. Then Drew and El put our bags in the guest room. Andre was so excited to see us, which made me so happy. Even though this wasn't my first time here, he showed us around the house. When we were upstairs the doorbell rang. I peeked out to see who was here and it was a guy I didn't recognize and I could tell by Drew's body language he didn't know him either. I excused myself and I went downstairs and stood next to my cousin. The guy looked slightly nervous as he explained that he sold this house to Tracy as a part of his divorce settlement. He wanted to know if they would be interested in selling the house back to him. Andrew was listening to his proposal, I bumped Andrew and I asked him where Tracy was. He said she should be home in a minute. He asked the guy to come back in an hour. But I could see the wheels in his brain were already turning. He called Uncle Dale, and I shook my head at him. I went back upstairs and then we heard Tracy calling up for help with her groceries. We ran down to the garage and it looked like she bought enough groceries for a month. Andrew told her to put her feet up and he would put the groceries away. She smiled real big and said thank you. I could see the wheels of Drew's brain thinking and trying to figure out an approach.

I told Tracy that El and I decided that we needed to invest in property out this way. Tracy smiled and said that was a good idea. Drew sat down and put Tracy's feet in his lap. Then he said, "I was thinking, where are we going to put the nursery? We shouldn't make Andre give up his room for the baby."

Tracy said she was thinking about the same thing, but they had time to figure that out. Then she asked me what type of property I wanted to invest in. I was going over my laundry list of ideas. El said he wanted to look at apartment buildings and places like that as well. Then the doorbell rang, Drew went to the door. They were talking for a few minutes and then Drew walked in with the guy. He was looking around taking in the house. "I love what you did with the house, I couldn't imagine all of this." He said, and then he explained his proposition to Drew and Tracy like he had earlier. Tracy's eyes danced between the guy and Drew. She asked him if he was serious, and he assured her that he was. He took out paperwork showing her what he sold her the house for. The current estimated value of the house. Then he offered her a hundred thousand over the market value. I could tell Drew was sold on the idea already, but Tracy got very emotional which caught the guy off guard. Drew took his information and said they needed a couple days to think it over. Drew explained that she was newly pregnant, and the guy said he understood. Tracy apologized like she was frustrated with herself for crying. I asked her if it was that bad, she looked at me and said she couldn't pull it back and she was trying with everything in her. Drew said we should go for a ride. We drove to Oakland and up the hill. I recognized the security gates. We parked by the trailer and Sharon and her brother Darren came out of the trailer. Andrew asked them to show us Malachi's house, which was almost finished. His circular driveway made me think of mine. The house wasn't finished, the floors and walls needed to be done, etc. Then we walked over to Chantel and Derrick's house. It was a community of mansions tucked away in the Oakland hills. Drew asked Tracy if she wanted one. She rolled her eyes at him while holding Andre's hand. I asked who else was up here. Sharon ran down the list. Amber and Malcolm, Malachi and Denise, Chantel and Derrick, Cyrus and Sherrell, Yussef, Jade and Sonny, a couple football players, a few baseball players, doctors and lawyers, etc. Andre asked his parents if they were getting a new house. Drew looked at Tracy and said it was up to her. Tracy said they needed to discuss somethings first. I could tell it was a done deal when they went in the trailer and looked at available lots. El knew by the look on my face I was curious. He shook his head no and said we already had a big house in LA and we didn't need two big houses that was just a waste of money. I knew he was right, and I knew Richard would have a fit if I tried to leave him in LA alone. Even though he moved out there by himself, but whatever. When I looked at the model of the community Amber and Malcolm's lot was the biggest one. Their lot was so big that Amber was having a multipurpose room placed on the property with its own kitchen and bathroom. When Sharon was explaining it, it sound like that's where we'd have family dinners, parties, etc. It was pretty big but on the display it looked small. My momma called me to ask if we made it yet. Then she proceeded to fuss at me for not checking in. Andrew said we'd come by as soon as they finished with Uncle Dale. That calmed her some. Tracy was quiet on the car ride over; I know she was trying to take everything in. When we got to my momma's restaurant she was talking to the manager. Travis and Sabrina were waiting by the car. I got out and gave them hugs, and then my momma asked where we were going to eat. When no one could think of anything Sabrina suggested Greek food. When Tracy said she's never had Greek food, my momma, Sabrina, and I got excited. We followed Travis's car down Ygnacio Valley Road into Walnut Creek.

Andrew kept smiling at us as I talked Tracy through the menu. Andre asked his dad what he was going to have. Andrew pointed it out on the menu, Andre said that his meal sounded good and he'd have the same. That tickled my momma so much. She said it was a trip to see Andrew with his miniature version of himself, and she couldn't wait to meet little Sassy. El put his arm around me and said he couldn't wait either. I smiled, what could I say to that?

Andrew told my momma that he and Tracy were thinking about moving to the hill with everyone else. My momma smiled, then she said she was considering the same thing. I got excited, "why are you excited?"

"Because I can stay with you when I come out. El says we can't have two big houses."

"Why can't you?" My momma asked.

"What purpose would two big houses serve? I'm open to a condo or something out this way. We have a condo in New York. But you live in the big house, you visit in the condos. We live in LA. We visit out here." El said matter of factly.

"Well I think you guys should move out here. You only moved out there to go to school. You've spent enough time out there, it's time to come back!" My momma said.

"Sophia our jobs are out there." El responded.

My momma looked at El, "you know as well as I do that you could do your jobs from out here. You guys travel a lot as it is. There's nothing keeping you planted in LA."

"We have our lives out there momma."

"You mean your father's out there!"

"Yes, and Richard's out there too. You're faulting me for wanting to be close to my father!"

"Yes! Yes I am! You belong out here, with me. With your family."

"Richard is my family too momma. And El and I are a family." I was trying to control my tone cause this was on its way to getting real ugly.

"You and El can be a family anywhere. I think you should move out here!"

"You're trying to tell me to move out here! I happen to like where I live. In the house that Poppa built for me, and my father secured."

"Your Poppa could have Uncle Dale build you another one next door to me!"

"Sophia!" Travis said sternly. "Stop doing Sasha like that. You're just mad cause you're not getting your way. What difference does it make where she lives? When she has her first child she's going to be in the house with us. Stop giving her such a hard time and look at the big picture."

My momma was breathing fire. "I am looking at the big picture TRA-VIS!"

"Uh oh!" Sabrina said shaking her head.

That stopped my momma from saying what she was going to say next. "Uh oh what?" She was looking at Sabrina.

Sabrina swallowed, "whenever you say daddy's name like that. It normally does not end well." Sabrina sank in her chair.

"You trying to be funny?" My momma asked.

"No ma'am, you're just beyond reasoning right now." Sabrina said scooting closer to Andrew away from my momma.

"Don't come over here. When she starts swinging, I'm ducking!"

My momma sat back in her chair smoldering, I hope Travis didn't have any plans of getting any tonight, cause she was in a mood. Everyone sat quiet for a little bit. Then Travis told my momma to step outside with him. We watched out the window as my momma's neck was wiggling and arms were flying as she gestured wildly. Travis said something and she crossed her arms and started pouting. He said something else and my momma tried to say something and he cut her off. My momma was so red I thought she was going to start sweating blood. Then I saw it, she lowered her head. Whatever Travis said made her back down, my momma doesn't back down. Tracy was smiling real big and then she said she wondered what he said. Andrew said he knew what he said, he put his foot down and she had to obey. Tracy and I rolled our eyes like whatever. Travis led my momma back inside, and then she apologized for going off. I smiled and then I gave Travis a big hug. She sucked her teeth and sat down. Then I asked her to tell me about the new house.

****

"I'M NOT COMING OUT!" Tanisha barked.

"Oh come on. We gotta see which one looks best."

"I CAN'T BELIEVE I SAID I WOULD DO THIS!" She yelled, and then she walked out of the dressing room.

I gasped as I put my hands over my mouth. Tears came to my eyes as I realized how much my sister really does love me. "Tanisha you look BEAUTIFUL!"

Tanisha was blushing and uncomfortable. "I can change right after the ceremony right?"

"NO! We gotta take pictures and I would love it if you stayed this way the entire night."

"Oh come on Sasha! It's bad enough you want people to see me like this, you want me to stay like this too?" She tugged at the dress.

"You look beautiful! If you were tore up I would tell you. You know I would. I don't know why you hide that body under baggy clothes? You don't like men, fine! But I don't know why you have to cover up so much."

"Says the recovering attention whore!"

"I'm recovered now, so that doesn't hurt me." I stuck my tongue at her. "Do you like the dress?"

Carina shook her head yes, "yes I do." Tanisha blushed again.

"Good! Cause I love it! Ava's going to wear the same color and fabric, but a different style. The rest of the girls are wearing this pretty tangerine color." I said pointing to three different dresses in my shade.

"Sasha?" I looked at Tanisha, "why are you having a rainbow bright wedding?"

"Shut up! My wedding is not a rainbow bright wedding. I like colors, bright happy colors. Even though it won't technically be spring, I'm hoping for spring like weather on my day."

"It's going to be beautiful!"

"Thank you Carina! See she knows, you just sit back and watch."

"What color are the mothers and grandmothers wearing?"

"Cream, watch it's going to be beautiful!" I said very confident about my color choices. Then she admired herself in the mirror even though she was trying to pretend that she didn't like it, Carina and I knew she did. Tanisha looked at me in the mirror. "DT!"

I frowned, "DT?"

She stood there waiting for me to get it. "Turan?"

"OH! DT got it."

"What did you say to him?"

"Nothing he did most of the talking. I told Richard everything. Why?"

"He came all the way out to find me. I don't know who he's sprung off more you, Amber, or Tina."

I smiled, "interesting. Did you tell somebody?"

"Yussef and Juan know."

"What did they say?"

"They'd talk to Malcolm," Tanisha eyed me.

"Was Yussef surprised?" They smiled, "what?"

"I told Carina at some point you'd ask about him."

"Whatever! He's very happy with his very ordinary girlfriend."

Tanisha smiled at me through the mirror. "I smell trouble in paradise for them."

"SHUT UP!" I leaned in for details.

"My momma went out to dinner with them before the engagement party. She's not feeling the stepmom roll." Then Tanisha explained how they got together before everything happened with his girls.

I felt bad for Yussef. I love El, but if he ever steps out of line Yussef is mine! I'd take those little girls and love them up. I don't care how crazy his baby momma thinks she is. She hasn't met me!

We ordered Tanisha's dress. I gave my consultant Nihjia my dress style choices for the tangerine dresses. I told her I'd come back with Ava to pick out her dress. Then I paid for my dress for Derrick's wedding and then I put it on to have it altered for the wedding. I told them I'd come back to try it on when I came out for Chantel's shower.

****

"We need to tighten up security. My family has to remain safe. Are there any questions?" Malcolm asked.

"You want all of the vehicles upgraded?" Clayton asked.

"That's correct."

"I'm just wondering how that's going to be done without raising alarm." Clayton said.

"Sasha and Chantel's cars are done already. Andrew maybe you spin the new house warrants a new car with Tracy. My LA cars are already done. This information is on a need to know basis. Wallace's, Secure your families, secure your families." Malcolm said.

"I'm sitting pretty, they could pluck a chickenhead if they want to." Darryl said sitting back in his chair.

"What about Kendra?" I asked.

"SON OF A! Malcolm!"

"Secure your families!" Malcolm repeated.

"This feels like pressure! I mean I care about her, but do I loop her in at such a traumatic time?" Darryl stroked his chin. "But they could use her against me." Darryl growled, "I'm not ready for such a commitment!" I couldn't help it I laughed at him. I imagined Malcolm glaring at the phone. "It's not funny Sasha! This just got serious!"

"Darryl!" Malcolm growled, "take your deliberations off line. Besides Jason has arrangements for his family."

"Derrick, take your wife on a nice honeymoon. Make sure it's kept quiet where you're going. I can see her celebrity status being exploited and used against us." Uncle Frank said. "Yussef, your sister. Her situation is very sensitive. We will speak offline about possible approaches. Joseph and Richard I want you in that conversation as well."

"I have information on Phineas' family and mistress." Carly said.

"Did you give that to Yussef?" Uncle Frank asked.

"Most of it, I have a few more details,"

"Well, what are you waiting for?"

"Uploading now."

"The bakery is moving along, Darren said it should be ready in a couple weeks." Andrew said.

"Push back, we need a little more time. I'll talk to Dale." Uncle Frank said.

I sat there listening to them play chest against their selves. "You guys know that DT is out here?" I asked.

"That's why Darryl is out there. Good thing is that Detective Dartnell is trying to have him assigned to something else. Bad news is that Detective White is being watched as a possible leak. All communication with him is on hold." Malcolm said.

"Timothy, how is Amber doing with your daughter?"

"Blood curdling screams, pleads for mercy, tough love I guess." Timothy said in defeat.

"Does your son have any tactical training?" Malcolm asked Timothy.

"Very basic to the point that I would say no," Timothy exhaled.

"Can he handle it?" Uncle Frank asked.

"Does he have a choice?" Timothy said.

"Andrew, Jeff, and Yussef, I'm going to need all of you to work with him. If he doesn't get it I need to know immediately!"

"How's security for the wedding coming?" My Poppa asked.

"Juan is in charge day of. Yussef and Richard are collaborating." Derrick said, "I've asked that no stone is left unturned, that's what I'm getting."

While they were talking Darryl was quietly arguing with himself. I put us on mute so that I could openly laugh at Darryl. He didn't appreciate me laughing at him but he was hilarious. His laughter was a much needed change of pace cause this meeting was intense. Even though I was just in New York checking out the Shylight lounge and I provided my findings, there was another inspection done by the city that has temporarily shut the lounge down. The findings have been escalated to the appropriate city officials. However Malcolm feels things are going to get rough from here. The San Francisco office got a female finger in the mail. There are a few possibilities, but no one has told Derrick that one possibility is that the finger could belong to his ex Brooklyn. Her family is looking for her, I never thought I would wish that someone is cracked out somewhere instead of the alternative.

"Ok, we will touch base next week."

Darryl stood up, "SASHA!!!! What am I gonna do? I don't think she's in danger, aargh!" Darryl fought the air. "This could be nothing and then I realize I don't want to be with her. But she's all in love with me, and hanging on my leg begging me not to go!" He shook his leg. "Get off me!"

"Or! What if it turns out she is the one and then you're all sprung and getting married like your brothers?" I smiled.

"MARRIED!!!! Are you kidding? What I look like getting married?"

"You look happy!"

"I'm not trying to be tied down like that. Look at my momma's life! Chasing a husband has gotten her three kids and heartache!"

"And Malcolm!" He shook his head, "no matter what he says. Or what he tells anybody. He knows my momma was going to get back with the pretty boy. He's marrying her just to keep her."

"If you look at it that way. I'd say he's marrying her because he loves her and he wants her to be happy."

"I guess!" He plopped back in his chair.

I watched him for a minute. "Darryl you're afraid of being hurt!"

"SSSHHHH!!! Watch what you say! I ain't scared of nothing!"

"Why is it ok for your brothers to marry and not you?"

"Me get married!!!! Please! I'd kill somebody!" He got up and started pacing. "I...." He paced some more, "I..." Then he frowned at me. "Dang it Sasha! I need to call Joanne! Stop messing with my head!" Then he walked to the kitchen to use the phone mumbling the whole way. I couldn't stop laughing, but I wanted an answer to my question. "Aw! Joanne! Come on!" I heard him say and I couldn't help but laugh. Darryl turned his back to me and he continued to talk to his therapist. He could stall talking to his therapist all he wanted to, but I saw them together. Plus she's Jason's daughter so her safety wasn't the question. Whether or not he wanted her with him was. Darryl isn't fooling me; I could see his love for her all over him. I got some work done over my laptop as I halfway listened to Darryl whine to his doctor. He was trying to convince her to agree with him that he wasn't afraid of anything or anyone. When she wouldn't agree he dramatically sighed and then he tried to re-argue his point. My puppies were sitting at the sliding glass window, relaxing and watching us mostly. Suddenly the dogs all looked to the left. Champ sent the other dogs to investigate, and Champ stayed posted by the door. I looked at Darryl thinking I would've needed to tell him to look but he was talking while he looked at the dogs. Darryl got off the phone then he walked to the door, he looked out. He was looking for a minute, and then he told me to go upstairs. I grabbed my computer and I went without asking any more questions. I shut my door and then I listened; now it was more than likely nothing. Aside from all of our drama, a few of the houses on my street have been broken into. It's the middle of the day, someone could be feeling Froggy. It's not like it's obvious that I have dogs, my dogs don't bark. Darryl called me down; he was looking at the monitor and laughing. The mailwoman was frozen in front of the gate after she entered. Darryl said the puppies let her in the gate, she took about five steps, and now they won't let her move. Darryl took the safety off his gun and put it in the back of his waist. "You ready?"

We walked out the house, and Champ came around and followed us but not closely. "Can I help you?"

"OH! Thank you JESUS! PLEASE CALL YOUR DOGS!"

"I need to see your ID first." Darryl said smiling.

She pulled out her Post Office Employee ID, "Your dogs don't respond to pepper spray."

"Puppy breath spray!" Darryl said proudly.

"Please sign." She said nervously.

I signed for the really thick and big envelope. Darryl told the puppies to stand down and then he told the mail lady to leave slowly.

There was a copy of a proposal I received from a developer offering to buy my house some months ago. And then there were tons of legal documents from the city that planned to invoke eminent domain on my property, well my block and the next two blocks over. I started cursing as I speed read the paperwork. Darryl was looking over my shoulder as I had my fit. El drove in the gate then he stopped when he saw me having my fit. "What is it?" He called out the car window.

"They're taking my house!"

"Who is?" El said marching over.

I gave him the papers; El hugged me as I cried.

When we walked in the door I called My Poppa and I cried to him. He told me to fax over the documents. He told me he'd ask Sonny to take a look at them.

When I got off the phone Darryl smiled at me. "You guys might as well prepare to move up the hill with everybody else."

"I'm not moving!" I pouted.

****

"Hello gorgeous!" Detective Turan said like it burned in him to say.

I frowned at him, "what do you want?"

"Turan is that you? You came all the way out here to see me?"

Turan frowned, "I thought I left you in Oakland."

"Come on now you know I'm everywhere." Darryl said, "what do you want?"

"To talk to Sasha." He barked.

"So talk!" Darryl barked back.

He looked at me, "this little boy is going to make me cause a scene!"

"What are you doing here?" El returned to the table.

Turan threw his hands up, "I thought you were on your way back to the office!"

"That's what you get for thoughting!"Darryl started laughing.

"What do you want with my daughter?" Richard said coming out of nowhere.

"Jesus! Is she on lockdown or something?" Turan barked.

"You know firsthand what our situation is. Don't act surprised. What do you want?" Richard barked

Turan stood there quiet for a minute. "Well played! I guess the Wallace's don't slip up no matter where they are." Then he looked at me, "you're the prettiest bait I've ever fell for."

I put my hand on El's arm because I saw that look in his eye. Darryl leaned back smiling. Richard told Turan to come with him. Turan didn't want to but when he saw the other four guys with Richard I know he didn't want to be drug out of this restaurant in front of everybody.

"I thought you were going back to the office too." I looked at El.

El was completely irritated. He took a deep breath. "Brielis called me. She said that my mum's losing a lot of weight and she's concerned. If something's going on with her she won't tell me over the phone. I need to go check on her."

"When are we leaving?"

He smiled at me and touched my face. "I love you, but you need to go to the Bay. Chantel's shower, talk to your Uncle. We've got too many things up in the air right now."

"Forget all that I need to be here for you!"

"Right and I need you to take care of business for us. I just bought a ticket out that leaves in an hour and a half. I need you to meet with the realtor this afternoon. If you like it I love it. Baby, I need you to take care of business." Then he kissed my lips. I could see worry all over his face.

I wanted to argue that I was going with him but he didn't want me to go. So I surrendered in defeat, but my gut told me whatever is happening with his momma was bad. Darryl didn't say anything he just watched us.

That afternoon we met with my favorite realtor Susan. Darryl and Bruce came with us. She showed me a few houses, but when she said she had a listing in the same building as Amber and Malcolm I got excited. The unit was on the fifth floor on the opposite side of the building as Amber's and I loved it. It made sense to have a condo out here anyways. My puppies would just have to come back to the Bay. There were a few things that needed to be updated, but I told Susan I wanted to make an offer. I didn't want to see anything else. I left El a voicemail, telling him we were downgrading to a condo.

When I talked to El that night he was thoroughly upset. His father has leukemia and contracted something through the blood transfusion he received. He said it was ironic that the very thing that was supposed to save his life is now killing him and his mother. I cried and asked him how long they've known. He said they've known for years but didn't want to trouble him. I could hear the anger in his voice. I wished I was there with him. He told me he loved me and he'd see me when he got back. He was going to stay longer than the few days he originally planned to stay.

Tracy

"Why are you pushing for this so badly?" I said trying to chew back my emotions.

"I think a new house would be a good idea. Think about it, a new beginning for us in a new house we buy together. PLUS!" He put his finger up to highlight the emphasis on the plus. "You can deposit, or whatever you would like to do with, the profit from the sale into your account. You put up your hard earned money to buy this place, do whatever you want with it?"

"I thought we were going to raise our family here." I said in defeat.

"Think about it Tracy, Andre has the room closest to our bedroom, where are we going to put the nursery? On the very end by the stairs? We could design our love nest together. My momma will be around the corner. You and Sherrell could ride to work together. Andre and the baby could go outside and play with their cousins. In addition to our personal home security we will be in a gated community. That will make me feel better whenever I have to travel for work, knowing that you're surrounded by family and completely secure."

"Yea but we'd have to move before the house was ready."

"I got that covered as well." He smiled, "Malcolm will move in with momma. They're practically living together now anyways. Darryl will stay in the loft until we move out." Then he kissed my hand, "this is perfect for us."

"Can I think about it?"

Andrew exhaled, "what is there to think about? It's a win-win situation."

I pointed to my non-existent belly, "hormones!"

Andrew blew irritated air. "I'll give you a few hours, but I want to call him back tonight with a decision." Then he stood up, "I'll go make dinner."

As soon as he closed the door I called Joy. I needed to talk to someone who understood my emotions about the situation without me having to explain everything from the bottom up. I needed to be able to be as dramatic as I felt without being judged for it.

"Hey what's going on?" As I spilled my guts crying and carrying on. She laughed cause

Andrew was calling Anthony for the same reason I was calling her, to be heard. I didn't tell her how much it amounted to but I told her what the buyer was offering and then Andrew's offer on top of it. "Tracy, you know I love you. You're my girl, and I say this in the most sincerest form of sisterhood." Then she cleared her throat, "ARE YOU CRAZY? Of course you're gonna do it! Think about everything you'll gain. Stop thinking about what you're losing. Property values are going down now is the best time to sell. And who gets a deal like that? Girl if you don't stop playing. You didn't even pay market value for your house. And the value has gone up, and then he's paying you above and beyond that! Even if there wasn't a brand new house in the background, you'd be a fool not to take it!"

I sat there shooting evil looks at no one around the room. "I guess I'm too emotionally attached."

"No, the fool that wants to buy the house is emotionally attached. You are making money hand over fist. If you don't tuck that money away and stop this nonsense." Then she laughed, "I wish Anthony would come at me with some stuff like that."

"How are things going on the job front?"

"The rumors are still floating around about layoffs. I'm trying not to stress about it. Anthony does enough of that for the both of us."

"Now I feel guilty." I said.

"Why?"

"Cause you gotta know, I'm hoping they do lay you off so you can join me and Sherrell in the bakery."

"What am I going to do in a bakery?"

"Manage it. I'm going to handle the baking. Sherrell is going to handle decorating. You could manage the business side. Keep my books in order, stuff like that. You couldn't possibly think that your services would stop at helping me design the layout of the bakery."

"Are you going to offer benefits?"

"Andrew is helping me put together a whole benefits package. If you tell me that you're in I'll go over money with Andrew."

"What happens if I don't get laid off?"

"Then I'll have to look for someone else. But the job will always be yours. Think about it, no more fighting for time off for service. You'll have more time with the kids. You could even have another baby if you want."

Joy started choking, "ANOTHER BABY?"

"Yes, you could have two more so that we'd have babies together."

"Uh NO! I'm good with the two I got. I've got one of each who could ask for anything more perfect. A boy for me and a girl for him. You can cover the baby making front for us from here on out."

Chantel

"Tracy's pretty cool, I don't know why you guys aren't best friends already."

I shrugged, "she's in her own world. She hasn't made an effort to know me."

"She could probably say the same about you. Technically you're the one who's always gone."

"Did she say something?" I eyed Sherrell.

"No, but I was thinking about it. I'm happy that we're close. Now you're going to have two sister in-laws, I can't be stingy." She smiled like she did her good deed of the day. "Besides all our babies are gonna be about the same age."

"Un huh, after you checked her out to see if you'd want to be bothered with her or not."

Sherrell laughed, "if she was annoying I wasn't going anywhere with ya'll." Then she cleared her throat. "You wanna call her now?"

"For what?" It felt like a set up.

"We should see what she's doing. Maybe you guys should rub your pregnant bellies together so your babies will look alike, we already know what mine is gonna look like. Another baby Rosa." She laughed.

"You are so goofy! Whatever, call her if you want to."

Sherrell called her on speakerphone. "Hey Tracy, it's Sherrell and Chantel."

"Hello ladies," then her voice got excited. "What are you guys doing right now?"

"We're sitting in my living room with our feet up. What you doing?"

"I'm with Amber and we're at this bridal trunk show in downtown San Jose. These dresses are amazing, you guys should come."

"I already got my dress though." I didn't exactly feel like it.

I could hear her smile, "I know but I need back up. It's like these sales people smell money and they are trying to convince Amber that these overpriced monstrous dresses will be pretty on her. **HELP**!"

We laughed and said we were on our way. Tracy gave Sherrell the address and we plugged it into the navigation system in my car. Little Rosa was so happy to be in the car. When we were close Tracy called again, her dramatics were cracking me up. She said Amber was in the dressing room trying on the ugliest dress ever made and they wanted seventeen thousand dollars for it. She said she'd meet us in the garage and she told Amber not to come out until we were all there. As we were getting out of the car I asked Tracy why Amber would go dress shopping without Jade, Sophia, and her Auntie Lauren? She said they were only supposed to be browsing but the salespeople here are pushy. I've never been to a trunk show so I had to take her word for it. When we walked into the banquet hall everyone yelled "SURPRISE!" I froze in place for a minute, and then I rolled my eyes at Sherrell and Tracy who were very pleased with their performances. There were cameras and photographers everywhere. I told everyone if I wasn't so tired I would've paid attention to Sherrell encouraging me to get dressed for no reason, and that baby girl was dressed and hair combed on a Saturday for no reason.

The room was decorated nicely with large pictures of Derrick and I when we were little and then pictures of me and Amber, me and Ms. Laverne, me and Grandma Rosa, me and Pearla, etc. My favorite pose from Derrick and I's pregnancy pictures. We're both looking down at my stomach. I noticed that all the pictures with Derrick in them never show his whole face except for when he was a baby. Dionne Derrick's grandmother came and gave me a big hug. I was happy she was having a good day, but then she called me Patricia like she normally does. I took pictures with everyone; Alexa and Meredith made it out. Sasha was even here. The food was so good. Sherrell told me that she helped Tracy decorate my cake. It was so cute, pink, white, and Chocolate. It had a sign that said welcome Baby Chanel. I loved it!

Then Carina announced that the entertainment portion of my bridal slash baby shower was about to begin. They sat my chair in the middle of the dance floor. I was nervous cause I didn't know what to expect. A group of guys in black suits, white shirts, and black fedoras walked in the room. I know my man's walk anywhere. I stood up and cat called to him. Derrick smiled as they approached. It was Darryl, Drew, Jeff, JoJo, Eric and my baby. They did a dance that I could tell was tastefully choreographed for us. Eric sang to me, while they danced. I love his voice and I keep begging him to go back in the studio with me. He always smiles and says he'll think about it. Then little Andre came in at the end dressed like the men. He danced just like them and he handed me a rose. I couldn't stop smiling. I thanked everyone for going through so much trouble for me.

Tracy

"Sherrell did this?" Amber asked smiling at the cake.

"Isn't she good!" I smiled at her handy work.

"I think the two of you together are going to be a force to recon with."

"I hope you're right."

The photographer came over snapping picture after picture of everything and she took special interest in the cake. I was starting to get antsy until Sherrell called like planned. I tried to sound as natural as I could. When we hung up, I told everyone to get ready cause they were on their way. I called the room upstairs and I told the men that Chantel was coming. I'd say I played my part very well. The shower went off without a hitch, Chantel was surprised and she loved the cake just like Sherrell said she would. As everyone was partying and having a good time, I felt tired and crampy. I sat over to the side trying to calm myself because immediately I felt alarmed. Amber was smiling until she noticed me sitting, she looked for Andrew then she told me to come with her. I never noticed how strong her hands were before. But I guess she felt like she needed to stable me. When we walked into the hallway I don't know where Yussef came from. "Are you ok?" His eyes were concerned.

"I'm ok, I think I need to lay down though." I said trying to hold back my dramatics.

"Can you stay with her while I go get Andy?" Amber asked as she handed me over.

"I'm fine Amber, I can tell him I need to go."

"No! You stay here." She said firmly then she walked away.

"Come sit." Yussef said pointing to a bench.

I looked at him, "it is so weird looking at you without your locs."

"Am I ugly now?" He laughed.

"No it's just different." I don't know why I felt embarrassed.

"My head feels so much lighter. Sometimes I feel like I'm gonna fall over cause I'm used to balancing them. This is the first time in life that I don't have long hair."

"Survey says? You gonna keep your hair short?"

He shrugged, "for now."

Andrew came out of the banquet hall completely worried. I told him I was fine I just needed to lay down and rest. He didn't believe me, but he agreed to take me home instead of to the emergency room like he wanted to. Andrew thanked Yussef for waiting with me and then Yussef walked away. Amber told us to go home and she'd keep Andre with her. Andrew held my hand during the car ride home. I had to remind him to breathe cause it seemed like he was holding his breath looking at me for signs of alarm. I kept reassuring Andrew that I was fine. When we got home he willingly kissed me, but he refused to go any further. I looked at him like he had to be kidding. He said he needed a doctor's note before he went there with me. I thought he was kidding at first until I saw his face. He wasn't joking. "Andrew! Seriously?"

Andrew exhaled, laid down, and put his pillow over his head. "Whatever!"

"Andrew?"

"Last night could be the reason you're all messed up today. My poor baby could be in there screaming for help and the beast is in there wrecking shop. I'm not beating on my baby."

I laughed, "you know that's not true."

"Maybe for the averaged sized man. Don't forget I've been blessed."

"What about me? What about us?"

"We can do other stuff, I'm not going in there!" He said sternly.

"This is ridiculous! To be so smart, sometimes I swear!" I reached for my phone.

"You gonna call my momma?"

I laughed again. "No! I'm calling the advice nurse cause you're being ridiculous. If you

can't perform your marital dues I promise this will be the ONLY baby I have!"
He looked at me sarcastically. "It's only sex Tracy."
I felt my anger boil, "don't make me hit you with this phone! ONLY SEX! ONLY SEX!"
Andrew started laughing at me, which made me angrier.
"Labor and delivery how may I help you?"
"Yes I need to speak with the advice nurse." Andrew told me to put the phone on speaker.
"That would be me, my name is nurse Sandra how may I help you?"
I froze in shock. "The same nurse Sandra from like five years ago?"
I could hear the smile in her voice. "More than likely. I've been the only nurse Sandra here over the past fifteen years. How may I help you?"
Tears poured out of my eyes. "My name is Tracy Thomas-Wallace, but you waited on me years ago."
"That's nice, when did you deliver?"
"I didn't I ended up miscarrying and being admitted because I lost an unusual amount of blood for a miscarriage. You were always very kind to me, and you convinced me to share my news with my parents but then I lost the baby. You held my hand during the whole thing. I'll never forget your kindness!"
She was quiet for a minute, "Tracy do you wear your hair curly?"
"Yes!" I said through my tears.
"I remember you baby. How are you?"
"I'm so much better! I got married he's here on the phone actually." I nudged Andrew.
"Hello," he said.
"How much longer is your shift?"
"I just started actually."
"Can I come by? I want you to meet my husband, and then I can ask my questions."
"That's fine baby."
"See you in a minute. I live up the street."
"Ok see you in a minute."
Andrew didn't want to leave but when he saw I was going with or without him, he came along. When we walked up to the nurse's station, she smiled as soon as she saw me. We hugged and then she told them we were going in Doctor Mann's office. We walked down the hall hand in hand. She peeked at Andrew, "he's handsome." She said congratulating me.
"Thank you," I said while Andrew blushed.
In the office she wanted to hear everything, how we met. How he proposed, about the wedding. She admired my ring and kept telling me that I've come so far. I thanked her and then I thanked her again for all the kindness she showed me those years ago. Then she reminded me that I was calling for the advice nurse. Andrew turned red as he sat back in his chair. "Today I was feeling a little crampy and tired, my dear husband seems to think that means we shouldn't have sex anymore. Needless to say we're not seeing eye to eye."
"You think you might hurt the baby?" She asked him.
"Yes," he said trying to control how hard he was blushing.
Nurse Sandra walked over to the diagram of the uterus, etc. She explained how well the baby was protected and that he'd hurt me before he hurt the baby.
We left the hospital smiling, and then I got my evening delight.

****

"Mr. & Mrs. Wallace your baby is fine, and Mrs. Wallace you are healthy. I just want you to try to keep stress to a minimum. As much as you can avoid it." Doctor Shabazz said.
"Easier said than done, she stresses about everything."

"Andrew! Don't talk about me like I'm not here! No stress ok, can I still prepare my bakery for opening?"

"It's fine if you still work, but don't stay on your feet all day. Make sure you sit when you can. Your contractions aren't uncommon but with your history we want to make sure we do everything to keep you comfortable. And Mr. Wallace no stressing about your wife's stress. All that's going to do is make her stress more."

"Thank you doctor!" I rolled my eyes at Andrew. "Is it normal to be so small?" I pointed to my barely there stomach.

"Your baby's development is normal. Trust me you will get to the uncomfortable part of pregnancy soon enough."

I relaxed a lot, but Andrew still looked stressed. "You're not packing the rest of the house. I'll have someone come do it tomorrow."

"Andrew! I can do it! I'm not helpless you know. You heard what the doctor said."

Andrew didn't say anything he just kept driving. When we got to his mom's house he was quietly sitting and thinking. I told Amber what the doctor said; she looked at Andrew and shook her head. "He's worried, you gotta appreciate that even if he has a messed up way of showing it." Then she looked at him. "Andy will you entrust Tracy's care to me next week?"

He frowned, "next week? What's next week?"

Amber blank stared at him, "your brother's wedding. Hello!"

"What does that have to do with her care?"

"The first night is just us girls. I was there when Tracy told you."

"Momma that was a long time ago. Derrick can't be ok with this! Malcolm's letting you go?"

Amber put her hand on her hip, "letting? Boy you are funny!"

"Whatever!" Andrew mumbled up at the ceiling. Then he exhaled, "you know what would make me feel better?"

"What?"

"There have been updates in safety features. I want to buy Tracy a new car."

I looked at Amber, and then I looked at her son. "What is wrong with you? You just paid for a huge wedding, first class honeymoon, and now this house. Is money burning a hole in your pocket? I cannot believe you can afford to keep spending like this without us ending up in trouble."

He looked at me like I insulted him. "Believe it!" Then he stared at me. I looked at Amber to back me up and she looked up at the ceiling. "What kind of car do you want?"

I rolled my eyes, "whatever Andrew. Since you're mister big spender, just bring me what you think I'll like."

He nodded his head; "you'll have it by the weekend."

"Malcolm's getting me a new car as well." Amber volunteered.

"What kind of car are you getting?"

She shrugged, "last time I let him pick out my car I got a silver bullet. You haven't been to the condo huh?"

"No, where is it?"

She smiled real big, "Beverly Hills!"

My mouth fell open, "you have a condo in Beverly Hills?"

"Yep, it's really nice if I do say so myself." She was somewhat defending her son. "You gotta go out with me one of these times. Maybe once everything calms down we can take a girl's trip out." Then she looked at Andrew, "you guys didn't discuss finances?"

"Tracy is scary." He said standing to see who was pulling up to the house.

"Whatever Andrew!"

"Scary?" Amber asked.

"Talk to her," then Andrew walked out the door.

"What does he mean by saying you're scary?"

"What if he starts thinking I'm about the money?" I said in my defense.

"What if something happens to him and you need to take care of his money for him? If you aren't aware of one, how he manages it, two, where it comes from, and three, what needs to be paid how are you of any value? I understand being nervous about it, but you can't let fear stop you from doing anything. You need to know as much as he's willing to show you."

"Do you know all of Malcolm's financial information?"

"Mostly, but there was a time when he needed me to handle business for him as well. Malcolm's never hidden his money from me, and I doubt Andy would do that to you. You're his wife! Besides you need to know how well you're being taken care of so you can relax. Remember the doctor said no stress. And stressing about money is not something you need to do right now."

Andrew came in the door carrying a big box, with Malcolm behind him with another. Both of their faces were serious and holding the same expression. "Tracy," Malcolm said acknowledging me and then following his son up the stairs.

Yussef

"Auntie!" Sydney said excitedly through the intercom. "Can I go down to meet her?"

"You can wait for her next to the elevator." I told her as I buzzed Latia in.

Syd bolted out the door and down the hallway. Sylvia nervously stood in the middle of the floor. I smiled at her and told her to relax. Syd came in the door holding Latia's hand with big eyes. Lewis walked in the door behind them. Sylvia's eyes got big just like Syd's. I told her Latia was coming over today, I didn't mention that Lewis was going to be with her. I introduced Sylvia and Sydney to Lewis. He said hello, the whole time Latia was watching Sylvia. Sylvia said hello to Latia, and then she asked Syd to help her put out the appetizers Syd made for her auntie. Lewis said he definitely was going to have to carry a gun with two more beautiful nieces.

The thing is that if Sylvia wouldn't have been plotting and scheming all those years ago the fact that Latia is with Lewis wouldn't have been shocking. The mood lightened a little after a while. Then Syd volunteered to make each person a sundae for dessert. When Syd took Lewis in the kitchen to go over his options, Latia invited Sylvia out on the deck. She closed the door behind them and they turned their backs to me. Latia was gesturing with her hands. When Lewis sat down with his mountain of a sundae he looked out the window with me. He said *Oh Boy*! when Latia's neck started wiggling. Latia was doing most of the talking. He whispered and asked me if we should rescue Sylvia. I shook my head no; I had Syd put their ice cream in the freezer. Then Lewis raved over Syd's dinner, he said that the girls were going to have to cook for him after the wedding too. Syd smiled at the thought of it. Then I saw Latia and Sylvia hug. Then Latia called me out on the deck. "How you going to take Sydney away?"

"Is that what she said?" I looked at Sylvia.

"No, she said that she owes you blah, blah, blah. She has no parental rights now?"

"Latia like I said I'm aware of how much I hurt him. I'm not trying to get with him, but I do want to be here for him any way he needs me to be. He has complete control."

"And like I said he doesn't need that much power. You apologized, and humbled yourself to hear his grandma and me out. It's done isn't it? How many times can you apologize?"

"Latia I appreciate the concern, but I know how wrong I was. I'm completely fortunate that he's accepting my friendship right now." Latia looked at her long and hard.

"I know right!" I said knowing my sister was testing her by defending her to see how she responded.

"Ok, well you can bring her to the wedding. If it turns out that this whole thing is a put on... **GIRL!** It sucks to be you!"

Sylvia lowered her eyes, "you guys still doubt me?"

"I want to believe you. I feel the need to put the disclosure out there." Latia said.

"I understand." Sylvia said looking at the lake across the street. Latia went back inside. "You don't believe me? Do you?"

"I want to, but everyone keeps saying otherwise."

"By everyone you mean Melissa and Angela? Melissa doesn't want you to be with anyone except her. Angela can't handle that you were ever with me. The women closest to you don't say what they're saying. Here's the thing, I'm not asking to be with you."

"Then why were you throwing yourself at me?"

She shrugged, "that's all men want from me anyways. I just want to take your mind off the pain."

"I think we're fine being friends."

Her whole face lit up, "you consider me to be a friend?"

"We've got Syd, we gotta be something."

Chantel

"I'm your friend girl, but I've got a job to do!" Caprice said with sadness in her eyes and then she grabbed my neck and started choking me. I was fighting for not only my life but the life of my unborn child.

Then I felt Derrick's touch as he grabbed me to calm me. I woke up completely drenched in sweat, and our bed looked like a tornado hit it. I must've kicked the covers off during my fight. I laid there crying and trying to catch my breath and focus on the room to make sure I was awake. Derrick kissed my forehead as he rubbed my arms. I guess I woke Chanel up too, cause she was kicking me like crazy. Derrick rubbed my stomach and gently told the baby to go back to sleep. His voice is as calming to her as it is to me. She calmed down immediately, and then he hugged me and started telling me a random story about a training day with Malcolm. Drew was trying to prove he was better than Malcolm, Darryl was complaining, and he said he was about to complain when a car rolled up on them. He said he had no idea who any of these guys were or what they wanted. Suddenly no one was tired anymore, no one was complaining. He said they stood there side by side like a wall. He said the guy who he still doesn't know who he was thought Malcolm was vulnerable because he was with his sons. He spared me the details but they walked away unharmed and finally the things Malcolm had been telling them started to make sense. Just the sound of Derrick's voice calmed me. I told him about my dream, and he told me I was safe. I melted in his arms, "even though my wicked aunties are going to be at our wedding?"

He laughed, "I don't care who's there. As long as you say I do! I can't wait for the morning after we're husband and wife." Then he laughed, "I just remembered how surprised my momma was when I told her I wanted a wife and family when I grew up. I guess because everybody calls me little Malcolm she thought I would be like him in every way. One thing we all agreed on is that we did not want to end up like Malcolm. But somehow we've all repeated his mistakes in one-way or another. I'm just glad I'm not forty something trying to finally get it together."

I swallowed, "are you sure I won't end up like my mother? She loved my dad so much. That part I get it, I understand."

He rubbed my stomach, "I have every confidence that you will love our children more than you think you love me. We are not our parents, remember all those sessions with Joanne that we needed just to understand that?"

"Yes, sometimes I need to hear you say we got this."

"Chantel, we got this." Then he kissed me.

Yussef

"This nigga was running top speed and I was like SLOW DOWN!" Darryl said while everyone was gasping for air. "Then here comes D-Rick smooth as butter! He looked at them and asked why they running like he don't see the dog! Milton you's a stupid somebody I swear!" Everyone was cracking up.

"That's alright! I know how to fix you. I'ma tell Auntie Lorraine you came to Richmond without stopping by." Milton said.

Darryl's smile dropped, "I hate niggas that fight dirty! You getting whooped so you gonna pick up auntie and throw her at me." Then he huffed, "we grown men." Then he smiled, as he pulled out his phone. "I'll see your auntie threat and I will bring the trauma back to you." Milton looked worried. Darryl scrolled through his phone. Then he held it out to Milton, "what color is this dress?"

Milton looked at the dress, "black and blue." He shrugged like it was no big deal.

Darryl smiled, then he showed us the picture and to me it looked white and gold, a few others agreed. "Milton I haven't touched the picture, what color is the dress?"

Milton looked at the picture again and then he became visibly shaken, "ON TOP OF EVERYTHING ELSE YOU DO WITCHCRAFT NOW TOO?" He screamed as he covered his eyes.

Everyone was cracking up again, as Darryl showed the same picture to everyone. To some it seemed to change as well. It was still white and gold to me. Milton was so shook up he covered his face as Darryl accused him of crying. "Threaten to snitch on me! I got something for your monkey behind! Who's idea was it to go play laser tag?" Milton raised his hand. "Figures! Laser tag is for those who don't know nothing about the real thing." No one had anything to say to that.

Derrick was in the corner checking in, making sure Chantel was ok and taken care of before he started drinking. Watching Derrick with Chantel was always like seeing a different side to him. Derrick's brother in-law Cyrus and I were sitting over to the side watching Darryl and Ryder cut up. I agreed that it was dumb to go play laser tag until they presented the challenge. All of them against us (Derrick, Darryl, Drew, EJ, Eric, Cyrus, William, Jeff, Joseph, Hubby, Dude, Ryder, and Me). Then we were going to EA aka Elegant Affairs for a private party. Most people forgot I wasn't at Drew's bachelor party. So they keep saying you remember. Um yea! I wasn't there.

EJ was telling Derrick and Jeff something, when Derrick told me to come rap to him. "So Sylvia?"

"What about her?" I tried not to sound defensive.

Derrick looked at me for a minute. "Can you handle that?"

"What are you saying?" I knew what he was saying so I don't know why I asked but I did. It's not like it was a secret what happened.

"You know what I'm saying."

"I'm battling myself." I said in defeat.

"Love will make you do that."

"Love?"

"Come on, I was there. I know how in love with her you were." Jeff said.

"That was then."

"So then what are you doing? You've got two little girls watching." Derrick said.

"I keep throwing fire balls at her. I'm waiting for the old her to surface."

"How's that working out for you?" Jeff asked.

I shrugged, "she's taking it all. But at the end of the day, she did what she did."

"Right, we've all done the unthinkable at some point." Derrick said pointing his eyes at me.

"I'm not as mad as I used to be. I don't exactly understand how I feel." I said honestly. "How's Angela?"

"Haven't spoken to her since we broke up."

"So you're in love with one woman and you got a married woman pulling at you. And another woman who did the unthinkable waiting for you." Jeff said.

His words hung over my head with a bad taste on them. "Right! There's nothing I can do about Angela. I will not walk away from my girls over anyone. In the end it's like she's only loving one part of me. I honestly thought she was the one. Oh well."

"It's your choice who you end up with, you're the only one who has to live with it. Just make sure you're choosing when you make your choice." Derrick said.

"Meaning?"

"Think it through."

When the limos came we piled in them and the rowdy debate about how our game was going to go, started. Darryl was pumping them up to think they actually stood a chance. While they were getting pumped our team was quiet. They were stupid but funny thinking there was power in their numbers. Drew met us at the laser tag place. The staff laughed first when they heard it was us against them. They were in a big huddle strategizing and being funny. Drew said V-formation and that was it. No other instructions needed.

The instructor informed us that we were outnumbered more than three to one; she smiled and said they were going to watch from the booth. She explained where each team's target was. How many hits would take you out before you needed to go to your charging station. You accumulate points by hitting the other team's target. Inside we took our places, it's already black with only a black light to see. Somebody threw down dry ice so the illumination was very foggy. I laid on the floor on one side while Drew was on the other. Anyone approaching our target was taken out. All you heard was cursing and swearing. They thought they had us. Derrick took my spot and Darryl took Drew's. Down low these fools couldn't see me coming. It was like always, I moved past them one by one like I was invisible. Drew and I tore up their target, they were yelling trying to find us. I bit my lip so I wouldn't smile and have my teeth give me away. Then we rotated again, the rest of our army took them out as they tried to get to our target. When the game was over we laughed at the scores. Ryder said he was putting our scores on a T-shirt. Milton the self-designated captain of the others was too mad about it. He started to fuss at the staff asking them why they turned on a smoke machine. They said they didn't have a smoke machine. They had no idea what he was talking about. The smoke in the room was thick enough to make us even but thin enough that the staff didn't notice. They turned on the lights in the room. Talking mess the whole time he was looking for something. When if he would've noticed Darryl's gloves, he might've figured it out. The ice was melted and gone. Milton swore up and down we cheated. There was no way we should've beat them, Darryl threw his hands up. He told him he was the main dumb one going up against the soldiers. He said next time just say no!

Drew asked me to ride with him to EA while the rest of them got it together. As soon as he closed his door, "what's up?"

"I could say the same to you. You were just as off in there. Good thing they were amateurs." I laughed.

"You first," he said.

"Nope, you invited me. The floor is yours."

He unloaded, he was nervous about Tracy and the baby. Then all this Phineas stuff was getting too close. I told him about Angela, and then everything with Sylvia. He said every time I mention her he cringes. I laughed, and then I told him she was coming with me to Latia's wedding. He blank stared at me for a minute. I started laughing, "you feeling her again?"

"I don't know. Shouldn't I be with at least one of the mothers?"

Drew sat back in his chair. "That's like if I had a child with Toya, and a child with Jennay. But Tracy's out there somewhere. I know if I didn't know Tracy I'd be torn. Who could choose, but if Toya's married I could see accepting being with Jennay. And until Tracy I thought Jennay was the one who got away. But there was something that made me drag my feet. If you're dragging your feet it's for a reason." Then he frowned, "why did I drag my feet with her?"

"Because she was a ridiculous flirt! She loved you but she needed attention, don't you remember all the fights!"

Drew laughed, "oh yea."

"Tracy never did anything like that." Drew eyed me, "look at me like that if you want to. You've got what I'm looking for. A woman who loves me to death and worships the ground I walk on."

He smiled, "she does doesn't she."

"What would you have done if she rejected your son?" Drew exhaled shaking his head.

"Exactly! That's why I'm not with Angela."

He shook his head, "Sylvia though!"

I smiled, "I guess it's your turn to ask why."

"Toya was.... Something I was going through. You're a late bloomer."

"Call it whatever you want, I guess everybody goes through something."

Chantel

"Are you excited? One more day until the big day!"

I was sulking, "I don't care about traditions and whatever. I want to be with Derrick!" I protested.

"Sprung much?" Sophia said, "it's not going to kill you to spend two nights away from the man you're going to spend the rest of your life with. Lighten up Chantel."

I realized I was acting like a brat so I decided to shut up and go with the flow. Tomorrow we were rehearsing in the evening after a full day of pampering. Mitigated staff was everywhere; they wouldn't open the limo doors until everyone was in position. I know paparazzi is annoying but this felt heavier than protection from commercial eyes. We were escorted past the lobby and directly into our suites. For those who weren't staying in my two-bedroom suite they put their bags down in their rooms and then they came to my room. An extra-long table and chairs were brought in so that we could have dinner together. The staff set the TV up at the head of our table. Then the segment on my shower came on. We were served dinner while we watched. "The world has been taken by storm. Chantel Shaw made her first debut on the scene on this awards ceremony." They showed a clip of me singing live. I admired how fresh and new I looked, and myself without the growing belly. They showed clips from interviews and clips from Lewis' movie where we were clowning. They showed a clip that showed the back of Caprice's head. I looked at Brandy with tears in my eyes. She rubbed my hand to calm me. The interview was nice and funny. "Now Chantel is taking on a new roll, the roll of wife and mother." I loved the way they made everything seem grand. Everyone said "Aw!" When they showed Amber and I hugging and being emotional. "Chantel will be related to this choreographer extraordinaire. Many may have forgotten about this dancing powerhouse... Amber Wallace!" Amber blushed as she sunk in her chair. They said so many positive things about her you would've sworn she wrote it herself. Her embarrassment let you know she was completely surprised. They said Derrick was her brother. Everyone started laughing and clapping when they said it. They showed a quick clip of the entertainment at my shower, and me being excited about little Andre breaking it down. Then the segment said that I was getting married sometime next year. We laughed again. Latia said they were trying to throw paparazzi off their scent just like that with her wedding, but Lewis' family talk too much.

The next day we had a wonderful breakfast, spa treatments, and bonding time. I was so happy that Ms. Laverne and Grandma Rosa got along so well. They were always having their own side conversations, and enjoying the time they were spending together. I sat back rubbing my stomach and looking at all the beautiful women in my family. It used to be just my brother and I. Now I have this huge family of people who genuinely loved me and took time out of their lives to wish me well as I marry the man who has consumed my entire being since I was a child. I sat there for a while taking everyone in.

Even though my father and Aunts were supposed to come for the rehearsal dinner only, they came early. Maria, my stepmother, said she tried to stall them as long as she could. She said they would've been here hours earlier if she didn't stall them like she did. I hugged and kissed her; I told her it was ok. I told her I had plenty of backup.

"Chantel this hotel is GORGEOUS! Exactly the kind of place a celebrity should get married!" My Auntie Deborah said with her eyes wide.

"Thank you."

"Chantel are you feeling okay? You look tired!" My Auntie Tania said taking a stab at me.

My dad who never hears any of it was grinning from ear to ear. "I love all of this!" He said looking around the hotel. "Where's the reception going to be?" He was bubbling over with excitement.

I asked the nearest Mitigated staff member to show them where the reception was going to be held. They hadn't started to set up the space so I warned that it was still basic right now, but Carina my event planner was working on it. As they walked away Yussef came out of nowhere, he was giving someone direction. I gave him a hug and I told him I had no idea he was out here today. He said Juan was on point for security tomorrow, but he did his own assessment tonight and he found a few things he wanted tightened up. Then he said he'd see me in a few at the rehearsal. He was in work mode, so he didn't have his normal relaxed look. I wanted to ask him what was wrong, but I decided to let it go.

"Auntie!" I heard a little voice say.

I turned around as my Babygirl Rosa ran top speed to me. She wrapped her arms around my legs. Cyrus was right behind her and he looked nervous. I gave him a hug and I asked him what was up. He tried to tell me nothing but I could see it all over his face. I stood there not budging, I wanted to know what was wrong. He looked around as he asked where Derrick was. I could feel my blood boiling. "So what! I don't exist anymore?" As soon as I exploded I realized I was overreacting, but he was disregarding me and that was irritating.

"Of course you exist." He said softening his voice. He put his arm around me. "I need to talk to Derrick about guy stuff. It's nothing against you."

"I'm sorry Cyrus, I'm emotional. Maybe I should go lay down for a bit."

He kissed my cheek, "why don't you do that and then I'll come check on you."

Derrick and Yussef were coming towards us as they were seriously talking about something. Derrick gave me a hug and kiss then he asked Cyrus what was going on. Cyrus asked Derrick who detective Dartnell was. Derrick grinned and then he told Cyrus to walk with him. Babygirl Rosa didn't appreciate being ignored by her uncle Derrick. She crossed her arms and started crying. Everything in Derrick changed and he picked her up and he apologized for not giving her a hug and kiss. Little Rosa smiled and gave him a big hug. Yussef volunteered to walk us back to my room. He looked at my stomach then he asked how I was feeling. I told him my moods are all over the place. He exhaled; I asked him what was wrong as we entered my suite. Ms. Laverne and Grandma Rosa were in the bedroom talking. Yussef said hello to them then he followed me in the living room. He looked at the window at my breathtaking view. "I just wonder when it will be my turn. I want the wife, babies, the whole thing."

"Angela seems nice."

"She is, but it's not going to work. She didn't sign up for my life, it's too many twist and turns and we were just starting. So it's back to the drawing board." He said sounding defeated.

"Yussef it's gonna happen. I never thought of myself as a wife or a mother. And here we are, every time I look at my stomach I can't believe it."

He exhaled, "Sylvia's coming tomorrow. Sylvia is my ex. She's Sydney's mother." He exhaled again, "I was so in love with that woman when we were together. I listened to no one until she broke my heart. I can see now that I'm not over it. I thought I was. She's been bending over in every way possible to tell me how sorry she is."

"Do you believe her?"

He exhaled, "yes. But I don't trust her."

"You don't trust who?" Ms. Laverne said walking around the corner.

"My ex."

"Yussef without getting too much in your business or putting you in mine." I swallowed, "in relationships sometimes you have to forgive the unthinkable in order to find your own happiness. Derrick and I have been through our own roller coaster. He's had to forgive me and I him. Two people with trust issues makes for a volatile relationship. Have you prayed on it?"

He smiled, "no."

"And why not?"

"God's going to tell me to forgive her. I can see the signs."

We all laughed, "Yussef baby pray on it and stop punishing yourself." Ms. Laverne said.

"You're right." Then he hugged Ms. Laverne. "Get some rest." Then he hugged me. "See you later." He hugged grandma Rosa. Then he gave little Rosa a kiss and then he left.

I don't remember falling asleep but that couch was ridiculously comfortable. I woke up to Derrick kissing me ever so gently. He showed me the picture he took of me sleeping. It was a pretty picture. He said it was time to go rehearse for tomorrow. I asked him if I should change, I had on a simple dress. Derrick told me I looked beautiful and that was all that mattered to him. Everyone was waiting with big smiles for us. Even Malcolm was almost smiling. Andre guided little Rosa down the aisle perfectly. I was so happy the weather agreed to allow us to have our wedding without a cloud in the forecast for tomorrow. Carina had tents on standby, but I didn't want that. As Cyrus and I walked down the aisle my aunts were buzzing in my father's ears. I could feel the drama coming. At the dinner both of my aunts kept shooting me looks and I did my best to ignore them. After the dinner Derrick and I were talking to Malcolm and Amber about the big day tomorrow, when my Auntie Tania rudely interrupted our conversation. "What is wrong with you Chantel! Why would you do this to your father?" She pointed at my dad who's back was to us. It didn't look like he knew she was interjecting herself in our situation. "Who are you?" Amber spit at her.

She opened her mouth to speak but Derrick cut her off. "Tania let me stop you there before you say the wrong thing to my parents and I have to get on you." She started to say something again. "Nope! I can see that you're stupid enough to keep going. So how about this." He waved someone over. A girl I didn't recognize walked over. "This is Chantel's aunt, that one too." Then he pointed at my Auntie Deborah. "They tend to be problematic, and you know my patience for problems this weekend. Put Carly on her and I want you on Tania. The first time they even sneeze like they're going to be a problem throw them out!"

Malcolm and Amber stood there side by side like they approved. My Auntie Tania stood there with her mouth hanging open like she didn't know if she should test Derrick or not. He was looking at her like he was hoping she would be that dumb. My Grandmother walked over. "What's wrong?"

"He just told this girl to throw me and Deborah out!"

I pointed my eyes at her, "is that what he said?"

"Hello baby how are you doing?" Grandma said to Malcolm as she gave him a kiss on the cheek. "Please excuse my children. I guess that one I lost and some of my grandchildren are the only ones who got an ounce of sense from me and my husband."

"It's ok Grandma Rosa. I don't want you dealing with them either. You deserve to relax as much as anyone else here tonight." Then he looked at the girl. "Tell Carly, and don't fail me!"

The girl hurried away and my auntie stood there like she was going to burst. Then she walked away to where daddy and Auntie Deborah were sitting. Malcolm frowned, "Ms. Rosa you sure you gave birth to that one?"

She sighed, "yep. I remember it like it was yesterday. You would think they were raised to be the way they are. I don't know what I did wrong."

"Ms. Rosa don't let them steal your joy! Come dance with me." Malcolm commanded.

The three of us stood there watching Malcolm and my Grandma dance. They had such a good time while my aunts shot daggers at me until Derrick saw them. Then they convinced my dad that it was time to go.

Derrick and I took Andre with us up to Cyrus' room where all my brothers and Darryl were. We spent the next couple of hours laughing so hard. Andrew and Tracy came up and the group became even more lively. I could tell that Tracy and Sherrell really hit it off. It helped that their due dates were a couple of weeks apart, and they had older kids to keep up with as well. All three of us were about to pass out. So we took baby Rosa back to our room and we told the men we'd see them tomorrow. Derrick and Darryl walked us to our room. Derrick and I shared one final kiss as single people.

Sasha

"You know what I would really love, and I know it's probably simple." Tracy sat on the edge of her seat waiting for me to say. "A white cake with fresh strawberries."

"HHHMMM! I'll have to see if I can get fresh strawberries in March. But you're right that's simple enough. Do you want the whole cake that flavor? Or do you want another flavor as well?"

"I want everything to be bright and airy. Maybe lemon, and peach if you can find them." I said thinking.

"Tell me what you think of Derrick's cake, it's a peach Bellini cake."

"What does that mean?" I said trying to imagine what I think that would taste like.

"Champagne and peach. It's kind of hard to describe but you tell me what you think when you taste it."

"Deal!" I said, then I turned my back to her, "can you zip me?" It was time to get going for the wedding.

She zipped me then she stood for a minute steadying herself. "I'm sorry." She said looking embarrassed.

"Are you nauseous?" She looked a little green.

"Just a little. This feeling comes and goes. It's the only sign besides my missing period that I'm pregnant. Otherwise I'd think the doctor lied to me."

"I can't wait to be right there with you guys."

"It's gonna be your turn soon enough." She said.

I can see why Andrew is so gone over this girl. She has nothing but love and admiration for my twin-cousin. She's down to earth, and completely ignorant to the things that happen around her. I don't mean that in a bad way, but she's got that live and let God handle it type of personality. Nothing like any of us are used to. I see how Andrew can take delight in that peacefulness at home.

As we walked down through the lobby, I looked around Mitigated was everywhere. I still had a little piece in my purse just in case I needed to be ready. I walked with JoJo, but I found myself looking at Yussef, fortunately he was ahead of me so it wasn't like I was turning my head to do it or anything.

After the pictures I saw Alexa lurking, I sat next to Pearla and Liz; we watched the whole scene play out. Yussef's girls were too cute in their overprotectiveness of their dad. When we ate I watched the girls walk over to a woman. She was pretty, not prettier than me, but pretty in her own right. After secretly studying her face I came to the conclusion that she was the girl's mother. Did he get back with his baby momma? Or was she just here? Thank goodness El was preoccupied with Derrick's cousins that he met the other day, I could sit here and dissect them in peace. I asked Pearla who the girl was and she said she was on her way to ask Yussef. I looked at Yussef at the same time that he looked at me. He grinned at me and I smiled back, I had to check myself. I'm almost a married woman. I went and sat myself next to my momma. When Andre and Yussef's girls came over I introduced myself. I noticed immediately their reaction to me was different than Alexa. I smiled really big inside, they sat down and talked with me. They had the cutest laughs, and they were really good girls. "Your hair is so pretty," I said to both of them. "Did your mother do it?"

"My mom did mine and her mom did hers." Yesmina said proudly.

I was confused, "I thought you guys were twins?"

"We are!" Sydney said proudly.

"But we have different mothers." Yesmina said.

"Is that lady your step mommy?" Andre asked Yesmina.

"No just her momma."

"I have a twin too." I said with a big smile.

"You do?" Andre said with his eyes extended big.

"Yep, your dad!" I smiled.

Andre sucked his teeth like he understood I was tricking him. "Nana isn't your momma, Auntie Sophia is. And Poppa isn't your daddy. You're Sabrina's big sister."

"You're Sabrina's big sister?" Sydney said with big eyes. "She's so cool!"

"She got it from me."

"Wow!" They said in unison.

Then Ryder and Malachi's girls came over and asked them to come dance with them. Yussef was watching my interaction with the girls, he smiled at me again.

When it was time for cake, I was in love. It was moist, with the right amount of peach flavor. I wanted to be greedy but that cake was gone. I guess everybody else had the same idea as I did. I gave Tracy a thumbs up, and then I danced the night away with my man.

Yussef

"Good morning daddy!" Yezzy said with the biggest smile. "Mommy did my hair special do you like it?" She twirled so I could see the whole thing.

"I love it! Did you thank her?"

"Yes!" Then she looked at the car, "Sydney's momma is going too?"

"Is that a problem?" I said giving her a look.

She looked down at the ground, "I guess not." I looked up at the window, and Melissa was looking out.

I sat on the step, "come on sit down. Talk to me." I patted the step next to me. "You don't like Sylvia?"

"She's always nice to me." Then she looked up at the window, she scooted in closer. She lowered her voice, "my momma gets so mad. She always asks me what we did, who was there, everything. Then she gets mad when I say Sylvia was there. She starts asking me a bunch of questions like she doesn't want me to like her. I don't want to be mean to Sydney's mom."

I put my arm around my baby. "Your momma is mad at me. I'm sorry that you have to see it."

"Why is she mad at you?"

"I was very young and dumb. And I pray that when the time comes you pick a man that is smarter than your daddy was back then." I exhaled, "although I had loving feelings for your momma I told myself we were only friends." I thought about it for a minute. "You know those dolls that Angela picked out for you?" She shook her head yes. "What if I only brought one, and it was the doll that you have and love but you had to watch Sydney play with it all the time? That wouldn't make you feel good would it?" She shook her head no. "Then, you can see that Sydney doesn't take care of the doll like you would. All you want is the doll but it belongs to her. Then your momma puts a special doll for you on layaway. It's not the same doll but very special in its own right. Finally you have your own doll, but you still remember the doll that Sydney had right?" She shook her head again. "I'm that doll. I shouldn't have let her see how poorly Sylvia was taking care of me. She loves your step dad very much otherwise she wouldn't have married him. But she still looks at me like that doll she never got a chance to truly play with. Does that make sense?" She shook her head yes, "I'm sorry that you have to be in the middle and see all of this, none of this is Syd or your fault. I want you guys to always be close no matter what. I will talk to your parents and hopefully smooth things out. Does Sylvia ever make you feel badly?"

"No she's always nice to me even when you're not in the room."

"Is someone mean to you?"

"No, but Angela would stare at me and Sydney whenever you weren't in the room. Sometimes she would look mad and most of the time she would look sad."

"Why didn't you say anything?" She shrugged, "baby girl if someone ever does something to make you feel uncomfortable I don't care who it is you tell me. Ok?"

"Yes daddy," she smiled at me. "You gonna beat them up or something?"

"Of course! But if it's a girl, I know your momma got it." I smiled, she laughed. "You ready to go?" I said standing up. As Yezzy and I walked to the car Melissa shut the kitchen window.

My chatterboxes sat in the back going back and forth about some of the kids at their school. Sylvia asked me if everything was ok, and I told her it was fine. We had breakfast, and then we drove to Half-moon Bay for the wedding. I asked the girls to hang with Sylvia after they got dressed in the dresses I picked out for them. We had a one-bedroom suite, Sylvia and the girls were in the room and I planned to sleep on the pullout bed in the couch. I put on my first tux without my locs. I stood in the mirror trying to see my own face. I saw glimpses of me, but to no avail, it was like I was looking at my father. I did my rounds around the hotel. I studied the floor plan of this hotel, every cellar, every back door until I knew it like the back of my hand. Between Richard and Juan I knew security was on point, but I still felt the need to know everything for my own peace of mind.

While we clowned around in the waiting room Carina was running around cracking her whip. Malcolm asked everyone to sit. Then he looked at Derrick, "I'm so proud of you! I know most people say you act like me, but we both know you were born serious. Whether I was in your life or not you would still be this magnificent man before me right now. You've got a good woman who loves you, and I'm so happy that you and your brother haven't taken after me. To be so smart I've been dumb about so many things. One thing I've never been wrong about is the value of my sons. Today you marry your queen, cherish her and always keep her safe!" Then they hugged.

"THAT'S IT?" Darryl hopped out his chair like it was on fire.

Malcolm and Derrick looked at Darryl with the same blank expression. "What?"

"Malcolm you had us on the verge of tears at Drew's wedding! It's ok cause it's my turn." He shooed Malcolm to sit. Malcolm sat while Derrick continued to stand and hold on to his blank stare at his little brother. "After today it's just me, Yussef, and a few others on the single man's tour. The four of us couldn't be more different, but we're all the same. What most of you guys don't know is that I've been going behind all of you and patching up the hole you've made with your women, especially you Derrick! This fool is so stubborn! Derrick has been in love with Chantel since the first time he laid eyes on her. It took you forever to make a move and even that move was SLOW! I could never understand having that much self-control with someone or something you've wanted as badly as you wanted her. I've watched you guys grow up together. Mister stone face in love is a sight to see, he smiles, he's affectionate. That's how I knew she was the one for him, cause he was never in as deeply with anyone as he has been with Chantel. She out stubborned you and made you grow up. So just in case you didn't figure it out, I'm the reason we're all here today." Everyone laughed, "Derrick please tell them. If I wouldn't have betrayed you and made you go to The Place Where Jazz is Played that night, you and Chantel would've probably taken too long to get back together and we may not be standing here right now. I'm happy for you big bro." He gave him a hug.

"My turn." Cyrus said, "for the longest time it was just me and my skinny little sister. No family, barely any friends, just me and her working towards one goal. Our freedom. Then my sister met you and I didn't know what to make of you. I questioned her almost daily making sure everything was on the up and up. Derrick always handled my sister the way I felt she deserved to be.... with love. I kept telling her he liked her but she wouldn't believe me. You stepped in and changed her life for the better. Everything I wanted for her you've done. You even got her to be excited about marriage and family. If any of you know my sister, she doesn't change her mind about things she thinks strongly about very easily. Thank you for loving my sister, I wish you guys the best."

"My turn," Chantel's other brother said. "I'm Dan or DJ as Chantel calls me. I just wanted to say. This man has been the coolest cat since we met him. Mario and I have looked up to him since we were kids cause he was always the man about everything. He took time out of his busy schedule to teach us something, and most importantly you showed us how a real man conducts himself. I'm so happy we're officially brothers today. You've been my family since the day we met."

"Yea, what he said." Mario said not wanting to make a speech.

"Thank you all for agreeing to share with me and my lady our most special occasion, this outside of the birth of our daughter, this day is a dream realized and each one of you are back here with me because of everything you've meant to our lives." Derrick said, "our family is huge, and it keeps on growing. Thank you all for standing with me today."

Carina popped her head in and told us it was time to take our places. It was just before sunset just like Chantel wanted. I escorted Liz down the aisle; my girls were all smiles as we walked past them. Derrick smiled as Cyrus walked Chantel down the aisle. Her father did not look happy, and I didn't understand why he wasn't giving her away, but it was none of my business. Chantel was a beautiful bride and they said their vows under the sunset on the bay.

Chantel

In the morning Tracy, Pearla, and Sherrell disappeared to put the final touches on my cake. I was now curious to know what it looked like, but they wouldn't say. When a different photographer followed us around all day I asked Carina what happened to Angela? I really liked the pictures she got at the engagement party. She shrugged and said

Angela backed out. Then Carina introduced me to Olivia, she said that Olivia and her partner Paula covered my baby shower and a few other gigs. Then she said they were professionals and I would appreciate their work even more. Tanisha's mom Rosalind did our makeup. She was really good; she made my pregnant nose disappear. I admired her work in the mirror. The day flew by, and I found myself tearfully thanking everyone for being here for me. Everyone hugged me and Sasha helped me fix my makeup before I ruined it. She told me to dab, I knew that but pregnancy brain had me messing everything up. When Grandma Rosa and I were alone, I tearfully asked her if she thinks my mother would've liked my dress and everything. She held me and we cried together. Then she helped me calm down, she sang to me, her voice soothed me. Her voice was smooth and strong and I ate every second of that moment up. When Carina said it was time we walked down through the lobby and out to beautiful green and luscious grass. The silver chavarri chairs had white cushions with burgundy and black ribbons tied to the back that danced in the slight breeze over our ceremony site. Cyrus told me I was beautiful and that he was so happy for me then he kissed my cheek. I tucked my arm under my big brother who has always protected me and stood up for me when I had no one else in the world. As we glided down the aisle my dad looked like he had been robbed and my aunts were angry. I didn't care it was my day executed how I wanted it. Derrick smiled at me really big when I got to him. When the judge asked who gives this woman away to be married, my brothers, father, and grandma stood forward and said they do. We sealed our commitment under the sunset just like I wanted. We took a ton of pictures with the sunset as our backdrop. I've never seen Derrick smile so much, no one has.
"Congratulations Chantel," Malcolm said.
I knew he was saying welcome to the family officially, but you've always been like a daughter to me so this is just a formality. "Thank you Malcolm." Then I kissed his cheek. Malcolm walked away. Then Pearla and Sherrell led us inside to the banquet room for our reception. Tracy was standing in front of the cake table. When she stepped out of the way I gasped. It was better than I imagined. The cake was four tiers and it was decorated in our colors. Derrick and I loved it. Tracy looked relieved that we did. My dad and aunts opened their set by singing the song that Derrick wrote for me. They did a good job and I appreciated the effort, but no one could rock that song like Derrick and I could. They played for everyone while we ate and the beginning of the dancing portion of the evening. They got the clue to stop when my Aunt Tania tried to sing a Tina Marie song and held on to a note too long. Darryl and Ryder fell onto each other belly laughing. I turned my head trying not to laugh but it was hilarious. Then Derrick played "isn't she lovely" by Stevie Wonder for the father daughter dance. My dad looked excited to be acknowledged. I smiled even though I would've rather have danced with Malcolm to this song cause he's always looked out for me like a father would. Even if it meant telling me to slow down with his knucklehead son.
When they put on Momma by Boys II Men Derrick danced with Amber. Malcolm danced with Ms. Laverne, my dad danced with my grandma, Andre danced with Tracy, Andrew danced with Auntie Lorraine, Jeff danced with Auntie Lauren, Ryder danced with his mother Sharon, Eric danced with his mother Jenise, and then Dionne asked me to dance with her. She had the biggest smile on her face as she danced with me. I wondered if she was with me or if she thought I was someone else. At the end of the song she rubbed my belly and asked me if the baby was a good baby? I told her she was. Then she said,
"David was a good baby too. He loved me so much, and I him. All of his boys remind me so much of him. Doyle's the only one who got that bad gene."
"Doyle?" I've never heard that name.
"Yes, that's right. He's your brother in law now. But you might not want to meet him. He tried to be good, but he got that bad gene like David's father."
"Who's his mother?"

"Patricia of course! The only other woman David's ever loved." Then her eyes glazed over. "Patricia you gotta leave David alone he has a new family now." She made her voice stern.

I looked at Derrick and he and Amber came over quickly. "What's wrong?"

"She just said you have a brother." I watched Derrick's eyes.

Amber covered her mouth. "What?"

"Did she say anything else?" Derrick asked as he held his mother's free hand.

"David, I was telling Patricia to leave you and Amber alone."

"What's wrong?" Auntie Lorraine said coming to check on her sister.

"She said Patricia has a son." Amber said.

Auntie Lorraine shrugged it off. "Dionne says all kinds of off the wall stuff. I haven't seen Patricia in ages, and I never saw a baby."

"She said his name was Doyle." I think she was telling the truth, she was clear in that moment.

"My sister says a lot of stuff, like calling you Patricia. Please don't let her ruin your night. Come on Dionne it's time to go." Auntie Lorraine said removing her sister from our huddle.

Malcolm and Andrew walked over with the same expression. Both of them had their eyes locked on Amber. She did her best to suck it up especially since they were watching her now.

Yussef

While the wedding party took pictures that singer Alexa was lingering. I saw her looking at me, but I wasn't thinking about her. Come on, she left the engagement party with Dwayne Reed. I hope she's not looking at me.

"I don't think we've met," she said sticking out her hand. "I'm Alexa."

"Yussef"

"It's nice to finally have a chance to talk to you."

Yezzy and Syd hurried over, I saw Sylvia pretending like she wasn't looking. "Oh my goodness!"

"Hello pretty lady, what's your name?"

"Sydney, and this is my twin sister Yesmina."

"Nice to meet you. Would you two mind giving me a couple of minutes to talk to this guy and then I will come and chat with you personally." She said with the fakest nice voice, it was that sugary sweet my momma does but bubbled down for her fans.

"O….k….," Syd said.

"Daddy, can you come dance with us?" Yezzy said, not taking her eyes off Alexa reminding me of her mother in that moment.

"Daddy?" Alexa said realizing she messed up.

"Excuse us," I said walking away with my daughters.

After that Yezzy was on defense and all the available women were on offense. I found it interesting to say the least. Even though I danced to a couple songs with my girls they were between me and Sylvia the entire night. None of them seem to question or care to ask if I was with Sylvia. I liked the dress she was wearing, it wasn't flashy or like she was trying to draw attention to herself, and when men approached her she politely turned each one down.

Part of me wondered if Angela was going to be doing the photography for tonight, but they used someone else. The photographer came in about business, and the way they structured some of our photos you knew they meant business. I sat and chatted with Tanisha for a while, she said she couldn't believe Derrick was married. I tried not to let it bother me that even my stepsister knew my family longer and better than me. I found myself in a mood, it was no one here's fault that I didn't have long memories of my family.

Liz, Paulette, Pearla, and I sat over to the side chatting. They wanted to know who Sylvia was and what happened to Angela. I explained that she was Syd's mother, and then all that happened with Angela. Pearla told me to delete Angela's number and I deserved better than that. Pearla asked if it was ok if they went and had a "talk" with Sylvia. I told them that was fine, and they were excited, I scanned the room and made eye contact with each Mitigated staff member who was on point for our evening. Then I made my way to the bar. A couple of drinks later I was relaxed. The kids were on the dance floor breaking it down. Tracy and I nodded hello from across the room just like Sasha and I. The DJ called out the last song of the night and it was a slow dance. I made eye contact with Sylvia and I motioned for her to meet me on the dance floor. She was still talking with my cousins and they were all smiles. Sylvia came over as she was told and I danced with her. I could tell she wanted to melt like she used to, but she didn't know what to do. Sydney was dancing with a cousin and Yezzy was standing on the side watching us. I told her to come join us. She smiled really big, I told her to stand on my feet and to put her arms around Sylvia. She did and the cutest Latia giggle kept erupting from my baby girl.

When we went back to the room Sylvia and the girls changed into their pj's while I sat in the chair. They sat on the couch with Sylvia in the middle and they both fell asleep on her. I carried Syd and Sylvia carried Yezzy and we put them in the bed together. Sylvia asked if I was going to bed yet, and I said not quite. She asked if it was ok if she hung out in the living room with me. We weren't finished with our movie so I was fine with it, I moved to the couch. Then I went in the bathroom and put on my pajama pants and wife beater.

When I came out the bathroom Sylvia was sitting Indian style on the couch with a piece of cake. I asked her how she was going to have private stashes of cake. She said the cake was *SO* good she had to get another piece and then ducked out to put it in our fridge for later. She bounced her leg and hummed while she ate it. It was that good, but she had to know she was sharing. When I reached for her plate she turned away from me. She tried to keep it away, but I knew she was enjoying me touching her. I wanted some more cake, but I was enjoying the free feels I was sliding in as well. Finally she shared her cake with me, but only once we were kind of wrapped up in each other. She asked me again if she could kiss me, I hesitated. She promised that she wouldn't hold it against me if I let her kiss me. When I didn't say anything, I looked at her she got up and put the desk chair under the knob to the bedroom door so we'd know if the girls tried to come out. She turned off the light and only the TV was illuminating the darkness. She sat across my lap and then she kissed me as passionately as she could. I could tell she had been holding that in for a while. Sex with Sylvia was always good, but now I know better. Even in the almost dark I could see she wasn't expecting me to have her like this. I worked her all over that living room, and I only stopped when I ran out of condoms, which I know she was thankful for. Her body shook so much I bet she thought she was having a seizure. Sylvia laid there catching her breath staring at me like she never seen me before. Satisfied with myself I told her she needed to go sleep with the girls.

Episode 12

Yussef

Sylvia didn't come out of the room until the girls were showered and dressed. When she finally came out of that room her eyes were big and fixed on me. I smiled at her and she smiled back. When we went down to the restaurant to have breakfast a lot of the family members were down having breakfast as well. People kept saying our family was so cute.

The first time someone said it Sylvia looked at me for a reaction. When I thanked them and continued talking Sylvia looked completely confused. After breakfast I put our luggage in the car and then we went down to the beach. The girls were playing with Malachi and Ryder's girls and it looked like Malachi and Denise were having a needed conversation. "How come I keep ending up on beaches with you?" I smiled at Sylvia who nervously smiled back. Suddenly an alarm went off in my head. "Did I hurt you?"
She spoke slowly, "no. But you were never like that before."
"Is that good or bad?"
"Both, we always had fun. But last night..." She looked away. "Even though I know you weren't making love to me, and that's all you used to do. I wanted more, are you like that while making love too?"
I laughed, "like what?"
"I know I have no right to beg you for more. I want to do that again. I need to make sure last night wasn't my drought pumping everything up. Only if you want to." Her eyes pleaded with me to say yes.
I smiled, "it was that good huh?"
She laughed embarrassedly, "I cried!"
"Something tells me you're exaggerating."
She grabbed my shirt and pulled me close to her. "I wish I was!"
I smiled and backed up cause the girls were watching. "That's sweet." I said dismissing her claim and changing the subject.
The rest of the day served as confirmation that anything I wanted from Sylvia all I had to do was vaguely imply it. It tickled me at first but then I didn't like it. I could see her driving herself crazy behind running after me like that. After we dropped Yezzy home I came inside Sylvia's place. Syd gave me a hug and kiss goodnight and then she happily bounced up the stairs. Sylvia sat on the couch like a dope fiend bouncing her leg wondering if I came inside to give her another hit or not. I sat on the other end of the couch I couldn't stop smiling. "You are really tripping aren't you?"
I could see her getting frustrated with herself for having a reaction. "It's like all this time I've been carrying this guilt with me. I still feel horrible about everything, I don't know if that will ever go away. Then last night..." She closed her eyes, and then she swallowed. "I never thought you could turn the tables on me."
"Was I horrible in bed? Is that what it was?"
"No, you were always good. If I have to put my finger on it, I guess you loved me too much. Does that make sense? Whenever we had sex there was an element of gentle loving-kindness. Last night you didn't care, you didn't hurt me. Everything was just enough. The way you pulled my hair, smacked me, bit me. I felt drunk and I didn't drink a lick last night."
"Who would've ever thought my problem was that I loved you too much." I looked at her in disbelief.
"I'm not explaining it right. Last night I couldn't predict anything with you. And then you kept going, and going!" Her leg shook harder.
"Women are weird. You claim you want someone to love you, treat you good, and be there for you. The moment a man acts like he doesn't care you're willing to bend over backwards for him." I looked her in her eyes. "You asked me to kiss you and I did. Now what you think I'm supposed to keep sleeping with you?"
She bit the inside of her mouth, as she twirled her hair. "Please don't stop sleeping with me!"
We laughed, "so what happens when I meet someone?"
"I won't tell if you won't."
"Sylvia, how could you sink so low?"
She put her head down and tears poured out of her eyes. "I know what I did. I know how

I behaved. When I tell Sydney the stories about us it makes her so happy to know that she was conceived in love. But then I feel horrible, I know I messed up. I was young and dumb, thinking pretty was enough. Until we happened to run into you I was drowning. Men only wanna trade sex for favors. They don't love me; they just wanna use me and wear me out. No one cared how I was doing, or how I felt. No matter how pretty I may have been there was always someone prettier. Someone who didn't have a child, someone with good credit. Our baby is gorgeous, but I don't want to raise her like I was raised. Beauty is not a weapon, it's not enough to be pretty. I want to spend the rest of my life making it up to you. I'm so sorry Yussef! I did love you, but I wouldn't allow myself to be weakened by it any more than I had to."

"Sylvia we all make mistakes. One of the painful parts of life is trying to forgive. I'm trying to forgive you, but now you're making me feel guilty for turning you out." I laughed.

"WHAT? NO! DON'T FEEL GUILTY ABOUT THAT I LOVED IT!"

I laughed again, "stop acting. It wasn't that good."

She sat up straight, "I'm not acting, kidding, joking, or exaggerating!" She looked me in my eyes.

"Ok…" I looked away. "Well this isn't healthy. Sydney will pick up on your behavior and think that's how you're supposed to behave."

"What's wrong with her seeing her mother love someone?"

"She might think we're going to get married and then I flash cause I had a flashback. Last night wasn't even supposed to happen."

She scooted closer to me. Then she put her arms around me. "Did you have fun last night?" She said as she started sucking on my earlobe.

I took a deep breath, "are you trying to game me again? You got the baby you wanted. You trying for another one?"

"I will have as many babies as you want me to." She started kissing my neck.

I could feel my brain freezing over. "Nope, nope, nope!" I said standing up. "Ain't right!"

"Please Yussef, I will do whatever!"

"Get up and go sit over there!" I pointed her back to the corner she started in. "You can't just be a booty call, my daughters are watching. I can't see marrying you after what you did." She lowered her head. "I want a wife, I want babies, and I want to go back to service. You're in the way! You can only offer me companionship, and more children. I can't say I still wouldn't feel cheated. When I look at you I remember how much I loved you, I can feel what it used to feel like to be in love with you. I'm not in love with you. It feels wrong to trust you. I only have your word that you're sorry. And you know what… I still feel uneasy about trusting you."

"I'll do whatever it takes!" She said through tears.

"I had my own trust issues. You made them worse!"

"I know, I understand."

"You don't know!" Then I walked to the door. I cursed then I walked out the door. I paced around my car trying to think. I couldn't think straight. I drove to the store, and bought a box of condoms. I lightly tapped on Sylvia's front door. She opened the door with red eyes, but she looked relieved that I was back. She didn't say anything as she sat back on the couch. I went up the stairs and Syd was fast asleep in her bed. I kissed my baby girl goodnight, and then I booby-trapped the door. When I came back down Sylvia was still sitting in her corner unsure of why I returned. I took my jacket off and laid it on the futon, and then I jumped on Sylvia.

Lanie

I had the door shut to my office, Brian McKnight was singing, "my shattered dreams and broken heart, are mending on the shelf...." over my computer speakers on repeat as I stared at my fingers. I couldn't focus on my work, I was too depressed. "Ms. Wallace?" The receptionist said buzzing my phone.

"Yes?" I said very dryly...

"Dorian is here to see you, he doesn't...."

"SEND HIM IN!" I didn't mean to scream it, but suddenly energy flash through me. I stopped the music, jumped up and tried to smooth my already smooth ponytail. I pulled at my sports jacket as if my clothes could be wrinkled and I tried to get it together. Dorian's eyes were sad when she showed him in. He stood by the door and waited for her to disappear. "Would you like to have a seat?" I pointed to the chairs in front of my desk.

"Since when do you stop fighting? I've been waiting for the backlash." He said standing by the door with his hands in his jacket pocket.

"Backlash?"

"Don't play dumb, you know you're crazy. I expected you to trash my car, or I come home one day to a burning building. My bank account zeroed out. Something! You always do something."

"I..." Don't get emotional Lanie! SUCK IT UP! SUCK IT UP! "I know what I did to you was wrong. I finally understood what you meant. My guilt was pain enough for both of us. Please have a seat."

He stared at my stomach, "are you pregnant?"

"Is that your way of trying to say I look fat?"

"No! But you are wearing all black and you never do that."

"I'm not pregnant, were you trying to get me pregnant?"

He finally took his seat, "I don't know. I would be lying if I said no, and I wouldn't feel right saying yes. I guess if I wasn't trying to do anything to prevent it...." He let that ride on the air. "Why aren't you pregnant?"

"I don't know, I actually thought I was. I came clean with my momma. You should run if you see my daddy." I forced a grin, he didn't. "I was relieved and depressed all at the same time. Relieved that you wouldn't think I was trying to trap you, and depressed that you were done with me."

He put his hands out on my desk and waited for me to give him mine. When I did he rubbed my hands with his thumbs. "I love you Elaine, but we are going to be the death of each other. Look at you, your vibrance is gone. What happened to your natural flair for excitement? I don't want this for you. I'm sick of this life, let's go back together."

I released his hands and I sunk in my seat. "You want me to go back there after all of this? Everybody knows that your disappearance has everything to do with me. Dotty will look at me and I will beat her down right there in front of everybody before she has a chance to say anything. That wouldn't be respect for our place of worship."

"There are other congregations."

"All of them know who we are. I can't Dorian. When you go back in there they're going to fight over you. Probably to the death. I need you to film April getting socked in the eye for me. I wanna see it. I'm not what you need Dorian. I get it now."

He squeezed my hands; "I will never forgive you for making me leave you behind."

"Good! It will be easier if you hate me."

He got up and paced the floor. "Come have dinner with me. Come straight to my place after work."

"I don't think...."

"SHUT UP AND JUST DO IT! DON'T GIVE ME NO EXCUSES! IF YOU EVER LOVED ME YOU WILL BE THERE!" Then he walked out.

I closed my office door, I turned Brian back on and then I put my head on my arms as I cried. Brian sang like five times, my door opened. I didn't move. The person walked up behind me and then they poked me in my sides. "Wake up!"

"Hi Darryl…" I said not lifting my head.

He grabbed my ponytail and pulled my head back. "OK! I'M WORRIED NOW!"

"Why?"

"You were barely there at D-Rick's wedding. Ryder and I carried the responsibility of entertaining everybody. You didn't even react when Chantel's auntie killed our eardrums with that Teena Marie song. We were expecting you to boo her off the stage or something. Everybody noticed when you didn't react. Tell me about it, what did Dorian do?"

"Nothing it was all me."

"You sure he didn't do the unthinkable, break your heart, and then get mad when you equally do something as bad like oh I don't know dig out his best friend. BUT IT WASN'T MY FAULT! I'M A SEXY GUY! PANTIES DROP WHEN I WALK IN THE DOOR! NOW SHE WANNA BACK IT UP! DROP IT! LET ME TOUCH IT! JUST TO TAKE IT AWAY! BUT WHAT I DID WAS SO MUCH WORSE! THE MAN IS ALWAYS THE DOG!"

I tried to hold back my laughter as Darryl went off; I reduced it to a smile. "No, it's more like he wanted to marry me but I wouldn't agree to go to service. So he broke up with me. Then when he was weak I took his virginity, broke him down like he was a girl. Then he got a little practice and came back and broke me down showing me what I passed on. Now he wants me to have dinner with him cause he wants to go back to service and I don't want to go."

Darryl looked horrified, "he still wants to marry you?"

"If I'll go to service. Now I can't go!"

"It was you!"

"Me what?"

"You're the one who's been in KB's ear advising her on how to make me out to be the female in this relationship! I should've known one day a Wallace was going to turn on a Wallace."

I laughed, "No it wasn't me. Maybe she taught me. Clearly she's got a few tricks up her sleeves."

"She ain't got no tricks, maybe that's why. Good old fashion turned out by yours truly."

"Sounds like you turned yourself out."

"I may have strangled myself with the same whip I used to tame her…" he sat back. "Her glorious booty!" He smiled off into the distance.

"You act like her butt is bigger than it actually is. Yes, Kendra's booty is irrepressible, but I've seen bigger."

"Bigger *NATURAL* booty? I beg to differ! KB's got cakes on top of cakes. Her booty so big you can see it from the front." He drooled at the memory.

"Your exaggeration is hilarious. My booty is bigger than hers."

"EEEWWLLLL!" Darryl screamed as he hopped out of his seat. "Don't talk about nothing on you when I'm thinking of my woman. You trying to make me sick?" He held his stomach.

I cracked up, "thank you D. I needed this laugh."

"Well what thanks I get, you have disturbed my soul. I don't want to think about your grossness."

"I take it back, Kendra's booty is the biggest."

"Thank you, I smacked it myself."

I laughed harder, "why are you here?"

"Because you been tripping. I haven't seen you and then you were acting all zombie like.

Don't let anybody take your crazy feistiness away. In the end it may be all we have."
"Got it, I'm gonna need you to remind me of this tomorrow."
After work I did as I was told and I went straight to Dorian's. He tried to hide the take out boxes in the kitchen and act like he actually cooked for me. I told him it was nice to be able to use the front door for a change. He smiled, and then he poured our homemade Beautifuls. He said he made them doubles cause it was all we were getting tonight. Then he said it could always be like this. We could come home to each other, no more sneaking around. I didn't say anything I just smiled. He asked me about my day, and I told him about Darryl's visit. He said he was sorry he missed him; he could've used another smile today. Then he said my agreement to dinner was the first smile he's had in months. I apologized again for what I did. He put his hand up to stop me. He told me he knew I wasn't going to take no for an answer. He shouldn't have drunken anything that night. When I finished eating he turned my chair out from the table, he got down on one knee and he begged me to say yes. When I shook my head no, he said I was missing the big picture. He stood up and took his shirt off. He told me to look at what I would be getting, all of his beautifully sculpted body for the price of one yes. I smiled at him, "what am I going to do if I can't kiss those lips." Then he unbuttoned my blazer and opened it. "These are my breast, they've been waiting for me." Then he massaged them. Then he took off my shirt and bra. "MINE!" Then he stood me up, "why would you deny me?"
"I'm not what you need. You'll end up hating me."
"More than I already do?"
"Yes, more than you already do."
"Ok, I didn't want to have to resort to this. I think we should make love so you can feel how wonderful it feels. Think about forever like this." Then he kissed me and led me into his bedroom.
"No Dorian, you're going to hate me more." I held on to the doorpost.
"Please Lanie, if you hold on to your no. I can't have the last image of you walking out of here in tears as the final time I touched you. We owe it to each other to make love at least once."
"Don't try to knock me up."
"That's half the fun! Come on!" He joked, when I only smiled. He opened his nightstand, "I have condoms." He showed me.
He undressed then he undressed me, he kept whispering, "you're mine!" in my ear. He kept looking at me watching my face, and kissing me. There was no fast hard tempo this time. This time it was me and him, I guess the way it would've been. Every time he wanted to start again, I wouldn't let him in until he put a condom on. When he finally fell asleep hard, I quietly got up. Dressed, gently kissed his cheek and then I left.

****

"I am here! Lemon Drop me!" I announced to my sister as I arrived at our second Wednesday of the month location.
"I got you covered." Erica said moving my glass closer to me. I took a sip when a guy approached our table.
"Excuse you." He said looking me up and down.
"Excuse yourself." I returned his look.
"How you gonna walk past me like you didn't see me?"
"Like I did. Why would I care about looking at you?" My eyes continued to go up and down his body.
"Cause I know you saw me, and I'm letting you know I see you."
"Yes, but I also see that your pants are sagging. Sorry, better luck next time."
"You got a problem with swag?"
"I have no problem with swag, but I do have a problem with sag. Be original, try walking

around with your pants pulled up."

He smiled at me, "give me your number."

"Pull your pants up." Ok so this guy was cute, and nothing like Dorian. It's a pet peeve of mine that all these idiots emulate a ridiculous fad that was started by a lifestyle most of them claim they ain't with. If you ain't with it, stop dressing the part.

"Why do my pants bother you?"

"They confuse me. If you want me then you should dress the part of a man interested in a woman. If you want a man, continue dressing like you do."

"Write your number down."

I looked at his pants, "no. Maybe if I see you again, you'll be wearing a belt and I won't be confused. Not gonna happen today, sorry." Then I turned my attention to my sisters who were smiling.

He smiled at me, "you better be worth it." As he walked away our waiter came over and greeted us all by name. I saw mister soggy pants notice our interaction.

****

"I would like to call this meeting to order." Darryl tapped his glass. "I'm going to let it slide that the two of you have let the funny go temporarily. As long as you promise to never let it happen again."

"But D, Lanie's not so much funny as she is rude. Does she belong here?" Ryder said.

"I think the rude can be harnessed into comedy, what do you think?"

"Maybe if we give her some drills, she could show potential." Then his phone rang. "Ok, fatherhood calls."

"What? We just got here!" Then Darryl looked at me, "you gonna abandon me as well?"

"I'm here." Then I looked at the girl staring in our direction. "Who is this?"

Darryl shook his head, "the chickenhead also known as Brenda. That's my KB stand in."

"Why would you have a chickenhead stand in for Kendra?"

"Cause she's acting crazy right now." Then he waived the girl over. Ryder laughed and told D to be nice. Then he left. "What you doing?"

"Wondering why you're here without me." She focused on D.

"You see I'm here with someone." He nodded towards me.

"Yes." She didn't look at me.

"I guess she chose to ignore me. You know how I feel about being ignored."

Darryl smiled, "I do."

"Hey KB wanna be, stop staring at us and let us enjoy our evening. D will call you when he feels up to it."

The girl looked at Darryl with sad eyes then she walked away and out the door. "What up D? Long time no see." Mister soggy pants said as he came to greet Darryl. I noticed that his pants were pulled up, he better had listened to me.

"What up man, you chasing chickens tonight?"

"I'm here with my cousin, this you D?" He asked him without looking at me.

"Which cousin?" Darryl said ignoring his question.

"You remember Martin? He was a couple classes ahead of us."

Darryl looked over to where soggy pants was gesturing. "Oh Martin, right. What's your name again?"

"Bilal."

"Right, you're Allee. Did you have a baby by… by…" Darryl was trying to remember the girl's name.

"Debbie, yeah we had a little boy. We haven't been together since six months after he was born though. It just didn't work out."

Darryl looked at him, "right. So what you up to now? You into making babies and not taking care of them? Have a seat tell me all about it."

"Is it cool if Martin comes over?"

179

Darryl looked at me, "is that ok with you? This is supposed to be our time."

"Oh my bad, you on a date?" Bilal asked.

"It's fine." I said watching Darryl take him in.

Bilal waived his cousin over. They sat in the two available chairs. "D! Man! Where you been? I haven't seen you in ages." He shook Darryl's hand.

"Graduated from college, hit the ground running, what about you two?"

"College, nice! I'm doing what I gotta do to make it." Martin said.

"How many kids you got now?" Darryl asked him.

"I got two."

Darryl rolled his hands, "and...."

"What you CIA? How you know?" Martin laughed.

"I can smell that new baby smell all over you. So what's up?"

"I got one on the way, and this other girl tryna say her baby mine, but I'm not buying it."

"Allee what about you?"

"I got my junior, I'm straight." Bilal looked away.

Darryl looked at me, "Aw come on Allee you ain't gotta lie to kick it. You smell just like your cousin. New baby smell oozing out of your pores and what not."

"That ain't my baby!" Bilal got a little hot under the collar after the declaration.

Darryl smiled, "did I strike a nerve?"

"What about you D, what you been up to?"

"Nothing, working, partying. Met up with her for a change of pace tonight. Sometimes you gotta change it up."

Martin looked at me, and then he looked at Bilal. "D is this your woman?"

Darryl looked at Bilal, "so tell me the story."

"Story?"

"I saw you notice her, I know that's what brought you over. Tell me the story." Darryl sat back with his drink no smile on his face.

"I approached her a few weeks ago, been looking for her ever since."

"You didn't give him your number?"

I shook my head, "his pants were sagging."

"Oh yeah, she don't like that. Don't you call it soggy pants or something like that?"

"Yep, I told him it confused me. Didn't know what team he's batting for."

Darryl smiled, "and he took that as an invitation to keep flirting? Wow!" The waiter asked them if they wanted to order something to drink. They placed their orders. "So you feeling a little bold approaching me not knowing who she is to me."

"You've always been cool, I figured if this was your woman you would just say so. I didn't see her all up in your space like a female who was checking for you would be."

"Either way it feels like a test, I don't like tests. Even though I always pass them with flying colors. What you think?" He asked me.

"D, he pulled up his pants."

"He did didn't he.... How you know he didn't do it when he saw you?"

"You would've called him out on it." Then I looked at him. "I don't like being lied to, tell me why the kid ain't yours?"

"All due respect, that's really none of your business."

I smiled, "that's cool. Well we don't want to keep you. You two go ahead and enjoy your evening."

Darryl started laughing.

Amber

"Room service is twenty-four hours a day. Good looking out mister Latour!" I looked over the menu book on the desk. Malcolm was laying on the bed staring at the ceiling.

He's been very quiet since we got out here. Not that he's ever been a chatterbox; I normally do most of the talking. But he's definitely been a fish out of water on this trip. "You wanna see the menu?"

"Just order whatever sounds good."

I ordered breakfast even though it was almost midnight, then I went back to the room and I straddled Malcolm. "Are you ok? You're quieter than usual."

"Mind overload happening at the moment." He was still staring at the ceiling.

"Is something wrong?"

He exhaled then he looked at me. "Don't take this the wrong way." I didn't like that upfront disclosure. "I always knew that I wanted something more than what I had when I was young. Even though I was the youngest, Troy and I had this whole plan with Leonard and Fuzzy. All these moves we were going to make, we were going to be running things."

"You are running things."

"Yes, but running with a wife and kids changes your pace. Amber you are my Queen and I'd never change that. I can't be as reckless as sometimes I see things needing to be. There's always some person threatening our throne, wanting to take what's mine. What's ours because they feel some entitlement. Our family is getting bigger and bigger. That just makes for more moving parts, more what ifs, more possibilities. I never saw myself as a family man until Drew. Even with that you saw how I fumbled through that at first. Prison gave me time to research and learn. Except for when you were with that loser. I wasn't too concerned with him until you showed up with that ring. Why do you still have it?"

He locked his eyes on me, while I immediately felt like he threw me on the hot seat. "He gave it to me with all his heart. I was in love with the man who gave me that ring."

"What about the earrings?"

He was referring to the earrings that Dwayne gave me. I exhaled, "I was in love with the man who gave me those earrings." I heard myself say. I never said it out loud like that so it was weird hearing me say it, and weirder that I was saying it to Malcolm.

"What about now?" His eyes were burning a hole in my forehead.

"I'm with you Malcolm."

"I know you're with me. I'm asking about him. I wonder sometimes, about the way you remember things. Even though David did the things he did. You still let him work on Andrew."

"I did not!" I was offended and moving off of him.

"Moving on Amber. In the end I know your heart wasn't with him. The pretty boy on the other hand…" He looked like he was trying to burn a hole into me. "I have no tolerance for back sliding unless you're doing it with me."

"Malcolm, I'm here with you. I'm in love with you! Only for my babies would I wait this long to have us say our vows. I've wanted to marry you since I was thirteen."

"Remember that when we're at Latia's wedding and he's there with his little heart on his sleeve giving you puppy dog sad eyes." He smiled, "sissy!"

I waited a minute before changing the subject. "Have you chosen a best man?"

"Not yet." Then he looked at me, "have you asked Roz?"

"I'm gonna talk to her when we get back. She was pretty messed up about seeing Ben, where did you find him?"

"Was he ever missing? I've always known where he was."

"Does he want Rosalind back? Or was he messing with her?"

"You saw him following her around you tell me."

"I don't understand men. They had a family, why come back after all of this?"

"He was young Amber, we all mess up. If she takes him back I'll be happy for them."

"Did you believe I'd take you back?"

"Not at first, but I decided that you didn't have a choice we were getting back together. You could only say when."

"Oh Malcolm!" I blew air as I got off the bed.

Malachi

"What's up Malachi?"

"How was the vacation? You guys have fun?"

"Of course we did, she was with me. What's up?" Malcolm watched my eyes.

I couldn't keep it in anymore. "What you doing after?"

"Meeting Amber at some point. We'll send the others ahead and catch up to them in a while. Darryl or Ryder or both will get stuck in the sand pit eventually. Hold on." He motioned towards Derrick who was openly watching us. No words were exchanged, Derrick nodded and then he took our group ahead to start our day of golf.

I leaned forward and Malcolm mimicked my posture. In a low voice, I spilled everything. I held nothing back. When I was done Malcolm looked at me. "You can't let your wife hang out with this woman. That within itself is a time bomb waiting to happen. Quit your job! You need to get away from her! It's very interesting to me how she tells you she wants to move and then suddenly this huge company came up with the same idea. Quit! Abandon ship! Why are you working for someone else anyways? What happened to opening your garage?"

"The money!" I said remembering one of my goals.

Malcolm frowned, "you need money?"

"No! The money I've been making has been sweet!"

"Look at the trade off! And anything you're making there is probably only pocket change. You're going to have to tell her."

"Would you tell Amber?"

Malcolm chuckled, "only when I was ready to die! I'm not stupid enough to let any female get that close to my Queen. Your life is in her hands and she knows it. Quit your job! This is as good of a time as any to start over. Besides, you're going to need all the down time you can find to fix this."

"You're right."

"You guys need to go see Joanne."

"You keep saying that like she's a miracle worker."

"I got my Queen back didn't I?"

I thought about it and he had a point.

****

"Baby! Wake up!" Denise said as she nudged me awake. As my eyes focused she was holding a positive pregnancy test in front of my eyes. "We did it!" She said completely happy.

Seeing her smile made me smile, "congratulations baby. We did it." I gave her a hug.

"So the girls already ate. Amaya already took her bath and Jada's gonna take a shower right now."

I frowned, "you're leaving?"

"I have my class with your sisters, Jenise, and Grace this morning. Remember I told you." I sighed, "then I'm going to meet Cora for lunch."

"Baby let's keep our news contained to family at least until I've left the company."

She smiled, "ok," and then she kissed me.

"I will take a back seat to my sisters, but where's our celebration we did it sex? You need to come spend this rainy day in bed with me, tell Cora to kick rocks."

She smiled, "I know it's stupid." Then she got nervous like she didn't want to say. I rubbed her arms and asked her to tell me. "We've been together all these years. Aren't you tired of me? I don't feel sexy."

I exhaled, "baby you are more gorgeous to me today than you were when we first met. I can't get enough of you, and that's being honest. Is that why you pull away from me?" She started crying and immediately I felt like garbage. "I guess so. I'm going to be better ok. I'm going to be the wife you deserve."

"You are already more than I deserve. You deserve better than me!"

She looked at me in shock. "Malachi there is no better husband than you! You are a wonderful father and husband. Hanging out with your sisters has helped me so much. They've been helping haven't you noticed the difference?"

"I have, it feels like we're getting back on track. Before we can get completely there, we're going to need to talk." I swallowed, now is as good of time as any. "I need to...."

"MOMMY! AMAYA KEEPS THROWING MY CLOTHES ON THE FLOOR!" Jada screamed at our door.

"Amaya! Stop it!" Denise called out.

"Jada's being mean to me!" Amaya cried while hitting the door.

I exhaled, it's like those girls know when we need to talk and then they do whatever they can to stop it. Denise walked to the door. She checked both of the girls and told them someone better be dying before they knocked on the door again. I was surprised that she remembered to loop back around to me. This was new. She got back on the bed, and then she looked at the clock. "Malachi! I'm going to be late. Can we finish when I get back? I'll try to reschedule with Cora ok?" she said running into the closet to get her shoes.

I deflated, but what could I say? Denise ran out the door and my girls happily ran in the room and bounced on Denise's side of the bed. They want to go do something; I told them it was raining so we couldn't walk down to the park. The girls were looking to me to entertain them. We sat there in a stare down as my brain ran a mile a minute. I picked up the phone and I called Andrew to see what he was doing with Andre today. He said they were going to the kid's museum in downtown Berkeley and we were more than welcome to come.

Andre got so excited seeing his cousins. Andrew put his seat in the very back of my SUV. They were having their own kid's conversation as Drew and I talked. Drew told me about the proposal that they got from this guy to buy their home. He sounded as frustrated as I would've been when he was talking about Tracy's illogical attachment to that house. He said point blank that house had been compromised a long time ago, and this whole situation provided an opportunity for them to move on to a more secure location. I glanced in my rearview mirror again and that same car was following me. I told Drew we had a tail. He lowered the passenger side mirror like he was looking at his hair. He sucked his teeth and said that was detective Dartnell. He said she follows, she approaches, and then she follows some more. We parked in the garage and then we took the very excited kids inside the building. This place encouraged kids to explore and touch. They had an art museum where the kids could create their own watercolor masterpieces. Interactive exhibits. Tubes for the kids to climb through, etc. Parents were given ID bracelets that matched the kids they came with. I told Jada to keep her little sister and Andre with her at all times. Then they took off running. Every so many steps there were kids, you couldn't move without making sure you weren't stepping on a kid. The place was buzzing and the kids were having a blast. We followed the kids to the art exhibit, the facilitator for that room smiled real big when she saw Drew and I walk in the room. She gave the kids smocks and then she set them up on their individual easels. She was cute and young and overly eager. She came over to us; she said our kids were adorable. I saw the disappointment in her eyes as she saw both of our wedding bands. She talked to us for a little while longer, trying to save face and then she turned her attention back to the children in the room.

"Wallace's!" The slightly chubby white woman said. "Andrew long time no see, and

Malachi I don't think we've ever been properly introduced. I'm detective Dartnell nice to meet you."

"You know what doesn't make sense to me? Why after all these years you still feel the need to follow us around? How many different ways do you need to see that we are just a working class family?"

She clapped her hands, "that's the way you try to come off today. But I know better. I know you guys are still dirty, it's just a matter of figuring out how filthy you are."

I hit her with my smile, and she literally jumped which made Drew and I chuckle, "how dirty do you think we'd be with our kids right next to us? My nephew and I are family men and hard working. I can't speak for everyone else. Doesn't a trip to the kid's museum in Berkeley seem like a waste of your time?"

"What does your mistress think of your little family trip?" She said staring me in my eyes.

"You must have the wrong guy!" Drew said as if he automatically knew she had the story wrong.

"Your nephew doesn't know about Cora does he?" She said not taking her eyes off of me.

Andrew looked at me, and I know I turned red. I couldn't say anything, as angry as I was I could've knocked this woman's head off right here in the middle of the room with all these kids watching. "It looks like you've taken care of that for me." Drew sat back in his seat. "What's your point in blurting out my personal failings? You want to make me look bad? Done! Do you need anything else?"

"I just wanted to let you know I plan on approaching her with some questions. Who knows what your little pillow talk could have exposed her to."

"Do what you feel you have to."

"Should I do it before or after she hangs out with your wife again?"

I could see Drew looking at me in disbelief out the corner of my eye. "Why are you asking me what you should do? Do your job and be done with it. I'm trying to understand the point of your harassment today."

She smiled, "no real point. You've been very good about covering your tracks with her. You know as a civil servant I felt it was my duty to let someone know what was going on here. Have a good day Wallace's." Then she walked away.

"Uncle Malachi! Say it ain't so!" Drew said halfway playing. I couldn't look at him. I knew Cora moving out here would cause things like this. It was all bad from here.

I told Drew the whole story. He listened quietly just like Malcolm, and then he told me to leave the girls with him and to go talk to Denise immediately. He said this whole thing was about to blow up, and I couldn't let Denise hear from anyone other than me. He had a point. We let the kids play for a little while longer and then we took them to a drive-thru. The girls were excited to go over Andrew's; Tracy was with her parents so he said they could run wild around the house. When I got to Amber's school none of my sister's or Denise's cars were there. That's when I saw the missed call and voicemail from Denise. She said they decided as a group to go get something to eat at Gonzalez's, and that she'd be home after that.

Amber

"So my next project is burlesques themed. I wanted to use our time today to work out some ideas."

"Amber these pictures are beautiful! Malachi said he doesn't care where we go, but I've been putting it off too long. We need some alone time just he and I." Denise said blushing.

"Thank you, and vacations are what every couple needs. The beautiful Mexico backdrop was just what the doctor ordered for Malcolm and I. We cleared the air on a lot of things we hadn't talked about. I think the added incentive to not ruin our vacation is what made us have to dig deeper to talk things out."

"A vacation sounds so good. Timothy and I haven't gone anywhere alone since we were in school."

"Ethan and I go to Bora Bora, it's amazing. Every couple should go at least once." Jenise volunteered.

"You know all the husbands are going to be blaming you for the vacation virus that's about to spread." Jade said smiling.

"What do you guys think about inviting Rosalind to our next session?" I asked hoping they said yes.

"She's a part of the sisterhood, she should've been here from the start." I was relieved that Sophia felt that way.

After talking to Malcolm I realized that I wanted her in my wedding, but we definitely needed to talk and clear the air. Things felt stagnant around us and I don't know why. I gave each person their routine and then we went over it. We were cracking up laughing out of embarrassment at times, but we were having a good time and everyone knew we were in a safe place. No competition, judgment, or cattiness allowed in this class. Denise was full of smiles this morning and anxious to get back home. She said she and Malachi had a *conversation* to finish. I was so happy for her. When our class was over I thanked everyone for working with me. We synchronized our calendars for our next session. Denise looked disappointed when Malachi didn't answer his phone when she called him. Right after she hung up from leaving him a voicemail her phone rang, she answered it assuming it was Malachi. She put her caller on hold and asked us if her friend could join us for lunch. Everyone agreed and so Denise gave her friend directions to Gonzalez's our regular spot. At the restaurant Denise kept smiling saying she couldn't wait to get home. I found myself thinking about the romantic scene this rainy Saturday afternoon provided as well. I was going through my mind setting the stage for later on with Malcolm when Denise's friend walked in. Denise got up and greeted her with a hug, we all said hello and then returned our attention to our menus.

"What is this place?" Cora asked with a "she's too good to be here" tone.

"This is a little spot that we've come to since we were young. It holds a lot of memories for us." Jade said watching Cora.

When I saw that look in Jade's eye I decided to pay attention so that I would understand why she was looking at this stranger this way. "So, what brought you all out on this rainy day?" Cora asked.

"Sisterly bonding," Denise said still looking at her menu.

Cora frowned, "I thought you had only one sister?"

Grace looked annoyed, "what brings you out?"

"I thought Denise and I had plans, but I guess hanging with you guys was more important." She said frowning at the menu. "Did you ever try that recipe I gave you?"

"Yes I did, the girls loved it." Denise said.

"Your husband didn't?"

"He didn't get a chance to try it. He was busy that week with work."

"Have you tried to talk him into staying with the company? He's a huge asset there."

"He wants to leave."

"Tell him he can't, he should listen to you. You're his wife!"

"But I want him to do what makes him happy. He hasn't been happy there for the past few years, I think he's due for a change."

"That's crazy! He's really good at his job, he's happy at the company. Talk him into staying. He...."

"Why are you all up in their business?" Sophia asked.

"I was about to ask the same thing!" Grace said.

"She works at the plant with Malachi." Denise said.

"So what! Do you get paid a commission if he stays?" Grace asked.

Cora frowned again, "no. I'm looking out for him. Malachi is one of very few black men who has made it as far as he has. I'd hate to see him give it up on a whim of a notion."

"How is it your place to speak on it?" I said.

"I'm a friend," Cora said defensively.

"A quote unquote friend who's all up in their business! Do you have a man?" Sophia asked.

"Not at the moment." Cora said looking at Sophia.

"Denise first of all she's too comfortable being all up in you and your man's business. You don't let a single woman even look in your man's direction."

"Oh no! Cora's cool you guys." Denise said defending her friend.

Denise put her head down and we exchanged looks. I guess it's Malcolm and I's history but I don't have tolerance for any female getting too close to him. The fact that this chick has no filter and is like this in front of us. Is this her holding back? She's probably living through Denise and Malachi wishing she had a man like that. I shot Sophia a look telling her to calm down. We ordered our food and then whenever Cora would open her mouth, Sophia would talk over her saying whatever to Denise. Grace kept looking Cora up and down, Jenise openly stared, and Jade was sitting back in her chair looking annoyed. When Malachi and Darryl walked in all hell broke loose. The way this chick said my brother's name made me think of any female I've hated and how they responded to Malcolm. I looked at my brother completely disappointed.

Malachi

I went back to Drew's and Darryl was getting ready to leave as I was pulling up. I asked him to give me a ride to Gonzalez's; I tossed my car keys to Drew in case he needed to move it later. "What's up Uncle Mali you look stressed."

"I am! It's my fault so hey what am I gonna do?"

"You're always as cool as ice, so it's gotta be pretty bad if you're stressed off of it."

I blinked my eyes repetitively as I tried to make sure I was seeing straight. Cora's car was in the parking lot along with everyone else's. I cursed! What part of the game was this? Darryl looked at my reaction and then he parked his car. He was looking around seeing who was where, and I was trying to focus on what I needed to say.

When we walked in the door they were sitting at a table in the middle of the floor. I could see looks in the women's eyes in Cora's direction. She was sitting at the end of the table with her back to me next to Denise. Amber and Grace were sitting at the heads of the table, and Jade, Jenise, and Sophia were facing me. When I approached the table Cora turned to see who they were looking at. "Malachi?" She said in the wrong tone.

The look on everyone's faces as they looked at me made my skin crawl. "Hey baby, we decided to collectively come and get something to eat." Denise said getting up to kiss me.

"Denise there's a reason why I told you I needed to talk to you immediately." I said trying not to sound too abrupt.

"I called you, since you didn't answer I figured you were busy with the girls."

"Denise let's go!" I said, everyone else sat there motionless watching.

"Ok," Denise said not understanding what was going on.

"You can leave too!" Sophia said to Cora.

"You don't even know me!" Cora said defensively.

"And yet I don't like you. You're sneaky! AND! I don't like the way my cousin's name rolled off your tongue."

Cora rolled her eyes and sucked her teeth, "whatever! I'll see you later Denise."

"No you won't!"

Cora looked at me with pleading eyes, "Malachi please!"

Everybody sat up straight, "what?" Denise said not connecting the dots.

"Malachi?" Amber said looking at me with sad eyes just like my momma would've when she was disappointed in me.

I turned my eyes from her. "What?" Denise said looking at everybody who now held the same expression as Amber. "Malachi? What?"

"Let's go," I said as gently as I could.

"Where are we going?" She said as tears filled her eyes.

"Home, we need to talk."

"About Cora?" She stared at Cora's guilty expression.

"Denise, let's go."

All the women watched Denise like they were waiting for a reaction.

"Mal…" Cora didn't get my name out her mouth before Denise knocked her so hard she flew backwards.

No one at the table moved, if anything I could see Sophia holding herself back. Denise flew at her, "YOU CALLED YOURSELF MY FRIEND! TELLING ME HOW I SHOULD BE WITH MY HUSBAND!" I tried to grab Denise but she moved before I had her and she went after Cora.

"Denise!" Cora yelled jumping up. "I don't want to hurt you! I know you're mad, but I'm not going to sit here and let you hit on me!"

Denise tagged her in the face again as she lunged on her. I ran and grabbed Denise who was punching and kicking the entire time. "Let me go Malachi! Don't touch me!" She screamed.

Cora jumped up like she was going to do something and my sisters were right there standing side by side like a wall, waiting for her to do something. Darryl was talking to the manager while one of the workers put the closed sign in the window and locked the door. "Nephew!" I said tossing the six hundred I had in my pocket in cash to him. Darryl added it to the cash he was already handing over.

"Denise I'm SORRY!" Cora said with tears running down her face.

"YOU AREN'T SORRY! YOU JUST DON'T KNOW WHAT ELSE TO SAY TO ME!" Denise screamed at her.

"I AM SORRY! I TOLD HIM NOT TO TELL YOU!"

Denise cursed, "HOW YOU GONNA TELL MY HUSBAND WHAT HE CAN AND CAN'T SAY TO ME! I'M HIS WIFE! WHY WOULD HE LISTEN TO YOU!"

"BECAUSE I HAD HIM!" Now why did she say that?

Denise found the strength of four men and broke free from my grip. Grace stepped to the side so that Denise could charge her again. Cora punched Denise in the stomach, and all the women dove on her.

Darryl was standing next to the manager, "GET HER MOMMA GET HER! KICK HER SOPHIA!"

"HELP ME!" I barked at Darryl who was enjoying the scene too much.

"Mali, she the stupid one running her mouth when she see all these women about to pounce on her. I thought she was strapped honestly." Darryl explained as he casually walked over.

I grabbed Denise who was beyond furious! Darryl picked Cora up by her neck and let her feet dangle while he told the other women to stay back. I wanted to tell him to let her go, but I knew the women would turn on me too. "Darryl! Put her in her car!" I commanded. Darryl put Cora's feet back on the ground. After she caught her air, she grabbed her purse and umbrella. Darryl walked behind her out the door. As soon as the door closed all the women charged me. They were screaming profanity and smacking me! Denise was crying so hard she ran to the bathroom to throw up. "Malachi how could you?" Jade said with pain in her eyes.

I went to the bathroom and Denise was flushing the toilet. "SHE HIT ME IN MY STOMACH MALACHI!"

"Let's go," I said gently touching her arm.

"DON'T TOUCH ME! DON'T YOU EVER TOUCH ME! HOW COULD YOU MALACHI?" She held on to the sink to steady herself. "I know things haven't been perfect…" Her voice trailed off cause she was crying so hard. I felt like the smallest man in the entire world. Denise turned red as she tried to calm herself and stop crying. I tried to touch her again and she slapped the daylights out of me. I stood there waiting for her to hit me whatever she needed to do so that we could leave this bathroom. Jade came in the bathroom with fire in her eyes. She asked Denise if she wanted to ride home with her. I told Denise she was coming home with me, and I told Jade to get out! Jade frowned and turned on her heels. Darryl was at the door, he told us we needed to get going. He said the restaurant has been swept clean. I told Denise we had to go. When we walked out into the restaurant all the women were sitting at the table like nothing happened except they were giving me evil looks. Other customers were now in the restaurant and it looked like business as usual. Amber came and gave Denise a hug who was still bawling. I put Denise in the passenger seat in her car. She balled up in a ball in her seat crying and crying.

I kept taking deep breaths, when we got to the house she went in the guest room and shut the door. I knocked on the door and I could hear her crying. I stood there not knowing what to do. I felt weak and like a pathetic version of myself. I turned the knob and the door was locked, I kicked the door open. Denise stopped crying and looked at the door.

"STOP SHUTTING ME OUT! I'M HERE! I EXIST! I HAVE FEELINGS TOO!"

"She knows we were trying, she hit me in my stomach!"

"You kept attacking her, she will be dealt with. But what you think was going to happen if you kept jumping on her?"

"How could you let me hang out with her? Why would you let me befriend her?"

I sat on the bed next to her, "it was happening too fast. Think about it, I was not in favor of you guys being friends."

"When did it start? When was the last time? Why? Am I that horrible as a wife?"

"Denise I don't think we should have this conversation on our own. I think we need help."

"Wow! Now you can't even talk to me." She said shaking her head and staring at the bed.

"Denise we need help, I've been trying to talk to you for some time now. I haven't been as assertive as I should've been and I don't know how to give you what you need so that you'll understand me. I shouldn't have let you leave this morning." Then my phone rang, it was Drew. "Hello?"

"Are you ok? My momma is HOT!"

"We just got home."

"My momma wants to take the kids with her to spend the night, is that ok with you guys?"

"Yea that's fine. I'll figure out my car later."

"We can bring it to you when we bring the girls home. Word of advice, don't leave her side until she understands that you love her."

"Thanks," I said not knowing if that was possible.

Amber

When I got home I brought my nieces and Andre with me. Malcolm was in the office downstairs working on the computer. When I walked past the door he called me back. "What's wrong?"

"Malachi," I said with tears in my eyes.

Malcolm sat back in his chair and waited for me to say something. I told him what happened, how disappointed I was in him, everything. "Amber you're judging him and you don't know the whole story."

"What's to know? He cheated on her, end of story!"

"Think about who your brother is. How much he loves his wife, and his family. There's more to the story. Your brother isn't that shallow."

"So you're saying when you cheated on me you were being shallow?"

Malcolm cut his eyes to the left, "don't make their problems ours."

"I'm trying to understand what you're saying to me."

"Come here." He pushed back from the desk. When I walked around the desk, he pulled me into his lap. "I'm saying that they need professional help. There's more to their marriage than he needed to satisfy some selfish whim. Some people cheat cause they're selfish, some people cheat cause they can't get out of their own way, and that was me. Some people cheat when they get caught up, and I believe that's Malachi."

"So... what you're saying to me is that you knew about this and you didn't say anything!"

"Amber you're not going to get mad at me because of someone else's relationship. I'm here; I'm here every night and just about every day. I'm not cheating on you, don't let this consume you. This is something they have to work through, calm yourself." Then he kissed my lips.

Then Andre peeked his head in the office and the other two heads peeked in as well.

"EEEWWLLLL! Poppa! Nana! You guys are acting like my Mommy and Daddy!"

"EEEWWLLLL!" Jada and Amaya sang together.

"What's wrong with that?" Malcolm asked.

"I tried to kiss Monet and she slapped me. Hard!" He rubbed his cheek.

"Good! You're too young to be kissing on girls."

"How old were you when you kissed Poppa?"

Malcolm looked at me and smiled, "Boy!" I said embarrassed and not ready to have that conversation. "What are you guys doing?"

"Can we play basketball?"

"Of course."

"Where's my ball?"

"It's in your room in your closet."

"Come on you guys." Andre said running up the stairs.

Malcolm rubbed my butt; "I wish you would've asked me before you brought blockers home. I had plans for us."

I smiled at him, "sounds like we were on the same page." Then I kissed him.

"You got your dress yet?"

Ugh! I forgot, "oh right. I should have something in my closet I could wear."

"Procrastination has never been your style."

I exhaled, "I know. I've been trying to figure out an approach for this whole Tina thing. I wanna make sure I reach her."

Malcolm smiled, "you're gonna reach her alright. Reach out and choke her up."

"Why does everyone think I'm gonna put hands on this child?"

"You'll see."

****

"What's the dress for?" Tina asked.

"A charity event. You should come Malcolm bought a couple of tables and I'm sure there's room for you. Besides who doesn't like shopping?"

Tina half smiled, "I can't. I got plans."

"What could be more important than hanging out with me?"

"You gotta know I have a boyfriend." She threwing attitude.

"Why do I have to know that?" I said staring at her.

Tina's eyes bounced around the store, "I just figured you knew." She looked at a girl looking through a rack just a little away from us. "She's been in every store we've gone to." She whispered.

"That's just Shane," I whispered back.

"Who's Shane?"

"Her." I said pointing at her.

Tina rolled her eyes, "but who is she?"

"Shane." She looked at me and smiled. "Come here sweetheart, my niece wants to know who you are."

Shane walked over, "I'm Shane. I've been in charge of your safety for the past month."

"My safety?" Tina looked at me confused, "what does she mean?"

"You're a Wallace sweetheart, there's always someone watching." I said watching her eyes.

"Watching what? Andrew has the biggest mouth I swear!"

"Come again?"

"He met my boyfriend, and told my dad. Now everybody's been weird and ridiculous. If he would've just kept his mouth shut."

"Then what? You could continue with your shenanigans? The choices you make in your life affect more than just you sweetheart. You have no idea who you are."

"Why does everybody keep saying that? I know who I am, I'm Tina Wallace!"

"You don't even know what that means."

Shane moved closer to us, "I think we should leave."

Tina sucked her teeth, "we?" She put her hand on her hip.

"IF YOU DON'T BRING YOUR BRATTY BEHIND ON!" I said through clinched teeth.

"Just because some chick I don't know said to leave you're leaving? Nobody tells me what to do!" Tina wiggled her neck.

"Tina I don't have time for this, if someone tells you to go, you go!" I said grabbing her hand. Did this little heifer snatch her hand away from me? Shane took a deep breath. I felt my temper flash and I grabbed a fist full of her curls and proceeded to curse her out all the way outside to the car. People in the store were looking at us, but I didn't care.

"When I tell you to bring your behind you bring it! Get in!" I said unlocking the doors to my new car.

Shane got in her car, which was a couple of cars over from me. She followed directly behind me on the freeway. "Listen, maybe you don't value your life. I value mine; if you want to die let me know right now! Everyone can come and say their goodbyes and then you can go dangle out there until something bad happens. If you're trying to live like the rest of us then you're going to need to fix your attitude."

Tina was still pouting and rubbing her head where I grabbed her hair. "I don't know why you're putting on this whole dramatic scene! Nobody's concerned with us."

"So now you're calling me a liar?" I glanced at her and she shrugged. I backhanded her; "Timothy did you no favors by sheltering you this badly. I highly doubt this is what daddy meant for you guys."

"Why are you hitting and grabbing on me?" She said with tears pouring out of her eyes.

"Cause you're stupid and you have no idea how stupid you sound. You're a spoiled little ignorant girl. You can't even listen to what I'm telling you cause you're sitting over there thinking you know better. Only an idiot does that! By the time I was your age…"

She cut me off, "you had two or three kids."

"Stupid!" I said as I backhanded her again. I pulled over on the side of the 880 freeway on the shoulder. I took my seat belt off and I started hitting this idiot. "I am not one of

your friends! You better show me some respect or I'll beat it into you!"
Tina was screaming, "Ok! Ok! Ok!"
"I don't know who told you it was ok to talk to me like this! I know you aren't stupid
enough to try this with your momma! Tina I am not the one either!" Then I slapped the
mess out of her one more time for the road.
Then I put my seatbelt back on and calmly drove down the freeway as I lectured her
about her attitude. Tina stayed balled up in a ball in the passenger seat afraid that I was
going to hit her again. "Oh and in case you didn't know, you're going to the party. I got a
dress you can wear!"

****

"Daddy! I don't want to stay here! She's crazy! She keeps going off on me for nothing.
Please come get me!" Tina cried to her daddy over the phone.
Malcolm walked in the door, he looked at Tina and he smiled real big. Darryl walked in
behind Malcolm looking at him like he was crazy, more than likely because of the smile.
"DANG!" He said when he looked at Tina. "What happened to her?"
"Your momma!" Malcolm said still smiling.
Darryl looked at me in disbelief, "Momma why?"
"Her mouth!" I sat on the couch irritated by the sound of her whining.
"Oh," he said like I didn't need to say anymore.
Tina hung up the phone and sobbed loudly, "I want to go home!" She cried into her arm.
"It's not that bad over here." Darryl said.
"What do you know! I'm grown and she's over there hitting on me like I'm a little kid!"
Tina sobbed.
"Because you stupid enough to say stuff to make her hit you. She'd hit me too, but I
learned that lesson young."
Tina snatched her head off her arms. "You are not my auntie! I will fight you Darryl!
Don't forget I have a black belt!"
Darryl smiled, "and my belt is brown." He said showing her the belt on his pants, "you
don't want none Tina. You need to learn how to pick your battles."
Tina popped out of her chair; Darryl blank stared at her then he looked at Malcolm like
he was in shock. "I guess she's coming for you." Malcolm said completely tickled by this
display.
Tina gasped when Darryl handed Malcolm his gun, but then she went back to her stance.
"I guess my name supposed to be Ike now!" He said like he couldn't believe it. Tina
charged at Darryl, he slapped her cheek and swept her legs from under her. When she fell
flat on her back he grabbed her legs and pinned her. "AnaMae! Say sorry!"
"Get off me!" She yelled trying to free herself.
"Not until you apologize!" He fake cried, "It didn't have to be all this Tina. But you over
here no doubt disrespecting my momma like you don't know better when we all know
you do. AND THEN! Then you have the audacity to challenge me. Like something they
taught you in a class could ever save you from me! I may be your little cousin, but you
are the stupid one. Apologize!"
"No!" Tina refused.
Darryl squeezed her legs, "APOLOGIZE! *Eat the cake*!"
Tina screamed in pain, "Ok! Ok! SORRY!"
Darryl smiled, "say I'm sorry."
"I'M SORRY!"
"Yes you are, but why are you sorry?"
"DARRYL GET OFF OF ME!"
"Let her up!" Malcolm said.
Darryl popped her head and then he let her up. Malcolm gave Darryl back his gun. "Why
do you carry a gun?" She said with tears streaming down her face.

191

"This is grown folks business. Ask questions when you grow up." Darryl said waving her off.

"I'm older than you!"

"Yes, but every ounce of stupidity from you decreases your actual age. You're like a twelve year old kid right now."

Tina growled.

****

"Thank you for coming over." I said taking Rosalind's coat.

"When do you invite me over anymore? Of course I was coming." She said with a big smile.

"Have a seat," I said gesturing towards the living room. "I have been slipping on the invites haven't I."

"Girl, we all busy. Don't worry about it. What's up," she sat down.

I figured there was no point in beating around the bush, so I dove right in. "What happened to us? We've known each other since we were little. Now we don't talk, if it wasn't for the kids I wonder if we would even know each other."

"Whoa! Ok, no foreplay or nothing. You just going in I see." Rosalind smiled. "Like I said I think we've both been busy."

"Yea, but when have we ever been too busy for each other? I'm not saying we gotta talk every day, week, or month even. It's like we're strangers when we see each other now. I feel awkward when I see you."

Rosalind exhaled, "me too! I thought it was just me!"

"To me it feels like I'm holding back and not saying something that needs to be said."

"I feel like every time you look at me you want to talk about Troy." Then she slouched, "I can't always deal with that. Some days are better than others. I can't expect you to know the difference."

"I do want to talk about him, cause I'm still hurt about the whole thing!" Tears started pouring out of my eyes. "That could've been Malcolm, and I don't know how I would survive if that would've been him. I don't know how you're still standing. I admire that strength in you. Troy was like a brother to me, and you know you've always been a sister. Troy died and I lost not only my brother, but my man and my sister. THEN! My Poppa and NANA!" I took a minute to grab air between tears, "MELVIN!" Rosalind scooted closer and we hugged. "I lost everybody, and my DOGGONE HAIR!"

Rosalind started laughing, "You lost your hair?"

"Remember I was getting my hair permed back then. It started shedding and the next thing I know I had to cut it all off." I took a deep breath, "we haven't been right since then."

"I know, I'm sorry!"

"No, I'm not asking you to be sorry. I'm saying I want my sister back."

"The world don't seem right without Troy in it. I tried to replace him and we know that was a disaster. We were going to have babies; he had been on best behavior. He was back on Tanisha's good side, and Tanisha and I were going to move back in with him. He finally had the ball moving on Yussef, and a good read on Latia. Everything was coming together too perfectly and then...." She squeezed me as she cried; "sometimes I still hear the gun in my sleep. I still see him fighting to stay, trying his hardest not to leave me. I should've demanded that he stay with me instead of going out. He would've done it if I put my foot down."

"It's not your fault Roz!"

"Most times I believe that, but the other times I say I could've done something to stop the chaos. My Babygirl lost the only father she's ever known. Did you see that Benjamin is back?"

"Yea, what is that about?"

"Girl I don't know, he's been swinging from my nuts. Showing up at the shop, calling me all hours of the day and night."

I sat up and looked at her, I gave her the eye. "How did he get your number?"

She blushed, "I gave it to him, but only so he'd stop showing up at my job and messing up my head at work. One time I started a loc on a girl's hair that I was supposed to be braiding. It was an easy fix, but he keeps messing with me. I'm not that same little eighteen-year-old girl he kicked to the curb. I don't even understand why any of this has to be!"

"Are you going to give him a chance?" I was studying her eyes like the answer was going to show through them.

She blew air, "Tanisha would have a fit! She doesn't want me talking to him. She reminds me that he's not even like Malcolm. Malcolm never left you guys to fend for yourselves. Benjamin completely abandoned us, and now that Tanisha's grown he's trying to show up again? It doesn't work that way."

"That's how Tanisha feels, how do you feel?"

She started crying really hard. "I MISS TROY! I WANT TROY!" We cried together…

Kendra

I keep seeing this guy out when we're out. I've even seen him checking me out from time to time. He's cute and could be fine if he has any intelligence to him. I told Kalani I was going in. She nodded and watched from her seat as I approached this guy. He did a double take when he realized I was walking towards him. "Hey."

"Hey," He said with a smile.

I stuck my hand out, "Kendra."

"Shai."

"Shai?"

"It's short for Abishai, my parents are heavily into the bible."

"Definitely on the original side."

"Thanks, what are you drinking?"

"Seven and Seven."

He ordered another drink for me, and then he smiled. A guy walked over to us with a smile, "what's going on?"

"This is my friend Russell, Russell this is Kendra. She came over to say hello."

Russell looked surprised, "well ok! Nice to meet you Kendra."

Then a girl walked up to them, she looked like she just got here and was probably rushing. She looked kind of stuck when she saw me at first then she flashed Russell and Shai a look. "Latonya this is Kendra, Kendra this is Latonya."

"Nice to meet you, I said with a smile."

"Likewise, so what brings you over?" She asked like she was trying to figure out what was going on.

That's when I noticed her wedding ring. Neither Shai nor Russell wore one. "Honey, let's let these two get a chance to know each other." Russell said putting his arm around Latonya while walking away. Latonya looked back at us then she smiled at Russell, the smile seemed a little forced but she did it anyways.

Shai and I sat at the bar talking all night, he was cute, sweet, and I liked the way he didn't try to get up in my face. I've never been so bold as to approach a guy in a bar before, but this experience was good. I gave Shai my number when he asked for it. Then I went back to my sister while he went back to his friends.

****

"Kendra! This is crazy! I don't know what that punk D said to you, but I don't understand how you gonna take someone else's word without even talking to me. Your ex don't ever wanna see you happy with your next, please call me back give me a chance to explain at least." Everyday Raffy's been leaving me messages like this at least twice a day. It got back to Jason that I was keeping company with a known drug dealer. In my defense I didn't know, Kalani wants to blame it all on that girl Sonya. To let Kalani paint the scene Sonya found out that her cousin was hanging with us and she said something to her friend who said something to Andrew's wife, then Drew told Darryl and well Darryl ran interference. He gonna call my jumper a onesie! He knew I was looking GOOD and he had to make light of it to be a jerk.

My phone rang again, this time it was my momma. Kaleah's water broke and they were on their way to the hospital. I told her I'd come as soon as I finished up Ms. Agnes' house. Ms. Agnes got excited when she heard me say that my sister's baby was coming. She loves babies and little people; she started reminiscing on when she had her babies, then her grandbabies and now her great grandbabies. I finished cleaning while I listened to her talk about her babies. On the car ride over I felt irritable and I couldn't put my finger on why exactly.

Darryl and Milton's Auntie Lorraine parked next to me. She gave me the biggest hug and she told me she missed me. Even though she's religious she's cool about it. She doesn't beat you over the head with the bible like a lot of people do. I appreciate that about her. When we got up to the Labor and Delivery she smacked Milton upside the head instead of hugging him. He was expecting it so he took it and hugged her anyways. She asked him why he and Kaleah weren't getting married. Milton didn't say anything he just stood there rubbing his head. When I walked in the room Kaleah was in the middle of a contraction. Jason was sitting in the corner looking pissed with his eyes locked on Milton. When I asked where Micah was, they said he was in the cafeteria with Kalani. I gave Kaleah a kiss on her forehead after her contraction and then I put my head on Jason's shoulder as I sat next to him. He put his arm around me and kissed my forehead. As if he knew what I was feeling when I couldn't even understand it. He said that it would be my turn when it was time. The door opened slowly and then Dana popped her head in. She asked how things were going. I always liked Dana one of the long list of Mason women. She was older than me but always nice, unless you made her mad. But I guess that's the same with anybody. Dana is Milton's sister and the two of them fight all the time. If he's not starting it then she is. I honestly think they like fighting the way they do. Momma told her Kaleah had a little ways to go she was seven centimeters. She asked where Mikey was, so we told her he was downstairs with Kalani. She said all their cousins were filling up the waiting room as usual. Milton started to go out, but stopped in his tracks when he thought about it and looked at Jason. Jason was daring him to go. Jason wanted Milton right there with Kaleah going through all the motions with her. When the doctor came to check Kaleah again, Jason and I stepped into the hallway. "That idiot's still calling?"

"Yeah, he wants to explain."

"Explain to me how you didn't know what he did for a living?" Jason folded his arms.

I exhaled, "I didn't really ask. I was just passing time with him anyways."

"Kendra when are you going to stop rebounding?"

I shrugged as I looked at the ground. The nurse came out. She said Kaleah was going to start pushing. I went back in the room and Jason went to the waiting room. Milton was turning all kinds of reds and purple as Kaleah clawed him while she pushed. Kaleah was having a hard time pushing but the baby was coming. When his head finally came out you understood why, this baby's head was huge. The nurse said congratulations and that it was a boy as she laid him on Kaleah. Six pounds, eight ounces, twenty inches of new Mason blood. When I approached the waiting room everyone in there was cracking up. My heart sped up cause I knew that meant Darryl was in there. Everybody started smiling at me the moment I rounded the corner. I gave everyone the details; Darryl stuck his

hands out and told everyone to pay up. Then he shamed them for ever trying to bet against him. I sat next to Jason so Dana and Kalani could go see their new nephew. My nephew Micah was playing with his brother and sister, Milton's other kids. Darryl looked at me but he didn't say anything. One by one people went in the back to see the baby, when Dana and Kalani came out Jason and I went back in. My momma was crying as she snapped pictures of Jason and the baby. I could feel Darryl standing behind me without looking. Eventually he stood next to me. He stared at me and I acted like he wasn't there. When he looked at the baby he gasped and then he started cracking up laughing. "His head though! He got your dome Milton." Darryl was cracking up, "Kay-Kay I don't know if you'll ever be the same after that one! That is the biggest cone head I have ever seen!" Darryl caught everyone by surprise and one by one everyone gave in to the laughter they were fighting. Once everyone started laughing he kept it going, even the nurses were in stitches cracking up at him. I asked the nurse where the bathroom was and then I excused myself. As I was walking out of the bathroom Darryl was standing in my way. There was no smile on his face. When I tried to go around him he slowly pushed me back into the bathroom. He locked the door then he stared at me. The seriousness in his face was alarming. After a minute of blood curdling silence, I put my hands out. "WHAT?"
"You know what!"
"I really don't."
He watched my eyes. "How you gonna breakup with the square? And then! Not only do you not come back to me. You try to replace me WITH A FOOT SOLDIER! What is wrong with you?"
"You made me walk home!" I snapped.
"You took all my good loving and went home to a square. You dang skippy I made you walk! You don't appreciate me!"
"You don't appreciate me!"
"Please! I changed your name, went out of my way for you every chance I got." He moved in close to me, "I gave you my seed. What you do with it is up to you." I didn't think of it that way. "But you wanna be running around with foot soldiers who mess with all kinds of tricks and tramps. Are you still clean?"
"Whether I slept with Raffy or not is none of your business."
Darryl tilted his head at me, "none of my business?"
I put my hand on my hip, "you heard me."
He grabbed my chin, he wasn't hurting me but I wasn't expecting him to grab me. "You keep pushing me! I'm trying to hold back the crazy! You won't respect it until you see it! I don't want to hurt you Kendra. I don't want you to be scared of me, but keep on disregarding me like you have been and it'll suck to be you!" Then he kissed my lips. I slapped him as hard as I could, "don't threaten me!"
He scrunched his face up, and then he started laughing. "KB, you want me!"
"Kendra, and no I don't!"
He grabbed both of my wrist and moved in like he was going to kiss me again, I turned my face. "Yes you do!" Then he let me go, he exhaled. "I think I got a date tonight anyways. What is it about you and hospitals?" He laughed as he turned and walked out the bathroom. Kalani smiled at us, I rolled my eyes out of frustration. How he gonna tell me I want him? So what! I'm not giving in to it, I deserve better.
****
"What did all of that mean?" Ahjanae asked sitting on the edge of her chair.
"Nothing, he left the hospital without saying bye. He hasn't called me or anything."
"Kendra, please! My heart can't take this. Call the man! Go over his house! Go after him! Stop waiting for him to come after you."
I frowned, "I don't want Darryl!"
Ahjanae blew air, "you want him so bad you can't see straight. Anyone who looks at you

can see it. Why does he always have to chase you? Can you cut him a break? Goodness!"
"What if I go over there thinking he wants me and he really doesn't? I don't trust him, he's always gotta have somebody. Why can't he just be cool?"
"You're becoming just like him. Anton, Raffy, and now whoever this new guy is. Why can't you just be cool?"
"We're just friends, I can have friends."
"And so can Darryl."
"Yea, but he sleeps with his."
"So do you!"
"No I don't! I didn't sleep with Raffy either."
"Oh, I was just checking." Then we laughed. "Then that means you're all backed up. You could use a tune up."
"Darryl isn't just a tune up. He's an addiction that I don't need right now."
"At least go clear the air. So that when you're ready you two can mutually agree on how it's going down."
"I don't want to sleep with Darryl." I whined.
"But you're going to. Everyone knows it so go put your bid in. I got work to do."
I sat there feeling dumb for a minute. "You know Ahjanae, this whole thing about you sleeping with the enemy is not working for me."
She laughed, "Ryder is not the enemy."
"He puts his bid in for Darryl. They've poisoned your mind so that you poison me. You gotta see that's what they're doing." Ahjanae laughed as she thought about it. "See! You've been brainwashed too!"
"I do the same thing to Ryder. I promise it's an even swap."
I decided to drop by the office in the mall. Darryl travels a lot so he could be out of town. I had no idea of what I was going to say to Darryl if he was here. When I walked through the heavy glass door, the woman behind the counter smiled at me and asked how she could help me. When I asked to speak to Darryl. She picked up her phone, "Kendra's here for Darryl." I didn't know she knew who I was. A guy came from the back and he asked me to follow him. He showed me into a conference room.
"Why do you look familiar?" I asked the guy as he dialed a number on the conference phone.
He smiled, "you've seen me around."
"What's up Yu?" Darryl said answering the phone.
"I have Kendra."
"WHAT? What she want? Where she at? She look mad?" The guy laughed, Darryl paused. "I'm on speaker aren't I?" I laughed, "Yu! This ain't cool! You supposed to warn me."
"You two have fun." The guy said as he walked out and closed the door behind him. Darryl didn't say anything, and I felt dumb staring at the phone. "Where are you?"
"InMyOfficeInTheCity!" He said real fast.
"I thought you worked in Oakland."
"EveryOnceInABlueMoonButI'mNormallyOutHere!"
I laughed, "why are you talking so fast and running your words together?"
Then he whispered, "KB! You don't pop up at my job. I would think you were coming to tell me you're pregnant. Please don't tell me I gotta go kill a foot soldier! I didn't wake up feeling like somebody was gonna die. Normally I wake up knowing today is a day I'm gonna have to handle business. I didn't get that feeling. Maybe I'm slipping! I..."
I cut him off, "Darryl I'm not pregnant. I never slept with Raffy!"
He let out a dramatic sigh, "guess that means I broke his leg for nothing. Oh well next time he'll know better."
"You broke his leg?"

"And his arm." He said matter of factly.

"Why?"

"He put his arm around you. And his leg for stepping to you. Trying to act like he didn't know who I am! Everybody knows who I am! They gotta be square like Ant not to know me or know better."

"Are you serious?"

"As a heart attack!"

"So I guess I don't have to ask you if you still care?" I started shaking my leg.

"The issue isn't whether or not I care, the issue is you. You be wanting a nigga to go completely out on a limb for you and then you still act like it's not good enough. My name is Darryl!"

"I know what your name is."

"Then let me hear you say it!"

"Seriously?"

"As a freaking heart attack KB!"

"Darryl"

"No! No! Un un! Say it like you mean it!"

"Darryl!"

"You can do better than that!"

"Ugh! Darryl! Cut it out!"

"Now call me daddy!"

"Shut up! No!"

Darryl started cracking up. "What do you need?"

"I just wanted to talk to you, clear the air. I hate all the tension."

"Oh me too! Me too! I hate calling you anything other than KB! But how were you going to know I was still mad at you if I didn't?"

"Even though I tell you to call me Kendra."

"Call you.... You dating somebody else ALREADY!" He said like he was irritated.

"Um!" I said feeling guilty.

I could hear the phone fall, "she want a nigga to catch a case!" Then he picked up the phone. "Why must you torment me? You're back to Kendra! Leave me alone!" Then he hung up. I pressed the redial button. "Yu?"

"Kendra!"

"No! Have you no heart! Get off my phone woman!" Then he hung up again.

I know there's always truth in a person's joke, and Darryl especially. But I couldn't help but laugh. The guy opened the door with a big smile on his face. He had a phone to his ear it had to be Darryl.

When I got home, I showered then I made a sandwich. I was sitting on my couch with my feet up watching TV when I heard a key in the front door. I stared at the door; Darryl came in the door with a weird looking key thingy in his hand. He rolled his eyes at me as he walked in. I asked him what he was doing. He said I came to his job so that meant I wanted him and he came to give me what I wanted. I frowned at him and told him he was crazy, but when he kissed me I didn't fight it.

****

"I can't believe you're not going." My momma said.

"I'm so busy momma. With all the other weddings going on I can't squeeze this one in as well. Plus! Another dress? Please! Spare me! I don't know Latia, I understand Jason and her father were close, but I can't do it. That's a lot of time off work for someone I don't know." Kaleah gave the baby to me while she hurried to the kitchen to feed Micah. I looked at Keith who was full and happy. I want one! I want one so badly!

"Kendra you are beautiful in your dresses. For someone who never wears them, you come to life in them. It's like a whole new you when you wear them."

"I guess!" I said staring at my nephew.

"Plus! There's going to be a ton of celebrities there. Who's going to tell me who I'm looking at?"

"Jason can tell you." I said staring at my nephew and admiring how adorable he truly is.

"You know those things are contagious." She warned. "Don't have one until you're certain about your relationship."

"What does that mean?"

"Don't have any babies with Darryl until you two definitely have an agreement about when you're together."

"Why do you think it's going to be Darryl? It could be someone else."

"Oh right!" She said sarcastically, "what's this new guy's name?"

I rolled my eyes, "seriously momma? How come nobody gives Kalani a hard time? She dates different guys all the time."

"You know what's good for the goose ain't always good for the gander. You need to stop playing games. I don't understand what the holdup is? You know that boy loves you."

"Yep, he loves me. He wants to be my boyfriend forever, while he has all his sidepieces. Then one day he pulls a Jerry and I'm stuck with three kids all by myself. No thanks! He can't be alone. And! He won't leave me alone! His life is a mess so mine has to be as well I guess."

"You can't hold what Jerry did against all men. If I did that I never would've met and fell in love with Jason. Jerry doesn't speak for how all men are. You gotta let Jerry go."

"Jerry broke my heart momma! We could've been homeless and he wouldn't have cared. I'm glad you're over it, but I'm not. The likelihood of me ending up with someone like him is too high! I don't want that."

My momma was quiet for a minute. "Now you know I love Jason. It's like he was put on this earth for me, for us. It ain't easy over here. I've got my baggage and my ways. And he isn't always a picnic nor has he always been an angel. We fight hard, you've seen it. Sometimes I get so afraid because my life now is totally dependent on him. After all I went through with Jerry I never thought I'd trust another man like I trust Jason. Kendra you gotta watch what a man does in addition to what he says. Sometimes people change, normally that change isn't overnight. When you see the signs don't ignore them. Darryl has done some pretty bad stuff." She rolled her eyes, "but so have you."

"What have you been told?"

"My husband tells me everything." She smiled

"How does he know?" I said feeling embarrassed.

"He knows everything I guess." I put baby Keith on my shoulder and bounced him while my momma had a good time laughing at me. Kaleah came and plopped on the couch with Micah in her arms. Momma asked when Milton was coming over and she said after work. My momma looked at Kaleah. "No more babies!"

"Yes momma." Kaleah said in defeat. Then she looked at me. "Do you think you could give me a job?"

I frowned, "give you?"

"Yes, with two babies I need a little more than Milton can provide."

"Probably cause he got two other kids! Who's supposed to be watching your boys while you're at work?" My momma asked.

"I was going to ask you." Kaleah didn't see the problem.

My momma adjusted in her chair. "You sat up here and had two babies on purpose, and then you think I'm going to sit at home all day waiting for you?"

"Momma! I didn't get pregnant on purpose!"

"YES YOU DID! I made sure all three of you had what you needed to make sure babies happened when you're ready for them."

"Accidents still happen momma." I said defending my sister, but also thinking of my own past.

"Not when you're handling business! I told all three of you what to do to protect yourself, you messed up fine. You live here rent-free; I told you I would help you. I'm not taking care of two babies who are only eleven months apart and by myself! No! You better learn how to clip coupons or something. All my babies are grown! You want me to keep your babies during the day, and at night when you run the streets trying to keep up with your little boyfriend? No!"

"I'll put them in day care then." Kaleah said matter of factly.

My momma laughed, "Do you know how much infant care cost? You would be working just to pay the sitter. You need to stay home with your kids. You should be thankful that your situation allows you to stay with your babies."

Kaleah got irritated and walked out of the room with Micah on her hip. "You not gonna watch my baby?" I whispered in horror.

"That would be different. She's creating all these babies and then trying to unload them. She's going to have more, mark my words."

"What would be different?"

"For one, you live outside of my house! For two, you would primarily have your baby with you. So I wouldn't mind filling in here and there. For three, I wouldn't be paying for your everything and you still hollering it's not enough. She was mad cause she couldn't buy Micah some name brand shoes. That boy ain't even walking yet and she worried about the labels on his feet. She wasn't raised like that, and if you're gonna raise your child like that you should be able to afford it. Milton got four kids and he ain't even twenty-five yet. You think he's done having babies? She wasn't raised like this, but she feels the need to put herself in this type of setting."

"Momma when Jerry left us everything changed."

"So that's supposed to be her excuse for the rest of her life?"

"I'm not saying you give her that handicap. But remember she was the one who was traumatized the most, and you see how screwed up I am."

"Still, she has to take responsibility for her choices. And no one gets a pass cause their parents were messed up in this world. I'm sorry she feels some kind of way, but I'm not raising her kids."

****

"Kendra! Kendra! Kendra!" I heard my name and I slowly turned to see Ms. Tafoya standing with one hand pointing straight up to the sky, she was shaking her head yes, and stomping her left foot. "Come here girl! Why you ain't came to see me!"

I put one finger up as I put my groceries in my trunk. I pushed my cart back then I went over to hug her. "How are you?"

"Oh! I'm blessed! Beautiful! AND BLACK! Baby I CAINT COMPLAIN!" She started laughing like I said something funny.

"That's good, what brings you out?"

She put her arm undermine, and then she whispered as if anyone was listening. "I got a grandson, how you dealing with that?"

Great! He didn't tell her we broke up. I showed her my empty hand, "that's how I'm dealing."

"WHAT! WHEN DID THIS HAPPEN?"

"Months ago."

Ms. Tafoya threw her body against the nearest car. "NO!!!! NO! NO! KENDRA! KENDRA! KENDRA! You black! You caint let that white gurl take your man!"

"It doesn't matter what color her skin is, his heart is with her. I let him follow his heart."

Ms. Tafoya threw her body on the ground in the middle of the parking lot and she started rolling around. "NO! KENDRA KENDRA KENDRA NO! Don't do this to me! I was gonna sing at your wedding! I had so many plans! No! I thought I was blessed, but I guess I'm cursed! Oh lord WHY? EARTH WIND AND FIRE!!! AFTER THE LOVE IS GONE!! AFTER THE LOVE IS GONE! BRING ALL THE ELEMENTS! We need a healing!"

This lady is high as a kite and crazy! I had to laugh. "It's for the best."

"Who's best? Not my best! I WANT YOU BACK! MICHAEL JACKSON! You're the one I like! YOU!" She was still rolling on the ground crying.

"That's so sweet!" I helped her up.

"He's really back with that white girl?"

"I don't know who he's with."

Her knees started to buckle. "OH LORD! ITS TRUE! NO! I DON'T WANNA BELIEVE IT! CHAKA KHAN! I FEEL FOR YOU!"

"I'm ok."

She stopped, "why? Why are you ok? This is a tragedy of tremendous proportions!" She said wiping her eyes.

"Cause it's for the best. They can be a family, and I can have one of my own."

She straightened up, "oh. I see! You've already got somebody new. So you ain't worried about my son no more!" She stared at my face.

"Um, ok," I said wondering if I was that transparent that even the drunk high lady could see through me.

"Yea! Cause what woman breaks up with her fiancé who she loves and jumps right back on the horse? I just rolled on the ground for you!" She said like she was disgusted. "I guess I'm dying my hair blonde, bleaching my skin, and putting BLUE contacts in. Cause I don't wanna see another black woman either!" Then she stormed away. She stopped ten feet away from me and turned around. "LET ME TELL YOU SOMETHING ELSE!" She yelled so everybody could hear. "MY SON MAY NOT BE THE PRETTIEST BOY! HE MAY NOT HAVE THE LONGEST DICK! BUT LET ME TELL YOU WHAT HE GOT!" She put her hand on her hip. "CHERYL PEPSI AND DON'T FORGET THE RILEY! I'M THANKFUL FOR MY CHILD! THE LOVE I HAVE IN ME! IS THE LOVE I HAVE FOR HIM! THANKS FOR MY CHILD! THANKS FOR MY CHILD!"

Then she walked away singing the song.

Sasha

"I love you!" I said kissing El goodbye.

"I love you! I miss you already!" He said picking me up. "When you get home!"

I smiled, "you promise!"

We kissed one more time. Then El got into our rental car. I grabbed my bags and then I got in the car service. El was flying back to LA for work and I was going to work out here for the next week and get things done for our wedding. I got back on the phone with my momma, I was trying to convince her to take my puppies until El and I decided what we were going to buy out here. I was explaining how well they're trained and they don't bark, etc. Then my driver interrupted my call. "I'm sorry Sasha, Bart is experiencing thirty minute delays, so any train you get on at this point is going to be extremely crowded. The freeways are all backed up from people trying to drive in. What would you like to do?" The driver asked me.

Last thing I wanted to do was be on an overly crowded Bart train with my luggage. I told my momma I'd call her back and then I called Malcolm. He was already in the city sitting at his desk. He told me to go to the Oakland Kiosk and I could work from his office. He said he'd let Ms. Laverne know I was coming. I told the driver then I called my momma back. I told her I'd ask Ms. Laverne to give me a ride to the Bart station after work so that I could come to her house later. The driver grabbed my luggage and walked behind me into the mall. When I walked in the door Yussef was standing in the middle of the floor talking to Ms. Laverne. "Good morning sweetheart. I was just telling Yussef that you're working from this office today."

"Good morning," Yussef said taking my bags from the driver.

"Good morning, and thank you." I said as I watched Yussef take my bags to what I assume is Malcolm's office.

"Wasn't that a beautiful wedding? I had such a lovely time!" Ms. Laverne said like the memory made her feel all warm and fuzzy inside.

"It was beautiful. How are you this morning?" I gave her a hug.

"Oh I'm kicking!" She said with a smile. "And you?"

"I'm good, getting excited about my day as it quickly approaches." I said feeling excited.

Ms. Laverne frowned, "now Sasha. I don't know if it was a mix up at the post office or something, but I haven't gotten my invitation to your wedding yet."

I laughed as Yussef came back to the reception area, "We haven't mailed them yet. We barely set the date before we had to buckle down and focus on Derrick's wedding. But now it's my turn." I smiled.

The phone rang and Ms. Laverne answered it. "Yussef your girls are beautiful!"

He blushed, "thank you." Then he turned on his heels. "Have you seen the latest minutes?"

That fast he was in work mode, no more small talk. He said we had a conference call at ten, and to meet him in the conference room. I wanted to chat with him, but clearly Yussef was all about business. I had too many emails in my inbox. Nine-forty-five came before I realized it, I finished up my email and then I took a notepad and pen into the conference room. I took a seat and then Yussef walked in the room. He stopped in his tracks, he rolled his eyes at me and then he smiled. "What?"

"That's my seat." He said sitting across from me.

"Oh I'm sorry is there assigned seating?" I said giving him sass.

Yussef smiled but he didn't respond, he dialed the conference line and then he looked over his notes as he waited for the call to begin. I stared at him, "what is your problem woman?"

"It is so weird seeing you without your locs, I'm sure people tell you this all the time, you look exactly like your father."

"ALL THE TIME! My grandmother could barely stand to look at me when she was alive, I looked so much like him to her."

"I guess if I would've been a boy I would've had the same issue with my father."

He smiled, "you don't look exactly like your father. You are definitely his daughter, but not his twin."

I looked at him in amazement. "YOU ARE THE FIRST PERSON TO EVER SAY THAT!"

Yussef laughed and put his attention back to his notes. The conference call went as it should've, lots of back and forth and basically status updates. Two hours later I asked Ms. Laverne where she wanted to go for lunch. I hoped that Yussef heard us and invited himself or came out of his office so I could invite him. But I think he knew it so he stayed in his office until we left. Ms. Laverne asked me to tell her how I met El; I guess I needed that reminder to gush over my man. I told her how we met and how he was always special to me from the moment I met him.

In the afternoon Yussef left, he came back with his daughter Sydney. Her face completely lit up when she saw me, "HI SASHA!"

"Hello sweetie, how are you?"

"I'm good," she said smiling up at me.

"How was school?"

"Good, why are you in Malcolm's office?" She asked looking around.

"I was supposed to go to the city but it was going to be too much trouble so Malcolm told me to come and work here."

"Are you going to be here tomorrow? Yesmina wants to see you again too."

"She does? How do you know?"

She started blushing, "we were talking about everybody at the wedding today at school with all of our cousins. Everybody was saying how nice and pretty you are." She was totally embarrassed.

I could feel all the blood rush to my face, "give me a hug baby! Of course I will be here! I want to see Yesmina too."

Yussef stepped in the doorway, I guess Sydney is used to not hearing her daddy coming but it made me jump. "Daddy, can Sasha go to dinner with us tomorrow when Yesmina comes?"

Yussef looked as stuck as I did. "Um, isn't that special time with just the three of you? I don't know if that's a good idea." I shot Yussef a look telling him to help me out.

"But we want you to go. We don't get to see you very much." Sydney said giving me pleading eyes.

"You've bewitched my girls I see." Yussef smiled.

"Not intentionally." I said putting my hands up like I didn't want any problems.

"Syd, let me see if I can figure it out. I'm not making any promises for Sasha, she's a very busy woman."

"K!" Sydney said excitedly like her father just promised I would be there.

"Come do your homework and let Sasha get back to her job."

"Ok, bye Sasha!" Sydney said with her little happy voice.

"Bye baby!" I smiled the rest of the day.

When the day was over, I grabbed my luggage and headed for the door. "Sasha where are you going?" Little feet ran after me as I headed out the door.

"I gotta go catch Bart to my momma's house. I will see you tomorrow."

"You're getting on Bart with your luggage?" Yussef said.

"Yes, I do it all the time its fine."

"Nonsense, Syd and I will take you to your mother's."

"I'm a big girl Yussef, I can ride the Bart by myself."

Yussef took my bags and walked ahead, while Sydney grabbed my hand and smiled at me with the biggest smile. I exhaled cause this was absolute torture for me. Yussef didn't appear to be phased at all, but he never seems too phased by anything when it comes to me anyways. When I told Sydney I was going to ride in the back with her she giggled really loud. She got such a kick out of me riding in the back with her. When I called my momma and told her that Yussef was bringing me to the restaurant, I could hear the question in her voice. When we got to the restaurant Sydney asked me if Sabrina was here. I told her I wasn't sure, when Yussef got out of the car my momma and Sabrina walked out. "OH GOSH IT'S SABRINA!" Sydney said like Sabrina was a celebrity.

I laughed so hard and then I told Sabrina she had to come say hi to one of her biggest fans. I thanked Yussef for the ride, and then my momma invited Yussef in for a meal. He asked for a rain check, he gave her a hug and kiss just like he did with Sabrina, then he waved bye to me. My momma twisted her face, "you don't get a hug and a kiss bye?"

"I guess not." I said trying to shrug it off. My momma cut her eyes at me. "What? There's nothing to tell!" I avoided her eyes.

"Un huh!" She eyed me not believing me for one minute. We took my bags to my momma's house and then we went back to the restaurant to meet my Dan-Dan and some of my very excited aunties and cousins. Whitney wanted to know if I was going to have her walk with Darryl, her way of trying to make her idea come true.

"Sasha, Enna says that your man is real handsome." My Auntie Vicky smiled at me.

"Yea, and I hear he's got an accent? How did that happen?" My Auntie Tacorra asked.

I proudly took out my phone and sent them one of my favorite pictures of El and I. Both of them stared at the picture for a long time. "Oh lord Jesus this man is FINE!" Tacorra said as we all laughed.

"He ain't finer than Darryl!" Whitney interjected.

"Why on earth would she care if her man was finer than her cousin?" Auntie Vicky said staring Whitney down. "Your obsession with her cousin is downright disgusting sometimes. Why would you obsess over a man you never had?" She was waiting for Whitney to say she was wrong.

"Whitney baby, cut it out before I tell your daddy on you." Dan-Dan said, Whitney slouched.

"Dalenna, I noticed you and your husband at the engagement party having a good time. Are you two back on again?" My momma smiled.

Dan-Dan smiled, "I guess you can say that. Shoot that man ain't getting no younger. He would want to slow his happy go lucky butt down." Then she looked at my momma, "how are things with you and my son?"

"He's with his baby momma and I'm with Travis." Then she rubbed Sabrina's shoulder as she put her arm around her.

"He seems like a nice young man, but is that who you're going to be with?"

"Yes, Richard and I had more than enough chances to work and for one reason or another we never seemed to be able to get it together. I'll always have love for him; he gave me that beautiful powerhouse over there." She shook her head, "Richard and I are over."

My Auntie Vicky smiled real big, "YEA RIGHT!" She made everyone laugh, "you and Richie going to be on walkers chasing each other around the nursing home. Momma always tries to say this time she's done too. You see who was sitting at her side at your party." Everyone laughed, "then I try to drop by her house the next morning and she's telling me to go home cause I need to learn to call first. Excuse me! With Daddy's card blocking hers in the driveway. Enna can you do us all a favor and just stay together? Sheesh!"

I know everyone was poking fun and teasing each other, but I was sinking further and further in my seat. My malfunction goes deeper than my parents. I guess it's the fear that someone you love so much could fall out of love with you. I honestly think that's my parent's dysfunction. They love each other so much, and so hard that actually breaking up for good would kill them. So they've played this on again off again game for years. My father mimicking what he grew up with, and my momma... Well shoot she's just crazy. My Dan-Dan kept looking at me like she saw something but she was waiting. We went over wedding plans and the guest list. That was a lively discussion. Family skeletons falling all out the closet as my Momma, Sabrina, and I kept making conscious efforts to close our mouths as we listened to some of the stories. With so many people in our family some of them had no family honor. When we were leaving Dan-Dan asked me when I was going to come see her.

Yussef

When I took Syd home she excitedly told her momma that we gave Sasha a ride to her mother's house. Sylvia didn't look at me; she gave Syd a pained smile. I walked away; I didn't want to see that.

I called Drew, "I need help!"

"What's up?"

"My girls seem to be quite taken with your cousin. Syd used her cuteness to twist Sasha's arm to go out to dinner with us tomorrow. I don't want to disappoint my girls, but I don't want El thinking I'm pushing up on his woman."

"Are you?"

I blank stared until he saw it through the phone. "Get real!"

He laughed, "come have dinner with us."

"Tracy won't mind?"

"Of course not."

In the morning Jackson opened the door, the kitchen window was cracked so I knew Melissa was somewhere listening. "Good morning Daddy!" Yezzy said excitedly.

"Good morning Babygirl, you ready?"

"Yes," she smiled brightly.

"Thanks Jackson, I'll see you this evening." I said shaking his hand.

"Syd said Sasha's going to be working at your office today. Can we go by and say good morning to her?"

"You can say hi this afternoon when I pick you up. Now where are we having breakfast this morning?"

"Please daddy!" She hit me with the big brown eyes that I couldn't resist.

Jackson stood there laughing at me, "glad to know I'm not the only one melted by that look."

"Who taught her this? They need to be thrown in jail." I laughed, "I guess we're going through a nasty drive through then.

"Who's Sasha? If you don't mind me being nosey." Jackson asked.

"She's a VERY pretty lady, and she's so nice." Yezzy volunteered.

Jackson smiled, "well alright then. You two have a good day.

"I see her! I see her!" Yezzy said excitedly as she spotted Sasha walking across the parking lot. "SASHA!" She yelled sticking her head out the window. Yezzy used her charms to sucker Sasha into the car.

Sasha

As I was walking towards the mall I heard a little voice call out my name. I turned to see Yussef's car with a little head hanging out the window. "Good morning Yesmina." I said happy to see her.

"Good morning."

"Are you on your way to school?"

"Yes, Sydney called me last night and said we were having dinner with you tonight." She had the biggest smile.

I looked at Yussef, "if you can come. We can have dinner at Drew's."

I sighed a sigh of relief. "Yes I guess so."

Yesmina giggled excitedly just like her sister. "Can you ride with us to take me to school?"

"Um…" Darn it I couldn't think of a good reason to bow out. And Yussef looked as stuck as I did.

In defeat I got back in the backseat this time with Yesmina, who just like her sister talked my ear off. I thought I talked a lot. Yesmina gave me a hug and told me she would see me after school. "You gonna stay in the back?"

"Yes, this way I can feel like royalty as you escort me around." I said jokingly.

"I think this is the most I've seen you out here ever."

"Cause I was in school and what not. But El and I are going to move out here."

"You don't say, you guys going to have something built on the hill too?"

"That was the plan. It looks like Uncle Dale has completed phase one. So as soon as he has phase two ready we'll decide then. Meanwhile we're looking for a condo or townhouse, something that will make a good rental later."

"Good plan," He nodded his head.

"Your girlfriend is really pretty." I said watching his face in the mirror.

"Thanks?"

"Why the question mark at the end of your thanks?"

"That was random."

"I guess it was." I said feeling stupid, "here's an awkward question. Are you going to come to my wedding?"

As usual no visible reaction, he only paused. "Are you going to send me an invitation?"

"If you'll go, otherwise why waste the stamp?"

"If you send me an invitation I will come. Can I bring my girls?"

"Of course, and your girlfriend."

"Ok."

We walked in silence inside the mall and into the office, he went to his office, and I went into Malcolm's.

Yussef

At the office I stayed in my corner and I prayed that she stayed in hers. When I picked the girls up from school they seemed disappointed that she wasn't in the car. When we got to the office the girls abandoned me to hangout in Malcolm's office with Sasha. When I went to my office my Grandma was calling. She was excited because Arthur's granddaughters were coming over and she wanted to have her great granddaughters as well. I told her she could definitely have Sydney but I'd have to check on Yesmina's availability. When I called Jackson's number Melissa answered. I looked at my phone to make sure I dialed correctly. "Where's Jackson?"

"He grabbed my phone by accident this morning."

"I'll call him back."

"For real Yussef? I don't exist?"

I sighed, "Melissa you exist. I can't even deal with you."

"I heard what you said to Yesmina Saturday."

"No duh! You were sitting in the window listening like you have been."

"Thank you for defending me."

"You're her mother. What kind of father would I be if I put you down to her? I didn't do that for you."

"I'm sorry for everything Yussef. I wish I could take it all back, do it over."

"That's what everyone's singing lately."

"Are you and Sylvia back together?"

"Not that it's any of your business, but yes we are."

"How could you forgive her? After what she did to you!"

"Melissa, where's your faith these days? The Melissa I loved, loved the bible and was doing everything she could to align her life according to God's standards. If someone is truly repentant for what they've done who am I to continue to hold it against them. Vengeance is not mine, and she's been through a lot."

"Yes but you also have to suffer the consequences of your actions even if God forgives you."

"And what? You're over there plotting on her? You can't get anyone the way God can, give it to him and do your part. Love the man he's blessed you with despite how evil you've been with me."

"I know but...."

"But what? There's no but Melissa."

"What am I supposed to do? I don't want you to be with anyone but me." I exhaled, "I'm being honest." Her voice shook.

"Melissa, you're supposed to check your feelings at the door and do what's right for our daughter. Sylvia's coming to Latia's wedding. If you've ever loved me, if you love your daughter, most importantly if you love God leave her and us alone. Concern yourself with

Latia it's going to be her day. You ran Angela off with your craziness. Sylvia is the only person goofy enough not to care about you. Please let me have some peace instead of regretting you like I have been."

Melissa was crying, "the only time you choose me is when you couldn't have me. I have been in love with you since the day I met you. I..."

"Melissa, timing was never on our side. Put all the love you had for me into our daughter, and I will do the same. It's not ok for you to keep pouring your heart out to me like this when you are married. Love your husband. Be good to our daughter. Let me feel the love from you there. As far as you and I are concerned, we will not be together ever again."

"What Sylvia did was worse!"

"Not to me, I love you Melissa take care. I got to go."

"Yussef!" She exclaimed, I hung up.

Sasha

I didn't see Yussef again for the rest of the day, until both of the girls came with huge smiles into the office to say hi to me. They did their homework on Malcolm's roundtable. I watched in Aw as Yesmina helped her sister figure out how to do her math homework. Tanisha and I were like that when we were growing up. We were always helping each other understand something. "Sasha are you going to work here with my daddy every day?" Yesmina asked.

I sat there thinking about it, living out here meant I would need to come into the office. This office would be a wonderful commute, but I highly doubt El would be ok with me working day in and day out here. If anything El could work here and I could find another remote office. I didn't work in the Mitigated office in LA, I was a floor above. "That's a good question, I don't think so. My husband might work here though."

"Yay! That means we will still see you then." Yesmina cheered.

Yussef followed me to Drew's house. Drew and Dre were outside when we pulled up. He told us to park in his driveway. Andrew tiptoed over to us, "I forgot to tell Tracy you were coming until a little while ago. I hope pizza is ok with everybody." Drew said looking like he was in trouble.

"Pizza is perfectly fine." Yussef said.

"How about the women go inside, and the men will go get the pizza."

Andre mimicked his father's walk to the car, it was too cute. I wondered if El and our son would be the same way. The girls and I walked in the door. Most of the house was packed up. Tracy was sitting on the couch trying not to look pissed off. "Hey Tracy."

"Hey," she smiled. "I'm sorry you guys. He didn't tell me you were coming. I would've made something for dinner. Or at least cupcakes."

"Don't worry, this is all merely to please the girls. Apparently I didn't get on their nerves enough at the wedding." I smiled.

"You did see who they didn't like didn't you?" She gave me a knowing smile.

"Girl yes," I said sitting on the couch next to her.

"Ladies, what would you like to do, if you go up those stairs there's a room with toys in it. That's Andre's room. Make yourself comfortable and Andre will be right up? Or, I can turn on a movie or show for you."

They looked at each other. "Upstairs please," both of the girls said happily, and then they took off.

"His girlfriend is really pretty huh?" Tracy said.

"I said the same thing and he shrugged me off."

"There's a huge difference between her and Angela."

"Does he really have a type? Angela, the girlfriend, I don't know what Yesmina's momma looks like." I said

"You," She was smiling WIDE at me.
"YOU!"
She started laughing, "Andrew runs his mouth too doggone much!"
"I'll second that." I laughed as well.
"But you and the girl are on that same gorgeous level!"
"Please! I look better than her!" I spit.
Tracy laughed an embarrassed laugh, "yes you do, but I didn't expect you to say it."
"And please believe you look WAY better than Angela. She was VERY ordinary."
"Isn't that just like him. I don't think he looks at women the same way most guys do.
Andrew either for that matter. Today's man is supposed to love the skinny girl, and the
extra extra female. But Andrew married me; I'm not extra extra. And my skinny days last
maybe a month max. My weight never stays consistent."
"Your weight fluctuates? I didn't notice."
"All the time, watch by the time I have this baby I'll be five hundred pounds. I hope I
don't stay up there, Andrew says he doesn't care. He has to care, everybody else does. At
some point everyone cares."
"My man cares, but not like that. What made me love him is knowing that he appreciates
my appearance but he put it in its proper place. Yussef didn't respond period. I was
always attacking him. I think that's why he's always on guard around me now."
"Even though you're engaged?"
"We're here aren't we? When has Yussef ever been over for dinner?"
"Never." She said as she thought about it.
"Exactly!" Then we laughed. I guess I have conducted myself poorly whenever it came to
him. I wouldn't do that now, I'm almost married.
When the men came back we sat at the big table, chatting with the kids mostly. We didn't
stay too late; the kids had school the next day. When we left I gave the girls hugs and
then I told them I'd see them soon.

Yussef

"Good morning daddy." Yezzy said with her backpack in hand.
"Good morning Babygirl."
"Can I talk to you real quick?" Jackson stepped out the door.
The kitchen window was open so I knew Melissa was in earshot. "Sure, Yezzy. Syd and
Sylvia are in the car." Yezzy happily skipped to the car. "What's up?" I said looking at his
sad eyes.
"We're all adjusting, I think it's important to try to return or establish some normalcy.
Usually we take two family trips and then Melissa and I take one with just the two of us.
With everything that's happened I feel the urgent need to take my wife away."
I nodded my head, "I can understand that."
"Melissa's mom hasn't been feeling all that great and she normally keeps the kids for us."
I smiled at Jackson, "you trust me with your son?"
"I trust that you will be as good to my son as I have been to your daughter." He said
watching my eyes.
"Cool! Just let me know when."
"How about we get together when you have a moment free." He motioned his eyes
towards the window.
"How soon? We could hook up tomorrow before I get the girls from my grandma's."
"That works for me." We shook on it.
When we pulled up to my Grandma's house my momma was pulling up at the same time.
I was surprised she was alone until I saw the tears in her eyes. "Ladies this is my momma
Shonda. Momma these are my daughters Yesmina and Sydney. And just in case you

forgot this is my girlfriend Sylvia." Both of the girls looked at me with big eyes.
My momma squatted so she could see both of their faces, "they look just like you baby.
Your daddy's got some strong genes." She tried to put pep in her voice.
"I've never met you before." Yezzy said as an authority.
"No, but that's because I don't always behave like I should." She admitted.
"So you're the Grandma? You're G-Momma's daughter?" Yezzy asked.
"Yes, but I don't know about calling me Grandma, I'm not old enough to be ok with that.
Let's come up with something else." She said looking at both of the girls.
"Ok," they said together.
"Good morning Sylvia," she said standing up.
"Good morning."
"Why are you here? I know Grandma is not expecting you." Tears started running down
her cheeks. Sylvia took the girls inside.
"Yussef, I'm pregnant and Jarvis is acting a fool. He says he doesn't want it, but then
when I talk like I don't want it either he flips the script."
I frowned, "how you gonna start over now?"
"He's my husband, I could have a whole football team if I wanted to."
I rubbed my head, "I guess. Jarvis is a jerk you know that. I don't understand why you'd
reproduce with him. Your spawn could be deadly."
She got mad, "tell me how you really feel about me. Regardless, I'm still your mother,
you turned out just fine."
"No thanks to you."
Her mouth dropped open, "what makes you think it's ok to talk to me like this? I'm going
through enough over here."
"Am I supposed to be sympathetic? You know what kind of person you're married to. I
don't know what would make you think it's a good idea to reproduce with him. Every
marriage doesn't equal a family. Momma you act like a kid sometimes I swear!"
"It's done already!"
"Yea so it's done! Try not to screw this kid up like you did me."
"What are you talking about? You're fine!"
"No I'm not momma. I'm not fine! Everyone around me is married with families, and I'm
over here invisibly angry because of you. Go back to service momma, you're married
now. What's holding you back?"
"I hate being judged!"
"That's just your guilty conscience talking. Push through the awkwardness, cause
honestly momma, only God can help you."
After she got past being offended she listened then she went home to her man to work
things out. I told my grandma what she said and she cut her eyes at me and said I needed
to take my own advice.
I asked Sylvia where she wanted to go to eat. She looked at me like I needed to get
serious. She asked me to take her to the grocery store. So I did, then she said she had no
intentions of coming out of my apartment again.

Sasha

"So you don't care?" I said searching his eyes.
He blew irritated air, "Sasha! I'm being pulled in so many directions right now. Whatever
you decide is fine with me. I'm at capacity for making decisions right now." He slammed
the refrigerator door. "I can't even decide what to eat!"
"El are you even hungry?" I watched him.
"Yes!" Then he looked around, "NO!" Then he showed frustration, "I DON'T KNOW
SASHA!"

I knew he was beside himself with everything with his parents. His sister is no help and the burden of everything has fallen on his shoulders. I wish he would just cry and let it out, but instead he keeps exploding about the dumbest things. I grabbed his hand and he reluctantly followed me through the boxes to the couch. I sat on the couch and I made him sit on the floor with his back to me between my legs. I started massaging his shoulders. He was hard as a rock, I worked his shoulders, neck, head, arms everything until I felt some of his tension release. I kissed him then he took me in his arms and he apologized for snapping. He said he couldn't believe he was losing his "mum." He said he couldn't imagine a world without his parents. Then he asked me why everyone around him dies. We talked about when I lost my stepfather. I told him the pain of the loss doesn't go away. My family has been my source of healing. Then he told me I would be his only family. I told him Brielis and her son would need him. El shook his head no, he said look at how irresponsible she is with their parents alive. He said imagine her with an excuse to be the way she is.

I hated seeing him like this; I offered to postpone the wedding. And he said his parents are looking forward to the wedding. El being broken up about his parents did steal a lot of my thunder though. At a time when I should be my happiest and the most at peace with my relationship, my best friend was hurting and there was nothing I could do about it. I continued taking care of business. I packed up the things that were going to the condo here and labeled the pieces that were going to the townhouse in The Bay. Our big day was approaching and I was running out of steam. Fortunately Richard had enough enthusiasm for the both of us while I was here, and my momma had it covered in The Bay.

Yussef

"Why are you looking all nervous?" My grandma asked Sylvia.

"Everybody's going to be here." Sylvia swallowed.

"Sweetheart relax. If Melissa so much as spits in your direction I will yank her up by her collar."

"I'm not afraid of her. I can handle myself, I just don't want to make Yussef look or feel bad for being here with me."

My grandma looked at me, "what you been saying to this child?"

I shook my head and continued loading our luggage on the luggage cart.

"I CAN'T BELIEVE WE'RE GOING ON AN AIRPLANE! YEZZY GOES ALL THE TIME! BUT THIS IS MY FIRST TIME!" Syd said besides herself with excitement.

"Maybe we can manage to have you sit together. I think we're all on the same flight."

Syd squealed with excitement. We checked our bags and then went through security check; I raised an eyebrow at the Mitigated Staff on their FSA post. Arthur and I strolled over to the bar where Jackson was sitting not knowing he was looking at Malcolm, Derrick, and Darryl. Chantel and Amber were sitting in a booth over towards the back so that Chantel wouldn't draw attention.

Arthur kept looking at Malcolm as he spoke. Then he asked him where his family was from. Malcolm said Oakland, Arthur nodded but you could tell he was thinking. Latia was in heaven with her nieces and nephew; she paid none of us any attention. Grandma had Melissa and Sylvia involved in the same conversation but you could tell they were not talking to each other. Malcolm looked at them then he cut his eyes at me. He said this was going to be interesting. Latia, Sylvia, and I sat behind the kids in our three-seat row. Malcolm, Amber, Grandma, and Arthur rode in first class. Darryl and Jackson seemed to hit it off really well. Melissa tried not to pay us too much attention on our side of the plane. I was actually impressed with the measure of self-control she was displaying. I know it couldn't be easy, but I did it for years so now it was her turn.

When we got to New York, Arthur, Grandma, Melissa & Jackson went to a hotel. Latia came with the rest of us to Malcolm's place. His four and a half bedroom townhouse proved to be just what we needed. Darryl took up camp on the couch in Malcolm's office. Latia and Sydney shared a room, and the rest of the couples were in the other rooms. Sylvia kept saying how nice this place was as she took it all in. The difference between Sylvia and I's sex life now is that before she knew what to do to keep me spent. She enjoyed it, but it wasn't like now. My mission is always to get her before she got me. The best gift I ever gave myself was looking up some books on the subject matter and really honing in on my craft. Sylvia screamed into her pillow to muffle her sounds. I had her pretty much figured out in this short period of time. Seeing her strung out was a nice pat on the back for me.

In the morning, we met at the hotel and as a group we went sightseeing. Jackson turned out to be a lot of fun. He made sure Syd was included whenever he did anything for the kids. Melissa was mostly quiet and watching everything we did. Eventually Amber pried Sylvia from my side and she got her to open up a little. Melissa and Latia eventually departed from our group to handle wedding business. Derrick and Chantel opted to head in once Chantel started getting tired. She'd done a pretty good job of going unrecognized except by a few loyal fans.

"So Malcolm what is it that you do?" Jackson asked.

"What don't I do is a better question."

"Ok, what don't you do?"

"I do everything. What do you do?" Malcolm watched Jackson's face.

Jackson was quiet for a minute; you could tell he decided to let Malcolm's vagueness slide. He explained he was head of security for a large computer company. I knew Malcolm knew all this already but he listened anyways. "I guess you're not open to questions." Jackson said.

"No not really." Malcolm said staring at him.

"Got it," Jackson said. Then he changed the subject.

****

"We're missing the corsages!" Melissa said in complete frustration. She picked up her phone and marched over to the less occupied side of the room.

Everyone was excited about tomorrow. Most of Lewis' family were excited about the guest list more than they were excited about the actual wedding. I could tell Latia was not happy about the cameras following them around but she did her best to deal with them. Melissa walked over to Latia to update her on the flowers. Carina lovingly stepped up to help Melissa and Latia out after they were completely disappointed in the abilities of the wedding planner they were working with. Carina was working with the wedding planner to put out another fire. Latia marched over looking stressed with Melissa in slow tow behind her. I could feel the set up. "Yussef I need you!" I didn't like the disclaimer. She begged me to take Melissa to the florist to clear up the discrepancy with the flowers. She said we needed to get there as soon as possible as they would be closing soon.

I frowned, "Latia I can have someone take care of that for you."

"My paperwork says one thing and they swear theirs says another. By the time someone gets here and then there they'll be closed. Please do this for me!"

Melissa was already putting her coat on I guess it was known that I would do it. I sighed and put my jacket on. I pulled up my GPS and then I told Melissa to keep up. It was freezing outside and I immediately missed my locs. Melissa didn't try to hide her smile, she was cheesing from ear to ear. When we got on the subway it was packed and it gave her the perfect excuse to stand in my face. "How are you doing Yussef?" She said watching my eyes.

"Fine." I said uninterested.

"Can you believe this is happening? Latia is getting married."

210

"Yep."

"She's been running from Lewis for so long! I was starting to think this was never going to happen." When I didn't say anything to that she touched my shoulder. "Give me credit, I'm trying."

"This is ridiculous! You'd pull me away from my sister the day before her wedding just to have a moment alone? I appreciate you being civil with Sylvia but this still has me annoyed!"

"Sorry!" She looked away.

"I'm proud of her though. She waited until her heart couldn't stand it anymore."

"You're not thinking about marriage are you?" Her eyes begged me to say no.

I shrugged, "I want a family of my own. I'm not getting any younger."

"Sylvia? Yussef you can't be serious!"

"What's the difference between you and her? I can forgive what she did."

I could tell she never considered that I didn't forgive her. "You can't forgive me?"

"Please tell me why I should? It's not like you've conducted yourself like you've had any remorse for what you did to me. You just complicate things more. I haven't found anything pleasant in you other than when you bless me with keeping your mouth shut."

I could see the impact of my words. We remained silent the rest of the way to the florist. I guess the person responsible thought today was going to be a good day to decide the customer isn't right even when the customer had all their paperwork. Melissa tore into that florist so badly I cringed at the tongue-lashing she gave them. The cold part is that when she told her off, not one curse word crossed her lips. I was impressed, but I also knew she was taking out some of her frustration on the florist. When it was all said and done the florist not only was fixing the mishap but also adding extra arrangements that Latia wanted but turned down because they were above her floral budget. I walked slower on my way back. "Everything got out of control. I couldn't face you; I know that's no excuse. But it's the truth! I HATE seeing her with you, she doesn't deserve you. She had you and she threw it all away. With me, one day you stopped calling. That night we were together the thought never crossed my mind that I would get pregnant. Nothing crossed my mind really. Looking back I can see that was your way of apologizing. I missed my opportunity to have you all to myself. I liked the way you explained everything to Yesmina. I've been mindful to control myself since then. But you gotta know she's after the money. She hasn't changed."

"You don't know that, that's what you're hoping."

She sighed, "not that I'd wish that heartache on you. But I guess I am."

"Outside of the agreed upon child support I haven't given her one red cent nor has she asked for it. So far that other person doesn't exist. Not that it's any of your business. What's most important to me, she's good to Yezzy. She doesn't treat her any different than she does Syd."

"Do you love her?" Her eyes pleaded with me to say no.

"I don't know, once I know I'll make a declarative decision."

"Could you do me a favor?"

I looked at her out the corner of my eye, "what?"

"Stop acting like I don't exist. That hurts!"

"You chased Angela away! You must be punished!" I laughed.

Melissa smiled, "she wasn't right for you. She scares too easily."

****

Malcolm dismissed everyone, and I turned my eyes. El kissed Sasha's forehead and then he hurried off. Concern for El was all over Sasha's face. Darryl was on his phone making plans with someone. He looked at me and waved me over. "I'm going to go see my sisters, can you make sure Sasha makes it back safely?" I cut my eyes at Darryl, he smiled at me. "She's just a girl, you aren't scared of a girl are you?"

"Darryl it's late." Plus I didn't need the temptation.

Someone started talking on the phone, "hold on. Hold on, I'm talking to my cousin." He looked at me, "Yu, I trust you with my life, and therefore I trust you with hers. Sasha is just a girl, stop punking out." When I didn't respond, Darryl decided to take matters into his own hands. "Sasha! Yu's going to take you home." Then he patted my shoulder, "see ya'll tomorrow." Then he returned his attention to the phone, "which one is that? I don't want no skinny hungry model type. I needs a corn-fed big boned girl like the ones in Oakland!" Then he walked out the door.

Sasha didn't even try to hold back her smile, "I'm hungry. Let's go eat."

"Sasha!" I exhaled.

"You wouldn't deny me the opportunity to eat would you?" She quickly put on her coat, and gloves. When I held the door open so that she could exit the building Sasha smiled. "Yussef you're always a gentleman."

I opened the car door, "yep. Me and El are the last of a dying breed." I turned my eyes away as she bent over to get in the car. "Where are we going?"

Sasha clapped her hands, "I know the perfect spot." Then she spoke louder for the driver, "take us to Latour's in Manhattan." Then she smiled at me, "have you eaten here yet?"

"We had lunch there the other day."

Sasha lowered her eyes at me, "so. You're here alone?"

I looked her in her eyes, "no."

Sasha growled, "YUSSEF IF YOU DON'T WANT TO GET RAPED IN THIS CAR! DON'T YOU EVER LOOK AT ME LIKE THAT!" Then she tried to laugh off her frustration.

I chuckled, "how am I looking at you?"

"Come on! You know this is me and you. You run, I chase you, it's our thing."

I touched her ring, "this suggests otherwise. You know you have to stop that don't you?"

"I know," she said defeated.

"Besides, I like El. I think you two belong together."

"El is my best friend, at least he made it clear what hoops I needed to jump through to get with him."

"Timing was never on our side. I was in a very bad place. I just broke up with Sylvia. We never found the right time after that. You've always had too much going on. Some guy wanting to be with you. You weren't ready for me."

"Yussef I would've given everyone up to be with you. I was too pretty to value you?"

"Sylvia didn't," I laughed as I shook my head.

She turned my head towards her with her finger. She looked me in my eyes. "Our names may both start with S's but we are *nothing* alike. I've wanted you since you wouldn't dance with me that night. We never got our *dance*."

"Something tells me you don't mean vertically," I joked.

"Am I that transparent?" She stared in my eyes to let me know she was not joking.

"You're basically married," my brain was starting to freeze over again.

"I guess you're right." Sasha exhaled as she looked out the window. I stared at her neck for a minute. My weakness for her was getting the best of me for a minute.

In the restaurant, Sasha was quiet at first as she drank her glass of red wine. She kept staring as she moved her hand up and down her glass. "What Sasha?"

"Yussef, you are a beautiful man."

I blushed as I sat back, "thank you."

"How my momma never hooked up with your daddy is beyond my understanding." Then she smiled.

"So you're wishing we were siblings? You know you're disturbed."

"What I meant is, you look just like him and I can't control myself."

"So all of that happens because you like the way I look?"

"No," then she took another drink. "Are you ready to go?"

I could feel my brain freezing as my mind fought with my conscience. When we got in the car, it did not surprise me that Sasha kissed me. It surprised me that I allowed myself to want the kiss as much as she did. My moment of weakness continued to escalate. Sasha told the driver to take us to the nearby hotel. She got out of the car while I stayed put unable to think. I couldn't feel all the remorse that I knew was coming from this. The side eyes from Malcolm, my grandma, my cousins, Drew telling me he told me this would happen after he calmed down. Sasha came back to the car, opened my door and led me out. She led me to the room, and when the door closed it was too late. I couldn't stop this from happening even if I wanted to.

Sasha was too eager and I told her to relax. She looked at me with big eyes as she obeyed. She stood there as I slowly undressed her. Then she followed my lead and slowly undressed me as well. When she pulled my boxers down she smiled at my body and said an excited YES! I savored every moment of our encounter cause I knew I could never allow myself to be this weak again. Every thrust told me this was not the last time; every kiss confirmed this was my new life. I was now addicted to a woman who promised forever to someone else. As we laid at the foot of the bed spent I held Sasha in my arms as I stroked her hair. My ability to think had not returned yet. Sasha started to cry as she asked me what we were going to do. I was honest when I said I didn't know. She turned over on her back as she looked me in my eyes. "I'm pregnant."

My insides turned to fire, "why are we here if you're carrying El's baby?"

"It's yours," she watched my eyes as her stomach started to grow.

I backed up from her, "what kind of Sci-Fi channel movie is this?"

"I'm a Wallace, and you're you! The two most fertile families on this planet. I can tell El it's his, he'll be happy." Her eyes pleaded with me to say no.

Her stomach kept growing, "I'm sorry Sasha. I knew better than to give in to my weakness for you."

Sasha bent over holding her stomach as she screamed in pain. Sophia ran in the room and pushed me off the bed. She told me to put some clothes on. Sasha screamed as she pushed. Just when I was decent I heard a baby cry, Sasha sat on the bed happy as she could ever be. She said it was a boy. I looked at my son and there were no words. Sasha touched me and said we should name him Troy. I agreed. As I reached for him I started falling. I jumped so hard; Sylvia asked me if I was ok. I looked around the room for a minute focusing my eyes. It was all a dream, I exhaled. I laid there struggling with myself, why was I disappointed?

****

Sylvia sat there staring at me through the vanity mirror. She was putting on her makeup but stopped mid-stroke when she saw me. "You look so handsome!"

"Thanks, I like your dress." I sat on the bed.

"Your grandma is so sweet, I wish I would've realized it before." I didn't say anything, "and I really like Amber."

"Yea she's lovable, you see where her boys get it from."

"Derrick and Darryl are sweet."

"And Drew," I watched her eyes.

She turned to look at me. "She's Drew's mother too?" Her breathing got heavy, "does she secretly hate me?"

"Amber's not fake if she hated you, you'd know. Are you hiding your feelings about anyone here?" I watched her eyes.

"No, but I'd rather know who hates me and who doesn't. I know Malcolm doesn't like me."

"Malcolm doesn't like anybody." I smiled, "stop stressing. You're going to ride over with Amber. The rest of us are going over to get ready, I'll see you after the ceremony." I

213

kissed her and then I walked out of the room.

Derrick was attentively tending to his wife while Malcolm and Darryl watched by the door. I actually saw a little sadness in Malcolm's eyes as he watched them. Derrick kissed her and then we stepped out the door. Malcolm spoke with the six staff members on the house and then we got in the car.

"D-Rick is gonna be a daddy!" Darryl smiled.

Derrick smiled, "she's almost here! I can't wait!"

"I might have a kid or two." Darryl said.

"Children are forever, you better be sure." Malcolm said.

"You need to get the chickenheads out your system first." Derrick teased.

"A little cluck, cluck now and then is good for your health." Darryl smiled.

"What if you have a daughter you want her to see that? You want her to think that's what love looks like?" Derrick asked.

"It'll be ok if I have all boys like Malcolm."

Malcolm looked at him unamused. "Now? You wanna do this now?" Darryl opened his hands. "You surely know how to pick your moments."

"You're right let's wait until Drew gets in the car." Darryl said as we pulled up to the hotel. Andrew and his son got in the car. Darryl clasped his hands together and smiled, Drew blank stared as if he knew what was going on. Then Darryl quickly got Andrew up to speed on the conversation.

"Point blank, I expect all of you to be better men than me. So far you all have, except you." He said pointing to Darryl.

"Aw! Daddy what I do?"

We all started laughing except Malcolm. "You are so guarded that you miss the point sometimes. You can control a lot of things in life, but love isn't one of them. If these females are nobody then we can't have security details on them. Don't waste my time!"

When the limo pulled up Dwayne Reed was outside with Lewis talking to cameras. Malcolm smiled at Dwayne. "Looks like somebody has been working out."

"Yea, he's shooting a movie where he has to be about that big."

"You mean he's not thinking about flexing once and for all!" Malcolm sounded disappointed.

"Come on Malcolm he's not stupid." Darryl said.

"Yes he is, this is going to be fun!" Malcolm said getting out of the Limo first.

Drew looked at Derrick, "keep him calm this could be bad."

The head of security came over to us, and gave us play by plays of the mishaps this morning. We separated and did our own rounds of the grounds. Security was in every corner like Richard and I designed it. Once I was satisfied I gave my very anxious and nervous sister a hug and a kiss. She looked beautiful, and she glowed. Melissa looked very pretty as well, I nodded at her. Latia asked Melissa to give us a minute in the room right off of the dressing room for her and all her bridesmaids. Latia grabbed my hands, "can you believe all of this? I still can't believe that I said yes."

"Yes, and you're a beautiful bride. I'm very happy for you." I said kissing her hands.

"Lewis' mom and mine keep arguing, it's so horrible, but even that can't still my joy. I can't believe he loves me."

"Why wouldn't he love you?"

"Lewis is this big person, in the spotlight constantly and I'm just me. I'm not a model, an overly gorgeous celebrity, or anything like that."

"Latia he would've been a FOOL not to love you. Any man who waits as long as he did for a woman to make her mind up about him has to love you. You definitely took him down a peg or two. He's the lucky one not you."

She smiled, "next it will be your wedding."

"You think I should marry Sylvia?" I asked searching her eyes.

"I think you should marry the person you're in love with. Are you in love with her?"

"I don't know, I have love for her." Immediately I thought of Sasha.

"That settles it, you don't marry anyone until you're in love. Don't worry about how long it takes either. Take your time and make sure it feels right in your soul. Only you can answer that."

My sister and I talked awhile longer, for a minute we forgot we were here for the wedding. Latia's mother came barging in and making a big fuss over how beautiful everything was turning out, and how happy she was. I went out to the ceremony area and I caught a glimpse of Sasha walking with Amber. She looked really pretty but I also saw sadness in her eyes. When Amber sat her next to Sylvia I took a seat to watch their interaction. Sylvia was fine until Tracy came, she turned a little green and I knew she was uncomfortable. When I went back to the back to get ready for the ceremony Derrick and Malcolm were sitting to the side with their eyes locked on Dwayne. Dwayne was returning Malcolm's glare. Lewis kind of held his breath when Dwayne walked over to Malcolm.

"I hear there's congratulations in order."

Malcolm looked at Dwayne with a "So What!" expression.

"Can't we let by-gones be by-gones?"

"So, this is supposed to be like some scene off a movie or out of a book? We supposed to pretend like the past is the past and it doesn't matter? I know you're still in love with my woman. That entertains me, but just remember if you cross me you die!" Malcolm's expression and tone did not change.

"If she chooses me, you and your threats are the furthest from my mind. I'm glad to know we're on the same page." Then he walked away...

I leaned in to Drew, "did I miss something?"

"Same story different day, they'll be fighting over my momma until they're all old and grey." Drew started laughing, "can't you see them in a nursing home trying to beat each other with their walkers, taking their teeth and flinging them like ninja stars."

Lewis looked angry with his friend; they stepped out the room to talk. Darryl and I looked at each other and then we hurried to the door on the other side of the room. Darryl gonna shush me like I don't know how to creep on somebody. I told him to shush. We had to stop cause I almost laughed. We stood on the edge of the corner that they thought they were tucked away from everyone in. "WHAT WAS THAT?" Lewis was angry.

"I was congratulating the man!" Dwayne said sounding like he was laughing.

"That's my family! What upsets them upsets Latia!"

"Who's upset?"

"D! Don't be stupid! You gave it your best, let it go!"

"Whatever! She still loves me! We haven't gotten closure." He said convinced of his words.

"I don't know how you think that's possible."

"I know her! All of the things unsaid the last time we were together."

"And she still said yes when he proposed." Lewis sounded exhausted.

"It's complicated!" He said frustrated.

"Doesn't matter! Don't do this to me today! Today is about Latia and me. I will walk down that aisle without a best man if you can't get it together." They didn't say anything they were probably staring each other down. "I'm not playing!"

"Alright! Alright! I'll be good." Dwayne said reluctantly.

"This is my day man! I've waited a long time for this. Shoot I worked hard for this!"

"So you better not mess it up."

"Tell me what you did to Amber to get kicked to the curb and I'll just avoid that."

Dwayne frowned at Lewis, Darryl tried not to laugh but he did. They looked at the corner; I smacked Darryl and pushed him. "That was a good one Lewis!"

Dwayne was not amused, Darryl patted his shoulder. "You sure you ready to be a part of this family?" I asked Lewis.

Lewis popped his collar, "I was born ready."

Sasha

"Are you sure you're going to be ok?" El kissed my forehead.

"Yea, I'll hang out with Amber. I'll come over in the morning." I put on a brave face for him.

Lewis & Latia's wedding day was finally here. Latia was not happy that they weren't able to avoid the media circus, but Malcolm had the place on lockdown with extremely tight security. I followed Amber around like I was glued to her. "Did you guys meet?" Amber asked Sylvia and I.

"Not formally. Sasha nice to meet you."

"Sylvia, you as well."

"You two save me a seat, I'll be right back." Amber said walking towards the back of the auditorium.

We found seats just behind the family section, "Sydney talks about you all the time. She's quite taken with you."

"Both of Yussef's girls are adorable. I'm taken with them as well."

"So you're not family?" She said watching my face.

So that's what this is? I looked around the room and I saw Yussef watching, he had no expression on his face. "I'm not related to Yussef if that's what you mean." I looked at her.

Then her eyes landed on my ring. She smiled like she was relieved, "you're married?"

"Almost," then I looked back at Yussef. "So what's the deal with you and Yussef?"

She shrugged, "I'm waiting on him to tell me what he wants to do."

"You love him?" I asked still looking at him.

"With all my heart!" She said passionately.

"So why aren't you married? How come I never heard of you?" I asked her point blank because she was bold enough to ask me questions.

She deflated, "I messed up everything. Long story, but I'm doing whatever I can to make him understand how in love with him I am! There's no one like Yussef anywhere! I'll spend the rest of my life making it up to him if he lets me."

"He doesn't trust you?"

I watched her eyes dart around the room. "Not right now."

"Hello ladies!" Tracy said breaking the tension.

"Hey sweetheart," I said standing up to give her a hug.

"Hello," Sylvia said.

"I'm Tracy, you're the girl's mother right?"

"I'm Sydney's mother."

"It's nice to meet you. I'm Andrew's wife."

Sylvia swallowed, "nice to meet you." Then she looked at Yussef who was still watching but now he had a smirk.

After that Sylvia was quiet, I didn't know why she was so quiet but she was. Tracy noticed it as well and she asked me if she said something. I told her I had no idea. Amber came back with Chantel. I asked why she wasn't in the wedding. She pointed at her stomach, she said it was too much flying all the way out here. Chantel sat on the other side of Sylvia then she and Amber pointed out celebrities and important people in the business.

When Tiffany and Crystal came to our seats they were so excited to see Amber. They gave us all hugs, but they were beyond excited about seeing Amber. They sat in the row directly behind Amber and they talked her ears off about nothing. I thought it was so sweet of her to keep an open relationship with them even though she was no longer with their father. The place was packed out by the time the wedding started. Everybody looked so pretty and comparatively their wedding party was HUGE! Yussef looked delicious in his tux, I can say that without offending myself. Amber had no reaction when Dwayne Reed emerged from the back escorting a beautiful chocolate woman. He was so obvious; his eyes were locked on Amber until he passed our aisle. Latia was beautiful and Malcolm looked so proud as he escorted her. He winked at Amber.

At the reception Randi, my Uncle Jeff's wife and I were saying we couldn't wait to have babies. Then Sydney and Yesmina came over looking like little dolls. I told them they looked so pretty and how they did wonderful jobs walking down the aisle. Yesmina introduced her little brother Jackson to me. When he was extremely bashful and shy they teased him about having a little crush on me. I was sitting with Amber trying to keep my eyes down cause men were on the prowl everywhere when they started playing music. Little Jackson came over and asked me to dance. He was too cute! We danced to two songs and a younger woman caught Jackson's eye, so I left them to their fun. "Working that poor little boy like that." Yussef said smiling.

"What can I say?" I shrugged.

"Let's dance." He took my hand.

I looked at Andrew who was grinning at us from across the floor while he danced with Tracy. "Will your girlfriend be mad?" I asked since this was a slow song.

"Nope!" He smiled, "you look very pretty. Where's El?"

"With his family, you heard about his mom and dad?"

He nodded his head, "that's right. They live out here. I'm sorry to hear about them."

It was quiet for a minute, "thank you for the compliment."

"Has Drew been giving you that goofy look? What does it mean?"

"He's a nut, who knows." I didn't want to think about it.

"Well, thank you for the dance miss Sasha. Congratulations on the wedding. I'll be there with bells on." He smiled and then we hugged. Darryl came bouncing over, and then Jeff came bouncing, then Tanisha, then JoJo, then Derrick, and then Andrew. We always used to bounce together. It was our thing; at parties people would move out of our way. Since this was not our party, we did a muted version of our dance together. Then I danced with Darryl until I had to use the bathroom. When I came out the stall the girl Dwayne escorted was watching me in the mirror while she fixed her makeup. "I think my son likes you." She smiled but it wasn't genuine.

"Your son?"

"Jackson." She said watching my eyes in the mirror.

So this is the crazy chick. "You are?"

"Melissa." She turned to face me.

"Jackson is a sweetheart." I dried my hands.

"How do you know Yussef?"

"Why is that any of your business?"

She looked me up and down, "anyone who interacts with my children is my business."

"Yea, but Yussef isn't." I returned her look up and down then I walked past her and out the bathroom. Yussef was dancing with Sylvia and Melissa turned on her heels and went back to the bathroom when she saw them. Tiffany and Crystal were watching Malcolm and Amber dance with brokenhearted expressions. "What's up guys?"

"This is heartbreaking!" Crystal said, "she's supposed to be with our dad!"

"You guys are old enough to understand that the heart wants what the heart wants. She's been in love with him since she was a kid." I thought about Yussef, and that sinking feeling settled over me that I try to ignore. Shoot I try to fight it as much as I can. It's that Cardell blood mixed with Wallace that plagues in moments like this.

"Why doesn't he do something?" Tiffany growled in the direction of her father who had his back to the dance floor.

I rubbed her hand, "your father has done everything he could. Be kind to him, this isn't easy for anybody involved."

****

"I can't wait for your day to get here. I have been waiting too long for this." Mrs. Parsons said.

"Oh, well." I was rocking in my seat trying to hold back my tears. Mr. Parsons was not having a good day, and El was in the other room trying to be strong with his father. "Our day is almost here. I can't wait to see you in your dress looking gorgeous."

She touched my hand, "I have no doubt in my mind that you will be good to my baby. I am so happy that he has you, and I'm sorry that your marriage will be starting on this note."

"This is so unreal, I can't believe this is happening."

"It's better this way. I can't imagine life without that man, and he says the same. It's not fair to the children, but I like it better this way. I couldn't imagine another twenty plus years on this earth without him. He's the first and only man to be good to me. And between you and me, I don't wanna be stuck with his daughter." I didn't expect her to say that so it caught me off guard and I chuckled. "He spoiled that girl rotten. El says he's done with her, and I know it's for the best. She's been running with Zoila lately."

"I thought they didn't get along?"

"Honey I can't explain the dysfunctions of other people's brains. My son needs to stay as far away from my daughter as he can. She's only out for herself."

"What about the baby?"

"She found the father, once the test confirmed it. They've been fighting over custody ever since. He'll have it shortly though, and then she'll be free to run the streets. I think children should be with fathers that want them, don't you think?"

I thought about Drew. "I agree."

I told Mrs. Parsons that I was happy that they'd see our townhouse in Oakland. When we left I hugged both of them and told them the next time we see them would be on our big day and I was so excited.

Tracy

I couldn't stop crying. I looked around my empty house. I couldn't believe this was no longer home. I never thought I was going to leave this place. Andrew was doing one last walk through to make sure we had everything. He looked at me crying but he didn't say anything, he put his arm around me. I gave him my keys and he set them on the mantel. I loved living in Berkeley; it felt so much like me, free and peace loving. I would be lying if I said the occasional out of town business trip for Andrew didn't leave me a little nervous about staying in the house with just Andre and I.

Malcolm's house is beautiful, and nicer than mine. But still! Malcolm offered to have the house repainted for us, but I liked the colors he had. He had the house cleaned from top to bottom before we moved in, so it was like moving into a brand new house. Andrew said he never spent the night in this house so it was new to all of us. Every time I turned the corner to go up the stairs I remembered the huge picture Malcolm had of Amber at the top of it. It was such a pretty picture. Andrew tried to argue with him to leave it, but Malcolm wasn't having it. He said it was his picture and it went with him. When I looked at Amber she shrugged like she didn't know what to say to that.

Cain and Eve kept patrolling the house over and over, like they were staff securing the house as well. Andrew showed me all the not so obvious cameras around the outside of the house. There was a basement and a completely invisible room off the basement.

218

Andrew said if for any crazy reason he ever tells Andre or I to go to the attic, we needed to come in and make sure we shut it. He said it was sound proof etc. then he went over to the panel and gently pushed it. There were a bunch of guns neatly lined up and ammunition, I gasped and looked at Andrew. His face was completely serious. "This is only here for emergencies, this is the bread box. Got it?"
I started to feel uneasy, "why do I need to know this? You said your family aren't drug dealers."
"Is that the Richmond way of thinking? Drug dealers and then everybody else?"
"I don't understand living like this if you aren't dealing."
He shook his head, "just because our businesses are legit doesn't mean we don't play defense. I don't know how else to explain it." Then he looked at Andre, "these are not toys. When the time is right I'll show you how to handle each one. You don't know anything about this unless someone asks for the *breadbox* got it? That's the only way you show them!"
"Yes dad!" Andre said taking his assignment seriously.
"Come on, let me show you the rest of the house," he said to Andre.
****
"Ladies, I want to say thank you so much for doing this with me. It means so much to me that each one of you are here." I said looking around the table. Do you have any questions?"
"HOLD ON! HOLD ON! HOLD ON! This says if one of these college kids start feeling froggy I can't bust them upside they head!" Liz said in disgust.
I smiled at her and then I looked at Andrew who was too tickled. "It's not a question of can you, I don't want you to. I'm not putting you on detail. You're supporting Tracy, if you have trouble just press the panic button and my people will handle it." Andrew said from the corner.
"I'm just saying. I might want to bust somebody. I might not want backup to come save them. They over eighteen it's all legal! *OK*!" She said slapping hands with Pearla.
"Just don't kill anybody." I said.
"I make no promises." She smiled.
"My father will be the runner or delivery person between the bakery and kiosk. Paulette will hand out samples, Pearla will fill orders, and Liz will handle money. Any questions?"
"Nope, everything looks good here. Especially the pay, THANK YOU COUSIN!" Paulette said.
Andre gave everyone their black "Tracy's Tasty Treats" aprons with the electric blue to match my brand. "The Grand Opening will be Sunday at the Rockridge location, we'll see you guys then." Andrew said
Gwen and Jenise's firm has been talking up the Grand Opening; a few Radio stations are going to be there. She sent them cupcake baskets throughout the week to entice the staff who wouldn't be broadcasting to come on down. Chantel, Lewis, and a few of their other celebrity friends were coming to endorse my business. All week, Joy, Marie, Sherrell, and I have been preparing for the opening. Gwen said there would be thousands of people coming by through the day. And at first I didn't believe her. When I started hearing the mentions on the radio and seeing "Tracy's Tasty Treats" trending on the internet I was beyond elated, but scared all at the same time. I drove Andrew absolutely crazy; thankfully he started tuning me out. Saturday night, all hands were on deck. We made close to three thousand cupcakes. Even though I planned to sell cakes, pies, cookies, etc. Gwen said cupcakes were the way to go to introduce the bakery based upon public opinion.
My celebrity line-up was there, and the first few people who came out of curiosity got a free cupcake and their pictures taken with the stars and posted immediately on my

219

website. By midmorning the parking lot was packed and Mitigated staff had barricades set up to control the crowds. A couple of news stations came and interviewed me, I held onto Chantel so tight. I felt like an idiot. I don't know how she does this on a regular basis. Thank goodness she was there, she spoke so well for me. I got the nerve to say a few things but I mostly smiled. Then I watched each person take their first bite. Each person had the same reaction; they said it was **SO GOOD!** Not only did we quickly go through the three thousand cupcakes we made the night before. I prepared batters for at least another batch and a half of that amount. We told the public that the bakery and Kiosk would be officially open Tuesday. When we finally closed our doors at six that evening, I threw my arms around Amber's neck SO tight! I couldn't stop crying which made her cry. I told her this was all because of her, and I was so thankful for her gentle push. When I hugged Malcolm he expected it, but he still stood there like a fish out of water. My parents were so proud, and I hadn't seen so many cousins and relatives in years. Even people who were *mad* at me because they didn't get an invite to my wedding ESPECIALLY when word got out that Chantel was there, were there and acting like they were my main supporters all my life. We had dinner at Uncle Frank's restaurant across the shopping center; poor little Andre and Anthony could barely keep their eyes open. They ate and then they passed out. As Andrew drove us home I stared at him and told him how much he's changed my life for the better and how thankful I was that he chose me to love.

Episode 13

Amber

I don't know what's wrong with this girl. The gloves are off and she's constantly testing me. I asked Jade and Sophia if they deal with this with their girls. After they stopped laughing at me they said mostly when they were little so it didn't seem so violent. Then Sophia said Sasha was feeling herself one time in her teen years and she had to remind her who her momma was. When I walked up the stairs I could hear her in the room crying. I exhaled and knocked on the door. When she didn't respond I pushed it open slowly all the while knocking on it. She was sitting on the bed crying. "Why did I have to come back here?"
"I told you, you were coming back."
"Why do I have to be here? I'm not a child."
"Sweetheart I know you're not a child. You were sent here so that I could try and talk some sense into you. I had no idea that you would let your hair down and act this way."
"You haven't said anything. You keep hitting me." She said between sobs.
"You keep testing me. Why do you keep doing that? I know you don't talk to your momma like this."
"That's my mom."
"Let's try this, you give me the same respect you'd give your momma. And I will exercise more control." Then I hugged her. I didn't want her thinking she was sent here to be my punching bag.
I went downstairs to go in the office but Malcolm was in there working as usual. He was on the phone and looking at something on his computer. He had the phone on speaker and it was a female on the other end. His tone was normal Malcolm tone, she sounded too excited to have his attention for my liking. His eyes were watching me when I walked in the office. I looked at the phone and then I looked at him. He put his hands out to ask me what was wrong with me. I grabbed my laptop off the desk next to his, I rolled my eyes and then I walked out. I made myself comfortable in my bed then I checked emails and statuses on my invoices that I sent to a few labels. Just before I got pissed about him still being on the phone Malcolm walked in the room. He knows me too well. "So I can't work

from home now?"

"How many females work for you? I thought it was mostly men."

"Depends on the business." He sat on the bed.

"No late night business conversations with females."

"Ok, I can do that. But you need to wear different clothes when you're on assignment then."

"You can't be serious." I said looking at him.

"You're jumping around in little shirts and clothes that leave nothing to the imagination. Now I don't exactly care, but if you're going to start making rules that affect my business, then it's only right."

"Fine Malcolm! Let me find out one of those females is trying to talk about more than business.... It sucks to be you!"

He raised an eyebrow, "you're threatening me?"

"It's a promise not a threat." Malcolm chuckled like I tickled him but I wasn't playing. I set my laptop on my nightstand I sat up. "Did you find her?"

"Yes," he watched my eyes.

"Well? Does she have a son?"

"Yes," he said still watching.

"Where is he? How old is he? Is he David's son?"

"Patricia Walker has four kids."

"Ok, but I'm only asking about one."

"You should be asking about two. Doyle and David Mason."

My shoulders tensed up. "Two? He had two kids with her? How in the world is that possible?"

"Doyle is older than Derrick, and David was born after he died. He didn't know about David, I can't explain Doyle I wasn't around remember."

"Did you know about this and just not tell me?"

"Outside of my boys, explain to me why I would care to think anything about that fool? I could care less if he had fifteen kids."

"That's not a yes or no Malcolm."

"Before I answer that you tell me once and for all. Did you cheat on me with David?"

I blew air, "REALLY? After all these years he's still asking me. "How in the world would that have been possible?"

He looked at me sideways, "don't play dumb!"

"Malcolm I don't know why any conversations about David amount to arguments between us. My children have siblings they need to find."

"They're found."

"Where are they?"

Malcolm stared at me for a minute. "I can't do this with you. Ask Yussef." Then he walked in the bathroom.

"You're mad at me?"

"This is dumb Amber! The boys may have questions, but this is not your business. Unless they bring you into it, you need to stay out." He growled from the bathroom.

I could see jealousy all over his face. No matter what I said if I kept pushing we were going to be arguing so I let it go.

David sat there in the chair at his kitchen table; drinking whatever cheap rotgut drink he had in his cabinet staring at me. "What difference does it make? You got what you wanted!"

I couldn't stop staring at his drink, I never did figure out how many exact sips it took before he turned mean. He was in a mood when he poured this glass so it wasn't going to take much. "What do you mean?"

"You made me believe you loved me! We have a family! And all you ever wanted was to lay back under that black demon!" He swallowed the last of his liquor. "I loved you, I wanted to marry you!"

"You also beat me up!" Something I never confronted him on.

He stood up, "because you like to provoke me!" Then he charged me.

I screamed and started fighting for my life.

I awoke to the sound of knocking, and then I heard the door open. Malcolm was dressed like he was about to walk out the door, and Tina looked scared as she peeked in the room behind Malcolm. Malcolm didn't say anything he watched me for a minute, and then he came and hugged me while I cried. Malcolm told Tina to sit on the bed next to us. She did as she was told of course. Malcolm held me until I calmed down; he kept kissing my face and rubbing my back. Once I was calm I told him to go to work. Tina looked so confused. I looked around the room Nana provided for me and I felt it in my soul, it was time to move out of this house. Tina stared at me with her eyes stretched real big. I told her I was having a bad dream; I didn't have it in me to explain any further than that. Something in my closet caught Tina's eye. I saw her eyeballing my closet like Sasha would. I told her she could go in. She got excited and she took off. I heard the front door and then Darryl called up to me. When he came in my room Tina was excitedly moving through my racks like she was shopping.

He frowned at her, and then he invited us out to breakfast. Tina got excited and started moving faster. She pieced together a very cute outfit. I was still dragging my feet; my lemongrass soap did open my eyes a bit. I decided to go for comfort so I put on jeans. Darryl took us to another one of his unknown spots. He knew everyone there and they were excited that we were there. Even though there were only three of us, they gave us a large table towards the back. The place was pretty empty, but he said this was the down period they're normally packed at breakfast then from lunch onward it stayed pretty busy. Since Tina was on her best behavior today, I didn't see the harm in giving her, her phone while we were here. Darryl asked me what was wrong. Even though I was trying to shake off my dream it was still bothering me. I saw David and his old place so clearly, like it was minutes ago that I was with him. I didn't want to trouble Darryl with nonsense.

Saved by the bell Timothy called asking where we were cause he was at my house. I had Darryl give him directions to where we were. Tina was completely involved in her phone and oblivious to anything happening with us.

"You were saying?" He handed me my phone.

"I wasn't." Then I exhaled, "Malcolm said you have two brothers. I know it shouldn't affect me, but it does. How could David know about them and not do anything for them?"

"Momma you know David was twisted. From what I remember of him I don't know if it matters to meet them."

Tina was frowning when she put her phone down. Darryl asked her what was wrong, and she shook her head. She lost all color in her face when her parents walked in. "What are you doing here?" She almost yelled.

"Is that how you greet your parents?" Grace asked.

Tina sat there even more nervous, "what gives?" I asked her.

"Um! I need to use the bathroom."

"I'll go with you." Grace said eyeing her.

"No!" She tried to fix her face. "I'm not a child."

"You're acting real suspicious." Grace focused on her daughter.

With Shane in the front about four other Mitigated staff members came in the restaurant sitting at two tables close by. Shane and a guy looking like a cute couple, and three guys at the other table. Darryl sat back in his seat at the edge of the booth blocking Tina. His eyes danced around the room. Then a tall light skinned lanky looking guy came walking in. Darryl put his finger up and whipped it in a circle. I heard the restaurant doors close.

Shane looked at the guy then she looked at Tina, then she looked at me. Timothy who was sitting directly across from Darryl turned to see who was coming. The guy walked right up to our table, Tina's eyes looked horrified. "Come here!" He commanded Tina who had the nerve to look scared. Immediately I thought of David.

"Who are you?" Grace asked then she looked at Tina.

Timothy had fire in his eyes as he looked at him. "I'm here for her!" He gestured towards Tina.

"How you gonna walk up on our table and not even introduce yourself. Don't you have any manners?" Darryl said with a smile.

"This is not a social visit. I said COME HERE!"

Then Tina started to move and Darryl told her to stop. "Social or not you're rude. Pull up your chair, introduce yourself have some breakfast. Let me teach you some manners."

He glared at Darryl, and then Darryl smiled really big at him. I looked at Tina and she was visibly shaking. I reached out to touch her hand, I knew this look. "She's been avoiding me, and I told her what would happen the next time I saw her!"

"Why don't you tell me!" Timothy moved out of his seat and stepped in his face.

"Daddy!" Tina yelled.

He smirked, "this is your father?" Then he completely disregarded Timothy's white collar appearance and turned to Tina. "If I got to tell you one more time!"

Tina tried to get up again, "why do you keep getting up? He ain't gonna do nothing!" Darryl made her sit.

"Who you supposed to be? You cheating on me with him!"

"No! He's...." Tina started to explain.

"SHUT UP!" Darryl said to her.

"Darryl he's crazy!" She said completely afraid.

Darryl looked at her in complete disbelief. "Clearly we haven't met! I wear the crazy crown around these parts!" Then he stood up, "what have you done to my cousin to make her fear you?"

He smirked at Darryl then he turned his attention back to Tina. "Let's go!"

You heard Timothy's fist connect with the guy's face. Everybody jumped cause we weren't expecting it. Timothy didn't give him a chance to recover; you heard every hit and it sound like he was breaking stuff. "Daddy!" Tina screamed in disbelief.

"Timothy?" Grace said completely surprised. Everybody else sat back, you could tell this guy was used to hitting defenseless women. When he hit the ground Timothy kept booting him, even though Tina was begging him to stop. The guy reached in his jacket and pulled out a gun. Timothy, Darryl, and everyone else pulled theirs out at the same time. Grace and Tina screamed. "Timothy?" Grace called out.

The guy dropped his gun and everyone lowered theirs except Darryl. "Sorry, I don't take out my gun unless I plan to use it!"

"Darryl!" I screamed immediately knowing he was about to pull the trigger.

"Momma!" He sucked his teeth. Then he looked at the Mitigated staff. "I don't want to see him again!"

They picked up the busted up guy, Grace got off the chair and she ran to Timothy. "Since when do you carry a gun?" She put her arms around him.

"I always have!"

"What? Where did they take Luke?" Tina asked as she trembled.

"Tina come meet my Uncle Timothy. Seems like you don't know who anybody is!"

Malachi

"And there's the baby's heart beat." The doctor said.

"Do you think the baby is fine? I..." She looked at me, "I fell and we were wondering if that could've affected the baby."

"You heard that rhythm loud and strong? You've got a little soldier on your hands. But...." She said looking at the chart. "Your weight has dropped significantly since your last regular checkup. How are you feeling?"

Denise looked at me with angry eyes. "We are going through some tough times right now. I'm a little overwhelmed."

The doctor looked at me, "tough times?"

"Career change, we're moving, oh and the day she found out she was pregnant she found out about my mistress. Tough times is putting it lightly!" I watched the doctor's eyes.

"Whoa, ok..." She took a deep breath. "Are you guys getting help?"

"He doesn't want to meet with my doctor." Denise said.

"Don't know him don't want to deal with him."

"Mr. and Mrs. Wallace stress could affect your pregnancy. Especially if you continue to lose weight like this. You two need to come up with a compromise or solution and fast before it affects your family any further than it already has."

Denise rolled her eyes, "all we do is argue. I feel trapped! I don't want to deal with any of this. I just want it to go away."

"I don't know what to tell you. If you ignore it, it will come out in another way. Your baby deserves a fair start."

"Tell him to cave. I feel more comfortable with my doctor!" Denise said adamant in thinking she's right.

"Mr. Wallace please, I am concerned. You two have always been a lovely couple. An unhealthy child can put an even bigger strain on your relationship. If you won't do it for your wife, please do it for your child." The doctor pleaded.

"I haven't seen any results with this doctor and she's been going to him for years. She starts hanging out with my sisters and immediately I see results. If it wasn't a conflict of interest I swear we'd need to see Jade, my sister. I feel like it's a waste of time! You won't be satisfied until you see for yourself."

The doctor looked at Denise, "girl you better hurry up and call that doctor." Denise and I smiled at the doctor cause she broke her doctor character to tell Denise to hurry up. The doctor put her hand on her chest. "Oh my goodness! I'm so sorry!" Embarrassment was all over her face. She sat on the stool and started typing in the computer. "I want to see you in three weeks. Denise you can't lose any more weight, the baby is going to take what it needs first. You need to take better care of yourself."

We weren't out of the office good before Denise had her ear on the phone making an emergency appointment for tomorrow. We rode in silence, nothing but tension was in the air. Denise kept her eyes out the passenger side window; I could tell she was crying which made me feel horrible. When we pulled up to the girl's school, she told me we had an appointment tomorrow morning. Then we both put on smiles for the girls.

Dinner and everything else was just like it was before, cold and mechanical. If the girls hadn't seen us like this before I would've been concerned. They didn't seem to notice, I made sure I tucked them in at night and that I woke them up in the morning so that they wouldn't see me sleeping in the guest room. I used to demand to sleep in our bed no matter what, but now it was the last place I wanted to be. I tossed and turned all night not sleeping, my mind was racing all over the place. The guilt was in my face, but something in me made me want to fight back and not completely accept the blame in this. Yes I cheated, and no matter what I'm wrong for that. I can't take the complete blame for everything that's wrong here. I LOVE my wife! I'm starting to feel like it would probably be easier to let it all go than stand here and fight. Dealing with me is depressing her, we haven't told anyone about the baby. I think we're both afraid we may have to unexplain as soon as we explain. In the morning I cursed the world, and then I put on a happy face and went in the room to wake my girls. Today did not feel like it was going to be a good day.

"Hello I'm doctor Dobson, it's nice to finally meet you." He said holding the office door open. I nodded but I didn't say anything. "Have a seat. Have a seat." Denise sat in the corner of the love seat and I sat on the chair facing the couch and his seat. He had all these placards on the wall, and awards. He wrote a book or two or three and they were on his bookshelf looking like advertisements. He definitely thought a lot of himself with the subtle shrine he had. "Denise you don't look so good, what's wrong?" He touched Denise's leg, ok more like tapped it. I didn't like all the touching. Why did he hug her when he saw her?

"Doctor Dobson, we're a mess!" Denise said crying immediately.

"Clearly cause you actually got him here." He was talking to her like I wasn't there, strike two.

"I'm pregnant and then I found out he's been cheating on me! I can't eat, I can't sleep! I feel like everything is closing in on me!" She cried.

"There, there!" He tapped her leg AGAIN, and then he reached for tissue and gave it to her. "You're stronger than you know. You've survived your mother, you can survive this too." Then he rubbed her knee.

"Why do you keep touching my wife?" I tried to pull some of the bass out of my voice, but I was not happy.

"Does my touching your wife make you think about your intimacy issues?"

I looked up at the ceiling, this FOOL DON'T KNOW ME! "Did I tell you I have intimacy issues?" I burned a hole in him with my eyes.

This fool looked at the ground, "no. I'm reflecting on the conversations I've had with your wife."

I adjusted in my chair, "if we're here together, why would you rely on her explanation of who I am? How are you supposed to provide unbiased therapeutic help in this situation?"

He put his hands up, "ok Malachi please...."

"Un huh! If you're 'Doctor Dobson!' I'm Mr. Wallace!"

He exhaled frustrated air, "*MISTER WALLACE! PLEASE CALM DOWN!*" He said flustered.

I leaned back and smiled, "I am calm. Why aren't you?"

"Clearly we're getting off on the wrong foot. I am here to help you, not to judge."

"Interesting choice of words." I stroked my chin.

"**Malachi!**" Denise was completely embarrassed.

"You claim you're not judging me, but I am judging you! Quite Frankly, I think you're used to dealing with women."

"I can't disclose information about my patients." He started shaking his foot.

"Oh yea, you aren't used to having a man before you. I'm not a doctor but I know as a man, that you cannot rely on someone else, **ESPECIALLY** an emotional **FEMALE** to accurately describe another man to you. She's going to give you her emotional point of view about who I am." His eyes danced around the office. "Ah! Son, didn't anyone teach you that you look a man in the eyes? First rule of being a man is eye contact. You would do good if you teach your daughters that, but a man should live and die by this rule! You over there shaking like a FEMALE cause I'm making you uncomfortable. Don't they teach you how to treat a man in school? Or did you stop listening once you found a few faithful women who didn't know any better? I can see a woman who knows nothing about a real man being comfortable in here."

"Your wife is comfortable in here." He shot back.

I smiled cause he was all off guard. "Yes, well she needed the company of a lesser male. A dang near girlfriend to make her feel better."

"Malachi!" Denise said looking at me like she couldn't believe it.

"This fool is a joke and we haven't even been here ten minutes! He's stupid enough to follow me off script, and this is who you want me to open up to? If you want to meet with a man, we need to meet with a man. This woman in men's clothing isn't going to work for me."

"Mala… I mean MISTER WALLACE!"

"That's right! Matter of fact call me **SIR**!" I chuckled.

"WHAT?"

"You aren't even man enough to address me by my last name I've decided. So call me **SIR** or don't call me at all!"

He rolled his eyes and turned his body towards Denise. "Anyways, where were we?" He took a deep breath like he was trying to gather his thoughts; he looked up at the ceiling. He got an idea; he got out of his seat. He walked over to his bookshelf. Selected one of his books with his face plastered on the cover. I guess he was going for a pensive look, but he looked constipated to me. He opened the book and flipped through the pages as he walked back to his seat. When he found his desired passage, he handed the book to Denise and told her to read it out loud.

"*More often times than not, when a child has grown up in an environment when they have felt unvalued, unappreciated, and underestimated they seek out partners that continue to increase these feelings in their adult life…*"

"Stop right there Denise. You see, your mother has really done a number on you. She got in your head and really messed with your self-esteem. It's no wonder you ended up with someone who treats you the same way."

Denise looked at me, "uh Doctor Dobson I never said…."

"SSSShhhh! It's ok. I can see why you have felt the way you have."

I chuckled; I looked up at the wall. "Did you go to art and design school?"

"I don't understand?" The look on his face confirmed his ignorance.

"These diplomas can't be real! You're an idiot!"

"Good thing my definition of my job isn't dependent on the mediocre opinion of an inferior simpleton."

"Inferior? Mediocre? Simpleton?" I shook my head. "Right, because I make my living off of enabling false dependencies from people who truly come to me for help. You are a pathetic joke! You cop inappropriate feels on these poor women who honestly come to you looking for help. You've got all this unnecessary decoration around your office to try to subliminally drive in the point that you're an authority when honestly you read a few books, looked at a few case studies and then they gave you a diploma. All this is supposed to cover up the fact that you use this job to compensate for what you're lacking." I pointed at his shoes, "those little feet!"

"WHAT?"

I smiled at him, "I know you're mad cause I got fourteens and what are those a size seven or eight?" I chuckled, and then I looked at Denise. "Can we please go now? I'm not paying for this! I ought to sue you for malpractice!"

He stood up completely *ticked off*. I looked at Denise and her eyes were big. "Denise, I cannot work with your husband. He has anger issues and he lacks the ability to be civil. We can book another appointment for later on…"

"Denise you are not coming back here. Matter of fact, now that I know firsthand the things that happen here you're not practicing anymore. I hope you have a backup cause this scam is over. I'm doing the women of the world a favor."

"Denise, it's ok. You don't have to fear him. You're in a safe place. You let me know if he threatens any violence towards you. I will have him locked up faster than he can say Amen."

"My husband's never been violent towards me!" Denise barked.

I was so busy focusing on him I didn't realize that she was getting angry as well. "I know sweetheart, it's ok!"

"I never told you he has intimacy issues either! How dare you! I've been coming here for years and I've never seen you for who you are until my husband said it. You are a scam artist! You're always telling me how I feel and what I think; you don't let me explain anything. You're always reading passages from your books, but barely listening!" Then she looked at me, "baby I'm sorry!"

He put his hands out, "Denise? Really?"

"REALLY!" She spit; she stood up and reached for my hand. I felt a little warm and tingly, my baby's got a little spunk. "Baby, let's go!"

"You're letting him manipulate you!" He said trying to block her path to lead us out.

"Denise I have been here for you all of these years. How can you let a brief interaction with your husband change everything we've established?"

"I know he loves.... me!" She looked at me like she was just realizing it. Tears welled up in her eyes cause she was confused by the realization. "Malachi let's go!"

When we left I called Sonny.

****

"Imagine if it was your daughter!" Timothy barked.

"So now what?" Sonny asked.

"Grace is so turned on! The day I understand women!" Timothy said smirking. "Where is he?"

My big brother looked at me with my daddy's eyes, "he's gone."

"Timothy! Not right now! The situation is too hot right now." Sonny said.

Timothy looked at Sonny, "I don't care! That is my daughter! She's fearing this fool in a way she's never feared anyone."

Sonny shook his head cause he understood but the lawyer in him was going over all the angles. "Who swept the scene?"

"You gotta ask nephew all that." He said in defeat.

"And you, what's happening with Cora?"

I grimaced, "nothing!"

"Dartnell got to her after the Grand Smack Down!" Sonny smiled, "she's trying to press charges. But she has no witnesses. Be on guard!"

"What about Dobson?"

"He's losing his practice. He's had a few affairs with some of his patients, it'll come to light shortly."

I took that in, "ok."

"You do know that this does not let you off the hook. You guys still need to seek out therapy."

"Yea, yea, I know."

"For real, you guys can still survive this if you get help."

"We are surviving, we left Dobson's together."

"That was a step in the right direction, but you aren't fixed."

Chantel

"I'm sorry you feel that way daddy, but I haven't been avoiding you. I've been busy." I've been working as much as I can since we came back from Lewis' wedding. Derrick and Cyrus want me to slow down cause the baby's going to come soon. And I am tired, but I gotta get a few more things done. My maternity endorsements moved their photo-shoot and interview locations to San Francisco just so that I could work with them. I was extremely grateful, and happy that they felt satisfied with what I gave them.

"It seems like you have time for everyone except me." My daddy pouted.

"Seriously daddy? You sound like a girl!"

"I guess that's what you're reducing me to."

I rolled my eyes. "I'll talk to Derrick about going to Gus' this weekend. I can't promise you anything."

"Can't you tell him that you're coming?"

I exhaled, "fortunately I'm married to a real man. Sometimes I don't always get my way. I don't always like it, but I love that he's a man and I respect his decisions. So if he says we can't go, then we can't go. End of story!" Sophia smiled at me. "Daddy I have to go, I'm being rude. I'm handling important information right now."

"Ok well let me know." He said, "talk to you later. I love you."

"Love you too, bye daddy." Then I hung up the phone and exhaled.

"Your father doesn't advise you to go against Derrick does he?"

"My father is selfish, so he'll advise against anything that is in opposition to him." I took a deep breath.

"That can't be easy." Then Sophia exhaled. She returned to our previous conversation before my father's call interrupted us.

I told Sophia I wanted to do something special for Sasha since I couldn't be in her wedding. So Sasha knew that I promised to sing at her wedding. Sophia had Amber put a group together to perform. At first Derrick was getting huffy about me working so close to my due date. Amber assured him that I would be sitting the entire time we practiced and performed. And she meant it; if I stood up she was on me.

In the end we had a beautiful number together that Sasha and El would love. After the dancers left the studio, Sophia brought in the lunch she prepared for us. She was so excited for Sasha.

"How has Derrick been holding up? He's been avoiding me." Amber said.

I knew exactly what she was talking about. Derrick did his best not to be affected by his grandmother's comment. He said as soon as he heard it, he believed it. Yussef gave us until we came back from Lewis' wedding before he came over with the information about Derrick's brothers. When Yussef read off their names Derrick flinched when Yussef said the youngest was named David. Doyle is in and out of jail; mostly assault charges on women and drunken fights. David looked good on paper but who knows. Yussef had David's driver's license picture and Doyle's California ID picture. Derrick looked once then he sat there processing. I kept looking at the pictures to see if they favored at all. I couldn't tell by their DMV pictures. Doyle was older than Derrick, almost two years older. David was born almost nine months to the day that their father died. I could tell that Derrick was conflicted. Then Darryl saying that it was irrelevant didn't help Derrick at all. Andrew wanted to find them immediately. Derrick growled at both of them. He said he needed time to think it through and right now his family is his primary focus. I looked at Amber; "it's a very touchy subject with him right now."

"What is?" Sophia asked looking back and forth between us.

"Do you remember David's ex Patricia?"

Sophia frowned, "should I? Not really."

"We met her one time when the kids were babies. She was really pretty and brown skinned." Sophia shrugged, "anyways Dionne had a moment of clarity at the wedding. She told Chantel that David had a son. It turns out he has two by Patricia. Doyle and David."

Sophia gasped, "Why did he let her name her son David? Were they married?"

"David was born after he died, I doubt he knew about him. I don't think they were married, how could he justify breaking into my house to kidnap us and marry me if he was married to her?"

"But he knew about the oldest one?"

"I guess so, but how could he not say anything? He was so good to Andy. How could he be so horrible to his own son?" Amber said looking confused.

"Remember he wasn't good to anyone other than Drew. Or at least that's the way Derrick tells the story." I said.

"Is it wrong that I want to talk to her?"

"For what?" Sophia said.

"I don't want her to think I knew."

"Was she at the funeral?" I asked.

"I can't remember." Amber said still trying to think back.

"Why would you care what she thinks? That heifer ain't nobody to you or your family. Why would she have a second baby with him when he clearly didn't take care of the first one? After all those years she reset the clock, who does that? A lonely and desperate person. You don't owe them nothing!" Sophia said wiggling her neck the whole time.

"What would that say about me if we were together and he didn't provide for his son? I didn't know about him or of course I would've said or done something. I still find it hard to believe that David was this evil."

Sophia started giving her evil eyes. "You're kidding right! Please tell me you're kidding! Why do you become so weak when it comes to him? He was evil! He was manipulating you the whole time! You're being shown the whole picture and some how you're victimizing yourself because of that no good sorry excuse for a man." She exhaled then she looked at her. "What does Malcolm think about all of this?" Then she smirked.

"I HATE YOU!" Amber smiled, "he told me about the boys then he told me he doesn't want to discuss it."

"Cause he knows your goofy behind. Stop punishing yourself behind him!" Sophia said.

Amber glanced at me with an embarrassed look and then she looked away.

When I got home Derrick was working in his office. His eyes were dancing from screen to screen when I walked into his office. "How was practice?" he asked without lifting his eyes.

"Good."

His eyes locked on me, "what's up?"

"Your mom wants to know why you're avoiding her."

He huffed, "what did you tell her?"

"That you're focusing on us right now, and then you'd think about them later."

"Ok, so what's wrong?" He was still eyeing me.

"Was your father a bad person?"

His eyes turned angry, "Malcolm is my father!"

I tilted my head, "you know what I mean?" Then I sat in the chair in front of him. There was no negotiating in his eyes. "Everything you need to know about him you already know." Then he gave me that warning look to drop it.

"Derrick! I'm your wife, we can discuss anything. You know my family life isn't rosy. Please talk to me."

"I can't go there with you right now! I've got business to handle."

I rolled my eyes and I got up in a huff. I slammed the door shut on his office. I popped some popcorn grabbed my fleece throw and gallon jug of ice water. Then I went in the theater. I put on a movie and snuggled into my comfy couch. I didn't make it past the opening credits I was out. I awoke to Andre sitting in the theater chair next to my couch chomping on some popcorn and Derrick moving my feet so he could sit down. He gently massaged them as he held on to them. Then he asked Andre if he was going to get married when he grew up. Andre smiled real big as he said he was going to marry Monet when he grew up. My head popped up, and then I asked him who Monet was. He said she was his girlfriend. I asked him if his parents knew about her and he said yes. I looked at Derrick. Derrick told him not to promise forever to a girl until he finished college. Andre asked why not as he sat there processing what his uncle was telling him. He explained to Andre that sometimes people change when they go to college and not for the good. I looked at him cause I knew he was talking about Brooklyn. Then the action on the screen caught my attention. I asked Derrick what happened to my movie. He said it went off, then they both exclaimed *whoa* as some guy threw another guy across the screen. I was in no mood to watch their dumb movie so I left the theater. Feeling a little restless and irritated by Derrick's brush off I went in the music room. I picked up my guitar and started strumming. One of the many things I love about this pregnancy is that my creative juices flow at will. I've written so many songs, some have melodies and others don't. Today I was strumming along. I wrote at the top of the sheet, "SECRETS!" and that was it I had the melody. I sat there strumming asking the melody what story it was trying to tell. The chorus held no words yet, but I kept strumming. As I finished my first verse, here came the followers. UGH! He was not my favorite person and yet he's following me around the house.

Andre sat on the piano stool next to him. He showed Andre the basic chords, chord progressions, and then he showed him a simple one and he told him to follow that while I played my melody. I was not in the mood for a family moment, but I played along for Andre's sake. He had nothing to do with his uncle getting on my nerves. Andre smiled really big as his uncle congratulated his success on mastering the few chords he showed him. I loved seeing how patient Derrick was with Andre. I didn't expect that, but he was always patient with my little brothers as well. Which is why they always looked up to him. But he's so much like Malcolm; if you only look at them you'd think they're mean. If you watch what they do and what they're trying to show you, you understand they're not completely mean. Only when they throw you out of their office because they don't want to answer your questions.

When the intercom buzzed, I went to the monitor on the wall. It was Tracy she was at the front gate. I buzzed her in. Sherrell honked as she drove by to go home. Tracy pulled in my driveway. When she got out of the car she looked pale and exhausted. She was trying to rush out and get home but I made her come inside. She looked around the house with all smiles, she said she loved our house, and she couldn't wait to see the finished project for hers. I told her I was so happy to have another girl in the house, cause their boy stuff kept following me around. When she heard Derrick in the music room pounding away on the piano she said she forgot he plays the piano.

When the music stopped Derrick and Andre came into the living room where we were sitting with our feet up. Derrick's face became concerned when he looked at Tracy. He immediately asked her how she was feeling. She said she was fine just tired. He shook his head, and then he stood up. He informed us that he and Andre were making dinner. I had no complaints about that, and Andre was eager to help. I asked Tracy how things were going at the bakery. She said everything was going better than expected. She said they sell out every day. She said that was good and bad. Because the people who came after everything was gone made her feel so bad. I told her she couldn't keep up this pace for too much longer. She said she and Andrew were coming up with a plan of attack for the time she'd need to take off for the baby. Andrew came over a little while later and he had the same concerned look that we all had when you look at Tracy. He went in the kitchen with Derrick and created wonderful smells.

Kendra

I slapped the counter, "this is amazing!" I said taking another bite of my cupcake. I don't know how her stuff tastes so good. But this cupcake is amazing, Lanie shook her head in agreement as she hummed and ate her cupcake.

"Ooh girl, you gotta go to the bakery, the warm cookies are the bomb dot com!" Liz said wiping down the counters.

A student knocked on the door, begging Liz to open it. Liz told them the kiosk was closed and they could come back tomorrow or try to get to the bakery before it closed.

Student after student kept coming and she kept redirecting them. She told us she had to put our cupcakes aside, cause the kiosk always sold out as we could see. The bakery was right across from my office, but I felt like a dork just popping in. There was always a line in there and everything looked so busy. I've met Tracy before, but Darryl and I are not together so I feel DUMB trying to go in there like I belong in there or something. Paulette, Liz, and Pearla rode in the truck with Mr. Thomas as Lanie and I followed them back to the bakery. "So you're coming out with Kalani and I Friday night right?"
Lanie started dancing in her chair, "YES! I need to get out and release some stress. Where are we going?"
"Good question. I don't think we know just yet. Kalani will tell us before the night."
When I pulled into the parking lot I parked closer to my office.
"Come say hi to everybody." Lanie said, she looked at me funny when I hesitated.
"What?"
"Darryl and I aren't together. I feel funny about hanging out with his family."
"You feel some kind of way about hanging out with me?" She pointed to herself.
"Not you of course, but everybody else."
"Why? You're family."
"Not anymore?" I said realizing how much that actually hurt to say.
"What you mean? Once family, always family! You guys are stupid but you're in love."
"Um, how could we be in love if I'm dating someone else?"
"Hence the stupid! You guys make my butt hurt! One minute you're all I love you so much! No! I love you so much! No! I love you so much! YUCK! Then you're all; I'm in love with this random person. Well I'm in love with someone too…"
"HOLD ON!" Lanie paused, "Darryl's in love with someone?"
"That's not what I said." She said looking around.
My blood was boiling, "I heard what you said. Now answer the question!"
She frowned at me, "how come whenever Darryl is at stake, sweet and loving Kendra goes out the window?"
"LANIE IF YOU DON'T STOP PLAYING WITH ME AND ANSWER THE QUESTION!"
"Ok! Ok! You don't have to yell though, it's really not nice Kendra." She leaned against my car. "Darryl's a guy, right?" She shrugged. "He's been hanging around that girl, or I should say he's been letting that girl hang around him. I call her wanna be Kendra, she hates it so I call her that more."
"You call her that to her face?"
"Yep! You know I don't care!"
"Darryl doesn't get mad when you do that?"
"Please! He knows better. Anyways! She's been around for a while now. I think he might be feeling her a little bit. She's a stand in for you at best. But you know how you've been running from him."
I slumped into my car. "I have feelings about this! I need a minute to understand them." I said honestly.
"Take your time, well not too much time. Darryl's a guy, and they seem to forget you if you take too long and drag your feet."
"Fine! He forgets me, he's already forgotten."
Lanie stared at me. "You're not fooling nobody! Your feelings are hurt. It's all good though. It's not time for you two to get it right."
"Timing sucks though, I really want a baby."
"I think he's getting that itch too."
"WHAT?" I was getting pissed off now.
"Everybody around him is married or getting married or living like they're married. Everybody is having babies or got them already. The cheese stands alone!"

"What does that mean?"

"I don't know, it just felt like the right thing to say right then." We laughed. "Come say hi, ain't nobody tripping Kendra."

****

I took my lasagna out of the oven and set it on the stovetop. I threw my garlic cheese bread in the oven. "You want to pour the wine, we'll be ready in two shakes." I walked to his table and putting a potholder in the middle. I set the piping hot lasagna on top of it next to the salad. When I took the garlic bread out I cut it and set it in a bowl in the middle of the table as well.

"Gurl! This all smells so good!" Latonya said.

"Thanks, this is just a quick something to throw together." I was trying to be humble.

"Quick! Whatever, I don't cook. I can order like nobody's business though."

"And don't I know it." Russell said kissing her cheek.

Shai turned off the TV and put on soft music. He walked to the table with a smile.

"Kendra it smells great! I bet it's as good as it smells." He gave me a kiss on my cheek.

"I guess we'll have to see." I said taking my seat.

We sat down and then everyone dug in. Russell celebrated his meal too much for Latonya's liking so she just about cursed him out. Shai tore his plate up; "I can't believe you made this in my kitchen!"

It seemed like Shai and Russell were in a race to see who could finish their food first and go back for more. "Actually, you know cheese isn't all that good for you. Russell you might wanna slow down."

"Screw you woman! I'm loving this!" Russell said with a mouth full of food.

"Latonya stop hating! Kendra, this is a delicious meal. Thank you so much." Shai said.

"What's for dessert?" Russell blurted.

"I got a carrot cake from that new bakery."

"Carrot cake?" Russell and Latonya said in unison

"It was all they had left." Shai said.

"Pass! I don't like carrot cake." Latonya turned up her nose.

"Suit yourself! More for me. But I hear that everything from this bakery is really good." Shai said.

"It is actually. I have yet to not like something." I volunteered.

"I'll take your word for it. Cheese all over everything, and then she brings carrot cake. Guess you're not worried about a diet." Latonya snipped at me.

"I'm naturally this way, but if you gotta count calories to be on my level, I understand." I snipped back.

"Ooh!" Shai said, "That's enough of that. I need my best friend and my girl to get a long."

I liked the sound of that, Latonya didn't. "You're claiming her now?"

"You heard me," He shot her a look to tell her to calm down.

The rest of the night was good, Shai was sweet and kind. We watched a couple of movies; I sat in Shai's arms while we watched the movies. Latonya kept looking in our direction, but I chose to ignore her. Sometimes she's cool and other times she's a little possessive of her friend. Her man seems to make light of it, but he accepts it. Latonya and Russell are married, while Shai and Latonya who grew up together are best friends and work for the same company. I almost walked away from Shai because of how close he and Latonya are; sometimes it's too much. The three of them share this house together. They're all in each other's lives, but what can I say. Shai convinced me to stick it out. He's a sweetheart and a gentleman, but don't make him mad. It's been months and he doesn't push the sex issue. I've spent the night quite a few times and he doesn't try anything. He may spoon me or we make out for a long time, but we haven't made that connection. And it's not that I haven't wanted to either. When it got late, Latonya stood up and stretched. "So Kendra, you're spending the night?"

Shai smiled at me with approval in his eyes, "yes."

"Great! Fine! See you in the morning." She went up the stairs.

Russell smiled and got comfortable on the couch. Shai cleared his throat and nodded at Russell. "Oh!" He faked a yawn, "I'm tired too. Good night you two." Then he went upstairs with his wife as well.

I kissed Shai immediately. "That was some potent wine, I only had a glass and I feel tingly." I said with a smile.

"Dinner was so good. I think Russell and I got used to Latonya's non cooking ways we forgot that there's women who can cook."

"Is that why you do most of the cooking?'

"Pretty much, and it's pretty basic at that. You're gonna have to show me how you cook one day." He smiled.

"You wanna see how I cook?" I smiled, and then I kissed him.

When the kiss kept going and my hands were all under his shirt, he said we needed to talk. He told me he liked me and he really wanted to take his time with me. He said he grew up really religious, and he doesn't believe in sex before marriage. I asked him if he was a virgin, cause I got the impression he knew about a few things. He said he wasn't a virgin, but he had been through his share of letdowns. So he decided that he needed to go back to basics, he said the next person he connected with he wanted them to be his last. I'm not gonna lie, I was disappointed. I had no choice but to accept it. Especially since we agreed we weren't exclusive. So I'd see Darryl from time to time, and it was great not to feel guilty about it.

****

Shai was stroking my hair, "tell me something?" I looked at him. "Why don't you wear your hair naturally? Why do you still put chemicals in it?"

"I've had a perm since I was little. I never thought of my hair another way."

"I think you would look nice with your hair in its natural state."

"You're just saying that because Latonya's hair looks like that. She has mixed girl hair, my hair won't look like that in its natural state."

"How will you know unless you try?"

"I'd have to want to try first. It looks like a lot of work that I just don't have time for right now." I felt a little irritated.

"Talk to Latonya, I'm sure she could give you some pointers on how to do it. She helped me a lot when I had my locs."

"You had locs?"

He shook his head yes, "since I was twenty until about three almost four years ago."

"You got pictures, I want to see?" He went to the closet, came back with a photo album full of pictures. He picked the pictures he wanted to show me, but I wanted to see the whole album. Most of the pictures had Latonya in them and they were a lot younger in then. He had locs and they were long and pretty. From the pictures I doubt that Latonya has ever had a perm on her hair. Most of these pictures were of him and her in some kind of way together. "How did she end up married to Russell with you two being this close?" He smiled looking at the picture of them sitting side by side. It looked like they were arguing about something. "She's my best friend, I know her inside and out. Russell's a good guy, he could give her what I couldn't at the time."

"What's that?"

"A monogamous relationship. Besides it's better this way anyways. I didn't lose my friend, and I met you." He smiled, "I never would've thought you would've approached me. You completely surprised me."

"I surprised myself, I don't approach men." I exhaled, "I surely can pick them though. A guy who doesn't put out... whoopity-do! It's for the best anyways cause if we aren't

233

exclusive then we shouldn't go there."

"We're making good progress, you are special to me. I could see us going all the way. *Kendra Miller* has a nice ring to it if you ask me." He smiled.

"Yea, we'll see." I smiled.

He put his arms around me, he kissed my cheek. "Let's go to bed." When we went to his room he gave me a T-shirt to put on. When I got under the covers, he pulled them back. "I feel so conflicted. I want you, you have no idea how much." I smiled at him cause his internal debate was cute. He opened my legs, "I need to taste you at least. Don't tell them I gave in." I was about to ask him whom he was talking about, but the feeling of his warm mouth on me stopped me from speaking.

Tracy

"Are you feeling ok? You don't look too good?" My mom asked me.

We just barely said "Amen," and she made a beeline over here. I guess I look how I feel. I've been really tired this past week. Our trip to New York was a nice break but then we opened the bakery and it's been go time ever since. Andrew's cousins Gwen and Jenise definitely put the bakery on the map. The Tuesday after our Grande Opening there was a long line of people wanting sweets. I wasn't expecting that and it seemed like as soon as we got our cupcakes baked, cooled, and iced along with our cookies and other treats they were gone. Thinking that the fresh still warm out the oven cookies would be too much we were asking people to wait. It turned out that the warm cookies sold better than the still fresh but cooled cookies. Joy had a custom light made and whenever the light was on that meant we had fresh out of the oven cookies. Kind of like the donut place. I'm gonna tell you when that light was on; I'd have a line. We closed the bakery doors at six, and then Sherrell and I would prepare for the next day. That down time was spent cleaning the front of the bakery and then Sherrell would bake and decorate. Going at this pace was fine for the first few weeks. Now I'm starting to conk out. And Sherrell is right there with me. "I'm just getting a little tired, but everything is ok."

"Have you been cramping?" She asked searching my eyes.

"Um," I can't lie. I'm terrible at it, and especially in my place of worship. "Mom, I'm ok."

"Are you still coming over for dinner?" She put her hand on my stomach. I went from no belly-to-belly it seemed overnight. I was kind of relieved cause the lack of a belly was scaring me.

"Uh! A meal I don't have to cook or clean up after always sounds good to me."

"Is Andrew coming?"

"That's the plan, but he's been working more than usual these days."

She eyed me and then she said ok, she told Andre and I to come as early as we needed to. Joy told me to call her when I headed over, and she'd bring the kids. When we got home Andrew was on the phone and working away. He did a double take when he looked at me, he didn't even tell the person on the phone to hold or anything. He hurried to me and started touching my forehead, etc. asking me what was wrong. I told him my mom asked me the same thing. He said I looked a little pale, I told him I felt a little tired, but other than that I was fine. He told me to lay down and try to rest. I told him I wanted to get going to my parents' house so Andre could spend more time with Anthony and Veronica. Andrew told me to lay down and rest and that I couldn't drive myself, so I had to wait for him anyways. At first I protested cause I really didn't want to wait for him, but after he growled at me I decided to pick another battle.

I decided to take a bath to relax some and then lay down until Andrew was ready. I missed my old tub; this tub was nice, but not as nice as my old tub. Even though this house was a lot nicer than my old house, it still didn't feel like home to me. When I told my parents about the mansion Andrew was having built for us, my parents had the same reaction that I did initially. Then my mom in true her style got very excited. She likes to go look at the progress on the house more than I do. I showed her Derrick and Chantel's house and you should've seen how big her eyes got. When I showed her Sherrell's house she asked me why on earth was Sherrell working for me if she could afford a house like that. I told her Sherrell didn't need to work for me, but she did because she wanted to and liked what she was doing. Andrew and I agreed that our bedroom needed to be a haven away from the rest of the house. I can't wait to take a bath in the tub we're going to put in the master suite. Right now everything is in prints and layouts, his Uncle Timothy has a nice way of explaining things so that I understand them, and whatever Timothy doesn't explain Uncle Dale, his son Darren, or Ryder does. It still feels like a dream and unsettling. As I was soaking Andre yelled from around the corner, "KNOCK! KNOCK! MOMMY!"

"Yes baby?"

He refused to turn the corner I appreciated that. "Daddy said he needs to gauge how much time he has left. He said to ask you if the water is still hot or is it warm?"

I laughed, "Tell him it's hot warm."

"K!" Then I heard him run out the room to take care of business.

By the time I was lotioning up Andrew walked in the room. "Somebody is trying to make their presence known." He said as he touched my stomach. "When do we find out the sex?"

"A month or so, what do you have your heart set on?"

"A girl of course!"

"What if it's a boy?"

"Then next time it will be a girl."

"How many times are we gonna do this?" I wanted to hear what he thought.

"As many as you want but I wouldn't mind a whole clan. I'm thinking four at least."

"I'm one of four so ok. So we're talking five kids total?"

He got a thoughtful look, "maybe we should have five so that we have six total. When we take family vacations everyone has a partner."

"Oh my goodness Andrew really?"

"Yea, I'm serious. When we would take vacations I was normally the odd man out."

"I thought you said Malcolm didn't go?"

He exhaled, "he didn't. When my momma dated the pretty boy, we did a few family things. We try to keep up with the girls, but they still hold on to when our parents were together. It's hard to enjoy our time together sometimes, they're always rallying for their dad. Anyways, I guess we'll see when you get tired of having babies, deal?"

"Deal!"

****

"I love your resume. Chrystina we'll need to run a background check and if everything checks out, I'll call you shortly after to discuss next steps." I said

She looked like my reference to a background check caught her off guard. "Ok, well thank you for your time." She stood up uneasy. Paulette showed her out.

"What did you guys think?"

"She was ok, I just don't know why she reacted that way to hearing you say that you would run a background check." Joy said.

She was right, maybe she has a past that she's not proud of and she's trying to start over. "After the background checks we'll have our final candidates though so it should be good." I said as I started to get up.

"If you don't sit down!" Sherrell demanded.

"I'm saying!" Pearla co-signed, "You don't look good."

"We got to start baking guys. I'll sit." I felt like the child and not the boss.

Joy grabbed my hand and gently stroked it. "We're worried about you. We know you're used to Corporate America where things have to happen no matter what. You run this, it's ok to pull back and rely on us. We've got it all taken care of. Instead of waiting until you go out we should start the simple menu now. When you come back to work you can do the monthly specials like we talked about. But you are doing too much and we're worried. Don't push too hard." She said gently.

I looked at everyone who was surrounding me with love in their eyes. "Is this supposed to be an Intervention?"

Everyone smiled, "we got..."

We heard someone banging on the door. Liz ran out the door first. It was two young guys going crazy cause we were closed. Their eyes were red it looked like they had the munchies. Liz, Pearla, and Paulette immediately cursed the kids out so bad that my ears were bleeding. I didn't see the staff that was supposed to be outside. Sherrell called the shopping center security. The guys walked away and we went back in the kitchen. When I tried to help with the basic recipes Sherrell popped my hand. When I started pouting we heard glass shattering and then shouting. "WE JUST WANT SOME COOKIES!" One of the guys came running in the kitchen. Pearla grabbed a knife out of the wooden block. It was like he didn't realize what she had in her hand until she stabbed him. Joy and I screamed, while Liz and Paulette went after the other guy. The shopping center *Security* came in and he was scared. "Ma'am! Please put the knife down the guy said to Pearla. "Do you have a gun?"

"No, but..."

"I'm not putting anything down until somebody with a gun gets here!"

I could hear the other guy screaming. "Oh my god you guys!" The security guard exclaimed he was melting down worse than me. "They don't pay me enough to deal with this!" He was hysterical, "he's bleeding to death! And I don't want to know what they're doing to him in there! Help me!" He screamed.

"What you screaming for?" Curtis said standing in the doorway. The now crying security guard pointed towards the front and at the kid being held at knifepoint who was bleeding. "Stupid Mark! Don't soak your panties!" Then he looked at Pearla. "The police are on the way?" His voice was calm like this was an everyday occurrence for him.

Pearla looked at the still crying guard, "are they?" The guard shook his head yes while wiping his tears.

Curtis grabbed a towel then he took the knife from Pearla. He wiped the handle then he told the guard to take it. When he refused Curtis took out his gun and told him to take it. "I'm trying to make you the hero and you too busy crying like a little girl to get it!" The guard took the knife. Curtis told him how everything happened. That he fought the guy in the entry way and then he had to pick up the knife to defend himself against this guy. Then he told Pearla, Liz, and Paulette to leave.

I started getting light headed so I sat down, and as I rubbed my now cramping stomach. Andrew came in angry stepping on glass and everything while we were talking to the police. He was going to stand there and listen until he heard me taking deep breaths to calm myself. He looked horrified when he looked at my face. He told me we were going to the hospital to make sure I was ok. I was too light headed to protest even though I wanted to stay to make sure everything was locked up. When I stood up the room started spinning, Andrew grabbed me then he picked me up. Joy ran to get my purse. I kept telling Andrew I was ok, but he wasn't listening to me. He gave Joy the keys to my car and asked her to give them to Malcolm who was on his way. Andrew cursed all the way to the hospital and he was asking why no one thought to call for an ambulance. I told him I was fine the situation was stressful, and he reminded me that I was supposed to be avoiding stress.

Andrew parked all crazy in front of the emergency room entrance. He ran inside and he came back with a nurse and a wheelchair. The security guard tried to tell him he was going to have to move his car. Andrew used choice words as he told the guard to keep the car as he hit him dead in the chest with his keys when he threw them at him. Andrew looked like he was going to kill somebody. I asked him to please calm down. But he wasn't listening to me. My blood pressure was extremely high so they had me lay on my side, and eventually they asked Andrew to come away for a minute cause he was too nerved up. I needed to calm down, and when I finally allowed myself to cry my blood pressure started going back to normal. I let it all out and stopped trying to pull it back. It was all too much! My mom and dad, brother Terence and sister in-law came to the hospital. Since they were doing another ultrasound we hoped at least this time the baby would cooperate and let us see the sex, but baby difficult would not open those legs for nothing. Andrew finally laughed and said it had to be a girl cause she was a good girl like her momma and keeping her legs closed. I said it could be a boy and he looked at me, "now you know my son would have no choice but to sit with his legs open."

I shook my head as we did everything we could AGAIN to get the baby to move but baby difficult was being difficult on purpose. When the police came to the hospital to talk to me my blood pressure went up again. Andrew made them come out of the room and speak directly with him. My mom grinned as she watched Andrew handle them, "I guess it's safe to say my son in-law don't play!"

"Mom you have no idea." I shook my head. When the doctor came back to the room. Andrew told the officers to wait as he walked away from them mid-sentence to hear what the doctor was saying to me. She said since they had me there they were concerned about my iron levels and my pressure going back up. So they told me they wanted to keep me over night. There was a small debate over who got to stay with me. I thought my mom would back down because after all she was talking to my husband, but she would not. And well Andrew only backs down to his mom and me. Finally the doctor offered to have a cot brought in for my mom and she said they could both stay. When my mom went home to pack an overnight bag I had to calm Andrew down. I told him to imagine I was our daughter and her husband was telling me to go home. Andrew's eyes got big, and then he called my mom and apologized. By the time my dad brought my mom back Andrew was downstairs. Mom said he was going off on somebody.

****

"I can find a backup." Sasha was insisting.

"No! No! No! Please I can do this. Please don't take this from me." I

Sasha started crying, "I don't want you to hurt yourself just for one day. I will be ok, it's just a cake." She said

"No! It's not just a cake. It's my gift to you and it makes me feel special, wanted, and needed to be able to do this for you. Andrew's banned me from my own bakery, this is all I have!"

"Drew is going to be mad at me!"

"No he won't! I'll take all the blame, Sasha please let me do this for you!"

Sasha and I mapped out our plan to have me make her cakes at her house. I got to spend a lot of one on one time with Sasha, which was nice because we hadn't really had time, just the two of us alone. In a lot of ways she reminded me of Andrew, they called each other twin cousins so I guess there would be similarities in their personalities. She told me how hard Andrew was crushing on me way back in the beginning and all I could do was blush. Andrew has told me numerous times that he's always liked and wanted me. But I loved hearing the backup stories from others that support his claims.

Sasha

"Are you coming down with something?" My receptionist asked as I walked back to my

237

office.

"I hope not, my wedding is coming. I don't want to look sickly on my special day." I smiled as I walked into my office. I sat at my desk staring at the calendar. It seemed like a good idea to go off my birth control two months ago so that we could get this party started on our honeymoon. Now I sit here sick as a dog and afraid to take a test. The last time I took a test I got a false positive and it about broke my heart. I wasn't sick last time, but still I'm scared to find out. Plus, El is completely stressed with his parents right now; I don't want to burden him with another disappointment. I called my doctor to ask for a blood test. When I left a message for her with my symptoms she called me back in less than ten minutes. She told me to come in for the blood test and then to come see her directly. I took a deep breath and then I told my receptionist I would be out for the rest of the day. I called Malcolm and told him I was leaving for the day. He listened to my tone and then he said ok. He told me that Bonita was on me, and to call him if I needed him. I went to the lab and watched the technician take my blood. Then my phone rang it was Richard. "He's here!" I could hear nothing but joy in his voice.

"What room I'll come over in a bit?"

Richard was too excited which made me feel a little better, I don't know why.

My doctor squeezed me in, so her nurse assistant took me into the room. She looked me in my eyes, "Sasha where's your spark?"

"It's been a lot going on."

"I've been told I'm an excellent listener if you feel like you need to vent."

"It's a long story." I warned.

She sat down on the chair, "we got time."

I unloaded everything. I went all the way back to Hubby. I was in tears and a blubbering mess. Nurse Jasmine put her arms around me and told me everything was going to be ok. She warned me to stop looking back at Yussef. I told her I thought I was over him, but I still get tingles when I see him. She reminded me that I was marrying a man that I was in love with. By the end of our conversation she had me laughing so hard I was crying. Nurse Jasmine always helped me relax and laugh at things I normally wouldn't. When my doctor finally walked in she seemed confused by my red eyes and big smile. She looked at Nurse Jasmine with a big smile, "I see you've been working your magic again." Nurse Jasmine shrugged, "I do what I can."

"Can you pull Sasha's lab results for me while I check her out?" My doctor said. My doctor did her routine checkup to make sure I didn't have a virus while we waited for my results. Nurse Jasmine poked her head in the room and she asked my doctor to come out. My heart dropped I wondered if they found something, maybe I was dying. My doctor and Nurse came in the room. Nurse Jasmine held my hand and stroked it gently. My doctor had my lab results in her hands. "So Sasha I have good news and bad news." I exhaled; I looked down at the floor then back up at her. "I know how you like to plan things. The good news is that you're extremely fertile and you're pregnant, the bad news is that you'll have to be really careful about fitting into your dress."

For a minute I thought I didn't hear her right, but their smiles told me I did. I exploded in happy tears. Nurse Jasmine cried with me, I kept asking the doctor to say it again so that I knew I wasn't dreaming. My doctor scheduled my first prenatal visit then she gave me pamphlets and she told me which prenatal vitamins to get. I hugged Nurse Jasmine so tight and I thanked her for everything. As I walked to the Labor and Delivery side of the hospital I took inventory of my body. Everything felt normal and I was excited. Then I thought about Yussef, I guess this means I really am going to marry El. I love El and I look forward to being his wife, its that stupid blood in me that was kind of watching to see if he would step up at the last minute and change everything. This news makes everything final.

When I walked in the room as Richard was holding the baby with a huge smile on his face. His smile dropped a little when he looked at me. He asked me if I was ok and I told him I was fine. His girlfriend looked like she just got ran over by a truck. She didn't look happy or at peace. "Erica are you ok?"

"Yea, I'm just tired." She said with the sound of sleep in her voice. She turned her head to the side and knocked out.

I took a few pictures of Richard and my new little brother. He looked a lot like Erica but I could see Richard in his face. When Richard gave the baby to me he immediately started snapping pictures. When Erica started snoring we laughed. Richard said the snoring was new. "So Sassy baby what's up?" He said watching my eyes.

"Oh nothing much, pre-wedding jitters I guess."

He smiled really big, "I am so proud of you! If nothing else in my life turns out right, you are my biggest accomplishment." Then he kissed my forehead.

"Thanks, so.... What did you name this little guy?"

He smirked, "Richard of course!"

"Of course you did." Then I looked at him. "You gonna be ok leaving him behind for my wedding?"

Richard sucked his teeth, "he's coming! I got his baby tux already."

"Richard he'll barely be a month old then. Dan-Dan is gonna get you!"

"I don't have a choice. I'm walking you down the aisle. Erica refuses to stay behind knowing your momma is gonna be there. My family is going to be there, I don't have a choice."

"Why is she worried about my momma?"

He gave me a knowing look, "she's not stupid. Bless her little heart she was trying to keep up even with the belly."

I frowned, "why didn't you assure her everything was ok and that she had nothing to worry about?"

"She don't believe anything when it comes to your momma."

Erica's family came in droves; they kept asking if I was Richard's sister. And when he proudly said I was his daughter each one had the same reaction. I stayed for a while, but the obvious comments about money and how well Richard takes care of Erica were getting on my nerves. Reading my face Richard told Erica he'd be back. "Her family is ridiculous. You sure she's not about your money?" I asked.

Richard sighed, "it's the tradeoff I guess. I know she loves me. Would she love me if I was broke? Probably not. I'm going to have at least one more child with her. Would I be with her if your momma wasn't so stubborn? Probably not!"

"So that means you don't get to be with the person you love?"

He looked me in my eyes, "you know firsthand that you don't always end up with the person you love."

I blank stared at him, "I'm marrying my best friend!"

"I'm not saying he's not. I just know he isn't your first choice."

"Oh whatever! I am in love with El!"

"I'm not taking anything away from you and El. You guys are in love, but I'm your father. And Sophia is your mother, I know you!"

"Bye Richard!" I said huffing to my car.

As I pulled out of my parking spot a car pulled up and Richard got in. I didn't know if that was Mitigated or someone else. I turned the radio up as loud as it would go so that I wouldn't have time to think about my father's words on my way home.

El was home and on the phone with his parents when I walked in the door, his eyes smiled when he saw me. I went in the kitchen and made dinner while they chatted. I watched a cooking show while I cooked. I didn't want to allow my mind the chance to focus on Richard's words. When dinner was ready El came and gave me the biggest hug and kiss. He said he was going to miss me the two weeks I was gone before our wedding.

He said I've been his happy thought and force during all of this. We ate dinner and then we spent the evening wrapped up in each other. I laid on his chest listening to his heartbeat while he rubbed my back and kissed my forehead. He apologized for being so distracted with his parents. I told him not to apologize cause I would be the same way if it were my parents. I decided as I absorbed all the love he freely gave me to make our news my wedding gift to him. I thought about how excited he'd be and how long he's wanted this, and it was happening just as it should.

****

"When does El's parents come?" Amber asked.

"Next week, I'm so excited!" I could see Amber's knuckles turning white as she gripped the steering wheel. "Are you ok?"

She was trying to calm herself. "I hate the city."

"Do you need me to drive?"

"No, I'm ok. I can do this." She tried to control her breathing.

I looked back at Tina and her eyes were big watching Amber. My momma reached over and calmly rubbed her arm. Once we got to Cassondra's Amber was fine. I asked my momma what that was about and she said it was a long story.

"So Sasha are you excited for your big day?" Our consultant Nihjia asked me as she took us to the fitting room.

"I am! But I can't wait to see almost everyone in their dresses."

Tanisha was taking her seat next to Carina when we walked into my fitting area. "So do you want to go first or do you want everyone else to go?"

"Everyone else, especially since this will be my first time seeing Ava in her dress."

Nihjia gave each person their dress and they went in their dressing rooms. I leaned in to Tanisha and Carina and I asked how Tanisha's dress fit. She smiled real big and said pretty good. She said with the alterations it should fit like a glove. We high fived, and then one by one they came out. Each took turns standing on the pedestal and having their dresses pinned. I loved my colors they were nice spring colors even though it wasn't spring yet.

My dress was trumpet style with a sweetheart neckline. It hugged my body and left nothing to the imagination. I was so happy that it had rooshing, my stomach wasn't noticeable to everyone else and with the design of my dress I didn't see it either. I added a belt with rhinestones to match the brooch in the middle of my neckline. I was nervous about the fit. I didn't feel like I gained weight, but I wasn't sure. My dress zipped right up too easily though. Nihjia smiled and said I lost a couple pounds. It had to be all that throwing up I did. When I walked out everybody got weepy. When I stood on the pedestal I felt like the bride and I loved the feeling. Nihjia started pinning and I told her I didn't want my dress too tight. My momma kept shushing me and telling me the whole point of that dress was to be tight. Ava said we should definitely go with the side swept hair option. I got excited cause that was the one I really wanted. Then I tried on the dress options for Amber's wedding. They were all kind of whimsical in style to me. Since I didn't know what my body would look like then I ordered the most forgiving dress. Amber said she thought I would've picked the more form fitting style.

After the fittings we went back to our side of the bay where Amber relaxed. We went to Shylight lounge in Berkeley for dinner and drinks. Out of habit I ordered a glass of wine with my meal. I took a couple sips and then I let it sit on the table. My momma asked why I wasn't drinking my glass. I told her it wasn't agreeing with me. She looked at me then she looked away. I felt like I was going to get a whooping for not finishing. I was talking to the table while my momma kept checking me out. Then her eyes widened, she pulled me away from the table. "Sasha! How do you think you could hide something so huge from your momma?"

"I don't know..."

"Before you lie to me, I'm your momma and I know you! Nobody knows do they?" She asked staring me in the eyes.

I sighed, "no ma'am! I want it to be a surprise. Please don't say anything!" I begged.

"We have to tell my momma! And I will do my best not to tell Amber, but I make no guarantees."

"Momma!"

"The woman knows me like I know her. I'm just saying I'll try my best to keep it quiet." Then she hugged me like she was trying to squeeze juice out of me. "I'm too young for this! Oh well, I guess I can't tease Amber anymore." She smiled.

When we returned to the table Amber was watching us. My momma was avoiding Amber's eyes. I blew air cause it was only a matter of time before they were whispering. Ava asked Amber what her dress looked like and her eyes lit up. She explained it with so much love, I couldn't wait to see it.

****

"I gotta pee!" Tina said.

"Can you hold it, we're almost there?" My momma asked her.

"I've been holding it all this time, I'm about to pop!" She started dancing in her seat.

My momma blew air and turned into a hotel. "Sasha baby go with her."

"She's not a child!" I snapped.

"Come on, I'll go with you." Ava said.

"If you're going then I don't need to go." I snapped again.

"Stop flashing attitude Sassy and get your tail inside!" My momma barked.

Tina's eyes were big as she waited for me. "Are all the women violent in this family?"

I rolled my eyes, "what do you mean?"

"Auntie Amber goes off so easy!"

"You must be running your mouth too much! I've never had any problems with her."

I was fussing and following Ava. I stopped talking when I saw my cousin Sharon. Everyone yelled surprise, and immediately I felt like a witch for fussing like I had been. They put a glass of champagne in my hand, and then everyone came over to say hello. I was doing fine until I saw Mrs. Parsons. She traveled all the way out here early just to be here for my shower. I hugged her while I cried on her neck. I should've known they were up to something. My momma quietly took my glass from me. I could tell Amber and my Nana knew because they were full of as many tears as I was.

After my lovely and fancy shower we went back to my Nana's. My Nana pulled me away from everyone and up to her room. "My first grandbaby is going to have a baby!" She said holding my face as tears poured out of her eyes. "I am so happy for you!" She said kissing my forehead and then squeezing the life out of me. "How do you feel?"

"Other than moody, I feel pretty good. I miss El already and I just saw him yesterday. This is going to be a long two weeks."

"His mother is very nice. We've enjoyed her and her husband's company the past two days." My Nana gave me the run down. She said the Parsons were going to stay with them until Friday. Then Mr. Parsons would be with El and Mrs. Parsons would stay with me as planned. My Nana said my cousin Jennifer was in charge of their medical care, which is why they needed to stay in Sacramento for the first week, but she was coming to the Bay for the wedding.

Then there was a knock at the door, "who is it?"

"It's me," Mrs. Parsons' voice chimed in.

My Nana smiled, "come in Ruthie."

My momma and Amber were too nosey not to follow Mrs. Parsons in the room. "Sasha I love your family. I know my son is going to be in good hands." She smiled.

I hugged her. "Mrs. Parsons how are you feeling?"

"Oh I'm fine honey."

"Are you good at holding secrets?" I asked.

"Of course!"

"El doesn't know yet. I'm pregnant!"

She smiled really big, "that's why you didn't get smashed at your party. I expected you to get pissy." I love her accent. We hugged really tight and then she started crying. "When I get home I'm sending you everything! All of his awards, trophies, everything! Make sure you tell the baby about me!"

That did it; we all cried our eyes out. "Mrs. Parsons I think you should get a third opinion. I can't accept this."

"El says the same thing, we fight about it. I don't see the point in getting my hopes up."

"PLEASE! My baby deserves to know you. PLEASE!"

"Oh Sasha don't get fussy on account of me. We can talk about this after your wedding."

Tanisha came up to find out why we weren't downstairs with the smaller party of people here. As soon as she saw all of our red puffy eyes and runny noses she knew something was up.

****

"I told Malcolm you're working from his office in Oakland today." Amber said.

"You didn't have to do that. I could've gone to the city." I put my dishes in the dishwasher.

"That would've been too much. Fighting traffic to get over to the city, and then coming out here for your appointments. It's easier this way, and we'll see you this afternoon."

"Ok," I said in defeat, and then we got off the phone.

Ava came in the kitchen looking for coffee. I begged her to get dressed and come to work with me. She frowned and said no, I told her I was working from the office in the mall and she could shop while I worked. She swished the thought around her brain for a minute and then she got showered and dressed in record timing. When I pulled on the street I spotted my Mitigated tail right away. When we pulled up to the light the Mitigated car started flashing their turning signals first the right then the left then the right then the left. I told Ava we were taking the scenic route. I didn't know what was up, but I was following directions. Then Richard called I put him on speaker and I told him that Ava was in the car. He sighed, "Babygirl if you're going off script you gotta tell someone. Everything is fine go in. Good morning Ava." He sounded like a worried father.

"Good morning!" She said all bright and chipper like she normally does.

"Ok, love you. Talk to you later."

When we pulled up to the mall I parked next to Yussef's car. He got out at the same time we did. I introduced him to Ava. I told him she was going to be shopping while I worked.

"Ava I need a favor." Yussef said, she smiled. "My friend Darlene is coming in a few minutes to do some shopping as well. Would you mind if she tags along with you?" Yussef held the door open for us as we walked inside the office.

"Is she weird or rude?" Ava asked.

"No, she's good people."

"Of course but I'll have to drop off whenever Sasha's ready to go."

"That's fine."

I took Ava into Malcolm's office; Ava said it looked like dust was afraid to exist in here. A few minutes later Yussef was in the doorway with a beautiful woman. He introduced her as his friend Darlene and immediately I felt jealous. She was nice, but the way her eyes scanned the room I realized she was Mitigated staff. Yussef walked them to the front door as they chatted like old friends.

Yussef came back and asked me if I was ok as he handed me a water bottle. When I said I was ok he asked why did I look at Darlene the way I did. I told him I didn't know who she was. "Who else could she be? You know our situation is hostile right now."

242

"She could've been another girlfriend for all I know." I spit.

Yussef leaned against the doorway and put his hands in his pocket. "But you sound jealous."

Busted! "Come in shut the door." He stood up straight and frowned at me. I put my hands up, "I'm gonna stay seated." He came in and sat in the chair in front of the desk. I know this was the chicken way to do this but he had me up against the ropes. "Please keep my secret. I'm pregnant and I don't want to tell El until the wedding. My moods swing all over the place. I'm not blind; I saw the way she looked at you. I didn't like it!"

He frowned, "women!" Then he stood up. "Congratulations!" He spit at me.

"Ok now you sound jealous." I sat back in my chair.

He sat down. "I want that experience as well. The wedding, the news, the growing belly, the newborn, and watching my child grow. I didn't meet either of my girls until almost a year ago. The death of my grandmother brought on a new life and existence for me."

"You don't see that happening with Sylvia?" Inside I was hoping he said no.

"I don't know. I don't feel like that's the right option for us."

"Why? She obviously loves you. You have a beautiful family. Seems like it's all setup for you."

He exhaled, "there's more to it than just that."

"Why are you with her if you don't know?"

"Long story, but in the end. That's who I'm with. I can't see marrying her. She knows that, we've discussed it. Wouldn't be fair to have more kids just because. So I'm just here."

"You don't have to be with her. You're handsome, smart, and a good guy Yussef. Very marketable."

"I used to think so. But I don't have the stomach for the game. Angela..." His voice trailed off.

"Yea, the ordinary girl. What happened to her?"

He eyed me, "you trying to say she was ugly?"

"No, she wasn't ugly. But she wasn't HOTT! She must've been a really good person."

He leaned forward on the desk and clasped his hands. "She was to me."

"I guess! Beauty is in the eyes of the beholder."

"It is, and she was beautiful! Until...." He frowned and sat back, "until the baby momma's. It's not her fault, at least she knows she couldn't handle it despite my best efforts to assure her they didn't matter." He shook his head, "I don't know what happened."

"I'm gonna tell you what happened. She thought you were too good for her. I bet she never had a boyfriend as fine as you. She didn't present herself like," I was looking for the words. "Let's take me for example." He chuckled, "I wouldn't second guess why you were with me. That insecurity would not come across. What you would know and only you is that I would constantly check-in to make sure you didn't need something I overlooked. With her, she didn't look in the mirror with appreciation for who she is. So naturally she sees the baby momma's and immediately feels inadequate. You would've exhausted yourself trying to please her." He grinned at me. "What you need to do is ask yourself, does she have the **Sasha factor**!" He belly laughed as he blushed. "Is she confident enough to be with you. And I'm gonna tell you neither one of your baby momma's have it either."

"What?"

"At your sister's wedding both of them questioned me. Insecurities on their sleeves!"

"Can you blame them?" He smiled.

"Nope! But if all I had to offer was beauty I'd be nervous about me too. Shoot I'm the complete package!" I smiled, "but sometimes that isn't enough." I gave him a knowing look.

His eyes went around the room, "we had this conversation. I thought we were cool."

"We are cool until you start acting weird."
"How do I act weird?"
"You act more comfortable around Tracy than you do me, and that hurts!"
He slouched, "you know about that? Drew talks too much!" We laughed, "I don't know. Maybe because I had to be around her every day. I know her, you... you like to surprise attack people. I feel like I always gotta be on guard with you."
"How many years ago was that? I'm basically married."
He looked me in my eyes, "you will always be different."
Electricity shot up my leg. I started tapping my foot under the desk. "You too!"
He smiled, "I figured. How many times you gonna sneak that I'm fine in the conversation?" He smiled at me. "So, Malcolm put me on young Eldridge next week. When his family comes I'm taking them around sightseeing. He's not gonna try to push me off a ferry is he?"
I smiled, "El knows everything. He knows I was always the one."
"He can use my office when he comes. I'm gonna be working from home more." Then he stood up, "I'm gonna be honest." He took a deep breath, "I'm happy for you. I know you and El will be happy together. I was going to try and fake the funk and come to the wedding. I can't do it. I'll see you guys around."
I tapped my foot harder, "Yussef, I wanna say I understand. But that would be a lie."
"Timing was never on our side. I know you'll be beautiful. Take care Sasha." Then he walked out the door.

Chantel

I feel like I can't get any bigger. I move real slowly especially in the morning. We needed to get over to Sasha's wedding site pronto, but I could only move so fast. Sasha hadn't arrived yet so I went up to the room that Carina was keeping Sasha away from and out of, that contained my dancers. Carina had a camera set up so they could see the ceremony as if they were downstairs. They had plenty of food and drinks to keep them comfortable until show time. I told everyone they looked beautiful then I found a seat downstairs. Sasha's father was carrying his son around like a trophy that he was too proud to carry. His mother was getting on his case constantly saying the baby was too little to be out in the air like he had him. His mother was nice about it; I couldn't imagine Amber being that nice about her grandchild's health. I was thankful when they opened the tent so that I could take my seat inside and get comfortable. Malcolm felt the need to guide me to my seat. I did look like I was going to pop so ok.

Sasha

Rosalind did a wonderful job on my makeup. I loved it, but I dang near ruined it watching her do Tanisha's makeup. Each stroke and each brush conveyed how much Rosalind was enjoying this moment. She couldn't stop crying as well. Tanisha looked so beautiful! Ava did an amazing job on her hair, and then Rosalind lovingly enhanced her natural beauty with a few touches of makeup. I have NEVER seen my sister look like this. I snapped a picture of her initial reaction to her appearance. Tanisha stared at herself for a long time. Her eyes watered and she said she loved it. Since Tanisha was my surprise to everyone she got ready in her room. Carina was in charge of getting her outside at the last minute.
I was getting married at the Dupree Mansion at the very top of Oakland. The view of the city below was breath taking. In all my life in Oakland I had never heard of this place. But it was a classic beauty; high ceilings antique furnishing, floor to ceiling mirrors, pillars and columns. If the beautiful statues and a tree lined LONG driveway didn't get you on the way in, the house in all its Regal Grandness did. Our ceremony is being

performed under a beautiful white tent, which is huge and spacious enough to cover all of these Wallace's and Cardell's. I was so relieved that the weather cooperated with my request and gave us beautiful California weather to celebrate my nuptials. The ceremony began with Mr. & Mrs. Parsons strolling down the aisle. My uncle Philip escorted my Auntie Samira after My grandfather and Dan-Dan walked down the aisle. Derrick escorted my momma and then he went back to Chantel. My cousin Whitney was very disappointed when I had her walk with Drew. She just knew she was walking with Darryl. But Darryl was going to escort Tanisha; Brody was going to escort Ava. All of the guests took their seats inside the tent. Carina said everyone oohed and awed when they entered cause it was so big and beautiful inside. When Carina and I walked to the top of the stairs, Richard smiled a mile wide. When we got to him he squeezed me tight, then he kissed my forehead like four times. He told me I was breathtaking, and ok I know I've always given him such a hard time. But I loved this moment with just us as he admired me. When Carina rushed Tanisha past us he gasped, "Was that T?" I smiled at him and he had the most intrigued and curious look.

As we glided down towards the tent Darryl was jumping up and down very animatedly as he couldn't get over Tanisha. "WHO THE HECK ARE YOU?" He said beaming with pure excitement. Ava and Brody walked inside. "Tanisha you are stunning if I do say so myself big sister. Please keep this up! Even if it's only once a month, you deserve it!"

"The dress, the whole get up?" She frowned.

"No, being yourself and not hiding behind baggy clothes. I heard the stories."

"Oh brother!" She rolled her eyes.

Richard cleared his throat and they smiled at me. "There's my other big sister. If it wasn't for this wedding I'd say we should hit up EA tonight. Sasha, you are a beautiful bride I can't even believe it."

Carina cleared her throat to get Darryl's attention cause he was running off at the mouth. I didn't even have to see his face to know he was giving a toothy grin as he escorted Tanisha down the aisle. Richard kissed my forehead one more time as they opened the tent for us to descend. It was just like I dreamed, everyone smiling at me and taking me in as the most beautiful bride! I caught sight of Yussef and his family sitting with Malcolm; I knew Tanisha would make him change his mind. Everybody was smiling at Tanisha except Drew. His face was very serious without a real expression. He looked at her and then he looked away. El's smile couldn't shine any brighter as he watched me walk towards him.

After the ceremony, the guests were invited to have appetizers while the wedding clan went out on the lush green lawn and took pictures. I was so happy that my parents were being cordial, but they didn't have a choice their significant others were right there. I saw my momma looking at the baby, I could tell she wanted to hold him but she didn't ask. I understood why, it was still too new.

Drew didn't say anything to Tanisha all night. He looked at her a few times but quickly, Tracy gushed enough for the both of them. As everyone was taking pictures I pulled El to the side. "El baby are you happy?"

"This is the best day! Nothing could make me happier than I am in this moment." He said looking at me with love in his eyes.

"Are you sure, cause I could think of something."

He smiled, as if he was going to say yea right. I could see the idea light up above his head. "Don't play with my emotions!" He eyed me. I smiled and shook my head yes, "OH MY GOD! I LOVE YOU SO MUCH!" He said rushing me and picking me up as he hugged me and slightly ran with me. When everyone looked at us with questions, he yelled "SHE'S HAVING MY BABY!" Then he kept kissing me. So much that those who came over to congratulate us eventually walked away cause El was in his own world with me at the center of it.

Chantel

That night I awoke to stomach pains. I wasn't due for another two weeks. Derrick calmly called the advice nurse and they told him that I was probably in labor and to come in so they could check me. Derrick said he wanted to wait until the contractions were closer together cause it could be false labor. I wanted to slap the taste out of his mouth. If he felt what I was feeling he wouldn't be calmly talking about false labor. I went back to sleep. I woke up a few hours later with another contraction. This kept happening every few hours, which was annoying, it was like every time I would get to sleep real good, then here comes the pain. Amber called to check on us, and she called in the middle of a contraction. It seemed like she and Malcolm were there five minutes later. Amber came in the room, Malcolm stayed in the hallway barking at us telling us we needed to go to the hospital. When Derrick said they would send us home if I wasn't in active labor, Malcolm told him to pack me up cause we were going and they weren't sending me home. I tucked my braids in a knit cap and I made my way slowly to the doorway. Then Derrick picked me up, Malcolm told him he should've done that in the first place. I had never witnessed Malcolm and Derrick fussing at each other. I kind of forgot I was in labor watching them going back and forth. Both of them had to be right and have the last word. Malcolm called the hospital administrator and told them we were on our way and to have the wheelchair by the curb when we arrived. I didn't worry about anyone recognizing me cause if they did oh well. When I got in the bed in the labor and delivery room. Amber said all her babies were delivered in this hospital. Malcolm announced from the door that he was going to get my Grandma Rosa. We laughed cause he wanted nothing to do with being in the room with us. I wasn't pushing or being checked but he didn't care. Once I was in the bed my contractions seemed to slow down. At first we played cards, but then a nurse told me to walk around to move things along. I didn't feel like walking but I did it anyways. When Sherrell and Cyrus came I asked where my Babygirl was and Sherrell said she was with her momma. Another contraction hit me and it was a big one. I was done with walking I didn't care what they said. Grandma Rosa came in the room and walked past everyone. She put her hands on my stomach, "Grandma Rosa is here little one. Come on out!" She said rubbing my stomach. A few minutes later my water broke and then the **PAIN**! I told Derrick I didn't care what the birthing plan was I needed an epidural. He grabbed an innocent male nurse and brought him in the room by his collar. He told him to get my doctor cause I needed drugs. The nurse was so spooked he did as he was told. After they doped me up I drifted off into la la land.... and then I awoke to extreme uncomfortableness. The doctor said the baby was in position and it was time to meet my little person. Malcolm and Cyrus were in the waiting room with the rest of our family. First I felt relief then I heard her cry loud and hard. Derrick cut the cord, and then they handed him our baby girl. Amber, Ms. Laverne, and Grandma Rosa snapped picture after picture of Derrick and Chanel who were in their own little world staring at each other. I had to tell Derrick to give her to me. Amber was crying as she held onto her son. "She looks just like me doesn't she!" He smiled proudly. He was right; I looked at her face for a trace of me anywhere in there. All I saw was Derrick, and she was so tiny and precious. After they cleaned me up and removed all the gross parts, they let my huge family come in. Darryl held her and then he looked at Derrick then he looked at the baby. "I always thought you would make a ugly girl! I'm so happy I was wrong!" Malcolm smacked Darryl upside the head. So in hindsight the delivery wasn't so horrible that I wouldn't do it again. I just didn't know when. Malcolm commanded that Mitigated staff stay planted right outside my door at all times. The hospital staff was already too excited about me being there.

In the morning my grandma insisted that I take my shower early. When I stepped out the shower she was in the bathroom with bandages. She scared me cause I wasn't expecting her to be right there, and hello I was naked but she didn't care. She made me put on an interesting lotion like cream and then she wrapped me up almost like a mummy. She left my breast out for the baby, but almost everything else got wrapped. I told her this was going to make going to the bathroom interesting. She said a month from now I was going to thank her. When my doctor came in to check me out, she asked about the bandages. Grandma Rosa told her I would have my body back before my husband did. Derrick and I blushed; I couldn't believe she said that. She said people pay way too much money for stuff like this, but she guaranteed it worked.

Kendra

"KB!" Darryl was coming into my room. "She's here! Chantel had the baby! She looks just like D-Rick!"
"Congratulations!" I turned over to look at his excited face.
He was extremely happy, "how can something so small make so many people so happy?" He stripped down next to my bed.
"Babies always make people happy. That's what they're programmed to do."
Darryl got in the bed and got on top of me. "I can't believe both of my brothers are fathers now." Then he kissed me. "When are we going to stop playing this stupid game and have some babies of our own?"
"Game?"
"Yes! This is a stupid game. I'm not even holding back with you anymore. Do you even remember what condoms felt like?" He kissed me; "whenever you decide to stop taking those pills we can get this show on the road."
"I can't do that, I'm seeing someone remember?"
"KB! You better be happy I'm on a baby high right now. Cause talking about irrelevant people is a mood killer."
"Well…." That's all I could get out before Darryl went in. I promise it felt like he was trying to get me pregnant this time. He went in deep, he went in stronger, and he kept going all night. When I opened my eyes in the morning he was gone. I don't even know what that was. Our night together could've been a figment of my imagination.

Episode 14

Amber

"Honey there's nothing wrong with hanging with football players, celebrities, all that. But there's a certain way you need to conduct yourself. Especially if you're going to be in the limelight. Personally I didn't like that life. And if you choose to date someone in that light they have to be strong. They have to try to maintain some privacy."
"People barely remember who you are." Then she caught her tone. She put her hands up, "I'm SORRY!"
I eyed her a minute then I caught my reflection in the mirror. I could see my momma's eyes locked on her. Everything in me deflated. "I am happy that, that phase in my life is over. It's bad enough that now we have to have staff following us around all the time. Gwen has lived her whole life like this, she doesn't know any different. At least we know a little different. You can't be out there stirring the pot. What you do and how you conduct yourself affects us."
She looked at me with tear filled eyes, "where's Luke Auntie?"
"I don't know baby. Tell me something, why were you so scared of him?"
"He has a bad temper sometimes, and I know he was upset cause he was missing me. I didn't want things to go like they did. Now he's really going to be angry when he sees

me."

"If your momma gave you back your phone right now what would you do?"

"Call Luke."

"Why?"

"Cause I don't want him to be mad at me."

"Why does it matter if he's mad?"

"Cause he gets angry. And then it's bad."

I touched her hand, "honey what are you trying to tell me?"

"I'm not going to explain it right. All you're going to hear is that…" her voice trailed off.

"Does he make you mad?"

"Sometimes."

"What do you do when he makes you mad?"

"I don't say anything because it escalates."

"How did you meet this guy?"

"I was at this party with my girl. We were drinking and carrying on. The old guy who normally follows me around wasn't there, so we really let our hair down. This guy approached me and I wasn't interested. But he wouldn't take no for an answer. Luke swooped in and saved me. At first I wasn't feeling him cause he didn't really have any money, no car, etc. But he was really sweet to me. Before I knew it I was in love with him."

"Then it started with something like a push, or a slap didn't it? Then slowly but surely it escalated? And every time he made you feel like you did something to provoke him?"

"Yes but I know I have a smart mouth."

"You sure do! But you got it honestly. Out of the four of us, they say I act like my momma the most, and my mouth always got me in trouble. Unlike you I learned to curve it, I could never imagine talking to Auntie Lauren the way you tried to talk to me. But I guess I'm no different than, what's that boy's name?"

"Luke?"

"Yea, him. Tell me something why did you know it was wrong when I hit you, but for him it was ok?" She opened her mouth then she closed it. She looked at me confused.

"I've been there honey. It took my momma dying for me to remember that she was the only person who put fear in me. And that fool had nothing on her."

Her eyes were open wide, "Uncle Malcolm hits you?"

"ARE YOU CRAZY! ABSOLUTELY NOT!" I shook my head. "There was this other guy I dated that did that. The other morning when I woke up screaming, he was coming after me. It's been years since all of that transpired. But I still suffer from the residuals from time to time." Tina's eyes were big in amazement; she was hanging on my every word as I explained what happened with David.

"Auntie! That's it! That's exactly how I felt."

"The last time I saw him I finally accepted what everyone was trying to tell me. One day it wasn't just gonna be a bruise that eventually goes away. Or a busted lip, or whatever. I had to protect my family from him. He knew me as Amber, he had no idea who Amber Wallace was."

"Do you still see him?"

"No, eventually they found him dead."

"Who killed him?" She asked with her eyes completely wide.

"I don't know for sure."

"It was probably Malcolm."

She caught me off guard with her matter of fact accusation. "Why would you say that?" She shrugged, "he's very possessive of you. He's not bad with it or anything. He's like my daddy, if there's anything upsetting my mom, my daddy is determined to fix it."

"That's nice."

FINALLY! I was making some progress with this girl. She even agreed to come with me on my next video shoot. I told her she could see everything from the ground up.

We made dinner together, and then Malcolm came home. We sat at the table together and ate; Malcolm was quiet the entire time. A little more than normal for my liking. He was acting a little weird. Just before nine Yussef called he said he was outside, he wanted to know if it was ok to come in. I frowned at Malcolm, and then I asked him when he ever needed to get permission to come in my house? When he walked in the door his face was completely serious, and his eyes were locked on Malcolm. "Malcolm this isn't going to go away!"

"I know that. I told you I would get back to you tomorrow."

"Amber needs to know about this. We need damage control on this end."

My heart started beating a thousand times a minute. "What is it?"

"You are too eager, you think I wouldn't tell my woman?"

"That's not my point. I have to move on this tonight. I can't wait until the morning."

"You said it was in editing and proofing."

"They approved and sent to press."

Malcolm looked at Tina. "Go upstairs and shut your door." Tina very obediently did as she was told. Malcolm looked at me, "Amber please sit." I sat next to Yussef who set a folder on the coffee table. "It's Torrie, someone is stirring old drama."

"What do you mean by someone?"

"The story is somewhat accurate, it raises too many questions."

"Is it Torrie?"

"She wouldn't risk the negative effects on her good girl reputation." Yussef said.

"HA! Good girl my butt!" Malcolm watched me. "So who then?"

"It could be one or two persons or a combination of both."

"Like?" I said rolling my hands.

"Toya or Sonya or both." Malcolm mimicked me by rolling his hands. "Or the pretty boy."

I blank stared at Malcolm, "you won't be satisfied until you hurt him will you?"

He smiled at me, "no I won't."

I rolled my eyes, "leave him alone." Then I looked at Yussef. "Who is Sonya?"

"Nicole, Hubby's wife's friend. The girl Sasha beat up at your engagement party."

"Oh yea! The busy body. She wouldn't? Would she?"

"She has motive, we're going to find out." Then Yussef stood up, "someone's going to have to talk to Torrie."

My temper FLASHED! "By someone you mean him!" I pointed at Malcolm. "ABSOLUTELY NOT!"

Malcolm gave Yussef an *I told you so look*. Yussef huffed, "Amber, I know there's bad blood there. But it has to happen, we need to know what position her publicist is going to take."

I rolled my eyes at both of them. "No! Somebody else can do it! No! No! No!"

"What if he does it right here. Right now? On speaker."

"Very funny, very slick, nice try. NO!"

Malcolm sat back very tickled, "nobody seems to believe me when I say I know my Queen." He smiled at me. "Look Amber I understand how you feel. I don't like it either but this is what has to happen and it needs to happen now. So that there's no misunderstanding, I want you here when I call. Sit down and stop tensing up. This is for the family; it's bigger than just us. Yussef give me the number." Yussef looked at me with big eyes like he didn't know if I was going to go off some more. I sat down but he had to know this wasn't over. Yussef gave Malcolm the number and then he watched my face. Malcolm dialed the number and put the phone on speaker. "Hello?" The sound of her voice made me madder. There was a lot of noise in the background like she was at a club or something.

"Torrie!"

"Yes, who is this?"

"You need to go somewhere so you can hear me!" Malcolm's voice was deep and unaffectionate.

Torrie gasped and then I heard her telling someone in the background she'd be right back. She kept saying excuse me; excuse me as if she was walking through a crowd. Then a door closed and it was silent. "Hello?" She said with curiosity in her voice.

"Torrie!"

She gasped again, "OH MY GOD MALCOLM!!! Where have you been? You completely disappeared! I was just...."

"This is not a social call!" She whined like a baby. I shot daggers at Malcolm; Yussef's eyes were glued to my face. "The tabloids are about to run some pretty damaging stories about you, what position is your publicist taking?"

"He called me a few hours ago, but I wasn't sure. I thought you were him." She sounded disappointed.

"Call him now on three way!"

"Ok! Ok! Hold on!" She said messing with her phone.

She brought her publicist on the line and Malcolm and the guy discussed in detail his plan of attack on the situation. The guy asked why any of this mattered to Malcolm; he simply said this little rumor has bigger implications than they need to understand. When Torrie started shamelessly throwing herself at Malcolm, he looked at me and then he told her to cut it out. Yussef scooted back in his seat, trying to take himself out of the line of fire. When Malcolm was satisfied with the information he got, he didn't say goodbye or anything he hung up. I was pissed. He told Yussef he knew what to do next and then he prepared himself cause he knew I was about to go off! Yussef hurried out the door.

****

"Tony can you escort the new student to Ginger's class?" Jade said.

"Certainly," Tony walked with the single mother and her son to Ginger's class.

"How's she doing?" .

"You can tell. She's always taking everything in but she asks too many questions. I guess we're supposed to be stupid.".

"Emerald asked me why she wasn't assisting in that class anymore."

"What did you tell her?"

"I told her we pulled all our babies out of that class so that they could embrace other forms of dance. Andre didn't seem to mind or really care about the change in dance style, he seems to flow with everything." I couldn't help but be proud.

"Like his daddy." Jade smiled.

"Like his Nana!"

Tony came back to the receptionist desk with a smile. "I'll have those digits before I go home."

"If you're going to take on another girlfriend you're really going to need that second job." I joked.

Tony didn't laugh, "I quit that job." He said dryly.

"Oh really? When?" Jade asked eyeing him.

"A few months ago. It's not a big deal!" Tony said defensively.

His reaction made Jade and I stare at him for a minute, he was flashing major attitude and this was not his normal way of being. Jade turned her attention back to me, "I finally have the kid's passports. I'll give them to you this weekend."

"Going somewhere?"

I smiled really big, "I want to take a European Tour with everybody instead of just me and Malcolm for our honeymoon." Tony frowned, "what? It's just an idea at this point.

250

That or the Wallace's take over a cruise ship, either way we need everyone to have their passports."

"Does Malcolm know you're planning all of this on his alone time with you?"

"No, but as long as I'm happy he's happy." I eyed Tony trying to figure out where the attitude was coming from.

"A honeymoon is supposed to be you and your woman. Why would you make it a family trip?" He shook his head.

"Why does it bother you how they decide to spend their time together?" Jade asked watching Tony.

"It doesn't! I'm just saying that she should at least talk to Malcolm about all of this before she goes setting her heart on it and then it doesn't happen."

"Tony in all these years of you working here I guess you've overlooked an extremely important ingredient to Malcolm's world.... **ME**! If I'm happy, he's great! If I wanted to take the entire Wallace clan on a trip to the moon *my* Malcolm would make it happen for me."

"It must be nice! He does that for you, what do you do for him?"

I frowned, "he gets to be with me. DUH!" I said as a joke, but Tony didn't laugh.

"I wonder, with Malcolm's life and all the balls he has up in the air, why would he jeopardize all of that by having you all around?"

I started to respond and Jade pulled me into her office. I was going to get in his face and it was going to be bad. Jade told me he must be going through a dry spell cause he's been moody lately. When Jade thought I was calm enough for her to walk behind her desk, I hopped right up and snatched the door open. "Tony! If you're in a bad place today, tomorrow, or whenever DON'T YOU EVER IN YOUR LIFE DO THAT AGAIN! WHAT HAPPENS IN MY FAMILY IS NONE OF YOUR BUSINESS! SINCE I THOUGHT WE WERE ALL FAMILY, I ENJOYED SHARING WITH YOU! SINCE WE NOW KNOW THAT YOU CAN'T CONTROL YOUR PMS LIKE THE REST OF THOSE REJECTS, I WILL NOT BURDEN YOU WITH THE DETAILS OF MY LIFE AND FAMILY!"

"Amber calm down, I was just pointing out a fact. Sometimes the truth hurts!"

"Oh ok, well here's some truth for you. The reason why you keep ending up single is because you act like a freaking female! You set your sights too high and you're never content with what you have. You need to provide for yourself, what you want a female to come to you with and then things might start turning around for you!" His face completely dropped and then I was satisfied, I slammed the door.

When I turned around Jade was shaking her head. "You act too much like momma sometimes! I know what he said hurt your feelings but you could've let it go. He was stupid for going there but you just stooped right down there with him."

"I was happy, in a good mood. Who asked him for his two scents? He's just jealous."

"He was wrong, but you didn't have to go there too. That's all I'm saying."

"You're saying that cause he was talking about Malcolm. What if he was talking about Sonny?" I gave her a knowing look.

Jade's mouth clinched, "you already know." Then she laughed, exactly.

****

There is no feeling like holding your grandchild for the first time. Malcolm couldn't stop smiling when they told us her name, Chanel Dareese Latour Mason. Malcolm and Derrick hugged hard and manly, I guess that made him emotional. The two of them hugging it out had to be aggressive and loud. Malcolm even initiated the hug between he and Chantel. I kept looking at my baby's baby and remembering what it felt like to hold Derrick for the first time. He's my only baby that I purposely had, the only time I was excited to be pregnant. And now he has a family of his own. It seems like only yesterday he was born and now he's over here smiling with a family of his own. I hugged and kissed Derrick to the point of embarrassment. I kept telling him how well he's done and how proud I am of him.

Malcolm was sitting in a chair watching us and almost smiling, I walked behind him and put my arms around him. I told him our baby has a family of his own. Auntie Lorraine and Dionne walked into the room. Auntie Lorraine looked at me with my arms around Malcolm and then she focused on Derrick, Chantel and the baby. They took a bunch of pictures with both of them holding the baby. Dionne was having a good day and she cried while holding her great grand baby. It was so touching to see her understanding the moment.

Until… when she sat down. She sat next to Malcolm, and she asked him who he was. He said he was my fiancé, and she looked at me confused. Then she asked Derrick if he was back with Patricia, he told her that he was married to Chantel. Malcolm looked at her like he was waiting for her to reveal something he could use. Auntie Lorraine started getting their jackets and her purse. Then Dionne said, "See I told you he wasn't trying to kill you." She said to Derrick.

My heart dropped and I looked at Malcolm, he had no reaction he watched Dionne. Auntie Lorraine told her to hush and then she started apologizing for her sister. As if we didn't know the story, "She hasn't been right since she had that stroke. One time she was telling me how sad her own funeral was." Auntie Lorraine said nervously, because she was concerned about ruining the good vibes in the room.

"David you called me! Tell her I'm not crazy. Patricia you were crying in the background. It was the last time we spoke. You told me you are really sorry for everything. You told me to tell Amber that you were sorry, and to explain to her son that you understood he was protecting his momma. And you told me to tell Derrick and Darryl…" she was trying to remember. No one moved or made a peep, we were waiting for her to say. "You were sorry that they had to be related to you. Yes, you loved them but you knew they were poisoned by you the moment you laid eyes on them."

"What is that supposed to mean? My children aren't poisoned!" I said feeling every ounce of blood rush to my face. "My sons aren't monsters like he could be! How could he say that?"

"Amber, I'm sorry! We don't even know if this is true. Dionne isn't all there." Then she looked at Chantel and Derrick. Derrick was now sitting on the bed in Chantel's arms, "I'm sorry you guys. She doesn't know what she's saying."

Dionne looked at Malcolm, "my son wasn't the monster. He is! You killed him didn't you! Then you sit up and play daddy to my grandchildren smiling that the baby I birthed into this world is gone!"

"Would you believe me if I said no?"

"NO!" She yelled, "You never wanted David with Amber, and they had a family and were in love. That's why you killed him isn't it!"

"Would you believe me if I said no?" Malcolm repeated.

"I will cut you! Keep messing with my son! He and Amber are in love, deal with it!"

"What about Patricia?" Malcolm said sarcastically.

Then she looked at Chantel with tears in her eyes, "David is a good man. He doesn't mean it when he does stuff like that. Please don't call the police I will talk to him he will be better. He's going to come see you and Doyle just hold on ok sweetheart! He's going to be so happy to introduce all the boys, ok sweetie?" She said to Chantel who was now balling as she held on to Derrick who couldn't hide the pain on his face.

"Gram, can you tell David something for me?" Darryl stood.

She looked confused, "you mean tell yourself? You're trying to confuse me."

"NO! I'm Darryl! Dar-ryl! Tell David to leave us alone! Tell him we are healthy and strong now that he's not around. The best thing he ever did for us was to get in trouble and die! That way he could stop hurting us by hurting our momma! Tell him to get out of your head cause he doesn't live in mine! Tell him to stop making it hard for me to get to know you, because you're constantly mistaking me for a dead man. A man who I clearly remember grabbing my momma! The only real memory I have of him is angry and evil. Nobody messes with my momma! Tell him to leave her **ALONE!**"

Dionne started crying, "when Amber has the baby DON'T FORGET ME OK!"

"Come on Dionne!" Auntie Lorraine said crying her eyes out. "I'm sorry you guys!" I walked over to Auntie Lorraine and I hugged her, "I'm sorry baby."

"You told me to leave, it's not your fault. Even though David was your family you still looked out for me. I love you, please don't pull away now."

"She's making up extra kids and stories." Auntie Lorraine was embarrassed.

"This is your family too. If I arrange to have someone come look after Dionne will you and your husband come to our wedding? Don't answer now, sleep on it and answer when you're ready."

"Thank you baby, I'll call you." Then she walked out with Dionne.

Malcolm was watching me, but I was looking at the effects of Dionne's words on my babies. I walked over to Darryl and I put my arms around him, "even though she's crazy. You know he said it don't you."

"I'm sorry baby, I don't know if that's true or not."

"It's true, he said something like that to me once. I guess he was supposed to be passing on his evil." Derrick said still holding that pained look on his face.

"Both of you are better than him on his good days, on your worst days."

"I know momma, I just hate when she calls me by his name.".

"I guess she does that because you look like him."

Darryl blew air, "PLEASE! David wishes he was this fine! I know I look way better than him!"

"You are way more handsome than he could ever imagine to be." I smiled.

"I know it! I know she don't know what to say to me when she goes into her whole David! David routine! But I know what will fix it."

Derrick pointed his eyes at Darryl, "don't!"

Darryl put his hands up and walked back to his seat. I guess he was going to say something too silly for Derrick to handle right now. Then Andy, Andre, and Tracy walked in the door. Darryl shot out of his chair, "THANK GOODNESS YOU'RE HERE!" He said hurrying to the door. "Tracy I need you!"

She smiled, "you need me?"

"Yes, let me know what time you're leaving I need to come to your house. I need a red velvet STAT!" He put his arm around her shoulder.

Andy frowned at him, "why would I want my wife slaving in the kitchen for you?"

"Drew! Man! Dionne was here saying some stuff." Then he put his finger on his temples, "I'm hanging on by a string! I need red velvet to navigate this emotional roller coaster. Please let her do it for me man! I haven't begged about a red velvet in months."

"Sharon is on her way up, ask her."

Darryl gasped, he looked around the room. "Don't be mentioning this to her either, but I need one with some rhythm to it! Please man!"

"It's up to her."

Tracy smiled at him, "when are you going to tell her about us?"

"Never! She don't have to know."

"One day she's gonna wonder why you're not asking for her cake anymore. You're going to have to tell her eventually, I won't let you keep sneaking around with my cake."

"I'm gonna tell her, this time will be the last time we sneak, PROMISE!"

"Un huh, that's what you said last time." Tracy smiled.

Chantel

When everyone left the hospital Derrick was quiet for a long time. I didn't know what to say to him and I know he was thinking about everything that happened earlier. I could tell he was hurt by the things his grandmother said I just couldn't put my finger on how he was processing it. Early in the morning he was up changing Chanel and talking to her. "How's daddy's baby this morning?" I opened my eyes and watched him talk to Chanel. He looked at her with so much love in his face. His voice was gentle and full of love and appreciation. I know some characteristics are passed down from your parents whether you want them or not. However, Derrick's birth father doesn't sound like a good guy and I doubt he was ever this good with Derrick or Darryl for that matter. I don't understand everything that was said or that happened, but Derrick told me that it was a good thing that Drew wasn't here when she was talking like that. Malcolm and Drew are finally behaving like a father and son should. That conversation could've easily set them back, just because. I didn't ask Derrick what he meant, because the fact that he said that much was a lot. Derrick held Chanel and got comfortable with her on the couch. She was a daddy's girl already. He told her how much he loved her, how happy he is that she's here, and that he hopes that he makes her proud to call him daddy.

When she got fussy I sat up, I figured she was ready to eat. He helped me get her to latch on, he memorized everything the nurse showed us. Then he kept kissing my cheek, forehead, etc. and thanking me. As soon as Chanel finished eating, he took her and burped her. They went back on the couch. I watched them from the bed, kind of feeling like an outsider on their love moment. Grandma Rosa came in the morning, and I was happy to have someone. We took my bandages off so that I could shower. And then she wrapped me right back up in fresh bandages.

"So Grandma Rosa, when are you going to move in?" Derrick asked her.

She looked at me completely surprised. "You want me to move in?"

"Of course! Chantel needs her grandma, and you guys will eventually travel together. You could move into the house or you could have the three bedroom in-law cottage behind our house."

"What cottage? Your place is so huge, I don't remember a cottage."

"It's almost done. Until then you could move into the house."

"Chantel you knew about this?"

"No, but I'm so happy right now, it would be nice to have you right here with us. I know Cyrus would love having you closer as well," I said hoping that she would say yes.

"I guess you're right, I would love to have my own space so the cottage sounds lovely Derrick. I'll come as soon as you'll have me." She said with a gigantic smile.

I erupted in tears as I cried on my grandma's shoulder. She told Derrick my hormones were going to be all out of whack for a little bit and to bear with us. She told me she had a tea she wanted me to drink as soon as my milk starts coming in. She said it would help build my milk and balance my hormones. Derrick said they were going to release me tomorrow from the hospital and it would be nice to have her there as well. When she hesitated he told her he would have staff come and pack up her apartment. He said her things would go into the garage until the cottage was ready. They were talking out the details when Sasha called me. She thanked me for giving birth the day after her wedding and not the day before or of. Derrick has already sent her a ton of pictures of Chanel and she said she was beautiful. She said the media has already announced Chanel's birth. I guess they had to be happy about something cause when pictures from my wedding were released everyone was asking each other how we pulled it off without alerting the media and having cameras there.

My daddy and Maria came with my brothers and sister. I was counting the minutes until my dad asked when I was going back to work. I was impressed that he made it an hour in before he asked. By that time Cyrus was there. Cyrus told him I was taking the rest of the year off, only doing local things when I had to. I needed time to bond with Chanel. Plus my previous projects were launching throughout that time so my name and face would stay out there. When Grandma Rosa told my daddy that she was moving in with Derrick and I, my dad got a little jealous. He said he could've used her help with the twins. And she reminded him that she did come and help them with the twins initially, but he's a veteran dad. He should know exactly what to do. I'm a first time mom, and I needed her more than he did. It almost seemed like she was talking to a child. DJ and Mario looked at him like they were embarrassed. Derrick changed the subject and got my brothers engaged in a conversation with him. Maria smiled at Chanel while she held her. She asked me if I made barrettes for her like I did for little Rosa and Alex. I told her I made some, but I didn't know if she would have hair or not. Chanel had a head full of curly hair, I was happy she got her daddy's dimples.

Kendra

I was tired from my night with Darryl all day. I was going to bed early tonight. I stood in my kitchen frustrated. The hard part about cooking is that I don't know how to make a home cooked meal for one person. So out of frustration I normally make a sandwich or something. I ate my tuna sandwich, showered and then snuggled into my covers. It was barely seven thirty when I closed my eyes.

I felt someone sit on my bed. Darryl was in his boxers with a fork and a cake. I looked at him with a question on my face; the clock said it's after eleven. He smiled, "yes! Yes it is!" Then he put a fork full in my mouth. It was so good. I sat up and took Darryl's fork from him. We ended up fighting over the fork, so Darryl put the rest of the cake away. He was smiling but he looked upset. When he got in the bed, he put his head in my lap as he took deep breaths. He was upset about something and he was trying to work through it. He threw his body all over my bed. I didn't say anything, I waited. He got up and started kicking an invisible person. He was kicking the person in the face. He was having an inaudible argument with them and he was going off. Then he shot them. "He's dead! He's dead and I still wanna kill him!" He was completely pissed off. "He hurt my momma KB! He.... I HATE HIM!" He yelled. "My kids will NOT BE MASON'S! MALCOLM IS MY FATHER! MALCOLM IS MY FATHER!"

I got up and put my arms around him. "Darryl! Just cry! Let it out!"

"NO! KENDRA HE DOESN'T GET TO HAVE MY TEARS!" Darryl was shaking. His cellphone started ringing. "Hello?..... Momma!...... I know...... I know..." Then I heard the tears in his voice even though his back was to me. "I know I'm better than him.... Yes momma... It hurts!....." He exhaled, and then he looked at me with red eyes. "I'm not alone..." He tried to smile at me. "Yes momma, I love you too... Bye." He hung up and looked at me. He smiled at me and wiped my tears. "Why are you crying?"

"You don't cry Darryl." I said grabbing his hand and kissing it.

"Dionne came to the hospital calling us David. It was system overload. Tracy made that cake for me, but I needed the real thing. I'm glad you were home cause I was coming wherever you were. I NEED you so bad right now!"

"You need me to do it?"

"You're the only one who can do it right." I tickled his legs and he cracked up laughing. Then he put his arms around me. "Thank you for crying for me." Then he kissed my cheek.

"Was it that bad?"

"We were with the baby, everybody's happy you know. Dionne was fine at first."

I put my hand up, "why do you call your grandmother by her first name?"

"Not to her face, only when I talk about her. Keep up." Then he kissed me. "KB! Let's

stop wasting time. Stop taking your pill. Let's do this!"
This was going to start an argument so I didn't say anything.
In the morning as I put lotion on, my cellphone rang. It was Shai, Darryl looked at me.
He was going to flash if I didn't answer. "Hi"
"Good morning beautiful." He was smiling through the phone.
"Good morning, listen. Can I call you back? Now is not a good time." Darryl watched
me.
"Let's have dinner tonight."
I had no idea if Darryl was coming back. "Um, let me get back to you."
"Just say yes."
"Let me call you back."
"Ok, dinner and then you can spend the night at my place it sounds crowded over there."
He slightly chuckled.
"I'll call you back!" I said through clinched teeth.
When I hung up my phone Darryl walked over and picked it up. He looked at my phone,
and then his eyes cut me. "Shai? Who names their son Shai?"
"It's a nickname," I watched him cause he looked mad.
"Nickname?" Then he threw my phone at the wall and it shattered into pieces.
"For real?" I said annoyed. I dove across the bed and got his phone. I threw his phone just
like he did mine and it bounced off the wall.
Darryl started cracking up laughing. I got up, took his boot, and started beating his phone
with it. "A! A! A!" I kept going until his was broken. "I need that for work!" He snapped
at me.
"Like I don't need mine?" I rolled my eyes.
Darryl stared at me, "what you wearing to my parent's wedding?"
"I'm invited?"
Darryl jerked his head like I hit him. "I don't know how you figured it was ok for you to
miss D-Rick's wedding. I dropped the ball on that one. We gone fight if you miss my
parent's wedding."
I rolled my eyes, "you ain't gone do nothing!" Is it wrong that I was eating up this whole
scene?
He kicked my bed, "won't I!"
"Why don't you bring that girl you've been playing house with when I'm not around."
He picked up his broken phone. "Get real! Her booty ain't even big enough to hold my
attention." Then he picked up my landline and dialed. "I need info... She has him under
Shai... Everything!" Then he hung up.
I frowned, "what are you doing?"
He put lotion in his hands and then he rubbed it on me. "I'm not in the mood for you to
have friends right now! Just because you're stubborn you'll get him killed." Darryl's face
looked crazy and his hands were strong. "Your new phone will be delivered to your
office before you go out in the field." His hands were strong and deliberate. "KB! Don't
test me!"
I knew he wasn't playing.

****

Our host asked our group if anyone was celebrating a birthday. Darryl raised his hand
excitely and said it was not his birthday then he asked if that counted. The host laughed
and told us it didn't. Darryl snapped his fingers and said next time. "Uncle Mali tell her
how I'm your favorite nephew." Darryl sat back like he just knew his uncle would
comply.
"You are the craziest!"
Darryl smiled, but he wasn't satisfied. "Denise! Auntie!" He smiled, "who's your
favorite?"

She looked embarrassed; "I met you when you were so little. I don't think I ever chose a favorite."

"Yes! Auntie! You did, it was me you don't remember?"

She smiled, "I must've forgotten."

"You're our favorite Darryl." The biggest little girl said.

Darryl started blushing, "thanks Jada. I'm glad to know somebody loves me."

"We love you very much!" The other little girl said.

"Ok! Bring it in, give me the love ladies." Darryl put his arms out for a hug and both of the girls got up to hug him.

Denise laughed as she held on to her pregnant belly. I tried not to keep looking at her stomach but my eyes kept going there. Then Drew and his family walked in, his wife was very pregnant as well. Darryl thinks he's slick surrounding me with all these pregnant women. Drew smiled really big when he saw me. He told everybody at the table about the kickbacks we had at my house when my parents moved out. Tracy said she didn't realize I've been around as long as I have. When my drink came Tracy and Denise looked at my drink with longing eyes. Tracy told me to describe the taste. When I did she rubbed her belly and said she couldn't wait to drink again. I told them meanwhile I'd drink enough for all of us. When the chef came out to prepare our meal we had everyone around our table cracking up. Drew said I was just as silly as Darryl. Denise and I went to the bathroom; Tracy joined us a minute later. We were chatting for minute and laughing at my slurred words.

As we approached the table Drew stopped smiling and Darryl had a look I hadn't seen before. Then someone gently grabbed my arm. I turned to see Russell. I smiled and hugged him. Russell kept looking at the table; he asked me why I haven't taken any of Shai's calls? I didn't think Russell was talking all that loud. "Cause she ain't interested!" Darryl said pulling my arm to make me stand behind him.

Russell looked Darryl up and down. "You need to call him." Russell spoke around Darryl.

"I don't have his number anymore, but Rusty it's ok. We weren't serious, he can move on." I know my drinks were clouding my vision.

"You stumbled into the wrong room. If you value your life you'll run out of here." Darryl said looking down at Russell.

"You don't know me!" Russell said.

Darryl smiled, "but you know me. I can see it in your eyes." Darryl's smile disappeared.

"I get the feeling I'm gonna have to deal with you."

"Nephew give him a pass, we not finished eating."

"No, he's not cool." Drew said with a crazy look on his face.

"I know Drew! I know!"

"Nephew, scan the room. Come sit down."

The kids were looking at Darryl with big eyes; I don't think any of them have ever seen him in this space. I could see the reaction to the kids on Darryl's face. He continued scanning the room and then his eyes landed on a woman. "Did you send him in here?" He barked at her.

She had a mile wide smile on her face as she excitedly hurried over. "No, I didn't. This is so perfect!" She clasped her hands excitedly. "Don't let me stop you. Threaten his life, go ahead do something, anything! This is so perfect."

"Who are you?" I was trying to push my buzz aside to focus on what was happening.

"Detective Dartnell, Kendra you are a gem! This is perfect! Go ahead touch him Darryl! I always knew you were the hot head and trigger happy one."

"Detective? What do you want with Darryl?" I asked.

"She doesn't know who you are? Honey, you don't know who he is? Your little boyfriend is pretty ruthless. I can imagine that if I wasn't here, this guy's body would wash up somewhere." Then she looked at Rusty. "Let me see your ID!" She barked at him.

Rusty kept his eyes locked on Darryl as he handed his wallet to the Detective. "Russell Demetrius Payne! Hhhmmm nice name!" She kept moving his ID around in her hand, and then she looked at him. "Looks like I need to do some more homework, things just got interesting."

"What you see?" Darryl asked with a smile.

She handed the ID to Darryl, Rusty sucked his teeth. "You're not from California are you?"

Rusty squinted at her, "how do you know that from looking at my ID?"

"The number is a newer number. You haven't been out here all that long."

"This is a nice picture! What you do, sleep with the photographer to make sure yours is nicer than everybody else's?" Darryl said

"He's married." I volunteered.

"Kendra, go sit down." Darryl said to me firmly.

When I did as I was told, Tracy and Denise had the same horrified looks in their faces. Drew looked angry and like he was pulling calmness from everywhere. Malachi and the kids looked like they were taking the information in and processing it. Tracy touched my hand and rubbed it softly when I sat down, like she understood my confusion. Rusty walked out with the Detective, and Darryl pulled out his phone. Drew and Darryl stayed on their phones. Malachi tried to calmly point our attention elsewhere, but Darryl's anger was sobering.

In the car Darryl was hitting me with question after question about Rusty, Shai, and Latonya. When he asked me if I slept with Shai I felt uncomfortable even though I hadn't. When he asked me if it was because of me or Shai, I told him the truth that it was because of Shai. Darryl said he was putting a pin in that to come back to it later. He told me to show him where they lived; the house was completely dark when we pulled up. When Darryl said we were going in, as he put on leather gloves, my heart dropped. He stuck a card at the top of the door and entered something into his phone, then he took out the key thing he used on my door to unlock both locks. He cracked the door then entered something into his phone. Then the alarm beeped to say it was disarmed. Darryl told me to show him around the house. He kept asking me why a married couple would live with a bachelor. I kept saying that they all moved out here for their job, and then he flashed me a look. He told me none of this was adding up nor was I looking at the bigger picture. He said if Russell is married where was his wife earlier? He said if they do everything together cause they're relatively new to the area where was his wife and her best friend? I didn't know, and then he asked me if I ever saw Latonya and Russell kiss. If I heard them having sex? Other than them telling me that they were married and the fact that I saw them go in the same room at night what confirmation did I have that they were married? Did I ever see a wedding picture or anything? When I said no, he moved on. I showed him Shai's room, and he asked me if any of the clothes in the closet and drawers were anything I ever saw him wear, and I said no. Then we went in Latonya and Russell's room. There were no clothes in the closet, nothing in the drawers. It was like the room was staged to look like a room but it really wasn't. Darryl called someone and he said there was a dead fish in suburbia. He asked me if Shai ever asked me anything about him. I told him that Shai never came to my house because he could and would pop up at any given time so I wouldn't bring him there. Darryl said no one lives in this house, and that it was a staging area. When I asked him what that meant, he waived his hand and told me to be quiet. He was listening for something, and then there was a knock on the front door. Darryl took out his gun and told me to get in the closet, my heart started pounding. I didn't know he had a gun on his body. I was scared and trying to control my breathing so that I was quiet then I heard Darryl laugh. For a normal person that would mean everything was ok, but Darryl was not normal. When I heard him call me, I came out. There were guys all over the house checking things out, taking pictures, etc. Darryl told me we were leaving.

"You were going to sleep with him?" Darryl's face was stone.

"Yes."

"Why KB? Why?" He said shaking his head, "I'm giving you everything. And you keep looking for the next person to give everything to."

"You're still seeing Brenda and whomever else, how dare you question me!"

"Oh so this is return evil for evil? Stop playing this game KB and she's gone. Everybody's gone!"

"What game?"

"You're too hard to get. My name is not Jerry! I'm not going anywhere!"

Hearing him speak my father's name enraged me. "And I'm not Amber! I don't want a baby daddy for all of eternity!"

"KB! FOR REAL! Don't talk about my momma!" He was trying not to drive angry.

"Like I want to hear Jerry's name!"

"Let's have this conversation once and for all. This game you're playing is going to get someone killed. You're a weak link right now."

"I'm bringing you drama? Is that what you're saying?"

"KB! Listen! There's a lot you don't know. We need to talk about it."

"No," I said shaking my head. "I don't want to talk to you right now. Take me home!"

"You can't go home. Kalani isn't even at her house next door."

"THEN TAKE ME TO MY PARENT'S HOUSE! I'm not spending the night with you!"

"KB! Why?"

"IT'S TOO MUCH DARRYL! I WANT MY MOMMA!" I said as tears poured out of my eyes. My buzz wasn't completely gone.

"KB! We need to talk!"

"I want my momma, you know better than to bring Jerry up. And then you do it anyways! What if I brought up David?"

"OH SO YOU MUST BE PMS'ING CAUSE YOU TRIPPING! WHAT'S DOES HE HAVE TO DO WITH ALL THE TEA IN CHINA?"

"He is just as much a part of your malfunction as Jerry is mine. You don't wanna hear about David and I don't wanna hear about Jerry!"

"WELL THAT'S ALL YOU HAD TO SAY! BUT NO! YOU GOTTA GO FOR THE MOMMA'S AND THEN YOU BRING UP THAT FOOL! I'M TAKING YOU TO YOUR MOMMA CAUSE NOW I DON'T WANT TO BE AROUND YOU!"

"FINE CAUSE I DON'T WANT TO BE AROUND YOU!"

"Fine!"

"Where you going?"

He cut his eyes at me, "to your momma's house!"

"I wanna go to your house now!" I watched his face.

"KB!" He pounded the steering wheel. "YOU JUST SAID!"

"I know what I said, and I have the right to change my mind." I smiled at him.

He screamed, "I'm not playing this back and forth game with you!"

"Darryl you are so sexy when you're mad! I find myself completely turned on!"

He smiled at me, "this is what I get for arguing with a drunk person. I completely forgot about the fun those drinks were supposed to bring us."

"I'm on fire Darryl aren't you sizzling?"

"I'm snapping, I'm crackling, and I'm gonna pop you!" He laughed.

I rubbed my legs together, "hurry up Darryl! Hurry up!"

"KB! You are so crazy! I love you!"

"I love you!"

Lanie

"You guys frustrate me!"

"KB tell her as long as we make sense to each other it don't matter what no one else thinks."

"As long as we make sense to each other it doesn't matter what no one else thinks." Kendra blushed.

"Are you back together?"

"NO!"

"YES!" Darryl said at the same time. I threw my hands up in frustration. "KB! We discussed this, we're back together and you're going to have my baby. You agreed last night."

Kendra looked embarrassed, "drop it."

"No! You said yes, you said yes to everything. You even agreed to things I haven't asked for yet."

"Darryl!" She said through clinched teeth.

"Yes KB?" He smiled real big.

"Drop it!"

"No! You agreed." He winked at me.

She got fed up, "you can't ask me anything in the middle of a drunken orgasm and expect anything other than agreement from me."

"Well a yes should be my reward for hitting it so good last night." Darryl did a silly dance.

Kendra stormed out of the room in embarrassment. "Aw! KB! COME BACK!" Then he smiled at me, "I like when she storms away. I like the way her booty bounces." He raised his eyebrows at me.

"Gross Darryl!"

"What got you up so early? You know you're interfering with me going in again. If she don't end up pregnant it won't be for lack of trying."

"Is it your mission to gross me out until I leave?"

"Now you're catching on."

Kendra came back with a big T-shirt, and sweats on. Darryl watched Kendra wrap a blanket around herself and sit on the couch. "I want to know more about Bilal."

"You came over early in the morning to ask me about some nigga?"

"He keeps popping up everywhere, and I'm thinking about giving him a chance."

"Why?"

"He pulled his pants up."

"That's it?"

"Yes."

"You'd consider giving some guy a chance because he pulled his pants up?"

"All you knew about Kendra was that she had a big ole booty. That made you come back."

He smiled real big, "THAT! And she wasn't scared of me, but you're right it was mostly the booty. I wanted to touch it." He licked his lips at her. Kendra cracked up laughing like she was embarrassed. "However, I wasn't rebounding."

"No matter how long I wait you guys are going to say I'm rebounding with whomever I end up with next. Besides you guys were babies back then."

"What do you want to know, I thought I laid everything out for you that night in the restaurant."

I shrugged, "anything else you can tell me?"

"Not yet, I'll get back to you when I have more." Then he licked his lips at Kendra. She

rolled her eyes and turned her head. "You know I like it when you roll your eyes at me."
"Gross! Ok, I get it. I interrupted, I'm leaving."
"No, wait, stop, don't… whatever else I'm supposed to say to pretend like I want you to stay." He said as he pushed me towards the door.
Kendra and I laughed, "Darryl you are so wrong."
"I'll hit you up once I let her come up for air."

****

"There goes your boy." Zoey nodded in Bilal's direction.
Bilal was looking and I smiled at him. He looked a little confused for a minute, so I looked away. I filled my sisters in on what happened when I saw him with Darryl. Bilal kept watching us for a minute like he was debating on whether to come over or not. His indecision was getting on my nerves. We finished our dinner and he was still sitting at the bar watching me and whatever game was on. Zoey and I decided to go over to Shylight lounge and have a drink before going home. I was disappointed that he didn't man up and step to me, but I guess he might be fearful for his life.
Zoey and I danced a little then I saw him walk in. He hadn't seen me yet and now I know he's following me. Somewhat of a stalker, I smiled to myself. I pointed him out to Zoey and she shook her head saying this wasn't going to end well. We went to the bar got another drink and then we found space on the long couch. Bilal approached us looking around the whole time. "You're going to have to stop following me around. I don't want your Wallace man coming after me."
"Her Wallace man?" Zoey interjected.
"Sugar daddy, or whatever."
"So if you so scared for your life why you following me around?"
"It's not my fault you keep ending up everywhere I am." He smiled.
"Cute, what's your name."
"Bilal."
"And…"
"Bilal Talbot, yours?"
"Lanie Wallace."
His mouth fell open, "you're a Wallace?"
"Of course! Who else but a Wallace woman could make a man pull up his pants?"
He looked at me out the side of his eye. "And you're her friend?" He asked Zoey.
"Um! Look again! This is my sister, my twin soul almost." He looked so confused, Zoey and I laughed. "Look past the colors of our skins. You'll see the similarities."
Bilal looked between us, finally he gave up. "I don't see it, but I'll take your word for it." Then he sat down. "So D is not your man just your protective family member."
"You asking or you telling me?"
"You a feisty little thing aren't you." He smiled, "let's dance." He took me by the hand and to the dance floor. Real dance moves he did not possess, but he did his own thing and he wasn't afraid to do it. We were having a good time on the dance floor when I recognized the group of squares coming in the door. I continued dancing as I watched for…. Dorian to come in at the end of the group. He knows this is my family's house! Why is he here? I kept dancing as I watched, he was uncomfortable. So I'm guessing the group wanted to come and he was outnumbered. He was frustrated and I knew that meant he was going to end up leaving even if he didn't see me. When everyone sat, he sat on the end like he was going to jump up and leave at the drop of a hat. April walked over to him and started talking. "Who is he?"
"My ex."
"That guy?" Bilal said frowning at Dorian as if he was a punk.
I looked him in his eyes, "Yes!"
"So you're used to running all over fools? That's why your mouth shoots off like it

does."

"You should never judge a book by its cover. My man could never be a punk. He yielded to me out of love for me. He's not a punk."

Bilal frowned at Dorian and I was ready to sit down. When I sat, Zoey asked me if I saw who was here yet, and I told her I had. I'm not going to lie, watching Bilal be jealous about my pretty ex did tickle me. He was asking me all kinds of questions so I did like he did and told him it was none of his business. Dorian spotted us, I could tell by his eyes he wanted to know who Bilal was, but April was too happy sitting next to him. Dorian was still trying to find his way back to brother righteous. He didn't have that innocent glow about him anymore, and I'm sure that made those losers want him even more. Bilal moved closer to me and spoke in my ear as he asked me why Dorian was staring. I smiled and turned my eyes, I told Bilal all he needed to know is that we weren't together anymore. Bilal kissed my cheek and then he looked at Dorian who seemed to fly across the room. Zoey had a huge smile as she sat back to watch.

In one quick motion Dorian pulled me out of my seat and held my wrist while he asked me why I was disrespecting him. Bilal stood up looking hard as he told Dorian he needed to backup as he walked towards him. I didn't want Dorian to fight Bilal even though I know Bilal has no idea of what he's up against. I pulled Dorian back, I apologized and I asked him to calm down. All of his friends were looking with big scared eyes. I asked Dorian to go back to his friends. Dorian picked me up and kissed me, and then he looked at Bilal like he wasn't nothing. I was speechless, cause I didn't expect him to do that. I wanted Dorian so bad in that moment; I knew I had to leave. April was sitting there looking like she was about to cry. Dorian didn't return to his group, he walked out the door. Bilal asked me again if Dorian was my boyfriend and I said he was my ex. All Zoey needed was some popcorn; she was thoroughly pleased by the scene these two created. Bilal stormed out of the lounge and Zoey and I grabbed our purses. When I stepped out Bilal was looking to the right, then the left. There was no sign of Dorian anywhere. Bilal said I was nothing but trouble he could already tell. He walked Zoey and I to her car, and then he gave me his number and told me to call him when I was ready to date a real man.

Malachi

"This space is prime location for a garage. It has the square footage you were looking for. I think this could be a good fit for you Mister Wallace." She smiled a devilish grin.

This little girl needs to stop flirting with me. I've mentioned my wife and family I don't know how many times and she still continues. I took a deep breath as I looked around. The space was nice, but it wasn't as prime as I had hoped for. I was trying to distract myself from my sorry excuse for life, being at home I only seemed to be in Denise's way. Even though things are a little and I do mean a little better, it's still not enough to fix us. Then I gotta deal with this all day. Seems like females smell the dysfunction in our marriage and become bolder and come on harder. "This is nice, but it's not exactly what I'm looking for. I would prefer an office a little more in the middle of things."

"This space comes with a partially furnished apartment."

"Partial?"

"Yes, there's a bed and a sofa would you like to see it?" She raised an eyebrow.

Before I answered her a car pulled up, it was black with tinted windows. Then my Uncle Jeff stepped out of the passenger side. "Uncle!" I called out.

"Hey nephew!" He said walking over. "Looks like Allie here was trying to offer more than just an office." He looked her up and down.

"Have we met?" She asked as her womanly charm started to evaporate.

"You don't know me, but I know you." He said standing next to me. "Nephew why didn't you come to me or Uncle…" Then he looked back at her, "excuse you!" She was staring in his mouth. "How did you get here?"

"She picked me up from the Fremont house."

"Good!" Then he looked at her, "you've been dismissed! Tell your father if he ever gets this close to my family again I'll kill him!"

"You can't threaten me!" She barked.

"Trust me that is not a threat it's a promise. Tell him your client's last name, he'll put you in your place." He opened the rear passenger door. "Get in nephew."

When I got in the car, Dude was driving. "What's up?"

"Why didn't you come to me or your Uncle Frank? That skank was going to do whatever it took to get you to lease one of her father's places. Al is no good, but he knows his place."

"Small world!"

"And the more people you meet the smaller it gets." Then he bobbed his head to the R&B music on the radio. "Ok so I want to show you a building I own in downtown Oakland. If you like it, it's yours." Then he went back to the music.

"Does it need work?"

"Tons! Now that Darren has finished Tracy's bakery he can get it up to code and then whatever you need. Have you talked to your sister?"

"Which one?"

"Amber, she's going to have the fatty wobble her down the aisle." He blew air, Dude tried not to laugh. "He's gonna be out of breath just from the walk to meet her. Then down the aisle, he probably won't make it. He'll be puffing on an inhaler every three steps."

I laughed, "You ain't right! Why would you talk about your brother like that?"

"Cause she picked him." Then he exhaled, "but I'm dancing with her on the father daughter dance. Trying to pacify me. I know I'm in that space cause he couldn't keep up! You know it should be me walking her down the aisle, but NO! She's trying to have everyone involved!"

We parked on Broadway in front of a building that was so old it looked abandoned. He pointed out that he owned everything on this block, but he hadn't done anything with it in years. This space was just up ahead of quite a few car dealerships. Not far from the freeway, I liked everything about the space except how old and run down the actual building was. We went to lunch and I told him that the location of his property was prime it was close to Bart and the few surviving businesses in downtown. I told him he should maximize on his location. I suggested that he bulldoze the whole block; underground parking on one end, shops, and a leasing office on street level, and then luxury apartments above. I told him about Allie's mention of a partially furnished apartment above the garage didn't sound like a bad idea, hence the apartment building idea.

His brain was shifting and moving around. "Sounds good nephew. You and Darren talk out the design, if I like it, we'll do it. This block is just sitting here anyways."

As they drove me home after we had lunch, my old job called me. Since I left so abruptly, I agreed to consult for them from time to time, but only in extreme situations. They promoted Gerald to my old spot, which was a mistake in my opinion, but oh well. I knew they would be calling, and calls like this came in frequently enough to where I was making more money consulting than I was when I worked there.

"Malachi!" Cora's voice said.

Everything in me tightened up, "what?"

"I need to talk to you. Can you be here in an hour?"

I looked around the car like she was talking to someone else. "No!"

She moaned out of frustration, but it triggered something in me. "You need to talk to me it's important!"

"No!"

"It's about Turan."

"See you in an hour."

"What's going on nephew?"

I sang like a canary, I was tired of keeping it all bottled up. Instead of exiting towards my house Dude kept driving towards the plant. When we parked, I told her to come outside, she had a mile wide smirk on her face when she saw me. She looked really pretty and her perfume slapped my mouth. I led her to the car and she smiled anxiously as I held the door open. "What is this?" She said looking between my uncle and Dude.

"Cora they are the only ones holding me back from choking the life out of you! You raised your hand to my wife after you befriended her under false pretenses!" I felt my anger turn in my stomach. "Now you're calling my cellphone! I've never given you permission to call me EVER!" I growled at her.

Her eyes widened, "who are they?"

"Be a good girl and you won't have to know! Now what about Turan?"

My uncle and Dude stared at her. "I met him a few months ago. He says things are about to get real bad for someone named Malcolm. He always says it, so I never paid it any mind. Until he said the Wallace reign over Oakland was coming to an end. That's what caught my attention; I still had no idea that he was talking about you until he said something about your sister. He's obsessed with your family." Then she looked at me, "who are you?"

"I'M YOUR WORST NIGHTMARE! TOUCH MY WIFE AGAIN AND IT WILL BE THE LAST THING YOU DO! TELL ANYONE ABOUT THIS AND IT WILL BE THE LAST THING YOU DO! I don't love you! I don't like you! Stay away from my family! Don't call my phone ever again! Forget that you ever knew me. Step outside of any of that and it will be the last thing you do!"

"Malachi?" She looked at me in disbelief.

"MALACHI WHAT?" My voice rumbled through the car.

"I didn't mean to hit her. She kept coming at me."

"You befriended her under false pretenses what did you expect? If my child is born with even a birth mark that I think you caused...."

Her eyes got big, "she's pregnant?"

"Little girl you seem to be focusing on the wrong things. Pay attention!" Uncle Jeff said.

"Malachi I'm sorry for everything. I don't understand what's going on or who you really are at this point." She said looking from Dude to Uncle Jeff. "I don't want you to leave me!"

Dude chuckled as he turned back around in his seat. "Get out of the car Cora!" I demanded.

When I got home Denise was in the tub. I sat on the edge, "I don't want to get divorced."

"What do you want?" She stared at me.

"I want you to be happy. I want you to want me. I want my wife back. The one who used to love me, I never stopped loving you. I've got my own issues but I never meant to make them your problems. If you want a divorce and that will make your life easier, I don't like it and I don't want it, but I will do it if it will make you happy. Tell me what you want to do."

"I love you Malachi, I don't want a divorce either, I don't like you very much right now. My mother always said I wasn't good enough for you. I guess she knew better than we did."

I chewed back my anger. "Denise you need to let go of all the backward things that woman told you! She can't speak for me!"

"What am I supposed to think especially now? How do we fix this? I don't want to continue like this. I can't." She looked away.

"I don't know."

"Amber suggested that I call her doctor."

"Therapy!" I threw my hands up.

"She and Malcolm go separately, and not all the time. She said it has helped them."

"Black people don't do therapy."

"I'm not black Malachi." She looked at me with a "duh" expression.

"What? I ordered an African bride. What did you do with her?" I smiled.

"I sold her to the man who wanted to buy me." She smiled, "but Malachi in all seriousness, we need to do something or throw in the towel. We cannot continue like this."

****

"It's nothing against Denise. She's a nice young lady, but...." She gave me a look, "you always said you wanted someone like this." She pointed to her hand. "What happened baby?"

"Momma, she's brown. Why isn't that good enough? Most people think she's black anyways."

"Boy! You know there's a difference between brown and chocolate." My momma said. I lowered my head, "you don't like her?"

She looked in the window to my home. "You never introduced us!" She smacked me upside the head. "You don't even tell her about me. Are you ashamed of me?" She looked sad.

"No! Momma never! I love you! It's hard for me! You were the first person I wanted to tell about Denise. I wanted to know what you thought of her. I miss you!"

She looked in the window and then back at me. "She ain't chocolate!" She stared me in my eyes.

I woke up looking around my room. It took a minute to realize I was in the guest room. I sat there until I calmed down a little. I tried to go back to sleep but every time I laid down my heart started racing. It was only two o'clock in the morning, I needed sleep. I made my bed then I walked down the hallway. I peeked my head in the girl's room. Then I stood in front of my bedroom door. I took a deep breath then I slowly opened the door. When I closed it behind me Denise's head popped up. She asked what time it was and I told her it was after two. She asked me if I had another dream. I said yes, she pulled the covers back and invited me into our bed. When I laid down she put her head on my chest then her head popped up. She asked me if it was a nightmare, I told her I didn't know. Then she rubbed my head just like my momma used to. I held onto her like my life depended on it. I didn't go back to sleep but I laid there enjoying the idea of lying next to my wife.

****

I did not want to go see this Joanne lady. Especially after Dobson confirmed every assumption I had in my mind about this ridiculous field. They prey on the weak, pimp you for every nickel and dime. When she greeted us in the hallway I looked for her to be disappointed, to show some kind of ill feeling towards Denise and I for putting her colleague out of business. She told us to follow her back into her office. She gave Denise a footstool to prop up her feet. She asked me if I wanted one, so I agreed to it. She sat in her chair, no notepad, no voice recorder, no books with her pictures plastered, and no pictures of people in her office at all. Matter of fact her office was modest, neat, and clean. I still waited for the sneakiness to emerge. She introduced herself then she asked us how we met. Denise immediately smiled, she told the story happily. Denise was a waitress at a cafe that I stumbled into one night at the end of a date. She worked at night and went to school during the day. Denise noticed me before I noticed her. Denise said they would fight over who's station I would be sat in even though I was never alone. One night I had a horrible date, but I went to the cafe for pie and coffee alone. I found myself thinking about my momma, which always made me sad. When I sat at the counter Denise asked me what was wrong. That's when I saw her, she was young and cute, but I thought of her as a little girl. Denise says I patted her on the head, but I didn't. I just didn't think of her as a woman at that point. Whenever I came into the cafe alone we'd chat sometimes for a long time. Then one night I was on a date at a club and Denise was there and she wasn't in her uniform. I forgot about my date and our age difference.

Denise and I were all smiles remembering where we started. I had to keep reminding myself that Joanne was a doctor, and not an old family friend. She listened, she laughed, and she passed tissue when Denise cried. She messed up when she called me Tim. I deflated as I smiled at her, she didn't even realize she did it. "I remind you of him?"
"Of whom?"
"My father." She looked confused, "you called me Tim."
She put her hand over her mouth, "I am so sorry sweetheart I did not realize that I called you that."
"So I remind you of him?"
"Yes you do." She said embarrassed.
"How?"
"You're very cautious just like him. You're naturally likeable. I'm so sorry."
"It's ok." I liked the genuine apology in her tone.
Denise went right back to talking about the beginning. She had so many reasons why she fell in love with me. Some of the things made me feel like I couldn't believe how highly she thought of me. When it was my turn Denise squirmed in her chair as I went on and on about her. It was like it was hard for her to listen to me say positive things about her. She literally broke out in a sweat, Joanne gave her water. The water made her have to pee and when she stood up Joanne noticed her small belly. She didn't say anything until Denise came back. Denise was smiling, "so how did you sleep last night?"
The question jarred both of us. "Not well." Denise admitted.
"I didn't."
She turned her attention to me and asked why. I told her I keep dreaming about my momma. I couldn't admit to the skin issue. We talked to Joanne for hours, in the end barely scratching the surface, but when we walked out Denise was all smiles, and she put her arm under mine. My heart rejoiced that she willingly touched me.
As soon as we closed our car doors we turned to each other, "what did you think?" We said at the same time.
We laughed, "I liked her, did you?"
"Yes, and I love the smile she's put on your face."
She smiled bigger, "I think this will be good for us. Will you sleep in our bed tonight?"
"Yes," I said looking at her.
"Don't start rubbing on my booty. I'm not ready for that, but I haven't been sleeping well since you've been in the guest room."
"Ok."

Chantel

"Who misses their daddy?" Derrick's voice announced before he entered the room. Chanel searched the room looking for him. She started moving more as soon as she heard him. She's such a daddy's girl, and I love watching them together. Every time she starts hollering he takes her to the piano. He puts her in her bouncy chair and then he plays something for her. "How are you doing?" He said giving me a kiss.
"I miss you." I felt sad and weepy.
"I missed you two today too." He was not getting what I meant.
"No, I miss you."
"Oh!" He blushed, "miss you too baby. Two more weeks and then we're good."

266

"I CAN'T DO IT!" I cried.

He laughed, "why?"

"I miss you and I want to feel you. Everything has been about Chanel. I miss being your baby." I cried some more, "don't you want to?"

"Just because you're not bleeding anymore doesn't mean you're ready."

"Yes it does!"

"Chantel you're gonna mess around and get pregnant again." He looked at Chanel.

"So what, we planned to have more than one any ways. Derrick please!"

"No Chantel you need to be healed you could mess around and get an infection."

I sat up, "I'm clean! You're clean! It will be fine. Please!"

"Stop it! You're making me blush!" I rushed him and kissed him as hard as I could.

"Chantel! I am only a man! Stop it!" I kissed him again. "What about the baby?"

"Put her to sleep I need you!" I kissed his neck.

"You are so wrong for this!" He said rocking Chanel to sleep. "Where's Grandma?"

"She's having dinner with Cyrus and Sherrell." I said sending soothing thoughts to Chanel in hopes that she would fall asleep quickly.

"Did you set me up?" He smiled.

"I NEED YOU DERRICK!" I said desperately.

"Are you sure Chantel, I can wait." He said unconvincingly.

I smiled at him, like a good girl Chanel melted to her daddy's touch and was out. I took her from him and I put her in her bassinet and I moved it across the room. Derrick nervously asked me if we should use a condom. I ignored his question and I kissed him like my life depended on it. His nervousness was endearing to me. Derrick was so gentle and careful, I was happy that he indulged me. I don't know why I needed this sort of confirmation that he still loved me, but if he would've rejected me I couldn't handle it.

****

Grandma Rosa kept eyeing me; I kept giving her a guilty *what* look. "Why didn't you wait?"

"I don't know what you're talking about." I said looking around the room while she bathed Chanel.

"Chantel, I held you when you were this small. I know you! Why didn't you wait?"

Unless she confirmed that she knew, I wasn't owning up to anything. "I don't know what you're talking about."

"You had two weeks to go and you couldn't wait."

"Why are you saying this?"

"I know you and Derrick are making love again."

I gasped, "Why do you say that?"

"I saw the passion mark on his neck last week, and another one this week. You guys are ridiculous!" She laughed.

I frowned; I couldn't say anything to defend myself. "It's not Derrick's fault, I convinced him to do it."

"Baby why would you do that? Do you understand what your body just went through?"

"Yes, but I wanted him to focus on me only even if it was only for that little bit. I still need love too." I pouted.

"Derrick does a good job of showing you affection as well as the baby. You could've waited."

"I didn't want to. I missed my man!"

Then she chuckled. "That's how I ended up pregnant right away after I had your father." Fire hit my stomach, "pregnant?"

"You do know sex leads to pregnancy." She laughed sarcastically.

"Yes, but..."

She cut me off, "but nothing. You wanted your man so you jumped on him. I wished you

would've waited but hopefully everything works out for you."
She put the cutest little outfit on Chanel and brushed her hair. Pearla, Paulette, Liz, Sherrell and little Rosa came over after the bakery closed. Then after a while Brandy and Latia came over to see the baby. As soon as Brandy saw me she told me she hated me. She told me it took a whole year for her body to snap back after she had her son. I asked Latia how married life was treating her, and she smiled and said she had no complaints. Slowly everyone arrived, Tracy came over after Andre got out of school and she passed him off to Drew. Amber and Sophia brought the food, when Ms. Laverne arrived we sat down to a lovely meal just for the girls. We had a nice evening of just us while the men enjoyed their men's night out.

Yussef

"So...." Sylvia said trying to check her tone.
"So?" I said not wanting to get into it.
"You haven't come for me." She said searching my eyes.
"I know." I said focusing on my paperwork.
"Did I do something?"
"No," I said uninterested in discussing it.
"Then what? One minute we're together. The next minute I don't hear from you unless it involves Sydney. I miss you."
"I have been really busy with work." I continued to looking at my paperwork.
"Have you eaten? I can make dinner." She said looking towards the kitchen.
"Why aren't you at work?" I said out of frustration as I put my paperwork down.
"I've been trying to tell you I've finally paid everything off. Now I'm at ground zero." She was very proud of her accomplishment. "Now I can start rebuilding my life. I've never worked so hard before." She acted like she amazed herself.
"Whoopty-do!"
Sylvia swallowed then she looked down at her hands. I knew my lack of interest was bothering her, but I had a lot going on right now. There were so many balls in the air; I felt the pressure to keep everyone safe on my shoulders. I know it's not my sole responsibility, but those random kids pointed out a weak spot in the detail on Tracy's bakery. Of course it had to be Tracy that something like that happened to. The most delicate and fragile person always seems to get banged up the most. We met and Juan said we needed to go back to thinking about our protection practically. He said we've all been off our game with all these weddings happening. Fortunately we had only one more to go and then we could go back to business as usual. After I corrupted the file for the tabloid containing the article for Torrie's expose, I placed a virus in the magazine's computer system. Then I waited for them to reach out again. So far they haven't gotten very far they've been trying to rebuild what they had. "Yussef, " she said lowly.
"I thought you had to work, the girls are with my Grandma." I said looking at her.
"You want me to leave?"
"If you didn't have to work today, why are you just coming over? Where have you been?"
"I went to go workout."
"You've been working out a lot lately."
"Is it paying off? Can you tell yet?"
She was toning up nicely, but this certain interest in her appearance had me looking for the signs of the old her. "Why are you doing it?"
"I want to look nice for you." She was still waiting for my approval.
"I wasn't complaining about your appearance."
She exhaled, "I saw the way you looked at her, the way you danced with her, the way you

wouldn't look at her at her wedding. You used to be like that with me."
"So what is going to the gym supposed to do?"
She shrugged, "help."
I exhaled, "I've got work to do."

****

"Thank you Carly. Juan, anything new on your end?" Malcolm said.
"We need to speak offline Malcolm, I have nothing major to report to the group."
"OK, Richard?"
"Same here Malcolm."
"Ok, I think we have passports for just about everyone. So we're good. Does anyone have anything new to share with the group?"
"Darlene is on standby, I'll send her in as soon as you say so." Carly said.
"Ok, I'll be in touch in a minute. Everyone I'm giving you back twenty minutes to your day." Malcolm hung up, as everyone was saying their thank you's and goodbyes. Then he called Juan and Richard and put them on speaker. Juan told Malcolm that they checked, double checked and double-checked again and that the little boys who broke into Tracy's bakery were a fluke and they happened to hit at the right moment, but they were not affiliated with anyone. Curtis was not happy about wearing a uniform, but he was now personally inside the bakery the entire time anyone was there. Richard said that security was tight on Sasha while they were in New York. They flew back to New York with El's parents instead of going on a honeymoon. Juan reported about the failed attempts to come at us during Sasha's wedding. They played on the assumption that Sasha's wedding would be on the coastline just like Derrick's. That failed attempt cost Phineas a lot of man power. Malcolm said that he's reached out to Jonathan Myers in Mount Vernon. Juan paused for a minute, and then he asked if that was absolutely necessary. Jonathan was the Malcolm of New York. Malcolm assured Juan that the connection was clean, but it made him feel better to have extra backup while Sasha was out there. Richard said a quiet thank you. Then we got off the phone with them and Malcolm called Carly and told her to send Darlene in. Darlene came in the conference room with her eyes locked on me. I looked away, Malcolm didn't address it but I knew he saw it. She gave us a run down on the day to day with Sonya. Darlene's eyes kept darting to me whenever she could. After Malcolm asked everything and confirmed that I needed to pay Sonya a *friendly* visit he sat back in his chair and eyed Darlene. "So what's going on here?" Malcolm said watching her eyes
"Sir?"
"Darlene don't play dumb, it's not attractive. You know what I'm asking you. Why do you keep shooting my son goofy looks?" Malcolm almost smiled as he waited for her answer.
Darlene blushed, "I apologize sir. I've been trying to control it and keep it to myself. I think he's very handsome."
"You know my policy on interoffice dating."
"Yes sir, but according to the rules I don't report up to Yussef and we don't work for the same division. If he was into the idea we could date without any problems technically."
"Looks like someone did their homework." Malcolm said then he looked at me. "You still need to be more discreet." Then Malcolm went back to business. Darlene was working for the same company as Sonya. We went over the plan for tomorrow, and then Darlene left.
Malcolm asked me what was going on with Sylvia and I. When I didn't respond he said he knew I was curious about Darlene. I told him I was curious but not enough to do anything about it. He said he was always curious too, and then curiosity turned into frustration. And then... Then he asked me again what was going on with Sylvia. I told him nothing new; he eyed me for a minute. Then he asked me why I was settling. I

shrugged cause I didn't know what to say to the question. He told me to be careful and then he got up and went back to his office.

The next day, Ms. Laverne stood in the doorway extremely excited, which meant she had new pictures of the baby. Her excitement about Derrick and Chantel's child was refreshing. She referred to Chanel as her grandbaby. She shared her pictures and then she stood there beaming with pride.

Malcolm walked in holding papers in his hands looking back and forth between them. "It makes sense to expand this office taking over all of the space next door. Or we could relocate, but the logistics of that...."

"A temporary staffing office in the mall makes more sense. Especially since the headquarters are right across the bay. I vote to expand this space."

"I second that." Ms. Laverne said.

"Done." Malcolm said never taking his eyes from his paperwork. "What time are you leaving?"

"In a few." I returned to my computer. I looked over the layout of the office one more time.

On the way over I couldn't shake my frustrated feeling. I walked around the outside of the building. I piggybacked with some employees right onto the floor. As long as I walked like I belonged there I knew no one would question me. I saw Sonya talking to someone near the bathroom. Her gums were flapping so much that she didn't see me walk past her. Darlene texted me and said she was in the employee breakroom. I took the stairs down to the third floor and then I entered through the exit door, which was locked, but someone walked out so I walked in. Darlene was watching for me to come through the entrance. She smiled when I walked from behind her. "Very good mister Davis." She smiled.

Sonya spotted me walking to Darlene's table. "Pretty nice setup here."

"I guess, I'm hoping this is the end of this assignment. Most of the people around here are morons." She watched my eyes. "What do you need?"

"I need nosey people to keep their mouths shut."

She leaned forward and touched my hand. "What do you need?"

"I need a wife and family!"

She frowned, "why does everyone have to get married?"

"I thought most girls wanted to get married."

"Most, not all!"

"So why don't you?"

"I have no interest in it."

"Then you should turn your eyes, cause that's what I ultimately want."

"I guess that officially puts us in the friends zone."

Then Sonya walked over, "hey Darlene how you doing?" Darlene barely said hi before she switched gears to me. "Aren't you Drew's friend?"

"You are?"

"Sonya, I thought we met before." She searched her memory.

"You know him? Girl sit down."

When she did Darlene and I moved our chairs directly next to her so that our shoulders were touching on either side of her. "Put a smile on your face and your hands on the table like a good girl." There was no friendliness in my tone. She did as she was told; "now you can either talk to me." I smiled at her. "Or! You can talk to Malcolm." She slouched a little. "Go ahead and put a smile on your face for the onlookers." She did as she was told. "Cross me and I'm not responsible for what happens to you. Do you understand?" She shook her head yes. "Sonya are you a religious person?" She shook her head yes. "Then you know gossiping and meddling in other people's affairs is not cool. You know good and well what and who you're up against. Why would you do this?"

"I..." She started shaking her leg. "I didn't see the harm in talking about Torrie. Besides they came to me."

"You never stopped to think, why are they coming to you?"

"At the time my eye was swollen so I didn't care."

"See, a smart person would've considered that black-eye as a warning, but you are truly the stupidest person I know. Who sent them to you?"

"I don't know."

I looked at Darlene, "how did you explain your eye to Philip?" She asked.

"I told him what happened."

"Do you think he would be so understanding if something more permanent happened to your pretty little face. I wonder how long he'd continue to tough things out with you if you're now difficult and ugly!" Sonya swallowed. "Don't play dumb! It doesn't suit you!"

"How did you find me?"

"I ask the questions you provide the answers. Now answer my question."

"I'm sorry. I'll give back the money and I won't say anything else."

Darlene raised an eyebrow, "how much they pay you?"

"Two thousand," she let her eyes hit the table.

"Judas!" I said.

"You opened the door to drama in your life for pocket change! That ain't nothing!" Darlene said.

"Who?" I asked again.

"Toya."

I didn't believe her. She was hiding something, I could see it in her eyes. "So let me get this right, you willingly cooperated with Toya knowing how much we LOVE her! And somehow you didn't think this would come back on you?" She got nervous, "you aren't that dumb. You seem to be the Wallace Family historian. You were the one feeding Tracy all the background information on Drew and Toya. I have no doubt that you would've steered clear of her if she came to you directly!" I exhaled, "I don't like repeating myself, so... You can keep playing dumb. Life as you know it will end. Or you can tell us what you know, keep your little pocket change, then promise to never open your mouth again." She started to say something. "Aah! Think about it. Cause I'm going to have to convince Malcolm that it's ok to let you slide. You need to know the difference between when it's ok to open your mouth and when it isn't. Sasha punched you out for running your mouth but somehow you didn't learn your lesson. What do you think should happen now?" I looked at her.

Sonya exhaled as she looked at the table, she fidgeted with her hands. A tear fell from her eye. "Since she's decided to turn on the water works I think we should take this party outside." Darlene said.

"NO!" Sonya yelled and a couple people looked at us.

"Do you feel that?" Darlene said giving Sonya evil eyes. Sonya's eyes were stretched wide as she shook her head yes. "Yell one more time or draw attention to us in any kind of way and you won't have to guess what it is." Then she smiled, "I won't kill you, but your quality of life would forever change!" She winked at me, "now. You're going to follow my man out the door with a happy demeanor. If you mess this up, you don't wanna know what I'd do to you. Now go!"

I stood up, Sonya stood up tossing her hair and putting on a brave face. I took them out to the stairway and up one flight to a maintenance door. I ran my rigged up badge over the badge reader and the door unlocked. I pushed Sonya in. I told her the dumbest thing she could've ever done was open her mouth. I warned her that if she ran from me I would not be the person to chase her, and I was not responsible for what happened to her. I told her when the magazine came back to keep her mouth shut. Then I showed her pictures of her and her sidepiece, the horror that splashed across her face. I needed to do some checking to verify the information she gave me.

When I left the building Darlene called me and said she'd send her report right away. After I switched cars I went and picked up my girls from school. We went to North Star so that I could check things out. I watched Miranda teach my girls to be graceful swans for a minute. Then I walked around the building checking things out. The emergency exits, the basement, the secret panic room. I was checking everything out to make sure it was all ok. When I sat in Ginger's class she kept watching me when she should've been watching her class. I was looking for something, we still didn't know who sent her yet. That little girl Desiree kept looking at me too. When Ginger dismissed the kids for ten minutes I walked out the door just before the kids and instead of going to the right towards the main office, I went to the left and stood behind the pillar. The kids ran to the bathrooms, Ginger came out to see which way I went. When she went back inside her classroom, I went to the office. When I walked in Jade's office she was watching the monitor. She said Ginger was reporting in. I told Jade this whole thing wasn't sitting well with me. I told her the school needs to close for a while. What sense would it make for Dartnell to send someone here when they know this facility is clean. I said I had a strong feeling that she was working for Phineas. And if that was the case we needed to close. Jade said I was right. Then she called Amber. I told her today would be Yezzy and Syd's last day until we got everything sorted out. I went back to Miranda's class and Tracy was watching the class with a big smile. I swallowed my jealousy of her growing belly and I greeted her with a hug and smile. I whispered and told her she looked like she was doing a lot better. She whispered that she had to change the way she was eating and now she's getting more rest. When I sat next to her, she bumped me and asked me what was wrong. I shook my head and then she bumped me again. I told her something was missing and I couldn't put my finger on it. She smiled then she waited for me to ask why she was smiling at me. She asked me to come to service with her on Sunday. I told her to discuss it with Drew first. Then she told me if I went Andrew would definitely come. I thought about it, and it had been a long time since I had been. I told her I'd go in Richmond. Then she said we could all go and then go out to eat afterwards. She said Andrew hadn't been in a couple months, but she knew he'd go if I was going. I told her she had a deal, and then I wondered if Sylvia would go if she knew Drew was going to be there.

When I dropped Yezzy home Jackson came out. I told him dance classes were postponed for the time being. We confirmed what time I was picking Yezzy and little Jackson up on Friday. I told him that we would most likely go to service with my Grandma and Arthur on Sunday. Jackson smiled real big but that was the extent of it.

Sylvia and I pulled up to her place at the same time. She had her workout bag in hand and her clothes were soaked. She smiled as she left the door open for us. Syd gave me a big hug and kiss as she bounced up the stairs. I asked Sylvia if she had a good workout. She smiled and said she did. I told her that Sunday I wanted to take the kids to service. I told her I wanted to go to service in Richmond with my Grandma and Arthur. Her smiled dropped a little, and then I told her Tracy and Andrew were going to be there and it completely disappeared. "You don't want to go?"

"No." She said point blank. "Why do they have to be there?"

"Drew is my family, you do realize that being with me means you're going to see him."

"I do now. I don't like being around him."

"Because?"

She looked irritated, "you know why."

"If you want me to move past the past why can't you?" I asked matching her irritation.

"Come on Yussef you haven't moved past anything. You're still mad at me."

I looked at her, "so now you're the master of how I feel or what I'm thinking?"

"What are we doing here? You're still mad at me and now you keep putting me in uncomfortable situations to see how I respond. You're trying to see how much I can take before I break."

I looked at her for a minute. "Typical Sylvia!"

"What?" I insulted her.

"You were eating my dirty draws when you had no one. Your knight in shining armor. Now that you've paid off your bills, you're working out and feeling good about yourself, now you push back. What happened to whatever I wanted you would do?"

"Yussef I love you! That hasn't changed, but now you're trying to see which way I'll bend for you. You don't love me!"

"Again, you're the expert on how I feel."

"Admit it Yussef, you don't love me!"

"I do love you Sylvia."

Tears came to her eyes, "but you're not in love with me!"

"I never said I was in love with you. Isn't that what we're supposed to be working towards?"

"Yussef! How could you ever truly love someone when you're in love with her?"

"What?" Rage started turning in my stomach.

"I have eyes! I know how you were when you were with me. I can recognize it with someone else."

"So, you're not coming Sunday because I caught feelings for someone else?"

"Yussef your daughters are watching. I don't want them to think less of you, by making you stay with me."

"Because you don't need me."

"I'm not going anywhere. I'm still in love with you. But come on! That would be too much for everybody. Tracy doesn't know, and I couldn't stand for her to know."

"So we're breaking up?"

"No! I just don't want to go Sunday."

"So then we're breaking up." I watched her eyes. "We'll talk to the kids Friday night."

****

"Before we go out to dinner we want to talk to you." I said to the girls. Sylvia put her arms around little Jackson as she tried to fake a smile. "Sylvia is not my girlfriend anymore." Both of the girls gasped. "I'm sorry you guys, we tried, but it's just not going to work out." Yezzy put her arms around Syd as she started crying.

"Sydney I still love your daddy very much. It's not the right thing for our family for he and I to continue that way." Sylvia said crying.

Little Jackson sat on the other side of Syd and he put his arms around her too. "I, I, I...." She was trying to talk over her sob, which broke my heart. "I thought we were going to be a family!"

"We are a family Babygirl, but your mom and dad are not going to get married."

"Who are you going to marry daddy?" Yezzy asked rubbing Syd's back.

"I don't know yet, I haven't met her." Then I picked Sydney up, "I'm sorry Babygirl! I'm sorry!" I hugged her and kissed her forehead. She hugged me back so at least she didn't hate me.

"Where do you guys want to go for dinner?" Sylvia asked walking to the bathroom to get tissue for her nose.

Jackson and Yezzy looked at Syd with sad eyes. "Maybe we should order pizza and stay here." Yezzy said, "I don't think Sydney wants to go anywhere."

I looked at Syd in my arms. "You want to stay here?" She shook her head yes. I looked at Yezzy and smiled, "can you guys read each other's minds?"

"We're twins. I know how she feels." Yezzy said proudly.

****

"It feels weird every time I come here," Drew said standing in my living room.

Little Jackson came in the living room with his clothes all twisted. Andre immediately started laughing at him. "You need to brush your hair! Fix your clothes, why do you look like that?"

Little Jackson frowned, "my mom always brushes my hair for me."

"It's not hard, I can show you how." Andre volunteered, then he walked to the bathroom with little Jackson who was bigger than him in tow.

"Well don't you look lovely." Tracy said as the girls walked out the room together.

"Thank you," they said at the same time. Syd was still sad but she was coming around.

"We can all fit in my truck, you ready?" Drew said.

On the way to service I asked how things were going and Drew said they were fine. Tracy said Drew's been making sure that she gets what she needs daily, and things have been looking up.

Service was nice and my momma came and sat with me. I hated that it felt good to sit next to her. At one point she held my hand cause hers was trembling. I didn't think about how hard it was for her to be here. After service a lot of people came over. Some of them knew Tracy's family. Others remembered me growing up. Afterwards we went out to brunch and the kids had a blast making new friends, and discovering new family members as Arthur's kids and grandkids came along as well. Seeing Drew and his magazine family didn't help my mood though.

Episode 15

Amber

Kimmy was too excited when she called me bright and early. I knew she wasn't calling to ask about my wedding. She was trying to chitchat with me, and I told her to stop beating around the bush. She said the label wanted to do a segment on Corey, my Director friend. She had her business hat on, she said they want to feature all of his achievements and as they reviewed what made his work shine like it did it was me. I exhaled; as she went on she was trying to sell me hard on the idea. I looked at Malcolm who was laying there waiting for me to get off the phone. My mind was rolling over what she was saying. When I asked about the artist that they had in mind to collaborate with, Kimmy stammered. Instantly I was angry, I told Kimmy I had to go. She begged me to think about it and not to automatically reject the idea. I told her I wasn't desperate for work, and I picked and chose the projects I wanted to work on these days. That didn't stop her from pleading with me. When I got off the phone Malcolm asked me what she wanted. I told him and he asked me if there was a measure of professionalism that I could exert to make this work for me. I frowned at him; the idea of sharing the same screen with Torrie did not sit well with me. I wanted nothing to do with it. He asked me how I was going to let Torrie stop me from receiving the praise that I worked so hard for. He told me to forget Torrie and let them do the segment. I called Kimmy back and I told her, I didn't want to be interviewed in case I had to wash my hands of the whole thing. She was extremely excited.

When I got out of the bed Malcolm asked me where I was going. I told him I didn't feel like laying next to him anymore. He frowned at me as he watched me grab my robe and walk out of the room. Tina was home with her parents discussing everything they needed to talk to her about. I walked downstairs not really knowing where I was going, but I wasn't feeling being in that room. I threw my body on the couch and picked up the remote. Malcolm came downstairs completely naked. I'm used to kids running in and out of the house unannounced so the idea of walking around here naked was foreign to me. He took the remote out of my hand and made me stand on the couch. He took my robe off. He told me all that stuff was in the past, it wasn't us today and I needed to let it go. I told him it was easier for him to say that. He looked at me, and then he said is the pretty boy still alive, was he still breathing? He said the thought of him being in his space because he left the door wide open for that to happen follows him every day. It may be one person but the pretty boy was everywhere, and it didn't feel like one person to him. I relaxed a lot. He picked me up and laid me gently on the couch. There will never be another touch like "*MY* **MALCOLM'S!**"

****

Jade's voice was too calm, which made me kind of panic. She told me that Yussef thinks we should close the school. I told her I would discuss it with Malcolm. It was now to the point that the guest list for our wedding was very tight. Unless the person was family they got save the dates for a fictitious ceremony in Vegas that would take place months after our actual ceremony. To make that date seem legit we booked a venue, put Mitigated staff on the date and everything. We were making plans like it was definitely going to happen in Vegas. I had to turn down projects for the rest of the year. Malcolm asked me if I thought about retiring with all the grandbabies coming. The idea made me feel extremely old and I could see the regret on his face as soon as he saw my reaction. He was trying to find the words to correct what he said but I tuned him out. I'm not old! Just older!

****

When I walked out in my dress my Auntie Lauren started crying. I stood on the pedestal feeling exactly the way I imagined I would feel in this moment. Beautiful, sexy, regal, like a bride. "Amber! You look so pretty honey. Your momma would be crying right now too!"
Now I was crying! I took deep breaths to calm myself then I took myself in again. My daddy's skin as if it had been kissed by the sun permanently. My momma's eyes, and then this dress! My dress was a fit and flare dress with a nice sized train. It had lace and almost tightly laid on my body. The neckline was somewhat cowl necked with very thin beaded straps. The part I loved about this dress was that my back was completely open. The back was open all the way down to my waistline. This dress accentuated my butt and how small my waistline is. I LOVE this dress! And I know Malcolm is going to love it. Sophia tried on her dress, which also hugged her body nicely. As Rosalind stood on the pedestal getting her dress pinned she looked really nervous. She didn't wait for us to ask, "Ben has been on my phone every day! Tanisha is so mad about it."
"How you feel about it?"
"It's weird, I'm still in love with Troy. I don't want to end up alone either."
"You shouldn't get back with Ben just because you don't wanna be alone." Sophia said.
"Says the woman who still sneaks around with Richard on the down low!"
We all gasped, Sophia looked at her momma. "Momma, no I don't she's lying!"
Rosalind smiled, "just checking. You know he wants to be with you. No matter how many babies that chick has you know all you have to do is say the word and he would leave her in a heartbeat. You've got somebody waiting on you. The man I love was taken from me over nonsense. I can sit and wallow in my loneliness or deal with this man who relies heavily on blue pills to get going."
I had to ask her, I pretended like my Auntie wasn't sitting right there. "You guys have been intimate?" She shook her head yes. Everyone moved in close even Auntie Lauren. "And?"
Rosalind smiled, "first of all I remember it being bigger than that or maybe he shrunk. Then we had to wait for that pill to work. Then it was ok, Troy is the only man to make me see God!"
"But he's younger than Malcolm."
"And the same age as Richard." We looked at Sophia, "and younger than Travis."
"They don't need help?" Rosalind asked wide-eyed. We shook our heads no. "Mrs. Wallace?"
"Nope, Jeff is good. I gotta take my vitamins just to keep up." Auntie Lauren said, Sophia plugged her ears.

"He has high blood pressure so his medicines mess with him. At least that's the way he described it to me."

"That sounds about right." Cassondra said still pinning away.

"Your man?" I asked.

"No!" She said adamantly. "A girlfriend of mine though, but they changed her man's diet and got him exercising. They adjusted his meds and he was good to go again."

"I was going to say, cause we're not old enough to deal with pills and stuff." I said.

"Technically you are. It really depends on the man's health. Pretty soon you guys are going to start going through the change."

I looked at Tracy who was holding Chanel, "I don't want any more babies, but I don't want to feel too old to have them."

Chantel's door opened and she came out of the room posing. "I just want you guys to know! My Grandma is GOOD! I missed this body!" She said posing all kinds of crazy ways in the doorway.

We all laughed, "You are crazy! Why would you thank your Grandma?"

"You didn't see how she had me wrapped up like a mummy? From the top of my stomach to my ankles she had me bandaged every day. It was hot in there, but I got a waistline again."

"Momma how come you didn't do that to me?" Sophia asked.

"I didn't know about it. Sounds wonderful though. Look at you, you don't look like you just had a baby."

"Thank you!" Chantel said admiring her form in the mirror.

"Well we already know it's not going to be like that for me, so no comparisons please." Tracy said.

"Don't you worry sweetheart, you're going to come workout with me. When you're ready we can do Nana's diet together." I smiled at her.

"What's that?"

"Eating right and working out, when I had Andy I was so depressed. I was up fifty pounds after everything shifted and decided where it was going to fall. One summer with my Nana and she got me on track. I learned how to run," I hadn't thought about Tag in a long time. "I made better food choices, and I was breast feeding."

"But I won't look like that after eight weeks." Tracy said.

"Genetics has a lot to do with it as well. Chantel's father is not a big man."

"And my mother was small in frame too. She was tall and thin. Who knows if I will have it this good after I have another baby."

I turned my attention back to Rosalind, "so are you and Ben back together?"

She exhaled, "I can't say yes or no. Tanisha isn't happy about us saying hello. She doesn't know about him spending the night. Please don't tell her."

****

I sat on the couch next to Tina, my heart was pounding. Malcolm and Darryl hurried in the door. The opening credits started rolling. "It's starting!" Andre called out to everyone outside the theater. Chantel sat next to me and I took the baby from her.

The commentator welcomed everyone to this latest edition of *A Closer Look*. Then she asked the audience if they knew about the selling power of music videos. She said they started in the late seventies and really caught on in the early 80's. She highlighted Corey as the Director to get! They even had an interview with Corey that they layered within the segment. Corey being the standup guy that he is gave credit where it was due to the costume designers, makeup artists, choreographers, etc. the commentator said that there was one choreographer that he preferred to work with above everyone else, then she asked who that maybe. "Amber Wallace of course!" Everyone applauded, but I braced myself for something bad to happen. They had a million pictures of me, and clips of me dancing in videos and during awards ceremonies. They said the world took notice of me as the love interest in Mister MC's video. Then they showed clips of behind the scenes interviews with me for different artist. They named Corey and I as the main power drivers behind the mega star Torrie when she was most in demand. Then they showed me on the red carpet as the arm candy of tons of artist. The commentator made it seem like I dated all those people, I rolled my eyes. Then she said my most noteworthy romances were with Dwayne Reed and the rapper Comfort. They had behind the scene footage of Dwayne and I being silly. Dwayne trying to master a move from a routine. I remembered that like it was yesterday. The commentator said they couldn't get in direct contact with Dwayne due to his heavy filming schedule, but he issued a statement. "Amber Wallace is very smart, talented, and very charismatic. It has been an honor and a privilege to know her, and I wish her nothing but success on her future endeavors." Then the commentator went on to talk about Comfort. "WE WERE NEVER TOGETHER!" I yelled at the screen, everyone laughed. Based off of one beautifully stupid song they created a whole love triangle. I folded my arms and pouted. Tina was on the edge of her seat taking everything in. They showed the clip from the awards ceremony where they had me dancing on the big screen behind Comfort accepting the award that Dwayne presented him with. The commentator stated that was the last time Comfort and I were seen in public together. She said there were reports that I left the party that night with an unidentified man. Everyone laughed and looked at Malcolm. They said today I remain the powerhouse behind a lot of the major artists. Then they showed Chantel. They said she married my brother, everyone laughed. Then they showed my school where I occasionally taught classes.

"I had no idea you were such a big deal when I met you. You were only Andrew's mom."

"That's good, that's all I wanted to be." I smiled.

"One more wedding you guys then we can relax!" Sophia announced.

"Thank goodness!" Darryl said coming to take Chanel from me. "Her cuteness is calling me!"

I watched Malcolm who was quietly watching Darryl and Chanel. I grabbed my phone then I told Darryl to give the baby to Malcolm. Chanel smiled really big at Malcolm, and Malcolm melted. I snapped picture after picture of them. Sophia and Grace had Denise cornered with a plate of food. Malachi told us they move into their house next weekend. I couldn't wait until our house was done too.

When we got home Malcolm was thoughtful, I knew he was thinking about the baby. I just wasn't sure in which direction. I went in the kitchen and put a pot on to make some tea. Malcolm came in and put his arms around me. He kissed my neck, then he said he was thinking about how he never wanted a family because of all of the headache having obvious liabilities would bring. He said he looks at the family that I always wanted and he thanks me for knowing better than him. Then he said he hoped Tracy has a boy, he said we were getting too many girls. I smiled and told him he finally gets his little girl. He said he thought of that when he was holding Chanel tonight. Then he chuckled; he said he had no idea how my daddy dealt with him. If he held me as a precious baby and then watched me fall victim to a guy like him, the guy would be dead.

****

"Amber I know you hate the city, but we're going straight to the Mitigated office and then we're leaving." Gloria said.

I didn't say anything I looked at her as she headed through the tollbooth for the Bay Bridge. She explained that she had to physically get something from her husband and it couldn't wait until he got home. I looked at the Mitigated car behind us and I took a deep breath. We parked in the garage and then we walked to the building. Since I hated coming to the city, I've only been to this office maybe twice. The receptionist smiled real big at Gloria and I as she greeted us as we walked towards her desk. She buzzed us right in, and we walked onto the floor. People on the floor looked at us and whispered as we walked past them. It was one of those they all know who we are but we don't know them moments. Gloria was heading towards Juan's office as I looked at Malcolm's. There were two females in his office. He was sitting behind his desk, and they were sitting in the chairs facing his desk. I knew that look on their faces, and today was not the day. As if he sensed my presence Malcolm looked up and saw me coming through the glass. I watched his mouth to see if he said anything, but he didn't. He watched me walk towards them. I opened the door and closed it behind me. The woman who was talking deflated a little when she saw me. She stopped talking; I put my purse on the file cabinet behind his desk. I picked up a chair from the table in his office and I sat it next to Malcolm and then I sat down. Both of them looked annoyed at my presence. I told her to continue, she looked at Malcolm and he told her to go on. She continued on with her statement but now her body language was different. My pictures were all over this office as well. So I doubted that they didn't know who I was, but I wanted to know who they were. They were trying to persuade Malcolm to go into business with them. Some kind of fashion endeavor. I didn't like the setup, but really let me be honest. There was nothing wrong with their business plan. I just didn't like that they were trying to sell everything with sex attached to it. Their attire was very sexy, and the items in their portfolios were all sexy as well. They wanted to market to stick figures, when the average woman is not a size two. "So we'll leave this with you to look over and you can give your final decision next week." The brunette said.

"Thank you," Malcolm said reaching for the binder but I took it. Then I looked at him, "ladies this is my wife."

Both of them said fake hellos, so I just looked at them. "Malcolm, should we increase the lunch reservation to four?" The second chick asked.

I looked at Malcolm, "why is lunch necessary?"

"Uh, we wanted to thank Malcolm for giving us his time by taking him out to lunch. We know how busy he is."

"You wanted to take up more of his time to thank him for giving you some of his time?"

"It's only a gesture to say thank you." The first girl said.

I looked at Malcolm, "they said thank you. Now send them away."

"Thank you ladies for your information, someone will be in contact with you shortly."

They gathered their things; the first girl didn't look at me again, but the other girl looked pissed off even though she was trying to hide it. When they walked out I looked at Malcolm and he smiled at me. "This is business."

I pointed at the binder, "This is business. Their attire, and lunch was not! Turn it down!" I glared at him.

"Amber this is business, don't go and start flying off the handle." He warned me.

"This is one business venture you can pass on. You will not be hurting by passing up on this one. You wanna get into the fashion world I know a designer you should meet with, but not them! All they're selling is sex!"

"Where's Gloria, I thought you guys were hanging out today."

"She's in Juan's office. I'm not playing with you Malcolm!" I warned.

Malcolm buzzed his admin and told him to come in. Clive came in with a notepad, and sat in the chair in front of his desk. He said hello to me and then waited for Malcolm. "I need you to draft up the decline letter to the young lady's proposal." He handed him the binder, and told him to send it back with the letter. Then he told him to make lunch reservations for four somewhere nice in the city. Clive hurried back to his desk and did as he was told. "Are you happy now?"

"Very!"

Sasha

"So, I'm going to be a grandfather, I guess that's ok Sassy." Richard said looking like he had a problem with the fact that I was pregnant.

"You guess?"

"You just got married and you're pregnant already. Why wouldn't you give yourself some time to adjust to married life first?"

"The technicality of our marriage is now out of the way, but we've been living like we're married for years. It's time for the new chapter."

"I don't like the idea of you being vulnerable."

"Um, Richard how am I vulnerable? If anything El is more vulnerable than me at this point. His parents are excited and it's like they've gotten their second wind after learning about the baby. They've both taken a turn for the better. Are you over here acting up with your girlfriend?"

He looked out my office window, he exhaled. "Your momma still loves me. I saw it all in her face at the wedding."

They make me tired! "She's in love with her man Travis. You are my father, and there will always be love there, but please don't mistake that for more than it actually is. If she wasn't so against getting remarried, my momma and Travis would get married."

"Sassy, that's your momma and you love her. I get that; you guys are close blah, blah, blah. But you will never know your mother like I know her. She's still in love with me."

"Why does any of that matter? You didn't want to do what it took to be with her. You have a whole new family. I love Travis, he's a wonderful stepfather, and he loves my momma without trying to make her jump through hoops to prove her love back. Once you have my momma on the hook you always run from her. She would be a fool to take you seriously."

Richard didn't respond for a long time. "I guess Erica can succeed in getting pregnant right away. Why fight it right?"

"Is that what you want?"

"I wanted more kids and she's giving me that. It will do for now. I miss Sophia though."

****

I didn't have to open my eyes to know he was staring at me. "El baby why are you staring at me?"

"I thought you made a noise. I was listening for it again or for you to move." Concern and worry was all over his face.

I couldn't be annoyed, even though I wanted to be. I know how hard of a time he had with Zoila when she was pregnant. Everything was high risk and then to lose his child after all of that. I know he's traumatized, but I really would just like some peaceful sleep. I kissed him, "El baby I'm fine."

"I'm scared Sasha, we've waited for this for so long."

I sat up, "did you just openly admit to being scared?"

He shook his head, "yes."

I kissed him again, "we're fine baby. We are just fine."

He put his arms around me, "I love you so much! Thank you! This is amazing that you would do this for me."

"Do what?"

"Risk forever ruining your body to have my baby."

"Babies, don't forget the plural. We're having at least two for now."

"Don't you want to see how everything goes before you have another one?"

"I hated being an only child. Even though I was always with Drew, Tanisha, and my uncles. There were times I was all-alone, and I did not like it. I was so happy when Sabrina came along. I just wish we were closer in age. She understands the drama with my momma when no one else does. I want our children to have each other."

"I can understand that, I'm so happy you're willing to do this for me."

I kissed him, "this is for us."

He exhaled, "we need to decide where we're going to be though. Are we delivering up here or down there?"

"What would you prefer?" I asked.

"The tug of war between your parents is hard. In this situation I think your mum wins. Don't you think? Everyone is here, the only reason I'd reject being out here is because he's here. You're about to be fat so I guess it doesn't matter." He teased.

I laughed, "Are you kidding. I'll be even more irresistible with the extra weight and belly." I laid my head on his chest. "I love that I can tell you anything and everything about me and you still love me anyways. Girls like me don't always get to have that."

"Girls like you?"

"I'm not supposed to have a soul or feelings. I'm not supposed to care, and the moment I start caring my looks are supposed to fade. I guess even now I guess I'm supposed to blow up and just be a version of my former glory. I'm still gonna be my sassy self even after the baby. I guess I'm just talking out loud."

"You're scared about your body aren't you?" His voice smiled.

"Does it make me horrible if I say yes?"

"You will always be beautiful to me no matter what." He rubbed my back.

"I'm not worried about you. I don't want to see anything crazy! I'm pretty confident that you will love me no matter what. I want to still love me when this is all said and done."

****

"Hello Miss Sasha! How's the married lady?" Nurse Jasmine asked.

"I's married now! I's married!" I joked, and then I brought out my tablet. "You wanted pictures right?"

She very excitedly clapped her hands, and then she took the tablet from me.

There was a knock on the door and then El walked in. "Nurse Jasmine, this is my husband El." I said.

"Oh my God Sasha! Your man is gorgeous!" She blurted. El blushed and thanked her.

"Seriously, you two can't be together. This is going to be one ugly baby."

We started cracking up. "Why do you say that?"

"Oh lord! And he has an accent!" She fanned herself. "It's only fair that two good looking people have ugly babies. And ugly people have pretty babies, it's only fair. The world stays balanced that way." Then she watched the pictures and short videos on the tablet. When the doctor walked in Nurse Jasmine popped up and put the tablet behind her.

The doctor smiled as she shook El's hand, then she congratulated me on having such a handsome husband. Again El blushed. My doctor asked us if we had any questions and El rattled off question after question. One of his many good questions was how soon should I find a doctor up north since I planned to spend more time out that way and I would most likely deliver out there. My doctor and Nurse Jasmine tried to pull back their sad expressions. Then she said right away. She did her normal checkup and then the fun part as she called it. We were going to hear my baby's heartbeat. SWISH-A-SWISH-A-SWISH! It sound very fast and alien to me. El held my hand but he had a funny look. That's when I noticed the same looks on the doctor and Nurse Jasmine's faces. El squeezed my hand as he waited. My doctor looked at me, "I think I hear two heartbeats." I was horrified, "what?" They laughed at my reaction. "I didn't sign up for two. Please tell me you were mistaken and there's only one."

Everyone laughed again, but I didn't see what was so doggone funny. Do they have any idea what two babies at one time will do to my body? This was all El's fault! I don't know how but it just is. There's no twins in my family. There's Tracy's sisters, and Chantel's little brother and sister. The twin terrors, but they're not real twins just close in age. No real twins tied to my family! This isn't FAIR! My doctor sent us down to have an ultrasound. Nurse Jasmine found an excuse to come with us. She was too excited and I could tell El was holding back his excitement cause he could see I was truly pissed. I rolled my eyes as soon as I saw both of the jellybeans on the screen. I turned my head away from the screen, I wanted to spit fire. I called my momma as soon as we hit the outside I was in tears. She was alarmed at first cause she knew we were going to the doctor's office today. She didn't care about my tears; she was excited and called my Nana on three-way. I could barely talk I was crying so hard. Both of them celebrated in my ear, which pissed me off some more. El didn't say anything he just smiled and drove. I called Drew looking for sympathy. His happiness pissed me off too! Nobody was getting it! I sat in the passenger seat mourning the loss of my beautiful body when Tracy called me back. I almost didn't answer cause I had no idea what she was going to say. I didn't want to hear excitement. "Hello!"

"Hey sweetheart." She said cautiously.

"Hi!" I spit.

"Andrew just called me and told me the news."

"Please don't say congratulations! I don't need that right now." I started sobbing again.

"I was calling to check on you. I don't know what it's like to have twins, but I know what it's like growing up with them." She paused, "twins is a bigger deal than, oh look at how cute they are or dressing them a like. They're attention stealers!"

I shook my head, "they are! Cause everybody is all excited but they're not thinking about what this is going to do to me."

"I understand. When are you coming back? We can plan something, like a lunch for us not all these babies."

That made me feel better, "I'll be back next week. And I like the sound of that."

"Ok let's touch base tomorrow and we'll plan something. Take care Sasha."

"Thank you Tracy, you too." Then I sat up in my seat. El still had that stupid smile plastered on his face. "I hate you!"

"I love you too Sasha. Thank you!" He said still smiling.

****

"It's not that serious Sasha calm down." Jeff said.

"That's because you and Randi are only having one."

"Those hormones got you tripping." Then he looked at El, "you got a long road ahead of you!"

"Are you going to carry them the entire nine months or will you deliver them early?" Randi asked.

"We don't know yet. So far they're doing well so we'll see." El rubbed my hand telling me to calm down.

Jeff shook his head, "come have a drink with us." He said leading El out into the backyard. JoJo arrived at the same time as my momma, Travis, and Sabrina. Sabrina kissed my forehead, then she gently touched my stomach saying hello to the babies. The men went out back, and then my nana came back. She was telling me to keep my skin moisturized. I told her my doctor told me there was no way to avoid stretch marks, she hissed at me. She said she didn't get any with my momma or Jeff. She barely got any with JoJo and that was because she was tired on the third one. Randi sat up she was all ears. She told us not to scratch and if we itched to put lotion on it. She held up a jar, she said Shea Butter was going to be our best friends. She even gave a jar to Sabrina even though she had some at home already.

****

Twins or not I wasn't going down without a fight. I was running on that treadmill like my life depended on it. Between Carly and Darlene I know they get sick of following me to the gym. At least Darlene decided to workout with me since I was in here all the time.

"Can I ask you something? You can say it's none of my business."

I frowned, "I already know that. Which way are you trying to get into my business?"

"Why did you look at me like you did when we met? Were you feeling Yussef or something?"

I held up my hand, "I'm married, hello!"

She blank stared at me; "please don't try to play me for stupid. Your man is fine, but Yussef is Yussef!"

"You feeling Yussef?"

"YES!! Girl! If I could I would climb that man!"

My stomach turned, "is that right."

"Sasha please don't be fake with me. I know you like him. I'm coming to you woman to woman."

"Fine! I'm married so it's not like I can say anything if you guys date."

"We're not going to date. We don't want the same things. He's looking for a wife and a family. I don't want anything to do with all that. I just wanna hit it." She smiled.

"At least you're honest. So I guess that means his wedding is next." I exhaled. I could see him doing so much better than Sylvia, but if he's going to settle she's not a horrible choice.

"They broke up." She watched my face.

"What? What happened?" I took a drink of my water.

"Don't know, but she'll be here in a few minutes. She was coming here just before they broke up, but now she's here all the time."

"Trying to catch?"

"I don't think so. She keeps her head down and she lets these guys down gently."

"She dating somebody?"

"Nope, gym and home. She goes out from time to time with a girlfriend from work or her daughter."

"So what's wrong with her? Why did they break up?"

Darlene smiled, "how do you know it's not on him?"

"Are you kidding Yussef is great!"

"Yea, but he's still only a man. He PMS's like the rest of them."

Then we watched Sylvia walk in with her baggy gym clothes on and ear buds in. Just like Darlene said she kept her eyes low. If she would've looked up she would've saw us but she never did. She came in did her work out and left.

Tracy

"How many treatments is she going to need?" Andrew asked the doctor.

"Her labs have come back nicely, this should be the last one."

I received my final iron treatment and I was happy one less needle to have to experience. My doctor scheduled an appointment to follow up on my results shortly after. She reminded me to do my kick count and other things to pay attention to.

Andrew exhaled, things have been good since I finally started letting him take care of me. I've gotten my color back; I'm eating kale, spinach, Rainbow Swiss Chard, and greens all day, every day now. In addition to that I'm eating more red meat than I've eaten in a long time. The perfect excuse for a juicy burger. Oh burgers! Oh how I've missed you! Turkey burgers and bean burgers are good. Matter of fact I love Portobello mushroom burgers as meat alternatives, this one place makes the best one my mouth drools at the thought of it. However, Andrew makes the best barbecue burgers ever. They're so juicy and well-seasoned. The burger in its self is fine, but if I'm gonna do it, I gotta do it right. Pepper jack cheese, bacon, avocado, red onions, pickles, lettuce, and tomato. With garlic mayo, DROOLS! Garlic fries and a thick milk shake. That has become our Monday night dinner. Poor Andre rolls away from the table while I sit there in heaven.

I make sure I'm on the treadmill at least thirty minutes a day Monday through Friday. I go down to the bakery sometimes but they don't let me do anything major. We discuss business, I make notes about the sales, I write down flavor ideas. Pearla always leaves flavor suggestions for me. I appreciate that she makes suggestions but never tells me how to achieve them.

When we come home Andre does his homework. Yes, homework in kindergarten good grief! Then he does his chores, he says he's in training and he takes the puppies out back and they run all over the backyard. Andrew gave him a list of things to check every day when he gets home. And when Andrew comes home, Andre has to report what he's found. Andrew acts like he's preparing Andre for battle and I don't like it. I normally leave when they start sparring cause I can't take it. I'm mad every time I come home and I see a bruise or a cut on Andre. Andre thinks his battle scars are cool, I hate them. When his Poppa comes over he shows them proudly. Amber always looks at my horrified face and then she tells them to go somewhere with their manly crap. Malcolm always looks so proud, and then they go out back. Sometimes Malcolm and Andrew disagree about something Andrew is showing Andre. It can get pretty heated at times, but they suck it up for Andre's sake.

I asked Amber if this is what she had to deal with all the time? She said the number one argument between her and Malcolm was that she was going to make Andrew soft. She said it's not easy watching your baby come home hurt, but it does condition them to be stronger. I rubbed my stomach praying for a girl, but then I wondered if that would make a difference as I remembered Sasha laying out Sonya like it was nothing.

Amber and I discussed her cake, it took a lot of convincing but eventually she and Andrew were on board with me making the cake. Amber was being very tight lipped about the venue for her wedding and reception. She only shared that the reception would not be held in the same location as the ceremony. Then with sad eyes she said she was going to have to temporarily close the school. When I asked why, she said keeping it open has become too high of a risk. She said once it closes this will be the first time since Darryl was little that she wasn't working. I didn't understand why the school needed to close, but if she felt it was necessary I knew it was for a good reason.

****

Andrew had a last minute meeting that he could not get away from so he couldn't go with me to the doctor. I was ok with it, but he was really upset about it. My mom gladly volunteered to go in his place. I went to the lab to have my blood drawn and then we went to my doctor's office. The doctor sent me down to the ultrasound lab to have them measure something that was a little unclear previously. My mom was so excited looking at baby difficult on the screen. The baby had its legs closed again. The technician asked if we knew the sex already, and I told her that we called the baby *baby difficult* because it would not open its legs. The technician had an old school pager at her station and she asked if she could try vibrating the baby to see if that would get the baby to move. I thought it was a funny idea, but I agreed to it. She put the pager on the vibrate setting and laid it on the baby's back. The baby jumped and immediately started kicking. She moved the pager around and the baby immediately started fighting. And then we saw it as clear and big as day. It was a boy, my mom started crying and I immediately thought of Eve and I. The male numbers were growing against us, but I was happy all the same. The baby was fighting for a minute after the vibrating had stopped; he had the nerve to have a little temper. My doctor told me to continue all my healthy habits and to enjoy my last trimester cause the baby was going to be here in a couple of months. Andrew didn't give me a chance to call him. He stepped out of his meeting and called to check in. I told him everything looked good and the baby was a fighter already. He asked me what that meant and I told him the technician got baby difficult to fight and HE was kicking and fighting the whole time. I could hear Andrew's smile through the phone as he said it was a boy. I told him I knew he was disappointed that it wasn't a girl. He said that's ok; he said the next baby would be a girl. I loved that he wasn't acting like the world was coming to an end. At the end of the day we are a family and our family was growing. My mom was so excited she called everybody and told them I was having a boy. She was bubbling forward with so much excitement; she immediately started thinking of all the pictures she wanted Andre and the baby to take together. How cute they would be at Service together. When Andrew came home he was too excited. He told Andre to work on his homework and then he took me upstairs. He kissed me long and deeply, then he said we needed to seriously talk about names. I asked him what he had in mind. He smiled and said he wanted to name him Andrew. I gasped and asked him what about Andre? He said they discussed it before, but we could officially discuss it as a family. I said I had a suggestion but I'd wait until the family discussion.

We waited for Andre to finish his homework and chores, while Andrew made dinner. He kept smiling at me like he was so happy. I was worried that he was going to be disappointed that it wasn't a girl, he was so happy I don't think it really mattered, which is a relief. I on the other hand couldn't wait to hold my baby. I couldn't wait to see him and hear his voice. Andrew handed each of us a bowl of fruit salad for dessert. "Dre guess what!" Andre smiled at his dad. "Mommy found out what we're having today." Andre gasped, "What is it?" He asked with his eyes open wide.

"Mommy?" Andrew smiled at me.

"You're going to have a little brother."

"YES!" Andre said as he celebrated.

"You wanted a little brother?"

"Yes, and then a little sister, but a brother first so we could be the men." Andre said like it was a no brainer.

"We have to figure out a name for him." Andrew said.

"Andrew!" Andre said quickly.

"Ok, that's one idea." I said, "but what about Malcolm?"

Both of them looked at me with surprise on their faces. "Malcolm?"

"Andrew you should've seen the way this baby was fighting the technician when they got him to move. The way he's already behaving the name seems to fit to me. What do you think?"

Andrew frowned, "I don't know."

"You mean like my Poppa?"

"Yes, I really like the idea of a little Malcolm. Your daddy's name should've been Malcolm, they act so much alike."

"Ok but my next brother needs to be named Andrew like dad." Andre said.

I smiled at Andre then I looked at Andrew. He was thinking, "I don't know. I need to think about it."

Andrew remained quiet the rest of the evening. When we went to bed he couldn't sleep. I asked him what was wrong; he said he and Malcolm didn't get along most of his life. I told him that didn't mean that he didn't love him. Andrew rubbed my stomach, and then he said we should wait until we saw him. Depending on how he looked we'd name him one or the other. I told him that sounds good to me.

Yussef

I made sure the freezers were full of meats and breads. I checked the expiration dates on the can goods and put the new cans in the back and the oldest cans in the front. I stocked more water bottles, etc. I keep going over the trends I'm seeing and Phineas is up to something.

Although I wanted Malcolm and Amber to close the school immediately, they decided on a later date to not appear so obvious. I understand why, but at the same time I don't think it's safe not to move immediately. Something tells me I need to get completely prepared for the storm.

I keep stressing to the kids the importance of paying attention to their surroundings. I tell them just because someone is an adult doesn't mean they will protect them and care for them, always be careful and to look for exit strategies. It's become one of our games whenever we go somewhere. In case of an emergency how would you get out of this room and get to safety? That's what I ask them with every new place we go to. I challenge them to come up with plan B's and C's. I stress the importance of being quiet. I told them it's good to get in the habit now cause they never know when they'll need to be this way.

Tracy

Just because I couldn't bake in my own bakery doesn't mean I was going to stop baking. I had a taste for my lemon cream pie. I sent a pie with Andrew to work. I put two in the freezer and then I sent one to my parents, my brother, one for Andre, and I still had two extra. I dozed off for my afternoon nap when my phone went off.

Darryl: Tracy

Me: Yes Darryl

Darryl: Can I have some of ur pie

Me: I don't know what u heard

Darryl: I heard u passing out pies. I want some

Me: Who told u that?

Darryl: I'm wit Drew! The greedy peeps in his office ate all da pie! Hook ur bro UP!

Me: I'll think about it!

I laughed when my phone started ringing. "I'm trying to take a nap." I said with a smile.
"So just agree to hook your little brother up and then you can go back to sleep."
"Have you told Sharon about us yet?"
Darryl sucked his teeth. "Why you gotta be worried about her right now. I'm calling you to talk to you and you wanna be worried about what I'm telling her." He took his mouth away from the phone, "Drew man your woman be tripping! I thought I told you to check her!" I could hear Andrew laughing in the background.
"Andrew knows better, and you see he gets all the cake and pie a man can stand."
"That's until you have that baby. Then the cakes and pies are going to be on lock down for a while. I bet you he was the main one eating up all the pies and being greedy. Drew man! You knew I was coming how come you didn't save me none?"
"I'm not worried about you. I gets my pie on the regular, how you get yours is how you get yours." Andrew said.
I laughed, "Tracy! Girl let's stop all this foolishness. I want some pie, and I know you want to give me some pie so let's stop playing hard to get. When you gonna hook your brother up so I can be ready?"
"Nope, I'm tired of being your down low hook up. You gotta call Sharon first."
"Tracy! Don't be like that. I need some pie, and I need you to give it to me. Don't let someone else come between us and what we got." He pleaded.
"Call her on three way."
"Drew! See, if you handled business like I told you to. I wouldn't have to go through this right now. Please man! Check her!"
"Sorry man, siding with you might jeopardize my future cakes and pies, and I need to

continue to be broken off at will. If my woman say you gotta come forth with the truth then you got to."

"Tracy! I don't want to break Sharon's heart. Me and Ryder is close. You're talking about hurting someone I love dearly. Sharon loves when I beg for her cake. True my heart isn't in it no more since you started baking for me. I still love her, and it's not her fault that I fell for your cakes and pies. I'm asking for more time and then I will come forward."

"Darryl, you've had years and still I'm your best kept secret. I can't continue like this anymore."

"Tracy! You are not a secret! Everybody knows I love your cakes and pies!"

"Everybody but Sharon."

"Alright, if I call her when will you have a pie ready for me?"

"Un un, I want to hear it, call her right now."

"You don't trust me?"

"No!"

Darryl gasped, "you have wounded me."

"Darryl you have had how many years to come clean about us, and you have failed me. I need undeniable proof. Matter of fact meet me up at the development after you leave there. I want to be there when you tell her."

"Drew man! This isn't fair, I don't want to hurt nobody."

"I'm sure you will find a way to be gentle."

"My pain is funny to you!"

"When you hide what you feel for my treats, yes it is."

"Drew! This feels too much like real life." He exhaled, "you win." He said in defeat. "I'll break the news to her when you get there."

I smiled, "alright! Deal! I love you little brother."

"Yeah! Yeah! Yeah! Talk to you in a little bit."

I laughed myself to sleep. I woke up when it was time to pick up Andre from school. I packed a pie for Darryl. I parked in the model home parking lot and then Andre and I went in. Sharon smiled when she saw me, she was on the phone. I looked at the little Model of the development; all of the plots were sold out in phase one. Before Sharon got off the phone Ryder arrived. I asked him how everything was going and he said he had no complaints. His eyes kept darting to the pie box in Andre's hands. He asked me who the cake was for, and I told him it was a pie, but the receiver was only getting it if he handled business. He stared at the box, and then he asked me if I made it. When I shook my head yes he started looking anxious. He asked me what kind of pie it was. I told him it was a lemon cream pie. Ryder sat down and started bouncing his leg. Then he got up and moved to the seat next to Andre. "Dre, is the pie good?"

"It's delicious!" Andre smiled.

Then Darryl and Andrew walked in the door. "Who's the pie for?" Ryder asked.

"That's my pie! What you need to know for?" Darryl said giving me a hug. "Tracy! Don't tell another man about my pie. All that's going to do is make him want some, and I ain't sharing!"

"Well, it's not yours yet."

Darryl shook his head and started pacing. Ryder looked at him with a smile. "Tracy," he had a sneaky grin. "You're my favorite cousin-in-law, forget him and give me the pie."

Darryl froze in place and looked at Ryder like he was a traitor. "Ryder! You were as close to me as a brother could be, you would betray me over a pie?"

"You know good and well that's not just a pie! Tracy made that pie so its automatically heck of good! What would you do for a T.T.T. pie?"

Darryl was not amused, "I will shoot you!"

"I got a gun too, ain't nobody worried about you and your little pistol."

Sharon came out of her office, "Hey everybody. What's going on?" She said with a big smile.

Darryl swallowed then he walked over to Sharon and asked her to have a seat. "I need to tell you something."

Sharon's face turned serious, until she saw my smile then she looked at Darryl like he was up to something. "What is it?"

Darryl shook his head, " I don't know how to say this." He looked at the floor, and then he looked at her. He dramatically grabbed her hand. "I want you to know that I still love you and it's not that you did anything wrong. It's just that sometimes bad things happen to good people. I still love you the same as I always did. I didn't plan for this to happen. It just happened one day and it was beyond me to fix it."

Sharon matched Darryl's dramatic tone and grabbed his hands. "What is it baby? You can tell me anything."

Darryl took a deep breath, "I'm in love with another red velvet!"

Sharon dramatically gasped as she covered her mouth, "Darryl!"

He shook his head, "I know! I know! I didn't mean for this to happen. It's all Drew's fault really!"

"Man! Why it gotta be my fault?" Drew said laughing.

Darryl slightly turned his head towards Andrew. "Cause! If you would've never proposed to this woman she never would've had us over for dinner. Then she never would've made her..." He turned to face Sharon and he made his face dramatically tender. "Her red velvet."

"So what, you were going around sampling other cakes to make sure mine was the best?"

"No! No! No! She had us over for dinner. She was all proud of her little cakes and I thought I was just going to humor her and eat a little of her cake. I knew I was in trouble when that first fork full hit my mouth. I'm sorry Sharon; I was going to keep the charade going, but she's withholding future goodies from me until I come clean with you."

"So what does this mean for us? You don't want my cake anymore? I mean, I know my cake isn't all fancy, but it's still good cake." She laughed a little under her fake cry of disappointment.

"Of course I still want your cake. It was there for me in the beginning. Your cake got me through some pretty tough times, nothing could ever replace your cake."

"Well my cake doesn't want to share you. You're going to have to choose!" Sharon laughed.

"No! Sharon! Please don't do this to me! Please don't make me choose. Her cake comes with pies and cookies."

"Oh so her cake knows some tricks, it got some backup. My cake could have some friends too." Sharon laughed.

"Sharon! Listen to me! I still love your cake. I still want your cake. But, I'm going to have other cakes, pies, cookies, puddings, etc. This is not a reflection of what I feel for you."

"You're just greedy Darryl!"

He shook his head in agreement. "Yes, I am." Then he kissed Sharon's cheek. He got up, he looked Andrew up and down then he went over to Andre. He reached for the pie, and Andre moved like he was going to play keep away. "Dre! I will get a little kid too! Give me my pie!"

"You have to say please." Andre teased.

"You guys make me sick! Tracy you better had put your foot in this pie!" Then he exhaled, "Andre please give your uncle the pie before he loses his mind." Andre handed him the box. Darryl looked at the pie and then he started to jump up and down until he looked at Sharon, he grabbed his dramatic composure and stifled his excitement. "I'm going to go now. I will see you guys later."

"A! Let me get a piece." Ryder said.

"YOU GOT TO BE KIDDING! I'm not sharing!" Darryl said walking out the door.

We laughed for a long time. Darryl definitely made me feel like I knew what I was doing with my treats.

Yussef

Buzz! Buzz! "Open up FOOL!" Darryl's voice came blasting through the intercom. I buzzed him in and Darryl walked through the door with a pie in one hand and a spoon in the other. He sat on the couch and proceeded to go to town. "Tracy always be trying to hold out on the good stuff."
"She made that, what is it?"
"Some kind of lemon creamy goodness! I understand why Drew gotta have a treadmill right there in the house. That woman would make me fat."
"You're going to eat that whole pie right now?"
"Some now, and some in a bit. I'll eat something at the club." Then he looked at me, "yeah Jeff wasn't exaggerating. You look beyond stressed."
"I look stressed?" I sat down.
"Stressed, backed up, the whole nine. You're not making Sylvia spread them anymore?"
"We're not together anymore."
"What's that got to do with her spreading them? She'd let you hit regardless."
"My girls are watching. I can't send that message to them."
"You don't know how to creep? It doesn't have to be that complicated"
"It's not worth all that."
"Nothing is worth being as pent up as you look right now. We're putting a chickenhead on the menu tonight for you."
I exhaled, "I'm tired of the game. When you gonna settle down?"
Darryl froze with his spoon almost to his mouth. He put his spoon in the pie tin and put it down on my coffee table. He looked at the floor and then at me. His face was serious and he squinted his eyes, "how you gonna ask me some freaking feminine question like that! What is wrong with you?"
"It's a legitimate question."
"It's a female question! I will settle down when I settle down! It's too complicated right now. Besides I don't want to get married ever. The only woman who I'd consider, and I do mean consider long term with she's being goofy acting like she rejecting the Daddy Long Dick program. There's the main chickenhead, Queen Cluck! And then there's the others. I'm not settling down! Cause I don't settle! Look at my brothers and Malcolm. They all soft and tender, running around waiting on these women like that's what they were supposed to do. They disgust me!" He frowned like something tasted bad.
"I want that!"
Darryl looked at me in disbelief, "I had no idea you were such a girl. No wonder you and Drew got along so well."
"Darryl you can't want this forever. When does clubbing get old?"
Darryl sprang up, and started pacing. "STOP IT! STOP IT! If you make me think too much and not have a good time with all these cluckers dying for a piece. I swear! We fighting!" He stopped and looked at me. "This is exactly why a man should NEVER go this long without sex. You need to get 2 cc's of chicken-head-release pronto!" He took his pie in the kitchen, and put it in the fridge."Yu! Don't eat my pie!"
"You put it in my fridge, I make no guarantees."
"YU! I will shoot you! Don't eat my pie!"
"Don't put it in my fridge then! If it's in there and I want some, I'll have some."
"YU! You can't mess with another man's pie! I promise I will shoot you!"
"And I said, if I want some and it's in there. I'm gonna have some."
Darryl took his pie out of my fridge. "You won't hook up with Skanky Sylvia but you'll

eat my pie. If I say I'll shoot somebody I mean it! You know me! You know I don't kid about such things! But no! That's not enough warning! I'm putting my pie in my car then! I don't want to have to shoot you."

"If you feel that's necessary."

"This pie is that good! Meet you downstairs." He walked out the door.

I grabbed my jacket and I locked up. The limo pulled up and JoJo stood up in the sunroof. He was ready to get out and have a good time as well. We sat in our usual booth in the VIP section at Elegant Affairs. My eyes glided around the club to see who was here so far. That's when I saw her, Angela was here. She hadn't seen me yet, I debated whether I wanted to see her or not. I told myself to be cool and go with the flow. Jeff and JoJo went out on the dance floor. Darryl spotted his next victim and he was off. I watched Angela for a minute, she lost some weight. She looked happy with herself, but what was the point. When I decided one dance wouldn't hurt, I got up and started towards her when the stare of someone else caught my attention. She smiled at me from her seat. I stood still for a moment, I told her to come over. She smiled and got up. She joined me on the dance floor. We danced to a few songs, and then I told her I'd be back. Angela was now watching me, I sat down in the VIP then I stared back at her. She came to the entrance and waited as the guard looked to me to say yes or no. I told him to let her up. My dance partner sat down and watched us. "Angela."

"Yussef, aren't you a sight for sore eyes." Angela said, "how have you been?"

"Busy. You?"

She smiled proudly, "I've been working out."

I guess I was supposed to have a reaction to that. "You and everybody else." I looked at my dancing partner.

Her smile dropped, "how's Sylvia?"

"She's fine. You came up here to ask me about Sylvia?"

"What's your status? Are you guys together? Are you single?"

"Why does it matter?"

"Cause I'm trying to see you." She said sounding like a crack head looking for a fix.

"Like you would respect it if I was with Sylvia." I said feeling irritated.

"What's up Angela!" Darryl said walking up to the booth.

"Hey Darryl." She said standing and giving him a hug. "I've been hearing your name a lot these days."

"Is that right?" Darryl said sitting down. He looked out on the floor. "Yu! Who's that?" He said gesturing towards my dancing partner.

"I don't know, I danced with her a few minutes ago."

"Don't ignore the call of the cluck cluck." He laughed, "here chicky-chicky!"

"Darryl!" Angela said irritated.

"What?" He said leaning back in his seat.

"How you going to point out some other female when I'm sitting right here?"

Darryl faked surprised, "Angela I had no idea you were clucky too!" Then he started laughing.

"I'm what?"

"Why you over here messing with my cousin? His kids are still a prominent part of his life; they're not going anywhere. You think sweating it out in the gym is supposed to change something? He's over here trying to be a good father, and have a good woman in his life. You over here messing with him, cause you know he's a good guy. Yu, this is exactly why I don't understand why you be trying to love these chicken-heads. She ain't up to no good being up here. She ain't no Chantel, She ain't no Sherrell, she ain't no Tracy, and she for sure ain't no Sasha. Angela you were cool until your insecurities came bursting through. Yu, if you wanna break her off that's your business, but don't do this whole love connection thing she's trying to lure you into." Angela was glaring at him, so he stared back at her. Then he started laughing, "Yu! Send this chicken-head away! You've already tasted her nuggets. Move on!"

"Darryl! What did I ever do to you? Why would you talk about me like this?"

"Keep going and you're going to irritate me in a minute." He picked up his drink, "you mess with my cousin. You messing with me!"

"Yussef! Why would you let him talk to me like that?"

I exhaled, "Darryl."

"Yeah Yu!" Darryl said looking out at the dance floor.

"Please be nice to my Q.C." Then I smiled.

Darryl repeated the acronym to himself until he got it. I was referring to Angela as my Queen Cluck. He started cracking up all over the seat. "Alright, I'm quiet! I see my next dance partner." Then he went out on the dance floor.

"What does Q.C. mean?" She asked me.

"Why does it matter? Why are you here?"

"Cause I'm trying to see you. I miss you." She smiled.

I'm tired of fighting. "Hold on." I stood up; I walked down to the main floor. I walked to the table where my watcher was sitting. "What's your name?"

"Cassie, you're?"

"Yussef"

"You?"

"Yu-ssef!"

"Nice to meet you Yussef."

I took out my phone, "what's your number? I'll call you later."

"Who's that?" She asked gesturing towards Angela.

I looked at Angela who was watching then I looked back at her. "Nobody!"

Tracy

I know my family tried very hard to surprise me, but let's face it, I was the drama queen of the family, they were horrible actors, but I went along with the whole get up. My mom asked me to show her where Amber's school was because she was going to take an aerobics class there. They had a good storyline, but the acting... it was horrible. As if I wouldn't notice, that Marie was unusually quietly and cheesy. Then she didn't want me to park in the parking lot or even approach the school from that direction, I knew it was because everyone's cars were over there. When we walked in the doors, Auntie Jade was at the front desk to buzz us in. Jade who was a much better actor than my mom volunteered to show us where the *aerobics* class was going to be held. We walked down the hall, and then my mother told me to go in first. When I walked in the door everyone yelled surprise, and I smiled really big and acted like I had no idea. My mom would've been crushed if she knew she gave away the whole surprise. The room was decorated nicely with "It's a Boy!" banners and decorations all over the room.

My sisters were there, Sasha said the three of them flew in together. A lot of my Aunties and cousins came. More family showed up for my baby shower than they did for my bridal shower. A lot of them came dressed up like they just knew they were going to be on camera or something. I shook my head at them cause now there's this sudden attention to my life and me. The phony ones were literally following Chantel around, telling her how much they loved her music and her videos. At one point she said she was going to leave, but I begged her to stay. I told her it was fine that some people didn't know how to act. I told her I wanted her there as my sister, and it was ok with me if she ignored them. She was too nice to do that though, so she just kept putting space between herself and the fans. I had a wonderful time all the same. Between Amber and my mom, this baby wasn't going to want for anything. Andre even got a few nice things as they celebrated that he was going to be a big brother again. The gift that he absolutely loved the most came from Tara. She had a T-shirt made that said, *#1 Big Brother!"* Andre was in love with the shirt and he put it on immediately over his other shirt. He made sure we got pictures of him in the shirt as he smiled really big and proud. I thanked everyone for everything they did for us.

****

I awoke to Andrew kissing my lips. "Happy Anniversary baby!" He smiled really big. I smiled, "Happy Anniversary baby." I was happy he remembered cause he hadn't mentioned our day at all.

He rubbed my back, "I have the whole day planned for us. We'll do a few things as a family to celebrate. Then Andre's gonna spend the night with my momma, and then we have some adult things to do." He smiled.

I pulled the covered back, "this big ole belly doesn't get in your way?"

"Have I complained once about the belly? I just gotta be more creative about how I get in there, but I love a challenge you should know that. Besides," he gave me an evil grin.

"The rumors are true!"

"What rumors?"

"Pregnant loving is the best!" He kissed me again as we laughed. "I love you so much! Thank you for loving me!"

We went back and forth over the reasons why we loved each other. I love moments like this with my man. It's just me and him, verbally expressing our love for each other. I could never deny that my baby loves me. He shows it in everything he does, and he tells me often.

We had breakfast as a family, and then we went to see a family play in the city. There was something for everyone in this play. Andre was thoroughly entertained by the acrobatics, and Andrew and I laughed uncontrollably at the adult humor. We had lunch at a nice restaurant close by the theater.

When we went home we exchanged gifts. We gave Andre the bike he had his eye on for some time. He took the bike in the back yard to show us some of the tricks he learned on little Anthony's bike. Andre knew how to make the whole bike stand up on one wheel as he twist and turned. My heart sank seeing him doing it. He knew how to pop wheelies on the bike already. He said there were some other moves he wanted to master with AJ and now they could work on them together. He was so excited.

I told Andrew he was not easy to shop for, Andre cosigned. I told him I hoped he liked it and that it wasn't too simple. It took forever but Andre and I finally found the cologne that he wears. It was so fancy and expensive and rare. He smiled cause he knew we had to do a lot of investigative work to find it, and then we gave him a framed picture of the three of us from the wedding. Andrew gave me jewelry, an anniversary ring and a charm bracelet with a charm that had Andre's baby picture on it. He said when each baby is born we could add a charm for each one. I loved the gifts and I thanked him. When we got to Amber's house, she was sending Malcolm to the store to get the things she needed for dinner. The way they were acting it seemed like we were interrupting, but Amber said we weren't. I was stalling to double check, but Andrew did everything but carry me out of there. He told me this was going to be one of our last chances to be away overnight for a while after the baby comes.

Andrew drove holding my hand most of the way. I recognized most of the way at first, we drove over to the coast like we were going to Half Moon Bay, but we deviated a little bit and then a sign said "Welcome to Pebble Beach". We pulled up to a beautiful resort, the bellhop took our bags and we glided past the check-in desk to our suite overlooking the golf course and the ocean. He setup a fantastic dinner by candlelight in our room, with the ocean spray as the background music. He kept telling me how beautiful I am, and I needed every mention cause I definitely didn't feel pretty with this nose the size of

291

Candlestick Park and skin that couldn't decide what it wanted to do. At first my skin got light and then as my pregnancy progressed I returned to my normal brownness, and now I'm a little darker than normal. As we laid in bed catching our breath I knew I shouldn't but I had to. "Andrew?"

"Un huh?" Sleep was starting to pull him.

"Please don't get mad."

He flinched, "if you start the statement that way I'm already on defense. What is it?" He snapped

"I need you to be honest with me."

"Tracy! No! No drama tonight! We are in this romantic setting. I just laid you down nicely. I wanna bask in the ambiance of being the man for the night. I don't want to go on an emotional roller coaster tonight."

"Fine!" I said sounding weepy.

He turned over, *I sniffled*. He put his pillow over his head, *I sniffled again*. He pulled the covers over his head, and *I sniffled twice*. Andrew growled kicking the covers on the floor. "*WHAT TRACY!*" He whined.

"Are you going to be mad if I don't lose all of this baby weight right away?"

He sat up halfway, "Are you serious? Why would I be mad?"

"Chantel came out of the hospital looking like her old self just about. Now I would love to have everything snap back in place too, but I know it's not going to, but I'll work extra hard on it, I promise."

"Why would you compare yourself to Chantel?"

"Isn't that like every guy's dream? His wife snaps right back after the baby is born, and everything is the same as it was before the baby."

"So let's remember us before any babies. When we met you were a big girl, was I any less excited about you regardless of your size? As long as you don't change into some crazy person, crazier than these pregnancy hormones have made you we're good. You know my motto, if you don't like the way you look, I'll help you, but I love you, and I especially love you when you're content with who you are. If you want to snap back right away, I'll help you with that. Whatever you wanna do Tracy."

"Yea, but Chantel..." He cut me off.

"Chantel is a completely different person, body type, everything. Plus her job requires that she has to remain tiny. She gotta be that little to look normal on TV. Please don't compare yourself to Chantel or anyone else for that matter. I am in love with you, and it's upsetting."

"I love you Andrew!"

"I love you Tracy!"

Yussef

"You know what Yussef, you are alright with me!" El said laughing.

"Thanks."

Then he stopped laughing and sat up straight. "Man to man."

"Man to man."

"I know who you are, and I've been dying to ask you a question."

"You know who I am?" I leaned back in my chair waiting for whatever he was about to lay on me.

"How could you walk away from her?" He watched my eyes.

I exhaled, looked at the floor, and then I looked him in his eyes. "Man to man, timing was never on our side."

"You're a stand-up guy. I don't know how you do it, but I appreciate it. Oh and thank you for passing," he smiled.

"You're not welcome," I smiled back.

Malcolm and Richard walked in and sat at the table. "What's with the goofy grins?" Richard asked.

"Nothing, where's everybody?" El said.

Richard frowned at El, "what's wrong with you?" I asked him.

Richard didn't take his eyes off El, El smiled at him. "He's mad because his daughter's having my babies."

"Richard?" Malcolm said frowning at him.

"Whatever man!" Richard said, "you got boys. You wouldn't understand."

"They're married though,"

"Doesn't mean I have to like it." Richard said, and then he looked at Malcolm. "Can we get to the meeting?"

"Juan isn't here. I don't know how you can be upset with that man for doing right by your daughter. Look what you do to another man's daughter," Malcolm said.

"That's different!"

"How is it different? Sophia is Jeff's daughter. Your other baby momma is somebody's daughter. Every female you give it to is somebody's daughter, but you mad at him for loving yours."

"Exactly!" Richard was determined to be upset.

"See what I gotta deal with!" El said to me.

"What's that supposed to mean?" He was looking for a reason.

"You're so worried that Sasha is going to end up married to you. I'm good to that woman even when you make it difficult. Calm down Richard, I'm not going to dog out your daughter. I love her with everything in my being, and we're going to be together for the rest of my life."

Malcolm and I looked at Richard. I personally thought his speech was moving, but Richard didn't want to believe him. When Juan came we went over business. We were determining department heads, etc. to oversee business while we went on a hiatus after the wedding.

The school was shutting down; Amber wasn't taking on any new projects for the rest of the year. Chantel was going to bond with her baby for the same duration; Malcolm said we all needed to lay low. So now we've been planning for business during all of that time. The hardest part was deciding whether we stayed together or if we spread out.

"Why would we spread out Malcolm, together we are strong? Divided we fall!" Darryl said.

"You've got a point, sticking together will require more planning," Malcolm said.

****

"Are you avoiding me?" Dale said.

"No, I've just been busy with business and things." Dale was calling me about my house. When I started this paperwork, I had Angela in mind. I thought I'd surprise her as a pre-wedding gift or something. Now, I don't want to finish it. I'm not ready to move into that big ole house by myself.

"What do you want to do about your house son?"

I exhaled, "how much time do I have?"

"I can move your house to the end of the list for phase two. Or you can pick everything out, finish it. It's your house you don't have to move in just because it's ready."

I agreed to come down tomorrow and pick everything out. Then I turned my attention back to my girls. We were talking about our family vacation for this summer. Since Syd and I have never been, we decided that we would go to the happiest place on earth. Yezzy was so excited, she said that she and Jackson would be our tour guides all over both parks because they've been there so many times they know where everything is. I told them I would let them know as soon as I had the dates for us.

I took the girls home and then my phone rang as soon as I walked in the door, it was Cassie. We'd talked over the phone a few times, and we went on a couple dates. Did I see her as my future wife, not really. It was nice to talk to someone from time to time. Angela and I didn't talk anymore, when I saw her we smashed, and then I left or I made sure she knew it was not cool to stay.

Cassie asked me why she didn't know where I lived. I didn't have a real reason; I hadn't invited her over my house yet. I picked her up each time we went out and I dropped her off at home when our date was over. I guess the lack of interest in getting to know her physically was making her a little restless. In my opinion, I wasn't doing anything to make her think I was in love with her or even feeling her on that level. She seemed to get comfortable real fast, which wasn't cool. Just because I took her to a couple of my poetry readings and she seemed to understand my poems she seemed to think she knew me. Now when I talk to her she's telling me how I am, it was cute at first. Now it's annoying to put it bluntly. I told her there was no reason for her to know where I lived, we were just friends. She asked me if I was going to "*No Words*" tomorrow night. I hadn't decided, but her question made me feel like I didn't want to go cause she was probably going to be there stalking me. She told me to let her know and she'd come to support me.

****

Sharon told me I wanted the nicer fixtures, and I wanted the marble tile. She told me which kind of hardwood I wanted and the neutral color I wanted the entire house painted. She said the good thing about paint is that it was nothing to change it later. So I decided that when I moved in I would have the interior painted accordingly. She told me to pick a landscaper and then pick out a design so that I wouldn't be in violation of the Homeowner's Association. I walked over to my house and I smiled at it. It was huge and beautiful! Not bad for a young lad from Richmond. I decided once it was ready I would put my father's car in the garage.

****

I scanned the room and there she was. Ugh! Cassie was sitting front and center. Here goes nothing. "Show him some love! Give it up for the Invisible Poet!" The MC said. I went out, and recited my poem. When the crowd begged for an encore, I gave them one more poem. Cassie sat there looking stuck because she knew I was talking about her. She watched me say hello to some of the regulars. She turned her head for half a second and I slid out the back door. I got on my bike and I went over my Grandma's. She and Arthur were sitting down to an old Black and White movie. They invited me to stay, and I was glad cause I didn't feel like being home alone and I didn't want to give in to Cassie. Whatever happened to Baby Jane was a good movie, after the movie we sat around talking. My Grandma asked what happened with Sylvia. I explained my side of the story, but not even that helped me. She asked me why I got back with her in the first place. I told her it seemed like the right thing to do at the time. She exhaled and said as long as the babies were ok and we had a clean break there was no harm. I looked away and Arthur started laughing.

****

"Thanks for letting me come over," I said.
"No problem man, have a seat." Hubby pointed me to the living room.
"Is Nicole here?"
Hubby looked at me, "yeah, hold on." He said then he walked to their bedroom. I could hear him tell her to come out to visit with me. "What's new Yussef?" Hubby said as he and Nicole walked into the living room.
"I need to cover every detail, and leave no stone unturned."
Nicole smiled, "you mean this is not a social visit?"
"Not at all." I said watching both of their faces.
Nicole looked alarmed, and Hubby locked his eyes on me. "What's wrong?" Nicole

asked.

"Your friend Sonya," Nicole frowned, as she had no idea where I was going. Hubby looked at Nicole then back at me. "She's been running her mouth. Not completely accurate, but she seems to know a lot about the family. She named a source, but she is your friend."

"I know Sonya is a bit of a gossip, but she's been there for me in some pretty messed up situations. There's goodness at the heart of her."

Hubby watched my face, "that's not what he means." Nicole looked confused; "he wants to know if you've been running your mouth telling her about them."

Nicole looked surprised, "me?" She said putting her hands on her chest. "I don't know anything. She was always telling me about you guys."

"What did she tell you?"

"That time when Derrick kidnapped Tracy and I. She explained who he was to me. I hadn't ever met him before that. I'm not from Oakland I didn't know about you guys."

"Where are you from?"

"Albany and Berkeley."

"Ok so, little miss Berkeley. What else did she tell you?"

Nicole purged everything she could think of. I could tell she wasn't lying, and I was glad to see it. It was going to be really bad if Malcolm's question about Nicole pointed to her as a leak. When I was satisfied that Nicole was innocent Hubby sent her back to their bedroom. He asked me what was going on. I gave him a brief overview and he exhaled. He told me to tell him what I needed. Then he said he was in the doghouse for a long time after Sonya outed him and Sasha. He said he figured it was a good idea for them to lay low for a while. He said he didn't mention her because she was in LA and it wasn't like they went over a name-by-name roster of their ex's. I asked him why they broke up, and he said the distance and then he met Nicole. He said its no secret to anyone how much he loves his wife, I nodded in agreement. He looked away, and I told him Sasha infected him. He shook his head like I took the words out of his mouth. I told him she was pregnant, and he looked stuck for a minute.

Malachi

"I think you could've found bigger diamonds!" I said sarcastically.

"Do you think she will like it?" Malcolm asked signing the receipt.

"What's not to like? All women love diamonds!"

"You know your sister. I think she'll love it, but I was looking for confirmation from my best man."

"Malcolm it's coming from you, I think she'd love anything as long as it comes from you, but I feel the need to warn you. You need to step up your game. When have you ever showered Amber with gifts?"

Malcolm's eyes bounced around the room. "I wasn't worried about gifts because I was taking care of her. Even when she didn't like me."

"Ok, but now you've got her wide open. I'm not saying buy out this whole store. Don't forget to do those extra things she likes."

"My Queen has access to everything I have, our kids are grown, and it's just me and her again. She will never want for anything and you're telling me there's more." Malcolm watched my eyes.

"Yep! Now you gotta travel, take vacations, make sure she never has to guess about you." Malcolm blank stared at me, "what is it with you people and vacations?"

I smiled, "you can't tell me it wasn't nice to get away from everything. Just you and her, and everything and everyone didn't matter."

Malcolm's expression didn't change, "it was fine, but I have businesses to run, decisions to make, I can't run all over the world care free and think everything is going to be ok. I have to work."

"You have an empire. You can officially say you made it. Rags to Riches for sure, but you gotta ask what it's all for, if you don't stop and enjoy the fruits of your labor."

"Amber put you up to this?"

"No, I haven't talked to her. This is a best man to groom conversation."

Malcolm handed me the ring box. "Since you want to dig deep into my soul, what's happening with Denise?"

I ran my hand over my head, as my stomach grumbled. "Where you wanna have lunch?"

"Doesn't matter, I'm not picky."

We drove over to *The Counter* in Walnut Creek where you pick everything out for your burger. Everything was an option. Bun, or no bun, Turkey, beef, chicken, mushroom, meatless patty, etc. You checked everything off on your menu card. When I chose garlic fries Malcolm said I must not be trying to get any later. When I didn't respond to that he told me to answer his question. I downed my cocktail and then I ordered another. I told him things were a little better, but nothing to write home about. He asked me what I was going to do about it. I shrugged, I was at a loss. He watched my eyes for a minute. "How can you be Tim's son with an answer like that?" His question jolted me up straight in my seat. "You love her, and you know she loves you. Why are you sitting over here sulking like a punk?!" He shifted in his chair, "what's the root of this problem? You're holding back something."

"What makes you the expert, how do you know I didn't put everything on the line?"

"I can see it in your face." He sat back waiting for me to say.

I wrestled with myself for a long time, "Ideally I saw the picture of my wife differently." Malcolm rolled his hands for me to continue. "I envisioned being married to someone who looked like my momma." It took everything in me to say that out loud.

Malcolm sat back in his chair and let my words swish around the room. "I can't believe I'm getting married. I can't believe that I'm looking forward to being married. Troy and I would listen to Fuzzy and Leonard talk about their future plans and then we'd say we wanted the same but better. Right before I met your sister, Troy and I came up with a plan for our lives. True it was the plan of a thirteen year old, but not much has changed. I can't even put my finger on what made me look at her, but I was intrigued from the moment I laid eyes on her. I was gonna chop it up to nothing but then..." he smirked at the memory. "Her rage!"

"You were feeling Amber because of her anger issues?"

"Yes! I understood it immediately. People look at me as a color, and they did the same thing to her. Now if you ask me what I'm attracted to, after my queen of course it's always browner than Amber. I tried to replace her, shake her out of my mind. Do anything I could to be free of her, but there's no one on this earth like my Queen. Momma was exceptional, beautiful, smart, ANGRY!, but that was Tim's woman. She was a one of a kind masterpiece! Stop punishing that woman for what she has no control over. She can't be your mother. That chick you were messing with may have had the coloring, but she was lacking in everything else. She knows you have a family and that you love your wife. She was pulling on your mixed kid guilt."

"Mixed kid guilt?"

"Your parents did a very good job, not raising the issue for you guys. Many try, but not too many can pull it off like your parents did. You know who you are, and everything isn't some big huge question about where you belong and who you fit in with. I honestly think your Nana and Poppa had a lot to do with the success of that, but here in the prime of our lives you're torturing yourself over something you have no control over. Stop doing this to yourself. You love Denise, take your own advice and show her. Step out of your comfort zone to make her happy. Keep going like you're going and you're going to lose your queen. And you can't come stay with Amber and I. I'm getting mine all over that house."

I blank stared at him, "you're talking about my little sister!"

"No, I'm talking about my Queen." Then he looked at me, "and I'm talking to my best man." I prepared myself to be grossed out. "Let me state the obvious." He looked out the window; "I am so in love with that woman. I thought I was a man before, but it's right at this moment that I realize how I wasn't a man until we got back together. I have a family now. I have a meaningful relationship with all of my sons; I know all of my grandchildren. The cycle is broken, I didn't have a father. All of my sons know me; I've always been there for them. I'm more in love today than I was yesterday with their mother. Everything I have is better because I share it with her. I thought I hated the idea of getting married, just because it wasn't in me. But now, I'm counting down the days until she has my last name as she should've always had." Then he looked at me, "and I'm done."

I started cracking up laughing. "That's as emotional as Malcolm gets huh?"

He shook his head, "yep. Until I hold my granddaughter."

"You wanted a little girl that bad?"

"Troy used to say there was nothing like having a little girl. Even though he barely saw his, his heart would melt looking at her. I only had that feeling with Amber. Our little girl could never get here to the other side." He adjusted in his seat. "I've adopted some stand-ins Sasha, Tanisha, Sabrina, Emerald, Chantel, Tracy, Yussef's girls, but holding Chanel seeing her respond to me, I now know what Troy was talking about."

"Malcolm, you are in rare form today."

"So my point is that you need to suck it up. Do whatever that woman asks you to. Stop it with all this punking out. Look at what you have with the woman who loves you for who you are. Don't throw it away for some tramp who only wants to win. Are you having a mid-life crisis or something? Man up!"

"Cora's not a tramp, she's…"

Malcolm waived his hand, "you're missing the point. How is she worthy of you if she doesn't love herself enough not to be the reason your family hurts? Did you ever ask how long it took her to hook up with Turan after you cut her off? How does she have such intimate information from him if they only just got together? I know you don't see her like I'm looking at her. Listen to me Malachi, you were set up. That woman may love you, but she will never be Denise, and all she cares about is winning. I'ma need you to ask yourself, what would Tim do? He didn't love your momma because of the color of her skin. He loved her because of who she was, and what they shared. Stop being stupid and man up. You are letting them out play you." I sat there chewing on what he was saying. "Did you ever wonder how she tells you she wants to move, and then miraculously she comes out here? I need your head in the game when we have to do what comes next. If you're sitting over here ambivalent about a tramp." He shook his head. "You're going to end up messed up. Let me know if I need to have Darryl come explain what a chicken-head, as he calls them, is."

I shook my head taking in his comments.

****

"*Happy* Anniversary?" Denise said sounding so unsure of the happy.

I smiled, "Happy Anniversary baby." My conversation with Malcolm had been plaguing my thoughts actions and deeds. I keep watching Denise; she doesn't know how to take it. I made the arrangements to come out here to Carmel without discussing it with her. Jade took our girls for us and then we drove down here to Carmel for an Anniversary get away. Seeing Joanne has helped a lot. We needed to get past my initial hesitation of opening up to this complete stranger. I still haven't let go completely but at least I feel confident that she's not like Dobson. Denise and I are sleeping in the same bed at least and we're trying. Moving back to Oakland has already felt like a good move. Any couple is stronger than us right now, but we've been having lunch and dinner with family in hopes that some of what they got rubs off on us. The girls love the frequency that they get to see their cousins now. They think that Jade's daughter Emerald, and Sophia's daughter Sabrina are the coolest teenagers they've ever met. They actually get excited when they hear that mommy and daddy are going out for the evening. "Denise we need to talk, and for real."

She didn't look happy about it, "ok."

I looked her in her eyes, "Happy Anniversary!" She gave me a questioning expression. "We are going to get past this. I am so sorry for hurting you. I'm sorry for being so consumed in what I felt I needed that I allowed this to happen to us. I want you to be happy, but I want you to be Happy with me. We need to talk so that we can get past this. Unless you don't want to continue, because you do have the option to say you don't want this anymore."

She rubbed her stomach, "I keep hearing your hesitation about the baby. I didn't get it then. Were you planning to leave me for her?"

"NO! NEVER!"

She relaxed some, "I thought you wanted out, but hesitated because of the baby."

"Denise I want you, the children are added bonuses."

She relaxed even more, "It's not all your fault, but I am so MAD Malachi! I thought we waited so long to get married so that we could get all this cheating crap out of our systems. Our marriage bed was supposed to be sacred. Isn't that what we promised?"

"It is."

"Now I feel like there's so much to be said, to be explained. Can we even fix this?"

"Only if you want to. Otherwise if neither of us wants to it's pretty pointless to try. I want to, but you have to be honest with yourself and me, do you want to?"

"Aren't you tired of me?"

"Why do you keep saying that? Why on earth would you think I would tire of you?" I was trying to pull back some of my anger.

"Who stays together this long? Did you cheat because you wanted something different, because you wanted something new?"

"If my parents were alive right now they would still be together."

"But you said I don't remind you of your mother, so how is that comforting to me?"

I smiled, "that was until I saw you knock Cora like you did. I didn't realize you loved me like that."

"Like what?"

"To the point of rage. You're always so calm, wanting to use your words. I didn't know a fighter existed in you."

She was quiet as she thought about it. "What was your mother like?"

I took her in my arms, "she was my everything. She was strong and an advocate for what was right. Don't ever mess with her children or her man, cause then she was coming for you. Whenever I stepped out of line she would snatch me up. My momma was the most beautiful woman in the world! Jade looks like a lighter version of her."

"Amber doesn't look like her?"

"She does, but she looks more like dad. To let my dad tell it Amber is all momma. She does act the most like her, but she looks like both of them."

"Do you think she would've liked me?"

"I'm sure she would've loved you. She'd choke me out if she knew about this."

"She'd probably choke both of us." She looked around the room.

I smiled, "she had no problem getting after me when I stepped out of line."

"Should I have choked you out as well?"

I laughed a yeah-right laugh. "You could've tried, but we don't put our hands on each other."

"Do you want this baby?" She braced herself for my answer.

"I want every piece of you I can get my hands on." I exhaled, "do you want this marriage? I won't like it, and I can't promise not to fight you on it, but I at least need to hear it."

She swallowed and hesitated. "I don't want to say yes, we have so much to talk about and fix." She exhaled, "my mother said men will only want you for so long."

Fire turned in my stomach. "YOUR MOTHER'S STORY IS NOT YOURS! WHY WOULD YOU LISTEN TO HER? SHE'S NOT EVEN HERE AND SHE'S RUNNING YOUR LIFE! TELL ME WHAT DENISE THINKS! WHAT DENISE FEELS?"

"I DON'T KNOW HOW I FEEL! My mother was all I had for the longest time."

"Does your sister feel the same way you do?"

"I don't talk to her."

"Why wouldn't you talk to your sister but you talk to your mother who belittled our relationship?"

"I don't even know where my sister is."

"If you want, I can find her for you, but for right now, I need to know how **YOU** feel. Do **YOU** want this marriage? Do you want **ME**?"

"Malachi, I love you."

"That doesn't mean you want me. It's not a hard question."

She took deep breaths. "If I admit to you that I don't want to break up. That I wouldn't know how to live if I wasn't with you, will you use that against me? I don't want to keep going through this, we've already been here." Her face held pain.

"No I wouldn't use that against you. I want you to feel happy and safe with me."

"Everything has gotten out of hand. I keep letting you down."

"We both dropped the ball, but now we can fix it. Let's enjoy this time together, get back to where we were always meant to be."

****

"How was your trip?" Joanne asked.

"Wonderful!" I said thoroughly smiling.

Denise shook her head in agreement. "So I take it you guys talked everything out?" Joanne asked looking between the both of us.

"Mostly. I'm sure there's more conversations to be had, but we're in a good place." Joanne smiled as she looked at me and then her smile flickered when she looked at Denise. So I looked at her as well. Her expression looked very guilty as she stared at the floor. Joanne asked where we went trying to redirect my attention. I told Joanne where we went, and how much I thoroughly enjoyed our trip. We walked on the beach, romantic dinners, shopping for gifts for the girls. Denise's willingness to work through my indiscretion had me completely open to whatever she wanted. Denise was still holding back but I figured it was her ambivalence towards me, but as I see Joanne read something in Denise that I can't seem to see myself has me nervous. I sat back and waited for Joanne to draw out whatever it is that Denise is holding onto.

When we hit the top of the hour Joanne said we could continue, as she didn't have any other patients today. I could see it in her eyes, she needed to tell me something, but she was scared to death to say. I got quieter and quieter waiting for Joanne to draw it out. Joanne looked at me and asked what I thought about forgiveness. Assuming she was talking about me, I told her I was aware that there were consequences for my actions, but I was willing to do whatever was needed to make things right between us. When Denise started crying her reaction grabbed my attention. I looked at Denise then Joanne and I asked if there was something they knew that I didn't know? Joanne looked at my eyes and said she thinks so. Denise got really nervous but it looked like she was giving herself a pep talk. Time stood still as I waited for Denise to say. I didn't say one more word; I burned holes in her with my eyes. Denise could not bring herself to look at me. She started explaining to Joanne, I couldn't decide if what she was going to say was going to piss me off more or the fact that she couldn't look at me. That told me that whatever she was about to say was all bad.

She explained to Joanne, not me, how hurt she was when her mother's health took a turn for the worse. She explained to Joanne, not me, how alone she felt at that time even though I was doing everything possible to help her. She said my kindness was too much, partially because her mother was in her ear constantly feeding her venom in regards to our relationship. It was coming; I was waiting for her to get to it. She looked at me with tears pouring down her face as she apologized over and over for letting me down, and for betraying me. I looked at Joanne who had nothing but concern and sadness for me in her eyes. Denise was rambling but not getting to the point. "I AM AT THE END OF MY ROPE!" I stood up, "at this point all I need is a yes or no answer from you." I paced the floor, talk about flipping the script! "You cheated on me!"

Denise hung her head while tears poured out of her eyes. "Malachi, I know you're upset..."

I looked at Joanne like that was the dumbest thing she could've ever said to me. "Stating the obvious! What am I paying you for? How could I not be upset! You! YOU'VE GOT ME RUNNING AROUND HERE THINKING SOMETHING WAS WRONG WITH ME! I WAS REACTING TO YOU!"

"Malachi, you made your own choice. You cannot blame Denise for your choice." Joanne said sternly.

"I'm over here guilting myself, and I was responding to her!" Denise sat there with her eyes to the floor rubbing her stomach. "Were you ever going to tell me?"

"My mother told me not to." She said lowly.

"YOUR MOTHER BETTER BE HAPPY SHE'S NOT HERE OR I'D BREAK HER NECK!"

"Malachi!"

"DON'T SAY MY NAME WHEN SHE..."

Joanne stood up and walked directly in my face, she was angry. "Little Boy if you don't sit down! You are not without reproach here. I know you're upset, but you need to calm down! You will not blame your actions on her and she will not blame you. Take responsibility for yours."

This is not regular therapist behavior; Joanne was emotionally invested in this situation. Her command of the moment reminded me of my mother, and Denise gasped when I did as I was told and sat down. Denise has never had that power over me. "I'm not saying what I did wasn't wrong, but I'm sitting up here taking the blame for everything and she's letting me. The whole time she knew she was wrong as well."

"Malachi, I am sorry. I didn't mean for it to happen. I'm sorry!"

"Yeah! Yeah! Yeah! I GOT TO GO!" I stood up and walked out of Joanne's office.

****

I looked out the peephole, I sighed and then I opened the door. "Amber sent you!" I walked back to my bed.

"Momma talked to Denise, we're here to come get you." Andrew said.

"I'm not going anywhere!" I sat on the bed.

Malcolm exhaled, "Malachi we haven't tussled since we were kids and that was playfully. If it will make you feel better getting your butt kicked before you go I can help you with that."

"Nigga PLEASE!" I sucked my teeth.

"Real talk Malachi, you gotta come on." Andrew said.

"She tell Amber what happened?"

"I don't care what happened. My Queen is upset!" Malcolm growled.

"And pregnant women stick together." Andrew rubbed his head, "Denise is in the hospital."

I searched his face to make sure it was true. "What happened?"

"Let's go so you can find out!" Andrew said.

I grabbed my room keycard and my keys. I noticed how Malcolm and Andrew walked exactly the same, when we got in the elevator they had the same serious expression. "Is she ok?" Andrew wouldn't look at me, and Malcolm grabbed my shoulder, but didn't say anything. In that moment I felt it. We rode to the hospital in silence, as we walked inside I asked, "since when you guys start hanging out with each other?"

Andrew looked at me, "Uncle Malachi, I know you're hurting, but don't do that." He kept walking.

I continued to walk in huffy silence; I had no idea what I was walking into. Amber was coming out of the room with the water pitcher when we rounded the corner. She looked relieved to see me and then immediately I saw my momma's anger in her eyes. She thanked Malcolm and Andrew for bringing me, and then she told me to come with her. I was in no hurry to deal with what could possibly be going on, on the other side of that door. Malcolm and Andrew went to the waiting room while I followed her back to the elevator and out of the hospital. She was even walking like my mother so I knew I was in trouble, but at the same time it tickled me that my little sister felt the need to think she could say anything to me about this whole thing. We sat on the bench for the bus stop. Amber looked at me with hurt and anger and then she proceeded to curse me out so badly, my ears started bleeding. She would not let me get a word in edge wise. She called me a coward and a hypocrite. I didn't expect Denise to tell her everything, but apparently she did. She told me how dare I demand forgiveness when it was me in the hot seat, but as soon as the shoe was on the other foot I ran. She said they had to tell the girls I was out of town. I was so wrapped up in my feelings, I hadn't thought of my girls. Amber and I went back and forth, I told her I was ready to carry the blame and I was taking everything on cause this whole thing was supposedly *all my fault*. She should've came clean especially when my dirty laundry was out there. Amber calmed down and then she said she didn't care how, but I needed to go in there and fix it. She said they were talking about their mommas and Denise's was a lightweight Momma Shuga who poisoned her daughter with self-doubt, etc. until the day she died. She told me to go in that room and fix my relationship, to be the big brother that she's always loved and adored. Ok, that made me feel guilty. She said all this garbage that has been going on is not me, and not what our parents showed us.

I had to ask her, "does it ever bother you that Malcolm looks nothing like dad?"

She frowned as she thought about it. "No, because he's always had daddy's strength. Malcolm could never be like Daddy cause our daddy was one in a million. But, when I think about it. That same from the middle of your heart and soul love that my Daddy had for me, I get that from Malcolm but on a different level. I know he loves me."

"Do you think Momma would've liked Denise?"

"Yes! She would've made her come sit and talk to her, like she did Sonny. Or taken her under her wing like she did with Malcolm, and then she would be sitting here cursing you out just the same. No who am I kidding, Momma would've punched you in your face as soon as she saw you, guaranteed." She smiled at the thought. Then she stood up, "now go make up with your wife. Suck it up Malachi!"

"Where are my girls?"

"They're with Sophia and Sabrina. Sophia's finalizing paperwork for her Oakland location for the restaurant and then she's going over Sasha's, but all you need to be worried about right now is your wife."

As we walked back inside Amber told me I better be happy that she got to me first. She said if it wasn't for the fact that Denise had no one to turn to for help with the girls she wouldn't have come clean about being in the hospital and then she really wouldn't have said anything about what happened if we didn't keep asking where you were. She warned me that Jade was looking for me with Momma's fire and she might punch me when she saw me. I laughed but when she looked at me I knew she wasn't kidding. Tracy was sitting in the chair next to Denise's bed reading when I walked in. Tracy slowly stood up with her very pregnant belly and then she gave me a hug as she exited the room. I took her seat and I stared at Denise while she slept. She was on an IV and the baby heart monitor was playing my child's strong heart song. Denise still looked like my innocent little girl, she didn't look tainted. I kept adjusting in my chair as I tried to understand what position to take. This past week I've been in my hotel room going crazy. So crazy that I even saw Cora who was too excited to spend the night day and night again with me, until I kicked her out. I knew then I was coming back to my wife, Cora pleaded with me. I guess she could sense the true end of her physical reign over me.

Suddenly Denise's eyes opened and she tried to focus on the room. "Malachi?" she said as she tried to determine whether I was real or if she was dreaming. I didn't say anything, I waited. Her heart monitor sped up, "Malachi!" Tears started pouring out of her eyes. "So you felt guilty?" She shook her head yes. "You felt like you couldn't face me, that you let me down." She shook her head again. "And then the girls say something that perfectly makes you feel like crap because of your secret?" She shook her head yes. "Where is he now?" She shrugged her shoulders. "Was it Dobson?" She better say no! There's no way he could've kept it together in my presence if it was him, but I looked at her for confirmation. She shook her head no, my body relaxed as I asked myself if it mattered after that.

"Are you here to ask for a divorce?" Her heart monitor sped up again.

"No, but I honestly don't know what to do with this."

"See it's not so easy to know is it?" She said sitting up. "You wanted all these answers from me, and the whole time I'm trying to figure out how to tell you." She slowly adjusted in her bed.

"Why are you here?"

"I was dehydrated and I started having contractions, they gave me medicines to stop the contractions and I've been on IV's. What are we going to do Malachi?" She said sounding defeated.

"I don't know, I keep trying to ask myself how I didn't know? When did it stop?"

"Probably when you and Cora began." She said looking at her hands, "I didn't feel good about it. I wasn't trying to hurt you either." She exhaled, "I get it my mother was wicked but she was the only mother I had, and the only person until you who ever truly cared about me. If she said one day you would blindside me by leaving me just because you were tired of me, why wouldn't I believe her?"

"Because you should know me! The longer we're together the more I love you. I don't come from divorce so maybe that's why I don't get what you mean, or where your mother was even coming from, but now we have this whole aftermath to deal with."

She looked at me with sad eyes, "you want to deal with it?"

I stirred in my chair, "I've never been cheated on. I don't even know how to deal with this."

"Joanne seems to think that you love me enough to work it out. I was planning on telling her on the next visit that she didn't know what she was talking about." I exhaled really big. "How's Cora?" She fixed her eyes on me to watch my reaction.

"She doesn't understand why this doesn't mean that she and I are finally together."

"Are you guys going to get together?"

I locked my eyes on her, "no. She knows she won't see me again."

"How does she know that? You've broken it off with her so many times before, at least that's what you've said. Why would she think this time is any different?"

"Because it is."

"Right! Whatever Malachi." She said not believing me. "Are we going to continue seeing Joanne?"

"Do we have a choice?"

"Are you going to live in the hotel?"

"I'm coming home."

"Good." She exhaled.

Chantel

I keep telling myself I have no right. No right to flip out. I stared at Chanel as she laid there looking at me. I didn't want to move, my internal alarm was sounding and I couldn't move. My Grandmother knocked on the door and I told her to come in. Chanel and I didn't take our eyes off of each other. My grandmother asked me if I was sick, cause I'm normally up by now bumping around the house or in the studio at least by this point. I shrugged to say I didn't know. She laughed at me and told me to suck it up. I made my bed and now I had to lay in it. My doctor gave me the news yesterday; due to the ridiculous shock of it I haven't said anything to Derrick. I have no right to be surprised, my grandmother warned me, and still I didn't care. So what right do I have to react this way? Thank goodness Derrick comes home this afternoon so that I can figure out a way to tell him. I have no clue about how he's going to respond to this. We just had Chanel, and I was too excited about feeling and looking like my old self.

Chanel laid there watching me; I wonder what goes through her mind. She has a lot of her father's expressions. Like when the doctor gave her, her shots she frowned at her, but she didn't cry. Amber said she acts a lot like her father, but Chanel smiles. Especially at Malcolm, every time she sees him she's all gums and dimples. She stares at him like she's engraving his face in her brain. She hears his voice and she's looking for him. She doesn't react to my father that way. She isn't mean to him, but she's Malcolm's baby. Malcolm openly smiles at her too. In all my years of knowing this man, I've never seen him smile so much.

I sat up and my grandmother kissed my forehead. I don't know why my mother flashed across my mind and I immediately started crying. My grandmother picked up Chanel and then they both sort of watched me. I asked my grandmother how my mother reacted to finding out she was pregnant with me. My grandmother put her arm around me and told me I'm not my mother. Then she handed Chanel to me, I kissed her and started rocking her. My grandmother smiled through her tears and said that gesture was further proof that I wasn't my mother. I sat there listening to her tell me the truth about my parents and the things she knew about their relationship. I tell Chanel every day that I love her, something my mother never said until the end. I hold her, and keep her with me. I think that's something Derrick and I have in common. We don't want our child... I guess I should say children.... Gasp! To know the way our various parents treated us. I'm scared out of my mind! My pregnancy was relatively painless except for morning, noon, and night sickness. The delivery hurt, but it wasn't like other people's experiences, I don't mind.

The sound of the chime of the alarm for the front door pulled me out of my thoughts. Derrick called out to us. I looked at my grandmother with a *oh crap!* look and she laughed at me, then she told him we were in his room. She stood up with Chanel and headed for the door. I silently pleaded with her to stay and she told me to suck it up. She met Derrick in the doorway; he kissed her and the baby. My grandmother told him to come in as I pulled my knees into my chest and she shut the door. I put on a brave smile I couldn't tell what type of mood he was in. I asked how the trip went, he shrugged and said business is business. He took his suitcase in the closet. I could hear him unpacking.

When he was done he came directly for me and kissed me. When he started to lay me down I shut down. He backed up and asked me what was wrong. Then he asked me if I finally got my period as he then noticed that the bedding was white. He looked at me, "*surprise I'm pregnant.*" I said dryly and unsure of his reaction. He asked me if I was joking and when I said I was serious and my eyes filled up with tears, he smiled at me and hugged me tightly. I asked him if he was mad and he told me he was not, but he was concerned about the effect of back-to-back pregnancies would have on my system. I told him what the doctor said and then I asked him again if he was ok. He kissed me and told me as long as I was ok he was excited. I cried tears of relief; I told him I was so worried about his reaction. He said we needed to celebrate. I told him we needed a plan. The doctor said it was ok for me to continue to breast feed Chanel. I had advertisers waiting for me at the beginning of the year and I would be big and pregnant again. He exhaled, and then we called Cyrus and JoJo together. Derrick told them in a matter of fact tone that I was pregnant. They were silent for a minute and then JoJo started cracking up. He told Derrick he had no self-control. Derrick looked at me without a smile and said he never has self-control when it comes to me. I blushed then I kissed him. My grandmother brought Chanel in to nurse as I listened to them juggle things around. Derrick was adamant about no travel and the constraints of my engagements. Everything had to be done by the weekend before the fake wedding. JoJo said he and Cyrus would fill my calendar starting next week. And that fast I was back to work.

****

"Chantel, your Babygirl is beautiful! What did you name her?" My interviewer said.
"Chanel," then I smiled.
"Like the perfume?"
"I hadn't thought of that, but she's my mini me."
"Congratulations again. So tell us what we can expect on this album."
"I have a few collaborations, there's one song with Murphy." The audience excitedly applauded, "a song Alexa wrote for me. And many more, I'm very proud of this project."
"You did all of this while you were pregnant?"
"Pretty much, I don't know about others but I've heard some say it and I have to agree, inspiration and pregnancy seem to go well together."
"What are you performing for us today?"
"Murphy is here so we're gonna perform our song."
The audience went wild. They cut to commercial and they unhooked me from my mic. I went backstage, I kissed my grandmother and Chanel and then the program director hurried Murphy and I to the stage. Murphy said it was going to be nice to actually sing this song with me. We recorded in separate studios; this was our first time meeting. Pearla and Penny were in the green room waiting for me to bring him back. Pearla about died when I told her I was performing with him today. Murphy has been voted as one of the sexiest male performers. He wore a sleeveless T-shirt and ripped up enough to ask why is he wearing it at all jeans. He's a little taller than me, caramel brown with dark brown eyes and long hair that he normally wears corn rolled.
He looked at me and said I was really tall, I thanked him and then I looked down to see the markings on the stage to make sure I knew where my mark was. Earlier in sound check he told me I was pitchy. He irritated me beyond belief, then my grandmother told me he just wanted to have something to say. She said he didn't know how to handle a female who wasn't swooning over him. I told her with a man like Derrick who would ever worry about him. She agreed, but she said he's not concerned with any of that he's used to being handled a certain way. When my interviewer introduced us the music started and Murphy started singing. Our song was telling a story about initial attraction. Murphy kept walking around me and singing to me. I smirked at him cause I knew he thought he had some kind of an effect on me, but all I could think about is when I met

304

Derrick. When I sang I always sang to Derrick, and today was no different. The audience went wild when we were done.

When we went backstage I told Murphy I had a couple of fans who wanted to meet him. He smiled at me as if he thought I was one of them. My grandmother was following us with Chanel; I don't know what he thought I was going to show him. Penny was standing closest to the door when I opened it. They screamed and grabbed him by the arm and pulled him completely into the room. My grandmother and I smiled and then we closed the door. As I said hello to my Babygirl who seemed like she was taking everything in Murphy came out of the green room with Penny and Pearla following him. They said they were going to show him around The Bay Area. Then he asked me if I wanted to go, but the way he said it was like he just knew I'd say yes. I looked at my grandmother like he was a disease. Just because these groupies blow their heads up doesn't mean all girls are going to fall all over them because they have talent. Pearla muffled her laughter as I pulled myself together to say no as respectfully as I could. Murphy was stuck for a minute like he's never heard the word before.

Cyrus came down the hallway with his planner and looking at his watch. The expressions on my grandmother and my face slowed him down. He asked us if we were ready, then he looked Murphy up and down. Pearla let her laugh go completely, and we went on with our day. I didn't have to babysit them, everyday counts at this point.

We ran all around San Francisco, promoting, photographing, and networking. Chanel looked as tired as we did on our way home. Cyrus had my grandmother and I cracking up as he made fun of Murphy. Our laughter stopped as our limo pulled up behind another limo sitting in my driveway. I sat there letting Chanel finish eating under her nursing cover while Cyrus and my grandmother got out of the car. Pearla came bouncing out of the door and Cyrus told her I was feeding the baby. She waited by the door. Penny and Murphy walked out the door like they were completely into each other. Chanel finished eating and I burped my baby then I covered her up. Derrick came outside as I got out of the limo. He greeted me with a kiss and then you saw everything add up for Murphy. He apologized to Derrick saying he forgot I was married. When Murphy tried to say goodbye to my grandmother she waived him off as she walked in the house shaking her head with irritation. Derrick looked at Murphy, "you were flirting with my woman."

"I forgot she was married, won't happen again. She surely didn't seem to care about hurting my feelings when she rejected me though."

"Why should she?" Cyrus said.

Murphy walked towards his limo, "good point. Alright then. See you guys around." He hurried off.

Pearla fell on the ground laughing. "D-Rick you ain't right! Why were you punking him like that?"

"Like what? What did I miss?" I smiled.

"You know D-Rick being D-Rick."

"Well I liked him even though." Penny said.

"Cougar!" Pearla said.

"As long as we don't look like I'm way older than him, why should I care? He looks like a man, feels like a man, why care?" Penny said with her hands on her hips.

"Stay in your lane. I don't go cruising the old people lanes looking for my next baby daddy, and neither should you come down here."

"Whatever Pearla, you gonna learn the hard way to stop focusing on the man's age and look at the man." Penny said.

****

Already this pregnancy is totally different than Chanel. I haven't gotten sick once, but it is still early. I almost feel like the doctor was wrong, but the fact that my period hasn't come means that they were right about something. I feel sad when I look in the mirror. I just got my body back, and now it was going to go away again. I hope I still get it back after this baby. Derrick said we should wait until after the wedding to tell people about the baby. Although I see Amber raising her eyebrow at me with the sudden burst of work when I was supposed to be taking the rest of the year off.

I have been working my behind off to get promotional pictures, interviews, slogans, etc. done. Amber came up with the video concept for Murphy and I's song. We filmed for a day, which was nice, and then avatars were created of us. I thought the computer-generated version of me was way cute. They had to come up with something when I refused to kiss Murphy. I'm not an actress where it's my job to kiss random people. I wasn't going for it, and Cyrus told them he knew I wasn't going to go for it, but I guess they needed to hear from the horse's mouth. **HE-HAW**! We still had to record our movements like we were acting out the scenes, but we didn't have to be together for that part. I couldn't wait to see the final product.

Sasha

I sent the MLS number to my realtor, and I told her I wanted to see it as soon as possible. She instant messaged me stating that she would be ready by the time I got to her office. I grabbed my keys and I told Malcolm I would be back. I liked this two-bedroom two-bathroom ground floor condo. I've been talking to El's mom and she hates being on the other side of the country. If she lives beyond the birth of our children she probably wouldn't be able to travel and we for sure couldn't. So Mrs. Parsons and I decided to have a Memorial or Celebration of Life Service, if you will, for her and Mr. Parsons out there while they're alive and then they would live out their final days out here. Mr. & Mrs. Parsons were the only ones who liked my idea, everybody was angry and accusing me of taking over. El didn't like all of the drama my decision brought. "How soon can we get this show on the road? I need to close by end of the month so I can have it ready for my in laws immediately." She showed me the list price. I went over my offer, which I thought was more than fair. I called El to tell him about the condo which was perfectly located by our townhouse. He barked at me telling me to let it go cause it wasn't happening. So I went straight to the office. He didn't even look up when I opened the door to his office, he knew it was me. I put my hands on my hips and I went in. Then I heard Yussef and his girls coming. Their little smiles and amazement over my slowly growing baby bump amused me and I forgot that fast that I was in sass mode. Once Yussef called his girls I went right back in on El. I told him this is what his parents want. Needless to say enough even though he was irritated beyond belief, Sassy gets her way. On my way home Richard called me to check-in. He asked when I was coming home. I took a deep breath and I told him that El and I were going to live up here. Richard went off, I turned the volume down on my phone he was going off so badly. I tried to calm him down by saying that I'd get more of the help I needed up here since there was more family around. He said by family I meant my momma. Why did he do that? Then I went in. I told him "exactly!" My momma wasn't running around having new babies creating new families. If his girlfriend wasn't pregnant yet she would be soon. The few times I've been out there it's been Richie this and Richie that! Now he'd have the space to completely gush over the son he finally had, and maybe if he was lucky Erica could have a little girl and for once he'd know what it felt like to be considered a father and finally start acting like a father rather than a jealous older brother all the time. I told him respect doesn't come from how well you shoot, but your words. All I ever see him doing is threatening my man and it gets old. El laughs him off, it pisses me off! I talked about him from the top of his head to the bottom of his feet. He couldn't get a word in edgewise until I thought I heard him call me Sophia. And I ONLY slowed to verify what I heard before I went off AGAIN! I was going off so hard the room started spinning. So I hung up! I sat on the couch crying from my heart. My mouth was dry from fussing, and my jaw was tight like I had exercised it hard. I was having a Sophia moment for sure. It did feel good to let all of that out though. My momma, Travis, and Sabrina made sure I was included in everything. I felt like an outsider in Richard's home. Watching him be the father to this baby that he never was to me was too much. I love my little brother very much, I just hate that he has to have such a father.

I called my momma who was with Amber and they came right over. She told me not to get so worked up over him. I told her that was like the pot calling the kettle black. She said she's kept her distance since Drew's wedding. I said that was good cause Travis deserves better than that.

****

"How's work going?" Chantel asked.

"It's going, and why are you back at work? What happened to taking the rest of the year off?"

"Something suddenly came up. Anyways, Chanel and I would like to have our first public lunch sighting with you if you're game?"

"Of course, so you're telling me there's going to be paparazzi. Ok, let me get ready." I ran to my closet and I went to my sundress section. When in doubt I default to my favorite color Turquoise or Tiffany blue. I have four different sundresses in turquoise. I picked the one that completely camouflaged my stomach. I wanted to be stunning, but I didn't want to look like I was trying to look that way. I did my makeup nicely; I put on heels, grabbed my clutch and bounced happily out the door. I went to Chantel's house; she looked very pretty in her burgundy top, jeans that highlighted her curves, and heels. Her grandmother gave her the gold diaper bag that went perfectly with her outfit as she gave her instructions. Chantel didn't act like she knew it all which I appreciated, and I liked how her grandmother didn't talk to her like she didn't know anything. I guess when both of them consider each other's feelings and points of view it makes it easier to function. Chantel said Shasta was going to take her grandmother shopping to decorate her cottage out back, which was just about done. Ms. Rosa asked Chantel one more time if there was a spending limit on the credit card Derrick gave her. Chantel smiled at her grandmother and explained that Ms. Rosa takes care of their most prized possession, so with that she could have anything she wanted for her house. Ms. Rosa cried a little as she hugged her granddaughter. She asked if it was ok to make her house ridiculously fancy. Chantel told her to go crazy. I wondered what she meant by fancy, but it wasn't my business so I said nothing.

Then the doorbell rang, it was mitigated staff and they had the housekeeper and the service owner with them. "Hello Mrs. Mason, I'm Kendra Hutchins the owner of Immaculately Tidy Cleaning Service." She looked at her paperwork, she paused then she looked at Chantel. Her voice changed, her positive assertion wavered a little, "your husband Derrick..." She looked at Chantel. "I'm sorry, do you remember me? We've met." I peeked around the door. I smiled real big when Chantel looked at me I mouthed that she was Darryl's date at the engagement party, and they're Jason's girls. "Come in," Chantel said, and then she asked the mitigated person at the door if they needed to come in. They said no and walked away. "Have a seat." Chantel told them pointing to the room I was ear hustling in.

"I'm sorry I feel so dumb that I didn't put two and two together. This is my sister Kaleah, we will be assigned to cleaning your home." Then she smiled, "now everything makes sense. I just became affiliated with Mitigated Staffing Solutions and my clientele has tripled."

Her sister sat there star struck. "I can't believe it's Chantel Shaw. I love your music! I can't believe it! I can't believe it!" Kaleah said looking like she was spacing out. Then she looked at me. "Are you an actress or a singer too?"

"Nope, just her cousin."

"You're so pretty you look like you should be on TV as well." She said like she just had to say it.

I blushed, "can I put you in my pocket and take you everywhere with me?"

Kendra took a minute to gather herself, and then she put her business hat back on. She went over the contract then Chanel and I followed them around the house as Chantel showed them around and they went over expectations. When they were done with the tour I asked if Kendra only serviced big houses and businesses. I was thinking of Mr. & Mrs. Parsons' condo. They would need to have full staff cleaning, cooking, and nursing care. She said there was no job too small for them, and then she gave me her card.

When we drove out of the gate Mitigated staff was behind us and then Chantel pointed out the paparazzi, she exhaled then we went to the restaurant. I checked my face before I got out of the car to make sure I was on point, then we made our way inside. The guys stayed back so far snapping pictures of us the whole time. When we were seated Chantel stared at Chanel. She said she couldn't believe she came out of her. Chanel looked at both of us looking just like her father, and then she looked around the restaurant like she was trying to figure out where we were. Then she fell asleep; I admired Chanel's calmness. I wondered if I would be blessed with similar dispositions with my babies. I was telling Chantel about my plans for El's parents. The travel arrangements were set, and Carina was planning the celebration of life for Mr. & Mrs. Parsons so they could say their last goodbyes to their families. I looked up and here comes Richard and to make matters worse he was with Yussef. Now he's just being evil! I could tell by Yussef's demeanor that Richard manipulated this whole thing. He has no idea that Richard knows anything about my feelings for him. Richard was in full charm mode, inviting himself to our table, etc. If it wasn't for all these people I could've shot Richard and then apologized to my Dan-Dan later. I honestly think she'd understand. She knows how her son is!

"So Yussef, rumor is that you've got a new girlfriend? You are certainly enjoying the bachelor life." Richard smiled at him.

"I guess you could say that." Yussef scanned the restaurant.

"Who's this new girl? Did you meet her at service?" Chantel asked.

"It's not that serious, and no I didn't." He said dryly.

"Since when are you so tight lipped, where's all your idealistic ideas about the future with this new person? She could be your wife one day." Chantel said smiling.

He shrugged, "I'm getting tired."

"Yussef, don't settle. Remember we talked about this. Hang in there," I said.

"What did you talk about?" Richard asked Yussef.

"This conversation was between he and I!" I glared at Richard.

"Maybe I know someone, what are you looking for?" Chantel said trying to change the subject.

"I don't like blind dates, no thanks."

"I have an idea, if things don't work out with this girl we'll have a kick back at the house. I'll invite family and friends, and if someone catches your attention there then so be it."

Yussef laughed, "we'll need T-shirts for the family members. I'm still meeting people there's too many of us."

"Good idea. Ok so deal, all the weddings and nonsense dies down then we get together and celebrate family." Chantel said.

"Deal."

Chantel did her best to keep our lunch pleasant; I wanted to get away from Richard cause he was making me MAD! The fact that he was breathing was angering me. Yussef looked at me and gestured telling me to calm down. I guess my irritation was all over my face. I took a deep breath then I looked around.

"So what are you hoping for?" Chantel asked.

"Girls of course! What could be better?" I said.

"Why not boy and girl? That way you're done." Richard said.

"Cause I would prefer girls, but I wouldn't be mad about one of each." I wiggled my neck, "however! My husband and I may decide to continue our family. We never said we only wanted two kids. We're just starting off with a bang! So far pregnancy hasn't been too bad outside of these hormones. I could see having more." Richard looked like he didn't approve which sealed it for me. "I'm going to have more. It's just a matter of when!"

"Sassy, you have to remember that kids are forever, and when you and El go your separate ways you will have to raise all those kids by yourself."

"El is not Richard! We said 'til death do we part and we meant it. El has proven how much he loves me time and time again especially dealing with you. He's not going anywhere!"

Richard was beyond pissed off which pleased me. "Sassy I thought we got past all of this? Why are you going backwards?"

Chantel checked on the baby and Yussef sat there listening. Couldn't blame him we were doing this at the table so oh well. "At first it was cute, but now your constant challenges to my man are a joke and unrespectable. You're just mad that we're not coming back so you can keep a watch on our every move. Maybe when you start being on the up and up with Erica you'll stop worrying about the what ifs with me and my GOOD man!"

He cut me off, "how long do you really see this lasting when you're looking back at someone else!"

OH NO HE DIDN'T! "JUST BECAUSE YOU STAY STUCK ON STUPID OVER MY MOTHER, DOES NOT MEAN THERE ARE ANY REGRETS ON MY PART! I LOVE EL AND HE LOVES ME! I'M NOT SOPHIA AND HE IS NOT YOU!" I was talking about Yussef, and I could tell by his demeanor he was following us. "WE MADE OUR CHOICES AND LIKE ADULTS WE EMBRACE THEM AND STAND BY THEM!"

Richard put his hand up, "UN HUH! That's real cute and inspiring, but one day you need to deal with the fact that you are my daughter and you've got a lot of my ways whether you admit it or not."

"Unfortunately I may be your daughter, but he's not you! He always does the honorable thing!"

"People fall short!"

Chantel

Lunch was awkward to say the least, but we went back to Sasha's place as she worked on a few things while we chatted. She was working while Chanel and I enjoyed the down time in her townhouse. I wasn't sad when Cyrus called me last night and said I had the day off. I've been running like a chicken with its head cut off. I promised Derrick I would take it easy, and what was easier than sitting next to Sasha and talking to her while she worked. She said she kind of missed working in an office sometimes, but not completely. When Darryl came over he took Chanel from me. Then he started talking about an office space downtown. It was almost like they were speaking in code, cause I couldn't follow them. Especially when I thought they were talking about an office building but he was talking about breadboxes. All I could think was, "why would they buy a bread factory?" I shrugged it off cause obviously I was trying too hard to understand their conversation. Darryl stayed longer than he wanted to because Chanel did not want him to put her down. He said he was putty in his little cousin's hands and now Chanel was going to melt him up.

Sasha switched gears and told Darryl that his Auntie Lorraine confirmed that she and her husband were coming to the wedding. Darryl tried to shake it off, but irritation was all over his face. "Chantel would you go? Would you go to the wedding of DJ's dead son's baby momma?"

"It would depend on the situation."

"I guess, but they don't like Malcolm over there. As if being at your wedding wasn't enough, I don't know why they would want to come to this."

I frowned, "they weren't happy at my wedding?"

"They were overjoyed! All I hear is," he quoted them. "*My cousin Derrick is married to Chantel Shaw!*" He shook his head, "like we don't exist anymore."

"I'm sorry."

"No apology necessary. It's them!"

"Can I ask why that side of your family seems to bother you so much?"

"Auntie Lorraine is cool for the most part. I know she's never been warm and fuzzy about Malcolm, so I don't know why she would come to the wedding."

"Maybe it's not about Malcolm. She knows what your momma went through with David. Maybe she's supporting Amber even if it's a little hard for her." Sasha said.

I looked at Darryl, he seemed upset but I couldn't really put my finger on the emotion I was seeing in him at that moment. "Do you remember him?" He asked Sasha.

"Of course, one day he was just there as if he came out of nowhere."

"Dionne's always David this, and David that. Do you think I look like him?"

"Yes, but all three of you have so much of Amber in your features it's hard to remember."

Darryl smiled, "smart woman. I look like my granddad with my grand-momma's brownness all David is to me is a last name." Then he looked at Chanel, "I don't know why you have to be a Mason at all. They should've stopped at Latour." Then he smiled, "ok. I gotta go. Got places to go and people to see. Chantel," he said handing Chanel to me. "Stay black! I'm out black people." He threw us the peace symbol and he left.

"Does he act like David?"

"Nope, but neither one of them do. Derrick is little Malcolm, but really he acts like Uncle Frank."

"That's why they're so close." I said.

"Exactly!"

The front door opened and we could hear El laughing before we saw him. When he walked into the office, we all said at the same time, "Darryl!"

Episode 16

Yussef

"Can I come up? I need to talk to you." Angela said over the intercom.

I buzzed her up and then I sat on the couch. I was playing with the dance game on the girl's game system. I needed a break to catch my breath anyways. "Don't get comfortable I've got a game going." I said as she walked in the door.

She frowned at my comment then she continued inside. She barely had the door closed before she went in, "Yussef what happened to us?"

I rolled my hands, "you're going to have to give me more if you expect me to participate in this conversation."

"We were in love, now I've been reduced to booty call status?"

"You don't date men with kids, I've got two. In all fairness to both of us, I didn't know I had them, but that's not either of our faults. You were the one reducing us to where we stand now. You tried to work with me, but you had to be true to yourself. Where you messed up was that once every two weeks just to hook up crap, I let you get away with that. At the end of the day, I've got kids. Two beautiful girls that have been my world from the moment I found out about them. I prayed you would work with me, but you couldn't so now here we are."

"I think we should try again."

I laughed until I looked at her face, "oh my bad you were serious? AW HECK NAW! NOPE! NOT HAPPENING!"

She looked annoyed at my reaction. "Why does that warrant such a dramatic response?"

"Because there's no way we could work. I believe it's pointless to try. If you want off the booty call list, I can move you off of rotation, but no relationship for you and me."

"You don't love me anymore?"

"No."

"You're just saying that. You can't fall out of love with someone just like that."

"Suit yourself, you don't have to believe me. Just remember you asked and I answered." I shrugged, "I'm tired."

"Tired of me?"

"Tired of females who act like their feelings are the only ones that matter. I do recall begging you to work with me. Begging you to ride out with me, but you couldn't do it, so you couldn't do it. And then I talked to my girls," I shrugged again. "There could never be a future for me and you."

She looked hurt, "what did they say? I wasn't mean to them."

"Nope, you weren't mean, but you were never enthusiastic and they knew it."

"But I tried, don't I get points for trying?"

"You tried and you failed." I said coldly.

"Yussef, this isn't even you. Why are you being so distant?"

"This is Yussef when there's no love to be found. You might as well go back to calling me Jeremy, cause now that you're not in my heart you won't get to see it anymore. Now if you excuse me I'm trying to master some moves." I stood up.

"Just like that? You can't work with me?"

"Work with you how? I'm not giving up my time with my girls, and I don't let females who can't be around my girls into my heart. Oh and I've taken little Jack under my wings too." I stretched, "so that's now three kids and you can't handle one. There's really NOTHING we need to talk about." I turned on my system, "and since you're all caught up; I can't trust you. I guess this is the end of the road for us. Cause I can't let you be a booty call anymore either, but you understand." Angela stood up and took a deep breath like she was about to go there with me. "Think about it! Whatever your bleeding heart is telling you to do right now, shut it up. There's no love here, just leave and don't come back. Don't risk pissing me off and making me react to you. It could get ugly!" Then I put my eyes back on my television.

Angela huffed out the door. I almost felt bad for her, but a couple of songs later I was like Angela who?

****

I was clicking away on a roll on my computer when Sylvia called to remind me that it's the end of the school year and the girls have Open House at their school tonight. I told her I'd get the girls like normal and then we'd pick her up. Grab dinner and then head over to their school. Then I got back to work, clicking away. El scooted in his chair into my office. I sat there watching him scoot, and then he slammed his hands on my desk and growled. "Suncoast?" I said empathetically.

"Yes! Why are they so difficult? After we jumped through so many hoops for them to meet their criteria, now we're haggling over pennies!" He took an imaginary gun out of his pocket and shot himself.

"Don't you have someone who deals with stuff like that?"

"Yes, Henry is our numbers guy, but this has escalated to me. Richard doesn't want to help me any further than he has to."

I shook my head, "you married his daughter though. It's not like you guys are shacking up."

"Right! But we go through stuff like this all the time. He's always pulling guns on me. We've boxed a couple times, he's all over the place."

"I hope I'm not like that with my girls."

El swallowed, "what if I have two little Sasha's AND THEN THE BIG ONE!" He shot himself again.

"It's too late, you're stuck with her now. And I'm completely rooting for two girls. Identical clones of Sasha, personality and the whole nine yards."

"You're not funny. I can rest assured that if both of them acted like their momma her stomach would be jumping all over the place, at least these nine months would drive her crazy."

"If you were Richard wouldn't you be a little crazy too?"

"I guess, I'll just take notes watching you with your gorgeous girls. When are you going to let them date?"

"Not until they're married." I smiled.

El chuckled, "thanks." He exhaled, "I can go back to my computer now. I needed to shift gears for a moment."

"Any time," and then I returned to my computer.

When I picked up the girls, they got very excited because they saw Sasha's car in the parking lot as we came back to the office so I could finish up a few things. They gave Ms. Laverne the usual hugs and kisses and then they bolted for El's office to see Sasha. I could tell by her stance she wasn't getting her way about something and instead of letting it go, she came down here to try to make El change his mind. I could tell without even hearing one drop of their conversation. The girls were rubbing her stomach and she looked like their touches calmed her. El shot himself again when I walked passed the door while Sasha had her back to him. When I smiled, Sasha jerked her head to see El. I gave the girls a few minutes and then I told them to come on and to leave Sasha and El alone. El said they were fine, I laughed but I told them to come on.

We picked Sylvia up and then we got a quick bite to eat. Sylvia looked really pretty, a lot like she did when we were together the first time. She was glowing from the inside out, but the light would dim every time I tried to find an angle to make her and I work under. She couldn't handle being around Drew, and I spend so much time with my family these days. The woman I marry has to get along with my family it's important to me that everyone gets along. Our past were now bigger than the both of us. When we met up with Jackson and Melissa, Sylvia and Melissa eyed each other like they were taking in everything. Both of them were too done up for an Open House at an elementary school if you ask me. Jackson and I said hello and then I told them I'd wait for them to go over Yezzy's information with the teacher.

Sylvia and I walked into the classroom and I saw the teacher's eyes fill with appreciation for Sylvia. Sylvia ignored it and followed Syd to her desk. Syd proudly showed us her work. Mr. Jensen carefully approached us, most likely trying to check himself. He told us that it was nice to see us again. Then he said normally sisters aren't placed in the same class, but Sydney and Yesmina were exemplary in their conduct. Then he said, as we may know Sydney started off the year very well, she was excelling with the help of her sister. Sydney beamed with pride. Then he said they hit a rough patch for a minute, and Sydney confided that her parents broke up and she was really upset about it. Sylvia put her arm around Sydney, and then Sydney said that she's ok now. I felt like garbage, maybe I should've stayed with Sylvia just so Sydney could be happy. Mr. Jensen confirmed that Sydney is performing very well again. He said with the school year winding down he could only imagine wonderful things for her next year. Sydney smiled and said thank you, to her teacher. He glanced at Sylvia again; she was lovingly praising Sydney for doing well. He excused himself to go talk to another family.

Then Syd sucked her teeth, she told her mother that Max just walked in and she couldn't stand him, he was so annoying. This husky little boy was grinning at my daughter, I wanted to flick him cause he knew he was bothering her. I asked her if she wanted me to say something to him. Her eyes got big; she was going to ask me something when Yezzy walked in the door. She ran to her sister, I assume telling her what I said. They smiled at me like they were going over their options. Then Yesmina showed us all of her work. Melissa kept shooting Sylvia evil looks as she sat on the side waiting. Mr. Jensen said Yesmina was quite the helper and all around wonderful student.

While Jackson and Melissa went over Yesmina's folder the girls pulled me over to the side. They asked me what I was going to say to Max, I took that as my cue and I told them to watch. Max was so busy looking at my girls that he failed to notice that I was approaching him until I was towering over him. "Is this your mother?" I asked pointing to the woman who had her back to us.

"Yeah!"

"Is your father here?" The little boy shook his head no. The woman turned around, how did such a beautiful woman have such an ugly son? "I'm Yussef," I said extending my hand.

"Max."

"Both of your names are Max?"

She pointed to herself, "Maxine." Then she pointed her to son, "Maximilian."

"Ok well I'm Yussef and my girls," I pointed to my angels, "say that he continues to bother them. I need you to tell your son to stand down."

"You mess with those girls?" She asked her son even though I just told her that he does.

"No!" He said real fast, I could tell he was lying.

"You wanna tell the truth this time? I can see it all over your face."

He tried to look innocent, "mommy I'm not lying!"

I pointed out the door at the pole on the playground. "You can lie to your momma all you want, but if my girls tell me that you even looked at them again I'm stringing you up on that pole!"

"How you think you gonna threaten my son? How you know your girls aren't lying?" She got angry in defense of her son.

"I can see it in his face. Plus my girls aren't liars." Then I motioned for the girls to walk over. "Can anyone else confirm what you guys said?"

"Everybody. He's always messing with us." Yezzy said.

I looked at the mother, "ask anyone of these kids."

She frowned, "I don't need to ask anybody anything. I believe my child, you don't know me to be approaching me like this!"

"And obviously your son didn't know me to even look at my girls. How come your cousins haven't handled him?" I asked the girls.

"They've beat him up a lot, he's hard headed." Yezzy said.

The mother's eyes danced around the room, "just to shut you up." She walked over to a little shy looking little boy, and she asked him to come over. "What's your name sugar?"

"Randall," he said meekly.

"Randall have you ever seen my son messing with either one of these girls?"

He shook his head yes, "all the time."

"What do you know, they probably paid you. BYE!" She said dismissing the little boy. After she asked two more kids and they all had the same answer. "Out of the mouth of two or more witnesses!" I smiled, and then I reminded little Max of my promise with the pole. He shook his head fast in agreement.

****

"Hey Mister Invisible Poet, nice poem." Max said retaking inventory of me.

"Thank you." I said waiting on my drink.

"Where's your wife? She don't come to your performances?"

"I'm not married."

"Was she your girlfriend? I saw you leave with someone that night."

"My daughter and her mother."

"Oh your baby momma. Ya'll not together?"

"Nope."

"Does she know you guys aren't together?"

I smiled back, "she does. Why aren't you here with your husband, baby daddy, or boyfriend?"

"I don't have a husband or a boyfriend, and if I ever see my baby daddy again I'll break his neck."

"Why would someone so pretty be so violent?"

She smiled bigger, "you should join me and my friend's table."

I told the bartender I was going to their table and to bring my drink there. Max introduced me to her friend Cherry. I smiled but didn't say anything; I hoped that was a nickname for her sake. Cherry looked at me with wanting eyes. "This is a nice little spot."

"This is your first time here?" Cherry asked.

"Yep, Verbal Illuminations is the spot." Max said.

"It's alright." I like my spot better.

"Well it definitely wasn't your first time performing. Why aren't you at your usual spot?" Max asked.

"Stalkers!" I tipped the bartender as he handed me my drink.

Max smiled and then we listened to the other performers. Max was light skinned with almost shoulder length brown hair. She was very pretty, just thinner than I normally like my women, but maybe I needed to give up on thickness. I shrugged, I wanted to assess whether she'd be on my lap girl list or not. When Max noticed her friend shooting me looks she said, "not-un! This one is mine! Go find somebody else!" Cherry rolled her eyes and looked around the room. When Cherry walked away Max leaned in, "I've got a question. So both of those girls are yours?"

"Yep."

"You went raw dogging one chick to the next?"

"If you look at it that way."

"EEEWWLLLL! That's how diseases get spread." She frowned.

"I'm sure, but that was the only time I was with either of them like that. I stay covered."

"I've been celibate for six years."

"Good for you."

"How long has it been for you?"

"What time is it?"

She laughed, "seriously. How long?"

"That's a very personal question Max. I don't know you like that."

"Do you have a girlfriend?"

"No I don't."

"I think I'd like to date you." She watched my eyes.

"Just like that you decide? You don't even know me."

"But your eyes tell me what I need to know."

"What do you know about eyes? You couldn't even tell that your son was lying to you."

She laughed, "he did get over on me didn't he." She exhaled, "he's the only man I let get over on me anymore."

"If you say so." I finished my drink.

Lanie

"So this is the little girl I've heard so much about. How you doing young thang, I'm his dad." His supposed charm gave me the creeps. He let his lips rest too long on my hand, and I swear it felt like he wanted to lick me.

I took my hand back, "it's nice to meet you Mr. Talbot."

"My name ain't no Talbot! Yeah he can thank his no good mama for that!"

"So what should I call you?"

"Just call me Dougie. You know, they made a song about my dance and eerythang!" I couldn't help it, I laughed while Allee looked completely embarrassed.

"Dad! Can you be serious? She's going to think you're really like this."

"Oh she knows I'm just playing."

"Hey! Hey!" A girl knocked on the screen door and then she opened it. She stopped in her tracks and looked me up and down. "And what do we have here?" I returned her gaze up and down at her clothes. "Who's she supposed to be?"

"Lanie, this is my cousin Peanut. Peanut meet Lanie."

"What kind of name is Lanie?"

"You tell me Peanut."

"You sound like a white girl."

"Thank you for noticing. You lack diction."

She squinted at me, "what?"

I smiled and looked at Allee, "you want to explain that to her."

"I don't know who you think you are, but I ain't the one!"

"The two or the three, maybe you could be the tenth, but even that's a stretch." I laughed at her.

"Allee! Who's this trick you brought up in my Uncle's house? You betta get her before I handle her."

I chuckled, "you should never be that stupid."

Peanut stared at me with her mouth open for a minute like she couldn't believe that her loud mouth routine didn't scare me. She walked like she was about to walk away; I could tell she thought she was going to catch me off guard. I stepped out of my heels and took my hands out of my pocket. When she turned around to charge at me I kicked her in the face. Stunned she fell backwards and she held her face like she didn't know what just happened to her. Allee laughed, "oh yeah. She's a Wallace." He said matter of factly with so much pride.

"A WHAT?" She looked at him with fear.

"You heard me."

"What you bring her here for? You trying to get us killed?" She fussed at her cousin as she took her face to the kitchen.

He followed her, I put my shoes back on and I put my hands back in my pocket. "Nobody told you to come here full of attitude."

"Attitude is what I do, you brought her to show off." I agreed with her, she wasn't completely stupid. "Why you wearing your pants like that? You look like a loser!"

"She likes my pants like this."

"So just because she likes it you change it?"

"Yes!" I said even though I know she didn't want me in their conversation.

"Why is she here?"

"She wanted to meet my family."

"So she could look down on us? Have you met hers?"

"No!" I said daring her to say anything else.

"How you extend your leg like that? Peanut is way bigger than you." Dougie asked.

"Lots of Tae-Bo and practice."

"Tae-Bo? What's that? Some kind of religion?"

"It's kickboxing exercise, it was a fad for a minute."

"Sounds like a religion. What's your religion?"

I felt guilty; "I'm not practicing anything right now."

"You believe in God though?"

"Dad!"

"I know a lot of you young folks got new ways of thinking these days. My boy says he's an anchovy."

Allee came out of the kitchen, "Agnostic dad."

"Sounds better when I said it."

"Dad respect my beliefs like I respect yours."

"Mine make sense, yours is some old nonsense you read in a book somewhere to confuse you."

"Are you ready? You met my father, you met my cousin, you ready?"

"Nice meeting you Dougie." I said as I walked out the door.

"So now what you want to do?" He smiled at me in the car.

I shook my head, "I can drop you off at home."

"You coming up?" He smiled.

"No!"

"No? NO? You met my father, both of my cousins, what else is there?"

"I haven't met your son, I just found out today that you don't believe in God. I mean there's no point in coming up. You don't believe in God we could never have a future together. Without a future, there's no point in opening my legs to you. To put extra miles on my coochie? For what?"

He growled, "you got me jumping through so many hoops just to get next to you and all you say is no, no, no. You don't like the way I wear my pants, you don't like my chain, you wanna meet my family so you can kick my cousin in the face. I haven't met your family, but you all up in mine."

"That's because my father would break you down. He only gets to meet the worthy. You're not worthy!"

"You're trying to change me into that little loser aren't you? Like that could ever work! There's a reason why you're not with him. So you've got to let the idea of him go."

I didn't say anything; I wasn't about to show that his words hurt me. He had no idea of what happened with Dorian and I and how dare he try to act like he did. I started the car without saying a word. I pulled in front of his place and unlocked my door. When he got out of the car he got mad and he kicked my bumper as I slowly pulled away. I put the car in reverse and then I reached in my purse. He was walking away when I shot at the ground next to his foot. He jumped high in the air, "I'll send you a bill for the damages to my car." Then I drove away before his feet touched the ground.

Allee started blowing up my phone with all kinds of apologies. Yeah, yeah, yeah. I missed Dorian in the worst way. I went to Shylight and I sat at the bar. I ordered a beautiful and then I sipped slowly hating my life. I was sitting there for a long time watching my phone vibrate all over the counter when my cellphone rang with a different ring. Even though the number was no longer saved to my phone, I knew the number. I tried to pull back my excitement. "Hello."

"I'm requesting permission to approach the bar."

I spun around in my seat, my heart ached for him. I ran and hugged him tightly. Dorian kissed my forehead and then he squeezed me back. "What are you doing here?"

"Hoping to get a glimpse of you. I miss you!"

"I miss you!" I took him in, he was living clean again I could tell, but I liked this look on him better anyways.

"Let me get your next drink."

"You know this is my house, but if you want to pretend."

The bartender brought my next drink to me, and Dorian's usual. "I take it, your momma hasn't told you my news?" He didn't look at me.

Tears welled up immediately in my eyes. "No." I swished my glass around in my hand. "You came here to tell me?"

"I didn't want you to hear from someone else."

"April?"

He exhaled, "yep."

"How long before you're engaged?"

"I don't know, I guess this will all kind of happen pretty fast."

"Well, yeah! Now that you know what's on the other side, you're ruined forever." A tear fell, "I'm sorry."

"No you're not. You're almost perfect." I tried to smile. "Is there any point in begging you?"

"No, especially when you've actually stopped long enough to consider April. I mean April! The same chick we've argued about for years! The next Dotty in the making. I guess it hurts this way like it's supposed to."

"I love you Lanie, I always have and I always will."

"I love you Dorian, I never stopped."

****

"Your daddy's coming to service tomorrow, why don't you come?" My momma said as she cut up her fruit.

"I'll pass."

"Uncle Nelson will be there." She sang.

I love my Uncle Nelson, I love that he'll check ANYBODY when necessary too. "Ok, I'll go. Just remember you asked for this." Then I ran up to Erica's room and told her I needed to look stunning tomorrow for service. Knowing that Dorian was going to be there, I wanted him to see what he was going to be missing.

We picked out a nicely modest and shapely dress for me. A turquoise sheath dress with a tan colored belt and shoes. Erica convinced me to let her blow dry my hair. Ok, so it's no secret, I'm tender headed, I'm so tender headed that I cry when I comb my own hair. Which is why I don't wear it out too often cause I have more important things to do with my time than cry my eyes out working out the tangles. BUT! For the shock value I endured the torture. I washed my hair and detangled it. Then I let Erica blow it out. Then she put something on my hair as she twisted it and she said tomorrow we'd style my hair.

I talked to Oneika and I told her I was going to my momma's service she said she'd be there. As I drifted off into sleep Kendra called me. I invited her to come with me to service so she could meet my Uncle that I've always told her about. To my surprise she agreed to come. All night I tried to calm myself. I kept telling myself not to strangle April unless she said something to me.

After I dressed Erica finished my hair. It was long, shiny, crimped, and slightly curled. When Kendra came to my room she gasped. She said I looked so pretty. So we had to take a bunch of pictures in my room. I uploaded them but didn't post them. Once we were walking into service I posted them. Dorian wasn't too far from the door. He did a double take when he saw me and his mouth dropped. I smiled and walked to our seats in the back in the corner. My parents were going to sit on the end of our row. My momma put her books down then she went to make her rounds. My father sat down, then Dorian came over to say hi to my father. My father was not in the mood for Dorian so he gave him one-word answers. Dorian told him it was good to see him and then he smiled real big at me. When I put my hand out to shake his hand like he's always done, he slapped my hand away and he gave me a huge hug. Zoey was smiling and Erica was looking at daddy. Dorian said I was stunning, and then he asked what did he owe the honor of my presence to. I told him my Uncle Nelson was coming. He smiled really big then he asked if we were going out to eat after. Zoey volunteered a yes. Then he asked if he could come. Zoey pointed to April who was watching from across the room. She said she thinks he has plans already. Dorian huffed then he looked at me again. He said he didn't care and asked again if he could come. Zoey told him he was always welcomed with us. He smiled at her then he looked at me again. He smiled really big then he walked away.

He didn't sit with April, he sat so many rows ahead of her and then he kept looking back at me. Erica leaned in slowly and she said he just proposed to her. I asked her why she didn't tell me last night. She said she was trying to let him tell me, but it looks like he forgot. April wasn't wearing a ring. I asked where her ring was, and Erica said as far as she knew April didn't have one yet. Dorian don't care about that boring girl, I bet she asked him and he agreed. He was dying to buy my ring. Does it really matter if he agreed or he asked? When they marry she's going to be his wife regardless and I know he's going to honor that commitment. I stared at him the rest of service. He kept looking back and then April would look. Then my daddy looked at me and I turned my eyes.

After service I made a beeline to my Uncle Nelson and I gave him a big hug. Uncle Nelson made a big deal about how beautiful my sisters and I are. He hugged Shelby and the kids; from the youngest to the oldest we all love Uncle Nelson. Dorian came over like he was still in the family to get some love from Uncle Nelson as well. Uncle Nelson hugged him and then he told Dorian that he wanted to talk to him then he looked at me and said me too. I looked at my momma who turned her eyes away as if she wasn't watching the whole scene. Dorian walked over to April and said something and you could see anger all over her face. He walked away without any concern for her feelings. If it wasn't Dorian I might've felt sorry for her, but it is so I don't. I told Kendra I would catch up to them at the restaurant, Uncle Nelson told me we were riding with Dorian. I told Uncle Nelson to ride in the front and I got in the backseat. When Dorian attempted to start the car Uncle Nelson told him to hold on. "What are you two doing?"

"Sir?" Dorian glanced at me like he was looking to understand what I might've told him. I shrugged cause I haven't said anything.

"So you're not marrying my baby girl?"

Dorian exhaled, "no."

"Explain it to me," he rubbed his chin like he was irritated. "Cause I don't get you kids today. You spent all those years courting and the last year seems like you have lost your complete and total minds. I can look at the two of you and tell you that you're having the most ridiculous power struggle. Why you wait so long to do this?"

"Brother Wright it's like this." Dorian adjusted in his seat to freely gesture with his hands. "I love that girl with all my heart, mind, body, and soul. There's only one Lanie in this world, and that's the woman that was put on this earth for me to love. We fight hard, we love harder, but she don't respect me, she don't respect none of this. She wants to do what she wants to do when she wants to do it, and that's not going to work long term. I told her I would work with her on everything else but I need her to serve God with me. Be by my side every step of the way. Without God in our marriage what are we supposed to have? She knows I'm right, and it's not putting her outside of anything she knows to be here. I told her I'm not asking her to be a missionary or go in there and go hard. Just come with me twice a week, that's all. She said no, she can't do that. I can't marry her without at least that."

"There are plenty of marriages that function without God in the middle." I said.

"I don't want a functioning marriage, I want to be happy. These females come in here from all over trying to get close to me. That's not going to stop just because I'm married."

"So you want her there as a control for you?"

"I want us to be on the same page. I conceded and gave her a taste of what married life would be like. Did you like it?" He turned towards me; I looked down at my hands. "She loved it Brother Wright! Got me going against what I know and believe to try to bring us closer and still. The only reason she's here today is because of you. I know she's not here because she reconsidered, or even that she cares that that girl asked me to marry her." I KNEW IT! "I don't know why you'd rather lose me than work with me."

"Lanie?" Uncle Nelson turned in his chair. "I'm shocked, you're never this quiet. Is everything he said true?"

"Yes," I said lowly.

"So you don't care that he's going to marry someone else?"

"Of course I do, but I can't do this."

"Do what?"

"This! All of this! Do you have any idea what I went through last night to get my hair like this? The combing! The blow-drying! The torture! I gotta remember not to rub my eyes cause I actually have makeup on today. Standing too long in these heels is torture! I have pretty feet and I would like them to stay that way." Dorian and Uncle Nelson blank stared at me. "Look all you want, but this whole get up took a lot of thought and effort. Then you want me to do this EVERY Sunday, and EVERY Tuesday! Kill me! Kill me a lot!"

"This is serious Lanie." Dorian had no laughter in his face.

"I am serious! You want me to come here all the time when I only like so many people here. You think I don't hear the things they say about me. My temper and my inability not to curse them out in our Father's house will only reflect badly on you. You'll get tired of them telling you to control your woman. Like I could ever be controlled. You'll end up regretting me telling me to the day we die how much I don't respect you." Then I cringed, "I will admit that I was wrong for what I did, and it was messed up, but I do respect you. I know it's not easy to stand by what you believe. You're walking away from me because of it."

"What we believe." He corrected me.

"I'm not going to lie to you and pretend to be someone I'm not. I love you, but I know I can't be consistent like you need me to be. Go ahead and marry that boring girl who will never stand up to you."

Dorian looked at Uncle Nelson, "she's killing me! April wants to move to Southern California so we can have a fresh start. Obviously I failed the test today, so how can I argue that we need to stay here, when my job can easily transfer down there? I think I've compromised in every way I can just to try to stay."

"Why do you have to marry someone you don't love?"

"I don't have to marry someone I don't love, but if the woman I love won't love me back, am I supposed to remain single the rest of my life?"

"I can tell you firsthand how life goes when you marry someone you don't love. You end up the good old faithful uncle on the sideline who dies a little more every day. You shouldn't marry anyone while you're in love with someone else."

"You want me to wait until I've fallen out of love with her?" Dorian shook his head and started the car. "I'd die single then." He pulled out of the parking lot. "If I move away eventually she won't be the first thing on my mind when I wake up. Consuming my thoughts and actions all day, or the last person I think about when I go to sleep. I won't remain single just because she doesn't want me."

"It's not that I don't want you."

"You don't want me enough to do right by me. I even compromised for you, and still this is where we are. It would break my momma's heart to know what you truly think. She thinks this is all on me, and she's constantly telling me to wait for you. You and I both know there's no point."

Uncle Nelson shook his head, "Lanie you act so much like your grandmother it's not funny. You gonna end up with some guy who treats you badly for you to understand what you had in this young fella. Your grandmother may have ended up with a nice guy, but your grandfather was far from nice. Ask your momma."

Fire turned in my stomach, "he shot my momma!"

"Exactly! You won't wise up until you have your own version of Fred in your life."

The car started spinning and I couldn't believe how much my mouth wanted to go bad on Uncle Nelson! I unlocked my door and got out of the car at the light. I don't even know what Dorian was hollering about. I was mad and I couldn't stand another minute in that car. Fortunately we were across the street from the restaurant. Everyone was standing in the parking lot, slowly getting out of their cars. I saw my dad standing next to the passenger door with my momma. When I got out the car I walked in the opposite direction away from everyone. I illegally crossed the street and then I started walking. Dorian barely parked his car and then he ran after me. "Leave me alone Dorian!"

"Are you high? You don't ever jump out of a moving car just because you don't like what someone said to you!"

"Leave me alone!" I screamed at him, "you have no idea what he just said to me!"

"Nothing worth all this Lanie!"

"That's because you don't know. He knows what he said that's why you're here and he's not!"

"Well I guess if you're acting like this, there was some truth to what he said."

I swung wildly at Dorian and he grabbed my hand. "You don't know what you're talking about!" I took my shoes off. Then I threw them at him. He dodged one shoe while the other one clocked him in the head. "Leave me alone! Go marry your boring girlfriend and live the rest of your boring life out there, or stay here. Either way you don't have to worry about me. The only way our paths would cross is if I went in that place, and I'm not going back!"

"LANIE! Please don't stop going altogether. People are always going to say and do things that rub us the wrong way, they may even devastate us, but God didn't do it. Don't punish Him for what they did."

I was so mad I started screaming and stomping my feet! How could Uncle Nelson say that to me! My daddy walked over calmly, "Lanie. Get a grip!"

"Daddy! Uncle Nelson said I'm going to end up with someone like Fred!"

"How is standing here barefoot on the cement going to affect that? You're upset, ok, but this tantrum is unnecessary. Put your shoes on and I'll take you home." He started walking back towards the street.

Dorian handed me my shoes then he walked with me across the street. My daddy sent everyone inside, and then he looked at Dorian. "What kind of a man agrees to the term of forever to a question he'd never ask?" Dorian was quiet, "I'm not saying I understand. However, I thought the kind of man my daughter was going to marry would be a man about everything. A broken heart is never easy, but don't start punking out now. You're better than this." Then he looked at me, "you need to get a grip. So what if he told you something you don't like, you want to be treated like an adult then you need to act like one. Find your words or shut up. Nobody has time to be chasing you across the city cause you're mad."

I lowered my head, "yes daddy."

"Now, I would like to go inside and eat breakfast. Do you really need to go home or can we eat?"

Dorian looked at me, "we can go eat."

"Lanie so help me if you start acting up in this restaurant it's going to be me and you. Do you want that?"

"No daddy."
"Alright, let's go."

Yussef

"Dang! It seems like every time you come through here you got a different female on your arm." My cousin Bernadette said.
"Trying to find the right one that fits." I said.
"She alright, she's not like the other ones."
"Is that good or bad?"
"I don't know," Bernadette said sounding thoughtful. "I guess time will tell, she's a little rough around the edges. And I thought you like thick girls."
"I still do, but I guess I'm trying something else this time."
"I don't know if I see you working out with her though. I guess we'll see."
"I guess we'll see." I watched Max play cards with my cousins. It's been a couple of weeks, and it's been alright. I don't feel overly excited about dating Max but I'm not hating it. It is what it is right now. The girls do not like little Max and they jump him whenever they can. Max is always defending little Max and I told her she needed to let him deal with the consequences of his actions. He needed to learn how to interact with females. She babies him too much; maybe it annoys me because my mother was never like that towards me. I don't know, Max provides me with company when I don't feel like being alone. I don't feel like she's in my heart or anything like that.
"Where are my babies?" Pearla asked me.
"They're spending the night with Roz."
"I like that you still take care of her."
"She's my stepmom, I don't have a choice."
"Will I meet her?" Max asked.
"Maybe, let's see how you do in this circle first." I said, and then I bumped Liz who was quiet. "Survey says?"
"Which survey were we filling out again?" She gestured with her hands, "Chickenhead, Girlfriend, or wifey? Cause I'm stamping a big ole DENIED on the wifey survey right now. The jury is still out on the other two."
Max frowned, "what does that mean?"
"That you won't ever be calling me cousin!" Liz said with attitude.
Max shrugged, "oh." She didn't care.
"Interesting response. I don't know if I believe her Yu! Stay strapped up!"
Max laughed out loud, "this ain't that kind of party, but ok!"
Liz looked at me, "like I said interesting."
I watched Max hold her own with my cousins and I have to admit I kind of liked that. When I took her home she invited me in. Her sister was sitting comfortably on the couch when Max opened the door. She screamed and ran to her bedroom. Max said oops as she laughed at her sister. Her sister came back in the room fussing that Max couldn't bring men in the house when she was half naked." Macy you had on a pajama top and bottoms." Max said in her defense.
"But I didn't have a bra on." She said through clinched teeth.
"Like anyone would notice. You're still president of the itty bitty...."
Macy cut her off, "Shut up!" She swung at her sister, "hi you must be Yussef. I'm her sister Macy."
"Hi."
"Have a seat." Macy got comfortable on the couch. "So Max this one gets an invite up? Wow!"
"Is this new behavior?" I asked sitting on the couch.

"Yep no one's ever good enough. She seems to like you for whatever crazy reason."

"Even though he's rude!" Max said.

"How am I rude?"

She looked at her sister, "I told you how we met. He threatened to put little Max up on a pole."

"Oh yeah! Give me high five my brotha! That little boy needs a man to put him in his place." We high fived.

"Where is he?"

"He went to bed." Then she looked at me, "you actually like her?"

"She's alright so far."

"Ha! See I told you pretty don't get you everything." Macy said.

Max started down the hallway to check on her son, "he's here isn't he?"

****

"Sometimes I just wanna know what you did to that woman?" Jackson said laughing a painful laugh.

I shrugged, "you gotta ask Latia she came to me wired to go."

"She got fifty-million questions whenever the kids come home. Sometimes I don't know why I even bother." He sounded fed up.

"You can't give up on her now. I need you to keep her in check." I laughed.

"Seriously, I'm man enough to ask you. You're hung aren't you?"

I almost lost my air I was laughing so hard. "What guy asks another guy something like that?"

"The guy who's married to your ex. Are you the reason I fell in?"

I laughed some more, "stop talking about your wife like that."

"I'm exaggerating of course, but sometimes I wonder if I apply just enough pressure to her head will that pop you out of her brain." Jackson was frustrated.

"I'm sorry man. I tried to get her back, but she chose you. Thank you for taking that bullet by the way."

"Do you ever wonder how different all this would be if that morning after she chose you? None of the lying would've happened."

"But then the crazy would've come out another way. Besides then I would've never known about Syd and little Jackson wouldn't be here." Jackson looked so frustrated and defeated. From time to time we have these conversations about Melissa's craziness. He mostly talks and I listen. The whole time I'm thanking him for being the one, when I used to feel like I was cheated out of something. "Let's change the subject. This is important, I need you to pack full suitcases with at least the things you'd need for five days for all three of you." I gave him a key, and an envelope. "When I call you and say 'it looks like it's going to rain,' I don't care where you are. Even if you're at service, fill up the tank in your car. Then follow the driving instructions in the envelope. Don't tell Melissa about this cause she will ask too many questions and be too difficult to manage. You go there, and you stay there until I call you. Yezzy will be with me directly, but I need to make sure you guys are covered as well."

"This sounds serious, what am I supposed to do about work?"

"I will have it taken care of. As far as they will know you're having another crisis."

"My medication will be out there?"

"Yes, and a physician will be on standby, still pack what you think you will need. Pack right away, tonight if you can. Things are getting heavy around here, the family is about to fade to Black for a minute."

****

When I stepped off the plane I saw Carly and she said Malcolm wanted to talk to me. I know he wants to tell me not to come to him, I told her thank you and I continued walking at the pace of a man on a mission. As I quickly walked past everyone I spotted

Malcolm sitting at the bar blending in with the travelers. He wasn't surprised that I spotted him, but I could tell he wanted to be left alone which is why he's here. I walked over to him and sat down. Malcolm exhaled and told the bartender to bring me a drink. I didn't say anything, I just sat there. Malcolm kept exhaling like he wanted to say something but he didn't. We sat quietly for a few hours. Then Malcolm stood up to leave. As we walked, I told him when all of this is over he needs to go to Vegas and clear the air. Malcolm's eyes pierced me but he didn't respond. He didn't know whether he wanted to curse me just to feel better or what. He started walking then he stopped. He put his hand on my shoulder. "You look so much like him, sometimes my mind expects you to know the things that he did." Then he looked around still gripping my shoulder. "Fuzzy wanted her, he can keep her. I don't know that she's completely changed. I don't know what variables remain the same with her. I'm not subjecting Amber to her. You see how Darryl responds to Eugene, he would kill her."

"You're saying this based off of who she used to be. She's managed to stay off your radar for the past twenty plus years, maybe she's different. "

"She could never change so much that I forget. As long as I remember she will always be the same." Then he started walking. I followed him to his car. He looked at me then he exhaled again. He unlocked my door and we rode in silence. He drove to Berkeley and waited at the gate for access. The gate opened and then Jenise stood in the doorway smiling. I gave her a hug, and then she said Blu was in his office. Malcolm walked hard and labored. He knocked on the door as we entered. Blu looked at us, but he didn't say anything. "He went to Vegas today."

Blu looked at me then back at Malcolm, "is that right."

"You said nothing all these years." Malcolm's voice was controlled.

"I told you that day, you chose not to hear me."

Malcolm frowned as he looked at Blu like he was crazy, "what?"

"I told you that Fuzzy came early and that he was gone."

"Is this supposed to be pay back for Cat?"

Blu stood up, "think about that. What did she do?"

"I was doing research for the blackout when I found her. She's been laying low these past twenty plus years, not so much as a spit on the sidewalk."

"This was not payback for Cat, Fuzzy was at the end of his rope. He pleaded for her life, I told you she threw up. He came before I finished her, he needed her. This is between you two."

"All these years, and neither one of you said anything! This sounds like mutiny!" Malcolm roared.

My phone rang; it was a facetime from Fuzzy. "Fuzzy."

"You're with Malcolm?"

"And Blu."

"I'll call back on Blu's phone." Then he hung up.

He called back and Blu answered over his computer. "Malcolm, talk to me." Fuzzy pleaded.

"All these years and you said nothing! You've come back and forth and still you said nothing."

Fuzzy looked upset, "you two are all I have left. She's come a long way man."

"You let her manipulate you into thinking that she has. She can't change!"

"You changed, why can't she?"

Malcolm glared at Fuzzy, "you know she hasn't changed all that much. She's a pathological liar. She lies so much that she doesn't even know what the truth is."

"Malcolm she's sick, she's harmless."

"She's harmless to everyone but me!" Malcolm shook his head.

"Malcolm, please! It's just you and me man. You think I would've had her around my family if she didn't change? My children know and love her man."

"Wrong! It's not me and you! It's ME! Then there's you! You chose her over me! How you think Renee's going to feel about this? Or the others? You chose her over everybody!" Then Malcolm took a deep breath, "my wife. My children!"

"What do you mean?"

"The Pam I know hates me. The Pam I know doesn't want me to have anything. The Pam I know will cause problems for me just because she can. She may have behaved herself cause she knew I was done with her. I couldn't have Yussef put her down, but now my finger is itching. If she so much as sneezes in my direction, I'll do it myself!"

****

"Are you going to come up?" She asked watching me.

"No," I said shaking my head.

"Did I say or do something?" She asked.

"No, but this is all happening at the worse time. I'm really busy with work, and I need to focus." We keep doing this same thing, we hang out. It's cool; she invites me up, ok. Then… it's like she wants to know that I would get physical with her, but she doesn't want to. That's fine, it's not like I don't have other options. I'm not even all that concerned with having sex with her, but turning me on to turn me off is not cool. I don't want to play this cat and mouse game, besides I have things to do for my peace of mind for work. Like planning exit routes for everyone.

"I feel like you're mad at me." She said lowering her eyes because she was showing weakness.

"I'm not mad at you, but I don't see you and I ever being married. We can be friends, I'm fine with that."

"Friends who kiss?"

"I guess so. We don't have to do that anymore either."

"Do you have time? Can we talk?"

"Not sitting in this car. You wanna come back to my place if it's going to take a long time?"

She thought about it for a minute then she looked at me and agreed to come to my place. I've only invited her once and she looked like the thought was going to kill her.

She walked in slowly and she looked around like she was taking mental pictures of everything. I offered her a drink but she refused as she sat on the couch. I poured some apple juice in a small glass and she got nervous, asking me not to drink right now, I smiled and told her it was apple juice. She sat in the middle of the couch nervous as all get out. I sat there looking at her waiting for her to speak. She said her last sexual experience was traumatic. She said she was never a big fan of sex in the first place, and then her last experience was completely wrong. She said she didn't want to rehash it too much but he really hurt her, to the point where she's more terrified than anything else to go there with anyone else. She said I was the first person that she considered ever going any further with. I told her I was sorry to hear that. With all that said I told her she should wait for her husband before she gets involved with anyone that deeply again. I told her she needed to be in a warm and trusting environment. She asked me why I didn't think that I would be her future husband. I said for one she was too skinny, and she said that's what biscuits are for. Then for two we'd end up arguing all the time about her son. Then for three she was sounding like a virgin, even though we know she's not. I'm not a fan of virgins. Then she said we could have this time together and whenever our time was over it was over, but at least she could have the memory of a shared experience and not the one the she has now. I did a "yeah right" laugh. If I touch her breast she freaks out, like sex would ever happen. Then she took off her coat, "so you're staying?"

"Yes," she said shyly.

"Ready to go to bed?" I stood up.

"Can I have a drink? BUT! I need you to stay sober."
I put my hands up, "fine. Whatever!" I poured some Hennessy and apple juice in a glass and gave it to her. She downed the drink then she followed me to the bedroom. I took off my shirt and I heard her gasp, I did like that reaction. She said my body was beautiful, I thanked her. I stripped to naked then I laid on the bed expecting her to back out at any minute. She stood there staring at me for a minute like she wanted to back out, and then she exhaled and took her clothes off in one big gesture. I was surprised we were this far. She asked me if I had condoms and I told her they were in my nightstand. I waited for her to decide if she was going to back down. When she got on the bed I was surprised again. She kissed me and straddled me. I told her to let me know when she was ready. I still didn't think she was going to go through with it. As we kissed I reached for a condom just in case, I cursed my body for getting excited just because it looked like this was going to happen. She looked at the condom and then she looked at me. "YUSSEF! WHY DIDN'T YOU TELL ME?"
"Tell you what?"
"That is not average." She said pointing to my dick, "you can't just unleash something like that on someone and expect them not to respond."
"It's not?" I laughed.
"NO!" She said trying to back up
"Oh come on! You can't punish me for being blessed. I promise I thought this is average. No one has said otherwise." When she still looked unsure. "You get to ride. You decide how much you want." Then I put the condom on. "Or we could stop, this is not how I normally get down anyways. No foreplay," I shook my head.
"This is fine for now." Then she got back on me.
Like she said her space was no man's land. I watched her face and she looked embarrassed. Then she finished quickly. I was still at attention, I didn't know if it was ok to touch her yet. She realized I hadn't finished yet, she changed my condom and took me in her mouth. Now this she was good at.
I watched her lay there unsure of how she was feeling. When I put my arm around her that pulled her back into the room. She said thank you and then she snuggled into me. She fell asleep and I laid there feeling.... Empty.
****
"So..." Darlene said standing up from her car as soon as I got out of mine.
"So?"
"She finally spent the night." She said watching my eyes.
"Come here," she walked over. "I need to know if she was exaggerating. She was terrified saying I'm huge."
Darlene started smiling, "oh come on. You know you're blessed."
"Blessed doesn't equal hung to me. Why didn't you say anything?"
"I thought you knew. How could you not know?"
I shook my head, "I guess."
"Does this mean you guys are in love and going to get married?" She asked as we walked inside the mall.
"Not on my end. She's working through something."
"Well you don't look satisfied."
"I'm not."
"We on for tonight?"
"Definitely."
Once the thought was planted I couldn't escape it. Just because my father gave me magnums didn't mean anything, right? Then I thought about Shannon my first and only virgin, I guess she was too much of a newbie. How would she have known what hung looked like. All this power I've been using for good when I should've been using it for

evil since I was gonna end up here anyways. I swiveled in my chair as I tried to think of something else. Something other than a SD on my chest for *Super Dick*! I was cracking myself up. When Malcolm tapped on my door, "Uncle Blackie what's up?"

Malcolm cut his eyes at me, "you're gonna stop calling me that. Do you plan on joining the call?"

"I'm on it!" I dialed in, and then Malcolm announced that Johnna Moreno would be in charge while he was away.

After the call, I called my grandma to see what her plans were for today. She said she and Arthur were having lunch today with my momma. And before I could back down she told me to come. Buzz kill for real, I regretted calling.

I called my grandma to tell them I was outside. My momma had the biggest smile on her face when she came out like she was actually happy to see me. That made me feel weird. She sat in the front seat and leaned over and kissed me. "Good afternoon baby." She said warm and tenderly.

I blinked my eyes to make sure I was looking at the right person. "Who are you and what did you do with my mother?"

Everyone laughed, but no one laughed harder than her. "I can't be happy to see my baby?"

"Your baby?" I told myself to wait for it, she must want money.

"Yes my baby. My first-born. Momma loves her baby."

I looked at Arthur and he put his hands up like he wasn't in it.

Lunch was nice even though I sat quietly enduring all her loving references to me. Her behavior was confusing and I don't know why it made me mad. When I took them back to the house I asked her to stay in the car while my grandparents went inside. "Ok Shonda, what's going on?"

"Shonda? Since when do you address me by my first name?"

"What game are you playing? Stop messing with my head."

She rubbed her stomach; "I want to do a better job this time. Can we have dinner or something and you can tell me how horrible of a mother I am, so I can know what to work on for this one?" I was quiet, "I've never been to your place. Maybe I could come over and cook for us?"

"I don't trust you."

"I guess that's fair. You got plans this Saturday?"

"What about Jarvis?"

"He doesn't seem to care too much now that I'm fat."

"You're not fat, just pregnant."

"He doesn't know the difference. He keeps calling me his fat girl."

I smiled, "you two act too much alike."

When I got back to the office Malcolm was in El's office. Malcolm opened the door and told me to come in. Richard and Juan were on the phone. El looked beyond irritated and drained. "Princess Sassy..." El said

Richard interrupted him, "watch yourself!"

"You watch yourself! I'm talking to Yussef about my wife!" He glared at the phone. Malcolm almost smiled, and then El continued. "The Princess in all her emotional state is stressing about my parents moving out here. She's arranged for them to be seen by specialist out here for second opinions. We've got two more people to add to your detail. I'm sorry man."

"Malcolm?" I looked to him to say something they were on their last legs as it was.

"She's already talked to Amber. It's family." He said slightly frustrated himself.

I exhaled, "El you don't want your family out here?"

"It's not that I don't want them out here, it's just too much. We can talk about it later. Meanwhile we gotta make all this rubbish happen!"

Sasha

"I'm sorry about that whole scene." I said as sincerely as I could.

"All of that stuff with us was in the past. Why does he think it's an issue today?" Yussef asked.

"Because he thinks I don't know doesn't he?" El asked.

"Because he and my momma until a year ago were stuck on stupid over each other. I guess he thinks there's still something there."

El leaned back in his chair to match Yussef's demeanor. "I see."

I looked at him, "you see what?"

Yussef chuckled then he pushed his keyboard tray down and under his desk. He got up and closed his office door, then he sat down and locked his eyes on El. "El this is your wife, after that there's nothing that needs to be said."

"Sasha?" El said.

"Sasha what?"

"Are you with me?" His eyes were locked on me.

I chewed back anger, "seriously? You gonna let Richard get up in your head? He's miserable so he's messing with us. After everything we've been through if you're dumb enough to ask me anything..."

He cut me off, "I've had about enough of your tantrums! Talk to me like you've got some sense or we will tear this entire office apart!"

Yussef tried to fight his grin but he couldn't hide it. "I apologize, but..."

"Don't but.... Just answer the simple question, are you with me?" He said with controlled calmness.

"Yes!" I said through clinched teeth.

"Then stop giving that man emotional reactions whenever he comes at you like that. It makes you look guilty." I deflated, "we're all adults here. He's upset about his lack of control. And if you keep letting him push your buttons you'll end up messing up just because you got caught up. You don't have to prove anything to him." He exhaled, "watch them babies gonna come out angry and looking just like Richard if you keep acting like this."

I gasped, "I'll be calm! Please no!"

We laughed, "ok so back to business." Yussef brought his keyboard back up. "The timing of this whole thing couldn't be worse, but we have a plan." He gave El a folder containing details.

I looked over his shoulder. I smiled, "you guys upgraded the verification system?"

"Yep, green means good. Any other color is no good. Simple enough right?" Yussef said clicking on his computer.

"Yes, because the scanning was good but what if they weren't cool? They already got you."

"Sasha, no guns!"

"Ah! Come on!" I whined.

"Why would you bring a gun?" El asked.

"In the words of my Uncle Tim 'you never know where the day might lead you!' I gotta be prepared."

"So you carry a gun when you travel?" El watched my eyes.

Yussef smiled at me, "um!"

"Um?" El frowned.

"She's strapped right now." Yussef snitched.

"Yussef!"

"Sasha? Why would you feel like you need to walk around like that?"

"Should I go?" Yussef said still grinning.

"No! You bust me out you stay." I put my hand on El's. "Baby, you married a thug. I don't know how else to say it." I smiled.

El started laughing, "yeah right!"

"What do you think this is all about?"

"Phineas," he said matter of factly.

"Right, a white collar thug flexing his white collar muscles, but we're from The Bay! Educated gangsters who keep beating him at his own game. That's why he's so mad." I rubbed his hand, "you married a thug."

He started laughing and then Yussef and I pulled out our guns. He stopped laughing. Then Yussef showed him a couple of the ones stashed in his office. He frowned, "duped by you again woman!" Then he laughed.

I laughed at his laugh, "you're going to be searched extra hard either going or coming back. Stay clean! You got bread boxes out there, you'll be fine." Yussef said.

Yussef

I waited outside the elevator for her. Her eyes were wide; she asked me how I got my father's apartment? Then she answered her own question and said it must've been rent controlled and he willed it to me. I didn't say anything. When she walked in she said she liked the upgrades the owner made to the apartment. She stared at a spot on the hallway floor. Then she smiled at me and said that was where I was conceived. I made a grossed out face and she laughed. Then she said no wonder I could afford to live so nicely on a temp's salary. She looked disappointed when she looked in the girl's room. I explained that we were waiting until we moved into a bigger house to decorate their room. I told her it was done up before but we gave all the furniture and decorations to Sydney for her room. Then she looked in my room. She told me where my father had his bed and how the room was setup back then. When she looked in the bathroom she said it was completely different. She said she liked my place. Then she pulled out her list of the groceries she needed. She looked in my cabinets to see if there was anything she could check off. I asked her if she wanted to pick up a cake for dessert. She smiled at the thought, so we went to the grocery store next to the Rockridge shopping center. I saw Max's friend Cherry following us around the store. For her sake I pretended like I didn't see her. We loaded the groceries and then we walked over to Tracy's Tasty Treats. Tracy happened to be there with Andrew and Andre. I introduced everyone who hadn't met her. All of their eyes dropped to her stomach. Tracy came and hugged her, and told her it was nice to see her again. Then everyone did the same. We got a chocolate raspberry cake and then we went back to my place. My momma was in full cook mode when my intercom buzzed. "Yes?" Even though my gut told me it was Max.

"Yussef, I need to talk to you." Max said.

"Now is not a good time."

"Please Yussef!"

"You should've called I'm busy."

"I know you're busy alright! Open the.... Thank you." Someone most likely left while she was buzzing and let her in.

My momma asked who was coming and I shook my head. Max turned the knob then she knocked on the door. When I didn't answer immediately she started banging. I snatched the door open, "I DID NOT INVITE YOU HERE! WHY ARE YOU HERE?"

"Is that your baby? Why wouldn't you tell me?" She had tears in her eyes.

"Max I told you! I told you, you couldn't handle this." I looked at my momma who was standing in the kitchen. I opened the door and Max stepped inside. She held her breath as she looked at my momma. "Max this is Shonda, Shonda this is Max."

"Ok, but who is she?" My momma said.

"I'm his woman who are you!" Max said with a ton of attitude.

"You heard what he said." She stood up straight and looked Max up and down. "I'm Shonda! I see you've spent so much time talking about me."

Max looked at me, "is that your baby?"

"Why does it matter? You were only concerned with you remember."

"Yeah but a heads up would've been nice. I didn't know I would feel like this."

"Like what? Like exactly like I said you would. You should've listened to me and kept your legs closed." Then I exhaled.

I started to say something and my momma put her hand up. She rubbed her stomach, "so what if this is his baby? What was barging into his apartment supposed to change?"

"Nothing, but he couldn't hide the truth if you're right there."

"Oh I see, you're still of the school that all men are liars." Her neck started wiggling and that finger came out. "My son is not a liar! You need to get it together! Even if the truth hurts, only be in relationships where the truth can be expected!"

"Did you say son?" She said pulling back her tears.

"Yes, but I hope that's not all you heard."

Max dramatically threw herself in the chair next to the table. Sweat started popping up as she released her hurt feelings. "I heard you." She said sounding relieved.

I lifted her by her arm, "you got your answer. We're still not in that kind of a relationship. You weren't invited so I'm gonna need you to leave." I said guiding her to the door.

"Yussef!" Max said as she walked.

"Yussef!" My momma said when I didn't respond to Max.

"Bye, bye!" I said as I closed the door in her face.

My momma laughed, "you act just like him!" She returned to her meal. "Yussef baby, I have to ask you, what happened with the girl who took the pictures?"

I exhaled, "when we met she told me she doesn't date men with children. I didn't know I had kids. She couldn't handle having you and Linda as baby momma's, or me having baby momma's period."

"You couldn't find a way to make things work out?"

"I tried, I tried to the best of my abilities, but it couldn't work. I'm tired of women and their emotional games!" My sudden outburst startled me too. "I was in love with Sylvia! The night we met felt right, the way I thought she loved me felt right. I loved her so much I didn't allow myself to see the truth. She was begging for Sydney, and all I wanted to do was finish school. Once I finished school I was going to marry her and we would have our own basketball team right now if she wanted. She was my future! I'll admit that I was stupid about Melissa but there was something that wasn't right about her. She was a different kind of crazy, unlike you in ways I've never encountered. Now I'm glad something was always in the way. I wasted a lot of time waiting for her, thinking her husband's next trip to the hospital would free her and then we'd be together." I laughed a little, "I'm so happy he's alive and well."

"That's your problem you're always holding back baby, when do you ever live in the moment and just experience life?"

I thought about Sasha, if I could rewind time… "Timing wasn't on our side."

My momma's eyes got big, she stopped stirring the food, and then she stared at me like she just saw a ghost. "What did you just say?"

"Timing wasn't on our side." I watched my momma freak out for a minute.

She stared at me with tears pouring out of her eyes. Then she started crying really hard. She cried and she rocked herself until she calmed down. "Troy…" then she took a deep breath to calm herself. "The last time I saw him. Before he informed me that he was taking you to live with him, he told me he was going to marry that woman. I felt so hurt, so betrayed. I never married anyone because I naively thought someday he was coming back to me. When I asked him how he could marry her and not me he said that to me. It broke my heart," then she looked at me. "You have no idea how much of a trip it is to be standing right here with you looking, sounding, and gesturing just like him. Then to hear the very words he said to me come out of your mouth." She wiped her tears; "time is never on anyone's side. The time is always now! Stop waiting for the right time, cause it's never the right time son. I'm not telling you to go back to anyone, just be present today. Sometimes love makes you do things that hurts other people. Sometimes it's ok to be selfish."

"Is this what you told yourself when you moved us from place to place? I never existed anywhere, I was always invisible."

"I get it, I'm the queen of selfish. I know you don't agree with all of my choices, but I never went without an opportunity to have what I need because I was being selfless for people who were being selfish. I know you don't like Jarvis and thank goodness you're grown and I don't have to be concerned with it. But, I wanted Jarvis so I have him. I don't always like him, but I love my husband. I'm not sitting over here angry because I let someone get away from me. If you don't fight for Yussef, who's going to? Stop waiting for people to return your goodness. That's not the world we live in. My momma and the rest aren't always going to like or agree with your choices. My point is, it's your life, make declarative choices for you."

When dinner was ready, I prayed over our meal, something I don't do as often as I should. Dinner was delicious, and we sat at that table speaking as real as we could with each other. She admitted that she still thinks about my father every day. She apologized over and over for everything. She told me things about him that I hadn't heard before. I told her about how she was a horrible mother, and I hoped she'd do a better job with this son.

Tracy

I know we said we'd wait until we saw the baby to decide whether he would be named Andrew or Malcolm, but my heart is already set on naming him Malcolm. My heart says this is his name. Andrew blank stares at me when I refer to the baby like he already knows what my heart wants. I don't want him to set his heart against it so I don't push the issue. My baby has been trying really hard when it comes to his father and I'm so proud of him. Malcolm is trying as well. If Andrew doesn't go to service with Andre and I, lately we may come home to Malcolm and Andrew talking or Andrew may be at his mother's house with his parents.

Guaranteed good times are when Joy and family come with us over Derrick and Chantel's. The kids call their selves explorers as they go out back and play whatever crazy games they play. Yussef comes whether he has his girls with him or not. I knew he was silly, but when all of the men together we are definitely in stitches. Whether they're playing dominos, cards, whatever.

This time Sherrell wanted to play a getting to know each other game. "Okay Tracy it's your turn." Sherrell said as we all calmed down from the hollering, crying, and gut busting laughter as Darryl relayed the last whoopin he got from his mom. Hearing the way they describe Amber isn't any way I know her to be. She's always mild even when she's irritated so I always listen with intrigue. Especially when they talk about her beating up Toya. I try not to cheese when they share those stories. Sherrell shook the box then she handed the box to Darryl who picked the question and he handed it to Andrew to read. "Tracy, name one thing you wanted as a teenager, but for whatever reason you didn't get it." Everybody looked at me.

Joy smiled cause I'm sure she could think of a laundry list of things I complained about when we were younger. "My dad said when I got my license I would have a car. And true to his word I had a car before I had my license. But, he didn't ask me what kind of car I wanted. I was happy just to have a car period so it didn't matter, but I wanted a blue Chevy Camaro with the beat in it."

Darryl laughed, "I knew you were a thug."

I wiggled my neck, "I'm from Richmond."

"The car you have now has a nice system in it." Joy said.

I looked at Andrew, "yes. My baby always gives me the best."

Sherrell shook up her box of questions, "Malcolm you're next." Everyone oohed.

Malcolm's expression was unamused, "I'm not playing." Then he returned his attention to Chanel.

"Aw! Come on Malcolm, this is just like cards. Cards with feelings." Yussef said.

"Yeah Malcolm." Everyone else chimed in.

"Fine!" He didn't look happy about it. He sat Chanel up in his lap with her back to him. She frowned at everybody just like Malcolm.

Sherrell handed the box to Chantel to pull a question. Chantel pulled and handed it to Amber. Amber opened the question and smiled. "Good question." She prepared to read the question out loud. Everyone leaned in, "if you could be any celebrity, who would you be?"

"Me!" He shot back quickly.

"You're a celebrity?" Amber said scoffing at his answer.

"All ya'll need to recognize who I am! What makes a celebrity a celebrity?"

"Hold on! I think we need the white board for this. Who's willing to be our Vanna Black?" Darryl asked

Chantel volunteered and went to the board. She wrote, "Celebrity Details" at the top.

"Number One, people look up to you. Do people look up to me?" Everyone shook their heads yes, "thank you. Chantel put a check next to that. Moving on, Number Two. Money! I got that." Everyone agreed, "thank you. Put a check next to that one. Number Three, people want to be me."

"That's only D-Rick!" Darryl blurted out.

Everyone started laughing, "shut up! No I don't!" Derrick was not laughing.

"If you can think of at least one person who wishes they were me point proven, put my check and let's move on." It seemed like everyone knew at least one person so no one disputed it. "Number Four, I have the woman that everyone wishes they had. So that makes me the ultimate man!" Amber blushed, while all of us girls said aw! "Number Five, everybody knows who I am, and I don't have to explain who I am. Check mark and I'm done."

"But you're not on TV." Anthony said.

"The question was about a celebrity there was no television requirement stated, so I stand by my answer. Next person." Then Chanel started laughing. That actually made him smile.

We moved on with our game. All of the men including Anthony, little Jackson, and AJ went to pick up the pizza. Malcolm was the only man to stay behind. Veronica, Rosa, and Yussef's girls sat around Malcolm asking him questions and getting so tickled by his monotone answers. I asked Amber why I was the only one to be scared of him when I met him. Chantel chimed in that if it wasn't for Ms. Laverne it would've taken her forever to understand Malcolm. Both of them explained that Malcolm could be very charming when he wanted to be, you just had to pay attention otherwise you'd miss it. Joy asked Amber what made her fall in love with Malcolm. Sherrell and I leaned in cause I don't know about her but I definitely wanted to know. We went in the kitchen and Chantel opened a bottle of wine and a bottle of sparkling cider. She poured wine for Joy and Amber, and cider for the rest of us. We all leaned in on the counter hanging on to Amber's words. She said she loved spending time with him, she said she knew that the things he did with her he didn't do them with others. Like his favorite place to go was the Berkeley campus libraries. She said they would spend hours there talking about books, and whatever she could get him talking about. She said he always made sure she knew that she was special. She said she would question it sometimes. Then she said as strong as he is, she loves that he's always weak for her.

Then we asked Chantel the same question. She said if it wasn't for Darryl she wouldn't have known other than the things Derrick said. She said like Amber she loves to listen to him talk about anything. She said they have a lot of fun together.

Then we asked Joy about her and her man. She said point blank that he doesn't play around when it comes to her. She said she wants for nothing. He's always strong for her so she doesn't have to be overly powerful even though sometimes she has to regulate. We laughed.

Then we told Sherrell it was her turn. She said she loved the way he took care of his sister. Then she smiled at Chantel. She said they had lots of drama in the beginning of their relationship, but she knew he needed time to get it together, so she worked with him. She said in all honesty she was in love with him after the first day they met. She said no matter how many times she cried, and how hard it was she said her heart would tell her to hang on just a little bit longer. Sherrell gushed about how much she loves her man and how good things are.

Then they said it was my turn. I said Andrew's excitement about me was always above anything that I knew. I told them how I've never been with a man who has my back like he does. He's always rallying for my best interest, and I matter to him. He's never made me feel insignificant or like I should worship the ground he walks on just because he's a guy.

Then we all got quiet as we sat there smiling and thinking about our men. When Chantel opened another cider Sherrell told her she could have a small glass of wine and then she could pump and dump. Chantel smiled an embarrassed smile, as she shook her head no. Amber and Sherrell looked at her funny when she did it.

When the men came with boxes and boxes of pizza, Yussef's girls hurried in the kitchen and said they wanted to bring Malcolm some pizza and a drink. Yussef put his hands up and asked him what about him? They told him that they would bring him pizza next and to sit at the table. Yesmina took charge, she put Sydney in charge of serving the pizza, Veronica in charge of the forks, and Rosa in charge of the napkins, while Yesmina served the drinks. Chantel's grandmother came in while we were eating and having a good time. Chantel's father followed her in looking for the baby. Malcolm still had her while they sat in the living room on the lounge part of the couch. Mr. Shaw looked a little jealous when Chanel kept looking for Malcolm while he held her. Then she frowned at him like she was tolerating him. Mr. Shaw held her for a few minutes then he gave her back to Malcolm. Then he picked up Rosa who was way more tolerant of him. He stayed for a few minutes then he left. Chantel's grandmother went in the living room with Malcolm and Chanel. I was stuck watching them have a whole conversation in Spanish; Malcolm spoke fluently as far as I could tell. I had no idea he knew Spanish and could speak it so well. I don't know why things with Malcolm surprise me anymore. Sydney heard them and came in with a smile. She said something to Malcolm, and when he responded Sydney laughed and Chantel's grandmother smiled. Yesmina stayed seated next to her father but she watched them talking and carrying on. The expression on her face was like her dad's when he was thinking hard about something.

"We're going to need a bigger car." I said to Andrew as we got in the car to go home.

"A bigger car or a Camaro?" He smiled showing me his dimples.

I laughed, "that was when I was a teenager and had no responsibilities. A two door car wouldn't even be practical for me right now."

"I hear you, but Malcolm has this Lamborghini." He blew air, "I've always thought that car was the cleanest car. I was going to buy one after I bought a house, but you're right it wouldn't be practical." Then he drove us by our house. The house was coming together nicely; the plan is to have the house done before the baby comes. I don't know if that's gonna happen cause its completion date is so close to my due date.

"Whoa!" Is all I could say when we drove around to Amber and Malcolm's house.

"Malcolm didn't hold back on anything huh." Andrew said smiling at the house.

"He really loves your mom." I said taking in the house.

"Why do you say that?"

"We were talking about why we love our men tonight, when I didn't even really know your dad I could see that he was crazy about your mom. Now that they're together love for her is all over him." I reached up and rubbed Andrew's head, "and I can see how proud he is of you too."

He glanced at me with half a smile, "you think he's proud of me?"

"Of course! I see him watching you with Andre, especially when I'm having a fit about your drills. He looks like he approves of it all, when I want him to side with me and make you guys stop." Andre laughed, "I don't like seeing my baby hurt."

"I'm not hurt mommy, I'm learning."

"Learning doesn't have to be so violent."

"Sometimes life is violent. Sometimes you have to do what comes next. Andre is a Prince he must be trained like all the other soldiers but better."

"Poppa is the King?"

"He's one of them, Uncle Jeff, and Uncle Frank are Kings too."

****

"Hello Tracy, how are you today?" Jennifer the receptionist said smiling at my belly.

"I'm ok, how are you?" I said as I walked to her desk.

"I'm good." Then she leaned in, "can you convince him to let us go home early?"

I smiled, "I'll see what I can do." I handed her the pastry box and people were standing at their cubicles watching her with the box.

I was almost to Andrew's door when Lisa came waltzing by. "Oh my goodness! Look at you!" She said with fake happiness for me laced with venom, "you are getting so big!" She fake laughed.

I didn't smile, "I thought I told him to fire you! Keep talking!"

"Oh honey, don't let those pregnancy hormones make you overreact." She reached out to touch my shoulder.

"Don't touch me! I don't like you! Never have and I never will! Until you're fired, do me a favor and don't speak to me. I have enough to deal with, without your dose of fakeness." Then I rolled my eyes and opened Andrew's door.

Andrew's eyes were focused and he was on a conference call. He waived me in and told me to hurry up. I kissed him then I sat in the chair in front of him. "Is she there yet?" Darryl's voice said, I thought this was a Cooper Financial Business call.

"Yep, she's here." Andrew said staring at me.

"Tracy what a little brotha gotta do to have Pastries delivered to my desk?"

"You keep eating all them pies and cakes, and you gonna end up like Uncle Frank." Yussef said.

"You're right, I should continue to walk from my car to the storefront. Never mind, cancel my delivery." Darryl said.

"Focus," Andrew said redirecting the meeting. It seemed like everybody was on that call. I couldn't put my finger on whether his Uncle Malachi or Uncle Timothy was speaking or it could've been both of them for all I know. Yussef kept stressing urgency to take action, and Derrick was agreeing with him. I stared at the phone in disbelief as I listened to Darryl's about business tone. No jokes, no silliness, no *N* bombs. I was impressed and wondering if it was really him until they conferenced in Tanisha. "This is Seaver."

333

"If it isn't Miss I'm-Too-Sexy!" Darryl said.

"Hello Darryl, who else is here?" Her tone didn't change.

"Everybody, and we were wondering when you were going to wear another dress for us."

She ignored him, "hello everyone. What's up?"

"We're checking to see how everything is on your end. Any news?" Derrick asked.

"Nothing new here." Tanisha said, "I'll reach out to you if anything changes."

"Alright, and Tanisha…"

"Yes Derrick."

"When you gonna wear another dress for us? I demand an Encore!" Derrick said with a smile in his voice.

"BYE YOU GUYS!" Tanisha said chuckling as she hung up.

Andrew smiled but he didn't say anything. They spoke some more and then they got off the phone. "To what do I owe the honor of your presence?" Andrew said looking at something on his computer.

"Amber got back early so she said she wanted to pick up Andre from school. I was hoping we could have an early dinner." I watched him multitask.

"I got a lot of work to do here before my sabbatical. Every moment counts." He said not looking at me.

"Ok, my heart wasn't set on it or anything." I sighed, "it's not like I drove all the way over here to Hercules from the Oakland hills to have dinner with you. I'll just hit a drive thru on my way home, and peacefully enjoy my me time alone."

He finally looked at me, "such a drama queen. Where are you dragging me to?"

"The Dead Fish!" I smiled.

He frowned, "really?"

"I want their lasagna." I smiled; Andrew shrugged and returned his attention to his computer. "Can you email Jennifer and tell her to whisper to everyone except Lisa to leave early?"

He chuckled, "I can do that."

"I thought I told you to fire her! Fair is fair Andrew!"

He laughed again, "he lives. He breathes, she can keep her job."

"That's by default Andrew, my feelings don't matter to you!" I heard myself say. Ok these pregnancy hormones are no joke. I don't like her, but I was grabbing onto this situation a lot harder than I needed to.

Andrew looked at me for a minute like he was thinking about how to respond. He typed something into the computer, "let's go." When he came around the desk, he put his arms around me. "Tracy, I work here keep your hands to yourself."

I chuckled cause the thought to smack her did cross my mind. When we walked out the door, people were smiling and shutting down their stations. Some were already heading out the door. Jennifer put the completely empty pastry box in the trash, then she mouthed thank you as she grabbed her purse. Andrew drove my car in silence, when we got to the restaurant they gave us an outdoor table that was overlooking the water and the Vallejo/Crockett bridge. Andrew took a deep breath, and then he looked at me. "I don't want to keep rehashing all of that. First of all this is California and although she is an at will employee if I act on your hormones the company could be liable to be sued. So obviously I'm not going to go that route. Despite her ridiculous crush on me that I don't encourage she's good at what she does. You will not walk up in my office telling me who gets fired and who stays. If you want to cause problems with me and my family bring this topic up again."

I looked away at the water. I was wrong for bringing it up, so I said nothing until the waiter came. We placed our order and then I think we smelled it at the same time. The smell of cigarettes invaded my pregnant nose. We looked at the door when a guy with a very serious face came out coming directly for our table. He said it was time to go.

Andrew dropped two hundred dollar bills on the table and he told our waiter to cancel our order. He grabbed my hand and told me I was ok. The guy walked behind me and Andrew walked ahead while still holding my hand. He and the guy walked me to the passenger side. Then the guy ran to the car waiting in the lot. My heart was pounding as I watched Andrew drive at a normal speed away. His phone rang and the car said caller ID unavailable. He told the phone to answer. The guy started talking, he told Andrew to pull into the parking lot of the Rodeo grocery store. He said the police should be calling in a minute to inform him about his car. Then the car said "Hercules Police Department." The officer informed Andrew that his car was targeted in a random act of violence. They asked that he came quickly and told no one as they didn't want this incident to get out to the media and blown out of proportion. When we pulled into the parking lot there was an ambulance, Andrew's car surrounded by yellow tape, and two other cars. Andrew's car looked like someone took a hammer to it, all over the car. I was trying to see who the paramedics had. Then Andrew said it was Lisa. I asked him how he knew; he said her car was still here. Andrew told me to stay in the car and lock the doors when he got out. I did as I was told; Andrew was met by an officer as he walked towards the ambulance. The car called out Darryl as Andrew looked down at his phone. He told me to answer it. "Hi Darryl, Andrew's talking to the cops right now you want him to call you back?"
There were no jokes in his tone. "Who's hurt?"
"I think one of the employees here, although I don't think it's too bad. She's standing up now."
"How are you doing? Are you ok?"
"I'm ok, once my nerves calm down I'm sure I'll be hungry again."
"You'll be there for a minute, I'm already in root. Tell Drew I'll see him in a few."
I texted Andrew and told him what Darryl said. He shook his head while looking at his phone. A little while later a car I didn't recognize pulled up. Darryl got out with a bag. When I rolled down my window he handed me the bag and told me to eat, then he walked away as I called out thank you. I started salivating when I saw the Dead Fish logo on the bag. I had forgotten about my hunger until the bag was in my lap. He brought everything just like I ordered it. And my lasagna was just as good as I remembered. After I finished I felt bad that I didn't even try to save Andrew any cause he should be hungry too.
An officer walked up to the car and tapped the window. My heart started pounding I looked at him and said yes? I sent Andrew a blank text. The officer looked around while he was telling me to roll down the window. I told him I could hear him just fine through the glass. Andrew looked down at his phone, and then Darryl asked the officer what he needed. I reached in my glove compartment and I grabbed a clean napkin cause I used the ones Darryl brought with my food. I wrote down his badge number while he was talking to Darryl. Darryl redirected him to the group of men with Andrew who represented the company. The officer looked frustrated but he went over with the group. Darryl told me not to open my door for anyone except Andrew. Then Darryl fell to the background again. The paramedic's left, Andrew gave a statement. Then a tow truck came, Yussef rode up on a motorcycle. I didn't know he rode a bike, and I wondered if it was safe for him to be vulnerable on a motorcycle right now. He walked around snapping pictures of everything. Then he spoke with Darryl towards the back of everything. They walked around looking around the edge of the parking lot, and at a creek that led out to the bay waters. Hours later Andrew came to the car, he asked who brought me food. I said an embarrassed Darryl. He laughed at my reaction then he told me that I needed to eat and it was ok. I gave him the napkin with the officer's badge number on it, as I told him about when the officer came to the window. I asked him what happened, I said it looked like an angry ex came with a hammer. He said those were bullet marks. My eyes got big when I asked him when was he going to tell me his car was bullet proof? He said all of our cars are. I let the statement run all over my head. We pulled up to Amber's house and I asked

him why we needed bulletproof cars. He looked at me and said because he's a Prince. Malcolm was in the office and Andrew went directly in and shut the door. Amber asked me if I was ok. I told her I was fine. I asked her if she had anything to make a sandwich or something cause Andrew hadn't eaten. We left Andre in the living room and then she took everything out in the kitchen for me. I asked her if she knew what happened, she said she didn't. Then she told me they would let me know what I needed to know, and to always do as I was told.

****

This one car stuff is no fun. I couldn't come up with any excuse to avoid this play date with Will and his kids so I had to come. Will smiled big and said he was starting to wonder if it was true that I was pregnant since he hadn't seen me pregnant once. I smiled and then I watched Andrew pick up the little girl who not only had walking down, but running was a must for her. She smiled at Andrew then she looked at me. She had Andrew put her down then she smiled at me as she came for me. She was adorable BUT that evilness from her momma was in her eyes. Her hair was in a bunch of cute ponytails. I told Will he did a good job, and then he said his girlfriend did her hair. He said she was coming to meet us. Andrew told him it took him long enough to get back out there. He said he wasn't exactly ready but he felt like this woman was worth the adjustment. He said she was a little older than him, and although their relationship was still new he felt she could be the one to inspire him to give marriage another try. Andrew said he was happy for him. I asked how she got along with the kids. He said the baby gets a little possessive sometimes but other than that it was fine. I looked at her imagining her being just like her mother. Will said Toya's mother met his girlfriend and she didn't like her so he took that as a good sign. We were talking for a minute then I saw her. You could never say Will didn't have a specific type. She was pretty and she was chocolate like Toya, her hair was short though, she had a tight little body and a big butt. She hugged Will then he proudly turned to us, "Andrew, Tracy, this is my girlfriend Cora."
She smiled; I smiled, "nice to meet you two. I think what you guys are doing with the kids is beautiful."
"That's between them, I tag along some of the time."
She smiled at the baby, and the baby rolled her eyes. I told her the baby has a lot of her mother in her. She said she was going to say the baby acted like her grandmother, just evil. Even though I think the baby has her mom's eyes, she doesn't know this child to say she's evil. I flashed Andrew a look. He smiled and then he took a picture of the baby. Andre and little Will came over to drink some of their sodas. Will introduced Andre to Cora. Andre looked at Cora for a minute then he said hi. The boys took off and the baby started crying cause she wanted to go. Andre came back and grabbed her hand. I started to get up and Andre told me to relax just like his daddy would. I was tickled as I watched Andre in his big brother space. Cora was impressed by our little man. Then she said Andre looked exactly like Andrew with his little cute self. I looked at Andrew again cause was she calling Andrew cute? I KNOW my baby is fine, but I also feel it's disrespectful for her to speak on it. Andrew motioned for me to calm down with his hands. I guess she felt my anger cause she took off her jacket claiming she got hot all of a sudden. "How did you meet?" I asked to distract myself from my growing; *I don't like her,* feeling.
"He was in line ahead of me at the movie theater. I noticed him and his kids, and they seemed like a cute little family. I expected his wife or girlfriend to join him, but then I heard him buy two tickets. I didn't see a wedding ring, but you know how men don't always wear them. I bought my ticket for my chick flick and then I got in line for popcorn. He put his little girl down and she took off running for the candy section. His little boy was in front of me trying to balance his popcorn. It touched my heart seeing him trying to manage them all by himself. I told him I'd help the little boy so he could go get

the baby. He looked at me and I knew I was in trouble."

"Do you have any children?"

"No, my husband and I divorced before we had the chance."

"Do you want children?"

She blew air, "I don't know, I guess I hadn't thought about it."

I looked at Andrew like her answer didn't make any sense. "I don't want to feel like I'm interrogating you. Tell me something about you."

"Will has put a smile on my face for the first time in a long time. If we stay together, I think we'll have our hands full with his two. He's already got one of each, I think we're good."

I looked at Andrew and his eyes were now glued to his screen, like he was reading something fascinating. The server came with the pizza and Will went and got the kids to have them come eat. Andre had the baby in his arms; I was very impressed with his big brother skills. "You are such a good big brother Andre." He blushed and said thank you as he put the baby in her high chair.

"Yes you are," then she looked at me. "Feel free to drop him off if you two ever need a night off."

"Thanks, but Andre stays with family." I said.

My comment offended her, but it shouldn't have. "Isn't the whole point of this set up to keep the children together so that they grow up knowing each other? Hence family, hello!" She said waving her hand.

I swallowed my irritation like dry cereal. "What would you know about this set up, you've been here five minutes. Honestly, I don't know about you. You're comfortable too fast in this situation without knowing all the details. Just because you and Will like each other doesn't make you family. Slow down, you're acting like you're running things already."

"O…K…" She said frowning at me. "Excuse me for trying to be helpful."

Andre's eyes darted between us as he ate his pizza. Andrew smiled at Will, "my wife ladies and gentlemen."

"So yeah, Drew I guess it's back to just me and you for occasions like this." He said with a smile.

****

With the wedding right around the corner I keep making little sample cakes to make sure I have my flavors spot on. I nervously write down any changes I make that I like. Amber said she couldn't taste any more cakes or else she was going to have to keep dancing twenty-four-seven just to fit in her wedding dress. And she forbid Malcolm from bringing it home any more cause she couldn't not eat it. So up next was Sasha, who outside of her very little baby bump looked the same. We were sitting at the table talking about our men. Both of the dogs were laying on the floor by our feet hoping that we dropped crumbs. I liked talking to her about Andrew because I didn't have to hold back with her. She knows her twin cousin inside and out. And when she says he's going to say or react a certain way, sure enough he does. He shakes his head when I tell him Sasha told me he would say exactly what he said. He told her to stop giving me pointers on working him.

"Would it be too much to have two cakes at my shower?" She said putting a fork full of cake in her mouth.

"No, do you know what kinds you want?"

"Nope, but here's my vision." She sat up straight in her chair and smiled. "Two Tiffany blue gift boxes, surrounded by bling!" She looked up at the ceiling with a smile. "I want to arrive in a limo. Ooh! And I want to walk on red carpet with rose petals at my feet."

"Oh my goodness Sasha your wedding was bad enough. Who's paying for this?"

"My parents and grandparents of course. And you know how you guys had pictures of Chantel and Derrick blown up? I want that, but I can't decide which picture I want to use so we'll probably use multiple pictures..." Sasha went on and on about her big and fancy ideas for her shower.

My job, just like everyone else's was to report back everything she tells me to Carina or Tanisha for her surprise shower. Although it was months away and my own baby would be here by then, we had a whole committee formed to hit all of her wants. This girl is truly loved and spoiled. With her spoiled ways and my dramatics I can see why Andrew just walks away from us sometimes. "I really enjoy these moments alone with you. I know you and Chantel are a lot closer, but I'm glad we all get along."

"I've known her longer is all. Thank Andy for that!" She rolled her eyes.

"Don't be mad at him. My drama was pretty big, he was juggling so much." I swallowed nerves; "please tell me if this puts you in a bad situation. You don't have to answer if you feel like you need to tell Andrew I asked cause he withdraws whenever it comes up."

"It's something about David, shoot."

"Did you hear about the other brothers?"

Her eyes got big, "other brothers?" She leaned in.

I leaned in and whispered as if we weren't the only people in the house besides the dogs. "David has two more sons. Dionne dropped the bomb about one at Chantel's wedding. Yussef told Andrew there's two actually. There's no way he could've known about the second one, he was probably conceived the morning before he died, but he had to know about the oldest one. Why was he so good to Andrew, but horrible to his own kids?"

"Who are they? What are they like?"

"We don't know. Andrew wants to reach out of course, but Derrick is on the fence, and Darryl says no."

"I don't know why he was like that. Andrew loved him so much. Now as an adult I can see the game he ran on Andrew but as a child...."

"What game?"

"Some men will come directly at you and others will come at you through your kids. While others won't want your kids or the ones who want you only to get at your kids. He knew Amber ate it up watching him play daddy to Andrew. He played the game like he was so innocent and loving until he couldn't take it anymore. At first they said he killed my stepdad, but then that theory disappeared."

"Do you think he was capable of doing something like that?"

"Yes, when he came to the house he was crazy! Screaming at everybody looking for Amber. All the men came for Amber that night, but when we were little he would be nice to us. He would play with us and he was really nice. He taught Andrew how to play basketball, but playing against Malcolm is what made him Good at it!"

I smiled at Sasha cause it didn't look like talking about this was easy for her. "Thank you."

She shook her head trying to shake off the icky feeling. "Let's change the subject."

"Ok, but this conversation stays between me and you."

"Of course! Andrew would have a fit on both of our parts. You think this is why he kept us separate?" She asked.

"Probably, but it's too late now."

Sasha

"I get it! But I hate this!" She leaned in, "I'm coming in two weeks."

"You're the only one allowed." I whispered back to El's auntie

Brielis was having her fifteenth break down on her daddy's lap. "They might just have a total 360, getting away from that girl. She's been impossible. Even though she doesn't have her son they're leaving the house and everything to her. You'd think she'd be happy."

"She's still losing her parents." I said feeling sorry for the brat.

"So then why not make your last moments wonderful? Giving them the blues until they're gone makes no sense."

"Brielis makes no sense!" We laughed.

She hugged me, "take care of yourself. Have a safe flight."

"Thanks."

The nurse told Brielis we had to go. Her cheeks turned red then her eyes searched for me. She got up quickly and started charging at me. I stood there smiling with my hands in my pockets. She didn't see Teresa right next to me, but why would she? Teresa clothes lined her and then returned to her magazine. It happened so fast people were asking Brielis what was wrong while she laid on the ground holding her neck. Mr. & Mrs. Parsons wouldn't turn their eyes to look. Their nurses pushed them through the security checkpoint while El and I went through the normal check. The agent at the X-ray machine kept looking at our bags. Over and over, El looked at me with a question. I slightly shook my head letting him know it was nothing. Irritated they gave us our bags and we waited for our plane. His parents held hands from their wheelchairs as they smiled. El put me in a bear hug and thanked me for making this happen. When we sat in our first class seats Mrs. Parsons looked back at El and I, "thank you for saving us!"

Kendra

I was in the dressing room trying on my dress. I was admiring my sexy appearance. The neckline was sweetheart with a plunging V-neck combination. My dress was knee length and hugged my body. When I turned around I knew Darryl was going to die, and so would Jason for that matter. Jason gave us a whole speech about how he was tired of the only dresses I wore being too sexy. In the end I made no promises to change my behavior. I was admiring myself in the mirror, when I opened the door to walk out; Shai pushed me back in the room and locked the door. "Where did you come from?" I said completely surprised.

He kissed me like it was killing him not to. "I've missed you!"

"Shai you can't be here!" I was trying to grab my sense. "I don't know how you got in here, but you've got to go!"

"Kendra!" He stared me in my eyes. "Little girl! I'm in too deep, I can't just walk away from you!" I looked away because his stare was too intense. "I'm in too deep."

"I don't even know who you are. I didn't lie about who I am. I don't even know you." I felt stupid, "besides our time together was very short. I don't understand what you mean."

"What I mean about what?" He said still staring at my eyes.

"You're in too deep, what does that mean?"

"You love him?" He asked me.

I looked away again, I kept inhaling and exhaling. "You gotta leave! I don't want anything bad to happen to you."

"I'm going to work something out where we can talk and clear the air. I had to look in your eyes though, see if it would even be worth the trouble." Then he kissed me. I didn't want to give in to it, but Shai is a good kisser. Then he walked out of the room and he walked out the back of the store. I stood there for a minute gathering myself and trying to understand what just happened. When I walked out Ahjanae and Kaleah smiled at my dress then they immediately asked me what was wrong? I played it off saying I didn't know what bra I was supposed to wear with this dress.

When I was alone in my car I called Darryl. He didn't answer which meant he was busy cause he always answers my calls. I don't know why I was scared to go home, but I was. The whole scene didn't sit well with me. It's not like Darryl sat me down and explained everything to me or anything for that matter. All I could see was drama coming from this. I went to my parent's house. My momma and Kaleah were fussing as usual. Kaleah didn't see the big deal. She was out until six o'clock in the morning, but she put her boys to bed before she left. Momma kept asking her why Milton didn't send her home. And she said he tried but she wasn't having it. Momma kept reminding her she better not bring any more babies home. Kaleah rolled her eyes in irritation and went in her room. When Jason came home from work he went straight to momma for his hello kiss. It was like he couldn't focus on anyone or anything else until he got his kiss. Both of them were too into the kiss if you ask me, I turned my head in disgust. Jason shook my leg and said hello then he went back to his room to put his things away. Jason walked back in the room with his phone to his ear and nothing but seriousness on his face. When his eyes darted across the room to me, I instantly broke out in a sweat. I took out my phone and called Darryl again. He didn't answer and then the doorbell rang. Momma came back with Aunrey. I was so happy to see him, cause I hadn't seen him in forever it felt like. He gave me a huge hug and kiss on the cheek. When Jason got off the phone he told Aunrey to go with him and they went in his office and shut the door. I tried calling Darryl again, and then the doorbell rang again. This time it was Darryl; he had an interesting look on his face when he hugged me. I told him I needed to talk to him, and he told me we'd talk in a minute. The doorbell rang again and the guy from the office walked in behind Darryl, he said hello to my momma and gave her a hug. He said hello to me and then he followed Darryl to Jason's office. I asked momma if this happened often and she said no. Curiosity was killing both of us. We wanted to know what was going on. Then I heard my name, when I walked in to Jason's office Jason was the only one sitting. "Yussef put this under the same code as Tracy." The deep voice over the phone said.

"Will do," Yussef said clicking away on his phone.

"Babygirl, do you trust me?" Jason asked me.

"Of course."

"There's going to be a bunch of things happening shortly and I need to know all the inner workings of your business."

"Ok."

"Aunrey is going to be with you on your day to day assignments." The deep voice over the phone said.

I looked at Aunrey, "we get to spend time together? I haven't seen you in seems like forever!" I smiled at him.

Aunrey smiled, "we get to catch up."

"Tomorrow I'm going to sit with Ahjanae, I need you to tell all of your elderly customers that you may have to send someone out to cover for you in a bit." Jason said.

"Why would I do that?" I asked.

"Because you're going to be at a seminar to help your business grow." Jason watched me.

"Aren't seminars one to two days max?"

"Yes, but they won't know that. There's going to be some changes happening pretty soon. We need you to stay alert." The deep voice over the phone said.

"Darryl, I've been trying to call you all day."

Darryl took out his phone, "I don't have any missed calls from you. Call me right now." I took out my phone and called him and it rang and rang. Yussef called Darryl and it went through. I tried to call Jason, and my momma and it wouldn't go through. Yussef took my phone, he started punching in numbers and watching my screen. "Her phone has been compromised."

"Where did you go?" Jason asked me.

"I got my dress, before then it was working fine."

Was your phone out of your sight at any point today?" Yussef asked.

"When I went out of the dressing room my purse stayed behind." I was scared.

"What is it?" Darryl asked watching my eyes.

"Shai…"

"SHAI!" Darryl spit before I could say anything else.

"Let her finish," the voice said over the phone.

"Shai was there, I don't know where he came from or where he went. That's why I've been trying to call you. The whole scene made me nervous." I kept my eyes on Darryl as I told them everything that happened.

Jason was pissed and saying he wanted Kalani and I pulled immediately. "How did this happen Malcolm?"

"We've got Aunrey on her now. We didn't have a full detail on her."

"Why they always gotta go through the women though. For once can one of these fools be a man and come at you straight up?" Darryl said.

"Women and children are liabilities, I've always told you guys that. That's why if you choose to have someone you gotta know stuff like this is going to happen." The voice said.

"Why can't they pluck a chicken-head though? Why it gotta be all this? Putting his nasty filthy slobber all over my woman!"

Yussef looked at Aunrey then they turned their heads, they were trying not to laugh.

"Kendra you're going to stay here." Jason said.

"Um No! She's going with me. Aunrey can pick her up from my place in the morning." Darryl said.

Jason frowned at Darryl, "and I said my daughter is staying here!"

"And I said my woman is going with me!"

Aunrey smiled real big looking between the both of them. He sat up big like he was waiting to see how this was all going to play out. Jason and Darryl were going back and forth neither one of them was going to back down until I chose. I raised my hand and everyone looked at me. "Jason am I in danger if I go with Darryl?"

"I don't think you'll be in harm's way. I just don't want his ego getting in the way of taking care of you like you need to be."

"My ego?" Darryl blew air.

"Yes your ego! Tell me you weren't thinking of dangling my daughter like bait to taunt this guy."

"I'm not gonna say that the thought didn't cross my mind. I'm also not gonna say that hearing you say it made it sound dumb."

"Darryl are you really that basic?" Malcolm said.

"He's still a kid." Jason said

"Kid or not, my boys gotta be smarter than that. Now that you've poured acid all over Darryl's childish plan I can vouch for Darryl and say your daughter will be safe if she goes with Darryl tonight." Jason frowned at the phone, "I understand you're her father and it wouldn't be easy to let her go."

"Don't look at him, do you want to go?" Jason asked me, while his eyes wanted me to say no.

"Yes," I said watching Jason.

"ALRIGHT!" Darryl started doing the cabbage patch.

"DARRYL!" Jason barked he was beyond irritated.

"I know! I know! You'll end my life! You'll skin me alive!" Darryl said smiling at me.

"This better not be what I have to look forward to." Yussef shook his head. "I'd have shot you a long time ago."

"He has shot me!" Darryl said in irritation.

Jason waived him off, "it was only a stun gun! Don't act like it was a bullet."

"I was hurt all the same Jayman!"

"Mess with my daughter again, next time I'm bringing bullets. I don't care who your father is!" Jason said full of venom.

"Daddy! He's threatening me again!" Darryl said like he was tattling.

"Kendra's his daughter, deal with it."

When we went back to Darryl's house he made dinner, and dramatically pulled out all the stops. I didn't get much sleep that night; again Darryl asked me when I was going to stop taking my pill. I didn't want to start an argument, but it didn't go unnoticed when someone called he sent them to voicemail, and then proceeded to text them for twenty minutes too long. Even if there's no condom between us I don't trust him all that much.

Episode 17

Amber

"Remember we are Royalty on this set. How you treat your subjects says a lot about you as a Queen. You don't ever want to treat anyone like they're beneath you. That is useless Diva behavior, you want to conduct yourself responsibly and be selective about everything you do. Your reputation says a lot about you in this business." I explained to Tina on the plane ride to LA. We were going to my last major job before my wedding. My other gigs before the fake wedding date were local, rehearsals at the school and filming in the Bay Area. Tina was excited about this job because I told her about the celebrities I've been working with on this project. I choreographed a movie about dance. This project was huge and I had assistants, etc. They wanted so many different facets of dance, I was so proud to say that I had most of them covered, and I could to back up my claim. Ryan and Sonny went over the paperwork and the money for this deal was, "BEAUTIFUL!" My assistants flew out to Oakland to work with me on my clock on my turf. We came up with game plans as the studios decided on the scenes they wanted. I know how this goes through, all the routines we prepare for and shoot won't be included in the movie. So I try not to get too emotionally involved with any of them. Tina was so excited though, because a lot of big named celebrities were going to be around the set even if they weren't filming. I told her the hardest part at this point is rejecting all of the negativity and self-doubt her last relationship poisoned her with. I told her it was an honor and a privilege to be associated with her, but it was up to her how she enforces that thinking. I kept telling her when in doubt watch what I do.

I felt like a proud momma watching Tina interact with the staff. She certainly was paying attention to her auntie's words. At about a week and a half into shooting Malcolm came down to the set, something he rarely does. He sat over to the side watching and taking everything in but not saying much. If he was here that had to mean something brought him. I had a pep talk with myself and then I told myself to keep moving forward. When it was time to go Malcolm said he had a car service bring him so he rode with Tina and I. We had dinner at The Vine and we had nice conversation. Malcolm asked her how she was doing and she said she really missed Luke, but she was starting to understand why her father wouldn't let her see him anymore. Malcolm told her to hold on to that understanding because she'd get it more and more as time passed. When we got home the doorman greeted us, Malcolm put money in his hand and kept it moving. Tina took a shower then came and hugged and kissed us goodnight.

I watched Malcolm waiting for him to share what brought him out here. We were having a stare down of nonverbal communication. Then he said he was looking at this project and they were still adding people to the roster for this film, I said ok. Then he looked at me and said his flight left in the morning, I said ok. He asked me if I could handle it, he told me to be honest. I put my arms around his neck, "I am so in love with YOU! YOU are all that I've ever wanted and needed. Nothing could cause me to doubt us right now unless you did something. We have grown up so much, why would we need to worry about anyone else right? I'm with you! I'm in love with you! I only want you!" Then I kissed him. "Thank you for checking, it was fun giving my little speech." I smiled at him. Of course that almost meant I got served up deliciously with no room for fantasies about needing more.

In the morning, I kissed Malcolm goodbye before I left and then I met Tina at the door. She had the goofiest grin on her face. I asked her what was wrong with her. In the elevator she leaned in, "I heard you guys."

I was horrified, "WHAT?" I turned completely red.

Tina couldn't contain her laughter. "I couldn't hear you from my room, but I went to get water and I thought I heard something. As I was coming back towards my room I realized what I was hearing and I ran in the room, shut the door, and put my pillow over my head. You guys are worse than my parents." She smiled big.

All I wanted to do was die; memories of Momma and Daddy's bed plagued my mind. I told Tina to shut up and not to look at me for the rest of the week. The only sound during our early morning car ride to the studio was Tina's gut busting laughter. She'd calm down, look at my face and start laughing again. I wanted to slap her to make her stop, but I knew that was wrong so I turned on the radio and turned it up LOUD!

When we got to the studio, I noticed the additional trailers outside. More people were arriving today; I had a pep talk with myself. Get the job done go home, don't be cold. But don't be open. Mid-morning we were shooting and I was keeping time on the sideline. Tina was being adored by some of the cast members when the caramel shadow cast across my light. He was smiling before I looked at him. I said hello and then I returned my attention back to my job. He didn't hover; he started conversing with the crew. He disappeared for a few hours and we moved along with filming. Tina mouthed and asked me if I was ok, I gave her a thumbs up.

The director decided that Dwayne needed to be present in some of the dance scenes. Writers were scrambling to make changes and people were dancing around Dwayne. I knew he put someone up to giving him more time on the set during the filming of the dances especially.

The caterer set up the lunch table while they were filming the acting scene on the basketball court set, before the actors decided to have a little dance off, and then Dwayne's character is supposed to come and discover his son dancing with the girl. I grabbed a salad and half a sandwich from the table. "So the wedding is coming up?" Tina was openly watching us. "Yep! It's almost here."

"I tried to offer Malcolm my congratulations, but you know Malcolm." He watched my eyes.

"I sure do." I grabbed napkins. "It's good to see you Dwayne, take care." And then I started to walk away.

"Hold on Amber, you're just gonna walk away from me like I'm nobody?"

I stopped walking and frowned at him, "who are you getting loud with?"

"I'm not just some guy…"

I cut him off, "you've been married, twice at that! You know exactly why I'm walking away from you. Don't take it personal Dwayne."

"Everything with you is personal to me."

I walked back to the table, "this is business. Check your personal feelings at the door." He frowned, "so that's it? When our paths cross from now on, you're gonna act like my name is Ramell? Amber don't do me like that."

"How about this, we respectfully say our hellos and then we keep respectable distances. I know your dating someone right now, and she wouldn't like to know you're demanding anything from me. My husband would prefer if we never spoke again. I acknowledged you because you were always as good to me as you could be. I am grateful that we shared a season together, but that was in the past. I'm not jeopardizing what I have today for anyone! You have to understand where I'm coming from."

343

Dwayne looked at Tina who was only missing a bucket of popcorn as her eyes stayed glued to us. "How you doing?" He said in an irritated tone.

Tina nodded hello and continued watching, "If this is too much for you, I will resign from this project, but I was hoping we could be professional about this whole thing."

"I'll settle for an opportunity to talk to you alone." He looked at Tina.

"That's not a good idea. We've said everything we need to say. Now we both can move on, knowing that we had closure the last time we spoke."

He frowned, "we did not have closure the last time we spoke."

I turned around and walked away from him, he was making me mad and if I got mad he'd accuse me of caring. He knows I care; he was always good to me. It wasn't his fault that I broke up with him, and if I wasn't raised differently I would've took him from his wife when I was alone all those years. I did a good job of avoiding him. Today, Malcolm is back, and it's unlike any other time with him. This time it's just me and him, no extras, no blind eyes, no nonsense. I hate that it has taken this long to get to my happily ever after, but I'm happy it's here all the same. I don't want any misunderstandings, so I choose to walk away to save his life. I filled my water bottle and then I sat next to Tina with my food. She put her arm around me and rubbed my back, I pretended not to be affected by that.

The next few days were interesting to say the least, Dwayne didn't push too hard, but daily he was trying to have any kind of conversation with me that he could. It was time to wrap up and finish this project. When I saw Derrick walking on the set, I figured Malcolm heard something he didn't like and he sent Derrick to shut it down. Like Malcolm, Derrick sat over to the side watching and taking everything in. When he came over and greeted me, I asked him how long he was here for. He told me he was flying back with me. Which meant he wasn't leaving until I left. Then he asked me point blank how the pretty boy was holding up? I told him it was hard for him, but he was doing as good as could be expected.

My last scene, was taking its final take so I walked away. I saw Dwayne make his way over to Derrick, they chatted for half a minute. Then they retreated to their corners. I felt bad for Dwayne, he did nothing wrong. I'm never stupid enough to fall for dumbness though. When the director said we were good I hugged my team and then I smiled widely at Derrick. Then we both looked at Tina who was chatting with one of the producers. He was completely taken with Tina I could see it. She even appeared to be blushing and open to the idea. I shrugged at Derrick, when Derrick returned my shrug I knew there was hope for this guy. Derrick quietly took pictures of them and then he sent them off.

A few minutes later Derrick got a response and he gave me a thumbs up. When Tina and the guy were still talking long after I confirmed our flight out early in the morning I invited her friend out to dinner with us. Donovan gave Tina his number so that she could call him with the restaurant location. Tina was so giggly and excited on the way to the condo. She talked the entire way, and then she literally ran into her room to shower. Derrick laughed at her and he said he wondered if Chantel ever acted like that over him. I looked at him in disbelief. I told him she still acts like that over him. He got the biggest smile. I excused myself to go take my own shower, since Sasha hasn't been around to take my clothes I've actually held on to a few things. The lightweight knock at the door told me it was Tina. I told her to come in. She had on a robe and her hair was nicely curled. She said she didn't like anything she brought and she was hoping I had something she could wear. I told her she wanted to wear something just sexy enough to peak his curiosity, but she didn't want her business hanging out. She stood there hanging on my every word. I gave her a dress that would caress her, but not cling to her. She asked me if I thought she looked nice, and I did. Then I eyed her; I asked her why was she cooperating with me all of a sudden? She smiled and looked me in my eyes; "I just realized you got Malcolm eating out of the palm of your hand for one. You guys started when you were a baby and he's still sprung stupid off of you. AND THEN you got Dwayne Reed begging you for a hello. I figured you gotta know something." I laughed so hard I had to sit down. She sat next to me on the bed, "why did you and Dwayne break up? Didn't you love him?"

"I have loved Malcolm since I was a child. No one has hurt me deeper, than he did. Over the years we've battled like you wouldn't believe over things that in hindsight weren't as important as we made them out to be. Do you remember Uncle Troy?"

"Vaguely, but yes."

"When we lost him the world seemed to stop spinning for a minute. We both shut down, even from each other. I hadn't laid eyes on Malcolm for a longtime when Dwayne came along. I didn't get with Dwayne for the right reasons at first. I mean you've seen him. Do you believe a man who is that gorgeous when he tells you that he's had a major crush on you before you even knew he existed? I took him as a playboy and I never thought we would get as serious as we did, but no matter how serious we got all I wanted was Malcolm. Dwayne never really had a fair chance. I broke up with him because I felt I was standing in the way of his family being whole again. His ex-wife wanted to get back together, and to my disappointment they did get back together and remarried. Malcolm and I didn't end up together until now."

"Does he know about all those years you were single?"

"I don't know, but it's spilled milk now."

"Did you love him?"

"I did, but not like I loved Malcolm. I've always been possessive over Malcolm, but I was never like that with Dwayne. Women were always throwing their selves at him everywhere we went. Dwayne was the one to pump up my head though."

"Because you had a man that fine?"

"No, although that helped. He constantly told me how beautiful I was, and he always made me feel like I was the most gorgeous woman alive. I mean look at the way he's still acting. How could you not feel pumped up over a man that fine treating you like you would treat someone on his level? The hurtful part is that I know it comes from the heart, and he's not trying to gas me up, but I'm in love with Malcolm and he's all I want. I don't want to continue hurting Dwayne. I've successfully avoided him all these years and BOOM! He's everywhere I go this past year and a half. It was getting hard though, that's why I'm glad that Derrick showed up. Derrick tolerated him, but you remember he was never really a fan of Dwayne."

"I remember, but he was nicer than usual today."

"I guess that's a sign that he's growing up as well. Matters of the heart are always sticky. And anyone who thinks it's easy to let go of someone you love, especially when it may not be right to love them is a fool!" Then I pulled my dress over my head. I smoothed my ponytail again then I told her to come stand next to me as we looked at ourselves in the mirror. "I want to apologize for going completely Annette on you in the beginning. I never knew or understood why my Momma would come after me like she did until you. Girl your mouth!" We chuckled, "I'm so happy we're past that."

Her eyes watered, "THANK YOU! Sasha told me to stop provoking you. I didn't realize the part I played in all of that until she said that. I'm happy we're past that too. I actually like you again."

I laughed, "that's good to know."

"Now I'm kind of taking notes, cause like I said. You've got Malcolm eating out of your hand, that's amazing within itself. So how should I be during dinner? I'm nervous."

"Just be yourself, you definitely don't want to pretend you're one way when you're not, but listen to the things he says and does. Remember you have a choice, you don't have to be with him."

Derrick was on the phone when we came out talking to Chantel and Chanel. I smiled at my baby as his tender side was all exposed. When we got to the restaurant Donovan was already sitting at the table. He looked very appreciative of Tina's appearance. Derrick asked him who else was joining us. He said Dwayne Reed in a matter fact tone. By his demeanor he had no idea that wasn't a good idea. Then the host showed Dwayne to our table right on cue. Derrick looked at Tina who was horrified, and then he asked me if I was ok. Donovan asked if there was something wrong. Derrick told him we wouldn't be staying for dessert. Dwayne didn't smile he looked like he was trying to read whether I was leaving or not. He sat on the end closest to Derrick.

"What am I missing?" Donovan asked referring to the tension at the table.

"I'm engaged to be married, and Dwayne and I used to date."

"Yep, she didn't even discuss breaking up with me. She decided and that was that." Dwayne sounded irritated.

"You're family needed you."

"My family needed you! The only person excited about Michelle and I getting back together was Michelle. My girls still struggle to understand." Then he looked at Derrick, "you've talked to the girls. Darryl has as well. You're getting married to someone else but you haven't closed the book with me."

My face started stinging. "Right here in front of everybody?"

"You're not going anywhere alone with him." Derrick shot me a look.

I looked at Donovan, "I'm sorry sweetheart. You guys will need a do over, I'm sure this is not what you had in mind for this evening." Donovan nodded to say it was ok. I looked at Dwayne and he was completely focused on me. "You were a playboy, you weren't supposed to change up. I was not trying to hurt you or lead you on, but I warned you not to fall in love with me, cause I was not going to fall back in love with you."

Dwayne frowned at me, "that disclosure is so weak. We're not little kids. We agreed to always be honest with each other, but when it comes to love you always lied to me."

"Ok so in all honesty, I was always in love with Malcolm." I said, not wanting to give in to his request to hear me say it.

"I never questioned whether you loved him, but you would never be honest about your love for me."

"You always want to push the dumbest issues! The ONLY reason we were ever together is because Malcolm wasn't around at first. He was going through some things and he needed time."

"Even still you're dancing around the issue."

"You were supposed to be my fling, my distraction while Malcolm got it together. I never intended for you to be more than that."

"But I was." He watched my eyes.

"You were a playboy, and you were never about just me."

"How would you know, you never asked. In the beginning, our relationship was open, but in the end I was only about you. I had the ring and everything, but you just left. You cut off all communication with me. You just left! Now you're sitting over there like it's my fault that I feel anything, like I did something wrong. I didn't fall out of love with you, or even break up with you. That was all you."

"So what, this is unfinished business?"

"What else would it be?"

"I told you she was going to get pregnant and you let it happen." I took a drink of my water.

"You set me up." He almost smiled.

"NO! No you will not, you will not blame me for you being irresponsible. When I would've come back you were married and increasing your family. I told you what was going to happen and you punked out and fell on the sword. Now that you're divorced you wanna keep popping up everywhere. I'm sorry your marriage ended but stop doing this to me. Your time to fight for me has come and past. It ended when you got Michelle pregnant, and then you remarried her. What was I supposed to do with that?"

Dwayne sat back in his chair; I could see the hurt all over his face. Our waitress brought our food out and Dwayne and I didn't touch our plates. "Miscommunications can cost a fortune! You shouldn't have left me without discussing it with me."

"If you pledge your allegiance to someone you should stand by that. Malcolm is the only man to make sure he didn't spread his seed elsewhere."

"You didn't want to have any more kids. You wouldn't even talk to me. You were avoiding me, and literally running from me."

He caught me at the grocery store one time. I thought I was safe in Oakland, when I saw him I grabbed my purse and ran. Left my cart in the middle of the aisle and ran around that parking lot with him on my heels the whole time until the Mitigated person pulled up in a car that I jumped in and we left. I cried myself to sleep that night; I couldn't stand hurting him like that. "If we were going to be together, I may have considered it, but I really didn't want to have any more kids. So it worked out for the best. All of your children have the same mother. That's an achievement you can hold your head high about. All this me and you stuff is over and done. Please respect my relationship and let this die here."

"I didn't know you were single all those years, this is the first I'm hearing of it. No one could've kept me from you if I would've known."

I sighed as I drummed my fingers, "doesn't matter now. Please respect my relationship and let this die here."

"If for some crazy reason you and Malcolm don't work out…"

I cut him off, "that's never going to happen, but if it did, you'd be married and not hearing about it." I smiled.

"Low blow." He painfully smiled back.

Derrick grabbed my hand under the table. "So this is done. Stop stalking my momma!"

"Stalking?" I asked.

Derrick looked at Dwayne, "I wiggled my way on this project once I heard you were on it."

"I thought it was odd that you were there. I didn't remember seeing you on the cast list." Dwayne looked at Derrick, "ok."

"So what does this mean? In the future you act like strangers?" Tina asked, I could tell she was trying to understand.

"Out of respect for me and my relationship our paths will only cross when it naturally happens professionally. And when that does happen we will be cordial, but there's no conversations we need to have. No closure that we need, we're done." I looked at Dwayne.

Dwayne's eyes pleaded with me to say something else, to add a "but" to the end of my statement, anything. When I looked away no one said anything for a long time. Then Derrick whipped out pictures of Chanel. He started talking about his Babygirl, Dwayne looked at Derrick in amazement. He told him he's never seen him smile before. Derrick held on to his smile and he continued to share pictures of his pride and joy.

****

"All of you have shown promise. I am very proud of your progress. Jack and AJ you haven't been a part of the regular drills but you will benefit from today's exercise as well. Even though today maybe fun for you, I need you all to focus because this is about more than fun. Do you have any questions?" Malcolm asked the kids.

Andre raised his hand, "Poppa it's kind of warm out here, do I need to wear this jacket?"

"You are all soldiers in training and those jackets are part of your gear for today. Do any of you know why we're out here?" All the kids shook their heads no. "Do you know where we are?"

347

Carey Anderson

Yesmina raised her hand, "this is a race track."
"Right, we're at the Sonoma race track cause we need space for today's drills." Malcolm
waived his hand and a truck pulling a trailer drove over on to the grass. I got a knot in my
stomach. "Today you're learning how to ride and drive."
"Drive like a real car?" Sydney asked.
"Yes!" Emerald, Sabrina, and Yussef got out of the truck. They looked like their own
biker group especially when Sonny junior and Emmanuel joined them. "Tim and Tina,
this part of the drills applies to you as well. Your bikes are in the trailer but Yussef is
going to explain the basics to all of you. If you need to take your jackets off for now,
that's fine, but everyone wears their gear while they're on the bikes. Yussef's going to
take over." Malcolm walked to the back of the group while I sat and listened to Yussef
explain to us the basics. The clutch, gears, brakes, accelerator, and RPMs. I was happily
sitting amongst the kids cause I never learned how to ride a motorcycle either. When I
heard Malcolm and Malachi talking about today I happily invited myself to today's drills.
All of the kids were engaged in the information asking a lot of the same questions I had.
Uncle Jeff, Jeff, and JoJo rode around the track having too much fun. Yussef explained
that riding motorcycles is very dangerous, however they felt that everyone should know
how as part of their basic education. Then he told the kids today was basic education so
no tricks. When they started loading the bikes off the trailer they had little miniature
bikes for Amaya, AJ, and Jack. Yussef explained that the bikes were only little and they
were still actual bikes. They had all the kids practice starting and stopping on the little
bikes. Then they unloaded dirt bikes. Once everyone was on their bikes we went around
the course a few times getting the hang of our bikes. The kids were screaming and
laughing they were having so much fun, but they kept us at low speeds the entire time.
Another truck and trailer pulled on the grass while we practiced, I expected at least one of
the kids to look scared or be wobbly on their bikes, but all of them rode like they'd been
riding for a while. I was impressed with how nicely they picked it up. Jackson was
wobbly, he doubted himself too much. Even little Amaya was telling him to get it
together. Then the big kids, myself included, got on the real bikes. Malcolm had all of us
going around and around on the track getting used to our bikes. He said next time would
be target practice while on the bikes and the kids got excited. We celebrated each child's
accomplishments, Darryl told me Malcolm was getting soft cause they had to be spot on
or they were wrong when Malcolm was training them. I said they had girls with them this
time. Darryl reminded me that they had Tanisha and Sasha with them a lot of the time.
Then they brought out go-carts. Malcolm explained the only difference with the carts
verses the bikes was the balance and that the clutch was on the floor and the gear shift
was in their hands. He said they were not driving bumper cars, so they needed to steer
clear of each other, but to have fun for a few laps. The kids were out and burning up the
track all you saw were teeth when they were called in and took off their helmets.
Malcolm told them that they did good, but now they had to do four laps in reverse. It was
hilarious, Sydney and Jada actually had the best reverse driving, but they all needed to
practice. We spent the entire day and most of the night on this track, Darryl and Yussef
showed the kids where they would eventually end up. They flew around the track doing
all kinds of tricks on their bikes. The kids were so fired up, screaming and carrying on. I
knew every one of them was going to pass out when they got in their cars. Malcolm got
on a bike and road around the track for a few laps. I stepped on the track and put my
thumb out. He slowed down and I told him I wanted a ride. All the kids cheered when I
got on his bike, I asked him why he didn't need a helmet, and he said he was Malcolm.
****

It was almost moving time; Malcolm had staff come to help me pack up the house. I was
fine for the most part packing up the kitchen, office, guest room, but when I got to
Andre's room a lot of his baby stuff put me in a remember when... place. Then when

348

they started bringing things down from the attic memories of when my babies were little flooded my mind. Some of those memories were attached to David and others were laced with memories of Dwayne. I was doing a good job of sucking it up, until I found a picture of Malcolm holding Andrew as a baby. Malcolm was a baby himself, I can see that now. He was actually smiling at Andrew and it looked like Andrew was smiling back. I took that picture and the ones like it to a camera shop. I wanted photo albums for each of my boy's to share with their families and then the pictures I had of Momma and Daddy and us while we were growing up I made copies of those for my siblings.

Certain pictures I wanted blown up HUGE! Like the picture of Malcolm and Andy. There was a picture of Malcolm talking to Andrew and Derrick all of their faces were serious. The hilarious part of the picture was that I had my back to them with Darryl on my hip. And he had his hand in full swing like he was about to smack Andrew upside the head, and he had the goofiest grin on his face. My silly baby has always been himself, it's like he was laughing at us when I was pregnant and we were let in on the joke after he was born. Andrew came over as I was sitting on the couch lost in my thoughts. He needed a minute to think because Tracy was being emotional and paranoid. I asked why was she paranoid and he said it was the whole idea of everything. She didn't like that it was necessary that we needed people to have our back twenty-four hours a day. She says it's beyond ridiculous that we need to have bulletproof cars. I told him this is exactly why you make sure that the person you choose understands the life they're signing up for. I asked him if she was ok and he said she's having dramatic fits but she's ok. Then Malcolm called he told me to get dressed cause he wanted to take me to dinner. I really didn't feel like going out, but Malcolm was insisting so I sucked it up. I confirmed my appointment at Raynel's for a practice run on my hairstyle for the wedding then I got dressed.

When I came downstairs I fussed at Andy for not going home and for letting poor Tracy wallow in her emotional state. He exhaled as I continued to fuss he told me that Malcolm was planning a romantic evening for he and I, and Andy needed to deliver me. Then he told me to act surprised when I stood their smiling. Andrew said women make it difficult to surprise them.

I quietly and happily sat in Andy's car as he drove me to Berkeley to a beautiful hotel, which I've never paid attention to before. I proudly walked on Andrew's arm and when the banquet doors opened women yelled, "SURPRISE"! My entire face turned red. My Auntie Lauren took my arm away from Andy and then she shooed him away. "This is why no one came to help me pack! Very clever distracting me like that!" Everyone laughed. Then Auntie led me to a golden throne, that I had to walk up three steps to sit on, in the middle of the room. Sophia brought a gold crown with jade and Emerald jewels, and Jade gave me a purple cape that she called my royal robe. I looked around the room and all my family and friends were here. They even had my Momma's sister Emma here. I waved hello to everyone.

"Welcome to your Bridal Shower Amber!" Auntie Lauren said into her microphone, then they dimmed the lights and the projector began its slide show. "For the record, did everyone remember to take note that we got no tears from Amber with our surprise?" Everyone laughed, then her voice shook. "She will be in tears when we are done with her."

The movie began with my baby picture. Then I heard my mother's voice. "I thought Malachi was my strong willed baby, but Amber changed the game." Jade held my hand, "she had those sneaky expressions. I ran behind that girl so much as a baby I didn't need to do anything extra. Running after her I lost all my weight." Everyone giggled. "All of my babies are special to me. And each one has their own special place in my heart. Timothy is my oldest and first born, and Malachi who really should've been little Tim, my beautiful Jade who's strength always amazes me, and then my little Amber. Emma pointed out that she acts just like me. Imagine the horror." She laughed, "your wedding is coming up. I am so happy for you. I'm so sorry that I couldn't be there for your special day, but your Auntie Lauren has my instructions, and I know she's going to carry them out for me just like I would. I bet you thought you chose a lace dress on your own." I could hear her smile. "I feel pretty confident that you've stuck with your original choice and you and Malcolm are getting married soon." She laughed, "it wasn't until I saw how giving he was with you that I opened my heart to him. And once I did that Malcolm has always felt like one of my own. I'm happy that you two have finally gotten it together and are making your family whole. Lauren please take good care of my baby." The only thing missing was to hear my daddy's voice as well.

Jade and I were hugging and balling our eyes out. Then Auntie Lauren joined our hug. Once we gathered our composure then she resumed the video. Pictures of me growing up and very few pictures of Malcolm when he was little. The few they had I could tell came from pictures of other people. Any pictures that reflected happiness were from my family. By the end of the slide show I was in all out tears.

Then Auntie Lauren gave the microphone to Tracy. "Congratulations Amber. I know in the timeline of things I am the newest addition to the family. However, words cannot express to you how happy I am for you. I am so thankful for you."

Then Chantel got the microphone. "I wanted to meet you so badly. Derrick couldn't introduce us fast enough. Like Tracy I want to thank you for always making me feel like I belong."

Then Bernadette got the microphone. "Malcolm introduced Amber as his girlfriend. A title he never gave anyone before or after that time. He gave me strict instructions to make sure she was protected at all times. He didn't want her fighting no matter what. I thought that meant she couldn't fight." She smiled at me, "that girl hits hard and on target. The one time we were going to fight she kept knocking me down, but she wasn't trying to fight me. I was so confused by that because in our family we were taught to fight first and ask questions later." She pointed to that girl Renee who was standing next to her shaking her head in agreement. "Amber having you in our family changed the dynamics. We started communicating and thinking first. It drove some people crazy. Imagine a family working together to achieve something better! You've been my cousin since that day we met, I love you and I'm so happy for you."

Then she handed the microphone to that girl Renee. "Amber I hated you so much! Many times I plotted evil things in my mind for you. Then without any reason you came through for me when I had literally no one to turn to. You even convinced my own family to help me. I can never repay you for the lesson you taught me that day. Thank you for never holding my ignorance against me. Thank you for hanging in there with our knucklehead cousin, but like Bernie said you've been family since we were kids. This upcoming ceremony is just a formality." Then I hugged them both.

"You guys all know her as Amber the fighter but I knew her before she defended herself. I was her protector." Rosalind said, "I've known her since before time began. I know how much you love Malcolm, and how much you mean to him. I am so honored to be a part of your celebration and to be here for you just like you've always been here for me and everybody else. Congratulations."

"My turn!" Sophia smiled at me. "My sister! You deserve it all congratulations." Then Sophia gave the microphone back because she was getting emotional. Everyone who knew Sophia and knew how much she spoke her mind, laughed. To witness her at such a loss of words was endearing.

Jade was too emotional she couldn't take the microphone.

Then they turned the screen back on. Sasha had on intellectual glasses, a news reporter navy blue suit and her hair pulled into a bun. The camera was only showing her. "Hello everyone good evening. At this portion of our evening I'm going to interview the men in

Amber's life." Everyone started applauding as the camera panned across her panel of men and introduced them. "We have her oldest brother Timothy!" Grace catcalled to him. "Her brother Malachi! We have Yussef who is a dead ringer for his father Troy!" Then she turned the camera to her face. "I bet some of you thought that was him, but it is his clone and son Yussef. Then we have her oldest son Andrew, her most serious son Derrick, and her youngest son Darryl. Her cousins Jeffrey Jr.," Jeff stopped smiling. He told her to call him Jeff. "And her cousin Joseph." Then she zoomed in, "this is her baby daddy soon to be husband Malcolm!" Everyone applauded, I wondered how they got him to agree to this silliness. "You all know why you're here."

"Yeah! Somebody thought they could actually have a party without me!" Darryl said shaking his head.

"You're here to play our television version of who knows Amber best! In order to answer you must hit the buzzer in front of you first once you've written down your answer. If you answer incorrectly you're out. Malcolm will only participate in the lightning round. Does everyone understand?" The men smiled and said they agreed.

"Here's your first question. How old was Amber when she first met..." Sasha looked at all the men with their markers in the air. "Troy!"

That was not what they thought she was going to say. When Darryl tried to look at Derrick's answer he turned his back to him and covered his answer. Malachi hit the buzzer first, and then they all hit the buzzer. Sasha told them to show their answers. Darryl had eight but then he crossed it out and put 13 like everyone else. Then Sasha asked where Timothy met Malcolm. They sat there scratching their heads as they sat there thinking for a minute. Timothy wrote his answer and he tried to flip over his card before anyone saw, but they were climbing over each other trying to see his card. Andrew saw the answer, and then everyone copied his. Sasha asked for the answer and they all said, "Pizza Joint!" Sasha threw them a curve ball, "when did Malachi and Malcolm fight?"

Even Malachi looked stuck. "Uncle Mali's still a live so she can't mean like we're thinking." Darryl said tapping his marker on his face.

"Oh! I know when she means!" He hit the buzzer. "That time at school when that fool was messing with Jade and he tried to jump me and Sonny. Malcolm and Troy had our backs." He looked at Yussef, "you remember don't you!" Then he laughed, "that was also the day I found out about them."

"Sasha you know what would work better. Malcolm sitting over there like he knows and we're wasting energy. It should be us against Malcolm." Darryl suggested.

"Suit yourself, you're still going to lose!" Malcolm said.

"Ooh! The challenge, ok." The camera cut away, and it was now everyone facing Malcolm. Darryl was stretching on the floor, saying he was ready. "Alright, what's Amber's favorite color?"

Darryl hit the buzzer, "Purple! Who knows they momma?" He said putting his hands out for everyone to congratulate him.

We sat there thoroughly entertained as the men tried to challenge Sasha's ability to challenge them. The final question for them, Sasha asked. "If Andrew had been a girl what did she plan to name him?"

The men sat there quiet for a minute, Malcolm smiled at them as they got irritated cause he seemed to know and they didn't. "How could you know? You guys didn't discuss names for me. My Grandmamma named me." Andrew said.

"Because I know my queen you guys are playing catch up." Malcolm said confident that he knew the answer.

"Ok! Ok! We got a list of three names, Malcolm what you got?" Darryl said.

"The name!" He said nonchalantly.

"Ok Darryl show us your list." Sasha said.

"First we have Malachijia! Because we all know how close she is to her big brother!"
"Mala what?" Sasha said cracking up.
"Mala-Kai-jah! Malachijia!" He smiled
"For the record we did not agree to that. He chose that on his own." Derrick said.
"Uncle Mali you can use that name if you like, I've got more. Anyways! Then we have Timothina. Tim-Moe-Thina! Cause she loves her daddy and her oldest brother."
"Again! Let the record reflect that both of those names came from Darryl!" Joseph said.
"Last but not least our final answer is Jade. Because we know how much she loves her big sister." Darryl said as he dropped an invisible mic to walk away.
"Did you guys agree to this?" Sasha asked the group.
"That's the only name we agreed to. The rest of that hot mess was all Darryl!" Timothy said laughing.
"Ok, Malcolm your answer?"
"Annette." He said tisking them.
"Annette? You better be happy you're a boy! You'd never hear the end of it if your name was Annette!" Darryl laughed, "ok so. Sasha tell him we're right."
Sasha smiled, "sorry guys Malcolm's right."
Malcolm threw his hands up in celebration. "I KNOW ALL THINGS AMBER! WHY WOULD YOU EVER DOUBT ME???" Everyone erupted into laughter as they watched Malcolm's victory celebration over all the sore losers.
I looked up as Tanisha tried to rush past me but I grabbed her arm. "Why are you avoiding me?" I said in her ear.
Guilt was all over her face, "no I'm not." She kept her eyes to the floor.
"I want to talk to you and you better not make me come looking for you." I said, she quietly agreed then I released her.
The rest of the evening was lovely and everyone congratulated me over and over again. I was so happy to see all of my family as they were happy for me. When it was time to open gifts, it was like everyone was competing to see who could give me the raunchiest lingerie. We had so much fun and I assured them that I would wear each item with pride.

****

"Let me explain!" She said putting her hands up. I didn't say anything; I sat there watching her. "That whole conversation was embarrassing and I think I was caught in some stupid emotional thing."
"Tanisha! Don't even! You're avoiding me on purpose. You felt something on the day your ex was getting married, been there done that, but then you spring your amazing body on everybody at Sasha's wedding. Shame on you for burying those curves. Anyways, then you fall back. Now you're avoiding me. Talk to me."
Tanisha exhaled, "I feel so lost right now. My momma is dating my father. Everybody acts like I should be happy about it but I'm not. I know she's not even feeling the situation like she's pretending to. I'd rather she missed Troy forever rather than pretend she's happy with him. He doesn't deserve her, and I'm not going to make it easy on him. I can talk to Sasha and Latia about this and I do, but Drew was the main person I turned to when I needed to whine about my father. Now it doesn't seem right to talk to him at all. I don't want to hurt Tracy, I actually like her. I've never liked anyone that he was with before."
"Not even Jennay?"
"Nope, didn't like her either." She exhaled, "I know why you called me here." She rolled her eyes.
I smiled really big and clapped my hands with excitement, "good! Make it purple and I want all the accessories. You should've came clean and just agreed to be in my wedding like I asked you in the first place."
"I need to tell you something." Her eyes filled with tears. "I haven't told my momma yet so please don't say anything." She swallowed, "I need to move away."

I gasped, "WHY?" I immediately thought of how devastated Rosalind would be. I knew Tanisha wasn't talking about a short car ride away either.

"I can't take it anymore! I need to sort out my feelings."

"What about Carina's business?"

"She's not going with me."

I closed my eyes; I needed a minute to understand what she was saying to me. "What or who are you running from?"

"Myself!" She looked at me with sad eyes.

"I don't understand."

"He should be married to me. Who knew he'd grow up before his father? I can't take seeing their family, like I said I like Tracy. I don't want to hurt anybody I've got to go. Things have been strained between Carina and I since the wedding anyways. She might be happy to be free."

I touched her face, "your momma needs you. You're telling me you guys are moving?"

"If she wants to go."

Very clever, but it hurt me to know she was making her mother choose between her daughter and her ex-husband. I didn't doubt the other things she said but her motivation to go was to get away from her father and she was hoping her mother would go away with her. She said she was leaving right after the wedding with or without her mother.

****

I couldn't stop smiling! It was beautiful! As we walked up the street to our massive home I grinned from ear to ear. The house it's self was a matte eggplant purple and dark and light greys with various stones outside. Even the pavers up the driveway were custom made with purple and dark grey with sparkles in them. I liked the fountain that captured your attention and then the water flowed down through a bubbling brook to a small pond. Malcolm said he was going to put Koi fish in there. The roadway from the street kind of reminded me of Uncle Frank's although the hill was not as big. Malcolm said the landscapers were bringing trees to align the driveway kind of like Uncle Frank and Ethan's houses. I asked him if we were getting dogs too? He didn't look enthused about it, but he said if I wanted them we could have them. I missed my dogs. Darryl took them away without discussing it with me and my house always felt off without my other babies. As I opened my mouth he said they would stay outside, they couldn't live inside. Even though I've walked through this house many many times before, this time when Uncle Dale opened the double doors my heart sang. Custom ordered tiles sparkled at me from the floor, happily greeting us and welcoming us inside. My pale lavender walls immediately relaxed me while making me smile. I grabbed Malcolm's hand then I climbed in his arms smothering him with kisses. He smiled as he allowed me to excitedly kiss him.

We went from room to room looking at everything. Turning on lights, flushing toilets, running faucets, slamming doors. Realizing there were surprise rooms and closets off of certain rooms. There was a hidden basement, and even that room had a secret room off of it. This house was so huge it felt like we'd be living in a hotel more than a house. Every time I took out my phone, Malcolm told me to wait. Then he'd have Uncle Dale show me another feature of the house. I was dying to call Shasta my interior decorator even though she was scheduled to come later I wanted her to come now. I guess Malcolm wanted my undivided attention before I went crazy with filling this beautiful place with furniture. I couldn't wait I was so excited.

We were walking around the finished attic when Timothy came up. He said there was a representative from Immaculately Tidy who was waiting for us by the front door. I looked at Malcolm and he said housekeeping as he continued his conversation. I made the long journey down to the front door; all this space was going to take some getting used to. Kendra and another young lady were standing by the front doors and they were looking around in Aw of the space. I immediately smiled at her. She nervously said hello and then she told me the house was beautiful. I thanked her, and then she reintroduced me to her sister. I reminded them that we've all met at least at Ryder's baby shower. I asked how many people was she going to have on the house? I warned that Mister Latour was very meticulous so they would need the people with the biggest case of OCD on our property. Kendra said that she and her sister Kalani would personally handle our home. I told her that the guesthouse and multi-purpose rooms would be finished soon. I advised that we value our privacy so we only really needed someone to come once a week to dust, vacuum, and shine the floors. Kendra did a good job of assuring me that our home would remain as clean as it is today. I liked her professionalism; even though we've partied together she was about her business, which I appreciated. She didn't act overly familiar with me. I held back from asking her why I hadn't seen her since the engagement party, but as much as Darryl hollers he's not getting married I figure he pulled back. Kendra seems like she would fit in just fine, I told myself not to pry.

We were in the kitchen when Darryl and Ryder walked in. "Hey momma." Darryl said with his eyes locked on Kendra.

"Hey baby, Ryder. You guys come to see the house?"

"Yep," Darryl said being unusually quiet.

"But you said you were coming to watch her interact with your mom." Ryder said smiling the entire time.

"Man!" Darryl said giving Ryder an irritated look.

"Payback is a mutha ain't it!" He smiled real big.

"Oh so you wanna start that game with me. Oh it's on!" Darryl shook his head, "don't start none. Won't be none." Then Darryl looked at me. "Momma tell her I'm your favorite son, and that it gets no better than me."

I smiled, "Darryl is one of my favorite sons."

"I am the favorite, she's just being modest."

"Good for you." Kendra said.

Then Kendra's sister stood up straight and nervousness was all over her face as she watched Malcolm walk into the kitchen. "Kendra," He said as his way of acknowledging her. Malcolm looked at her, "I don't want to know that dust exist. Can you handle that?"

"I feel pretty confident that we can. We will keep your home looking beautiful."

Malcolm looked at Darryl, "what?"

"Tell her I'm your favorite son." Darryl said.

Malcolm looked at Kendra, "Darryl is the best."

"I can't believe you said that." Ryder said.

"My son is a reflection of me. There is no one better than me so of course that makes him the best."

"But I asked you to tell her I'm your favorite."

"He is one of my favorite sons." Malcolm said standing next to me.

"Now you sound like her."

Malcolm looked at me, "shouldn't I sound like my better half?"

Darryl blew air, "see what marriage does! She already said yes. Would it kill anybody to stroke my ego?"

"That's why you need a wife of your own." I said taking my phone out to call Shasta.

"No thanks, I don't need a wife for that."

"You don't need a wife for anything." Kendra said with her eyes locked on Darryl.

Everyone looked at Darryl. He started stammering, "remain professional! Stop putting me on the spot!" He blushed.

I smiled looking at my baby at a loss for words. Mister never wants to get married is weakening. "Mister and Misses Latour, it was nice seeing you again. We will schedule an appointment to come back once you're moved in."

"Ok thank you," I said putting her card in my pocket.

Darryl and Ryder followed them out then I quickly dialed Shasta. Malcolm was all hands while I told Shasta to come from her hotel over now. Malcolm and I were lost in our kiss when Darryl and Ryder came back in the kitchen. "You're too young to be worried about a wife."

I frowned, "why is he too young?"

"Because he is. Just because his brothers are married off doesn't mean he has to hurry and settle down. Darryl's not ready to be anybody's husband." Malcolm said.

Darryl stood there listening. "I don't know about not being ready, but I thought you were against marriage?" I said.

Darryl shrugged, "Kendra's not a chickenhead. I don't know what I'm against anymore." He spun around, "WHAT IS THAT WOMAN DOING TO ME? Ryder! We going out tonight! I can't have this! This ain't me! I've got to get my cool back! Pronto!"

Ryder smiled, "you wanna hang with Ahjanae and the kids?"

Darryl shook his head in disbelief. "If I'm running from the idea of marriage why would I want to be with the Wallace's?"

"Running isn't going to save you." Ryder said.

"Why can't Kendra be like Jen? Jen is happy not being your actual wife right?" Ryder frowned, "RYDER! NO! DON'T!"

"Everyone's last name is Wallace except hers. She puts on a brave face, but how long will that last?"

"Exactly," Malcolm said.

"Malcolm how come it's ok for him to think about marriage but not me?"

Malcolm put his hands over my ears, even though I could still hear. "You're not off the chickenhead diet, it'll kill you faster than fast food."

****

"That is huge!" I said looking at the specifications for Andrew and Tracy's new bed.

"I know! I look forward to having more space to stretch out."

I raised an eyebrow, "is that all?" I smiled. Tracy rubbed her stomach as she blushed.

Chantel was too quiet sitting next to Tracy. "What's up Chantel?"

"Huh? Oh nothing." She said trying to focus her attention.

"You've been acting very suspicious." I said taking in her sudden nervous energy.

She shifted in her chair; she opened and closed her mouth. Then she exhaled, "I've got a lot on my mind." Then she looked embarrassed so I let it go.

"Are you guys going with us during our down time? Malcolm said you guys might veer off."

"I don't know Derrick tells me." Then she exhaled.

Tracy looked at her, "you're married why does it matter?"

Chantel narrowed her eyes at Tracy. "What are you talking about?"

Tracy rubbed her stomach, and then she looked at Chantel. Chantel looked at me like I needed to get Tracy. I looked Chantel up and down she had no patience. "You're pregnant?"

Chantel threw her body backwards in her chair. "Fine! Please don't tell ANYBODY! Not even your men!" She said rolling her eyes at Tracy. "Derrick didn't want to say anything until after your wedding."

I gave her the biggest smile my mouth could muster. "Sweetheart I'm excited, but are you ok? You just had a baby. Your body can handle this?"

Chantel exhaled, "apparently cause it's happening."

"Are you mad?" I asked because her attitude seemed like it.

"No I'm happy, but..." She started crying suddenly and hard. "I don't want to be my mother. My grandmother said that I'm not but I'm scared. My mother was as sprung if not more than I am off of Derrick, off of my father. She had me and Cyrus back to back, but she didn't want us she wanted the man."

I moved next to Chantel and I rubbed her back on one side and Tracy was crying and rubbing the other side. "I used to think my momma hated me. I used to tell myself I would never come after my boys like she came after us, but then I found myself ready to box my boys just like she did us, but the worse is when I was going after Tina. I've never understood so much about my momma until I had to pull my own self off of that girl. At times there are going to be things that you do like your parents. Just keep in mind that you have a choice in how bad it gets. We are not our parents even if we do things just like them. You are a good mother, don't doubt that. Matter of fact, I'll need to come over more often because Malcolm always hogs Chanel. Don't cry sweetheart."

"I gotta cry! I wanted to punch Tracy in her face for outing me and I'm not mad at her. I gotta let it out."

Tracy sat up and cut her eyes at me, to say she didn't appreciate the comment. "Ok, I think this room is too small for all the pregnant hormones in here. How about we go beat the heat with some ice cream?"

Malcolm had the baby in his arms, while he listened to Derrick and Andre pounding away on their piano. Andre was focused and following his uncle's directions exactly. I asked them if they wanted to break for some ice cream. Derrick looked at Chantel, and then he smiled at her. She went to him and put her head on his shoulder. He kissed her cheek and told her it was ok.

When Malcolm and I went home that night he asked me how far along was Chantel. I stared at him and he said it was obvious, I told him I didn't know. I grabbed my granny gown and I walked towards the bathroom. Malcolm frowned at the gown. I told him we agreed to pull back right before the wedding. Malcolm bucked his eyes at me as he told me I couldn't be serious. I told him if he couldn't control himself I could go stay with Andy until the wedding. Malcolm looked completely pissed off.

I got in the shower and when I came out the bathroom in my granny gown Malcolm was sitting on the bed naked. I rolled my eyes at him and then I reached for my lotion on the dresser, it was gone. He held up the jar and asked me if I was looking for that. I laughed and told him to stop playing. He asked me what I was willing to do to get it. I put my hands on my hips as I said *nothing*. He told me that was not the good girl answer. He stood up and kissed me, he told me that he would compromise with me and we wouldn't have sex the night before the wedding. I told him he wasn't slick cause we weren't spending the night before together anyways. He hadn't considered that. Then he said that was his compromise, and I had to deal with it. So I told him I would see his compromise and raise him one, the week before the wedding he had to go stay with Derrick and I'd go with Andy. He frowned at me; I told him to tell me which one he wanted. He said he needed me now, so he would do the no sex the week before the wedding. We both laughed cause we knew he was lying.

****

"Kendra you did a fabulous job. It looks just like it did when I moved in." I said. I couldn't believe this would not be home for me anymore. With tears in my eyes I put the keys in Yussef's hands. He put his arm around me and rubbed my shoulder. He assured me he would take good care of my house. I asked him why his house was just sitting; he exhaled and said that house wasn't ready to be a home yet. I signed Kendra's invoice and then she left. I sat on the beautiful hardwood floors that were sparkling clean next to Yussef. I bumped him and told him we hadn't been alone in a long time. He nodded in agreement, but I could see the wheels of his mind turning. I told him to spill it. My poor baby was frustrated with his life. He told me that Angela was supposed to be it. She told him she couldn't date a man with kids, he didn't know about the girls until his heart was invested with her. He said their breakup wasn't anyone's fault, but you could hear his heartache behind it all the same. He said he was really trying to make things work with

Sylvia. He knows she loves him and he has a measure of love for her, but they both couldn't move pass the past. He said when they broke up the first time, she broke his heart, and he hadn't really moved past it. I rubbed his back and I told him to cheer up. Then I asked him about this latest girl I've seen around. I told him she's pretty, but I don't know if she was what I envisioned for him. He shrugged like a little kid and said it beats being alone. We laughed about his girls and little Jackson beating up her son. I laughed cause that little boy don't know how to keep his mouth shut, and his girls show him no mercy. I asked Yussef if he loved her and he said no immediately. I told him to breakup with her, the more time that passes the harder it was gonna be. I could tell he was holding something back, but I didn't press him to talk about it.

Yussef and I picked up his girls from school. He brought them back to the house and they squealed with excitement as they ran around the house they said it looked so different without my furniture. They picked their rooms and he told them after the wedding they were picking out furniture. Then they took me to Sophia's restaurant. Sasha and Sophia were outside when we pulled up. The girls jumped out of the car with excited energy before he came to a complete stop. Yussef blew out frustrated air; he got out the car and told the girls to never do that again. The girls apologized then he told them to come so that they could go. Sophia told him he was staying for dinner. Yussef tried to growl and say he was leaving, but Sophia growled louder and told him he was staying. They went back and forth for a minute. I put my arm under Sasha's as we watched them go back and forth. It was impressive watching him handle Sophia. Sasha started breathing heavy and I asked her if she was ok, she turned her eyes and then she told the girls to come inside while their father and her momma worked it out. As we walked inside Sophia was calmly talking to Yussef. Sasha kept looking out the window, I smacked her bottom and I told her to stop looking at that man like that. Sophia stayed on the floor and ate dinner with Yussef while my bridal party was in the banquet room enjoying our feast. Bernadette, that girl Renee, Tiffany, and Penny came out to say hi to Yussef when they saw his girls. I bumped Sasha and I asked her what was up. She shook her head to say nothing, so I bumped her again. Her eyes pleaded with me not to make her say. I hugged her, and then I rubbed her head. Sydney and Yesmina stayed stuck to Sasha like she was a magnet. Kind of reminded me of Malcolm with the boys. If I didn't know any better you'd think they were hers.

Yussef stayed longer than I thought he would. Travis came to the restaurant and they were having a good time talking at their table. I was happy that hanging with Travis pulled him out of his funk. Once I saw that he was feeling better and he gave me a big hug thanking me for listening I relaxed and started having fun with my girls.

Sabrina and Emerald and all my under aged ladies were coming up early Friday morning. Tomorrow and Friday were pamper days in the hotel spas. Sophia, Jade, and I passed out my goody bags for all of my bride's maids. Sasha squealed with excitement when she saw that the bags were Michael Kors totes and everyone was going crazy over the items I had in the bags. The bags were purple with gold hardware. This particular tote came with a scarf, but Carina found these beautiful Jade colored silk scarves that we placed on the bags instead and they became the perfect keepsake. I put expensive soaps, lotions, and the stuff I normally use in them. Sasha screamed when she found the Tiffany box. Everyone got a gold bangle that said, "Thank you for the support. Love Malcolm & Amber" on the inside. I loved the appreciation everyone had for my gifts, but if they were excited about this, I couldn't wait until they saw what else we had in store for them. Because security was so tight on this whole thing none of them really knew where we were going. Everyone was getting on party buses with overnight bags. Malcolm and the groom's men were staying at Derrick's and then they would be brought out. I knew they were most likely going to Andrew's club Elegant Affairs for the bachelor party and then recovering at Derrick's before they came out for the rehearsal dinner. We kissed the girls,

Travis, and Yussef goodbye and then we boarded our huge party bus.

Jade addressed everyone on the bus, "hello everyone, we are thrilled that you were able to make it. The ladies in the leather jackets are our personal escorts on this leg of the trip. There's no reason to be alarmed, their loyalty and ability to protect us have been proven. We are in good hands. With that said, we need to ask everyone to turn off their cellphones, place them in your purses, and the staff is going to make sure you aren't carrying bugs that you may not know about. We will be boarding another bus shortly. We will have more instruction at that time. Meanwhile indulge in the free flowing champagne." Everyone cheered as they did as they were told.

In Vallejo we got off one party bus and on to the next bus. After everyone was thoroughly checked we were on our way again. "Now let the party begin!" Sophia said addressing everyone. "What happens from this point onward is not to be discussed, and no one is to be judged. We are going to check-in to our rooms. The itineraries will be on your beds. If you are not in the designated spots on time then it will be assumed you do not want to go and you will be left behind."

Everyone gasped as we pulled up to the hotel. Carina and Tanisha were waiting with bellhops who were armed with carts to escort each guest to their rooms. As each person stepped off the bus Carina checked off their name, she put their room card keys in their hands. Then their bellhops led them to their rooms. I was the last person to get off the bus, "Mrs. Latour right this way." The bellhop said, but I was stuck with the realization that this was *FINALLY* happening. Sophia and Jade hugged me immediately and on cue we screamed. People looked at us like we were crazy but we didn't care. I told them this is it! It was FINALLY happening. I jumped around giggling like a big ole kid! Yay me! The bellhop laughed at us as he pushed our bags to my suite. I called Rosalind and asked her where she was once I was in my suite, she was staying with us, but I didn't know where she went. Everyone else had their own rooms. She said Gwen and Jenise kidnapped her, but she'd be up in a minute. We ran around the suite like little kids taking in the whole room. It was beautiful! It was two bedrooms Sophia and Jade claimed the second room with the two queen sized beds. So that meant Rosalind was bunking with me in the master suite.

I put my black bride T-shirt with a white bride sash on with my crown. I put on jeans and heels. Cassondra, Rosalind, and Gwen came to the room in jeans and heels with their Bride's Maids T-shirts. We cracked open a few bottles in the mini fridge to start our party off right. As we assembled in the lobby, we greeted each person with smiles and laughter as they came down in their T-shirts, jeans, and heels.

We went to a nice restaurant and had a lovely dinner in the banquet room where we ordered drinks and had a great time. Malcolm called and they had him videoconference us, "Amber! Remember that you are my good girl, behave yourself!" He said trying to look as mean as possible.

I blew him a kiss, "I will be as behaved as you are!" I yelled everyone cheered.

"You know what that means! All bets are OFF! It's going down tonight!" Bernadette yelled.

Malcolm smiled, "have fun. I love you Babygirl!"

When everyone said, "Aw!" Malcolm blushed and then he hung up. He didn't say goodbye or anything. After dinner we got back on the bus, and we went to a club. It was a strip club and our tables were reserved in the front of the room by the stage. There were other brides in the room, but we walked in deep and like we owned the club. Everyone was looking at our party, cause of our grand entrance. That girl Renee leaned in and said, "Look alive we got haters all around the room ladies."

The owner went up on the stage and he greeted everyone. He said we had four brides in the house tonight, and tonight was ladies' night. He asked all the brides to come to the stage. He asked each bride to state their name. "Callie, Melinda, Calindra, Amber!" each group cheered for their bride, and of course my group was the loudest. The owner said he wanted to know who was the BADDEST Bride in the house tonight. I cut my eyes at him cause it wasn't fair. He wanted to have a dance off, my group laughed. Callie and Calindra had no rhythm poor babies. But Melinda knew what she was doing, and she was watching me to see whether she needed to pull out the big guns or not. The owner thanked Callie and Calindra and they went back to their seats. If this girl was any good and it looked like she was I was going on the pole.

Normally I shy away from stuff like this and I'd let the other person have it, but this was MY weekend. I deserve to win for that reason alone. Melinda went over to the DJ and she picked her song. The beat came booming over the speakers, "My milkshake brings all the boys to the yard!" Melinda was good and she worked the crowd. I went over to the DJ while she did her little dance. I chose my song then I waited. She finished her little dance by hitting the splits. She just knew she had it in the bag. She actually looked at me and said I had been served. I smiled; while my people sat there quiet containing their annoyance cause she was doing too much. I told Melinda to get off my stage, when she left like she was doing me a favor I told the DJ to go. "She had them Apple bottom jeans! Boots with the fur!" My group stood up as I worked that stage. When I flipped upside down on the pole and I slid down slowly. You heard the whole room scream! Still upside down I busted the splits and then I slowly rolled on the floor. I twisted from a front split to a sideways split and then I rolled forward and put my face on my hands as I rested on my elbows. The owner said hands down I won. My group stood up and cheered. Then I went to say no hard feelings to Melinda but she was not having it. So I shrugged and went back to my seat. The show started and the men were good. By the end of the evening we were all beyond tipsy and having a blast. Of course she wasn't as fantastic as me, but Gwen got up and did her little thing on the stripper pole, but everyone and I do mean EVERYONE was shocked when Jade got up there and did her stuff as well. When we looked at her with our mouths hanging open, she smiled and shrugged. She said that she's been married for a long time and there was a reason why. We had a complete blast, but the pregnant women needed to rest. They hung with us for as long as they could. The rest of my wedding party went back to my room. We acted like teenagers as we played "I never" as a drinking game. I started with, I never had a daughter. So everyone who had daughters had to take a drink. Jade said she never cheated on her man. I didn't count being with Malcolm as cheating while I was with Dwayne but Sophia told me I better CHUG so I did. Sophia said she never had sex with a celebrity; Gwen and I were the only ones to drink to that until I told Tina football players count. Pretty soon we were all wasted and almost everyone passed out where they laid. Rosalind and Gwen were having a deep conversation when I heard Rosalind say, "you are so twisted it's hard to still be mad at you."

Gwen was crying and slurring her words, "I've got issues. I need to go back to therapy, I mean who does this? My man knows my past and loves me anyways. I can't believe I'm doing this to him."

"I can, you got issues!" Rosalind said slurring her words as well.

I put my arms around Gwen and I rubbed her back, "what's going on?"

"I've been seeing Tag!" She blurted out.

I took my arms from around her and Jenise's head popped up, "What?" Then I looked at her, "how long?"

"Gwen!" Jenise sounded so disappointed.

"I don't know the past two years at least." She said still crying.

"EEEWWLLLL! EEEWWLLLL!" I said scooting away from her, "he was still trying to get with me until I changed my number when Malcolm and I got back together."

"But that was a little over a year ago." She said.

"I know! That's what I'm saying. He was sleeping with you while he was still begging me to get with him."

She sat up and looked at me, "why didn't you ever get with him? He's far from ugly!"

"His approach never sat well with me. I couldn't ever be more than his friend. He would always go from zero to sixty with me. We weren't even dating and he proposed. Who does that? Why can't you leave him alone?"

"It's like we understand each other's dysfunctions. We don't ever have to talk about them in detail but we understand. And the release with him is unlike anything with my husband. With Tag and I it's always raw and uncut! My Martin loves me too much! He wants to make sure I'm happy all the time. Sometimes I want him to take me by the hair and bend me over. Pound the life out of me and not apologize for being rough later."

"But you know your father will kill him if he ever finds out."

She sighed, and then she looked at Rosalind who looked like she was about to explode.

"I'm sorry for hurting you like that. There is no excuse for how much I hurt you and your daughter. I know it changes nothing, but I went after Troy. It wasn't his fault."

I looked at Rosalind and tears poured out of her eyes. "I lost time with my man, because you were mad at someone else. Hurting about something I'll never know! You chose your pain over the pains you caused us! At least now I know that you are too twisted for words, but please excuse me if sometimes I flash. My forgiveness is a work in progress." Then she stood up and went in our room and shut the door.

"Gwen, you have to stop seeing him. I have a bad feeling about this." I pleaded.

Gwen didn't say anything she kept crying.

****

In the morning Auntie Lauren came with her daughter in-law Randi. Everyone was trying to get it together and get hydrated. Everyone spent all day in the spa getting pampered and treated like the true royalty that we are. When I sat in the chair to get my pedicure, Auntie Lauren sat next to me in a chair then she handed me a sealed envelope. It was addressed to me and it was from my mother. I immediately started crying. I put the letter in my pocket and I sat there quiet as the torture of what the letter could possibly say drove me crazy. When my pedicure and manicures were done, I went up to my room before my facial. I took off my slippers then I sat in the middle of the bed with my legs crossed. I nervously opened the letter.

My sweet baby girl Amber,

I love you so much, and I am so sorry that I couldn't be there for you on your special day just like I was for Jade. But I want you to know that I have looked forward to this day for a long time. I hope that too much time hasn't gone by and that you and Malcolm have gotten it together sooner than later. However, as my illness continues to tug at my health, I see more and more confusion stirring for you two. Here's something you always need to remember with Malcolm and you will be fine. He loves you from the bottom of his heart. He doesn't know love like you know it, and your love is the first genuine love that he's ever felt. He's used to people coming at him with an agenda. Continue to be patient with him, keep showing him that you love him, and eventually he will come around.

Now as for you... my beautiful Amber baby. In order for you to read this, you've finally learned to put your foot down and ask for what you need to be happy as well. I am so happy for you, and I don't want you to lose that. I could see how unhappy you were with David, and I know about the issue you had with him whether you admit it or not. Don't worry I didn't tell your father, and it's up to

you whether you ever share it with him. That boy isn't forthcoming and he has a lot of hurt in his heart. I'm so happy that you realize you deserve better.
I should've named you Annette junior. You are the perfect combination of your father and I. You act like me, and you look like him. I am so happy for you and I love you so much. I hope you never think or felt as if I didn't love you because that was NEVER the case. I love all my babies and I wish you all the best.
I gave your Auntie Lauren some of my things to incorporate with your wedding look. I know you will be a beautiful bride just like Jade was. I love you forever more, and I have every confidence that you and Malcolm will be very happy together just like your daddy and I.

Loving you forever more,

Your Momma
Annette Wallace

I laid down for a while thinking about my Momma and missing her dearly. As much time as I spent running from her cause I didn't understand her. The time we spent together actually getting along is the time that I hold dear to my heart. When I finally pulled myself together I went back to the group. My massage was so relaxing, Jade made us all continue to drink water to push all of our toxins out. Auntie Lauren kept hugging and kissing me and telling me how happy she was for me. Every time she hugged me I thought of my Momma, which made me emotional.
Once we were all relaxed and lounging by the pool I was explaining to my bridesmaids that the ceremony was going to be here at the hotel, and the reception site is a surprise. We were having a good time as everyone tried to guess where the reception was going to be. Carina called and said the men were on their way so we needed to make our way upstairs. So Auntie Lauren, Cassondra, Rosalind, Sophia, Jade, Grace, Jenise, and Gwen went upstairs with me. Everyone else went up to their rooms.
We were sitting in the room sipping on water with lemon hydrating and preparing for tomorrow night while we were all letting go and having the time of our lives. There was a knock at the door like it was the police. Gwen opened the door, and then she said it was her daddy. Uncle Frank came in the room with a very rarely seen smile plastered on his face. He hugged Gwen then he picked me up in a bear hug as he kissed my cheeks. He told me he was so excited for me and he was so proud to be my father's stand-in and walk me down the aisle tomorrow. Gwen turned red to match her hair. Where I should've felt extremely happy and felt loved by my uncle's rarely seen emotional state I couldn't stop looking at Gwen. She was on fire. I asked her what was wrong, and Gwen shook her head as she fought with herself to get it together. I looked at Jade and she and Sophia shared the same disgusted expression. Uncle Frank's face returned to its normal seriousness as he looked at his daughter. He asked her what was wrong with her. Gwen stood there shaking her leg and fidgeting with her hands. Jade marched over to Gwen and went off. Even Uncle Frank leaned back as Jade went off. "Can we ever do something as a family without your drama! Why can't you be happy for Amber? Everything is not a competition!"
"You weren't this excited about my wedding! You've always been more invested in Jade and Amber than you have been with me your only daughter! Amber gets pregnant before she can even drive, but I'm an adult and it's all out murder because I was pregnant before the wedding. Now you're here hugging and kissing her when you only said hi to me

when you walked in the door. You act like you wish they were your daughters instead of me! You've always been more fond of Uncle Tim's kids then me and my brothers." Uncle Frank didn't say anything he stood there glaring at Gwen.

"My point to you is why do you have to do this right now? Your issues with your father are your issues with your father. Why would you do this to Amber?" Jade said as my usual protector.

"Amber, I'm sorry!"

"No you're not! Don't you lie and say you are. You're the same selfish little girl that you've always been. No one else's feelings matter more than yours. You act so much like your mother it isn't even funny." Then Auntie Lauren turned to me. "Amber I know it's your day, but I think you should really reconsider whether you even want her in your wedding on your special day. Look at the drama she's bringing and you haven't even rehearsed yet."

Everybody looked at me. Then Uncle Frank took me by the hand and led me out to the balcony. He put his arm around me and he apologized for his daughter. He told me he wouldn't be offended if I told her that she couldn't be in my wedding. He exhaled and then he went back into his excitement for my special day, and how honored and touched he was that I chose him. He told me I could never know how much it means to him. Even though Gwen was sitting there watching us I hugged my Uncle and enjoyed his excitement for my day. He exhaled and said he's so disappointed in his daughter. I tried to keep a straight face. He looked at my face, and then he said he knows. Then he said she's not new to this life, she knows how it goes. He didn't understand how she could possibly think that she could hide anything from him. He said her husband is soft and weak; he's not even concerned about him. He exhaled; he said he hates that kid. He was referring to Tag. He asked me why I never dated him. I told him there was always something about him, not that I could ever consider myself as a good judge of character. I told Uncle Frank when he and Gwen dated I couldn't go behind my cousin even if she didn't care. He exhaled and looked at Gwen who was staring. "Genetics!" Then he asked me for a moment with his daughter. Gwen couldn't wait to get out there with her father; I didn't even have to tell her that he wanted to talk to her. We sat on the couch watching them talk; Auntie Lauren said Gwen acts so much like her mother it wasn't funny. Sophia asked what happened to her mother, and Auntie Lauren said a guilty "I don't know." No one believed her but we let it go. Gwen backed away from her father and he had that crazy look in his eyes, Jade popped up and she went out to him. She told Gwen to go for a walk, and then she hugged Uncle Frank. He was livid and the look on his face told Gwen she better run. Gwen moved very quickly through the suite and out the door. Jade rubbed Uncle Frank's back as he spoke leaning on the balcony, I went back out there and I stood on the other side of him. Jade was telling Uncle Frank that each person has to choose who they're going to be, and Gwen has a choice in how she lives her life. Uncle Frank put his arms around us and he told us that he was so proud of us. Then he told us again how much he always wanted to hold us when we were born. He said he's always loved us so much, and he was proud that we never let anything hold us back from moving forward. "Have I told you two the story about when I met your momma?" Jade and I smiled, but I don't think Jade remembered any more than I did. "Everybody was scared of me, and she was the only little thing who wasn't. I wasn't in the mood for her sass that night and she didn't care." He chuckled, "she reminded me so much of my wife I could've strangled her. Your momma was always strong even when other people thought she was weak. She was good to people even when they didn't deserve it. As long as they didn't make her mad." He rubbed our shoulders, "she fit right on in with us as if she had always been a part of our family and she didn't know it." Uncle Frank took a deep breath, "family is so important. I know I don't have to tell you all this. Amber you tell me if he gets too big headed. I can step in at any time as the honorary Tim."

I kissed my uncle's cheek. "Thank you, but I know we got this. You might wanna offer your services to my daughter in-laws. My sons always seem to want to show their butts." We stood out there for a long time, until Carina respectfully came out and lightweight scolded us for not getting ready.

I showered then I put on my purple satin sweetheart neckline knee length cocktail dress. This dress hugged every curve and left nothing to the imagination. Again, it was my weekend and where I would normally back down this was my opportunity to not care for once. I put on my jade accessories from Jade's wedding, and then I grabbed my gold clutch. I gathered my hair into a side ponytail. Rosalind made sure my makeup was everyday nice and then Auntie Lauren snapped pictures of us. We were in our own remember when world. Carina came to check on us again. You could tell she was pleased that we were ready and still on time. Auntie Lauren held my hand as we took the elevator down to the lobby. I don't know why I was nervous about seeing Malcolm. Andy and Tracy were the first to see us. Andy smiled really big at me and he came over and gave me the biggest hug and kiss on my cheek. Then I hugged Tracy as well. They looked so nice, and I was happy I didn't have to tell anyone exactly what they needed to wear tonight. Uncle Jeff told me it wasn't too late to tell Uncle Frank to sit down and let him handle everything. I hugged him and I thanked him for being a good sport about this whole thing. He looked at me out the corner of his eyes to say *yea right*. Carina led us to the grass and gazebo area. Malcolm was talking to Darryl and Yussef with Andre who was standing next to him and mimicking his Poppa's stance. When Malcolm turned around and looked at me he smiled really big. Again everyone said, "AW!" and he blushed as he walked to me. He walked directly to me and threw his arms around me and kissed me deeply. Public displays of affection weren't really Malcolm's thing, so this kiss made me extremely weak in the knees. Uncle Jeff told Malcolm to hold on for one more day. Malcolm held on to his smile as he rested his forehead on mine and told me he loved me. Suddenly I didn't know if I would make it to tomorrow myself. When I saw Gwen hurry out I tried to decide if I even wanted to deal with her. If she acted like this today, how would she be tomorrow? Malcolm was talking to Uncle Jeff when he stopped and looked at me. He followed my eyes to Gwen, and then he asked me *what*. I shook my head to say nothing. Carina was trying to direct everyone to their places and Malcolm told her to hold on as he pulled me away from everyone. When we were to the side he asked me what Gwen did. I knew he wasn't going to let it go. So I told him about what happened and what Uncle Frank said. He asked me if I wanted her in the wedding. I told him I did, I said outside of men including her father, we were close and I loved her very much. I said I honestly thought the drama would be from the pregnant women and their hormones, I wasn't expecting Gwen to be the one. Malcolm called Gwen over, and it seemed like everyone froze. She came over with sad eyes. "So my Queen just informed me about your little melt down upstairs. Are we going to have a problem with you?"

"Amber I'm sorry. My emotions ran away from me. I will try my best to be on good behavior."

Malcolm shook his head, "Gwen that doesn't work. Either you're going to behave or you're not. There's no room for try. Only because she loves you will you get a chance to *try* that again. Because as far as I'm concerned that answer right there just put you on my radar. And the last place you want to be is on my radar. I'm not your daddy, I won't handle you with loving regard."

"Gwen, you know how long I've waited for this. Please don't be the reason for the drama. I need my cousin to be there supporting me and walking down the aisle with me. Please Gwen!"

Gwen hugged me and apologized again, she promised to be on best behavior. Uncle Frank was watching us, but he didn't say anything. Malcolm told Gwen to go away and then he told me it was up to me, but he didn't want her in the wedding anymore. I told him that we should see how the rehearsal went and then dinner and then we could make a decision then. He agreed, although I know he already made that hard decision already. I didn't want her to be out. We practiced the wedding march a few times. I didn't care that my procession line was long. I needed all my closest loved ones in the wedding. Then we had the rehearsal dinner in the restaurant at the hotel. Malcolm stood up, "I would like to thank each one of you for being here for us. All of you know firsthand how special this woman is to me. How much we've fought over the years, and my plain ole ignorance that has delayed this day until this moment. It means a lot to us that each one of you could be here with us. Thank you for all of your support and help getting us to get to this day. Especially my boys thank you to each one of you for being better men than I could ever be. Watching you love your mother and then the women in your lives has helped me grow up as well." Everyone Aw'ed! Darryl's eyes moved around the room, I wondered if he felt left out with that comment. So I went over and kissed his cheek, and then I hugged Yussef. Everyone stood up and said congratulations to us, and lots of people snapped pictures. Malcolm kept kissing me and my heart fluttered, I could definitely get used to this.

My Aunt Emma came over and hugged Jade and I. She congratulated me on my big day tomorrow. When she stepped to the side the people who were with her but behind her stepped forward to hug and congratulate me. I looked at Jade cause I had no idea who they were. The man smiled at me and said I looked so much like my father. I looked at Emma for help cause I had no idea who he was. She smiled and said the man was my Uncle Elmer Jr. Jade and I were a little taken back, cause outside of Aunt Emma my mother's family was off limits to us. I was confused as I looked at him, he didn't give me the creeps like the others did. Aunt Emma said I probably didn't remember him at my father's funeral. Apparently we were introduced and everything, but that day was such a blur to me still. Malcolm zeroed in on my confused expression and he came over and introduced himself. Aunt Emma reminded Malcolm that my Uncle Elmer and my Aunt Anne ran the store in New York, and her nieces ran the store in Atlanta. I asked Malcolm what store she was talking about. Malcolm shook my Uncle Elmer's hand and said it was nice to actually meet him in person. My uncle introduced his wife, children and grandchildren. Then my Aunt Anne introduced her family as well. Then cousins I never knew I had were introducing their selves to Jade and I. I looked at Jade confused because my Aunt Anne was as fair skinned as I was. My Uncle Elmer's skin looked like clay it was so smooth and slightly bronzed. Malcolm looked at Jade and I as he explained that my father jointly owned my Aunt Emma's stores with her and my momma. When they passed away they left their shares in the stores to him. He said Emma runs the businesses basically and she brought in my Aunts and Uncles. Then Anne said that their youngest sister died in a car accident some years ago, and so her girls took over her roll of running the stores in Atlanta. Malcolm said that my Aunt Emma consults with Jenise and Gwen regularly for their marketing needs etc. I was still confused as to how they were related to us. My Uncle Elmer explained the whole story, how we were related. I didn't know very much about anything with my momma before my daddy. One by one my boys came over and protectively introduced their selves. Although Derrick remembered them and he asked where the other Aunt was, and they told him she died in a car accident. Darryl asked Derrick how he remembered them. He said they were at Daddy's funeral. Darryl was quiet for a minute, and then he apologized for not remembering them. Uncle Elmer said it was ok, that day was too emotional for everyone; he said everything happened so suddenly. Derrick asked why no one reached out to us when my Aunt passed away. They said they had had back-to-back deaths in their family and they were tapped out. Then my Aunt Emma said it was her fault for not contacting us, but she honestly didn't think we remembered them. I looked at my Uncle and Aunts, all links to my momma that I didn't realize I had. Tonight was not the night for it, but I wanted to understand more about these strangers linked to me by blood. I could tell Jade wanted to know as well. Timothy and Malachi came over and met them. When Malachi stood next to Uncle Elmer there was a resemblance, we talked about that for a long time. Malcolm led me around our banquet room as I said hello to more family members and close friends. Then we sat down to enjoy more of our meal.

When we finished eating Malcolm asked me to take a walk with him. Everyone gave us a *Yeah-Right!* Look when we said we were going for a walk. Malcolm held my hand as he led me to a fountain over to the side away from everyone. He had me sit in his lap and then he had my lip locked in a kiss that seemed to go on and on. We sat down there for a long time kissing and not saying one single word. Eventually he said we had to stop cause he was on the verge of taking me to his room. When I didn't protest the idea he told me I had to get away from him cause I was melting his resolve to wait one more day. As he walked me back to our room he asked me what I wanted to do about Gwen. I told him unless she did something before the ceremony I wanted her to stay in. He said he figured that much. He kissed me one more time and then I went in my room. Auntie Lauren, Rosalind, Sophia, Cassondra, and Jade were sitting at the table talking and waiting for me. Auntie Lauren had a box in front of her. They all smiled at me as I sat down, I blushed and told them to stop staring. Auntie Lauren took out my Momma's pearl necklace, earrings, and bracelet, a brooch, and a fascinator hat with a veil. She told us how my momma picked them out and she held onto them for me. She told Auntie Lauren to make sure my dress was lace, and how to encourage me in that direction. I told Auntie Lauren that Raynel and I had a different plan for my hair. She said she already talked to her and she was on board. She also said that was why Raynel wasn't here tonight preparing my hair for tomorrow. My style would be so much simpler now. When I felt a little tired I excused myself, and then Cassondra and Auntie Lauren went to their rooms. Rosalind and I talked for a little while giggling and carrying on until we fell asleep.

****

I woke up and my heart was pounding out of my chest. This day was FINALLY here! I laid in the bed staring at the ceiling for a while. This was really going to happen. I could hear movement outside of my bedroom door and Rosalind was already up and out. Sophia came in my room with two cups of coffee and a big smile. She gave me a cup then she asked me how I slept. I told her I barely slept, but I felt GREAT! We sat and reminisced about the good times over the years. Jade came in and the three of us laughed over Sophia and I's ignorance in my youth when all this began with Malcolm. Jade said she never understood why I would take so many chances knowing who our Momma was just to be with Malcolm. She said she used to think I was crazy, but she confessed that she was fortunate that Sonny moved slow otherwise she would've been in the same kind of trouble.

Sophia shared that Richard came alone to the wedding. Her eyes stayed on the floor. She said she had no intentions of allowing anything to happen between them. She said everything has been wonderful between her and Travis, and she doesn't want to jeopardize that. She sighed and said Richard is hurting cause Sasha moved back to the Bay and their relationship has fallen apart. I asked her what did she do to that man to make him so sprung. She shrugged and said once upon a time she loved him. Now she doesn't know how she feels about him, but she knows she's in love with Travis. Jade put her hands on Sophia's shoulders, "Travis is a good man. AND he's good for you. Richard is creating more and more chaos for his life. Keep moving forward don't get caught up looking back."

After our massages and pamper morning. Raynel came to do my hair. She created a textured pulled back look for my hair. I liked it better than what we originally had planned. Rosalind made sure that my makeup was waterproof, and she said that since Malcolm was completely open and affectionate we used smudge proof lipstick. I loved

365

my look as I looked in the mirror. I thanked her as I clapped my hands and I jumped around. Cassondra and her girls came just in time. She said all of my maids were dressed and I was last on the list. The photographer Paula snapped away as I hugged my girls as I became overwhelmed with emotion. This was really going to happen. Malcolm finally belonged all to me, and I him. I looked at my dress on the hanger and my heart fluttered. Auntie Lauren came in the room and she said this was our moment alone. She opened another envelope from my Momma.

"Dear Babygirl,
You are a beautiful bride! I am so happy for you, **(kiss both her cheeks).** *"* So my auntie did. *"Remember that today is your day and you deserve to be happy in each endeavor.* **(Help her put her lace dress on. Hug her for me, and tell her how beautiful she is**.*)* *"* So we did as we were told and I put my dress on. I looked at my bareback in this dress and I smiled and thanked my Nana again. Auntie Lauren put my Momma's jewelry on me. *"Amber Wallace remember that you are a child of love and you deserve every happiness that life can give you. It's ok to love your husband and make his happiness a priority. But don't let that man run over you because he will if you let him. It's ok if you put your foot down from time to time just to remind him that his primary job is to keep you happy. Remember your Momma and remember that you fear no one!* **(Give her a hug and kiss, then put the hat on her**.*)* *"* Full of tears my auntie did as she was told. *"Congratulations Amber Wallace you are now Amber Latour! I love you Babygirl, enjoy your day!"*

Auntie Lauren and I fell on each other's necks. I blew my nose then I told myself to get it together. This was it! Auntie Lauren let the photographers in and they snapped all kinds of pictures of us. Raynel made sure my hat was secure. All of my maids were in my room looking like a sea of purple. Everyone looked beautiful; we took pictures of me with each person. All of us together, groupings of us. There was finger food in the room, but I was too excited to eat anything. I was so excited that I kept saying goofy thing after goofy thing. Bernadette said she always suspected that Darryl acted like me, but today was undeniable proof.

When Tanisha came to get everyone she looked beautiful in her dress. Rosalind looked at me and shook her head like she knew what I was thinking. I had the photographer snap a ton of pictures of me and my baby. Latia helped her usher everyone including Gwen down stairs for the ceremony. Everyone left Uncle Frank and I alone, his face was very serious as he took me in. I asked him if he thought Malcolm will like my dress. He told me I could come down in a potato sack and Malcolm would love it. Then he told me that since his kid brother wasn't here he felt as though the fatherly responsibilities should fall on his shoulders for the four of us. I told him that we were covered between him and Uncle Jeff. Tanisha knocked on the door and told us it was time. Uncle Frank held his hand out, and I laid my hand on his.

When we stepped on the elevator a little girl and her mother were riding down with us. Both of their eyes got big when they saw me, then the little girl said I looked beautiful. I thanked them as the little girl looked up to me with stars in her eyes. Uncle Frank led me to the double doors. I smiled as I took in the scenery. There were gold chavarri chairs with purple cushions and a purple runner down the aisle way. There were green and white flowers all around that stood tall outside of purple and gold vases. The gazebo was now gold and purple and green ribbons floated on the breeze. Everyone was looking my way but I could tell they didn't see me yet. Yesmina, Jada, Erin and Sydney walked down the aisle together and everyone ooh'ed them. Then Andre my ring bearer and Amaya my flower girl walked down the aisle as Amaya dropped white rose petals for my feet. Then the music changed and everyone stood. Malcolm and all of my men had mile wide smiles as soon as they saw me. Everyone in the audience smiled as I approached. But when I passed them you heard them gasp and ooh my dress. I rolled my eyes at Gwen cause I knew her tears were not for me. Uncle Frank proudly passed my hand to Malcolm who stared at me in appreciation. He kissed my cheek and told me I looked beautiful. Everyone sat down. My cousin Landrell officiated the ceremony. He was hilarious and he even made Malcolm laugh. Landrell smiled at me and then he asked out loud, "who gives this woman in marriage?" Andy, Derrick, Darryl, Malachi, Timothy, Uncle Jeff, Uncle Frank, Uncle Dale, Auntie Lauren, Jade, Sophia, and my Aunt Emma all stood up and said, "WE DO!" As if they had this moment planned. They stood long enough so that I could see each one of their faces and their sincere APPROVAL of my union to this man. I smiled at each of them, but when I looked at Andy a couple of tears fell from my eyes. Malcolm wiped them and then he kissed my cheek. Having my family stand for my parents was almost the same as having them here. When it was time for the rings I turned to Jade and handed her my bouquet, while Sophia handed me Malcolm's band. Everyone laughed as Malcolm took my hand twirled me around while holding his chest. Everyone laughed as he shook his head and said I was too much. He kissed me quick and then we got back on script and placed our bands on each other's fingers. All of my diamonds sparkled so bright you would've thought they were dancing. Malcolm kissed me long and deep when Landrell gave him permission to kiss his bride. Everyone applauded loud and hard for us. Then Tanisha thanked all the family and close friends for attending. She said transportation to the reception site would leave in thirty minutes, however they encouraged everyone to get their seats now because there was no room for anyone extra to ride with the wedding party. My old neighbors the Halls and Ms. Connie came over and hugged me and posed for a few pictures with Malcolm and I. Everyone cleared out and we took tons of pictures. Malcolm kept his eyes on me, and whenever I turned to see if he was watching me walk away. He was watching me with a smile of appreciation. The guest had been gone about thirty minutes when horses and a carriage arrived. The carriage was white with gold hardware and the insides were red and plush. There were two additional horses with riders on either sides of the carriage. When Malcolm said that the carriage was for us and the kids, all the kids erupted in excitement. Darryl said he needed to come with us to supervise the kids. When Malcolm stared at him he said, "Aw! Daddy don't be like that! This is your day and I'm just trying to make it less stressful." Then he smiled real big. To everyone including Darryl's surprise Malcolm said ok. Malcolm helped me in the carriage first, the back row was for us. Then he helped the girls, Andre and Emmanuel into the middle of the carriage. He and Darryl got in last. Darryl explained how everyone needed to waive to the peasants as we rode by. Then he said that they needed to keep an eye out for anyone who may look froggy as well. If anyone felt like jumping he would put them down.

The coachman told the four horses pulling our carriage to go and they started their stroll. People in the hotel came out to see us off. Darryl and the kids waved to people as they pointed and waved at us. The girls excitedly waved while the boys sat with serious eyes looking at everyone. The cars that passed us looked into our carriage to see who was occupying one lane of traffic while they passed in the second. Our photographer pulled on the side of us and one of them hung out the car taking candid shots of us in the carriage. I told Malcolm this was an over the top surprise to our day. When we pulled off the road into a driveway the bus drove ahead. Malcolm's only concern was kissing me, and showering me with love and attention. Even though it's only been a week, it felt like we hadn't been together in forever. The Coachman told the horses to go again and they trotted up the hill. All the kids and Darryl gasped when they caught sight of the castle.

All of our guests were out and on the grass cheering us on as we arrived in our carriage. The wedding party was waiting as they aligned the walkway and little drawbridge. The children walked ahead of us as we walked inside the courtyard, which was beautifully decorated with my colors. Everyone oohed and awed the castle as they came inside the courtyard taking the whole scene in. The photographers snapped pictures of everyone as they entered.

The brick walls complimented the decorations perfectly. Each table had a shimmery gold tablecloth, with a deep purple overlay, then there were Jade accents and napkins on the table, for all of our guests. The head table was covered in gold with purple and jade accents. Everyone's purple dresses and vest popped when we sat at the table. The lighting was strung across the tops of the castle once the sunset the lighting would make it appear as though the lights were a beautiful chandelier hanging from the sky. The photographer's jobs were clear. I wanted at least three good pictures of every single person there. So they were making their way around the reception taking pictures of everyone. When we sat at the table Malcolm rubbed my leg under the table. He couldn't not touch me. As the sunset the guest oohed the lighting cause it was really pretty. I also noticed the Mitigated Staff that were up high watching everything as all the Wallace's and Latour's came together to celebrate. Malcolm stood in the middle of the dance floor and he called me as the music started to play for our song. As soon as "there'll be no darkness tonight, lady our love will shine, lighting the night...." Played fireworks went off in a big BOOM! Everyone jumped; all of my boys were reaching in their clothes. **"DANG IT MALCOLM YOU CAN'T BE SURPRISING EVERYBODY WITH BANGS! WARN A BROTHA!"** Darryl yelled as even Malcolm chuckled. Our dance was beautiful and everything I dreamed it would be. For the father daughter dance Uncle Jeff was too excited. We didn't do a two-step. We danced a waltz around the dance floor. He smiled very proudly at me the entire time. I was very impressed that he learned this just for me. Everyone stood up one by one and wished us well and told us how happy they were for us. To everyone's surprise Malcolm stayed on the dance floor with me most of the night. People kept saying they didn't know he could dance, but when they played New Edition how could he not dance? Our evening was perfect!

Episode 18

Kendra

This wedding was over the top and fabulous! I don't ever think I've had more fun in a dress. Darryl kept screaming "OOWW!" at me whenever I turned my back to him. After a while I learned to back away from him and try not to bump into anything or anyone when I did. It was kind of a buzz kill when I saw the sadness in Ahjanae's eyes; I think she's getting to that breaking point. Ryder's been hinting around about having another baby, and I know she wants to do it. She's battling with herself about what she wants more the baby or the man. She doesn't want to admit it to me but I can see it all over her. Ryder can see it even though he's trying to pretend like he doesn't. I can't ask Darryl about it cause we end up arguing about the relevance of marriage, but I mean come on! I know the wedding is just the show, and this show was over the top! But everything he wants with me I want with him, but I want no, I need that paper. How could he not look at his parents and see how important that sort of commitment is. The time that I've spent with his momma recently has been amazing. Darryl is a momma's boy and she loves him dearly. Anything momma wants she gets, but she's the same way with her boys. She always has their backs even if its tough love and telling them to get it together when they step out of line. As for tonight!!! It was all about Amber and Malcolm. I didn't know Malcolm had teeth or that he even knew what a smile was. That man is so sprung off Amber, it's cute and amazing to see. I wonder if Darryl will ever grow up? If he'll ever be that man that I need him to be.

A fancy car pulled up for the happy couple. Darryl was hugging his momma and feeling his drink. "I'm so happy for you momma. You stuck it out, and here you are."

"Thanks baby," she said kissing his cheek.

"Momma!"

"Yes baby?" She was looking at him with so much love in her face even though her groom was ready to go.

Darryl had his back to me while he held on to his momma. "I love her, I always have." Amber looked at me. "But she's never taken me seriously. She wants me to say I'll marry her, but she hasn't done her part. I don't want to marry nobody who's a flight risk momma. Momma! What do I do?"

"Darryl!" His father said looking completely annoyed.

"Yes daddy?" Darryl said with a drunken smile.

"You're drunk, my wife is tipsy. I got plans for us that don't include you. You're not ready to get married so stop trying to force the idea. Let it go and release my woman!" Malcolm said

I wondered if Malcolm was tipsy cause I saw him throwing them back as well. When he smiled that's when I could tell he was toasted as well. He patted Darryl on the back loud and hard, and then they hugged. Amber started crying when Drew and D-Rick came to hug her. Yussef was standing to the side and she called him over demanding a hug from him as well. Amber said a tearful thank you to everyone as Malcolm pulled her to the car. She was calling out thank you's, and stuff like that. Her dramatics made me think of Darryl at his silliest. Darryl called out, "Momma can I go with you?" Malcolm stopped smiling and cut his eyes at Darryl as he told him to stop playing. Tired of the whole tug of war Malcolm picked Amber up and gently put her in the car as she continued her acceptance speech. I teased Darryl and told him his momma was getting pregnant tonight. Neither Darryl nor his brothers thought that was funny. So I reminded Darryl that he said the same thing to me when my parents got married. Then he looked at his brothers and told them this was his fault.

"AW! SHOOT!" Darryl said taking my hand and leading me to the dance floor.

"This song is for the newlyweds." Chantel said as she caressed the microphone.

"And before we begin, gentlemen.... you're welcome!" D-Rick said, then he put his saxophone to his lips.

I looked at them in amazement. I've never seen Chantel Shaw perform live, how does all of that come out of her little body! And who knew that D-Rick knew how to play anything? I LOVE this song, and I remember watching her sing it on TV. Darryl stared me in my eyes as our bodies swayed to the music. As a waiter walked past us, Darryl grabbed a champagne glass off their platter, "drink up Kendra." He smiled at me.

"You trying to get me drunk?"

"If that's what it takes for you to spend the night with me, yes. How you trying to play a brotha? You don't kick it with me no more."

I exhaled, "I don't want to talk about this now." I said looking up at the beautiful star lit sky. The way they placed these lights it didn't seem like we were outside. It seemed like we were under the most beautiful ceiling ever.

"Right so drink up baby. I need you to be open to us tonight. Even if it's only for tonight." He kissed my bare shoulder." When I attempted to say something he took a drink of my glass and then he kissed me. "Bump this fancy soda stuff. We need the real liquor! Where's my auntie Grace or Jade, they got the real stuff you need to be drinking right now!"

"Can we finish the song first, I love it."

He pulled me in close, "fine! But I'm getting you drunk tonight! Jayman is just gonna have to be mad at me."

When he asked his Auntie Jade about her stash, she pointed at the open bar and said a very tipsy "no stash needed." Darryl led me to the bar, "how you doing my friend?" He smiled at the bartender. "My lady needs a few drinks, I need each drink to hit her like a heat seeking missile. BUT! I need her to enjoy the experience. Can you handle that? Do you understand what I'm saying?"

"Hhhhmmmm, let me think." She said putting her finger up to her chin.

Darryl looked at the other bartender. "My man can you help me out? She's too new I need an OG, can you handle it?"

The guy nodded, "I got you!" He started mixing. "We'll call this," he put his hands up for dramatic affect. "**EXCLUSIVE**!"

Darryl started laughing, "*exclusive*! I like that. Here you go baby tell daddy if you like it." I took a sip and it was good. I gave them a thumbs up. "Hold on let me taste." He took my glass. "KB! This is like a fizzy Kool-aide with a kick!" Then Darryl leaned in. "I'm gonna need another one like that, AND two more but in manly glasses. Don't put the pineapple and umbrella in it."

The bartender smiled, "I got you." Then he showed the other bartenders how to make his drink.

Darryl said the other girly drink was for Ahjanae cause she needed to mellow out. I told Ahjanae she had to try this drink. She loved it; we gave my momma, Lanie, and anyone who wasn't pregnant one. The music was bumping the drinks were flowing. We were slurring our words and having a good time.

Lanie

Thank goodness Lynn couldn't make it cause Eric and my cousin JoJo were my only partners in crime. Everybody else came hooked up. This Donavan character seemed ok and Tina was totally in strong like over him. Erica brought Josh of course, probably taking notes for her own wedding. I tried really hard, but as I drank and the wonderful feeling of my alcohol came over me so did the sadness. I miss Dorian so much, and he would've loved tonight.

Watching Darryl drool all over Kendra was hilarious, but eventually it was too painful to watch. EJ and Shelby were all over the dance floor. My brother takes sprung to a whole other level, but then again he is Ethan junior, my daddy may be quiet, and a little mean, but no matter what; he's so sprung off of my momma like nobody's business. You know it's bad when your parent's relationship makes your heart hurt. I blinked my eyes really hard as I watched my Grammy on the dance floor with Frank. I've never seen her look at him the way she was tonight. Frank on the other hand was reminding me a lot of my dad. When he approached her I didn't think anything of it, cause I have seen him around Grammy a lot more since her mother died. After Grampy died Gram held on for a few years, but they have been *interesting* since Gram's passing. I was standing there openly watching when my Aunt Gwen bumped me with her drink in her hand. "What's up kiddo?"

"I don't understand what's happening."

She exhaled and then she took another gulp of her drink. "They're still married, I guess this was bound to happen sooner or later."

"Married?" I blinked my eyes at her.

"Yep! They got married a little after your father was born. I don't know why they broke up exactly, but I'm the bastard that's kept them apart."

"Auntie, you're not a bastard. Frank raised you, you're more like a loose cannon if anything."

She smiled, "I am, aren't I."

I looked at her, "that's not a license to go crazy. We need you here, and we need you sane."

Aunt Gwen looked at me, "am I that transparent? I've been good all these years, constantly fighting with myself to be better. Why can't I just be myself? I'm tired of conforming."

I shook my head, "I know what you mean. Everybody's always telling me to calm down and trying to convince me that I'm not a baby. I feel like this, if someone does something to rub me the wrong way I should be allowed to call them on it. My dad keeps telling me I can't run around killing people. Running people over, Stabbing people, or shooting them. I don't think it's fair, but what are you going to do?" I shrugged.

Aunt Gwen started laughing hard at me, "your mother is right. There is something wrong with you."

I shook my head no, "nope. Nothing more than the average person. I just say and do the things that people only think about but don't have the courage to do. I know it's hard but I do see the benefit sometimes of toning down my reactions. It's not only for other people's protection. It's for mine too. If you let go, you're going to hurt a lot of people."

"Who's said something to you?" She stared at me.

I smiled, "nobody has said anything to me. I've got eyes and I've been looking at your family. Uncle Martin just looks sad. Normally he looks sprung. I need him in my life, and I can only imagine how much Peyton and Paige need him. He's a good dad, husband, and you actually got you a FINE man following you around after all these years and child birth three times. I imagine after you delivered Perry's big ole head he falls in, but he still loves you anyways. Stop acting like your daddy and be good to him. Uncle Martin deserves your love."

"It's not my daddy's blood that plagues me."

"Can you for once tell me what happened with your momma?"

She shook her head real hard, "can't!" Then she kissed my cheek, "remember to take your own advice." Then she walked away. I looked at my grandparents looking like my parents on the dance floor and I shivered in disgust. It's bad enough watching my daddy act sprung, this was just not right.

Drew and EJ took a break from dancing with their women. Tracy had her feet up while she rubbed her stomach. I walked over as Shelby was saying all these babies were making her want another one. I sat down as I asked her if she would have anymore. She shrugged and said she wouldn't mind and she didn't think EJ cared. Tracy asked Shelby what congregation she was in. I didn't realize Tracy went to service. She said she'd have to visit her cause it would be nice for Andre to interact with more family that went to service. "Verses family that doesn't go?"

"When we go to service it's always nice to look up and see family is all I mean."

"We're all in the same congregation." Shelby said moving her hand in a circle.

"I don't go anymore."

"It's never too late to come back. Yussef comes to my congregation from time to time." Tracy said.

Instantly my sadness was gone. "He does? Is he regular?" I looked around the party for him. He was sitting by Jeff laughing about something.

"Not yet." Tracy said like she didn't understand my sudden change.

"Any news?" I asked Shelby. She knew I was talking about Dorian.

"I haven't seen either one of them. After I told Dorian's mom I wasn't thinking about even considering going to the wedding she hasn't mentioned another word about it. "

It felt like my throat was going to close up. "Do you think they're married?"

"I honestly don't know, but I haven't seen either of them in a minute, and Dorian hasn't missed one service since he came back."

I got up and searched the sea of people until I found my momma. She was dancing with my daddy. I didn't care I walked up to them on the dance floor. "Mmmooommmmaaa!"

My momma jumped and then she frowned at me. "What is wrong with you? You see me and your daddy grooving!" They continued to dance.

My father looked at me with red eyes and then he smiled. I knew he was gone. "Momma did Dorian get married?"

She moved her head in irritation. "Why do you care? You didn't want him no how. Acting like a complete spoiled brat that last time he was STILL begging you to reconsider! It's not like he was asking you to do something foreign to you. You like to fight too much, and you lost this battle. I don't know how you could think you would ever find someone better than him."

My mouth dropped open. "Momma are you high too?"

Irritation flashed over her face. "I'm completely sober! You're real quick to tell someone else how it is, how things go, but then you expect me to sugar coat it when you mess up? That boy wanted to give you the world! He's been in love with you since his first wet dream. You wanna tell him no, make him compromise everything and then act like the spoiled ingrate that I never raised. You better be happy your daddy came to your rescue cause you'd still be walking funny if I came over there! Now I'm enjoying the evening with my man that I happened to be smart enough to appreciate and love him for everything that he is. You can't be so dead set on getting your way that you miss out on being a part of something beautiful! You blew it Elaine!"

I wanted to scream! Did she go there? Right as I felt my anger blaze she stopped and looked at me with that look that I never like seeing. If I did or said anything she was going to take me out. "Momma! You just broke my heart, and now you gonna beat me up? How come you don't threaten violence with Erica or Zoey?"

"Cause you're the brat!" My daddy said as he dropped down and bobbed his head at my Momma's stomach to the beat.

My momma smiled at my daddy and went back to her dancing. When I stood there looking at my momma all hurt. I walked outside the courtyard and leaned against the wall. My world is crumbling before my eyes. Yussef looked at me as he hurried past me to the bathroom. When he came out he said this was a happy occasion and there was no room for sadness. Then he put his arm around my shoulder, I could smell alcohol on his breath. He told me I needed more **EXCLUSIVE**! in my system immediately. I told him drinking was just going to make me sadder. He looked down at me. "What's wrong with my little cousin?"

"Maybe it's the fact that we aren't family and you refuse to see me as a woman."

Yussef jumped and took his arm back. "What?"

"You've gotta know that I've always liked you."

"Yes but as a cousin." He looked at me seriously.

"We are not blood related and I've always wanted you."

He smiled, "you've always had a boyfriend."

"We've been broken up for a long time. I guess I should've come running."

"Lanie," he paused searching for words. "Your brothers are like brothers to me. Your sisters are like sisters to me. I've only ever regarded you as family, please don't do this to me."

"Do what?" I stepped closer to him and he backed up.

"This! We're family. We're cousins, come on!"

"How come Sasha's not family?"

He frowned, "so you want to pass me around the family?"

"No cause I would never let you go." I watched his eyes; I needed him to understand how serious I was.

He was quiet and thinking for a minute. Then he stared at me like he was looking at me for the first time. He walked in my face and pointed to my right eye in the corner. "Your eyes betray you. You think I'm handsome; you may even have a crush, but you are in

love with your ex. We wouldn't work out, I've got parent issues and you're spoiled." Then he ran his hand over his hair, "besides Sasha isn't out of my system. I haven't admitted that to anyone, so if it gets out I will know it came from you." He reached in his pocket and gave me a sour apple candy. "Let's go dance and tomorrow you're going to get back with your boyfriend."
"He got married."
"I'm sorry, maybe she'll get sick of his love for you and divorce him. You're going to have a happily ever after."
"Can't you at least kiss me?"
"No! A dance is the best I can do for you."
"Why?"
"I like kissing, no I love kissing. I can't kiss Sasha's cousin. I just can't."
"You have to know I'm a determined brat. I'm not giving up so easily."
"We can start our war tomorrow. Tonight let's dance." Then he led me to the dance floor.

Kendra

It was last call for the shuttle and then as all the drunk people loaded on the shuttle Darryl and his brothers and their cousins JoJo and Jeff entertained us with dancing and silliness. Eventually all the men were dancing, it was absolutely hilarious when Darryl's mean looking uncle even danced. I was drunk and loving every moment of it. On the shuttle Darryl was all in my space and all over me. I told him to control himself cause children were on this bus. And as soon as he was about to open his mouth to say he didn't care Sabrina and Emerald (the teenagers) sat up in their chair and faced us. Darryl didn't smile at them, but they had huge grins at him. They wanted to know if the party was in Darryl's room. Darryl's mouth stayed open with disappointment. I couldn't stop laughing. He looked at me for help, so I told them to come hang out with us. Darryl's mouth literally fell open as he looked at me in disbelief. Sobering up just a tad he said he knew how to fix me. He sprang out of his seat and made those getting on the bus wait until he got off. Then he ran back inside the castle real fast. He came back with a big box and a big smile. Everyone cheered him on. Darryl gave me an evil laugh as he sat down with his box.
All the teenagers came to Darryl's room. He had a ton of water brought to his room along with food and sodas. He kept alternating water and drinks with me, while entertaining the teens. Around four in the morning I was still pleasantly drunk and having a dance off with Darryl when his Auntie Jade came to our room to gather the teens. Darryl sarcastically sighed along with the teens as they left. Poor Emmanuel barely got out of the door when Darryl shut it and clapped his hands together with the biggest smile. When I yawned Darryl deflated, he asked me if I was tired and I shook my head yes. Darryl told me to undress and get in the bed, as he looked rejected. I got naked and got in the bed. Darryl was huffing as he got in preparing to leave me alone. It tickled me so much so I kissed him. He was holding back cause he thought he was going to bed. He rolled on his side and put his back to me. I kissed the back of his neck and he didn't react. As I went for his ear I reached around him and massaged him to life. He said he was putty in my hands as he allowed me to excite him. When I asked him if he had a condom, he laughed and said I had jokes. I was so used to not having a barrier between us I wondered if I could go back. This was my show so I wouldn't let him tire out on me. I kept bringing him back to life just like he showed me. The sun came up and we were still going. When we finally finished Darryl very weakly reached for the phone. He called the front desk and told them we were keeping the room one more night.

Malachi

Denise called out to me, asking if I was going to eat breakfast. I sat on the edge of the bed telling myself to get it together. My baby sister is married; her wedding was everything she dreamed it would be. Denise called out to me again as Jada slid out the bedroom door. "Good morning daddy!" She said with a big smile, and she put her arms around my neck and kissed my cheek.

"Good morning Babygirl. How's daddy's angel this morning?" I tried to find a smile.

"Good," I could tell she wanted to ask me something so I waited. "Mom said I had to ask you. Can Amaya and I go have breakfast with Emerald and Sabrina? I promise I will keep an eye on Amaya."

I exhaled, that meant I would be alone with Denise. And that wasn't my favorite thing to do these days. She wouldn't say or do anything, but my emotions are pretty all over the place. I looked at my Babygirl who was completely excited about hanging with the big kids. "Of course you can go, but don't leave the hotel."

"What about the grass right outside? If we go out can we go there?"

"You have to stay on the hotel grounds, no further than you can hear me call your name if I step outside the door. If there's water where you are you have to watch your sister more closely understood?"

Jada smiled real big, "yes daddy!" She gave me another kiss on my cheek.

When she went back in the room I heard the girls celebrate. Then they came out, told me I was the best dad ever and then they took off. I stared at the floor telling myself to get it together. I heard Denise come out of the room. She sat next to me rubbing her stomach. She asked me if I was hung over. I told her I could use some water but I wasn't hung over. She brought me water then she sat again. I drank then she told me to get showered so we could have breakfast. I got showered and dressed on autopilot. Timothy and Grace joined us on the elevator, perfect timing. Timothy and Grace were all love struck after the night they shared. Timothy said the alcohol was flowing, his woman was looking good, and then the icing on the cake was Derrick and Chantel's impromptu performance of their song. Timothy said they barely made it in their room. Grace blew Timothy a kiss. Grace asked Denise how our night went. Denise started stammering saying that I gave her and the girls the room. Grace flashed Timothy a look. Timothy pointed at the kids who were happily congregated in the banquet room enjoying their breakfast together. He said the kids were gone why were we downstairs? I looked at him and I told him I would rather be down here. Denise tried to change the subject but Timothy waved her off. He pointed at Denise, "there's your wife. What's the problem?"

"We're sorting through some things." I said taking a drink of my mimosa.

"Are you getting a divorce?"

"No" I said dryly.

"Then I don't see what the problem is. The rest is just details. You're in a five star hotel, and you're not paying for any of it. Malcolm has set the mood for everyone to get some this weekend. Why are you acting gun shy?"

I looked away, "Timothy it's my fault. I've put Malachi through a lot. It's understandable that this is where we stand." Denise said in my defense.

Timothy looked at me with my father's eyes. "You gonna let her speak for you?"

"We are not you two." I barked.

"All I'm saying Malachi is that Grace and I have been married for a long time. We've been here." He pointed at the table. "Fight for your wife, fight for your family. Don't do it for them, do it for you. You love this woman, and she loves you. All that other stuff, you guys can work out later."

"I'm here! I didn't leave."

Grace rubbed Denise's back. "You love him?" Denise shook her head yes. "Why do you keep waiting for him to come to you? Waiting for him to make a move? He needs to feel wanted and needed just like you do." Denise put her eyes on the table. "Girl look at your man! Although he's not as fine as mine you've got quite a catch over there. Are you waiting for someone to steal him?"

"Please Malachi is way finer than Timothy." She smiled at Grace.

Grace blew air, "please girl! It doesn't get any finer than mine. Timothy stand up and show off what your parents blessed you with!" Timothy smiled, stood up and hit a few muscle poses, and then he winked at Grace and kissed at her from across the table. "See all that fineness! It don't get no better than that!"

Denise smiled. "Please! Malachi, stand up please." So I did, "first of all my man's skin holds that caramel clay look all year long. That thick wavy black hair gives my baby beautiful dark features. Then they're about the same height so ok, but my baby's chest is bigger, broader. His arms are bigger, my baby has a better body." Denise said smiling at me.

"In your dreams!" Grace said standing up. "Baby take your shirt off!" Then she started laughing.

"What's next? You two gonna have us unzipping our pants?" I asked amused by the complete mood shift at the table.

Denise came over by me with a smile. She kissed me softly, and then she smiled again. "And my man tastes better!" She said wiggling her neck at Grace.

Grace cracked up, walked over to Timothy and kissed him deeply, and then she licked his lips. "My man always tastes GOOD!" Then she kissed him again, and then Denise kissed me. "My man is the best!" Grace argued.

Denise looked at me like she was feeling the effects of my mimosa. "Nope! Mine is!" Timothy put up a dizzy finger, "I..." He cleared his throat cause his voice cracked. "I have an idea. How about we see if Emerald and or Sabrina can keep the girls and if that works out we stay out here for a while. I think this competition stuff has just swung in our direction bruh. What you think?" He said not taking his eyes off his wife.

I asked Denise if she wanted to stay with my eyes, and she eagerly said yes. "Sounds good to me."

Timothy bumped me while raising his eyebrows at me as we walked towards the banquet room. I asked the girls if they would be willing to help their uncle out, I told them I would make it worth their while. They excitedly said they'd check with their parents. Timothy bumped me again; he said he bet I was feeling different now. I had to admit it was nice to have Denise look at me like that. Even if Grace had to draw on her competitive side to change the way she saw me. I guess when it all boiled down to the issue for me, it was Denise's lack of interest in me. I never wanted to cheat on her. And she's right; we promised not to bring this stuff into our marriage, but then again I'm not the only guilty party here. I can't seem to deal with the fact that she cheated on me. Why would she do that? I was on best behavior at the time. I didn't want to ruin the vibe so I sucked it up. Ethan and Jenise came down just like Timothy and Grace did. I shared with them that we were staying and before I could get my entire invite out Jenise was happily accepting.

Jade found us in the banquet room with all the kids. She wanted to know what the plan was. So I told her that the girls could stay at my house for a few days if it was ok with her and Sonny. She said the kids were all planning to hang out at Derrick and Chantel's house. Random, but ok. She said as long as it was ok with Derrick, my kids could stay with the girls at Derrick's for the week. I asked her if she and Sonny wanted to join us, but Jade said she had to keep the facade up, so she had to go to North Star tomorrow like nothing happened this weekend. Derrick said it was fine and to take all the time we needed.

When we went back to our women we told them it was all set up. Timothy asked if we wanted to stay at this hotel or move to another. Like a group of teenagers we went to the computer room and looked up the neighboring hotels. Grace said nothing less than four stars, but five stars was the preference. Anything less would compromise the mood. I couldn't help but notice when Denise put her arms around mine. Or when she kissed my shoulder, or when she.... when she acted like she loved me and wasn't afraid that I was going to hurt her... Break through! Timothy reserved three honeymoon suites at a hotel and spa just up the street. We told the women to relax while we went to gather our bags. Since Timothy and Ethan have grown children they literally went to their rooms picked up their bags sure that they left nothing behind. Where I was getting body wash out the showers, toothbrushes, and brushes left out and putting them in the appropriate bags. Ethan and Timothy sat on the couch too excited about the next couple of days. I thanked Timothy and I told him just spending this little bit of time with them in the morning has made a world of difference. Timothy smiled, "baby brother, Trust me. I've been there. You don't want to know how many times Grace and I came close to divorce. Moving back to California was a last ditch effort to get back on track. And you see where we are today."

"Does it ever bother you that your wife doesn't look like Momma?" I had to ask. Timothy took a deep breath, "honestly in the beginning it did. When I first met Grace I wasn't fooling with her. Although Momma never said if she can't use your comb don't bring her home, that's kind of how I felt, but then I realized that was dumb because our father was white so why would she put a limitation on her children like that? I always thought I would marry someone as chocolate or darker than Momma."

"ME TOO!"

"Even to this day my head may almost turn when I see chocolate just because Momma was my first love, but I had to learn that I couldn't fight that I loved Grace. She may not look like her," he exhaled hard. "But boy does she act like her! I love my wife for who she is, and how hard it's been to stick by me at times, but she's hung in there. And now that this chick realizes I'm packing...." He made exaggerated movements all over the couch. "All I gotta do is give her a look and the panties drop! Had I known that was all it would've taken all those years ago, when I was trying to invent ways to turn her on..." He blew air while he chuckled.

"How were you married all this time and she never knew?"

"Good question! That woman was clueless." Ethan interjected.

Timothy cut his eyes at me, "Ok! Ok! I know when it comes to the kids it's me, the squarest, Jade, square, you oval, and then Amber and Sophia the Ghetto twins!" We cracked up for a few minutes.

"I like how you threw Sophia in there."

"Yea, but when dad died, especially when dad died I boxed all that up. I was mister corporate America in Chicago. Beautiful wife, two kids, living the squarest life ever. When dad picked us up from the airport he kept asking me what was wrong with me. The *me*, I've always been only came alive around dad. I know I took it a bit overboard, my son.... A lady's magnet he may be, but a Wallace man at heart.... that remains to be seen. No matter which way you spin it there's regrets."

I sat down and unloaded everything with my big brother and cousin. They listened and then Timothy told me about when he cheated. He said Grace is CRAZY and she left him with the reminder of why he didn't want to go there ever again. He said her message was received. He said sometimes we lose sight of what's truly important sometimes. He said from where he was sitting Denise and I were even, so why were we sulking about it? I didn't have an answer for that, but I agreed with him.

The next two days were like VERY old times between Denise and I. We enjoyed each other's company. We flirted with each other. We shared each other until we had nothing else to give. I kept looking at my wife with happiness in my heart. I just hope she doesn't leave me again.

Yussef

"Daddy can we go with Sabrina and Emerald and Erin and Jada and Amaya over D-Rick and Chantel's house?" My girls said too excited.

I wanted to spend the day with my girls but they were too excited about leaving me. I sucked up my jealousy and told them I needed to talk to Derrick first. They got excited about my unspoken yes. Derrick told me to come over as well, he said a few were coming over but the girls could spend the night and the week if that was ok with their moms. Since I had nothing better to do I shrugged and agreed. I texted Malcolm and told him that the soldiers were about to pull out. I didn't expect a response from him cause I expected him to be completely gone and nose open. When he responded as I was loading up the car I smiled. He simply said "thank you for everything." I imagined him experiencing a feeling that these lap girls will never give me. I asked myself what I was doing with Max. The idea of her surprisingly irritated me. That sealed it. She and I could not continue.

I gave the girls their suitcases when we got to Derrick's. Chantel's brother Cyrus was walking up. We leaned against my car for a while talking about poetry and that led us to God. Talking to Cyrus was always interesting and thought provoking. Cyrus is a good man and a deep thinker. I asked him if he wanted to check out service. I told him I'd go with him, and maybe we could tag along with Tracy and Drew. He said he'd discuss it with his wife and then he'd get back to me.

The kids mostly played in the pool outside. We were playing pool and Chantel wasn't drinking. I told her that I read that drinking beer helps produce more milk. She looked at Derrick and he nodded. Then she told us she couldn't drink because she was pregnant. Everyone froze and then we erupted in excited congratulations. Drew followed me to the kitchen. I poured another shot and he eyed me. We stood there looking at each other for a minute. As if we just had an in-depth conversation about my feelings we started walking back towards the game room. Drew patted my shoulder and told me it was going to happen for me.

Sasha

"How was it?" Ava asked.

"The wedding was beautiful! And my hair held up nicely!" One drawback to moving back to the Bay is that I have to fly back to LA just to get my hair done. I normally make a day of it when I come. I'll schedule all in office visits on this day. I still have my office space out here. So I keep my calendar private to keep my secretary on her toes. She never knows when I'm going to pop up, so it's in her best interest to stay on top of her job.

"Ok so you're tense, what's going on?" Ava said reading me.

I tried to decide which story to go with. Tell her what I've uttered to no one except my sister Tanisha or Richard. Of course I chickened out and went on an all-out rant about Richard's horrible behavior at the wedding. He actually said to my mother in front of my Poppa, Nana, Travis, El, and Randi that, that day should've been theirs. Before my momma could say anything Travis spit fire at him. Everyone was surprised cause normally everybody ignores the things Richard says, but then again he's never that direct, so he directly said and Travis directly clowned him. None of that seemed to faze Richard. Richard asked my momma to step outside, and my Poppa grabbed Travis' arm and shook his head. Then he told Richard to walk with him. My momma put her arms around Travis' neck and then she kissed him. I followed them and my Poppa spoke at the bottom of his voice. "Leave my daughter alone. You've already made your choice now deal with it! You just had a baby. You've got another one on the way. Sophia doesn't need all that in her life."

"Jeff I have been in love with that woman since I've understood what love was. I..."
"I hope that's not true cause you've got a funny way of showing it. From where I sit you're always punking out and not standing up to your responsibilities. You had your chance and you blew it. I don't care what your excuse is for all the reasons why you've done what you've done. All I know is the heartache you've caused behind running. Had Sasha calling someone else daddy. Had my daughter married to a boy she didn't love. Then building both of them up when you ran again! YOU BLEW IT! Leave my daughter and Travis alone or else I will personally end you! The only reason you breathe is because of Sasha!"
I peeked around the corner, both of them were standing straight like they were wishing the other would be crazy enough to swing. JoJo put his hand on my back cause he was ear hustling behind me. "I can understand how you feel. If it were my daughter I would say and do the same thing, but with all due respect, I know your daughter better than you do. She will come back to me, and I will not back down!"
"She might have until you started popping out babies all over the place."
"My children won't matter in the end. Mark my words!"
"Your words?" My Poppa was irritated.
JoJo hurried around the corner trying to look casual. "Richard, just let it go. We've got a party going on. Dad, momma wants to dance. I promise both of you will have another opportunity to fight over Sophia. Let's let this rest for tonight."
Darryl's goofy laugh echoed off the wall. I didn't see him standing in the corner.
"Richard, you know Uncle Jeff was about to put his foot up your butt! Uncle I haven't seen you throw them in a minute. I was about to say hold on so I could get some popcorn. Sasha over there listening."
I emerged from my hiding place. "Richard my momma is in love with Travis. Let it go." Richard looked at all of us in disbelief. "None of you know her."
"I know my cousin is looking mighty comfortable over there with her baby daddy." Then Darryl put his arm around Richard. "Come on Richie Rich! Don't bring the rain clouds to our sunshine party. My parents *FINALLY* got married and I know that makes you reflect on your life." He put his hands up to paint the scene. "What does it mean? Where's it all going?" Then he smiled at him, "that type of reflection is done best in private. Don't come over here upsetting my Uncle. You know how he gets, and without my granddad to calm him down. I'll have to shoot you because he told me to."
"Please! Why would I care about a bullet?" Richard said.
"Cause they hurt!" Darryl said laughing.
Uncle Jeff chuckled, "they do don't they."
"We're a family Richard. Don't become a threat." Darryl warned him.
Ava stopped combing my hair her mouth was open. "Darryl shoots people?"
I laughed cause I forgot who I was talking to. "Girl please! He's from Oakland. Any ways, Richard calmed down after that."
"I didn't know Richard's girlfriend was pregnant."
"Girl! Me neither, but it's not a surprise." I didn't like thinking about it. Richard was probably hoping for a little girl to replace me with. "Thank you for fitting me in before your vacation." I smiled.
"Thank you! We didn't get around to taking a real honeymoon. This is above and beyond anything we could've afforded to do on our own. A European tour is something I've always dreamed of doing." She said with a big smile.
"I'm gonna miss you, take lots of pictures and videos I can't wait to see everything when you come back." I said trying to pull back my emotions.
"Sasha!" She said hugging me. "When do you find out what you're having?"
"I don't care as long as they're healthy." I lied. It was killing me not to know what's inside my body.

"Yea right! I know you want a girl at least."
I laughed, "it doesn't matter. We're gonna do this two more times. If I don't get my daughter this time, there's always next time. We plan to have four at least."
"Girl! You do realize those babies become teenagers?"
"Yes, but it's ok." I smiled as I imagined my little family with El.

Chantel

Who would want to come back to reality after the fairy tale wedding Malcolm and Amber had. Talk about doing it up big. Our wedding was pretty extravagant and the bill was high. I have no idea how much they spent on their wedding. Do I think it was worth it? I can't imagine waiting that long for Derrick and if I did he better pull out all the stops just like Malcolm did. Car service to and from the wedding was a nice touch. I had no idea that this whole time we've been using Andrew's limousine service.
My grandmother and Derrick's Auntie and Uncle hit it off really well. I thought Ms. Laverne and her husband already knew them as well.
No one has heard a peep from Amber or Malcolm since the wedding. When they drove away we all waved goodbye to their car and then we went back to partying. Derrick and I performed our song for everyone, I love performing with him.
****
Cyrus was on the phone looking at my calendar and talking hard. I didn't know what he was saying but he was being firm with someone. The photographer was going to town taking pictures of me, so I was trying to focus. As soon as the pictures were finished they rushed me on set. I changed, and then we shot footage for my final video. Everything has been so crammed together; don't ask me what day it is. I don't know whether I'm coming or going. Derrick comes along when he can, but with everything going on right now he can't always be there. My grandmother is so proud of me. She said all of her family back home knows about me, and they can't wait to meet me. I smiled out of courtesy, but I imagined a bunch of people just like my dad and aunties. I'd go because it means a lot to her, but I wasn't gonna be excited about it.
Cyrus held my cup for me while I nursed Chanel under my cover up. "Do I have to ask you?"
Cyrus exhaled, "the label wants. Actually they're demanding that you perform at the awards ceremony next year. You'll be at the end of your pregnancy and Derrick wants you to rest."
"Couldn't I sit on a stool for my performance?"
He looked at me sternly, "you still gotta travel out there. It could be done, but why have you travel that late in your pregnancy unnecessarily?"
"Well it sounds necessary."
"Not yet, we'll see."
I gave Chanel to Cyrus to burp while my grandmother ate and I ran back on set. We only had a little time left before my baby bump was completely noticeable. Derrick told me not to tell the world yet, and to the best of our ability we wanted to keep this pregnancy as private as possible. I didn't exactly understand why the secrecy was needed but I did as I was told.
Each pregnancy is different and that's the truth, I've only gotten nauseous once, but this baby makes me mean. We're only in the beginning and a few times already I have felt my mouth and anger running away with me. Derrick has had to walk away from me twice cause I was pushing all of his patience buttons. I've had a couple of phone sessions with my therapist Joanne, because I couldn't work out the time to go see her in person. I told her about how mad I got at Tracy for outing me, and how I keep making Derrick angry. Cyrus has even stared at me and then laughed an angry laugh as he walked away from

me. This pregnancy is going to be a long one for sure.

****

"Where are they sending your family?" Latia asked.

"On a world tour, they're taking the ultimate family vacay. Are you and Lewis still coming with us?" I asked.

"Yes, but you know how this goes. I don't know when we're leaving. I just know we're going."

"Do you know?" I asked Brandy.

Brandy looked at Sasha, "I don't know the itinerary. Do you?"

"Derrick is making your plans. I know you want to know, but you should really wait on him to tell you. Derrick is trying to accommodate your grandmother during the blackout cause he knows she wants to take you guys home, but I'm not a part of the planning for that."

The four of us were enjoying our little visit; I told them that I was happy to have some notice this time. The last time I was under a blackout it happened suddenly and it was not fun to only have two outfits to choose from. I sent lots of clothes ahead this time, especially since no one knew or was saying how long this was going to last. Yussef's sister Latia was fun and silly just like her brother, I enjoyed being around her. The fact that she and Brandy got a long really well helped too. Especially since Brandy was married to Lewis's bodyguard. They spent a lot of time together. I cracked up when Latia realized that Brandy was on assignment watching after her. I told her I had the same reaction when they put her on me. Brandy is a lovable person so I imagined that they got along just as well as Brandy and I did. I asked Latia if she and Lewis were going to have any children and she said once things calmed down they were going to. I told her she was smart as Sasha and I rubbed our belly's. Derrick and Yussef came home, they said a general hello but their faces were serious. They were about business and then they disappeared into Derrick's office.

****

"Daniel I cannot hold your hand through this nor do I have time to keep reminding you that your actions can and very likely will jeopardize the safety of your family." Yussef said firmly.

"All I'm saying is that you're asking a lot." My daddy said.

"Daddy, don't be ridiculous! You can go the duration of this period without performing."

"Chantel! Music is my life! I would expect you to understand that."

"I do to a point. He's not telling you not to play ever again. It's only temporary."

"Yes, but no one can answer me when I ask for how long. It don't feel temporary to me." He was getting angry.

I could feel my anger boil. "Yussef send him out there on his own! Your protection is only for those who understand that their life is at stake here! You go be stupid by yourself! You..."

Derrick put his hand up and I stopped talking immediately. "Daniel," he exhaled like he was tired. "I can understand that as a man it has to be difficult for other men to come in and tell you how your life is going to go for the next however long, but you have to understand my position. My wife loves you; if something should happen to you she's going to be torn up about it. You're a man and you have a choice. So here it is. Do you choose to live and follow instruction? Or do you choose to go out like a man? These aren't some little around the way thugs who will stop at twisting your cap backwards. If you don't follow instruction as it's given to you, you will die! That's a guarantee."

My daddy sat there like there was something to think about. Maria came out of nowhere and slapped the mess out of him. My brothers and I jumped, Derrick and Yussef smiled. She told him to stop being so stupid. I've never seen Maria assert herself, and I know she's never struck him before. She told Yussef that she and her kids would do whatever he tells them to do. Now he was embarrassed, so he went off. "Seems to me this is a dispute with this guy and those Wallace's. I don't know why my life has to turn upside down as a result!"

"Daniel! Derrick has taken care of us, protected us, and loved us. I can't believe you! I will not die with or for you. I have children who need me to be here for them as long as I can be. Yussef," Maria said with tears pouring out of her eyes. "I can't trust him not to get us killed! Please separate us."

You could've heard cotton hit the floor. Everybody was looking at my parents in disbelief. Yussef looked at Derrick, Derrick rolled his eyes and then he looked at me. DJ and Mario were shaking their heads. There was no honor in being this man's children. "Send him with his sisters," then I got up and hugged Maria. My grandmother!! "When Cyrus and I found you it was like a dream come true. That monster was not my real father. I will hold on to the memory of those first few years of getting to know you before the real you surfaced. Before the real you broke everyone's heart. My grandmother who's already buried a husband is going to be heart broken when she finds out that her son is gone. And Alex and Ria, little Rosa and Chanel will never know you, but at least you can say you died like a man! I'll try not to hate you for being so stupid! I'll try to remember that I love you, but you always continue to let me down. So I guess it's for the better this way." I started crying and I squeezed Maria. "You will have love in your life, you are a good woman! It's a shame you had to be hooked up with such a guy!" Maria kissed me and squeezed me.

"DJ that makes you the man in charge. I know this is hard but you've got to watch over everyone. Make sure you follow instructions. Yussef's going to give you full briefing in a few minutes." Derrick said watching Maria and I.

"Dad?" DJ said looking at my stubborn father who wasn't budging. "This is serious! It's not a game!" Our father moved his eyes around. "You want to leave us! You've been looking for a way out this whole time! Put some money in your pockets and you're ready to leave us high and dry like this?"

"You're leaving me! We don't have anything to do with some feud between them Wallace's and this guy. Why would anyone be concerned with us?"

"BECAUSE OF ME!" I screamed! "You are so selfish and stupid! Caprice is gone daddy, because of me! Wade is gone because of me! You don't get it! This is about me just as much as it is about them! We are a family! They brought Cyrus and I in when we had no one. If it weren't for them I wouldn't know you! Still this is how you act! I'm done talking about this! Derrick I want to go!" I yelled standing up.

"Sit down Chantel!" Derrick said calmly which made me angry. When I was still standing he pointed his eyes at me and repeated himself. I sat down, "I know this is stressful, but please stop pleading with this grown man. No one else even look in his direction. He's dead, he's gone, and we're done with him. Moving on, it's time for what comes next. DJ if you can't handle this let me know right now. I know Mario can do this if you can't." Mario sat a little taller.

DJ kicked the wall, yelled and then he said he was ready. Yussef explained when he called him they had to drop whatever they were doing and move. He said he had to reorganize something's now that our father wasn't going, but he would contact him immediately so he needed to be ready. Yussef told him no drinking or smoking while he was on point. Yussef told him he could do this and he had faith in him. From this moment on DJ was going to have to be clean and sober. Yussef got a text. "Daniel your car is outside." He said matter of factly.

When my father stood up it felt like my heart was ripping in my chest. I cannot believe I came from this man. He bent over and kissed Maria, then he told her he'd see her in a little while. Um, did he forget he had children? He walked out the door without acknowledging any of the rest of us. I looked at Adon and he was mimicking Derrick's demeanor. I asked him if he was ok, and he said yes our father had a choice.

Yussef

Armed with pictures of their rooms the girls marched to the bedding section. Little Jackson tried to mimic his father's walk as we slowly strolled around the store. We just picked out furniture for their bedrooms. This time both of the girls went with day beds and trundles. Yezzy said when little jack comes she'd sleep in Syd's room. Even though their mothers were clearly tolerating each other, the girls kept cross-referencing with each other. I had to tell Melissa I would not buy new blinds for the windows in Yezzy's room. I saw Sylvia drop the sample she had in her hand. I chuckled a little, and then they both came with curtains and other girly things to dress up even the windows. Jackson laughed at me as I gave into them.

When all four of them approached me with two carts overflowing with things for the girl's rooms I exhaled. I wasn't surprised I've been shopping with both of their mothers before, but it looked like a lot of stuff. I was impressed and marked it as progress when they showed me their collaboration on the girl's bathroom decorations. At the cash register I asked the cashier not to tell me the total, and to just put it on my card. Melissa asked Sylvia what she had planned for something in the cart. Sylvia excitedly explained it. Melissa's eyes got big, she asked Sylvia to show her where and then they informed the cashier that they would be back with more stuff. I told them if she reached the bottom of their pits before they came back I wasn't getting it. All four of them ran, Jackson and I cracked up. The cashier laughed and she said it was nice to see a blended family who all worked together. Jackson said today was a good day but we were making our way. They came laughing, arms full of things that they dumped into their respective carts. I told them no more. When we got to the house Jackson took out his tools and went from room to room putting up curtain rods, shelves, mirrors, etc. I wanted no part of that as I heard the women saying it's not straight or whatever. I went around the house installing my micro cameras and alarm triggers, testing them and making sure they not only worked but were unnoticeable. I took little jack with me outside and we walked around the house. I told him to pay attention to everything even how the grass laid. He frowned cause he didn't get it. I pointed to a patch, and then I stepped on it. I told him to notice the subtle bend on the grass from my footstep. Little Jack nodded, but attention to detail was not his strong suit, my girls would understand better than he would. He helped me set up the irrigation for my grass to a very slow leak. This would insure that my grass was always green, and also that the grass was always slightly wet, equaling footsteps and prints. Dude was next door visiting his mother when he came over to say hey. He said it didn't seem right that Amber wasn't living next door anymore. I told him I knew what he meant. Then Sylvia came to the door to ask how much longer before the furniture was delivered cause they were getting hungry. I told her to order pizzas for everyone.

"Yu! That's you?"

His eyes were big, "that's Sydney's mother."

He whistled, "why aren't you together?"

"Long story short, we couldn't get it straight the first time. Second time, first time bad taste still lingered." Then I looked at him, "what about you? You dating anybody?"

"Naw, I've been on Darryl's chickenhead diet." He shook his head.

"And how's that working out for you?"

He smiled, "I'm suffering from malnutrition."

I looked him in his eyes, "it wouldn't bother you to go behind me?"

He shrugged, "everybody can't be first. You think she'd go for me?"

"No," then I laughed. "But you have my blessing." We shook hands.

"I feel nervous. How should I be? What should I say?"

"Be strong, you know what to do." Then I invited him inside. Sylvia didn't look twice at Dude. Melissa noticed Dude before Sylvia did. And when Sylvia did it was out of courtesy, nothing more. Syd noticed Dude's attention towards her mother and I could see her eyeing him. Then she looked at me, when I smiled at her. She came over to me and led me outside by my hand. We sat on the stairs on the porch. She asked why Dude was looking at her momma. I told her that I think he likes her. She asked me why that didn't make me mad. I shrugged and told her that Dude is a good guy. I asked her if her mother deserved to be happy. She looked confused even though she was trying to understand. I made a mental note to ask Dude to lay low in front of Syd. When we came inside Sylvia grabbed my arm taking me back outside.

"What's up with your friend?" She asked with her hands on her hips.

I shrugged again, "I think he likes you."

She narrowed her eyes, "why would you be ok with that? I'm Sydney's mother!"

"You're her mother, you're not dead!"

"I told you, if I'm not with you I'm not with anybody. I know exactly what he wants and I'm over being used."

"Ok so you're not interested. It's not like I'm hooking you guys up. He asked me if I was ok with him stepping and I said yes I didn't..."

Her eyes filled with tears as she cut me off. "Why would you be ok with it? You don't care about me? Or what you think you can pass me around now? Is that what you want me to do? Do whomever you say?" She was pissed.

"I'm not your pimp. Shoot! Pimping ain't easy, and I got my hands full at work."

"This is not funny!"

"Ok, ok. Isn't this what you were killing yourself at the gym for? To get your body back and hook another big fish?"

"I can't believe you just said that to me. I go to the gym to do something good for me. I wanted to feel good about myself."

"There was nothing wrong with you the way you were."

"I happen to like myself like this."

I exhaled then I put my arm around her shoulders. "Dude is a good guy. I wouldn't let someone shady raise an eyebrow at you. I'm not telling you to go for him, I'm just saying I'm ok with it if you do decide to give him a chance."

"Meaning you're not coming back to me?" She was still crying.

"Truth?" I looked at her, "my heart is still broken from our breakup." She started crying harder. "Don't stress about it. You've done all you could to prove how sorry you are. I just wish apologies could rewrite history." I exhaled, "I don't wanna bore you with how our lives would be right now if I originally dated the Sylvia you are now. I still want to strangle the old Sylvia! She was heartless and cruel! The new Sylvia deserves the love and protection of a good man, I'm just sorry it can't be me." I rubbed her shoulder cause she was still crying.

"It's too weird, I can't do it!" She said between tears.

I busted Melissa peeking out the window. I told her to come out. She eyed me as she stepped out the door. "Sylvia has cold feet about moving on. I figured she should talk to an expert minus the keeping my daughter from me part."

"I wasn't trying to..."

"Don't lie, since you're all up in our business. You might as well make yourself useful." Both of them looked at me funny. "Whatever!" Then I walked inside leaving them on the porch.

Dude looked at me to ask what was up. I told him to hang around later so we could chat.

Tracy

I get the feeling that things are going really well between Tia and Brody. Every time I talk to her there's a smile in her voice. I think my parents are hearing wedding bells. Honestly I can't see why they wouldn't. I told them I would see them this weekend after everything was said and done.

The doctor came in the room, "Mrs. Wallace your pressure is extremely high. We need to get you over to triage and see if we can get it to go down." My doctor said.

I took a deep breath, as I looked at my mom for help to keep calm. "It's that bad?" I said rubbing my stomach. I had to do some major convincing to get Andrew to agree to not miss a day at work just to come to this doctor's appointment. I thought it would go according to plan, but it appears that baby Malcolm has his own plan. My mom asked what would happen if they couldn't get it down. They said they may have to induce me. I tried not to stress, I said a quick prayer in hopes that everything would be ok. They gave me cold water and had me lay on my side. When I felt calm I called Andrew. I tried to make my voice sound upbeat, "hey babe."

"What's wrong?"

"I didn't say anything was wrong. I was calling…"

He cut me off, "you're too calm Tracy! Stop it! Are you at the hospital?"

"Yes, but.."

"I'm on my way!" Then he hung up.

I looked at my mom in disbelief as she cracked up. She said she was glad he knew me so well cause she was just going to turn around and tell him to come over any ways. I don't know if he teleported to the hospital or what, but it seemed like we just hung up and there he was looking stone faced and concerned. The doctor explained to him what was happening. They did another ultrasound and they said the baby was measuring bigger than only thirty-three weeks, which was a good thing. They said he was at least five pounds already so he was good size in case they needed to take him early, but my pressure went down nicely. They told me to go home and to relax as much as possible. When we got home my mom, Andrew, and I got into a big argument. They wanted me to stay home this weekend and I wanted to go to service to be with my family. My sisters were coming in the night before, Tia and her fiancé Brody were coming I wanted to see everyone before they left. Andrew was sending them on vacation and they were going to go to service all over the world. It sound like so much fun to meet our brothers and sisters in different lands, I was kind of jealous that I wasn't going.

My parents almost called the whole thing off when they realized that I would be delivering without them here. Unfortunately they realized this after Andrew paid for everything and nothing was refundable. Or at least that's what he told them and I had to go along with it. If my parents had even a clue about this whole blackout thing, they would never leave and I needed my family to be safe.

Since I couldn't have my own mom with me during my delivery and I was being a team player about that, I put my foot down and told them I was going to service on Sunday and they could squawk all they wanted but I was going. I stayed in bed all day Friday and Saturday. Andrew worked from home on Friday and he used the blood pressure monitor he bought for home to keep an eye on my pressure. He talked to his cousin Jennifer and she gave him a meal plan for me, and reassured him that one outing wasn't going to hurt me. I thanked her for having my back, and then when she was off the phone I asked Andrew which one was she? She was one of his doctor cousins, and then I felt even better.

Sasha came over Sunday morning while Andre and I got ready for service. She and Andrew were in the office working away, which surprised me. I figured with the fit he pitched about me going to service that Andrew would go with me, but no he was too busy being lost in his twin world with his cousin talking about stuff I don't know about or understand. I know I was feeling a little jealous, but MAN! Normally I don't mind their closeness, but for whatever reason today I wasn't feeling like sharing my man with anybody. Andrew and Sasha were cracking up about some story he was telling her when I walked into the office. I smiled and waited for them to calm down before I spoke. They smiled at me with similar smiles. I told them Andre and I were leaving, Andrew hopped up an gave me a big sloppy kiss. Then he walked Andre and I to the garage. He gave me another hug and kiss then he told me he'd see us in a little bit. I cut my eyes at him as I said yea right. He frowned like he didn't understand what I meant. I got in the car, and Andre and I sang with the radio on the way to service.

I sat in the row in front of my parents cause we came in a few minutes late. Then not even five minutes later Yussef walked in with his girls, he was looking at me smiling in his suit. My mom's bible study's head whipped in Yussef's direction. I smiled and then I focused on the morning service.

After service the bible study made a beeline over to Yussef and I. Tara watched my face cause again I was annoyed by the presence of a female. I have no claim to Yussef other than we are *family*. It irritated me all the same, I didn't know this girl, and even though my mom speaks highly of her, all of a sudden it doesn't seem good enough.

My mom told me to invite Andrew to brunch, so I called him. I rolled my eyes when he answered the phone still laughing, what is SO FUNNY? I told Andrew we were going to brunch and my mom said he better be there and she wasn't taking no for an answer. He said he was in the car with Sasha, and I told him to bring her. Andre and AJ chatted in the back about the latest tricks AJ has mastered on his bike. When I pulled up Andrew met me at the car with a big kiss. He asked me what was wrong. I told him nothing and then I walked on. At the table Tia informed everyone that she and Brody got their marriage license yesterday and they wanted daddy to marry them here so that they could have a ceremony in Paris when they got there. I tried not to cry, but tears streamed down my face. I wanted to be there when my sister got married. Even though technically I would be I was bummed out. I excused myself and went to the bathroom. I sat on the chair in the powder room before the bathroom and I rested my head on the counter as I cried into my arms. Tia was right behind me rubbing my back; she said she didn't think I would take it this hard. She said she thought I was closer to Tara as if that meant I didn't care what happened to her. We had a sisterly bonding moment as I told her how much I loved her and that she meant the world to me.

Our mom came in saying that Andrew was outside the bathroom pacing because we were in the bathroom for so long. He was worried that something might be wrong. I asked her to tell him I was fine and I was talking to Tia. Sasha came in the bathroom armed with a blood pressure machine. She looked embarrassed and forced to ask me to let her check me.

Yussef thinks he's so slick. He slid out before my mom could demand that he come to the house with us. Then Sasha said she was going to pick up El and come over. They had me lay down until it was time for the ceremony. I laid in the guest bed that I spent months and months crying about the baby I lost, rubbing my stomach and assuring this baby of how much I loved him.

I couldn't wait to see him. I wondered if he would look like Andrew at all. What if he looked like me only or just like Malcolm. Would he be light like Amber or dark like Malcolm or browner like me or lighter brown like Andrew. By the way he's always fighting these days when someone touches my stomach, I'd say his temperament won't be like sweet little Andre. I'm hoping I'm misunderstanding and he's the sweetest little thing. I woke up to feeling comfy as Andrew spooned me and kissed my neck. He slipped the cuff on my arm to check my pressure. I couldn't say he wasn't concerned. When my pressure checked out I asked him if the door was locked. He frowned at me and said no. I told him to lock it and to come back to bed. He chuckled and said I was a freak. He said we could wait until we got home, but I didn't want to. I got up and locked the door. He laughed and said he wasn't gonna do it, which made us both laugh cause we both knew he would.

Sasha

"How are you feeling today?" I asked Mrs. Parsons.

"I'm good," she said with a smile. Then she rubbed my belly. "How's my babies doing today?"

"They're good." I said rubbing my little stomach. "All my dreams of a cute pregnant bump like my momma had with Sabrina flew out the window. I look at Tracy's real stomach and I can see my fate."

"Which one is Tracy again? There's so many of you guys it's hard to keep track sometimes."

"Tracy's the one who's married to my cousin Drew. She's brown and has the curly hair."

"Oh! Right! They have a little boy who looks just like his daddy?"

"Right. You're gonna be fine and in the end you're going to have two beautiful babies who look just like me." She smiled.

El came in the room; he put his arms around me and kissed my neck. "I feel like we've been running since the wedding. I haven't babied my baby in a minute." Then he sucked on my neck.

His mother blushed, "um. Your momma's right there." I said embarrassed.

"My mum knows she's got a happily married son." Then he winked at his momma.

"Tomorrow night, we're going out. I don't know where, but it'll be somewhere nice."

I got excited, "ok!" I gave him a quick kiss. He came in for more. "El, your momma." I said walking away. Mrs. Parsons laughed as El gave me that look and followed me out of the room. Mr. Parsons was sitting on the couch with his sister who decided to stay out here with them. El was all hands following me out to the car, which I parked in the garage. I asked him what had gotten into him, and he said he was happy. Then he closed the garage door behind him. I thought I was getting in the car to go meet up with Drew but my baby decided he had to have me. And who am I to make him go the whole day without Sasha loving even though I served him nicely this morning before we got here. Feeling completely high and sprung I drove to Andrew's. One look at my face and he was cracking up at me. He said it was that kind of morning and then we laughed together. Drew was all blushy and he couldn't stop smiling. We kept looking at each other and laughing, talk about nonproductive. Tracy came in the room to say bye to Drew. She looked pretty in her dress, even though it looked like she'd rather hang out with us.

When Drew came back I asked him if happy juice was swimming in the air. He said it had to be. At that moment I saw an unsavory thought flash across his mind. "Do you think I would've felt like this with Jennay?"

"I didn't really know her, we barely met, but from how Tanisha described her I doubt it." He frowned, "how did she describe her?"

"No one will ever be as bad as Toya. Jennay needed a lot of attention."

"You know how bad I was, she was just acting out."

"Either you accept it or you leave it. That's why Tanisha stopped messing with you."

He shook his head, "I didn't cheat on Tanisha! Why doesn't she believe that?"

"Did you end up with Toya?"

"Only after she rejected me." He had way more emotion than he should have behind it.

"Well it's not like it matters now. You've all moved beyond it." I watched him as he now sat irritated at the desk.

"What if I ended up with Hubby? Do you think I'd be happy?"

"No!"

"Why do you say that so strongly?"

He cut his eyes at me, "what's a marriage without sex?" I let that ride on the air, cause I was not about to come clean about anything with him in this mood. "It's bad enough you kissed him." He shook his head.

If he only knew I did more than kiss him, but why re-examine the past? We went over business for a while and then he asked me to take him by the post office so that he could check his box, and then swing by both of the bakeries. He was shuffling envelopes when he got in the car. An old school jam came on so we turned the radio up and had our own little dance party. We were cracking up trying to chair dance our routine and then Tracy called. Her mother was demanding his presence for brunch, so he told me I was coming. He asked me if El ever got into it with my momma. I immediately thought of Yussef. I told him mom's don't stop being momma's just because their babies get married.

Andrew dropped an envelope and started cursing. I looked at his face it had to be only one person who would get that reaction from him. I told him to forget about it, we're about to go have brunch and he could open it later if at all. His eyes turned red that fast. He was cursing and fighting the air "what does she want" he yelled. I told him not to think about her right now. I grabbed his hand and told him to calm down. He locked and unlocked his jaw the rest of the way to the hotel.

I told him to leave his mail on the floor and he could get it later. We stood outside the hotel waiting for everyone as he tried to calm down. When Yussef pulled up first I felt like I was going to need calming, but as soon as I saw my girls with their mile wide smiles I was calm again. If I was ever feeling unloved or un-liked, these girls definitely knew what to do to stroke my ego. I kissed both of their foreheads and asked them where they came from. They said they went to Tracy's service this morning. I about wanted to die looking at Yussef in his suit, he looked like he stepped off a magazine cover. I turned my eyes out of respect for my husband. I said a very happy hello to Tara and Tia, even though El and I saw them last night for dinner in the city.

There was another girl with them and I immediately sized her up. I didn't like the way she was... Her! She was hiding something, and then it didn't help that she had that goofy for Yussef look all over her. It was like she didn't notice anyone else at the table she was into him. Everyone noticed it even the girls, but they didn't seem to mind. I guess I was the only person throwing an internal fit about it. And so ok! She's not a shrinking violet like that other girl. She's not extremely ghetto like that last girl, but he wasn't really into her anyways, I could tell. When Drew shot me a look, that's when I knew I had to calm myself down. Andrew slid next to me when Tracy excused herself to the restroom. I could tell he was trying to compose himself so he took a minute to say anything. Then he told me to get up and follow him. He excused us from the table and I followed him out the back of the hotel onto the marina. He put his hands in his pockets and he walked closer to the water. His face was serious and he cut his eyes at me. "Did you sleep with him?"

"No!" I said like he was ridiculous for asking.

"Then what?"

"Nothing!" I kicked the ground.

"Something, you're not even trying to be discreet."

"I'm a married woman!"

"Well, you're not acting like it. I'd break Tracy's neck if she acted like you. From what I know of El, he's cool, and Yussef fears God more than he does any person. So the only wild card here is you. What are you doing?"

"How am I acting? I'm not doing anything!"

"Nothing but staring and lingering. Let's not be our parents ok!" That was UNCALLED-FOR! I went completely off. Drew stood there stone faced as I called him on EVERY scandalous thing he's done. Running around here talking about he was nothing like his father acting completely and totally like him. The only reason he married Tracy was so he could say he wasn't like his father. As long as he gets winded behind letters from Toya, or suddenly starts sulking and acting wounded when he sees Tanisha in a dress, then he had no room to judge me for having a crush on the only man that I ever wanted to be with more than El. I didn't care that Yussef was his cousin, he's not mine! Drew folded his arms and let me get it all out. When I was done explaining that I was not my mother or my father and their ridiculous and scandalous escapades were their history not mine! He almost grinned at me, "Feel better?" I rolled my eyes at him cause I did. He patted my arm, "good. Now suck it up and cut it out!" Then he started walking back towards the hotel.

I really hate him sometimes, I did feel better though. The kids were looking in the fountain so I opted to stay out there with them. Andrew came with a blood pressure monitor and he asked me to go take Tracy's blood pressure, his eyes were worried. I looked back at the table and Tara and that girl were talking. I told myself to suck it up and to let that girl hang herself. Whatever she was hiding would come to the front eventually.

I left to go get El so he could be present for his best friend's wedding.

Yussef

"How come you didn't tell me you were coming? You guys could've sat with us." Tracy said giving me a hug.

"Last minute decision." I tried to hold my breath so that her perfume wouldn't dance in my nose. Didn't work!

"Come meet my sister's fiancé." She invited us.

As we followed I saw someone notice us out the corner of my eye. It was the cashier from the store yesterday. "Small world!" She said with a big smile as she approached us.

"Yes it is, how are you?"

"I'm good. I've never seen you here. Do you go here?"

"No, I'm just visiting." I said

"I've just recently started having bible study." She looked embarrassed.

"That's cool, I'm just making my way back." I pointed at my girls.

"What's your name?"

"Yussef, and you are?"

"Sandreen, nice to meet you Yussef."

I looked at Tracy who did not look amused; I bucked my eyes at her cause I could tell she didn't realize she was looking at us like that. She fixed her face, "I don't think we've met either. I'm Tracy I'm his... Cousin?" She looked at me like she didn't like the way that sound.

"Ok, and that's your little man over there?" She pointed to Andre who was talking with AJ and my girls.

"Yep, that's my baby."

"Do you know what you're having?"

"A boy, another boy."

"You have any kids?" I asked her.

"Not yet, one day I will though."

Then Tracy's family came over and said hello. I made a mental note of who dressed like what. Tara had the side ponytail and a little more sass then her sister Tia who had her hair down and stars in her eyes for her man. Tracy's momma asked how Sandy and I knew each other. Tara leaned in as Sandy explained that we saw each other yesterday but this was our first time meeting. "Are you married?" Tara blurted out.

"No," Sandy said as her eyes landed on each person.

"Stop that!" Sister Thomas said shaking her head at her daughter. "Yussef you're joining us for brunch aren't you?" She asked but she was telling me to come.

"Yes Ma'am."

"Tracy call your husband and tell him to meet us. Tell him I won't take no for an answer." Then she took Sandy by the arm and walked away.

I looked at Tracy, "what was that?"

"I'ma start calling you Georgie." She smiled.

"Kissed the girls and made them cry." Tara said joining in her big sister's fun.

I frowned, "why?" They were making fun of me and it was annoying.

"You didn't see it?" I shook my head no, "you guys will be married by the end of the year." Tracy said matter of factly.

"How you know he won't break her heart?" Tara asked.

"Yussef's not a heart breaker. He's looking for a wife anyways." Tracy said.

"Thanks for the vote of confidence." I was feeling uncomfortable by the topic. Tracy's brother Terence came over and I was happy to change the subject to whatever subject he wanted to talk about.

When we pulled up to the hotel, I took a deep breath. Drew was waiting with Sasha. I just saw her last weekend I did not want to see her today. I stopped so the girls could bust out of the car, then I parked. Drew read my demeanor as I approached. I focused on him then he raised an eyebrow. "Sister Thomas!"

"You see I'm here, I'm not getting in trouble." He chuckled.

"Hey Yussef," Sasha said with one of my girls under each arm.

"Sasha," I said then I turned my attention to the Thomas' as they approached. Drew hugged his mother in-law on his way to his wife's car. When we sat down Sandy sat across from me and Sasha sat by Drew on the end. Sister Thomas was so excited that another one of her girls were getting married. Brody asked Sasha where El was and she said he was spending time with his parents and Auntie.

Sandy seemed cool, well as cool as could be expected under the circumstances. They were watching all of our interactions.

That night I did think about her. I thought about her enough to convince myself to go back to the store to get her number.

I left work a little earlier than I usually leave to get the girls so that I could swing by the store. I casually walked in and she was up front ringing customers up. She didn't see me walk in the front. I stood over to the side watching for a little bit. She was as cute as I remembered, I guess I was distracted Saturday and I didn't notice. When her coworker took over her register, I dropped back. She went in the back; I told myself it would be creepy if I appeared back there. So I looked at the time, I had time. When she emerged from the back she had a cart full of towels. She made her way past me without even noticing me. She walked over to the rainbow wall of bath towels and started folding towels. An elderly couple came over to her cart and asked her where something was and she helped them with a smile. Then she went back to folding. I looked at the time and it was leaving me, I had to make my presence known. As I walked towards her cart she smiled, "it took you long enough." She said cutely.

"Long enough for what?"

"To surface, why didn't you get my number Sunday?"

"We were on display, that's not my style."

"Un huh," she said eyeing me while she continued to fold.

"Why don't they call this place beyond the bathroom? This wall is insane," I said looking at all the color options.

"You can get everything here."

"And my girls did. Their bathroom and rooms are so girly."

"I liked most of the stuff their moms picked out. I bet it all looks amazing." She smiled.
"It does." I looked at my phone.
"Can I see your phone?" She said sticking out her hand. I handed it to her, "unlock it please." She handed it back to me. I unlocked it then I gave it to her. She pressed on the screen. "Now you can call me when you feel like it. I'm sure you have somewhere to be by the way you keep looking at the time."
"I gotta go pick up the girls."
"Yea, something like that." She smiled again.
We chatted for a few more minutes. Then I saw a kid eyeing me out the corner of my eye. I looked at him and he turned and walked away fast. I felt heat on my neck; I didn't need no drama today. I said bye to Sandy then I walked out the door. This kid knew nothing about creeping. I knew he was behind me and he called himself creeping up on me. I put my hand in my jacket pocket; it looked like I was grabbing my keys. As the kid charged I turned around and zapped him. He wanted to scream, but his body dropped and he was on the ground shaking. I looked at him on the ground looking stupid. He looked familiar, but I didn't have time to get reacquainted. "You need to be in school getting an education! You better be happy all I did was shock you! Next time it could mean your life. Stop messing with people; get a job and work for yours! Be smarter than this!" I said then I chirped my car. Before I shut the door I looked down on him on the ground still coming down from the shakes. "Move your feet, I will run you over."

Tracy

I felt that tingling feeling in my arms and legs. I know they say high blood pressure is a silent killer, but I can feel it. I turned on the machine and sure enough it was high still. The doctor told me to check it first thing in the morning when Andrew called last night. I called the doctor and I read my numbers and she told me to come so that we could come up with a plan of attack. I got in the tub and took deep breaths, when Andrew came upstairs he looked at me then he told Andre to get showered and ready cause we were going to the hospital. I could hear Andrew on the phone, he sounded nerved up. He was telling someone he needed the floor swept and security on point. Then his other phone rang, I could tell he was talking to Yussef when his tone calmed and also because I heard him say "Yu."
When I was dressed I sat on the bed trying to understand how I was feeling. I was scared, regardless of whatever, if I have to deliver now it's too soon. Is my baby going to be ok? I felt like I let Andrew down even though technically it's not my fault, I felt guilty. Andre came in the room excited about the possibility of the baby coming today. When we pulled out of the garage Andrew nodded at the guys around the house as we drove away. Andre was assuring Andrew that he got up and took care of his chores this morning and the dogs were fed and had fresh water. When we pulled up to the hospital Amber and Malcolm were there waiting. Amber asked me how I was feeling, and I tried to smile and say I was ok. Malcolm got in the car with Andrew to go park. Then Yussef gently grabbed my other arm as we walked inside. He scared me cause I didn't know where he came from. I told him to let go of my arm, I was fine and I could walk on my own. He and Amber smiled at me and then I apologized for snapping at him. When we got to triage they had me lay down immediately, as soon as I saw the numbers pop up on the screen I knew I wasn't leaving this hospital pregnant. They did another ultrasound measuring everything they could while little Malcolm moved around being difficult.
The doctor explained that my blood pressure was too high and both the baby and I weren't safe remaining that way. They said the baby is about six pounds and I was beyond thirty-five weeks so everything should be ok. Nurse Sandra came in the room and the funky cloud around me lifted. I started crying as soon as I saw her. She hugged me

and assured me that everything was going to be fine. She had a room for my inducement. She checked me in and then she chatted with us for a while, while they stuck needles in me and hooked me up to monitors. Amber came back in the room laughing at Malcolm she said she had to convince him that nothing was happening yet for him to agree to come in the room. When he walked in the room the baby responded to the sound of his voice and started kicking the monitor. Andrew told everyone to be quiet and to let only Amber and I speak. The baby moved a little but normal baby movement. Then Andrew said something and the baby moved more. Andre said hi to the baby and the baby moved more. Then Malcolm said hi and the baby went crazy. Andrew said either the baby was going to be all over Malcolm like Chanel or running from him. Sasha, Sherrell, and Chantel came in the room. After a little while Chantel started looking sick. She asked out loud what did she do? Everyone had a good laugh at her expense.

Amber asked Sasha if she was going to have a vaginal delivery or were they going to take the babies at a certain time. She exhaled and said they hadn't decided yet.

Sherrell asked me if I was in any pain, and I proudly said no. I was relieved and figured maybe I'll be one of those women who just spit the baby out. Then she asked me if my water broke yet, and I said no. Then she rubbed my shoulder and sat down. I was so happy I had Roz braid my hair last week in preparation for anything. Andrew and Malcolm set up a chessboard and Andre was watching them play and they explained each move they made to him. Malcolm kept telling him to remember to watch his opponent. Check his ability, is he the kind that would sacrifice his queen to win, how he uses his pawns, stuff like that.

We were all listening when I felt a gush, and then the feeling of cramps coming on. The cramps grew in a matter of seconds and then I was holding my stomach in pain. Amber asked me if I was ok, and I told her it hurt. She rubbed my back and then nurse Sandra came in the room. I told her I felt a gush and then the pain. Malcolm was heading for the door and he had Andre in tow with him. She pulled the covers back and she said my water broke. She wanted to know what my pain level was on a scale of one to ten and ten being the worst. I was sweating profusely and every time one contraction slowed down another one hit me. I couldn't think about measurements, I grabbed nurse Sandra's hand and I asked her how long I needed to endure that pain. It didn't grow to this intensity it started here and I couldn't hang. She asked if I wanted the epidural, and I said, "YES! FOR THE LOVE OF GOD YES!" Everyone was speaking calmly explaining things and at that point I would've agreed to anything as long as they took the pain away. Everyone except Andrew had to go out while they stuck me AGAIN! This time it was for the good stuff. One hit of the good stuff and I was out.

I was enjoying my slumber when I felt the warmth of Andrew's touch. I slowly opened my eyes and concern was on his face. He asked me how I was feeling, I told him I was doing much better once my drugs started kicking in. I asked him what time it was, and it was two in the morning. Amber was knocked out on the little pullout couch. I asked him if everyone went home, he said Sherrell and Chantel did, but Sasha, Malcolm, and Andre were out in the waiting room. I asked about El and his parents and if she needed to get home to them. He said she talked to El and it was fine. I asked him why he wasn't sleep, and he said he was too worried to sleep. I asked him why was he worried, and he said he wants it too badly. He said next time he won't be as worried for sure, but it's hard when you don't know what to expect. Then he kissed my forehead, he told me he loved me and he thanked me for going through all this just for him. That felt really good to hear, I told him he was welcome. Then I fell asleep again. I awoke to pain and pressure in my uterus. When I stirred everyone in the room stirred. Nurse Sandra came in the room when Andrew called her; it looked like she had been sleeping. She said the head was right there. She called the doctor to come quickly cause I was ready. They transformed my bed and the delivery team came in my room. The baby's doctor and nurse came as well as mine. I held on to Andrew for dear life, and I bared down as hard as I could. They told me I did good. The doctor said they needed one more like that to get past the shoulders. I thought I was still pushing when they said *congratulations mom* and they laid the baby on my chest. He looked at me then he cried a little. They took him over to the side to check him out. "Oh Andy! He looks like you and Andre." Amber said as she cried, and they held each other. The nurse called out six pounds eleven ounces, twenty inches. The baby doctor told Andrew that the baby was about two weeks early, and that he was on his way to being a big boy if he stayed put. They gave the baby who was not crying anymore to Andrew. Amber snapped picture after picture of them in their little moment. When they had me put together, Amber left to get everyone from the waiting room. Andrew put the baby close to me so I could see him. "What you think? Who does he look like, a little Malcolm or a little Andrew?"

I looked at my baby and I was no longer sure. Looking at him he looked like Andrew, but my heart kept saying Malcolm when I was pregnant. "Baby, you decide. Whatever you say it will be." I said feeling a little exhausted.

Andre came in the room, washed his hands, and then sat down so he could hold the baby. No one had to tell him what to do. Sasha cried as soon as she saw him; she said he was too precious. Malcolm smiled at the baby and as soon as Andrew stood up from giving the baby to Andre they hugged. Amber and Sasha snapped pictures of them hugging as we all sat there with big eyes. Were either of them going to shed a tear? "So is this little Andrew?" Amber asked.

Andrew looked at me smiled, and then he looked at his mom. "No," he looked at his father. "He's little Malcolm."

Malcolm's face turned to stone, "what?"

"Our next son will be little Andrew, but this one is little Malcolm." Andrew said.

Malcolm looked at Amber who was boo-who'ing like a baby. "Drew! You don't have to do that."

"We want to." Andrew said looking at his father.

Malcolm looked at the baby, and then he asked to hold him. He smiled real big at the baby, "this is too much! You guys are trying to make me weak with all these babies. First little Chanel, and now this!"

Yussef

"I told you this street don't go all the way through. Yu, you don't listen! And you call yourself alert!" Darryl said.

"I know this street doesn't go through, I drove this way on purpose. Shoot! I'm from Richmond I know which way to go." I said trying to cover up that I forgot.

We pulled up in front of Auntie Lorraine's house. I opened the back door for Chantel, while Derrick and the baby got out on the other side. Amber and Malcolm got out of his car behind us. Darryl ran up on the porch knocking hard. Auntie Lorraine looked surprised to see everyone, she told us to come. Darryl pointed to grass across the street. He said that's where he met Kendra when he hit her with a football on accident.

The women sat and we stood. Auntie looked nervous as she asked what was up. Amber explained that the family was going black for a while and that we needed to relocate her. Without even listening Auntie Lorraine shook her head no. She said she couldn't leave. She said Dionne couldn't handle being moved from place to place. Amber and Chantel pleaded with her. Auntie Lorraine said she couldn't hide with Dionne. Dionne's reaction to the stress would make them targets anyways. She did have a point. Malcolm told her that they had a plan B. He said it would require relocation for a week while they made some upgrades to her house. Since it wasn't time for them to go black yet it wouldn't be the worst thing if Dionne acted out right now. He said once they came back home they couldn't go back out. Malcolm explained that her immediate Family would be under a sort of house arrest. He said only certain Mason's would have access to come and go. He said the Baker Family was going to be on point to watch over them. He said they weren't logistically trained but that was the best he could offer. Derrick and Darryl were quiet not saying too much. When she agreed Amber said there was one other thing. She told Lorraine that David has two more sons. "What?"

"They ran a background check on Patricia and she has two sons Doyle and David Mason."

"What?" She said like she didn't believe it.

"What difference does it make? That's two more people cursed with his DNA." Darryl said frustrated.

"What do you mean?" Auntie Lorraine said turning to face Darryl.

"He means two more people with anger and disconnection issues. I don't know if I ever want to do anything with this information, but since it's your family as well, we felt you should know." Derrick said pointing between him and Amber.

Auntie Lorraine looked confused, "she was telling the truth?" Tears welled up in her eyes. Then she looked at Malcolm, "about everything?"

Malcolm showed no emotion, "I don't know everything she's told you, but right now you gotta ask yourself what matters. If you wanna sit down and talk we can do that. As for right now we've got more pressing issues. We should get your house ready. Yussef are they coming?" Malcolm asked me.

I looked out the window, "Darren just pulled up." I opened the door.

Darren measured all over the house and wrote down everything we needed.

As we drove away Darryl was in a mood. He kept getting frustrated as he tried to call someone. "What's wrong with you?" I asked.

"She's not picking up! What could be so important that she doesn't answer when I call?" He acted like he was choking the phone.

"D! Calm down, she could be working." Derrick said with no patience for his little brother's emotional state.

"Skip it! Yu! You coming out with your boy?" Darryl looked at me with pleading eyes.

"I'm not in the mood for a club."

"How about a lounge?"

"A relaxed club."

"Come on Yu! Work with me. I'm gonna call this chickenhead, you wanna see if she has a friend?"

"If you gonna bring a chickenhead what you need me for?"

"I need to blow off some steam, take the chickenhead out, let her feast on chicken feed like I just did something great for her. When I'm ready, blow my top a couple times until I feel relieved. That's my plan for her, but I need to kick it with my cousin since D-Rick's whimpering for his woman's attention already."

"Whatever! You know I can't deal with you right now." Derrick said looking out the window.

"Fine!" I said in defeat.

We dropped Derrick and Chantel home; we got in Darryl's car and made our way to a lounge in Albany. I had never been here, but Darryl always pulls unknown places out of his hat.

Brenda was pretty, and completely goofy over Darryl. She was eagerly waiting as we pulled up. We went inside and found a table in the corner. Brenda was so excited to see Darryl her mouth was going a mile a minute when Darryl shushed her. She didn't like it but she took it.

Darryl and I were talking when Darryl grabbed my shoulder like he was about to lose it. Kendra walked in with her sister. They sat at a table and I could tell Darryl wanted to ditch Brenda who was now pouting cause she saw Kendra as well. Aunrey sat over to the side in the background as if he wasn't here, we nodded hellos. Darryl took a deep breath when a guy walked in. The guy looked nervous but happy to see Kendra. Her sister hugged him but Kendra didn't stand. I asked Darryl who we were looking at. Darryl said it was the guy who couldn't pay the bill. I told Darryl not to go over, and to let them have their moment. When the guy touched Kendra's arm even though she looked at him crazy Darryl was out of his seat. "This is why you couldn't answer your phone!" Darryl said angry.

Kendra looked around the room trying to see where he came from. When she saw our table she stood up and put her finger in Darryl's face. "Don't question me about my life when you ALWAYS have somebody on the side!"

"I wouldn't need someone on the side if you'd answer your phone!"

"Don't try to blame her on me! You always got to have someone. You can't ever just be cool. I can't trust someone like that."

"You always trying to make these irrelevant imbeciles feel like they have a chance when you know you're in love with me!"

"Um, I'm her...."

Darryl cut him off, "I'M TOLERATING YOU! DON'T MAKE ME HURT YOU!"

I got up cause Darryl was about to lose it, and that meant someone was going to bleed. I guess Brenda thought that was her cue to get up as well, she followed me over. "D! Let's go, you need to calm down, in a quiet place after the day you had." I put my hand on his shoulder.

"What happened today?" Kendra looked at Darryl.

"Yes, take him...." The guy's gesture suggested that if he finished that comment it was going to be bad.

Didn't matter cause Darryl punched him in the head and his body went limp.

"DARRYL!" Kendra screamed, her sister smiled.

"Darryl what? I warned him! Didn't I warn him?" I shook my head yes as I walked away to take care of the manager or owner whoever this was who was watching in horror, Aunrey had the biggest smile as he watched the scene; thank goodness it was early and barely anyone here. I made the call to have Mitigated staff sweep the spot.

Darryl and Kendra kept fussing, when Darryl kissed Kendra, Brenda lost it. Next thing you know Darryl had Brenda by her hair and he's telling her to stand down cause she tried to charge at Kendra. Kendra was telling him to let her go, and her sister was begging him to let Brenda go. I didn't need this drama tonight, I needed to go home and relax. Not sitting here watching these two fight it out in some dramatic lover's quarrel. Darryl wouldn't leave until Kendra got in her car and left, Aunrey followed her. We left Brenda inside with the guy Nursing his head.

****

I pulled up to the house, and I was greeted by dogs. I looked the main dog in his eyes he growled and I growled back. "Sitz!" I commanded. The dog did as he was told, "Hier!" The dog came to me, "Braver Hund!" I said as I patted the good doggie. The dog started wagging his tail.

"Why you out here punking my dogs?" Amber said standing in the doorway., with a smile.

"Not punking, coming to an understanding." I gave her a hug. "How are you?"

"I'm good." She stood back and looked at me. "What's her name?"

"What makes you think there's a her?" I said blushing.

"Momma knows her babies, spill it!" She said tapping her foot.

My insides bubbled over, "momma?" I said just above a whisper while I grinned at her.

"You heard me! Stop deflecting! Spill it! Who is she?"

I wish Amber was my momma. "It's still new. Nothing to write home about."

"If you say so sweetheart, but I'm looking at you and you're glowing." She said with a big smile.

"Amber," Malcolm called out from his office. His voice echoed off the walls. "Let the boy come in, we're waiting for him."

I followed Amber down a hallway and into Malcolm's office. It was huge. I saw Drew, Derrick, Juan, Sasha, Jeff, JoJo, and my eyes landed on Darryl. "I AM SO DISAPPOINTED!" Darryl said shaking his head.

I smiled, "what?"

"Who's the chickenhead?"

I shrugged, "she's not a chickenhead."

"It's a real girl?" He asked in shock.

"Yep, not a lap girl."

"Whatever! Now that Yussef's here let's talk strategies." Malcolm said.

Richard, Uncle Jeff, Uncle Frank, Tanisha, Blu, and a few other Mitigated folks were on the phone. We were planning for our black out period. Sasha kept looking at me and looking away like her eyes were betraying her by looking at me. I put my focus on Malcolm; I didn't need no more problems. Max started blowing up my phone while I was in the meeting. She was acting so ugly I turned the ringer off. I told her I couldn't see her anymore, and of course she flipped. She tried popping up at my apartment, but I've already rented that unit out. I got a call from Pearla saying Max was sitting outside her house waiting for me to show up. Max didn't take too kindly to me sending Darlene to deal with her. When she blew up my phone that night, I told her our time had passed and I didn't want to keep playing with her. I reminded her that I warned her that this would happen. Now she leaves me alone for about a week and then she starts blowing me up. I told Malcolm that the safe house was ready, the location and information was with Juan. Juan said he already sent his family away to avoid the mass exodus. Tanisha informed us that she wasn't going to stick with the group. Malcolm stared at the intercom with serious eyes as he asked her why. Sasha had shock and disbelief all over her face. Then he told her to call him back ten minutes after we dismissed. Malcolm stood up and paced a little behind his chair. He was mad, he told everyone to take a break. He needed to talk to Tanisha and it couldn't wait until later. He said he would call everyone on the phone back. He told everyone in the room to go take a break, and that he'd call us back in the room in a minute. "Tanisha if this is about me teasing you cause you looked pretty in your dress, I won't say another word." Darryl said.

"Not now Darryl!" Malcolm barked.

Derrick kept looking at Drew who was unusually quiet. Derrick called his big brother outside. Juan called Darryl, Jeff, and JoJo to the table. I walked into the living room to sit forgetting that Sasha was even here.

Sasha

What did she just say? I stared at the intercom like I didn't hear her right. Did Tanisha just say what I thought she said? Her off the wall comment put me in an "I don't care" mood. I couldn't wait to get out of this house to talk to her. Malcolm kicked us out of his office so he could talk to Tanisha. I sat in the living room watching Yussef's happy-go-lucky looking behind unknowingly walk towards me. As soon as he crossed the invisible line I went in on him. The day he backs down to me means he doesn't care. Even though I like getting my way, I like it when he puts his foot down.

Yussef

She was quieter than normal as well. "It's that girl who was at the brunch isn't it?" I didn't say anything. "She seems nice enough, but she's hiding something."

"Ok, but we're still getting to know each other."

"I was just warning you. From what I hear, when you get involved you dive head first which is a good thing, but I'm just cautioning you to pump the breaks a little bit."

"Your husband loves you."

"I know."

"So focus on him, and stop worrying about reading the women in my life."

"I just want you to be happy."

"Says the married woman." I shook my head.

"Your happiness matters whether you believe me or not."

I stood up, "right Sasha." Then I started walking away.

"What?"

"You're married! Are you trying to have an emotional conversation with some guy who isn't your husband? You're married and carrying your husband's children!"

"Since when has being the other man bothered you?" She raised an eyebrow.

LOW BLOW! I was angry and in her face, "you're just jealous cause that wasn't you!"

She cut her eyes at me. "You've always had a man and worried about what I'm doing and what's going on with me. You aren't trust worthy! Focus on your man! Don't worry about the secrets of the woman I'm seeing." I could smell desire all over her breath.

"I'm sorry, I'm just saying she's not the one for you!"

"You're gonna say that about every female in my life. Stop provoking me to these emotional conversations. This is no different than you climbing on me and kissing on me. Control yourself, and show your husband some respect!"

"What's going on?" Amber whispered.

I pointed at Sasha, and Sasha put her head down. I left them to talk while I walked down the hallway. I was pissed off; she just wants me to argue with her so she can get up under my skin. Maybe I need to move away! Take my girls and work remotely from somewhere else for a while. Sasha is not going to be the death of me! I waited outside the office for Malcolm and Tanisha to finish talking. I could hear the low grumble of Malcolm's voice through the door. Max called again and I answered, "I'm working!"

"I'm pregnant!" She said immediately.

Everything in me went blank, "what?"

"I've been trying to tell you, I'm pregnant!"

"By whom?" I asked, this girl had so many issues that the only way she got me off was in her mouth. I never had a chance to get her pregnant in my mind. This felt like Shannon all over again.

"What do you mean by whom? You know I haven't been with anyone but you!"

That much had to be true, but I wasn't buying it. "I'm working I'll call you back!" I hung up.

Derrick and Darryl approached me, "what's up Yu? You look like you just got spooked." Darryl said.

"Max just said she's pregnant." I was getting angry.

Derrick watched my face, "you don't believe her?"

"NO! I stayed strapped!" I clinched my jaw, "it's stupid to even say we have sex! She has too many issues. She's trying to hold on cause I told her that her time was up."

"Oh I see, the chickenhead feather hold!" Darryl was shaking his head to say he agreed with himself.

Derrick and I looked at him, "the what?"

"The chickenhead feather hold. Feathers have no real grip, but they try to hold on with a fake pregnancy as a last ditch effort to hold on. Yu, this is what you do. Take a pregnancy test over there. Make her piss on the stick in front of you. When its negative just walk away."

"Could she be sleeping with someone else? It could be theirs." Derrick said.

"I highly doubt there's someone else, like I said she's got issues."

Darryl shook his head, "that don't sound like fun at all. I don't know how you did that."
"Me neither!" I said in frustration.
Derrick cut his eyes at me, "uh I think her name is Darlene."
"YU! You hit that? Nice! I guess I'm taking her off my future hit list."
I smiled, "right."
Drew walked up, his eyes were fixed on me. "What did you say to Sasha?"
"I reminded her that she's married and to stop provoking me to have emotional conversations with her."
All three of them stood there reading me, Darryl whistled and patted my shoulder. "It's a doggone shame!"
I didn't ask him what he meant, I knew already. I counted backwards; I wanted this meeting over so I could get out of this house. Malcolm opened the door then he told Darryl to get everybody. Andrew and Sasha sat next to each other holding the same expression. Once everyone was back on the line, Tanisha said, "so I thought I was transferring but Malcolm has spoken." Then she chuckled.

****

That meeting couldn't finish fast enough. I had no idea they had so many options for pregnancy tests. I was frustrating myself trying to decide. One of the workers asked me if I needed help. I pointed to the rows of tests, and asked her which one would she trust her future to. She helped me pick out a two pack. I bought a gallon of water and then I banged on Max's door. I gave her the water and I told her to drink. She tried to hug me and I refused. I told her to drink; she did as she was told. When she got up I put the test in her hand. She looked at me with pleading eyes. The truth was there, she lied, but I made her take the test any ways. Both test were negative. I washed my hands and headed for the door. "Yussef PLEASE! Don't do this to me!"
"Max I don't want this. How could you lie about something so serious? You do realize that I do know how babies are made. I got two to prove the point."
"I love you!" She screamed.
That hurt cause I knew she was telling the truth. "If you love me why would you lie to me? It's never ok to lie to someone you love." Then I felt guilt pour all over me, but not for her.
"I didn't know what else to do. I can't believe you'd leave me hanging like this."
"I know you're going through a lot, but you keep forcing things, I told you this wasn't a good idea, and you agreed that when our time was over it was over. It's over Max. That doesn't mean try to manipulate your way into my heart. That will only make me hate you. I wish you no harm, but I can't pretend with you."

****

I went back to Malcolm's and I waited for her to get in her car. I openly followed her. She got on the freeway, and she took us through Berkeley, then Richmond, over the San Rafael Bridge all the way to the Muir Woods parking lot. I didn't know what I was going to say, but the fact that she took us here meant she knew. I leaned against my car as I waited for her to get out of hers. She leaned on her car with tears streaming down her face. "I LOVE MY HUSBAND!"
"I know!" I felt confused.
"EVERY TIME I THINK I UNDERSTAND, I REALIZE THAT I DON'T!"
"I know!"
"I DON'T WANT TO BE MY MOMMA! AND YOU ARE NOT MY FATHER!"
"I know!" I said, "Why Sasha? We never slept together or even close. I like El; he's a good man. He trusts you."
Sasha shrugged, "maybe Richard is right about something after all."
"He's not right about this. You are in love with your husband, I've hated the look of it from the first time I saw it." I wanted to come around that car. **God is watching**!

"What is it about you?"

"I was the first person to tell you no and to stick to it."

"It's more than just that."

"It doesn't matter Sasha, you're married and I like Sandy. This ends today." I heard myself say.

"How?"

"By being honest with each other, is it all of this because I continue to reject you?"

"No, I love you." She said in complete embarrassment.

"Ok well," I took a deep breath. "I love you and it's not because you're pretty even though that helps, but you were the first person to see me. Not too many people can see me. This ends today. Go home to your husband knowing you made the right choice to honor him. You're free to go be the wonderful wife I always knew you'd be." The kind of wife I need.

"Yussef! You can't tell me you love me and expect me to walk away like you just told me my shoes are cute. I love you, and you love me? You really love me?" Her eyes were big and pouring out tears like a river.

I kept telling myself that **God is watching**, stay behind this car. "You're married."

She dropped her head, "El is a good man."

"You are his everything."

When she looked at me with that pained look my feet started to move towards her. I told them to replant on the asphalt. "I love El, he's my best friend. Maybe it's the pregnancy hormones that won't let me hide what I've always felt."

"I like El, he's a good man."

"You don't want to hurt him, I understand cause I don't either. This isn't fair Yussef! It literally hurts to exist like this. When you passively speak to me that makes me angry." She moved around the car. "You always push me away."

"What am I supposed to do? You're never single." I smiled and move two big steps away from her. She's trying to quietly get close to me. Although I want to mess up her hair with the juicy kiss I've always dreamed of laying on her, I know I have to retreat. Lord knows how hard it was that night with Tracy, this feels ten times worse. Like if I allowed her to get as close to me as Tracy was that night, nothing could stop me from going in. Nothing except, the reminder in front of her that she belongs to another man. I stopped moving away as she moved closer. Sasha was standing in front of me with red eyes. I touched her face, "I love you Sasha. Please go home." Then I rubbed her stomach with my other hand. Sasha kissed my arm as I put my forehead on her head. "Please go home Sasha."

"You love me?" I nodded my head yes against her forehead. "You want me?" I nodded my head yes again. "Kiss me!"

"I can't!"

She moaned a frustrated moan, "why not?"

"Cause I won't be able to stop. You have the power to completely undo everything that I've stood for all my life. If you love me you will go home to your husband."

"What about me?"

"You got me!"

Sasha cried, then she walked back to her car, blew me a kiss from across the car; I smiled even though my heart seemed to ache. We got in our cars, I assumed she called El and I called Sandy. I followed her back to Oakland, and then she went her way and I went mine. That night I sat on my bed confused. My admission freed me, it felt better than the feeling I had when I initially started dating Sylvia. I was trying to put my feeling on it for a long time. I exhaled, transparency recovery in progress. Telling her the truth made me feel seen. I like El and I never want to disrespect him, and most importantly **God is watching**.

It seems like everyone has been telling me not to do the right thing. Like I've earned the right to be selfish for once. I never want a redo on that moment, but I am SO PROUD of myself! We never have to speak on it again. Regardless of what happens now, I could die knowing that the woman I love loves me. She's willing to walk away from everything for me. I will always live on in Sasha's heart like my father lives in Roz's.

Sasha

After I talked to Yussef, I couldn't tell you how I felt. I drove home on autopilot. When I came home I laid on the bed with my shoes and everything still on. When El came home he asked me if I was sick. He was touching my forehead etc. searching for indication of a fever. I told him the babies, were fine and it was their trifling momma who needed help. My best friend let me admit everything on my heart to him. He didn't say anything; he let me get it out. When I was done he had sad eyes, but he kissed me and thanked me for telling him. He admitted that sometimes he gets caught up in looking back at Zoila too. He said moving to the west coast was the best thing he could've ever done. He exhaled, "when this whole episode is said and done with your family and my parents are gone. We can't work for Malcolm anymore. And we got to move."
I cried harder, "where are we going? Zoila and your sister are in New York."
"And your father is in LA. Where does that leave us?"
"Atlanta?"
"Or somewhere in the middle. We'll start posting out after the babies are born." He said calmly.
"You're not mad at me?" I asked wishing he would say yes.
"Sasha, you were so patient with me. It's my turn to return the favor." He kissed my forehead.
"It hurts though?" I asked knowing that it does.
"Of course it does! None of my natural reactions are going to change or fix anything. You're all the family I've got. I'm not letting go."
****
"Everything has gone according to plan. El's parents are in place." Darlene said.
I watched her eyes, she was in work mode. "D?" She looked at me. I shrugged, she sucked her teeth. "It's just sex. Why do you keep trying to make it into something else?"
"You're still seeing him?"
"No," she sighed. "He says he's been going back to service and he's trying to rely on God for strength to move on. Blah, blah, blah!" She rolled her eyes. "It's a shame cause he was good at what he does." I frowned, "you asked. I thought he'd at least want a top off before you guys went in, but I guess you guys will have to deal with backed up Yussef."
"Tracy delivered early so he'll have a buddy in the struggle." I sighed. "What name are they under?"
"Edwards and Pfifer." She gave me all the information for El's parents. They were in the same care facility but admitted separately under different names. I thanked her. Then I walked to my car. Darlene was on her phone calling it in but I spotted the car already. I waited for her to tell me it was ok to go.
I picked El up from the office and then we made our way to the airport. I told him there was a car following us. He couldn't really see the driver. As we sat at the gate waiting for our plane to board Detective Dartnell sat next to me. "What is going on?" She asked as she leaned in.
"What do you mean?" I asked her.
"Everything is hot right now, and you guys are behaving so well. It's a setup isn't it?" She searched my eyes, "are you guys going to kill everyone at Malcolm's wedding? I can't put my finger on it, but I know you guys are up to something. And let me be honest,

as soon as I throw your grandfather and Uncles in jail I'm retiring! I don't care who your great grandfather was. If you want me to go easy on you, you'll tell me what's going on."
"Oh right, cause I see what cooperating with you got Toya."
"NOBODY TOLD HER TO GO AROUND ATTEMPTING HER OWN MURDERS JUST BECAUSE SHE WAS COOPERATING WITH ME!"
"Why are you yelling?" El and I looked at her with frowns.
"Where are you going?" She asked.
"Why is that any of your business?" El barked.
"And why are you following me around making me paranoid?"
"Nice accent! Where are you from? I'll deport you as soon as I lock this pretty little thing up!"
"Dartnell?" She cut her eyes at me. "Didn't your momma ever teach you that you can catch more flies with sugar than you ever could with vinegar?"
"Are you trying to say I'm not nice?" She looked between El and I; we shook our heads yes like kids. "I'M NICE! I USED TO BE A FREAKING LADY UNTIL THIS FAMILY CRAP! I'M TIRED! I WANT TO RETIRE!" She huffed, "there's only a small group of people I can trust. You guys keep turning everyone out. Turan was a good man. You didn't have to do him like that."
"Like what?" I had no idea what she was talking about.
"I can't prove it, but you guys got him strung out. I don't know what he's on, but he's on something. And it didn't happen until he ran out there to LA trying to talk to you. You Wallace's are WICKED! You should've just killed him, but making him an instant addict is heartless." She whistled.
"You're lying! You know we didn't do anything like that." I said standing to board my plane.
"Ok, don't believe me if you want." She shrugged and stood up, "you two have a nice flight out."
I grabbed El's hand and I told him that she was messing with our heads. We landed at LAX without incident and we went straight to the hospital for my appointment. I had the release forms, etc. ready to transfer my prenatal care up north. Before we did that we were having one last ultrasound. El couldn't stop smiling as we looked at our children on the screen. I could tell they were good babies already. The technician took a picture, in the picture she pointed to baby A's labia. In the second picture she pointed to baby B's labia. "I wanna name one Sasha!" I blurted out. El started laughing at me. They were too precious and immediately I started thinking of all the clothes they were going to have. The technician took pictures of all the other important stuff that she needed, and then we went up to the doctor's office. El couldn't stop smiling; he said they looked so healthy and strong. I told him our girls had his head. Neither one of us could stop smiling. The doctor said everything looked good, both babies were healthy. She said it may be touch and go once we hit the thirty-week mark and my doctor will be monitoring me to determine next steps, whether I'll deliver early. And whether that would be vaginally or by C-section. I thanked El for being the best husband ever, and I told him I couldn't wait to raise our family together.

Yussef

"So like I was saying Mr. Davis, that top unit has a leak in the bathroom, and the floor needs to be fixed, etc." My property management said.
"Ok, sounds pretty straight forward. I'll swing by in about an hour." I said as I walked towards my car.
"Ok, thank you sir." The guy said as we hung up.
I chuckled to myself, he called me sir…. ok. Whatever. "Yussef!" My momma called out.

I exhaled and hoped for once she did what she needed to and not what she felt like would cause more drama or mess. I looked at her, "you're asking me to leave my husband behind."

"Momma you have a choice just like everybody else. You can hang around here and take your chances or you can go to the safe place I set aside for Grandma and Arthur, but Jarvis can't go."

"What if something happens to him?"

"Momma he's so stupid that he'll be like the cockroach that survives everything. He will be fine; I am concerned with your safety only. Even if you stay behind put the baby in the car with Grandma, when they leave its done. And they're leaving in a few minutes."

"Yussef?" She was scared and rightfully so, but I didn't have time for indecision.

Arthur came out the door carrying the baby carrier in one hand and my Grandma's hand in the other. "Shonda you coming or not?" He asked with a smile.

I told them I was sending them on an all-expense paid vacation, I apologized that it was so last minute but I told them they had to go now. Arthur watched my eyes for a minute and then he said they'd go wherever I sent them. My momma asked me to go out in the backyard. She asked me what was going on, and I told her I needed everyone to lay low. I told them to leave their cellphones and to only really take their medications. The car service was waiting for them. I hugged everyone and then I gave Arthur a clean phone. I told him to leave it off and not to turn it on. I'd turn it on when I needed to call them and only at that time. They didn't get it but they didn't argue either. Arthur and my Grandma got in the car, they asked my momma one more time if she was coming. She hugged me and then she got in the car. Immediately I felt relief when she got in. I watched the car drive off.

When I got to Oakland, I went by the apartment building and I talked to my tenants in the apartment with the leak and the tenants below who were affected by the leak. When I walked out Max was waiting. I exhaled and then I told her today wasn't the day. She begged me to tell her what she did wrong. I told her she's trying to force something that wasn't going to work. I reminded her that we discussed this. I told her from the beginning that we weren't going to work as a couple. She said she thought I'd change my mind. I asked her what happened that would make it seem as though I had a reason to change my mind? She said we made love. I put my arm around her shoulder, and I told her that I appreciated the fact that she opened up to me in a way that she hasn't with anyone in years, but I warned her before we went there that it wasn't a good idea. Out of frustration she screamed at me. She said everything that she thought would hurt me. Then she told me she was going to have someone beat me up and that I had no idea who she was. I chewed back my smile and pretended like her threat was serious as I told her I apologized. I know she was hurt and probably embarrassed so she acted like this. I waited for her to leave, and then I drove up to my house. I took a deep breath as I approached it. I put my nice car in the garage next to my father's car and my bikes. I hadn't walked through the rest of the house since I got the keys. I secured everything then I walked over to Derrick's. We chatted for a little then he gave me a ride to my bucket at the mall kiosk. I sent word to Juan that just about all the ducks were in a row.

Episode 19

Lanie

When I stepped out of the elevator Dorian was standing in the lobby. His eyes looked so sad when he saw me. I approached cautiously, uncomfortable with whatever he was about to say. "What?"

He shook his head, "I thought I could do it. I tried, but I can't!"

"Whatever Dorian! I'm not going to be a party to you cheating on your wife." I started walking, "I know I did you wrong and I'm sorry. I'm sorry that my momma didn't go off on me sooner. I...."

"I'm not married."

I don't know why that made me nervous. "Why are you here?"

"Cause I couldn't marry her. I've got to go away for job training for six months. Can you get it together by then? I can't be without you."

"Define getting it together."

"Go to service."

"Ok."

He lowered his eyes, "but?"

Tears forced their self out of my eyes. "I thought you married her. I knew you were gone forever. I will go, but I do not agree to relinquishing my bratty ways."

Dorian put his hands in my hair, "I wouldn't have you any other way." Then he kissed me.

I wanted the kiss to go on forever. Dorian said when he came back he wanted to have dinner with our families. I agreed, as long as I have my man back, I agreed.

Amber

I AM MISSES MALCOLM LATOUR! I keep saying it because it feels too good to be true. I keep plowing Malcolm with love, this is exactly the way I should feel married to the man that I love. All Malcolm has to do is inhale and I'm all over him. Even when my body was begging me for a rest I still kept coming after him. I had no real interest in coming up for air. Then reality hit when I would think about how good the good feeling felt and how wonderful it would've been to go away on our honeymoon right away. I'd talk myself out of feeling bad by saying that we'd have forever to make up for not taking it right now.

Jade said that the staff at North Star is all really excited about my upcoming wedding. They were even more excited about the paid time off while the school was closed. So I went down to the school to pop my head in. Tony still had his little huffy attitude. I came out and asked him if he was mad because I didn't ask him to be in my wedding. I didn't understand what all the attitude was for. He rolled his eyes and said if I wasn't paying him to be in the wedding he didn't care. I told Tony he needed to take a Midol and calm down. The rest of the staff was excited about my wedding and they were telling me about the dresses they found. I told them they could wear any color other than purple cause that's what my wedding party was wearing. Ginger couldn't have been sent to be invisible because the way she watched us was so obvious. Tony said he didn't like her and she was too quiet for his liking. In her classes she taught the children like she was hired to do, but the rest of the time she was sitting there listening and taking everything in. She didn't even fake a personality or like she was an interesting person. If I didn't know she was a mole she'd still stand out as weird to me. Desiree got really happy when she saw me. She hugged me tight and nuzzled her head into my stomach just like Darryl used to do. She said she missed me, and I hugged her and told her I missed her as well. I told her after my honeymoon I would have more time to come to the school and spend time with the individual classes. She squeezed me tighter.

I took calls at the school from the Vegas vendors for the wedding day. Everything was going according to plan.

Yussef

I really like this girl. She's cool, funny; the fact that we can have bible discussions is a plus. Sasha telling me that she was hiding something struck a nerve though. I saw that, but I haven't given her a chance to trust me so I stay mindful. Other than that it's been great. I told her I'm going to have to go out of town for a while so I wouldn't physically see her for a minute, and I would call her when I could. I figure since we hadn't really had any interactions that would link us she should be fine.

****

"Hello?"

"Jackson, it looks like it's going to rain."

"OH SHOOT! SERIOUS? WHERE ARE YOU CALLING ME FROM? NEVER MIND! NEVER MIND! SHOOT! OK! I'M GOING!"

I hung up and then I waited. Jackson and Melissa came out the door fussing at each other. Melissa was asking too many questions and she had her purse on her shoulder. Little Jack ran out the door with a juice box in his hands. Jackson stopped when he saw the black car blocking the driveway. They didn't notice me leaning against my car across the street, "pop the trunk." I called out.

Both of them jumped. "Yussef what's going on?" Melissa asked.

"We need to lay low, you guys gotta disappear for a while." I said calmly.

"Why?"

"For more reasons than you could understand. Melissa I don't have time for twenty questions. Your husband and I have discussed this. Either you get in the car and live, or you stay back here and take your chances."

"I'm just trying to understand…."

Jackson cut her off, "Shut up Melissa! Get in the car and SHUT UP! This is happening, you're going, and I swear to God if you say one more thing I'ma snap your neck! Get in the car! Get in the CAR!"

Melissa looked so shocked, I tried not to laugh, but I couldn't help it. Jackson was at the end of his rope with this crazy broad. I patted him on his shoulder, like he did well. Then I took Melissa's purse from her. I told her he packed everything she needed. I took his phone and little Jack's phone. I told him not to turn on the phone I gave him, and I'd call him only when I needed to reach him. He gave me a pound, and then he got in the car. I watched the car drive off. I exhaled, and then I drove to Hubby's.

Nicole was running around grabbing her last minute things. Hubby told her to leave her purse and phone like I told him. They were ready in record time. I followed their car to Ms. Connie's house. She was ready and happy to be going away with her boys. I took a deep breath then I asked Nicole to come with me inside Sylvia's place. We could hear Sylvia singing as we approached her apartment. I was happy she was in a good mood. I knocked on the door and she opened with a smile when she saw that it was me. She frowned when she saw Nicole, but she invited us in. I took a deep breath, "Sylvia I need you to pack enough clothes for the next two weeks. You've got ten minutes." I looked at my phone.

"What?"

"Here I'll help you." Nicole said, "I just packed my stuff."

"You're going?" Sylvia asked.

"You're going with her."

My words swished around her, "as in you're not coming with us? Where am I going?"

I put my hands on her shoulders and looked her in her eyes, "do you trust me?"

"Yes," she said wholeheartedly.

"Then I need you to pack now, answers later."

"Ok," She said as she ran up the stairs taking Nicole with her. I could hear them moving really fast up there. "Yussef? What should I pack for Sydney? Did you pack for her already?"

"She's taken care of."

403

She came down with her purse; I took it off of her shoulder and put it on the couch. She frowned but she accepted it. "One more thing Sylvia, Syd's gonna stay with me."
"Say that again?"
"You're going to go with Nicole and Hubby, and Joy and her family. Hubby's mother will be there."
"WITHOUT SYDNEY? FOR HOW LONG?"
"I don't know how long."
"No! You didn't even let me say goodbye. Yussef! You can't do this!" Sylvia screamed.
"Sylvia, do you trust me?"
"You're making me question why."
"Remember although I'm not in love with you, I do love you. I won't let anything bad happen to you. I need to have Syd with me right now. You will see her soon enough. Trust me, please!"
Tears poured out of Sylvia's eyes, she wanted to tell me no, but she didn't, she did as I told her. I kissed her forehead and then I put her in the car.
****
I rang the doorbell; Roz was surprised to see me. She said she thought I was Ben. When I told her it was time to go she hesitated. She said she didn't understand why it had to be so sudden. I told her Tanisha was supposed to explain how this was all going down. She asked me about Ben, and I told her that Tanisha didn't make arrangements for him. When she started to fix her lips to say she was going to wait on Ben, I surprised myself when I snapped. I told her I don't know Ben and from what I knew he was never around, and when he was around all he did was hurt her and Tanisha. "You don't know Ben, you only know what Tanisha's told you." She said defensively.
"Roz, I can't handle this. You are the one person I was sure of, and the one person to actually sound like you're going to tell me no." She exhaled like she was going to tell me she hated to disappoint me. "ROZ! He's not my father! Leave him! If he's here when you come back ok! You don't owe him any loyalty! He left you years ago, he pops up twenty something years later and you are willing to risk your life for him! Would he do the same?" I stared at her.
Her eyes got big, "I swear it's like looking at your daddy." A tear fell, "I'll go get my things." She said as she hurried away.
I made a mental note of how badly I was going to lose my religion when I give Tanisha a piece of my mind for setting me up like this. She knew I was the only one who could get Roz to come without her Ben.

Kendra

I awoke to the sound of my phone ringing. The darkness in my room told me whoever it was, was going to rub me the wrong way. "Hello?" I said with sleep in my voice.
The person hesitated. "Kendra? This is Megan."
I exhaled, "ok? And you're on my phone because?"
"I know it's early but I couldn't sleep." She sounded like she was crying.
"So that means I don't sleep?"
"Anton came home with some crazy story about how he got his concussion. I'm assuming you were involved some kind of way."
"Why do you ASSUME that?"
"The only time he lies to me is when you're involved."
"What is the point of this phone call? I'm sleep!"
She cried harder, "please leave Anton alone. We have a family."
"Tell Anton to stay off my phone. I'm not going after him. He's the one coming after me. Talk to your man!" Then I hung up, that was how long ago?

I tried to go back to sleep but I was irritated. I sat up and tried to catch my breath. That little scene was hitting me in a funky way. I met up with Anton cause he was harassing me and he wanted to clear the air. No one told him to drink courage juice and ever think it was ok to pop off to Darryl. I could've sworn he knew better. That one hit gave him a concussion? Whoa! I mean you heard it, but I don't think Darryl hit him as hard as he could have. When my phone rang again I got irritated! I am not going to deal with ridiculous females on my phone crying over their man. I snatched the phone, "HELLO?" The static on the line made me look at the caller ID; it was a bunch of zeros.
"Kendra," Shai said.
"Shai? Where are you calling from?"
"A portable phone. We don't have much time. I need to see you."
Jason would wring my neck even if I said I was cool off Darryl. Shai is off limits, I don't understand why, but if my father says no, I have to respect it right? "Shai, I can't!"
"Kendra, listen to me. There's a lot of things happening right now. I need to see you, I need to make sure you're safe."
"I'm safe Shai, my father makes sure I'm safe."
I could hear Shai wrestling with himself. "I'm in too deep! Kendra, there's things you don't understand. What time are you off today?"
My fill-in staff pretty much has everything else covered. Kalani and I personally take care of Amber & Chantel's houses only. And today was COOKIE DAY! After Chantel's house I'd be free. I guess I could meet him since he's making it seem urgent. "I could meet you after four."
"There's no way you could come sooner?"
I felt weird; Jason was going to kill me for disobeying him as it was. "I can try for three but that's pushing it."
"Ok, ok. I understand. Get a pen and paper." I did, "meet me at the Pasta Pelican Restaurant on the Waterfront in Alameda. I'll be waiting for you just inside the door." He gave me the address and he told me to put it in my phone, and to come as early as I can.
"Shai what's so urgent?" I said feeling nervous.
"I'll explain everything, come alone."
"If I have to drop off my sister it's going to take me longer to get there."
"Fine bring her, it doesn't matter. You promise you're coming?"
"I'm coming.".
When we got off the phone I now had nervous energy. I needed to clean something, so I cleaned my already clean bathroom. I showered and then I went next door to Kalani's. She was knocked out snuggled up in her covers and drooling. When I sat on her bed she jumped. "Don't sneak up on me!"
She asked me why I was up so early and I told her about Megan's call. Kalani shook her head at the whole thing. She was pumping me up to want to call that girl and go off some more. Then I swallowed and I told her about Shai's call. "I agreed to meet him."
"You're kidding!" Kalani stood up. "Just because Yussef sent momma and Jason off does not mean you act like he's not here! Aunrey won't let it happen. Why would you say yes?"
"It sounded urgent, and I don't know. I'm not seeing Darryl anymore so why not?"
She rolled her eyes, "for now! Everybody knows you two are getting back together. You guys are the only goofy ones who pretend like your quote unquote break-ups mean anything."
"I'm serious!"
"I'm sure you think so, and then.... You remember how Darryl loves you and puts it down. Please tell me where this brotha is lacking and why you have to be so difficult?"
"So it's all on me? I'm the reason? You know what he did!" I said frustrated.
"Oh so he's forever wrong? Are you forever wrong too?"

I got angry, "SHUT UP KALANI! You're supposed to be my sister! Is he paying you?"
"Kendra!"
"I don't want to talk about this anymore. Get dressed, I'm making breakfast!"
I went in the kitchen slamming pots and pans. Aunrey knocked on the door as he came in. He asked why I was up so early. I told him about Megan's call, and as he was digesting that I told him about Shai. He was going to find out anyways, I might as well be honest and forth coming. He was on his phone making calls while he ate, then he went outside. He said he was waiting for confirmation whether I was coming home or not cause I wasn't meeting Shai. "What? Why?"
"He's never been to your house, how he get your landline number? The whole thing is not sitting well with me."
"It sounded important."
"Yea, he wants to give it to you and we're blocking. Let it go Kendra. As soon as I find him he won't be calling you no more. "
I didn't know what he meant but I didn't want to find out either. Kalani lightened the mood by being silly and getting us to laugh. When she did her time check, she said it was time to go to Chantel's. We looked at each other and smiled, COOKIE DAY! Aunrey told me to call him when we were ready to leave. He said he'd have instruction for us at that time. Then he followed us to the security gate. Once we were inside he drove on.

Sasha

"How are daddy's babies doing this morning?" El said talking to my stomach. He kissed my stomach and then he kissed me. I keep waiting for him to flash, to get angry about something stupid as a guise for how angry he is with me, but he keeps looking at me with nothing but love in his eyes. He's choosing not to deal with the reality of my emotional affair. The reason he kept us on pause in the first place, neither one of us were emotionally ready. I thought I was over Yussef, I had no idea I would still feel like this. El has to hate me, there's no way he couldn't. I honestly believe he's so focused on this pregnancy that he can't see much else. I know how important being a father is to him, I feel horrible. "Baby girls even though your mum and I can't agree on names for you, you are my princesses!"
"Seriously El? One of them has a name. You just want to give one some old lady name. My name is Sasha! Sasha! Her name can't be Eleanor! Eeewwllll! I want her to like her name."
"You want to name the other after your nurse."
"Which sounds better Sasha or Jasmine. I'd rather have a junior. Jasmine is my compromise." He shook his head, "I'm compromising all over the place here. I put my foot down. Eleanor is not happening."
"You put your foot down?" He smiled, "I know how to change your mind."
I smiled cause I knew what that meant.

Amber

Jade and I looked at each other. We could hear them coming down the hallway. "LET ME GO! LET ME GO!" The little voice screamed. When they rounded the corner it was the little girl Desiree looking like a wild animal as Ginger unforgivingly held onto her.
"Let her go!" I said having a flashback of the way teachers used your anger against you in situations like this.
Ginger released her, "HOW COME YOU DIDN'T GRAB HER! I WASN'T THE ONLY PERSON FIGHTING!" Desiree yelled.
"You were the aggressor so I had to remove you." Ginger said calmly.
Jade gave Desiree tissue for her mouth. "Where's the other student?" Jade asked Ginger

as she stood there eyeing Desiree.

"I'll go bring her down."

Tony handed Jade the incident report. Jade looked at it and then handed it to Ginger. "No need, Tony will go get her. We'll contact the parents, just have your final report here at the end of the day."

"Alright," Ginger said as she turned on her heels and calmly walked away.

Jade looked at me, "even if I didn't know, her behavior would be alarming to me." Jade whispered. "Desiree come here child." Jade said lovingly.

Desiree frowned cause Jade's tone put her on guard although it shouldn't have. Desiree grabbed my hand as she walked past me. I took my hand back and told her it was ok, and to go talk to Jade. Jade stood in her doorway waiting. Desiree pleaded with me to come with them, and then I heard a loud boom from outside. When I looked out the tinted window a car was coming full speed at the building. I grabbed Desiree's shirt and I screamed, "JADE!" At the top of my lungs I threw Desiree to my left and reached for Jade. Jade hit the alarm and jumped over the counter just in time. The car crashed through the front door and through the receptionist area. I started to fall and then Jade steadied me and told us to run! All of the other classes except Ginger's were on the other side of that car. Tony came to the door with big eyes! He yelled telling us to hurry! The kids inside the class were screaming. You could hear guns going off. Which only made the kids hysterical, rightfully so. "Where's the box?" Tony asked

"It's not here!" Jade told him, "alright kids. We need everyone to listen up and pay attention. I need everyone to remain calm and relax. BUT! It's important that you follow instructions." All the scared kids looked to Jade. "Everyone calmly and quietly follow Tony to safety!"

"Ms. Amber please come!" Desiree begged.

"Jade!" I said looking at Desiree.

"I know! I know! Let's go!" Jade said, "Ginger you make sure no child gets left behind!"

"What?" Ginger yelled.

Desiree shot daggers at Ginger with her eyes! Tony led the kids through the alternate emergency exit. Instead of going out to the street it took us to the basement. When the last child entered and Ginger was not directly behind them Tony locked the door. All of the other classes were now here and Tony ran to the other door and secured it. I hugged Andre as I saw Jade hugging her babies. "Where is the box?" Tony asked Jade.

"I don't remember!" Jade yelled.

"I need it!" Tony yelled.

"Children!" Jade said loudly. "We need everyone to follow Miranda to the closet. Please babies no matter what don't scream and remain as still and quiet as you can!"

"Come on!" Miranda said as calmly as she could but she was freaking out like the rest of us.

The kids started following her, "Ms. Amber please come!" Desiree said again.

"Desiree please go!" Then I noticed that Andre was sticking to my side calm as all get out watching everything. "Andre! You go too!"

"He has to ask right." Andre whispered to me. I was confused, "he has to ask for the Bread Box!" He whispered quietly in my ear.

"You know where it is?"

"Only if he asks right. My daddy said only if they asks right. Nana you can't help him."

"Ms. Amber! Let's go!" Desiree had tears streaming down her face.

I had a sinking feeling. "Jade! Let's go!" I yelled.

"I'm trying to remember!" She said stressed.

"Jade!" I yelled.

"Forget it! Tony let's go!" Jade yelled as she ran to me.

"No," Tony said calmly as he started to open the door.

Jade cursed and we ran. We shut the door to the closet then I hit the panic button which blasted cold air at us, then it opened another heavy door. Some of the kids screamed but you couldn't blame them this was scary. As the last of us hurried through the door it closed on its own. It was a heavy and thick door, it sealed off the room. Then a light came on; there were chairs and couches. I told Emerald to help Miranda and the other teachers do a head check and make sure everyone is here. Andre told me not to worry cause his daddy and Poppa would be here soon. I hugged Andre then I hugged Desiree. I kissed them both on their foreheads. I didn't know what was going on but I knew to be patient and everything would work itself out.

Yussef

I heard the front door chime. A kid was in the lobby but the way his eyes moved around the office, I knew he wasn't as much of a kid as he appeared to be. I asked him how I could help him. He asked where the woman who helped him last week was. She told him to bring back a resume to go along with his application. I told him I would take it and he hesitated. Someone sent this kid I could smell it all over him. I took the paper from him and I looked him in his eyes as I told him someone would be in contact with him. When he walked out I watched him walk and he kept turning around to see if I was watching him. I locked the door to the office; I was the only person there. El called in, he said he needed time with his woman, Ms. Laverne was sent ahead with her husband and Roz. Malcolm had a meeting in San Jose. I went to my office and I brought up the cameras, the kid reported to a brown sedan. I couldn't see the driver. I ran the plates, while I scanned the kid's face through the system. The sedan was owned by City News and Graphics, this company used to be affiliated with Access before Mitigated took it over. All roads led to Phineas, I started checking on everyone, something had to be up if he was this out in the open. I sent a text message blast out to everyone to "look alive, the frog was turning green." Then I saw Andrew walking across the parking lot; I unlocked the door for him and locked it back. He had that look like he was about to explode on his face and an envelope in his hand. "You bring me a love letter? Don't worry I feel it too!" Drew didn't laugh at my joke. He marched in my office, then he handed me the unopened envelope. He said he couldn't open it, but he needed to know what it said. I took the envelope and it was from Toya. I looked at him and he threw his body in my guest chair. "You sure?" Drew nodded yes. I sat on the edge of my desk and opened the letter. "Toya has nice handwriting." I smiled, but Drew wasn't in the mood.

Dear Drew,

I'm not sure that this letter will make it to you, but it's worth a try. By now you're probably married to that ugly fat girl and trying to erase me from our son's mind. After all that we've been through I can't believe this is where you put me! I feel the need to clear my name since I'm sure Malcolm still paints me as the villain in everything. I didn't send Kevin after Derrick. I didn't start all that crap with Zack and Darryl. I hate that ugly fat girl, because she stole you from me. Of all the people Drew! Really? A fat girl? I don't care how much weight she lost she will always be fat to me. I want to see my son; he needs to know I am his mother, not that fat girl! I haven't heard from Will recently, can you check on him and make sure my children are ok. I know how you've always wanted a daughter, and I'm sure that fat girl will or has started blowing up again so your chances of having a baby with her are very slim. So, I named my little girl Amber after your mother for you. Will won't know about it until he has to look at her birth certificate. I did it for you, for us. Her name is Amber Ladrina Alissa Martin. I love you.

I don't understand why you keep sending people to talk to me. I already told Malcolm everything. I can imagine that the only reason I'm still alive is because Malcolm felt I had nothing, so I don't know why it has to be all this? Would you really hurt my mother? You moved your girl from her little job, and you don't stay in that house no more. I'm not a threat anymore so I don't understand why all of this has to be?

I know you don't believe me but I love you. I always have, and I wish things could've been different with us. Like what if my mother would've let me keep that first baby. How different our lives would be right now. I want Andre to know that I didn't forget about him. Please tell him the truth, make sure he knows I do love him, I just couldn't be his mother. I didn't know how, I guess the fat girl serves some purpose.

I love you,
Toy

I looked up from the letter, "you know Toya. She's trying to pull at your heartstrings, you've been sending people out there to talk to her?"

Drew frowned, "no."

I called Derrick, "D-Rick. You with Malcolm?"

"No Juan is, I'm with Darryl."

"Have you sent any one to talk to Toya?" I asked.

I could hear his frown, "no. What happened?"

"How does she know Tracy left her job and that you've moved?" I asked Drew.

He looked like he was thinking. "Will could've mentioned that he hasn't been to my house."

"Where is Will?" Darryl asked.

"Haven't seen him since he showed up with Uncle Mali's side piece." Drew said.

"You haven't talked to him?"

"We've been focused on the blackout."

"Something stinks!" Darryl said.

Drew took out his phone to look at his call history. "I have missed calls from him on the day of the wedding, but I didn't think anything of that."

I pulled up my computer, and I pulled up Drew's phone records. "He never blows you up like that."

"We're out here towards Hayward. We'll check him out and let you know." Derrick said.

Drew and I stayed on my systems. Drew told me to let him know if I found anything interesting. Then he left to get back to work.

Then Bernadette called me; she said some lady came to her door asking about Latour Enterprises. I pulled up the camera and it was the same car that was here earlier. If they found Bernadette they had to have everyone else. I gave her exact instructions, I told her to leave her phone and purse. I told her to take her new van (she's always driven one) and casually pick everybody up. I told her to make them leave their personal belongings wherever they are. Then Curtis called, he said there was a car approaching Andrew's house and it looked suspicious. I told him to tell everyone it was go time. I called Drew and he told me to set off the alarm there and he'd call Tracy. He asked me to go there first since I was the closest and she was too weak to do anything yet. I grabbed my backpack and briefcase. I threw laptops, files, and pictures in them. Then I set the office to torch in a couple hours. I called Derrick and Darryl I told them and then they hung up. I threw on a hat, shades, knuckle bars with gloves, and a casual looking leather jacket. I went out the back doors as I looked at my cameras. My bucket Bessie was being watched. I set the count down on Bessie. I casually walked through the mall, I popped an apple candy and then I got to Driscilla on the other side. She started up and we were off. I took my jacket, hat, and shades off. I called Darlene, Bruce, Todd, and any other staff I could think of. I told them to all look a live cause it was go time. Bernadette's van was moving so she was good.

Lanie

Ring, Ring. The screen on my phone said unavailable. I looked at my parents. My father told me to put it on speaker. Since we've sat down to lunch my phone keeps ringing and then there's silence. I was trying to tell them about my last conversation with Dorian. When I told my momma Dorian wasn't married she tried to act like she was surprised.
"Hello?"
"Lanie!" The caller's voice was coming in and out.
"Who is this?"
"Can you come out?"
"Out where? Who is this?"
"Bilal."
"Uh! No!"
"Please!"
"Why are you on my phone? Can't you get a hint?" He was trying to say something. "I can't understand you, your phone's breaking up." Then I hung up.
My father frowned as two guys approached our table. "Ethan we need to go."
I swear my daddy's eyes turned black. "My girls are in the restroom. As soon as they're here we'll leave. You have someone on them?"
"Yes, but you gotta move. Can you casually start walking?"
My momma's eyes were stretched and locked on my daddy. My dad took out his phone and put it on speaker. When Eric answered he told him to hold on then he called EJ. "Eric and Ethan you there?" They both said yes. "This is not a drill, it's go time!" Then he hung up.
"What does that mean?" I asked him.
"Put your phones in your purses and give them to me." We did then he picked up Erica and Zoey's purses and handed all of them to the guy. "Wait a minute my car keys are in there."
"Your car is at the house. Walk casually and come on."
Erica and Zoey were frowning and looking backwards as we walked towards each other. As they passed the front door you heard the pop and the glass door shattered. My daddy threw momma and me to the ground and then he ran to my sisters without any concern for himself. As soon as my daddy was visible outside they shot again. He picked up Erica and Zoey and brought them by us. One of the guys who came to get us was down on the ground and he wasn't moving. The other two were squatting looking for the shooter. Daddy looked at us and told us to stay low and to go back to the kitchen. One of the men had their phone out. They were talking to someone. Daddy told us to go. When we got to the kitchen, daddy told us to hold on. He took out his gun, I told him mine was in my purse back with them. He told us to hold on, he opened the backdoor fast and started shooting. POP! POP! POP! Someone returned fire and my daddy fell backwards while he shot again. My momma took two steps towards the door then she grabbed me cause I was on my way to him. My daddy stood up fast and looked around. Our car was right outside the door. My daddy opened the door then he told us to run. We all got in the back all

piled on top of each other. My daddy grunted. "Ethan!" I could hear devastation in my momma's voice.

"Baby I'm ok, today was a good day to wear my vest. It still knocked the wind out of me. Hold on to something." Then he stood on the gas and peeled rubber towards the front of the parking lot. "Put seat belts on!" He said as someone lit up the car. We did as we were told; Zoey and I fastened ourselves into the same belt. It seem like as soon as we clicked the belt a car crashed into us full speed on my side. My face hit the window hard. My daddy glanced back at me and the blackness in his eyes turned blacker. He tried to roll down the window, but it was cracked and stuck. My daddy opened his door and shot over the car at the car that hit us. Then he got back in the car and grunted then he drove.

"Call…"

"Incoming call from Jeremy…" The car called out.

"Answer!" He grunted again.

"Are you ok?" The voice said.

"I have a vest on, but it still hurts."

Hearing my daddy admitting to pain made all of us silently cry. "Can you drive? Do I need to come get you?"

"Zoey, can you drive?" Zoey's hand started shaking, she tried to speak and she had no voice.

"I'm coming!" I unfastened my belt and then gave it back to Zoey to fasten. "Pull over!"

"We can't afford to stop." My daddy said.

"Hold the steering wheel, and move over!" He did as I said, and I slid into the driver's seat. "Are we going home?"

"No! You have to go to the safe house. Are you being tailed?"

"No, but the car is all crashed and shot up, we can't drive around forever without drawing attention to us." I said looking around.

The voice told me to turn corners, and which lights to gently run. When we got to this ordinary looking building he told me to go down to the bottom of the parking garage and to pull into the last parking space against the wall in the corner. He said leave the motor running and once the car communicated with the sensor the door would open and go through it. He said to give our names to the clerks and to have Jennifer check out my daddy as soon as possible.

When we got out of the car my momma dramatically got out the back of the car, and opened my daddy's door. He looked at her and told her not to do this right here. My momma started jumping up and down as she cried at my daddy who was visibly hurting. He stood up and walked tall. I didn't see blood. The woman said hello and she opened the elevator for us. When we came out the other side my momma started screaming for Jennifer. Jennifer was already hurrying. My daddy told her to calm down and she was making the whole scene worse than it was. Then Erica told him to SHUT UP! She said she just watched her daddy get shot and if her momma wanted to scream to let her scream. My daddy didn't say anything. When Jennifer took his vest off, his skin was purple. The vest was caved in where the bullet hit him, like it used all its strength to protect him. Jennifer touched his side gently and my daddy frowned. She told my daddy to go up to his apartment and she would be right there.

Tracy

I can't believe he's here and someone so perfect came from me. Baby Malcolm and I laid on the bed having an all-out staring match. We did this very often. He would stare at me taking me in and I would do the same with him. He's about Andrew's complexion and his ears suggest that he will probably be browner like me. He looks just like Andrew and Andre, but he has my nose and that brow line like my father and the men in my family.

His hair is curly but I don't know if that hair will fall out or not. I have no doubt that he's my baby, but I don't know about his temperament just yet. Like Chanel he doesn't cry much. He has no patience when it comes to eating though. When he's ready to eat I better be ready or else he's fussing. My mom made me promise to stay in the house for the first month. She said no running around doing too much like most of these young moms these days. Since we still only have the one car, it wasn't hard to stay in. I couldn't believe I was finally a mom. I mean Andre made me feel like a mom, and you wouldn't know from him that he didn't come from me. However, now I have the whole experience. I keep kissing my baby and telling him how much I love him and how happy I am that he's here.

Nicole came over the other day and she couldn't get enough of him. She didn't want to leave when Hubby told her to step away from the baby cause it looked like she was catching the baby-germs. I told him that they had been married long enough, and it was time. Nicole smiled at Hubby and he proceeded to have an all-out melt down. He told her he was not ready to share! Then he insisted that they leave. Andrew was cracking up as Hubby told Nicole she needed to take a shower as soon as she got home to wash away the baby smell. Andrew said Hubby takes sprung to a whole other level. I told him I was happy I got to see Nicole before the blackout. They were leaving the next day with Hubby's mom, Dude, and Joy's family. I thanked Andrew for protecting my friends and family. He kissed me passionately and told me it was the least he could do.

I was breast-feeding little Malcolm when Cain and Eve jumped up and started growling. I didn't pay it any attention until a red light flashed in the room one time and Cain slowly walked out of the room in defense mode. Eve stood in the doorway at a low growl. The red light flashed one more time and my heart dropped. I didn't know what to do. I felt vulnerable all alone with my baby. Andrew called my cellphone; his voice was so deep I thought it was Malcolm at first. I whispered that a red light flashed twice and Cain went downstairs and Eve was standing guard in the doorway. "Tracy! I need you to use your head. Don't freak out on me. I'm coming! But I have to get there. Baby I'm coming ok?" I swallowed, "ok." I said lowly.

"I need you to keep the baby quiet. Lowly call Cain once. If he doesn't come take Eve with you in the TV room. Go in the closet and shut the door. It's going to be dark. Feel the wall on the right it should be smooth. You will feel texture like paint over one spot press hard there. That's going to open a door. Be careful cause it's going to be dark going up those stairs. They lead to the attic. Remember I showed you the attic when we moved in. Wait there quietly for me. Leave this phone on the bed. Do not take it with you. I have stuff for the baby already. Do exactly like I say ok?"

The red light flashed again. "Ok, the light flashed again." Cain started barking and then growling. "Cain's barking!" I tried to hold back my tears.

"Go! Don't call Cain! Keep the baby quiet! I'm coming! I love you!" I could hear the worry in his voice.

"I love you!" Then I put the phone down.

Eve was still posted and Cain was going crazy. I picked up the baby, and I let him continue to eat. My heart was pounding. I covered my mouth to muffle my cry. I walked past Eve and she stood in front of me in the hallway growling. I went in the closet with Eve like Andrew told me to. I was feeling in the dark for the spot like he told me but I couldn't find it. I opened my mouth so I wouldn't cry out loud. As soon as I found it the closet door opened I wanted to scream! It was Yussef. He put his finger up to tell me not to scream. Eve went back to the doorway growling. Yussef gave me a baby carrier that he strapped on me so fast. We put the baby in the carrier, I put the blanket I had over my left breast covering the fact that I was feeding the baby, now went over the baby's head. Yussef looked out the window. Then he backed up. He looked me up and down. I was barefoot and fortunately I had on sweats and a very loose fitting shirt. If this would've happened an hour earlier I would've been completely embarrassed. "You trust me?" He looked me in my eyes. I shook my head yes. He whispered, "go out this window. Lay down under the window, keep the baby quiet. Andrew is coming ok?"

The thought of going out the window sound ridiculous to me, but Cain's barking had stopped and Eve was about to attack. Yussef slowly opened the window and then he helped me climb out. The air was warm out, I could hear people moving on the ground but I didn't look out. I laid down like Yussef told me to. Little Malcolm was patiently waiting for me to feed him again. I fed him and put the cover back over him. Eve was going crazy barking and probably biting. I could hear bumping inside, I wanted to scream cause I was scared for Yussef. I heard a car speed past the house. Minutes later Yussef opened the window and told me to come but to close my eyes. His face was serious so I didn't ask any questions. Yussef said something to Eve and then I recognized the touch. I whispered, "Andrew?" He told me to keep my eyes closed. He kissed my cheek. Yussef told him to take me in and I heard his hurried footsteps away from me. I asked Andrew if I could open my eyes and he told me no. Then he slipped shoes on my feet. Eve started crying and he told her to come. I asked where Cain was. Andrew didn't say anything he squeezed my hand. He put me in the car and then he let Eve in through his door. He told me to open my eyes as we pulled away from the house. The passenger door on the watcher car was open but I didn't see anyone. I started crying for my puppy. Andrew reached over and rubbed my back. I didn't pay attention to where we were going until we were going down into an underground parking garage. Andrew parked in the far corner by the wall. I asked where we were and then another garage door opened. He drove in and parked in that lot. There were a couple of cargo vans and then cars. I noticed Andrew's car in the far corner. I didn't recognize the girl at the security desk. She looked at Eve and asked Andrew if the dog went as well. He looked at her like that was a dumb question. She pressed a button as she handed Andrew keys and the elevator door opened. It went up one level then it opened on the opposite end. We stepped out into a courtyard. It had a playground for the kids, a pool and fake grass. Directly across from us was a glass elevator that took you to level two or three. It looked like an apartment building with a huge courtyard. The lights at the ceiling were structured to mimic sunlight. Andrew said everyone with small children got bottom units. He said his Uncle Frank, Uncle Jeff, and Malcolm etc. had units on the top level. Andrew put Eve out the sliding glass door off the kitchen. She laid down sad and she cried a little which made me cry some more. I asked Andrew if Andre was safe. He said Andre was with Amber and he should be fine.

Chantel

Our house has become the summer hangout spot for the kids. Sabrina and Emerald are really good with the little ones. Denise walks over sometimes just so she can see her girls. Amaya is the only person who knows how to make Chanel crack up and her little laugh is so cute. The first time it happened Derrick and I looked at Chanel like we didn't know what was wrong with her. She laughed for a long time too. With all the kids here Grandma Rosa gets to relax in her place.

Her place was decorated so nice. We told her no limit and she went for it. Everything inside her place was fancy and nice. She smiled from ear to ear as she gave me a tour of her three-bedroom place. She got real crystal, really nice silver for her silverware, custom made china. A beautiful custom made curio with track lighting to display everything. Her tablecloths were silk blends with coordinating napkins and table decor for each set. She changed that set up weekly and she said she had a few options for when she had guest. So I knew that meant eventually she planned to have her children over. Everything in her place was top of the line and high quality. When I told Derrick, he shrugged and said she

413

takes care of Chanel so it was fine. I know I shouldn't have but seeing how far she took things I told him he should put at least a monthly limit on the card, so that her spending didn't get out of control. Once the bills started rolling in he understood what I meant, but even then, she still had a five thousand dollar limit MONTHLY on her card. Then Derrick put three thousand twice monthly in her checking. She has no expenses cause we pay for everything, but Derrick kept reminding me that she takes care of Chanel and she does it happily. So as far as he was concerned she could have whatever she wanted. I knew he was right I just wonder sometimes where my father's personality comes from. Now that I'm finished with work for a while I hang out with the kids or my Grandma. We hang out here, the stand-in driver for Tracy's dad brings us fresh pastries in the morning. I LOVE the apple coffee crumb cake. Yesmina, Sydney, and I go for that one first. Then we'll get a fresh cake, cookies, or cupcakes in the afternoon. We all act like kids when it's COOKIE DAY and the cookies are still warm. Yummy! All you hear is warm cookies being devoured and cold milk being slurped. Derrick stumbled across our warm cookie delivery one day. And now even he's here on cookie day. We had to increase our order when he came cause that meant Darryl would hear about it.

We were out in the backyard playing tag when Derrick and Darryl came out both of them were looking around and walking quickly. Darryl asked where Andre, Emerald, Emmanuel, and Sonny were. I told him they went to the school with Amber this morning. Derrick called everybody in the house. Even though he looked calm, there was urgency in his voice. The girls came inside; I asked Darryl if he high-jacked the cookie truck. He flatly said no, everyone looked at Darryl cause there was no joke in his demeanor. Darryl told us to put our phones on the coffee table. The doorbell rang and Darryl told us not to move. My heart started pounding, my grandma asked me what was going on. Derrick was upstairs running around. Darryl came back with Kendra and her sister. He told them to sit.

"Why is he being so scary?" Kalani asked.

"How am I being scary?" He asked with a serious face.

"Your lack of a joke is alarming!" She said.

Kendra watched him, "why are you here?" He asked her.

"We always come on Wednesday. It's COOKIE DAY!" She said with a smile.

"I've never seen you on cookie day." He said.

"Probably because you're too busy getting your cookies from all over the place."

"You took your cookies back." He exhaled. "Doesn't matter cause you just saved me a step." Derrick gave him a thumbs up. "Kendra and Kalani if you would be so kind to put your cell phones on the table with everyone else's."

Kalani looked at Kendra for direction cause you could tell she didn't want to, but she did it slowly and her sister followed her lead. "Tell them to leave their purses too." Derrick said running from room to room downstairs.

"My whole purse?" Kalani asked.

Kendra didn't take her eyes off of Darryl as she nodded yes to her sister.

"Girls come with me. Grandma & K girls go with Darryl." Derrick said holding the garage door open.

"We're leaving? I need to get the..."

Derrick cut me off, "leave it!" Derrick took Chanel from me and strapped her in her seat. He told Sabrina to sit behind me in the SUV and Darryl got in my sedan. Then Derrick smiled at the girls and all of their eyes stretched wide. "I need everybody to do me a favor. It needs to look like I'm in this car by myself. So I need everyone to sit on the floor. I need you to move quickly. Jada make sure Amaya is comfortable." Then he looked at me, "you too!" He flashed a serious face. I saw Kendra and everyone doing the same in my other car. My heart started beating and I had a flashback of Kevin holding a gun to my brother's head. "Cyrus?" I tried not to panic.

Derrick reached down and touched my hand, "he's coming. I promise!" He said calmly. He turned on the radio and hummed along to the music.

The car called out, "call from Malcolm!" Derrick told the car to answer. Derrick immediately told him he was on speaker and he had the girls. Malcolm was quiet for a minute, and then he asked who has Amber? Derrick said JoJo was in route there and he was right behind him after he secured us. Malcolm said he was on his way there. Derrick held back a swear, Malcolm was breathing hard. Then he told Derrick he'd call him back. We swerved hard and the girls said whoa. Derrick told everybody to hold on. His face was serious; I focused on his face telling myself to stay calm. He swerved around a corner, and then he threw the car in reverse. We went backwards down a hill, and then he yelled at someone to move. I heard tires and then he drove calmly. He parked and started playing percussion on the steering wheel like it was the only thing calming him. Then he told us we could sit up as he drove into a garage area. There was a security guard at the elevator. Derrick kissed me and then he said go with Nikki. I asked him who Nikki was and the guard raised her hand. Derrick ran to the sedan and he said JoJo was naked. They hurried in the car and out of the garage. Sabrina told the girls to come with her and their parents would be here soon. Her calmness was appreciated because I was freaking out. Nikki told grandma she was with Derrick and I. She told Kendra and Kalani they were with Darryl. Then she told Sabrina to take the girls with her to her place until their parents came. Apparently Nikki knew each person by face. We asked her if anyone else was here. She said Tracy and a few others were here, but until everyone showed up we should go into our units. She gave us our keys.

Malachi

"Your dad was pretty tight back in the day!" I said to my niece and nephew who were sitting there drinking up our stories.

"You fool! I ain't lost it!" Timothy said.

"You fool?" Tim said.

"I ain't?" Tina said.

I looked at him, "see what going to Stanford does to a brotha!" I smiled at him.

Tina frowned, "daddy you were a lady's man? How?"

We laughed, "what do you mean how? Look at him!" Grace said.

"Daddy?" Tina said like she was scared.

We laughed some more. I looked at Denise and she looked so happy. I could never repay my brother for what he's done for me. Grace and Jenise have taken Denise under their wings, they do their female thing and then Denise comes back more at peace. It's even better when Jade and Sophia come with their men. I guess whenever Amber and Malcolm come up for air they can join our party.

"Babygirl you are beautiful because your daddy is FINE!" Timothy smiled real big.

"Excuse you!" Grace said.

"And your momma is gorgeous! You had no choice in the matter." Timothy said.

Denise grabbed my arm and rested her head on my shoulder as she lovingly ran her fingers up and down me. I could definitely get reacquainted with her responding to me like this. I loved the feeling. Bruce walked into the restaurant with urgency in his walk. I looked at Timothy, and he looked and then he said it was time to go. We paid the bill then I watched Bruce's quick pace as he walked to his car. We piled into my SUV, as we prepared to head over to Derrick's. Traffic on the street suddenly slowed down and there was a cop directing traffic in the middle of the street. When we approached the intersection, Denise looked at me and told me she loved me. Everyone said "AW!" Then a pop noise hit the windshield. The fake cop was spraying my windshield. I cursed as Bruce tried to return fire from behind my car. When Timothy rolled down his window I reached for my gun. I hit the guy in the leg and he went down. Timothy hit the guy coming from the right. I stood on the gas. I called my Uncle Frank; I immediately asked him where my girls were. He started to say something then he said there was commotion outside of his home. He said Derrick knew what to do, and to tell Darryl to bring me in. Then he hung up. I called Darryl and he said the board lit up, he and Derrick were on their way to the girls. He told me to make sure I didn't have a tail and then to meet him at the hill in an hour.

I got on the freeway. "WHY ARE THEY SHOOTING AT US?" Tina yelled.

"Tina, just sit back! I can't explain this to you right now!" Timothy barked as he watched behind us. "Far left five back!"

The car was coming up on us, "I got it!" I said switching hands with my gun.

"Grace switch seats, Mali I got it!" Timothy said climbing over his wife.

"Naw! I got it!" I was watching the car in my mirror.

"Just worry about driving!" Timothy said.

As the car got closer I saw a woman and grey hair. "Timothy stand down!"

"Bump that! They're going down!" Timothy said rolling down his window.

"Timothy! Look at the driver. They're not hitters." I dropped my speed.

Timothy was almost out the window, gun in hand when he looked at his elderly target who saw him at the same time. She screamed putting her hand on her chest and stood on the gas. Timothy and I laughed as I dropped back more and switched lanes so I could get off the freeway. Timothy and I laughed. Timothy said he hopes she had her diapers on cause she definitely messed herself. I looked at Denise she was frozen in fear, then I looked in the rear view mirror and Tim and Tina were covered in sweat. Grace's eyes were locked on Timothy and he was busy looking for our tail. I reached over and touched Denise, "the windows are bullet proof?" She asked staring at the dings in the windshield. "Yes."

"I would be dead right now!" Her voice shook.

"Denise you're safe." I grabbed her hand. "Don't leave me! Stay with me!"

She looked at me, "what?"

"You've got that look. Stay with me, don't leave me." I pleaded.

I parked in the lot of the Wild Cat Canyon park in Tilden. It was still and warm out.

"Daddy?" Tina asked sounding like a child.

Timothy looked at me, "something must've tipped them off. This is early."

I was quiet trying to think of the answer to that. Grace was quiet as she kept staring at Timothy. Denise kept squeezing my hand but she was quiet. "I'm mad!" Tim blurted out. "Why?"

"This means that everything you said earlier was a watered down version of who you are. And if that's the case why wouldn't you make sure I knew something?"

"What did you think you were doing when you go rock climbing with Uncle Malcolm, bike riding, all those drills?" Timothy said.

"I thought we were messing around. My little cousins are better than me! Darryl's calling shots. This is so embarrassing!"

"This is not a competition son. I wanted a different life for you and your sister. But your sister...."

"I'm sorry daddy!" Then she gasped and put her hands over her mouth. "Daddy! What happened to Luke?"

Timothy turned his back to Tina. He looked straight ahead with fire in his eyes. "T!" Grace said getting Timothy's attention. "You shot that man in the middle of a busy street. We gotta ditch this car!" Timothy nodded. "T!" She said again. When he looked at her, she lunged on top of him.

"Grace!" I yelled in disgust. "Control yourself woman!"

She kept kissing all over Timothy. "You saved our lives! You shot a man!" Then she stopped, "you made an old lady piss herself." She laughed, "I am so HOT for you right now!"

Everyone in the car gagged. "Grace come on!" I said laughing. "Control yourself woman!"

"Gross! Mom!" Tina said.

"Oh shut up! How you think you got here?"

Grace snuggled into Timothy's chest. We sat in silence for a while. Then a car sped into the lot and swung next to us. Darryl and Derrick got out the car. Timothy and I got out the truck. Darryl said police are looking for this truck. Then he took the plates off. He told everyone to give him their phones and purses. Yussef called on the car phone he was asking for an ETA. Darryl asked Grace if she could drive. She said of course, I gently helped Denise out of the truck. I put my hands on both sides of her face. "Denise," she looked around. "Denise, look at me." Her eyes were looking at me but she wasn't seeing me. "Denise! Look at me!" She looked at me and her eyes lit up. "I love you! Grace is going to take you to our girls and the safe house. I will be right there."

Her eyes filled with tears, "you're coming for sure?"

"I'm coming home to you! I promise! I have to go get my sisters."

Sasha

I woke up to the phone ringing. "Hello?"

"Why do you sound sleep? It's almost one!" My momma said.

"El and I had a long morning." I said nudging him.

"You guys took the day off? Isn't that sweet, now get up! I'm around the corner." She demanded.

"Ok momma dang!" I huffed, "my momma's coming." I said tapping El.

I ran in the shower then El got in as I got out. I told my momma I would be right out. I decided to go for comfort since today was a low-key kind of day. I put on a pair of El's sweats. El was dressing as I went out to my momma. The phone rang again and my momma came over to greet my belly with a smile. The caller ID had all zeros. "Hello?"

"Sasha!" Yussef's voice stole any calmness in my body.

"Yes?" My momma stared at my face.

"They're moving early. They almost had Tracy. Leave your purse, phones, etc. Carefully get in your car and go. Darlene and Todd are going to run interference."

"Ok, I've got El and my momma."

"I know, Derrick has Sabrina. They should be there when you get there."

"What about Travis?"

"Jeff has him and your grandmother. Get going!" Then he hung up.

"WHAT?" My momma yelled as I hung up.

"We gotta go, something's happening." I ran to the bedroom with my momma on my heels. When I opened the door El was fighting shirtless!

"NOT TODAY!" My momma said running away from the door. I couldn't get around them to get to my gun. My momma came back with a knife. She stabbed the guy in the thigh; she was going for his pressure point. When he turned towards momma El hit him so hard he flew backwards. The guy was out cold, I started to go for my gun and El told me to leave it. Then I told them to come on. When I got in the driver seat El looked like he was going to say something, but I shot him a look like this is not the time. The garage opened and we were off. I was looking for Darlene and I didn't see her, but her car was there. I didn't see Todd either. I had to get to Hollis Street in Emeryville without a tail. The car started shaking and then BAM! The back of the car fell and I saw my tire roll away. Panic hit me as I thought about our phones that we left inside. "Call from Yussef" the car called out. "Why aren't you moving?"

"We're sitting ducks! My tired rolled down the street."

"I got you! Hold on!" He was quiet for a minute.

I felt relief when a police car rolled around the corner. That relief left me when it wasn't Tanisha. "Yussef who's approaching us?"

"Describe the car."

"It's a cop."

"Stay put!"

The cop got out his car and then he looked around as he approached our car. I got a sinking feeling. He told me to roll down the window and I told him it was stuck. My momma whispered asking where his badge number was. Another cop car came around the corner. The guy turned red and then he started walking towards the second car. That was Tanisha and she was on her radio. When I saw the guy reach for his gun I told everyone to get down. It sound like hail hitting the window. Then we heard a screech! Tanisha tapped on the window and told us to come on the other car was gone. El ran with his arms around me. Tanisha looked at El's face, "you're hurt?" His face was starting to swell.

"I'm ok," he said looking me over.

"You're hit," she pointed to his shoulder.

"It's fine! I'm fine! He almost missed me."

"You got them?" Yussef's voice played over the speakers.

"Yes, El's shoulder is grazed but he's ok. The fake cop got away; I'll call in the car after I drop them off. Who's got my momma?"

"She's there already. Remember she was going last night anyways. She's with Carina and Cyrus' family."

Tanisha said ok and then she drove casually. The office building was huge. You could see the lobby from the street level. People were moving about in the building without a clue that we were there. The garage was under ground and we drove to the bottom. Tanisha parked in the far corner and then a garage door opened. Tanisha let us out then she went back out.

Yussef

I told JoJo I was there, as I set up my laptop to survey the school and see exactly all that was happening. He said there were people all over and Phineas' men were looking for the students. He said they were trained and very reckless. I looked at the oxygen level in the safe room, I could tell the kids were panicked cause the levels were dropping faster than I would like them to. They still had hours' worth of oxygen, but if they didn't calm down it would keep dropping at un-estimable rates. I told myself to breathe; I have a way out for them. I just needed to make sure that everyone was in place before we got to the kids. Phineas' men would scatter and we needed the police there to capture anyone we didn't pick off ourselves. Jeff called in and said he was coming. I told him JoJo was on corner one and I needed him on corner two. Drew called and I told him to cover corner four. When Derrick called I told him corner three was still open. Darryl was in the background going off cause they had not only his nephew, auntie, and cousins, but they had his momma he was declaring that everyone died. I told him he had to be calm cause I had a way out. I needed everyone on point, we only had one shot and it had to be done right. Drew called and said Timothy was now with him and he needed me to hurry up cause he was about to lose it. I told them that the men were still searching; I needed confirmation that the police were on their way.

When Malcolm crept up on me I told Tanisha to hurry cause Malcolm was here and there was no holding him back. He was beyond angry, not even Juan could calm him. I showed them my screen. I told them everyone was in the panic room. He asked, "me how long

before they..." Malcolm stopped talking and I was rendered speechless as we watched Tony reporting in. I chirped everybody, "Tony is a double agent!"
Everyone was going crazy all over the line, while Darryl was promising a painful death. Malcolm's eyes turn the same color as his skin. That did it, Tony was gone. Juan said he was going to put trackers on their cars while everyone did their jobs, then he left. That way anyone who got away would clue us in to where Phineas has been hiding. Tanisha chirped in, she said boys in blue were in route we had three minutes. Malcolm said he needed one. Then he hurried away from me. I told everybody to go. Then I caught up to Malcolm. We were in his building across the street watching our men scramble as they picked people off. Malcolm chirped them, "TONY IS MINE!"
Then we hurried again, I warned Malcolm that if Tony found the breadbox it was going to be bad on the other side of the wall. Malcolm didn't say anything, he looked at the fork in the hallway as we approached it.. "Uncle Blackie this way!" I started jogging.
When we got to the dead end I entered the code on the wall and then we backed up. The ground started shaking and then the invisible door slowly opened. Then the door to the panic room opened from the opposite side that Amber and the kids entered. Kids were screaming as I called out to Andre who was opening the breadbox as I stepped in. His face was about business, I was so proud of my little soldier. Malcolm went to Amber and Jade and he squeezed them so tight. I chirped that everyone was ok. I could hear Phineas' people trying to figure out the panic room door. The fact that I could hear them meant they came more prepared than I had anticipated and we needed to move.
When I saw that little girl amongst the children I told Malcolm she had to stay. Malcolm looked at her then he asked me who was she. I told him she was Turan's daughter. She looked at me with surprise on her face. Amber looked at Malcolm and she pleaded. She told him that the little girl was trying to help them. The little girl looked at Malcolm, and he looked at me with evilness in his eyes. I told him she stays, anything that happened after that is on Turan's head for sending a child in. Malcolm opened the breadbox and he told me to take everyone. Then he told the little girl to sit down. I told the teachers to make sure they had all of their students and to move them out of the room. Jade put her arms around her sister and made her come out the room. Malcolm took everything out the box then closed it back. Amber screamed "No!" As she hurried back into the room and she cried like it broke her heart. "She was protecting me! We can't leave her! Protect her Malcolm!"
The little girl looked horrified but she didn't say a word, Malcolm told her to go to Amber. And the little girl bolted to Amber. Malcolm secured the doors then he told us to move. As I ran to the front of the group of kids, they screamed when the explosion from the panic room shook everything and our little tunnel collapsed behind us. All of the children and even the teachers had fear in their eyes as they tried to be brave. I told everyone they were safe and we'd make sure each one of them made it home safely. I told them once the police came we could go outside. We walked up the six flights of stairs back to where my computers were set up. I took the kids in the lunchroom. There were wall-to-wall vending machines. I showed the kids that no money was required and to help their selves. I gave Emerald a hug and I asked her if she was ok. She shook her head yes, but I could tell she was still scared. Amber had the trembling little girl in her arms and she was hugging her and rocking with her in her arms. Andre was standing next to Malcolm mimicking his stance as they watched Amber. "I hate to break up this love Fest but I gotta check her for bugs."
"Who would bug a baby?" Amber asked like I was being ridiculous.
I looked her in her eyes, "I have. You always bug the babies."
Amber reluctantly let her go. "Desiree, he's a good man. Go with him."
Desiree took off her belt and handed it to me. "And I need your shoes." I said, and then I looked at her. "Jade, can you run your fingers through her hair?" She had her hair in a

bun on the top of her head.

As soon as Jade took her hair thing out I saw the bug intertwined in the thing. I used my wand over her body to make sure there weren't any other clever hiding spots and that was it. I put her shoes, hair thing, and belt in the trash compactor to crush them and make the signal weak. Then I put them in the garbage shoot. Darryl chirped in that he had Tony. His voice was angry. Malcolm told everyone to pullout the queen was secure. Then he told them to take Tony to the warehouse. There were SWAT teams and every kind of police car and news media surrounding the school. Detective White called Malcolm. He said Phineas' men were claiming to have hostages, and there was a lot of commotion on the grounds. Malcolm told him if they still had hostages he wouldn't be on the phone. Malcolm asked how Phineas got this close to his queen. Detective White said they had inside help, and he was going to look into it. Malcolm said this was unacceptable!

Drew chirped and said it was all clear. Malcolm told Detective White to come get all these kids. We told the teachers to take the kids down to the parking lot. The teachers hurried the kids to the elevators. Desiree hugged Amber one last time and then she thanked her for saving her. Amber kissed her forehead and told her that she saved her first. Jade and Malcolm watched the little girl as she hugged Amber one more time then she nervously joined the other kids. Amber buried her head into Jade's shoulder as she cried a little more. Malcolm looked at Dre who was watching everything that he did. Malcolm told Dre it was time to take him to safety. We took the stairs down to the lobby. Malcolm told us to wait while he went to get the car. Dre asked me why we couldn't all walk out together. I told him we always have to be careful because we never know who's watching and why. When Malcolm pulled his SUV around we quickly walked out in the parking lot. I ditched Driscilla and caught a ride with Malcolm back to the safe house.

(To Be Concluded Soon!)

Author's Closing Thoughts

I know, I know! So many authors do this, and it wasn't until I did it that I felt badly about it (cliffhangers, bringing characters back from the dead, etc). I promise to get Season 2 out as soon as I can. There are so many loose ends to close up. It's just that this story was getting so long and I still have so much to tell you about the Wallace's that I stopped the story where my writer's block naturally kicked in.

I started writing this story when I finished No Regrets. This was supposed to be my sixth and final story. Kendra came up in this story and it kind of made no sense to gloss over their background. I had to tell you their story. THEN! I had to write At Last. THEN! I had to write Just A Friend. Every time I'd sit down to write the ending of this story another story would come up. Thirteen books (total) later and I've finally delivered this one.

So I'm making this promise to you now. Season 2 for better or for worst will conclude the Wallace Saga. HOWEVER! (insert a bunch of smiley faces) As you can see I don't let go of people that I know and love very easily. So fear not, in any future standalones or maybe even series you're liable to find a little Easter egg in there. You might find Darryl laughing at someone, or Yussef standing in the shadows. You never know with me. You may be reading a totally unrelated Carey Anderson new release (or unrelated so you think) and BAM! There's Amber or Malcolm or both of them.

I honestly believe that only six degrees of separation separate us from each person on this earth. You'll always see that reflected in my work. However, it will be up to you to put together who I'm talking about when a random person is thrown in the mix in future stories.

Thank you for reading the entire Wallace Family Saga and even this book. I'm sitting in Starbucks right now hoping that you forgive me. I'm working on the next part I promise. The conclusion to this saga is coming. It's coming! I promise.

MORE FROM THE AUTHOR

Thank you for allowing me to entertain you. I hope you have enjoyed reading Present the first Season in the Together We Are Strong Series. If you have not read Volumes I – VIII of the Wallace Family Affairs series, please do so. Click here for a list of all the background stories. Stay tune for more to come shortly.

Wallace Family Affairs

Volume I Tracy's Complications (Click here)
Beyond The Wallace's ~ Distorted Mirrors (Click here)
Volume II Part 1 Sometimes Love Isn't Enough (Click here)
Volume II Part 2 Love Is Just Enough (Click here)
Volume III Invisible (Click here)
Volume IV Look Beyond Your Eyes (Click here)
Volume V No Regrets (Click here)
Volume VI First You Laugh Then You Cry (Click here)
Beyond The Wallace's ~ A Heart That's Taken (Click here)
Volume VII At Last (Click here)
Volume VIII Just A Friend (Click here)
Beyond The Wallace's ~ Abandoned (Click here)
Beyond The Wallace's ~ Last Words (Click here)

Together We Are Strong

Season 1 Present
Beyond The Wallace's ~ I Knew You When (**TBD**)
Season 2 What Comes Next (Release **TBD**)

Standalones

Secrets ~ (**TBD**)
Anthology Short Story ~ (Sept/Oct. 2016)

Hopefully you've enjoyed all of the background stories for our lovely Wallace's and Latour's. Please tune in for more from the "Together We Are Strong" Wallace & Latour Family Episodes on Amazon.

www.ingramcontent.com/pod-product-compliance
Lightning Source LLC
Chambersburg PA
CBHW070800030726
47504CB00003B/625